THE
EXILE

ALLAN FOLSOM

A TOM DOHERTY ASSOCIATES BOOK
NEW YORK

This is a work of fiction. All the characters and events portrayed in this book are either products of the author's imagination or are used fictitiously.

THE EXILE

Copyright © 2004 by Allan Folsom

A Forge Book
Published by Tom Doherty Associates, LLC
175 Fifth Avenue
New York, NY 10010

www.tor.com

Forge® is a registered trademark of Tom Doherty Associates, LLC.

ISBN 0-765-34835-7
EAN 978-0-765-34835-7
Library of Congress Catalog Card Number: 2004010065

First edition: September 2004
First mass market international edition: May 2005
First mass market edition: February 2006

Printed in the United States of America

0 9 8 7 6 5 4 3 2 1

Praise for Allan Folsom's *The Exile*

"*The Exile* starts out like gangbusters and quickly engages the reader."
—Denver Post

"High-octane thriller writing with an almost visceral impact."
—*Publishers Weekly*

"Folsom can flat-out write an action scene." —*Kirkus Reviews*

"Fast-paced, exciting adventure . . . With a sturdy hero and a despicably clever villain, the novel grabs readers from the opening scenes and rarely lets them loose. It does exactly what it set out to do: deliver breathless excitement."   —*Booklist*

"Hold on tight—from the first scene Folsom spins a tale of page-turning suspense."
—W.E.B. Griffin

"Once you start *The Exile*, forget sleep. It's fierce, complex suspense is fast as a 9 mm slug and tight as a hangman's noose."
—Stephen Coonts

"Folsom returns with another winner. . . . Unexpected twists and catastrophe on a global scale . . . Folsom should have another best seller on his hands."   —*Library Journal*

"More twists and turns than a strand of DNA."
—William Peter Blatty, author of *The Exorcist*

"A masterful epic, *The Exile* has the sweep and power of *The DaVinci Code*—a global enigma of world-shattering proportions and a blistering pace that will singe your trembling fingers."   —Douglas Preston, *The New York Times* bestselling
co-author of *Relic* and *Cabinet of Curiosities*

"A sweeping novel, crossing California, France, Switzerland, and England as a young California cop takes on a criminal mastermind."   —Barbara D'Amato, Edgar Award-winning
author of *Death of A Thousand Cuts*

BOOKS BY ALLAN FOLSOM

The Day After Tomorrow
Day of Confession
The Exile

For Karen and for Riley,
and in memory of my father and my mother

CONTENTS

PROLOGUE

Two men sat alone in the private study of an elegant home on the Avenue Victor Hugo. They were old friends and successful businessmen of nearly the same age, somewhere in their early forties. One was Alfred Neuss, a Russian-born American citizen. The other, a Swiss-born British citizen, Peter Kitner. Both were tense and ill at ease.

"Get on with it," Kitner said quietly.

"Are you sure?"

"Yes."

Neuss hesitated.

"Go on."

"Alright." Reluctantly Neuss flipped the switch on an 8 mm movie projector on a table beside him. There was a flicker of light and the portable movie screen in front of them came to life.

What they saw was a silent, Super 8 mm home movie. The scene was the fashionable Parc Monceau on the Rive Droite, the city's Right Bank. A children's birthday party was under way. It was fun, silly, colorful. Twenty or more boys and girls pushed balloons and threw pieces of cake or shot spoons full of ice cream at one another while nannies and the occasional parent looked on, more or less keeping the fledgling riot under control.

A moment more and the camera panned away to another ten or so partygoers engaged in an impromptu soccer game. These were all boys and, like the others, ten or eleven years old. Soccer was their game, and they played it rough-and-tumble and with abandon. A miscued kick sent the ball beneath an overhang of trees toward a grouping of bushes. One of the boys chased after it, and the camera followed.

The boy was ten years old, and his name was Paul. The camera pulled back a little and stopped to follow him as he went toward the bushes to retrieve the ball. Suddenly another youth emerged from the foliage. He was older, taller, stronger. Maybe twelve or thirteen. Paul stopped and said something to him, pointing to where the ball had gone. And then, from nowhere, something appeared in the older boy's hand. He pressed a button and a huge knife blade snapped out. In the next instant he stepped forward and shoved it full force into Paul's chest. Suddenly the camera charged forward, bouncing as it went. The older boy looked up in surprise, staring directly into the onrushing camera. Then he turned and tried to run, but the person with the camera grabbed his hand and spun him around. He struggled wildly to get away but couldn't. Suddenly he let go of the knife and pushed away. The camera fell backward and dropped to the ground to come full on Paul, his eyes wide, lying motionless, dying.

"Stop it! Shut it off!" Kitner suddenly shouted.

Abruptly Alfred Neuss turned off the projector.

Peter Kitner closed his eyes. "I'm sorry, Alfred. I'm sorry."

Kitner took another moment to compose himself and then looked at Neuss. "The police are not aware of the film's existence?"

"No."

"Or the knife?"

"No."

"This is the only copy of the film?"

"Yes."

"And you have the knife?"

"Yes. Do you want to see it?"

"No, never."

"What do you want me to do?"

Kitner looked off, his face ashen, his stare vacant. Finally he turned back. "Take the film and the knife and lock them away in such a manner that only you or I may retrieve them.

Use whoever you need, include the family if you have to, pay whatever the cost. But whatever that price is, make certain that in the event I meet an untimely death the Paris police, in concert with the attorneys representing my estate, have direct and immediate access to both the knife and the film. How that is done, I will leave up to you."

"What about the—?"

"Murder of my son?"

"Yes."

"I will take care of it."

PART 1

LOS ANGELES

1

TWENTY YEARS LATER.

Amtrak Station, the desert community of Barstow, California. Tuesday, March 12, 4:20 A.M.

John Barron crossed toward the train alone in the cool of the desert night. He stopped at car number 39002 of the Amtrak Superliner Southwest Chief, waiting as a mustachioed conductor helped an elderly man with bottle-thick glasses up the steps. Then he boarded the train himself.

Inside, in the dim light, the conductor wished him good morning and punched his ticket, pointing him past sleeping passengers toward his seat two-thirds of the way down the car. Twenty seconds later he put his small carry-on bag into the overhead rack and sat down in the aisle seat beside an attractive young woman in sweatshirt and tight jeans curled up against the window, asleep.

Barron glanced at her, then settled back, his eyes more or less on the car door through which he had entered. A half minute later he saw Marty Valparaiso come on board, give the conductor his ticket, and take a seat just inside the front door. Several moments passed, and he heard a blast of train whistle. The conductor closed the door, and the Chief began to move. In no time the lights of the desert city gave way to the pitch-black of open land. Barron heard the whine of diesel engines as the train picked up speed. He tried to picture what it might look like from above, the kind of aerial shot you might see in a movie—of a giant, half-mile-long, twenty-seven-car snake, gliding west through the predawn desert darkness toward Los Angeles.

2

Raymond had been dozing when the passengers came on. At first he'd thought there were only two—an older man with thick glasses and an uneasy step, and a dark-haired young man in jeans and windbreaker who carried a small athletic bag. The older man had taken a window seat down and across the aisle from him; the younger man had walked past him to put his bag into the overhead rack a dozen rows behind. It was then the last passenger had come on board. He was slim and wiry, probably in his late thirties or early forties, and dressed in a sport coat and slacks. He'd given the conductor a ticket, had it punched, and then taken a seat just inside the door.

Under ordinary circumstances Raymond wouldn't have given it further thought, but these were not ordinary circumstances. Little more than thirty-six hours earlier he had shot two people to death in the back room of a tailor shop on Pearson Street in Chicago and very shortly afterward boarded the Chief for Los Angeles.

It was a train trip that had been unplanned, but a surprise ice storm had closed Chicago's airports and forced him to take the train instead of flying directly to Los Angeles. The delay was unfortunate but he'd had no choice, and ever since things had gone without incident, that was until they stopped in Barstow and the two men had come on board.

Of course, there was the chance they were nothing more than everyday early morning commuters on their way to jobs in Los Angeles, but it didn't feel likely. It was their physical manner, the way they moved and held themselves, the way they had taken up positions on either side of him, one in the aisle seat by the front door, the other in the dark behind. In effect they had boxed him in, making it impossible for him to go one way or the other without encountering one of them.

Raymond took a breath and glanced at the big, ruddy-faced man in the rumpled jacket dozing in the window seat next to him.

He was Frank Miller, a fortyish, somewhat overweight, divorced paper-products salesman from L.A. who wore an obvious hairpiece and hated to fly. Across the narrow table, Bill and Vivian Woods from Madison, Wisconsin, a fifty-something couple on their way to a California vacation, slept in seats facing him. They were strangers who had become friends and traveling companions almost from the moment the train left Chicago and Miller approached him as he stood alone in the lounge car drinking a cup of coffee, saying he was looking for a fourth for poker and asked if he'd like to join them. For Raymond it was perfect, and he'd agreed at once, seeing it as a way to blend in with the other passengers in the unlikely event someone had seen him leave the tailor shop and the police had put out a bulletin for someone of his description traveling alone.

From somewhere in the distance came two long wails of train whistle. A third came seconds later. Raymond looked toward the front of the car. The wiry man in the aisle seat sat motionless, his head back, as if he, like most everyone else, were dozing.

The ice storm and resulting train trip were troublesome enough by themselves, another kink in a series of meticulously planned events gone wrong. In the past four days he had been in San Francisco, Mexico City, then Chicago, arriving there via Dallas. In both San Francisco and Mexico City he had gone after vital information, failed to find it, killed the person or persons involved, and immediately moved on. The same maddening thing had played out in Chicago. Where he should have been able to extract information there had been none. So he'd had to move on to his last planned stop in the Americas, which was Los Angeles, or rather Beverly Hills. There, he was certain he would have no trouble whatsoever in garnering the information he needed before killing the man who had it. The trouble was time. Today was Tuesday, March 12. Because of the ice storm he was already more than a day late on what had originally been a precision schedule and one that, even now, needed to see him arrive in London no later than noon tomorrow. Still, while that was frustrating, he realized things had only been delayed and nonetheless remained workable. All he needed was for the next few hours to go off without a hitch. But now he wasn't so sure that was going to happen.

Cautiously, Raymond leaned back and glanced to his valise in the luggage rack above him. Inside was his U.S. passport, a first class British Airways ticket for London, the .40 caliber Sturm Ruger automatic he'd used in the Chicago murders, and two extra eleven-round clips of ammunition. He'd been bold enough to carry them past the sharp-eyed antiterrorist security detachments patrolling the station and take them onto the train in Chicago, but now he wondered if he should have brought them at all. The guns he'd used in the San Francisco and Mexico City murders he'd had sent in plain wrapped packages for pickup at Mailboxes Inc. stores where he'd earlier had accounts opened and where he had a numbered box with a key. In San Francisco he'd collected the gun, used it, then dropped it into San Francisco Bay, along with the body of the man he had killed. In Mexico City there had been a problem finding the package and he'd had to wait nearly an hour until the manager was called and the package found. He had another gun at a Mailboxes Inc. in Beverly Hills, but with his schedule already stretched to breaking because of the need to take the train and with the problem in Mexico City fresh in his mind, he'd decided to take the chance and keep the Ruger with him and not risk another foul-up that could further delay his getting to London.

Another distant blast of train whistle, and once again Raymond glanced toward the man dozing near the front door. He watched him for a moment and then looked up at the valise on the rack above him and decided to take the chance. Simply get up, take the bag down, and open it as if he were looking for something inside. Then, in the dim light, carefully slide the Ruger under his sweater and put the bag back. He was about to do just that when he saw Vivian Woods watching him. She smiled when he looked at her. It was a smile not of politeness or the acknowledgment of a fellow traveler awake as she was in the early morning, but of sexual longing, and it was hardly unfamiliar. At thirty-three, Raymond was hard-body slim and rock-star handsome, with blond hair and large blue-green eyes accentuating a face that was delicate, even aristocratic. Moreover, he was soft-spoken and extremely well mannered. To women of nearly any age the combination was deadly. They looked at him carefully and often and with the same kind of yearning Vivian Woods showed now, as if in an instant they would run away with him to anywhere he wanted. And once there, do anything he asked.

Raymond smiled gently in response and closed his eyes as if to sleep, but knowing she would continue to study him. It was flattering, but a vigilance that, at the moment, was most unwelcome, because it made it impossible for him to stand up and take possession of the gun.

3

AMTRAK STATION, SAN BERNARDINO,
CALIFORNIA. 6:25 A.M.

John Barron watched the string of early commuters come onto the train. Some clutched briefcases or laptop computers; others, paper coffee cups. Here and there someone talked on a cell phone. Most looked as if they were still half asleep.

Several minutes more and the conductor closed the door. Another moment and the train whistle sounded, the car gave a slight jerk, and the Chief began to move. As it did, the young woman in the seat beside Barron stirred and then went back to sleep.

Barron glanced at her and then down the aisle toward the line of passengers still waiting to find seats. He was impatient. Since first light he'd wanted to get up and walk past where the cardplayers were sitting and try to get a glimpse of their man. If he was their man. But it wasn't the tactic, so he stayed where he was and instead watched a four- or five-year-old clutching a teddy bear toddle by. A handsome blond woman followed, and Barron assumed she was his mother. As they passed he glimpsed Marty Valparaiso in his seat by the door. He was dozing, or pretending to. Barron felt sweat on his upper lip and realized his palms were wet as well. He was nervous and didn't like it. Of all the things to be, nervous was not one of them.

Now the last of the new commuters walked past looking for a

seat. He was tall and athletic, dressed in a dark business suit and carrying a briefcase. He looked like an eager young executive. He wasn't. His name was Jimmy Halliday, and he was the third of six plainclothes detectives assigned to take the cardplayer into custody when the Chief reached Union Station in Los Angeles at 8:40 A.M.

Barron sat back and looked out the window past the sleeping girl, trying to shake off his nervousness. It was the job of the detectives on the train to verify that the cardplayer was indeed the man wanted by the Chicago police. If so, they were to follow him if he got off the train before it reached L.A. or, if he stayed on board, as they suspected he would because his ticket was straight through to Los Angeles, to follow him off when it arrived. The idea was to sandwich him between themselves and the three other plainclothes detectives waiting on the platform at Union Station and quickly take him into custody.

In theory the concept was simple. Do nothing until the last second and then close the vise with as little risk to the public as possible. The trouble was, their man was an unusually perceptive, emotionally explosive, and excessively violent killer. What might happen if he sensed they were on the train and took action inside it, none of them wanted to guess. But it was why they'd boarded separately and had deliberately kept a low profile.

They—Barron, Valparaiso, and Halliday, and the three waiting at Union Station—were homicide detectives, members of the Los Angeles Police Department's 5-2 Squad, the famed hundred-year-old "special situations" section that was now part of the Robbery-Homicide Division. Of the three riding in car 39002, Valparaiso was oldest at forty-two. The father of three teenage girls, he'd been in the 5-2 for sixteen years. Halliday was thirty-one, had five-year-old twins and a newly pregnant wife, and had been in the squad for eight years. John Barron was the baby, twenty-six and unmarried. He'd been on the squad for a week.

Reason enough for him to have sweat on his palms and upper lip, and why the young girl sleeping next to him, the toddler with the teddy bear, and everyone else in the car made him nervous. This was his first potential live-fire situation in the 5-2, and their man, if he turned out to be their man, was hugely dangerous. If something happened and he missed a cue, if he screwed up in any way and people got hurt or killed—

He didn't want to think about it. Instead he looked at his watch. It was 6:40, two hours exactly before they were to arrive at Union Station.

4

Raymond had seen the tall man in the dark suit come on board, too. Confident, smiling, briefcase in hand, looking like a young businessman ready for a new day. But, like the men who had boarded the Chief in Barstow, his presence was too keen, too studied, too authoritative.

Raymond watched him as he passed, then turned casually to see him stop two-thirds of the way down the car to let a woman settle her toddler in a seat, then he continued on and went out the door at the far end of the car just as Bill Woods came through it the other way, smiling as he always did and balancing four cups of coffee on a cardboard tray.

Vivian Woods smiled as her husband set the tray on the card table and slid into his seat beside her. Immediately she took the coffee cups and handed them around, purposefully trying to keep her attention from Raymond. She turned sympathetically to Frank Miller instead.

"Are you feeling better, Frank? You look a little better."

By Raymond's count the salesman had been back and forth to the toilet three times in the last two hours, waking them all to some degree each time he left or came back.

"I'm better, thanks." Miller forced a smile. "Something I ate, I guess. What do you say we play a few hands before we hit L.A.?"

Just then the conductor passed. "Good morning," he said to Raymond as he went by.

"Good morning," Raymond said absently, then turned as Bill Woods picked up a deck of cards from the table in front of him. "You want to deal, Ray?"

Raymond smiled easily. "Why not?"

5

LOS ANGELES, UNION STATION. 7:10 A.M.

Commander Arnold McClatchy drove his unmarked light blue Ford through a dusty construction zone and stopped at a secluded graveled parking area just across a chain-link fence from track 12, where the Southwest Chief would come in. Less than a minute later, a second unmarked Ford with detectives Roosevelt Lee and Len Polchak inside pulled up beside him.

There was a brisk slam of doors, and the remaining three members of the 5-2 Squad crossed under an already hot sun to the track 12 platform.

"You want coffee, there's time, go get it. I'll be here," McClatchy said as they reached the platform, then watched his senior detectives, one tall and black, the other short and white, walk off and down a long ramp into the cool of Union Station below.

For a moment McClatchy stayed where he was, watching, then he turned and walked down the deserted platform to the end to stare out to a point in the distance where the tracks vanished around a bend in the bright glare of the sun. Whether Polchak or Lee had wanted coffee made no difference. They knew he wanted time alone, to get the sense of the place and how the action would play when the train came in and they went to work.

At fifty-nine, "Red" McClatchy had been a homicide detective for more than thirty-five years, thirty of them as a member of the 5-2. In that time he had personally broken one hundred and sixty-four murder cases. Three of his killers had been put to death in San Quentin's gas chamber; seven more still sat on death row awaiting appeals. In the last two decades he had been nominated to become chief of the Los Angeles Police Department four times, and each time he had brushed it aside, saying he was just a working stiff, an ordinary cop, not an administrator, psychologist, or politician. Besides, he wanted to sleep at night. Moreover, he was head of the 5-2 and had been for a long time. And that, he said, was enough for any man.

And obviously it was, because in all that time, through the scandals and the political and racial wars that had tarnished the name and reputation of both the city and the department, this "working stiff" had kept the long and rich tradition of the squad above reproach. It was a history that had involved incidents making worldwide headlines, among them the Black Dahlia murder, the suicide of Marilyn Monroe, the Robert Kennedy assassination, the Charles Manson murders, and the O. J. Simpson case. And all of it was surrounded by the aura, the dazzle and glamour, that was "Hollywood."

That the tall, broad-shouldered redhead with touches of white beginning to show at the temples looked every inch the classic frontier lawman only served to enhance his image. In his trademark starched white shirt, dark suit, and tie, with a .38 caliber pearl-handled Smith & Wesson revolver in a reverse-draw holster at his waist, he had become one of the most publicly known, respected, and influential personages within the LAPD, perhaps even the city, and was nearly a cult figure inside the worldwide law enforcement community.

Yet none of it changed him. Or the way he worked, or the way the squad worked. They were bricklayers. They had a job to do, and they did it day in and day out for better or worse. Today was the same. A man was coming in on the Southwest Chief. They were to apprehend and detain him for the Chicago police while at the same time guarding the safety of the public around them. Nothing more, nothing less. It was as simple as that.

6

Raymond took a sip of coffee and looked at the cards Frank Miller had dealt him. As he did he saw the Barstow man in the sport coat get up from his seat by the door and start down the aisle toward them. Raymond glanced at his hand, then at Vivian, and discarded three cards.

"Three, Frank, please," he said quietly.

The man in the sport coat walked past as Miller dealt him his cards. Raymond picked them up and turned in time to see the Barstow man pass through the door at the far end of the car. Just as the man in the business suit had done earlier. A heartbeat later the younger Barstow man got up from his seat midcar and casually walked back down the aisle and went out through the same door.

Slowly Raymond turned back to the game. If before there had been two, now there were three. Without doubt they were police and they were there for one reason alone.

Him.

"He's our man, no doubt about it." Marty Valparaiso stood with Jimmy Halliday, John Barron, and the train's conductor in the gently rocking vestibule between the passenger cars.

"Agreed." Halliday nodded and looked to the conductor. "Who are the others?"

"Far as I've been able to tell, just people he met on the Chief when it left Chicago."

"Okay." Halliday pulled a small two-way radio from his jacket and clicked it on. "Red," he said into it.

"I'm here, Jimmy." Red McClatchy's voice came back with crystal clarity over Halliday's radio.

"It's a confirm. We're going to sit tight as planned. Car number three-nine-zero-zero-two—" Halliday looked at the conductor. "Correct?"

The conductor nodded. "Yes, sir. Three-nine-zero-zero-two."

"We on time?" Valparaiso asked.

"Yes, sir," the conductor said again.

"On time and set, Red. See you in L.A." Halliday clicked off the radio and looked to the conductor.

"Thanks for your help. From here in it's our job. You and your people stay out of it."

"One thing." The conductor held up a warning finger. "This is my train, and the safety of the crew and passengers on it is my responsibility. I want no violence on board, no one hurt. You wait until he's on land before you do anything."

"That's the plan," Halliday said.

The conductor glanced at the others. "Okay," he said. "Okay." Then, with a tug on his mustache, he pulled open the door and went into the coach where the cardplayers were.

Valparaiso watched the door close behind him, then looked to the others. "Game's started, gentlemen. No further radio communication until we get there."

"Right," Halliday said. "Good luck."

Valparaiso gave a thumbs-up, then opened the door and followed the conductor into the car.

Halliday watched the door close behind Valparaiso; then his eyes went to Barron. It was he who had first learned of the young detective's meticulous and uncompromising work while in the Robbery-Homicide Division, breaking open a murder case long considered a dead end. Because of it he had brought him to the attention of McClatchy and the others in the squad and ultimately into the 5-2 itself. In short, Barron was in the squad because of him, and here on the train for the same reason. Halliday knew Barron would be nervous, and he wanted to address it.

"You okay with this?"

"Yeah." Barron smiled and nodded.

"You sure?"

"I'm sure."

"Then here we go."

7

Raymond had seen Valparaiso walk past and take his seat just inside the door, then simply sit and stare blankly out the window as the train drew closer to L.A. and the countryside became increasingly urban. A few moments later he'd seen the other Barstow man return to his seat a dozen rows behind him. He sat there now, head bowed, either dozing or reading, it was hard to tell. Then, after what seemed a carefully measured interval, the tall man in the business suit came back, reentering the coach and taking an aisle seat across from the lavatory at the rear to open his briefcase and take out a newspaper, which he sat reading now. It was about as tight a trap as could be.

"Raymond, are you playing?" Vivian Woods asked softly.

Raymond looked back to the game to see that the hand had come around to him and the others were waiting.

"Yes." He smiled and for an instant held her eyes the way she had his earlier, seductive and encouraging, then let go and looked to his cards.

If the three men on the train were indeed police as he believed, and were there for him, he was going to need every advantage he could get, and having Vivian Woods on his side was one of them. Middle-aged or not, in a pinch she might well do anything he asked.

"I'll play this hand, Vivian." Raymond's eyes went to hers once more, held just long enough, and then pulled away to look at Frank Miller studying his own hand in the window seat beside him. An overweight salesman with a nervous stomach who was afraid to fly—God only knew how he might react if the police closed in and things got tight. He could have a heart attack, or panic and do the wrong thing and get them all killed.

Raymond bet and Miller called his hand, pushing a stack of red plastic poker chips toward the center of the table. For the first time Raymond wondered whether Miller wore the hairpiece because chemotherapy or radiation treatments had caused him to lose his hair. Maybe he was ill and had said nothing about it and that was the real reason for his trips to the toilet.

"Too rich for me, Frank, I'm out." Raymond folded his cards. He might have had the better hand; he didn't care. Nor did he care if Miller was wearing a wig or even if he was ill. What he was thinking about was the police and how they had found him. He'd been utterly meticulous in the way he'd handled the killings in Chicago. There, as in San Francisco and Mexico City, he'd spent minimal time on the premises, disturbed almost nothing while he was there, and worn surgical gloves, the throwaway kind that in an era of public uncertainty about contagious diseases you could get in almost any pharmacy, meaning he'd left no fingerprints anywhere.

Immediately afterward he'd taken a deliberate zigzag of trails down the ice-slickened streets to the railroad station that should have been all but impossible to follow. It didn't seem thinkable that they could have traced him at all, let alone to the train. Yet here they were, and every passing moment brought him closer to a final confrontation with them.

What he had to do, and quickly, was find a way out.

8

UNION STATION. 7:50 A.M.

Detectives Polchak and Lee came up the ramp from the station toward the track 12 platform where McClatchy waited. Len Polchak was fifty-one and Caucasian; at five-foot-six, he weighed two hundred and thirty pounds. Roosevelt Lee was African-American, forty-four, and a foot taller, a towering, chiseled, still powerfully built former professional football player. Polchak had been in the 5-2 for twenty-one years, Lee for eighteen, and despite the disparities in age, size, and race, they were as close as two men could be without sharing the same birthright. It was a closeness that came from years of breathing in the same tedium, the same vigilance, the same danger, witnessing the same awfulness of what people did to each other. It was a familiarity fueled by time and experience that made knowing what the other was thinking and what he would do at any moment in any situation instinctual, the same as the inherent trust that told you he was protecting you at all times, the same as you were protecting him.

It was no different throughout the squad, where tradition dictated that no one man was more important than another, even the commander. It was a working, everyday mind-set that required a special breed of individual, and one was not invited to become a member of the 5-2 readily. A detective was recommended, then quietly watched for weeks, even months, before the others agreed on him and he was asked to join. Once he had been accepted and taken oaths of responsibility to the integrity of the squad and his fellow members, it was a commitment for life. The only way out was calamitous injury, death, or retirement. Those were the rules, the way it was. Over time the certainty of it fashioned a faith of brotherhood few other groups shared, and the longer one was there the more his blood became the same.

This was what they trusted in now as they reached the top of the ramp and walked down the platform toward where McClatchy stood watching them, each counting the minutes until the Chief arrived and their cardplayer stepped from it.

7:55 A.M.

John Barron had seen him clearly once, as he got up from the card game and walked down the aisle to use the lavatory at the end of the car. But it had hardly been more than a glimpse as he passed, not enough to get the kind of sense of him he wanted—to see the intensity in his eyes, or how quick he might be on his feet, or with his hands. It had been the same a few minutes later when he'd returned, walking past with his back to him and sliding in with the others on the same side of the coach a dozen rows down. Still not enough.

Barron looked at the young girl in the seat beside him. She

was wearing a headset and staring off, keeping time to whatever it was she was listening to. It was her innocence more than anything else that troubled him—the idea that she or any of the other passengers or train crew should even be subjected to this. It was potentially deadly stuff and no doubt the reason their man had chosen to travel the way he had, surrounded by innocents who were protecting him without knowing. It was also the primary reason they hadn't just grabbed him as he walked through the train.

Yet, for all the confidence he had that their man would be taken without incident, there was something else going on, something he couldn't put his finger on, and the closer they got to L.A. the more uncomfortable he became. Maybe it was the nervousness that had been with him most of the way. His concern for the people on the train went hand in hand with his relative inexperience compared with the others. Maybe it was his sense of wanting to prove himself worthy of the honor he had been given by being brought into the squad. Or maybe it was the volatile, "should be considered armed and extremely dangerous" profile put out by the Chicago police. Or maybe it was a combination of everything. Whatever it was, there was an increasingly unwelcome electricity in the air. With it came a sense of foreboding and the feeling that something awful and unexpected was about to happen. It was as if he knew they were there, and who they were, and was already two or three steps ahead of them in his thinking. Preparing for what he would do at the last moment.

9

UNION STATION. 8:10 A.M.

Red McClatchy watched people beginning to gather in anticipation of the train's arrival. A quick tally gave him twenty-eight persons on the platform, not counting himself, Lee, and Polchak. The area where they stood was where car number 39002 would stop. When it did, the two doors on the platform side would open and the passengers would detrain. It made no difference which of the doors their man chose. Halliday, stationed at one end, would be right behind him if he came that way. Valparaiso at the other would do the same if he came his way. Barron in the middle would back up either.

Across the track and behind the chain-link fence where their unmarked cars were parked was additional backup. Two black-and-white LAPD patrol cars with uniformed officers in each were parked out of sight behind three empty semitrailers using the area for temporary parking. Four more black-and-whites were positioned at strategic points outside the station in the unlikely event the fugitive somehow eluded them all.

A blast of train whistle made him turn, and he saw a Metrolink commuter train come in on a track two platforms away. The train slowed to a crawl and stopped, and for the next few minutes the area was alive with passengers. Then, as quickly, they were gone, filtering out to jobs across the city, and the platform was quiet again.

The same would happen when the Chief arrived. For a few crazy moments there would be concentrated activity as the train let loose its human cargo, and that was when they would make their move, stepping from the crowd as the cardplayer came off the car, handcuffing him quickly, and taking him fast across the tracks to the unmarked cars. As intense as those moments would be, the reality was that it would be over in a matter of seconds with few people even aware that it had happened.

McClatchy looked to Lee and Polchak; then his eyes swung to the platform clock.

8:14 A.M.

"Let's see what you have, Frank." Bill Woods chuckled, calling Miller's hand and pushing a short stack of the red chips toward the center of the table.

Moments earlier Raymond had dropped out of the game. So had Vivian Woods, and now she was looking across the table at him again the way she had earlier. That her husband was literally at her elbow seemed to make no difference. The trip was nearly at an end, and she was throwing herself at Raymond in some kind of desperate hope he might do something about it when they reached L.A. He let her do it, holding her eyes for just long enough, then looking off down the aisle toward the front of the car.

The wiry man in the sport coat was still in his seat by the door, his head turned, looking out the window. Raymond wanted to swivel around and look behind him, but there was no point. The man in the dark suit would still be sitting near the lavatory by the rear door, and the younger one, midway, in the same seat he'd been in since he'd come on in Barstow.

8:18 A.M.

Immediately he felt the Chief begin to slow. Outside he could see industrial plants, a convergence of busy freeways, and the concrete-lined drainage channel that was the Los Angeles River. They were in the final moments of the trip. Soon the other passengers would begin to get up and collect their belongings from the overhead racks. When they did, he would do the same, standing and taking his valise down like the rest, hoping his move would seem innocent enough alongside everyone else and giving him time to get the Ruger out and into the waistband under his sweater. Then, when the train stopped minutes later and Miller and the Woodses left, he would go with them, chatting personably, making his way toward whichever door they chose. It was then that he would make use of Vivian Woods's fantasies, taking her arm just before they reached the door. He would whisper that he was mad about her and urge her to come with him, leave her husband, everything, right then. She would be shocked and flattered at the same time. Long enough for him to take her down the steps and onto the platform, using her as a shield against the police behind him and the others he was certain would be waiting for him outside.

Timing, if crucial before, would be everything now. Bill Woods would come down the steps after them, making a loud fuss, wondering what the hell was going on. The police would use that instant to make their move, and when they did Raymond would open fire with the Ruger, killing as many as he could right off and in the process creating as much chaos as possible. A split second later he would duck under the train, cross the tracks to the adjoining platform, and go into the station.

Once there, he would lose himself in the swarm of people inside, find the busiest exit, and go out with everyone else. Then he would be gone, disappearing like smoke from the bloody pandemonium he had just created and vanishing into the endless tangle of the enormous city before him. As long as he had his timing and kept his head, it would work. He knew it.

10

8:20 A.M.

John Barron saw the door at the front of the car open and the conductor come in. Stopping, he looked out over the passengers and for the briefest moment let his gaze fall on Valparaiso in the seat directly in front of him. Then he turned and went out the way he had come in.

8:22 A.M.

Barron glanced at the young woman beside him. She was still absorbed with whatever played over her headset and was barely aware he was there. He looked over his shoulder and saw Halliday at the far end of the coach, then turned back and saw Valparaiso in his seat up front. Neither so much as looked his way. Barron's eyes went to his watch, and he saw the minutes ticking down. He took a breath and sat back trying to relax, one hand in his lap, the other just under his jacket, resting on the grip of the Beretta automatic in his waistband.

8:25 A.M.

"Jeez, one more time, Ray, sorry." Frank Miller was getting up again and squeezing past Raymond into the aisle. It was the second time in the last twenty minutes he'd stood and gone to the lavatory in the rear of the car. The last time he'd apologized openly, admitting that he had a bladder problem. And when Bill Woods told him he'd had bladder tumors removed twice and recommended he see a urologist as soon as possible, Miller waved him off, saying he was fine, that it was the long train ride that irritated things. The last made Raymond think he'd been right when he'd thought Miller's hairpiece might be àn indication that the salesman was ill. Maybe he had been in Chicago not on business but for treatment, and Bill Woods's reference to tumors had only made things worse.

Again he thought about the critical timing in the station, the split-second way things had to work once they reached it. It made him worry, as he had before, that whatever Miller's problem was, he would cause some kind of difficulty as they were trying to get off the train.

8:27 A.M.

The Chief began to slow even more.

11

UNION STATION.

McClatchy stood just down from Lee and Polchak, watching the activity on the platform around them build. By now the number of people waiting for the Southwest Chief to arrive had grown to fifty or more, and others were coming by the minute. Any crowd complicated things, and the larger it grew, the greater the potential for something to go wrong.

He glanced down the track, then was turning to look in the direction of the backup black-and-whites hidden beyond the chain-link fence when his jaw tightened. A troop of Girl Scouts was walking up the ramp from the station below. There were a dozen of them at least, ten- or eleven-year-olds in tidy, crisp uniforms. Two women in Girl Scout uniforms accompanied them, women McClatchy assumed were troop leaders. The situation was tense enough as it was, but put together a troop of Girl Scouts and an unstable killer stepping onto the platform who suddenly went crazy and started shooting, then what?

"Eight-twenty-nine." Lee came up to remind him of the time, but his focus was on the Girl Scouts, his concern as great as Red's. "We've got eleven minutes and counting."

Polchak joined them, looking from the troop to Red. "What do we do?"

"Get them the hell out of here."

8:30 A.M.

"Ten minutes to Union Station. Southwest Chief arriving track twelve. Ten minutes."

The train's public address system broadcast a recorded announcement, and the Chief slowed to a crawl. Almost immediately people stood and began to take down their luggage from the overhead racks, and Raymond started to do the same. Then he saw the young policeman stand midcar and reach for his own bag, blocking the aisle just as Miller was returning from the lavatory.

The policeman smiled, said something, then slid back into his seat, letting Miller pass. As he did, the conductor came in from the front car and stood in the doorway near Valparaiso. For a moment Raymond froze, uncertain what to do. He needed the gun, and he couldn't get it without taking down his bag. All around him others were still collecting their belongings. There was no reason he shouldn't do the same.

Abruptly he stood and was reaching for his valise as Miller reached him.

"Don't," Miller whispered, then leaned in toward the Woodses, his voice hushed and urgent. "I heard railroad people talking. They think there's a bomb on board. They don't know which car. They're going to stop the train before it gets to the station."

"What?" Raymond was thunderstruck.

"People are going to panic," Miller said with the same urgency. "We need to get to the door right now, so we can be first off. Leave your bags, leave everything."

The color drained from Bill Woods's face as he stood. "Come on, Viv. Let's go." His voice was anxious and filled with fear.

"Come on, Ray, hurry." Miller pressed as the Woodses moved into the aisle in front of them. Raymond looked at him, then glanced up at his valise. The last thing he wanted was to leave it behind.

"My bag."

"Forget it." Miller said quickly, taking him by the arm and forcing him after the Woodses. "It's no joke, Ray. That thing goes off, we're all in a million pieces."

8:33 A.M.

Valparaiso and the conductor saw the cardplayers coming. Behind them Halliday and Barron were suddenly on their feet, as surprised as they were by the foursome's move.

"What the hell?" Barron mouthed openly at Valparaiso.

"What are they doing?" The conductor was staring at the cardplayers pushing past people, heading toward the front of the car where they were.

"Don't move, don't do anything," Valparaiso warned.

Barron stepped into the aisle and started after them, his hand on the Beretta. Three steps and he felt Halliday's hand on his shoulder.

"Don't give him a reason to do something." Halliday pulled him back.

"What the hell's going on?"

"I don't know, but he's not going anywhere. Sit back down. We're only minutes from touchdown."

Valparaiso saw Halliday draw Barron down and into the seats the cardplayers had just vacated. In between the foursome kept coming. They were close together, squeezing past other passengers. He heard the conductor take a deep breath. A few more rows and they would be next to him. The train was still moving. Where the hell did he think he was going, the next car? Yes, of course. But after that was the engine, so the next car was as far as he could go, and they could handle that if they had to. As soon as they went in he would radio McClatchy and—suddenly the conductor was moving toward the cardplayers, blocking the aisle.

"There's been a problem with the ticketing," he said with authority. "Will you please return to your seats until it can be corrected?"

"Christ," Valparaiso breathed.

Barron was staring at the conductor, the Beretta out of sight under the card table. "Leave him alone, you asshole," he whispered out loud.

"Easy," Halliday said softly. "Take it easy."

8:34 A.M.

The conductor was right in their faces. Bill and Vivian Woods looked at Miller for help. They were scared and had no idea what to do. Raymond looked back toward his valise. The police were right there, in his seat, the valise in the rack directly overhead.

"I asked you to go back and sit down. Please do so and remain seated until we reach the station." The conductor continued to push them. Bomb or no bomb, Raymond thought, here was a man who truly believed this was his train and he was master of it. No one was going to march toward the doors until he gave the okay, especially a wanted felon. Suddenly it was all too clear who had alerted the police.

It was a move that was not only stupid but reckless. And Miller called him on it. For the second time in what seemed seconds he did the wholly unexpected.

"Stop the train," he said sharply. "Stop it now."

The conductor flared. "That's not possible."

"Yes it is." Suddenly Miller pulled a huge Colt automatic from under his jacket and shoved it hard against the conductor's head. "You have an emergency key. Use it."

"Jesus Christ!" Barron stood up fast. So did Halliday.

Raymond was staggered. He stood frozen, unbelieving. Bill

Woods pulled Vivian back tight against him. People stared, mouths agape. Then Raymond saw Valparaiso raise his arm. A 9 mm Beretta was in his hand, and it was pointed directly at Miller's chest.

"Police officer, freeze!" Valparaiso's eyes were locked on Miller's.

In the same instant Barron and Halliday made their move up the aisle from behind, their guns up and ready.

"Drop it! Or I'll kill the conductor right here!" Miller yelled at Valparaiso, then abruptly pulled back and swung the Colt at Barron and Halliday.

"That's all!" he yelled.

The policemen stopped dead where they were.

"Put the gun down, *now!*" Valparaiso shouted.

Suddenly Miller pivoted toward Bill Woods.

Booooom!

A thundering gunshot rocked the car and the top of Bill Woods's head exploded, showering his wife and the closest passengers with his brains and blood, his body collapsing to the floor as if he'd been poleaxed. Vivian Woods's screams were drowned by the shrieks of other passengers. Some, near the back, stampeded in horror toward the rear door, desperate to get out. Immediately Miller twisted the Colt toward Vivian Woods.

"Put it down, cop!" Miller was staring at Valparaiso. The car went stone silent.

8:36 A.M.

Barron inched forward, easing past terrified passengers, trying to get a clear shot. Miller saw him.

"You want somebody else dead?"

Miller's whole being was on fire, his eyes little more than seething dots retreating deep into his skull.

"Drop your weapon, Donlan!" Valparaiso barked, his finger easing back on the Beretta's trigger.

"Not me, *you!* All *three* of you, you bastard fucks!" Miller's hand flashed out, grabbing Vivian by her hair, dragging her to him, the Colt shoved tight up under her chin.

"Opleasegodno!" Vivian Woods screeched in terror.

"Drop your guns, now!"

Donlan! The named identification stabbed through Raymond like a dagger. My God, the man's name wasn't Miller, it was Donlan. He was the one they'd been after all along. Not him at all!

Valparaiso looked past the gunman to Barron and Halliday, then slowly opened his fingers and let his gun fall to the floor.

"Kick it here!" Donlan barked.

Valparaiso stared; then his foot slid out and kicked the automatic toward Donlan.

"Now you two!" Donlan shifted, his eyes going to Barron and Halliday in the aisle behind him.

"Do it," Halliday breathed. He let his Beretta drop first. Barron hesitated. He was standing sideways in the aisle, and he could see the mother clutching the little child with the teddy bear. The girl who had been sitting beside him was frozen against the window, her face twisted in horror. This was the dread he had felt coming, the awfulness in the air before it even started. But there was nothing he could do now without endangering more lives. He let go of the Beretta and heard it clunk as it hit the floor at his feet.

"Ray." Donlan was suddenly looking at his card-game companion. "I want you to pick up their guns and drop them out the window, then come back here to me." His order was quiet and exceedingly polite.

Raymond hesitated.

"Ray, do what I said!"

Raymond nodded and, with every eye in the car on him, slowly collected the guns and dropped them from the train window, then walked back to where Donlan stood. It was all he could do to keep from grinning. This was fortune from Heaven.

8:38 A.M.

Abruptly the gunman turned to the conductor. "Stop the train. Stop it now."

"Yes, sir." Trembling, horrified, the conductor took a ring of keys from his belt, walked down the aisle past Valparaiso, and fitted one of the keys into a slot above the door. He hesitated, then turned it.

12

Fifty yards ahead, warning lights danced across the control panel of the Chief's lead engine as the train's emergency brakes automatically engaged. At the same time a warning buzzer blasted over the engineer's head. He felt a jolt as the brakes caught; then beneath him came a tremendous shriek of steel on steel as the locked wheels slid forward over the rails.

Surprise, panic, fear, and total chaos reigned inside the passenger cars the entire length of the train. Luggage, purses, cell phones, laptops rocketed forward in an unleashed hurricane of airborne debris backed by a cacophony of screams and screeching steel. People were thrown against seat backs and headrests. Others, caught standing up, catapulted forward onto the aisle floors. Still others held on with all they had, braced against the monstrous forward pull of the half-mile-long train as the Southwest Chief slid and slid and slid. And then finally, mercifully, it stopped, and for the briefest moment everything was still.

Inside car 39002 the stillness was broken by a single voice. Donlan's. "Open the door." He was looking at Raymond.

Staggered by the turn of events, Raymond stepped around the conductor and went to the doorway and tugged on the emergency release. There was a hydraulic whine and the steps settled to the ground. He looked out. The train had stopped in a wide expanse of railroad yards at least a half mile from the station and in what looked like a large industrial area. Raymond could feel the thud of his heart. My God, it was easy. Donlan would flee; the police would go after him. All he would have to do then was retrieve his valise and walk away. This time he did grin, broadly and to himself, then quickly stepped back, expecting Donlan to rush past him to freedom. Instead, the gunman let go of Vivian Woods's hair and grabbed his.

"I think you should come with me, Ray."

"What?" Raymond cried out in disbelief.

Then he felt the cold jab of Donlan's Colt under his ear. He was horrified. God had promised deliverance, now Donlan was taking it away. He tried to pull free, but Donlan was stronger than he looked, and he wrestled him back.

Donlan spoke abruptly. "Don't do that, Ray."

He turned toward the conductor.

"You fuck," he said quietly.

The conductor's eyes went wide. A horrific chill enveloped him. He started to turn, to run. It was no good. Booming gunshots deafened everyone in the car as the Colt bucked twice in Donlan's hand. The conductor's body jumped in the air, then fell out of sight. Again Raymond tried to pull out of Donlan's grip, but it didn't work and he was dragged backward down the steps and onto the gravel beside the train. A split second later Donlan had him up and was half-dragging, half-shoving him across the tracks toward a distant fence.

13

8:44 A.M.

Barron leapt from the car door and hit the ground rolling. When he came up Halliday was past him and running toward a point where Donlan was shoving his hostage over a chain-link fence at the edge of the rail yards. Barron took off, running not after Halliday but back along the tracks beside the train. He saw Halliday looking back at him.

"You want to chase him unarmed, go ahead!" Barron was

sprinting, searching the roadbed in front of him, looking for their guns. It was nearly a quarter of a mile before he saw the first Beretta glinting in the sunlight. Then he saw the other two, twenty-odd feet apart on the gravel beside the tracks.

He scooped up one, then the other, then the last and cut back across the tracks at a diagonal, halving the distance to the fence Donlan had gone over. Halliday was to his left, just ahead of him, running full out. Catching up, Barron tossed him one of the guns. Seconds later he was at the fence and vaulting it with one hand. Halliday did the same behind him.

The land fell away quickly on the far side, and both men stopped. At the bottom of the hill two major streets crossed at a traffic signal.

"There he is!" Barron yelled, and they saw Donlan and his hostage run up to the passenger side of a white Toyota stopped at the light. Colt in hand, Donlan ripped open the driver's door and dragged a woman into the street. Then he looked at the hostage and said something. Immediately the hostage glanced back at the police, then ran to the passenger side, getting in just as Donlan was putting the car in gear. There was a sharp squeal of tires and the Toyota rocketed off across the intersection.

"You see that?" Barron yelled.

"They together?"

"Sure as hell looks like it!"

UNION STATION. 8:48 A.M.

"On our way, Marty!" McClatchy barked into his radio at Valparaiso.

Spinning dirt and gravel, Girl Scouts forgotten, McClatchy and his detectives raced the two unmarked Fords out of the secluded construction area across from track 12.

McClatchy drove the first car with Polchak beside him. Lee was alone in the second car, banging into the street right up McClatchy's tailpipe. A heartbeat later the two black-and-white backup units roared out behind them.

8:49 A.M.

Barron and Halliday stood in the middle of the street waving gold detective shields, trying to flag down any passing vehicle they could. It was no good. Cars shot by left and right. They kept it up. It still didn't work. People honked horns, yelled at them to get out of the way. Finally there was a wild screech of brakes and a green Dodge pickup truck slid to a stop beside Halliday.

Gold shield held high, Halliday yanked open the pickup's door, shouting at its teenage driver that this was a police emergency and they needed his truck.

Seconds later the kid was in the street and Halliday was sliding under the steering wheel into the passenger seat and yelling at Barron, "You're the kid here, you drive!"

In an instant Barron was in, slamming the door and shoving the Dodge into gear. Rubber screaming, he leaned on the horn and fishtailed through a red light, accelerating off in the same direction as Donlan's white Toyota.

8:51 A.M.

Two-way radio in hand, his feet slipping on the crushed stone lining the roadbed between tracks, Valparaiso ran full out across the rail yards toward the distant street. Two hundred feet behind him L.A. City Fire Department and LAPD rescue units banged over the same crushed rock, racing toward the stopped Southwest Chief.

"Roosevelt, pick up Marty."

Lee heard Red McClatchy's order stab over his radio above a scream of sirens and quickly chose the fastest route to the railroad yards, starting with a left turn at the intersection ahead. As he sped into the turning lane, he saw in front of him the McClatchy/Polchak car accelerating, taking a skidding right turn at the intersection and racing away, the red and yellow emergency lights in its rear window flashing violently. A half second later the two black-and-white units shot past in hot pursuit. It was all Code Three. Red light and siren.

8:52 A.M.

Lee caught sight of Valparaiso running toward a low fence twenty yards in front of him. Immediately his size-fourteen right-foot Florsheim pumped the brakes, bringing the Ford to a sliding stop just as Valparaiso vaulted the fence and ran toward him.

"Go!" Valparaiso yelled, climbing in. Lee's foot hit the accelerator even before Valparaiso closed the door, and the Ford shot forward with a shriek of burning rubber.

14

8:53 A.M.

Raymond looked at Donlan. The Colt automatic in his lap, the intensity and audacity with which he drove, cutting in and out of traffic, running traffic lights, turning abruptly down one street then up another, all with one eye on the road in front of them and the other on the rearview mirror—it was like being in some kind of action movie. Only this was no movie. This was as real as it got.

Raymond swung his eyes from Donlan and looked back to the road. They were traveling fast. Donlan was armed and obviously had no problem killing at the slightest provocation. Moreover, he was as observant as Raymond. Clearly he had picked up on the police on the train and they were the reason for his constant trips to the lavatory. It was his nerves, nothing else, as he tried to decide what to do. But his alertness and will-to-action meant that trying to make a move against him here and now would be foolhardy. That meant he had to let Donlan know exactly what he was going to do before he did it.

"I'm going to reach in my pocket and take out my wallet and cell phone."

"Why?" Donlan touched the Colt in his lap but kept his eyes on the road.

"Because I have a fake driver's license and credit cards and if the police get us I don't want them found. Nor do I want them getting my cell phone and tracing the numbers back."

"Why? What are you up to?"

"I'm in this country illegally."

"You a terrorist?"

"No. It's personal."

"Do what you gotta do."

Donlan took a sharp right turn. Raymond held on as the Toyota righted, then slid out his wallet and took out the cash he had remaining, five one-hundred-dollar bills. Folding them in half, he put them in his pocket, opened the window, and tossed the wallet out. Five seconds later Raymond threw out his cell phone and watched it smash into a jillion pieces against a curbstone. It was a gamble, he knew, and a big one, especially if he got away, because he would need credit cards and identification and a cell phone. But getting away from the armed and psychotic Donlan without the help of the police was unlikely, at least any time soon. And if the police got Raymond, they would question him. In questioning him they would have examined his IDs carefully, and if they'd run them, which they would have, they would've found out that his driver's license was fake and the credit cards, while real, had been issued by banks where he had used the license as identification, making them fraudulent as well.

For that reason, particularly in light of America's ongoing domestic security concerns, if they had his cell phone there was every chance they would do exactly what he had told Donlan, trace the calls he'd made on it. And while he had used third-party numbers and transfer stations outside the country to forward his calls, there was a possibility, however remote, that they would discover he had been in touch with Jacques Bertrand in Zurich and the Baroness, who was waiting for him in London. That they might uncover one or both was something he could not allow to happen, especially not now with their European timetable locked in and counting down.

What the police found on the train he could do nothing about. Eventually they would sift through the piles of scattered luggage and find his valise with a change of clothes, the Ruger, the two extra eleven-round clips of ammunition, the plane ticket to London, his U.S. passport, the sparse notes he kept in a thin, checkbook-sized daily calendar, and the three identically numbered safe deposit keys tucked into a small plastic Ziploc bag. He now regretted having brought the Ruger with him. The ticket was simply what it was. His notes would most likely mean nothing, and the safe deposit keys were equally nonrevealing, as he had angrily found out, because they had been stamped only with their Belgian manufacturer's corporate logo and safe deposit box number, 8989. The previous owners of the keys, the people he had killed in San Francisco, Mexico City, and Chicago, had had no idea where the safe deposit box itself was located. Of that he was certain, because he had inflicted enough physical pain on each victim to make any single human being reveal anything. So, he might have retrieved the keys, but he knew no more about them now than he had at the beginning—that the safe deposit box itself was in a bank in a city somewhere in France. But in what bank and in what city, he still had no idea. That information was vital, and without it the keys were useless. Getting it before he left for London had increased the necessity of his journey to Los Angeles a thousandfold, but that, of course, was something the police would not know.

What they would be left with, then, was his passport, and since he had successfully used it to get in and out of the country they would assume it was legitimate. The problem would come if they ran a check on the magnetic strip on the back. If they were astute enough to put things together, they would find he had been in both San Francisco and Mexico City on the days of the murders there and that he had come back into the United States via Dallas from Mexico City the day before the killings in Chicago. But that was assuming they had any information at all on those crimes, which was doubtful because the murders had been so regionally disparate and so recent. Moreover, sorting through all the chaos of luggage and personal effects that had spilled when the conductor had pulled the emergency brake on the train would take time, and that was what he was trying to buy now by getting rid of anything damning. If they did capture Donlan, Raymond could simply say all of his papers had been left on the train and hope they would take him at his word as a terrified hostage and let him go before they found the valise.

"Green pickup," Donlan said abruptly, his eyes locked on the rearview mirror.

Raymond turned and looked behind them. A green Dodge pickup truck was about a half mile back and moving up fast.

"There!" Barron yelled. Leaning on the horn, he mashed down on the accelerator. Passing a Buick on the inside, he cut sharply in front of it, then moved into the passing lane.

Halliday raised his radio. "Red—"

"Here, Jimmy." McClatchy's voice came back distinctly.

"We have him in sight. We're east on Cesar Chavez, just passing North Lorena."

Two blocks ahead the Toyota careened left across traffic lanes. Just missing a city bus, it accelerated off and down a side street.

"Hang on." Barron swerved around a Volkswagen Beetle, then cut across oncoming traffic and took the same left Donlan had.

Halliday lifted the radio. "We're left on Ditm— *Look out!*"

The Toyota was coming right at them. They could see Donlan at the wheel, his left hand outside the driver's window, the Colt in it. Barron jerked the wheel sharply and the truck veered right.

Boom! Boom! Boom!

Both detectives ducked away as the Dodge's windshield exploded in front of them and the truck swerved onto the sidewalk. It went up on two wheels, then slammed back down. Barron downshifted quickly, pulled a tight U-turn, and screamed off after the Toyota.

"We've taken live fire. We're okay. Back west on Chavez," Halliday spat into the radio. "Where the hell are you guys?"

"I see him!" Barron screamed. Ahead Donlan pulled around a delivery van, cut hard in front of it, and turned down another street.

"Right turn on Ezra!" Halliday yelled into the radio.

In the distance they heard sirens. Ahead they saw the Toyota slow, start right again, then suddenly turn left and race off.

"That's a dead end," Barron shouted.

"Yes it is."

Barron slowed just in time to see Donlan take the only way out he had. Smashing through a wooden gate, he drove directly into a closed parking structure.

"Got him!" Barron yelled exuberantly.

15

9:08 A.M.

Barron brought the windshieldless Dodge to a stop outside the parking structure's entrance, blocking it. A second later four black-and-white units arrived almost on top of each other. Uniformed cops jumped out, weapons up, starting toward the Dodge.

"Barron, Halliday, Five-Two!" Barron yelled, his gold shield shoved out the driver's window. "Cordon off the area. Seal any other exits."

"In process." McClatchy's voice came over Halliday's radio.

Barron glanced in the mirror. Red's blue Ford was right behind him. Red was at the wheel, Polchak beside him. Then the Lee/Valparaiso car rolled in behind Red's and stopped. All around more black-and-white units were pulling in.

"Go in." Red's voice came over the radio. "Stop at the first ramp. We'll follow."

Barron eased the pickup forward and into the empty garage, passing a sign at the entrance that read CLOSED MARCH–APRIL FOR STRUCTURAL RETROFITTING.

Halliday clicked on the radio. "Red, this is a retrofit. We got workers in here?"

"Stay put. We'll find out."

Barron stopped. The darkened structure in front of them looked like an empty concrete tomb. Scores of vacant parking spaces were illuminated here and there by fluorescent lights and broken up at measured distances by concrete support columns.

A minute passed, then another. Then Red's voice came back over the radio. "There's some kind of job action, nobody's been here for a couple of weeks. Move on in. But use extreme caution."

Halliday looked at Barron and nodded. Barron's foot touched the accelerator and the Dodge inched forward, both men's eyes scanning the area for the Toyota or a sign of men on foot.

Behind them came the McClatchy/Polchak car and then the Lee/Valparaiso car. Then abruptly and from above came the thundering roar of a police helicopter, its heavy rotor blades cutting the air as it hovered, its pilot acting as their eyes from above.

Barron turned a corner, reached the base of the first up-ramp, and stopped.

"Gentlemen." Red's voice came over Halliday's radio. "The outside area is cordoned off. No sign of the suspects." There was a pause and then Red finished. "Gentlemen, we have the go."

Barron looked at Halliday, puzzled. "What does that mean, 'we have the go'?"

Halliday hesitated.

"What's he talking about?"

"Means we don't sit and wait for SWAT. The show is ours."

Inside the unmarked Ford, McClatchy slipped his radio into his jacket and reached for the door handle. Then he saw Polchak looking at him.

"You gonna tell him?" Polchak asked.

"Barron?"

"Yeah."

"Nobody ever told us." McClatchy's reply was matter-of-fact, almost cold. He opened the car door.

"He's just a kid."

"We were all kids when we started."

Alert, automatics drawn and ready, Barron and Halliday stepped from the pickup. In the distance they could hear the crackle of police radios, and above, the heavy thud-thud of the helicopter's churning rotor blades. The others got out, too. Valparaiso walked over to talk quietly to McClatchy. Lee and Polchak opened the trunks of the two cars, then came forward to hand out flak jackets with the word POLICE stenciled on the back.

Barron slipped his on and walked over to where McClatchy stood with Valparaiso, his eyes searching the garage around them as he did. Donlan could be anywhere, waiting in the shadows, biding his time for a shot. He was crazy. They'd seen him in action.

"Donlan's hostage," Barron said as he reached them, "looked like he jumped into the Toyota of his own free will. He was also the one who collected our guns for Donlan on the train. Maybe they're accomplices, maybe not."

Red studied him lightly. "This hostage have a name?"

"Not one we know." Halliday came up beside them. "Have somebody check the wife of the man Donlan killed on the train. They'd been playing cards the whole time."

Suddenly a tremendous roar shook the entire building as the helicopter made a low-level pass, then pulled up to hover once more. As the sound eased, Barron saw Polchak lift an ugly short-barreled shotgunlike weapon with a huge drumlike magazine from the Ford's trunk.

"Striker twelve. South African riot gun." Polchak grinned. "Fifty-round magazine. Fires twelve shots in three seconds."

"You comfortable with this?" Valparaiso was holding a 12-gauge Ithaca shotgun.

"Yeah," Barron said, and Valparaiso tossed it to him.

McClatchy slid the pearl-handled Smith & Wesson revolver from the reverse-draw holster at his waist. "We'll walk it," he said. "Jimmy and Len, take the north fire stairs. Roosevelt and Marty, the south. Barron and I will go up the middle."

And then they were gone, Halliday and Polchak to the left, Lee and Valparaiso vanishing in the shadows to the right, the sound of their footsteps lost under the pounding thud of the hovering helicopter.

Barron and McClatchy, shotgun and revolver, walked up the main auto ramp five feet apart, their eyes scanning the concrete pillars, the neatly stacked piles of retrofit materials, the empty parking spaces, the shadows that the pillars and construction materials created.

Barron visualized the others climbing the fire stairs, weapons ready, blocking any escape path Donlan and his hostage/friend might take. He could feel the sweat on his palms, the charge of adrenaline. This wasn't the nervousness he'd felt on the train; it was something else entirely. Scarcely a week before, he'd been a cog in the wheel of Robbery-Homicide, and now here he was, a member for life in the famed 5-2 Squad, walking side by side with the man himself, Red McClatchy, closing in on an armed and extremely violent killer. It was storybook stuff. Dangerous as it was, the rush was enormous, even heroic. As if he were alongside Wyatt Earp as they advanced on the OK Corral.

"You might want to know a little more about our Mr. Donlan," McClatchy said softly, his concentration on the concrete and shadows in front of them. "Before he did his work on the train, before he had the misfortune to be seen in Chicago and have the Chicago PD put out an alert for him, he escaped from death row at Huntsville. He was there for the rape and torture-murder of two teenage sisters. Something he did exactly four days after he got an early release for good behavior from another rape conviction—easy." Red let his voice fall away as they reached the top of the ramp and turned the corner.

"Hold it," he said suddenly, and they stopped.

Sixty feet away was the white Toyota. It was parked facing a rear wall, its driver's and passenger's doors open, its emergency lights flashing.

Red lifted his radio. "Toyota's here," he said quietly. "Second floor. Come in slowly and with all the worry you've got."

Red clicked off the radio, and he and Barron stood listening, their eyes sweeping the area.

Nothing.

Ten seconds passed. Then they saw the dimly lit figures of Halliday and Polchak move in from the left, stopping thirty feet from the car, weapons raised, ready to fire. A moment later Lee and Valparaiso came in from the right, stopping at the same distance.

Red waited, judging, then his voice echoed across the concrete chamber. "Los Angeles Police, Donlan! The building is surrounded. There's no place for you to go. Throw your weapon out! Give yourself up!"

Still nothing. The only sound, the heavy overhead thud of the police helicopter.

"End of the road, Donlan. Make it easy on yourself!"

Red moved forward slowly. Barron did the same, his heart pounding, his palms slick with sweat as he grasped the big Ithaca. The others stood their ground where they were. Tense. Watching. Fingers resting on triggers. Polchak had the stock of the huge riot gun tucked against his shoulder, sighting down it.

"This is Frank Donlan!" The fugitive's voice suddenly echoed from a thousand corners.

Red and Barron froze where they were.

"I'm coming out! My hostage is safe. He's coming with me."

"Send him out first!" Red yelled.

For what seemed an eternity nothing happened. Then, slowly, Raymond walked from behind the Toyota.

16

Barron had the big Ithaca shotgun trained on Raymond as he stepped from the shadows and came toward them. Lee, Halliday, Polchak, and Valparaiso kept back, weapons ready, intent, watching.

"Facedown on the floor!" Red commanded loudly. "Hands behind your head."

"Help me, please!" Raymond pleaded as he walked forward. To his left and right and in front of him were the three policemen from the train. The others he'd never seen before.

"On the floor! Hands behind your head!" Red ordered again. "Now!"

Raymond took another step and then dropped to the floor, putting his hands behind his head as he had been told.

Instantly Barron swung the Ithaca from Raymond to the Toyota. Where was Donlan? Who knew if he was using his hostage as a cover to get in position to take one of them out? Or if he would suddenly burst from behind the car shooting at whomever he saw?

"Donlan!" McClatchy looked to the Toyota, the blinking emergency lights a distraction. "Throw out your weapon!"

Nothing happened. Barron took a breath. Up and to his left he could see Polchak adjust the heft of the riot gun.

"Donlan!" McClatchy shouted again. "Throw out your weapon or we're coming for it!"

Another pause and then an object flew from behind the Toyota and clattered across the floor, stopping halfway between Raymond and where Red McClatchy stood. It was Donlan's Colt automatic.

Red looked quickly to Barron. "He carrying anything else?"

"Not that we saw."

Red looked back. "Put your hands on top of your head and come out slowly!"

For a long moment everything was still. Then they saw movement behind the Toyota, and Donlan appeared. His hands on top of his head, he walked from deep shadow into the soft glow of the fluorescent light overhead. He was stark naked.

"Jesus Christ," Barron whispered.

Donlan stopped, bizzare-looking under the fluorescent light with nothing on but the hairpiece. Slowly he grinned. "Just wanted to show you I had nothing to hide."

The detectives came forward in a rush, Polchak and Lee taking up armed positions inches from the naked Donlan while Valparaiso moved in hard to handcuff him behind his back. Barron and Halliday went for the Toyota.

"Don't move. Don't talk." Smith & Wesson held in both hands, Red came up on Raymond. "Roosevelt," he said.

Abruptly Lee stepped away from Polchak and Donlan and came over to where Red was and quickly handcuffed their second fugitive.

"What are you doing?" Raymond screamed as he felt the steel close on his wrists. "I was kidnapped. I am a victim!" He was red-faced and suddenly furious. He'd expected they would hustle him to safety, interrogate him for a short while, then take a phone number and address and let him go. Not this.

"Nobody else, no weapons, it's clean," Barron said, as he and Halliday came back from the Toyota.

Red studied Raymond a moment longer, then holstered the revolver and looked to Lee. "Take this victim downtown and talk to him." He turned to Barron. "Find Mr. Donlan his pants."

Raymond saw the monstrous Lee bend toward him, felt his huge hands as he helped him up.

"Why are you arresting me? I did nothing." Now Raymond played it soft, the genuine innocent victim.

"Then you have nothing to worry about." Lee started him toward a fire door and the stairs down.

Suddenly his fears rushed back. The last thing he wanted was to be taken into custody and have them start digging into who he was and then find his bag on the train. Twisting in Lee's grip, he shouted toward Barron and Halliday, "You were on the train! You saw what happened!"

"I also saw you jump into the Toyota with Mr. Donlan with no encouragement at all." Barron was already walking off.

"He said he'd kill me right there if I didn't!" Raymond yelled after him. Barron kept walking, going for Donlan's clothes. Raymond swiveled toward Donlan. "Tell them!"

"Tell them what, Ray?" Donlan grinned.

Then they were at the steel fire door. Halliday held it open, and Lee took Raymond through it and into the stairwell on the far side. Halliday followed, and the door banged closed behind them.

17

Barron held Donlan's pants as he stepped into them, a task made awkward because of the handcuffs and because Polchak had the riot gun squarely in his face. After that came the socks and shoes.

"What about his shirt?" Barron looked up at Red. "He can't put on his shirt with handcuffs."

"Step back," Red said.

"What?"

"I said step back."

There was an odd quiet in Red's manner, and Barron didn't know what it meant. He saw the same calm in the faces of Polchak and Valparaiso, as if they knew something he didn't. Puzzled, he did as he was told. Then Polchak backed off as well, and for a moment time froze. The four detectives and their captive facing off. The only movement at all, the still-blinking emergency lights of the Toyota.

"That a wig?" Valparaiso asked of Donlan's hairpiece. "Looks like a wig."

"It's not."

"What alias did you use this time, Donlan? You know, for the people on the train, the people you played cards with," Red said softly. "Tom Haggerty? Don Donlan Jr.? Maybe James Dexter, or was it Bill Miller?"

"Miller."

"Bill?"

"Frank. It is my real name."

"Funny, I thought it was Whitey. It's been on your criminal records since you were twelve."

"Yeah, well, fuck you."

"Yeah, fuck us." Polchak smiled, then very deliberately set the riot gun aside.

Donlan's eyes swept them all. "What's goin' on?" he asked, his voice suddenly racked with fear.

"What the fuck do you think? Whitey . . ." Valparaiso was staring at him.

Barron looked to Red, as puzzled as before.

The next happened in a millisecond. Polchak moved in, grabbing Donlan by the arms and locking him where he was. At the same time Valparaiso stepped forward, a snub-nosed .22 revolver in his fist.

"No, don't!" Donlan screamed, his voice stark with terror. He tried to twist out of Polchak's grip, but it was no good. Valparaiso shoved the .22 against his temple.

Bang!

"Holy shit!" Barron's breath went out of him. Then Polchak let go and Donlan's body crumbled to the floor.

18

Raymond started and tried to pull up at the sharp report that echoed like a firecracker off the concrete walls from the floor above. Halliday shoved him back against the trunk of Lee's Ford, and Lee continued where he'd left off.

"You have the right to legal counsel. If you believe you cannot afford legal counsel—"

"We need a Scientific Investigations unit and the coroner." McClatchy had turned and was talking into his radio as Valparaiso handed the .22 to Polchak, then stood up and came over to Barron.

"Donlan had a twenty-two hidden in his pants. When we tried to take him downstairs he got one of the cuffs off and shot himself. His last words were 'This is as far as I go.'"

Barron heard, but it barely registered. Traumatic shock and horror overrode his entire being, while five feet away Polchak was unlocking one of Donlan's handcuffs and fitting the .22 into the hand, making it look as if Donlan had done exactly as Valparaiso said. All the while a dark pool of blood was seeping out from under Donlan's head.

That something like this could happen, and be done by these men, was unfathomable. Again, for the second time in his life, John Barron's world had suddenly become a dark and terrible dream. In it he saw McClatchy walk over to Valparaiso. "You've had a long day, Marty," he said gently, as if the detective had just come off a double shift as a bus driver or something. "Have one of the motor units take you home, huh?"

Barron saw Valparaiso nod a thanks and move off toward the fire stairs, and then Red was turning to him.

"Go back with Lee and Halliday," he said directly. "Book the hostage as an accessory until we can find out who he is and what the hell's going on with him. Afterward go home and get some rest yourself." McClatchy paused, and Barron thought maybe he was going to offer some explanation. Instead he tightened the screw. "Tomorrow morning I want you to file the report on what happened here."

"Me?" Barron blurted, unbelieving.

"Yes, you, Detective."

"What the hell do I put in it?"

"The truth."

"What, that Donlan shot himself?"

Red's pause was deliberate. "Didn't he?"

19

ST. FRANCIS SANCTUARY, PASADENA, CALIFORNIA. SAME DAY, MARCH 12. 2:00 P.M.—THREE HOURS LATER.

Jacket off, shirtsleeves rolled up, badminton racket in hand, John Barron stood on the lawn in the shade of a towering sycamore tree watching a shuttlecock sail over the net toward him and trying desperately to put out of his mind what had happened in the hours just before. As the shuttlecock reached him he hit it back in a high arc, sending it over the net toward two nuns on the far side. One, Sister Mackenzie, ran up as if to swat it, then suddenly stepped aside for the jovial Sister Reynoso, who moved in to deftly spike it back over the net. Barron swung and missed and lost his footing, taking a graceful pratfall that landed him flat on his back staring up at the sky.

"Oh, are you alright, Mr. Barron?" Sister Reynoso ran up and peered through the net.

"I'm outmanned, Sister." Barron sat up, forcing a grin, and then looked off to the side of the court. "Come on, Rebecca, two against one. Give a little help, huh? I'm getting creamed."

"Yes, come on, Rebecca." Sister Reynoso stepped around the net. "Your brother needs your help."

Rebecca Henna Barron stood in the grass watching her

brother, a soft breeze playing with her dark hair so neatly pulled back in a ponytail, the badminton racket in her hands held as if it were the most foreign object in the world.

Barron got up from the ground and came toward her. "I know you can't hear me, but I also know you understand what's going on. We want you to play with us. Will you do that?"

Rebecca smiled gently, then looked to the ground and shook her head. Barron breathed deeply. This was the thing that never changed, the sadness that wholly encompassed her and kept her from even taking the first steps toward having any kind of life at all.

Rebecca was now twenty-three and had not spoken or given any indication she could hear since she had seen their mother and father shot to death by intruders in the living room of their San Fernando Valley home eight years earlier, when she was fifteen. From that moment on, the bright, fun-loving, animated tomboy he'd known all his life had become a shadow of a human being, one wrapped in an air of tragic fragility that made her seem utterly childlike and, at times, even helpless; whatever cognizance and ability to communicate she might still have lay buried beneath a mountain of deep trauma. Yet behind it, in the way she held herself, in the way she perked up whenever he visited, was the sharp, funny, and intelligent sister he remembered. And from what he had been told by a number of so-far-unsuccessful mental health professionals, including her current psychiatrist, the very respected Dr. Janet Flannery, if somehow, in some way, her soul could be unlocked and the darkness lifted, she would emerge from her dreadful cocoon like a bright butterfly and in a very short while begin to live a full and meaningful, perhaps even rich, life. But up to now it hadn't happened. There had been no change at all.

Barron lifted her chin so she would look at him directly.

"Hey, it's okay." He tried to grin. "We'll play another time. We will. I love you. You know that, don't you?"

Rebecca smiled, then cocked her head and studied him. He saw a troubled expression cross her face and stay there. Finally she put her fingers to her lips and then to his. She loved him, too, was what it meant. But the way she did it, holding his eyes the entire time, meant she knew something had disturbed him terribly and she wanted him to know she knew it.

20

Barron was pulling into the parking lot of Thrifty Dry, the discount dry cleaners where he had his laundry done. He was going through the motions, trying to shake off the trauma of Donlan's murder and think logically about what he would do next, when his cell phone rang. Automatically he clicked on. "Barron."

"John, it's Jimmy." It was Halliday, and there was an edge and excitement to his voice. "The Special Investigations people who went over the train. They found Raymond's bag. Some victim."

"What do you mean?"

"The bag. There was a forty-caliber Ruger automatic in it and two full ammunition clips."

"Jesus," Barron heard himself say. "His prints on it?"

"There were no prints on it, period. None."

"You mean he wore gloves."

"Maybe. They're going over the rest of the contents now. Polchak's going to run his prints and photo past the Chicago PD to see if they have anything on him there, and Lee's going down and talk to him about it. Red's got this buttoned up till we know more. Nothing to the media. Nothing to anyone."

"Right."

"John—" Barron heard the change in Halliday's voice. It was the same concern he had shown on the train before the operation to take Donlan began. "What happened today was rough, I know. But that's the way all of us were introduced to it. You'll get over it. It just takes a little time."

"Yeah."

"You okay?"

"Yeah."

"I'll let you know if there's more on Raymond."

7:10 P.M.

One deep breath and then another.

John Barron closed his eyes and leaned back in the shower of his small, rented Craftsman-style house in the Los Feliz section of the city and let the water rush over him.

"That's the way we were all introduced to it," Halliday had said. All introduced to it? That meant there had been more. Jesus God, how long had this kind of thing been going on?

Was he okay, Halliday had asked.

Okay? Jesus in Heaven.

It had now been nearly fifteen hours since he'd boarded the Southwest Chief in Barstow with Marty Valparaiso, almost ten since, shotgun in hand, he'd walked up the ramp in the parking garage shoulder to shoulder with Red McClatchy, a little more than that since Valparaiso, father of three, had walked up to a handcuffed man and shot him in the head.

Barron lifted his face to the showerhead, as if the force of the water itself would make the memory and the horror go away.

It didn't. If anything it grew stronger. The sharp *bang* of the gunshot still reverberated. Along with it came the sight of Donlan's body crumpling to the floor. In his mind he saw it again and again. Each time it played slower than the last, until it became a delicate ballet of still-motion illustrating the sheer force of gravity once life ceased to exist.

Then came the rest, as faces, words, images flooded his memory.

"Gives his name as Raymond Thorne. Says his IDs were left on the train." Lee was in the front passenger seat of the detectives' car reading from his notes as Halliday drove them through the parking structure on the way out. Barron rode in the back, alongside their handcuffed, still-incensed hostage/prisoner, trying desperately not to let any of them see the feelings of shock and nearly unbearable horror that still pumped through him.

"Claims to be a U.S. citizen born in Hungary." Lee half turned in his seat to look back at Barron. "Resides at twenty-seven West Eighty-sixth Street, New York City. Says he's a computer software rep for a German company. Spends most of his time on the road. Said he was taking the train to L.A. because an ice storm in Chicago closed the airports. That was where he met Donlan."

"I don't claim to be a U.S. citizen, I am a U.S. citizen," Raymond snapped at Lee. "And I am a victim. I was kidnapped and taken hostage. These men were on the train. They saw it happen. Why don't you ask them?"

Suddenly they came into bright sunlight as Halliday exited the garage, and they were moving toward a wall of satellite trucks and media people. Uniformed officers cleared the way as Halliday approached, and then they were driving past them, turning onto the street and driving away, on their way downtown to police headquarters at Parker Center.

Barron remembered the solemn profiles of Lee and Halliday as they sat in the front. They had been on the floor below when it happened. He knew now they had known exactly what was going to happen the moment they took "Raymond" out of there and down the fire stairs. It meant that the execution of someone like Donlan was some kind of business as usual and they expected that, because Barron was one of them, he would simply go along with it. But they were wrong. Wrong as they could be.

Abruptly Barron turned off the water and stepped out of the shower. He dried off and went through the mechanics of shaving but paid little attention to it. His mind was still filled with unrelenting vignettes of things that had happened in the hours since Valparaiso pulled the trigger. Within them, two indelible moments stood out.

The first was of driving through the horde of media outside the garage and seeing the short, young man in his familiar rumpled blue blazer, wrinkled khakis, and horn-rimmed glasses move right up to the car and stare in as they passed. Dan Ford was like that, as aggressive as any reporter in the city. And when he stared the way he had, it was exceedingly obvious because he had only one eye. The other was glass, although it was hard to tell—that is, until he began to stare intently with the good eye, as if making sure he actually saw what he thought he was seeing. That was what he had done then as Halliday drove past. And seeing him that close and staring, Barron had hurriedly looked away.

It wasn't so much that Ford wrote for the *Los Angeles Times*, or that, at twenty-six, Barron's own age, he was arguably the most respected police-beat reporter in the city, a guy who told the truth in what he wrote and who knew detectives in almost every one of the city's eighteen police-community areas. It was because he and John Barron were best friends, and had been since grade school. It was why he had so quickly turned away when Ford approached as they passed through the media line. Barron knew Ford would see the shock and revulsion in his eyes and would know something horrific had just taken place. And it wouldn't be long before he would ask about it.

The second moment took place at police headquarters and belonged to Raymond himself. He'd been photographed and fingerprinted and was on his way to lockup when he'd asked to talk with Barron. As the arresting officer, Barron had agreed, thinking Raymond was going to protest his innocence one last time. Instead, his prisoner had asked about his well-being. "You don't look well, John," he'd said quietly. "You seemed upset about something in the car. Are you alright?"

Raymond had given the slightest hint of a smile at the end, and Barron had erupted in anger, yelling for the guards to take him away. And they had, immediately taking him through steel doors that had closed hard behind him.

John.

Somehow Raymond had learned his name and was using it to get to him, as if he'd guessed what had happened to Donlan and had seen or sensed how deeply shocked Barron had been by it. His asking to see him was nothing more than a way to test Barron's reaction and confirm his guess, and Barron had fallen for it. The tiny smile, the smirk, the grin at the end was not only outrageous, it had been done on purpose and gave everything away. He might as well have finished by saying "thank you."

And what would he do when Lee went down to talk to him about the Ruger automatic found in his bag on the train? How would he respond to that? The answer was that he would do nothing more than play the innocent. He would either have a legitimate answer for the gun—it was his, he was on the road a lot, and it was licensed, which Barron doubted—or he would deny any knowledge of it, especially when he knew there were no fingerprints on it, and claim he had no idea where it had come from. Whatever the case, the subject of Donlan would not come up in any manner whatsoever. That little piece of business Raymond would keep between himself and John Barron.

7:25 P.M.

Barron pulled on a pair of gray workout sweats and walked barefoot into the kitchen to take a bottle of beer from the refrigerator. None of it would leave his mind. The killing had been devastating enough. Raymond's arrogant cleverness made it worse. The rest was in what the others had done afterward: Valparaiso's coming up to him with the official story of what had taken place; Polchak's mechanical removing of the handcuff and planting of the gun in Donlan's cold, dead hand. Then there was the famed Red McClatchy—his paternalistic concern for Valparaiso that, in effect, patted him on the head and sent him home; his calm radioing for both an ambulance and a tech crew who would go over the "crime scene" and, no doubt, formally confirm whatever Red told them; his order demanding that John file the report on it. Aside from the killing itself, it was the last that was cruelest.

Like the others, Barron was already an accessory to murder by the simple fact that he'd been there. But by filing the report, typing it up and putting his name on it, he became a collaborator, his name right there on the bottom of the page as the police officer who certified the cover-up. It meant he could say nothing to anyone without incriminating himself. It was murder and he was part of it, whether he liked it or not. And whether he liked it or not, he was certain Raymond, no matter who he was or what he had been up to, knew what had happened.

Beer in hand, Barron closed the refrigerator door, his mind spinning. He was a cop, he wasn't supposed to be sickened or disturbed like this, but he was. The circumstances were different and he was older, but the shock and horror and disbelief twisting in his stomach now were the same as they had been that night eight years earlier when, at eighteen, he'd come home and seen the flashing lights of police cars and ambulances in the street outside his house. He'd been out with Dan Ford and some other friends. In his absence, three young men had broken into his house and shot and killed his mother and father directly in front of Rebecca. Neighbors had heard the shots and seen the three men run from the house and get into a black car and speed away. A "home invasion robbery gone bad," the police had called it. To this day no one knew why Rebecca hadn't been killed as well. Instead she'd been sentenced to a lifetime in Hell.

By the time Barron arrived, Rebecca had already been taken to a psychiatric hospital. And Dan Ford, seeing him paralyzed by the horrible impact of what had just happened and realizing that Barron's family had been insular and that he had no relatives or even close family friends he could turn to, had immediately called his own parents and arranged for John to come to their house and to stay as long as he needed. It was all a nightmare of police and flashing lights and confusion. Barron could still see the look on the face of the next-door neighbor as he came from the house. He was trembling, his eyes distant, his face the color of fireplace ash. It was only later Barron learned that he had volunteered to identify the bodies so that John wouldn't have to.

For days afterward he lived in the same mode of shock and horror and disbelief he felt now, as he tried to deal with what had happened and work with the various agencies to find a place for Rebecca. And then the shock turned to massive guilt. It was all his fault and he knew it. If only he had been there he might have done something to prevent it. He never should have gone out with his friends. He had deserted his mother and father and sister. If only he had been there. If only. If only.

And then the guilt turned to anger of the deepest kind and he wanted to become a cop right then and deal firsthand with these kinds of murderers. Those feelings deepened as days and weeks and months passed and the killers were never found.

John Barron had initially gone to college at Cal Poly in San Luis Obispo to study landscape architecture and follow a dream of a career designing formal gardens that he had held since he'd been a child. After the murder of his parents he'd transferred immediately to the University of California at Los Angeles to be closer to Rebecca and to pursue a bachelor's degree in English in preparation for law school, where he planned to study criminal law; he had visions of one day becoming a prosecutor or even a judge, choosing to enter law enforcement from that end. But with the money from his parents' life insurance nearly gone and Rebecca's expenses growing, he needed to find a full-time job, and he did—with the Los Angeles Police Department, academy to patrol cop to detective, all in rapid order.

Five years after joining the LAPD, he was a member of the renowned century-old 5-2 Squad, walking up a ramp in an abandoned garage side by side with the legendary Red Mc-Clatchy in search of an escaped killer. It was the dream job of every cop on the LAPD and probably half the other cops in the world and had been accomplished by a combination of hard work, his own intelligence, and a sense of deep commitment to the life he had taken on.

And then, in an instant, it all shattered, the same as his life had shattered that dark and awful night eight years before.

"Why?" he suddenly yelled out loud. "Why?"

Why, when Donlan was unarmed and already in custody? What kind of law enforcement was that? What code were they going by? Their own vigilante law? Was that why joining the squad was a commitment for life that you agreed to when you were sworn in? Nobody quit the 5-2 ever. That was the rule. Period.

Barron wrenched open the beer and started to drink. Then he saw the framed picture on the table beside the refrigerator. It was a photograph of him and Rebecca taken at St. Francis. Their arms were around each other and they were laughing. "Brother and sister of the year," the caption read. He didn't remember when it had been taken or even what it was for, except maybe showing up as often as he did to spend a little time with her. Somehow he'd done it today; tomorrow he couldn't even begin to think about.

Then, suddenly and from nowhere, a calm settled over him as he realized it didn't make any difference what the rules of the squad were. Never again would there be room in his life for cold-blooded killing, especially when it came from the police. He knew then what he had known almost from the moment Donlan had been taken down—that there was only one thing he could do. Find someplace far from L.A. where Rebecca could be treated and then simply take her and leave. He might have been the last to join the 5-2, but he was going to be the first in LAPD history to quit it.

21

Raymond stood at his cell door staring out at the darkened cell-block. He was alone and wore an orange jumpsuit with the word PRISONER stenciled on the back. He had a sink, a bunk, and a toilet, all of which were in clear view of anyone walking past in the corridor outside. How many other prisoners there were, or what their crimes had been, he had no idea. All he knew was that none were like him or could ever be. Not today, probably not ever. At least in America.

"You have the right to legal counsel," the huge and imposing African-American policeman had said, reading him his rights under law. Legal counsel? What did that mean now? Especially as the walls began to close in around him as he had known all along they would. It was a process that had already begun when the same huge, imposing African-American policeman had come to see him to ask about the Ruger. His reply had been what it would have been if he had been caught on the train and the gun found in his bag there—simply to lie. To act wholly surprised and tell him he had no idea at all where the weapon had come from. He had been on the train for a long time. Back and forth to the dining car, the toilet, just up taking a walk and stretching. Anyone could have put it there. Most likely Donlan, as a backup to his own gun. He had spoken to the detective seriously and in all innocence, still protesting that he was a victim, not a criminal. Finally the detective had thanked him for his cooperation and left. If nothing else, Raymond had bought himself a little more time.

The question now was, how soon would they realize everything he'd told them was false? When they did, their attention to everything else would suddenly ratchet up. How long would it be before they contacted the Chicago police to talk about the

Ruger and to see if he had a criminal record or outstanding warrants there? And no matter how many murders had been committed in Chicago over the weekend, how long would it be before the matter of the two men shot and killed in the Pearson Street tailor shop came up? Among other things, the caliber of the murder weapon would be discussed. How long after that before the Chicago police asked for a ballistics test on the Ruger? And even without fingerprints on the gun, how quickly would they start putting things together and wonder what the link was between the safe deposit keys, his recent travels in and out of the country, the men murdered in Chicago, his arrival and purpose in Los Angeles, and the plane ticket to London?

10:50 P.M.

Abruptly Raymond turned and walked back to his bunk and sat down, thinking of the odds against the incredible string of coincidences that had happened in such a short time. Somehow he had been on the same train, in the same car, and playing cards with a man wanted badly enough by the police that when it was discovered he was on the train, LAPD undercover agents had been sent to board it in the middle of the night to make certain he didn't escape. Then, of all the passengers on the coach, this same man had taken him hostage. And, in very nearly the same breath, the police had seen him jump into a hijacked car with his captor and assumed they were accomplices, which was hardly the truth, but nonetheless why he was here.

Raymond gritted his teeth in anger. It had all been so carefully thought out. He was one man traveling light, his weapons in place ahead of time. In his single cell phone he had all the communication he would need to stay in touch with the Baroness for such a short period of time. What should have been so simple had instead unraveled into an absurd and inconceivable series of events that, combined with his frustration at being unable to discover the French location of the safe deposit box, something wholly unforeseen because the instructions in the envelopes that held the safe deposit keys, which he had read and destroyed, were to have included that information but hadn't, was enough to— Suddenly he realized: These things were not accidental at all. They were inevitable. It was the thing Russians called *sudba,* his destiny, and what he had been prepared for and warned of since childhood—that God would test him over and over throughout his lifetime in trials that would tax his courage and devotion, his toughness, his cleverness, and his will to prevail in the most profound difficulties. Since his youth and up until this point he had prevailed. And impossible as his situation seemed now, this should be no different.

The thought gave him comfort, and he realized that for all the darkness surrounding him he had one thing in his favor: the mistake the police had made in killing Donlan. The why of it was not important; the fact that they had done it was. The single resounding gunshot had been enough for him to guess. It was a conjecture substantiated by the facial expression and body language of the young detective, John Barron, when he'd joined them in the police car moments later. Confirmation of it had come in Barron's quick and angry response at the end of the booking procedure when Raymond had questioned his state of well-being. So yes, the police had killed Donlan. And yes, Barron had been markedly shaken by it. How or if Raymond could use the information, he didn't know, but Barron was the key, the weak link. He was young and emotional and troubled by his own conscience. Barron was someone who in the right circumstance might well be exploited.

22

HOLLYWOOD COFFEE SHOP, SUNSET BOULEVARD.
WEDNESDAY, MARCH 13. 1:50 A.M.

"Let me go over this again." Dan Ford adjusted his horn-rimmed glasses and looked to the battered pocket-sized spiral notebook in front of him. "The other cardplayers were William and Vivian Woods of Madison, Wisconsin."

"Yes." John Barron glanced down the length of the diner. They were in a rear booth of the all-night diner they had nearly to themselves. The exceptions were three teenagers giggling at a table near the door and a silver-haired waitress chatting across the counter with a couple of gas company employees who looked as if they'd just come off work.

"The conductor's name was James Lynch, L-Y-N-C-H, of Flagstaff, Arizona." Ford drained the coffee from a cup at his elbow. "He'd been an Amtrak employee for seventeen years."

Barron nodded. Particulars about what had happened on the Southwest Chief and the names of the people involved, so far withheld from the press pending further investigation and notification of next of kin, were what he'd promised when Ford called him at home sometime after eleven. Barron had been awake, watching television after having spent the last hours trying to think through how to leave the squad and get out of L.A. Where to go and how best to do it with Rebecca. A call to her psychiatrist, Dr. Janet Flannery, had not been returned, and when the phone rang he expected it to be her. Instead it was Dan Ford calling to see how he was after his first real shift with the squad, and then to ask if he could talk about what had happened.

He'd started to ask if Ford had talked to Lee or Halliday or any of the others but caught himself. Dan Ford was his best friend, and at some point he would have to talk to him, and, if Ford was willing to leave Nadine, his pert French wife, who, after two years, he still called his bride and treated as such— this was as good a time as any. Besides, it got him away from thinking about the media coverage of the aftermath of the killings on the Chief and the chase and death of Frank Donlan that seemed to be on every TV channel. He'd seen the train, stopped in the rail yards, seen the bags containing the bodies of Bill Woods and the conductor brought off, over and over. He'd seen the parking garage and the unmarked Ford with Halliday at the wheel, glimpsing himself in the rear seat sitting next to Raymond, driving off through the army of media, seen the coroner's van bearing Donlan's body in the same setting, seen Red McClatchy at Parker Center standing alongside Chief of Police Louis Harwood, as Harwood reiterated Valparaiso's tale of Donlan's "suicide" for the cameras—Marty's version at once the official version, as Barron knew it would be.

"The so-called hostage identified himself as—" Again Ford looked to his notes. "Raymond Thorne, T-H-O-R-N-E, from New York City. He's being held in custody until positive identification is established."

"He has a hearing at eight-thirty this morning," Barron said. "He'll either walk or he won't. Depends on what checks out." It was clear that Red's order to keep silent about the finding of the Ruger automatic in Raymond's bag was in force, because if anyone outside the department could know about the gun, it would be Dan Ford.

Barron looked to the coffee cup cradled in his hands. So far he had done alright, giving Ford the information he could, not letting his emotions get the best of him. But he didn't know how much longer he could do it. He felt like a junkie. If he didn't get a fix soon he was going to jump right out of his skin. In his case the fix was looking Ford in the eye and telling him everything.

Reporter or not, Dan Ford was the only person in the world he kept no secrets from, who from the moment of his parents' murders had taken care of him like a brother even when Ford had gone off halfway across the country to Northwestern University.

Even then at long distance Ford had kept helping, working with Barron to fight through the impossible tangle of state and local agencies, insurance companies, and organizations, to make it possible for Rebecca to remain at St. Francis and to fund her considerable and ongoing psychotherapy as well.

And he'd done it all without grudge or malice toward the friend who had caused Ford to lose his eye when they were boys—ten-year-olds fashioning a short length of pipe as a rocket launcher, packing it with nails and BBs, then using two huge, illegal firecrackers for propulsion. Firecrackers an excited John Barron had ignited prematurely, blowing out a neighbor's garage window two blocks away and somehow propelling a nail backward and into the pupil of Dan Ford's right eye. The hell they had to pay for that had been purchased with half of his best friend's sight.

Now, sixteen years after that fateful afternoon, here they

were, huddled in a back booth of an all-night diner on Sunset Boulevard at an hour approaching two in the morning, with Barron expected at Parker Center at eight to make out the report on Frank "Whitey" Donlan's "suicide"—and Barron needing Dan Ford probably more than he ever had in his life, desperately wanting to tell him everything.

But he couldn't.

He'd known it from the moment he'd walked in and seen Ford already there and waiting. Right then he knew that if he shared the things inside him, he would put Ford in very nearly the same position he was in himself. Once Dan Ford knew, friendship would supersede his professionalism and he would say nothing. By his own silence he would become an accessory himself.

It didn't matter that Barron planned to quit the squad. Right now he was still a policeman and a member of it, and because of what the squad was and who Red McClatchy was, if the truth of what happened ever came to light, the scandal would be colossal and anyone even remotely involved with the accused would be under the glare of a hugely intense, public spotlight. Reporters, prosecutors, and legislators would look under every rock, turn every pebble, and there wasn't a Los Angeles journalist or detective working Central Division who didn't know about the long Ford and Barron friendship. A local television station had even done a story about them for the six o'clock news. No matter where Barron might be later, that day he had been a member of the 5-2 and had been in the garage when Donlan had been shot, and Ford would be asked what Barron might have told him about it. If Ford avoided answering, his circumvention would raise a red flag, and there would be little doubt the prosecution would call him to answer the same questions under oath. Barron knew his friend far too well to think that, even then, he would say anything. In denying what he knew, Ford would be committing perjury, or, if he took the Fifth Amendment, it would be the same as admitting guilt. Either way it would be the end of his career, his livelihood, his future. Everything.

So the only way out was to give Ford nothing more than the information he'd promised, then say he had to get some sleep and end the meeting as quickly as possible by calling the waitress for the check.

"Talk to me about Donlan."

"What?" Barron looked up sharply.

Ford had put down his notebook and was peering over his horn-rims. "I said, talk to me about Donlan."

Barron felt as if the floor had suddenly collapsed under him. He struggled like hell to keep his composure. "You mean on the train."

"I mean in the garage. For one thing, you've got four detectives and only one Whitey Donlan. And not just any four detectives—Red McClatchy, Polchak, Valparaiso, and you. The best there are. Now I realize Donlan had a lot of experience with guns and handcuffs, but suddenly he's got a hide-gun these four detectives missed?"

"What are you getting at?" Barron stared at him, his mind and emotions turned upside down, the way they had been the moment Donlan was shot.

"The details you gave me are available from almost anyone at Parker Center." Dan Ford's eyes, the glass one and the real one, crept up to hold on Barron's. "I was there when Halliday drove you away from the garage. You were sitting in back with this Raymond what's-his-name. You saw me, you looked away. Why?"

"If I did, I didn't realize it. A hell of a lot was going on."

Ford suddenly looked away. The waitress was coming toward them with the coffeepot. Ford shook his head and waved her off, then looked back to Barron. "What *was* going on, John? Tell me."

Barron wanted to leave right then, get up and walk out, but he couldn't. Suddenly he heard himself pour out Valparaiso's words almost verbatim, the same way they'd come out on television from Chief Harwood.

"Nobody knows. Somehow Donlan managed to have a snub-nosed twenty-two hidden in his pants. When we tried to take him downstairs he got one of his cuffs off, he yelled, 'This is as far as I go,' and there was the gun and—bang."

Dan Ford stared at him. "Just like that?"

Barron stared back, unwavering. "I never saw a man kill himself before."

23

Barron lay in the darkness trying to forget the way he'd lied to Dan Ford—Valparaiso's explanation of Donlan's murder erupting from inside him as if it were his own. His lie had horrified him almost as much as the murder itself, and he'd left as quickly as he could, forcing himself to look Ford in the eye and telling him he was bone tired, then giving the waitress a twenty-dollar bill to cover a four-dollar-and-fifty-cent check for the coffee, simply because he couldn't bear to stand there and wait for change. Then he was gone, getting into his vintage 1967 Ford Mustang and driving home through the empty streets.

Once there he checked his answering machine. There were two calls. The first had come shortly after he'd gone out to meet Dan Ford and was from Halliday, telling him Lee had visited Raymond at Parker Center and their "victim" had denied any knowledge of the automatic found in his bag. More than that, neither the weapon itself nor the two ammunition clips had fingerprints. All were perfectly clean, as if whoever had used them had either wiped them down thoroughly or worn gloves when handling them. "This guy is something, John," Halliday had finished. "What, I don't know but we're gonna find out. See you in the morning."

The second call had been from Dr. Flannery. It had been too late to call her then, and he knew he would have to wait for morning, the same as he would have to wait to do anything more about the logistics of leaving the squad. How he would do it and when and where he would go all centered on finding a facility for Rebecca, hopefully as far from L.A. as possible, and that was something he had to put fully in the hands of Dr. Flannery. So, with the second worst day of his life behind him, he had gone finally and gratefully to bed.

Sleep still refused to come. In its place was the slowly churning turmoil of wondering how he had become so alone as to have only one person on the earth he could talk to. His friends from the past, from high school and college, had gone their own ways, and his adult life, while still distantly focused on the idea of one day getting a law degree in criminal justice, had been directed by his responsibility for Rebecca. He'd had to find a secure job and do the best he could at it, which he had with the LAPD. And while there had been relationships among the patrol officers and detectives he'd worked with on the way up, none had lasted long enough to develop into the kind of genuine friendship that came from years of shared experiences. Nor were there the other people and resources that so many others had—relatives, clergy, even psychological counseling.

Both he and Rebecca had been adopted in infancy. Their adoptive mother and father had been from Maryland and Illinois, respectively, and their own parents were long dead. Rarely did they speak of, let alone have contact with, other members of the family, so if he had distant aunts or uncles or cousins, he didn't know it. Moreover, his adoptive father had been Jewish, his mother Catholic, and they had raised their children with no religious bent at all; therefore he had no pastor, priest, or rabbi in whom to confide. The fact that Rebecca was being cared for by nuns was only happenstance, reflecting the reality that St. Francis was the best, and perhaps only, place for her that was close by and that he could afford. As for counseling, in her eight years at St. Francis, Rebecca had seen five different psychotherapists, and not one, not even her current psychiatrist, the seemingly very capable Dr. Flannery, had been able even to begin to lift her from the plane of deep trauma where she lived. It made turning in that direction hardly an option with which he could feel comfortable.

So there it was, of the billions of human beings on earth, he had a grand total of two he felt close enough to open his heart to—Rebecca and Dan Ford. And for reasons most obvious, he could talk to neither.

3:57 A.M.

Finally he began to drift off. As he did and the darkness began to comfort, he saw a shadow rise and come toward him. It was Valparaiso, and he had a gun in his hand. Then he saw Donlan, standing terrified, clamped in Polchak's viselike grip. Valparaiso walked right up to him and put the gun to his head.

"No, don't!" Donlan screamed.

Bang!

24

PARKER CENTER. STILL WEDNESDAY,
MARCH 13. 7:15 A.M.

The 5-2 squad room was small and utilitarian, furnished with six old and scarred steel desks and worn swivel chairs to match. On each desk was a state-of-the-art computer and multiline telephone, while a shared printer near the door rested on a table under a large wall-mounted blackboard. A second wall was corkboard and filled with notes and photographs of people and locations of cases under investigation. Another wall was a bank of windows covered by venetian blinds drawn against the morning sun. A detailed map of the city of Los Angeles covered the fourth wall, and it was in front of this fourth wall that John Barron sat, alone in the room, staring at the computer screen on his desk. And what he had entered on it.

DATE: 12 March
FILE NUMBER: 01714
SUBJECT: Frank "Whitey" Donlan
ADDRESS: Unknown
REPORTING INVESTIGATOR: Detective II, John J. Barron
ASSISTING INVESTIGATORS: Commander Arnold

McClatchy; Detective III, Martin Valparaiso; Detective III, Leonard Polchak

Barron stared for a moment longer and then coldly, mechanically, began typing. Picking up where he had left off, doing as Commander McClatchy had instructed. Doing it for himself, for Rebecca, even for Dan Ford. Taking the only way out he knew.

OTHER INVESTIGATORS: Detective III, Roosevelt Lee; Detective III, James Halliday
OFFICE OF ORIGIN: 5-2 Squad, Central Division
CLASSIFICATION: Suicide by self-inflicted gunshot wou

Abruptly Barron stopped. Selecting the last, he hit the DELETE key, and "Suicide by self-inflicted gunshot wou" vanished from the screen. Then he angrily typed in:

CLASSIFICATION: Homicide
COMPLAINT: Execution of suspect-in-custody by Detective III, Martin Valparaiso

Barron stopped again. Selecting the entire document, he hit the DELETE key, and the screen went blank. A second later he sat back and for the fourth time in the last fifteen minutes looked at his watch.

7:29 A.M.

It was still early. He didn't care.

7:32 A.M.

Barron entered a small, brightly lit mini-cafeteria—a room with several vending machines, a half-dozen Formica tables, and a number of plastic chairs. A uniformed sergeant sat chatting with two secretaries in civilian clothes at the table nearest the door. Other than that the room was empty.

Barron nodded politely toward them, then went to a coffee machine and dropped in three quarters. Afterward he hit the MILK AND SUGAR key and waited as a cardboard cup dropped into place and began to fill. Cup full, the machine clicked off. He picked up the coffee and carried it to a corner table where he sat down, his back to the others.

He took a sip of coffee, then slid his cell phone from his jacket and dialed. On the third ring the phone was picked up and a familiar female voice answered. "This is Dr. Flannery."

"Dr. Flannery, it's John Barron."

"I called you back last night. Did you get the message?"

"Yes, thank you. I had to go out." Barron glanced up at a boisterous laugh from the threesome across the room. Immediately he looked back to the phone and lowered his voice. "Doctor, I need your help. I want to find another facility for Rebecca somewhere away from L.A., preferably out of California."

"Is something wrong, Detective?"

"It's—" Barron searched for the right word. "Personal, confidential—and," he added, "extremely urgent, for reasons I can't explain yet. I want to change some things in my life, and the first step is finding a place for Rebecca. I haven't really thought where, maybe Oregon, Washington State, or Colorado, somewhere like that. But it needs to be away from here and done as soon as possible."

There was a long silence, and Barron knew she was trying to understand what was going on. "Detective Barron," she said finally, "considering Rebecca's condition, I think you and I should sit down and talk."

"Hey, John!"

Barron looked up sharply at the sound of his name. Halliday had just entered the room and was coming toward him quickly.

Barron turned back to the phone. "Let me call you a little later, Doctor. Thank you." He clicked off just as Halliday reached him.

"There is no Raymond Thorne on Eighty-sixth Street in Manhattan," Halliday said emphatically. "The German computer company he claimed he worked for doesn't exist. His prints and ID came back clean from the Chicago PD, but we just found out they had two men tortured and shot to death in a tailor shop last Sunday not long before Raymond got on board the Southwest Chief. The murder weapon wasn't recovered, but the autopsies suggest it's about the same caliber as the Ruger found in Raymond's bag. They want a ballistics test done on it.

"That bag also had a first class ticket in the name of Raymond Thorne from L.A. to London on a flight that left LAX at five-forty Monday afternoon, which suggests he wasn't originally planning a two-day train trip to get here. I'm working with the Feds trying to get someone at State Department Passport Assistance to get us a readout on the magnetic tape on his passport. Polchak's setting up the ballistics test. You go down to Raymond's hearing at Criminal Courts and make sure the judge doesn't let him out on bail."

For the briefest moment Barron sat staring, as if he hadn't heard.

"John." Halliday pressed him. "Did you hear what I said?"

"Yeah, Jimmy, I heard." Barron was suddenly on his feet and sliding the cell phone into his jacket. "I'm on my way."

25

CRIMINAL COURTS BUILDING, SAME TIME, 7:50 A.M.

Dressed in his orange jumpsuit, his hands cuffed behind him, Raymond shared an elevator with two thickly built deputies in tight uniforms who had escorted him from Parker Center and were taking him to his hearing in a courtroom on an upper floor. This was the moment he'd decided on between the few brief hours he'd slept during the night.

The idea that he might use the young and uncertain Detective Barron as a way out still lingered, but time was passing quickly. His original purpose in coming to Los Angeles had been for a final confrontation with the arrogant and outspoken Beverly Hills jeweler, Alfred Neuss. That he had chosen to go to him last was integral to the operation.

The initial phase of the plan had been to quickly and quietly collect the safe deposit keys from the people in San Francisco, Mexico City, and Chicago, and then equally quickly and quietly eliminate the keys' holders. If that phase had worked as it should have, he would not only have the keys but at the same time would have learned the name and location of the French bank that contained the safe deposit box. Having that information, he would have immediately sent the first two keys by overnight express to Jacques Bertrand in Zurich. The third key would be sent the same way to the Baroness in London, where he would collect it upon his arrival on Tuesday. The following day he would travel to France and retrieve the contents of the box and then return immediately to London for crucial appointments the next day, which was Thursday, the day before they would carry out the deed itself—which was to be done in London on Friday, March 15, which was, most ironically, the Ides of March.

The second phase of the plan, and the reason for making Alfred Neuss his final stop in the Americas, had been to kill him—an act that would add immense leverage to their power base for what was to come on Friday. But his failure, even after torturing his victims, to learn the bank's name and location made him realize that the distribution of the keys had merely been a safeguard, and that without knowing where the box was, forwarding the safe deposit box keys to either Bertrand or the Baroness would be senseless. The truth, as he finally realized, was that only two men in the world knew in what bank and in what French city the box was located, and Alfred Neuss was one of them. It was a truth that greatly ratcheted up the game and made getting to him more urgent than ever.

From the beginning timing had been everything, and it still was. All the more so in light of the information the police would now have. It meant he had no choice but to take definitive action before he became implicated any deeper in the American judicial system.

7:52 A.M.

One floor passed, then two.

The deputies were staring ahead, not looking at him. Jaws set, pistols clipped into rugged belt holsters alongside nightsticks and handcuffs, radio microphones fastened to shirt collars, their bulging muscles and steely, detached attitude conveyed the obvious intimidation: They were fully prepared to take any action necessary in the event their prisoner became difficult.

Yet Raymond knew that despite all that bearing and bravado they were little more than city workers collecting a salary. His motivation, on the other hand, was immeasurably larger and infinitely more complex. Taken with the extent of his training, the difference was immense.

26

7:53 A.M.

Neither deputy saw Raymond turn his wrists nimbly behind him, nor saw him slip off one handcuff, then the other. Neither saw his left hand move forward to flip the holster loop covering the closest deputy's 9 mm Beretta. It was only in the nanosecond that followed that they sensed danger and started to turn. By then it was too late. The Beretta was placed behind the first deputy's ear and then the other's, one, two, with blinding speed.

The ear-shattering roar of the gunshots filled the tiny chamber, dying away just as the elevator reached its designated floor and stopped. Calmly, Raymond pressed the button for the top floor, and the elevator started upward again. One of the deputies moaned. Raymond ignored him, the same way he ignored the pungent smell of gunpowder and the blood slowly oozing across the elevator's floor. He stripped off his orange prisoner's suit and pulled on the first deputy's pants and shirt. Then he took the guns from both men and stood up, adjusting his deputy uniform as the elevator came to a stop.

Immediately the door slid open, revealing a broad hallway in a public building filled with people. Quickly he touched the button for the ground floor, then stepped into the hallway. A half second later the elevator doors closed behind him and he walked off into the crowd, looking for the nearest staircase.

7:55 A.M.

The Criminal Courts Building was two blocks down and across the street from Parker Center, and Barron walked the distance quickly, the core of him locked into the nearly overwhelming rawness of his own emotions, the rage and anger toward the squad, who they really were and what they had done so coldly not just to Donlan but to him. At the same time, the practical side of him told him it would take time to find a place to relocate Rebecca, and until that time came and he actually put her in the car and made the move, there was nothing he could do but play along, do his job, and not tip his hand.

7:58 A.M.

Dressed in the fallen deputy's uniform, the Beretta automatics of the dead officers tucked into his waistband, Raymond ran down one flight of fire stairs, and then another. Suddenly he stopped. A man in jeans and a black jacket was coming up the stairs. Who he was or what he was doing there made no difference. What Raymond needed was something to cover his uniform and the Berettas. The black jacket would do.

Immediately Raymond started down.

Two stairs. Three. Four. The man was right there. Raymond nodded as they passed. A half beat more and Raymond turned and went back up.

8:00 A.M.

The two Berettas tucked inside the black jacket, Raymond pushed through the stairwell door and stepped into a public corridor. This one, like the one he'd left moments earlier, swarmed with people.

He walked down it deliberately, trying to act as if he had some particular destination. Signs were everywhere. This court, that court, restrooms, elevators. The sheer number of people he had to move around slowed him, and that was troublesome because time was an ever more important factor. By now the bodies of the deputies would have been discovered, and with them his orange prisoner's jumpsuit. At any minute he could expect the building to come alive with an army of law enforcement officers looking for him.

"Hey, you!" A bailiff with a radio-microphone on his shirt collar was coming toward him. To this man the jacket did not hide his uniform. Instead it called attention to it. Raymond ignored him and kept walking.

"I said you! In the deputy pants!" The bailiff kept coming. Raymond looked back and saw him start to speak into the microphone at his collar.

Raymond simply stopped and turned, firing point-blank with both guns. The roar of gunshots shook the hall. The bailiff danced sideways, then fell backward, toppling over an elderly man in a wheelchair. People screamed and ran, ducking for cover. Raymond walked quickly away.

5-2 SQUAD ROOM. 8:02 A.M.

"We're on our way! Barron's there now!" Halliday slammed down the phone and headed for the door. Polchak was running and already halfway through it.

CRIMINAL COURTS BUILDING. 8:03 A.M.

Barron fought his way across the main floor against a torrent of panic. Terrified people coming from everywhere were trying to get out of harm's way, running from the cafeteria and the main corridor by the elevators, pouring out of fire-stairs doors. All he knew was what Halliday had radioed: The two deputies transporting Raymond had been killed, and there had been shooting on an upper floor.

"Christ!" he muttered under his breath, his personal monsters shoved aside by the immediate crisis and the rush of adrenaline surging with it.

Suddenly a man in a black jacket pushed past Barron in a crowd rushing from a fire-stairs door. It was another step before Barron realized.

"Whoa!" He whirled to see Raymond struggle through an emergency exit and take off, hurtling past the throng of people trying to escape him.

Barron's Beretta came up in his hand and he shoved his way toward the door, knocking people aside as he did. Outside he could see Raymond running down the long zigzag pedestrian ramp toward the parking lot. At the same time, uniforms were racing in from everywhere.

"Black jacket!" Barron barked into his radio. "He's heading down the parking lot ramp!"

Raymond hit the bottom of the ramp on the run. Using the crowd for cover, he saw the street and ran for it.

A split second later Barron bolted out the doors and raced down the ramp. At the same time, Halliday and Polchak banged through the doors behind him.

"You! Black jacket! Freeze!" A female voice barked behind a racing Raymond.

He whirled, his hand reaching under the jacket, a stolen Beretta coming up in it. A uniformed policewoman stood twenty paces away, her weapon pointed right at him.

"Watch it!" Barron screamed too late.

Boom! Boom!

Raymond squeezed off two quick rounds. The policewoman staggered backward and fell to the pavement, her gun firing once as she did.

Raymond glanced back toward the building, then dodged around a Cadillac and took off, ducking behind parked cars, running for the street. Barron pulled up hard at the base of the ramp, Beretta held in two hands, taking careful aim. Raymond saw him and twisted away just as Barron fired.

Searing heat tore in a straight line across Raymond's throat, throwing him off balance. He nearly fell, then recovered and half staggered, half ran on, one hand pressed against the wound at his throat. Behind him three black-and-white patrol units screeched into the parking lot. To his left he could see three more slide around a corner coming down the street toward him. At the same time, a taxi pulled up directly in front of him. A rear door opened and a middle-aged African-American woman got out, followed by a young African-American teenage girl.

Raymond pulled his hand from his throat. There was a little blood, but not much. The slug had merely creased and burned him. In five steps he was at the cab. His left hand flashed out and he dragged the terrified teenager to him. Spinning her around, he shoved a Beretta automatic tight against her head and looked up. What he saw was a dozen or more heavily armed uniformed police coming toward him. He could see them trying to find a way to shoot him without killing her. To both his left and right, more black-and-white police cars cordoned off the street. Then he saw John Barron push past the uniforms and come toward him. Two of the plainclothes detectives from the garage were with him; one of them had been on the train.

"Stop there!" Raymond yelled, his eyes going to the middle-aged woman who had climbed from the cab with the girl. She stood frozen in the middle of the street caught between him and the police. She was staring at him, horrified.

"Put down your weapon, Raymond!" Barron shouted. "Let her go! Let her go!" He and the other two were twenty yards away and still coming.

"One more step, John, and I will kill her," Raymond said loudly but calmly, his blue-green eyes locked on Barron's.

Barron stopped; so did Halliday and Polchak. There it was again. The familiarity, the cool composure.

"See if you can work your way for a side shot," Barron said quietly.

Halliday moved slowly left, Polchak right.

"No!" The woman was suddenly screaming. "No! No! Everybody stay away from him! Stay away!"

"Hold it," Barron breathed. Halliday and Polchak stopped where they were.

"Thank you," Raymond said to the woman. Then, with the gun still to the girl's head, he backed up until the two were against the cab. Inside he could see the cabbie hunched over, trying to hide from sight.

"Get out!" he commanded. "Get out!"

Like a scene out of a cartoon, the driver's door flew open and the cabbie bolted out.

"Run! Run away!" Raymond shouted. And the cabbie ran off toward the police. Then Raymond swung back to look at Barron.

"Please move the police cars, John, we're going that way." He nodded toward the street in front of him.

Barron hesitated, then looked to a uniformed sergeant behind him. "Let him out."

The sergeant paused before speaking into his radio. A moment later the black-and-whites at the end of the street backed up, opening the roadway.

The Beretta held fast against the young girl's head, Raymond shoved her into the taxi's front passenger seat, then slid in behind the wheel. The door slammed. There was a shriek of tires and the cab screamed off. Two seconds later it rocketed past the black-and-whites at the end of the block and was gone.

8:14 A.M.

27

CRIMINAL COURTS BUILDING. 8:15 A.M.

"How the hell could he get away? There are a hundred uniforms in this building. Fifty more outside!"

Valparaiso at his sleeve, McClatchy pushed angrily through a gang of uniforms, dismayed judges, and court officers. Shoving through a door, he went fast down the fire stairs toward the basement. McClatchy was angrier than Valparaiso had ever seen him. It got even worse as the word "hostage" came over their radios in a scramble of police-speak as they pushed through the door at the bottom and went into the underground garage, where Polchak waited behind the wheel of Red's unmarked Ford.

"What hostage?" Red barked at Polchak, buckling in beside him as Valparaiso jumped into the rear seat.

"Teenage female," Polchak told him. "African-American. That's all we know. Her aunt was with her, they're talking to her now."

"Where the hell is Roosevelt?"

Red light and siren, Polchak screamed up the ramp and turned into traffic. "Taking his kid to the dentist. His wife works," he said, nearly sideswiping a city bus.

"I know his wife works!" McClatchy was furious. At them, at the hundred and fifty other cops, at the whole thing.

"Christ!"

Five black-and-whites and one unmarked detective's car followed the United Independent taxi, number 7711, through the city streets in a slow-speed chase. Each car had its powerful roof lights dancing, but that was all; the sirens were purposely kept silent. Above, Air 14, an LAPD helicopter, had been quickly scrambled and was keeping pace. All along the route—South Grand Avenue to Twenty-third Street, Twenty-third to Figueroa, then south on Figueroa—people stood on the sidewalk waving and cheering as the 7711 taxi passed. The whole show was being seen live on TV as helicopters from three television stations followed the action from high above. Police chases were common in L.A. and had been for years, but they were still followed by a massive television audience that had station managers wishing they could have two or three a week just to boost ratings.

Barron and Halliday rode in 3-Adam-34, the lead black-and-white, commandeered from the mass of black-and-whites that suddenly descended on the Criminal Courts Building. This was no thrill-a-second movie chase; this was a solemn procession at twenty-five miles an hour. All they could do was follow, and try to project what Raymond had planned for the moment when it ended. If they had any advantage at all, it was that Red McClatchy was one of the best hostage negotiators in the business and that two of the following four black-and-whites held crack LAPD sharpshooters.

Halliday leaned forward in the passenger seat watching the cab tracking a quarter mile ahead of them, the morning sun glinting off the windows. The tinted rear windows made it especially hard to see inside, let alone determine if Raymond still had the gun at the girl's head.

"Who the hell is this Raymond anyway?" he said. "NYPD has nothing on him. Neither does Chicago unless something comes up with the ballistics test. It's going to take a little time for the Feds to get the readout on his passport, so who knows what we'll find there, if anything. If we hadn't found the gun in his bag and he'd given us a straight address, there's every chance he would've walked."

"But we found the gun and he didn't give us a straight address."

"Is that enough to make him start killing people?"

"He came here from Chicago with a gun in his bag. He had a plane ticket to London." Barron glanced at Halliday, then looked back to the cab. "Why did he come here first? Maybe to get laid, maybe to kill somebody, maybe to get a suntan, who knows? But whatever he's doing now, he's got to have a helluva reason."

"Like what?"

Barron shook his head. "He's been trained someplace, military maybe. The way he did the deputies in the elevator. The way he shoots—you saw him take down the policewoman. You don't pick that up in the street. Or that kind of balls, either."

"So what's he gonna do with the hostage?"

"He did all this trying to get away. We put him in a corner, he'll kill her just like the others."

Ahead, the taxi took a slow right turn onto Vernon Avenue. Barron followed; so did the parade of other chase vehicles. Air 14, the helicopter unit, crossed in front of them. Their radio crackled and they heard Red's voice.

"Central. This is McClatchy. Any ID on the girl hostage?"

"Affirmative, Commander, just came in," a female dispatcher's voice came back. "African-American. Darlwin Washburn. Age fifteen. Lives in Glendale."

"Anybody alert her parents?"

"Attempts have had no response."

"What is the status of the wounded policewoman?"

"She, ah . . . is, ah . . . deceased, sir. I'm sorry."

"The wounded deputies and court officer?"

"The, ah . . . same, sir . . ."

There was a long pause and then Red's voice came again, quieter this time. "Thank you."

Barron had to hold back from jumping on the accelerator. He wanted to race forward, box Raymond in between police cars, then force him off the road and take care of him. But he couldn't and he knew it. They all knew it, Raymond most of all. Whatever his plan was, he still had the girl, and there was nothing any of them could do about it except what they already were doing—follow and wait.

"There he goes!" Halliday shouted. Ahead of them the 7711 cab had sped up and was racing off. Barron jammed the accelerator down. The black-and-white shuddered, then leapt forward.

Halliday had the radio up and was speaking into it. "Three-Adam-Thirty-Four! He's taking off! Air Fourteen, what've you got for cross traffic ahead?"

In seconds Barron had cut the distance to the cab in half. Suddenly the taxi swung left, then cut back right directly in front of them and accelerated down a side street lined with apartment houses.

"Hang on!" Barron yelled. Halliday's hand went to the grip-rail above the passenger's window, and Barron cut the wheel hard. Tires screaming, the black-and-white slid through the turn. Barron spun the wheel back the other way, his foot hit the accelerator, and the car rocketed forward. An instant later he slammed on the brakes, bringing the car to an abrupt stop.

A half block away the taxi was stopped dead in the street.

28

Barron picked up his radio. "Red, this is Barron. The cab—"

"I see it."

Red's car suddenly pulled up beside Barron and Halliday. In the next instant black-and-white units cordoned off the far end of the street in front of them.

Barron glanced in the mirror and saw the two sharpshooter

pursuit units pull in behind them. Their doors opened and four men in flak jackets got out carrying rifles. At the same moment, Red and Polchak stepped from Red's car, their handguns drawn, their eyes locked on the taxi. A loud *click-clack* followed as Valparaiso climbed from the back door racking a 12-gauge shotgun.

Barron and Halliday got out, Berettas in hand. Behind them more black-and-whites pulled in. Overhead was the heavy thud-thud of the helicopter.

"Air Fourteen, what do you see?" Red spoke into his radio.

"A stopped seven-seven-one-one. Same as you."

Red moved back to his car, then reached in and lifted the radio microphone.

"Raymond!" His voice boomed from the car's loudspeaker. "Open the door and put your weapons on the pavement."

Barron and Halliday inched forward, guns up, ready to fire. Behind and to the side, the sharpshooters fanned out to take up clear-shot positions.

Polchak knelt beside the front bumper of Red's car, sighting his automatic with two hands. "Straight to hell, cocksucker," he breathed.

Nothing happened. The taxi remained as it was. Doors closed, windows up, the glare from the sun as harsh as ever, making it impossible to see inside.

"Raymond, open the door and put your weapons on the pavement."

Still nothing happened. Then, suddenly, the driver's window rolled partway down and the face of the young hostage, Darlwin, appeared.

"Momma! Momma! Momma!" She screamed with everything she had. Then her face disappeared and the window rolled back up.

"What the fuck's goin' on?" Valparaiso moved in behind Red. The sharpshooters inched up, ready to fire.

Suddenly the front door to the apartment directly across from the taxi flew open and Momma, a large African-American woman in jeans and tank top, was running from it straight toward the cab.

"My baby! My baby!" Momma was yelling, screaming, as she ran.

"Holy shit!" Barron yelled and took off at the dead run.

"Jesus Christ!" Red lunged forward.

Then they were all running. Momma. Barron, Red, Polchak, Valparaiso, Halliday, running with their weapons out.

Now the driver's door to the taxi was opening. Immediately Barron was on Momma, hitting her with a flying tackle, sending them both sprawling across the grass at the sidewalk.

Red took the cab door, jerking it open, his Smith & Wesson ready to fire.

"Freeze! Right there!"

Darlwin shrieked out loud, scrambling away from Red's gun in terror. Behind her the passenger's door was ripped open and Valparaiso jammed the shotgun forward, ready to blow Raymond to kingdom come! But all he did was send Darlwin screaming back across the front seat toward Red. Then Polchak wrenched open one rear door and Halliday yanked open the other.

There was no Raymond. Only a screaming, crying, very scared Darlwin.

Quickly Red motioned for the mother. "Momma," he said. "Momma."

Suddenly Momma was pushing away from Barron and running to the cab. And then she and her daughter were in each other's arms, holding each other, crying.

"Get 'em outta here!" Red yelled at Barron.

Barron moved in quickly, herding the women away from the cab. At the same time, Polchak and Valparaiso moved to the rear of the cab. Valparaiso leveled the shotgun and Polchak popped the trunk's lock. The lid flew up to reveal the car's spare tire and a few tools.

"April fucking fool." Polchak turned away, disgusted.

"It's March," Halliday said quietly.

Valparaiso tucked the shotgun under his arm. "When the hell did he get out? Where the hell did he get out?"

Down the block the sharpshooters lowered their rifles and moved back. Slowly heads began to appear in windows, doors started to open. People walked out onto the small lawns in front of the apartment buildings, gesturing toward the police, talking among themselves.

Red glanced up at the still-hovering Air 14 and ran a hand

through his hair, then walked to where Barron was trying to comfort Darlwin and her mother. "Tell us what happened," he said gently.

"Tell him, baby," Momma said, holding Darlwin's hand tightly, using her free hand to wipe away her daughter's tears and her own.

"We . . . just . . . barely left," Darlwin managed between sobs, "then the . . . Jack looks at me and . . . wants to know if . . . I knows how . . . to drive . . . I tell him sure I do. He says, 'Then get behind the wheel and drive yourself home. Don't stop for nobody and don't open the door till you gets there.' Then he got out . . . I sure wasn't gonna fool with no crazy Jack like that. So . . . I did what he said."

"Where did he get out, do you remember?" Red McClatchy's manner was easy and calming, as if he were talking to his own daughter.

"Where did he get out, baby?" Mama urged. "Tell the man where."

Darlwin looked up, trying to hold back tears that wouldn't be held back. "Like I said . . . we just barely got started . . . down the block and around the corner . . . from the courthouse . . . Don't know which street it was exactly." She shook her head. "He just stopped and got out."

"Thank you, Darlwin," Red said. He glanced at Barron, then turned and saw his other detectives grouped together, waiting expectantly, as if he were about to tell them where Raymond was and thereby remove the huge cloud of embarrassment that hung over them all. What they got instead was his own not inconsiderable frustration as he came toward them.

"Down the block and around the corner from the courthouse, gentlemen. The few seconds he was out of sight, he used. He stopped the cab and got out. Told the young lady to drive herself home."

Red glanced at his watch, then looked abruptly to Polchak.

"He's got more than an hour on us, and we've got to make it up. Put a 'citywide most-wanted and extremely dangerous' out for him. I want every available detective and black-and-white combing the area between Criminal Courts and the Santa Monica Freeway, Alvarado Street to the Santa Ana Freeway. Get his picture to the newspapers and TV and have it faxed to every air, bus, and train terminal, taxi company, and car rental agency in the city with a request to notify us immediately if he shows up. Or if he already *has* shown up. And just in case he slips us entirely, get his picture and description to the London police so they can keep a lookout for him getting off any incoming flights."

Red glanced up at the still-hovering helicopter, put his hands over his ears, and turned to Valparaiso. "I'm going deaf with that clatter up there. Send Air Fourteen home, but tell him to hang fire just in case. And put a priority on finding out who the hell this Raymond is! Find out where the hell he was in Chicago and why! Christ!"

He aimed the next request at Halliday. "Get Darlwin's story, and be gentle; she's had a rough day already." Then Red was turning and looking at Barron.

"Let's you and me go for a ride."

9:19 A.M.

29

"Talk to me." Red threw the unmarked Ford into reverse, swinging around a parked black-and-white, then accelerating off, heading back toward the central city.

"About what? Raymond? I don't know any more about him than—"

"About Donlan." Red looked at Barron carefully, his anger and frustration of seconds earlier suddenly quieted.

"What about him?"

In front of them an intersection light changed from yellow to red. McClatchy touched the siren, punched the accelerator, and went through it anyway.

"We picked us a fine young detective in John Barron. One

who brought down a killer nobody else in the whole damn department could get a handle on."

"I don't know what you're talking about."

McClatchy's eyes swung to Barron.

"Yes, you do, John. You're troubled by what happened with Donlan. I saw it yesterday. I still see it today. He was already in custody, so you say why, what was the point of it? Why did you do it?"

Barron didn't reply, and McClatchy looked back to the road.

"I say okay, let's find out."

30

THE WESTIN BONAVENTURE HOTEL,
DOWNTOWN LOS ANGELES. 9:44 A.M.

Raymond had a luxurious two-room suite complete with TV, writing desk, wet bar, microwave, refrigerator, and coffeemaker. He also had new clothes and a new identity, and would have until someone realized the New Jersey automotive design consultant Charlie Bailey was missing from wherever he was supposed to be and the police started to look for him.

Happening on Charlie Bailey had been luck created by circumstance and sheer need. Escaping the police at the Criminal Courts Building, Raymond drove the stolen taxi at top speed, knowing he had no more than ten to fifteen seconds before the police were on top of him. Immediately he'd asked his kidnap victim if she knew how to drive, and when she'd said yes, he'd simply pulled to the curb and stepped out, telling her to drive home, and staying there just long enough to see her put the car in gear and speed off. Then he'd walked away, praying he'd frightened her enough to do as he said and not stop for anyone, especially the police.

Wearing the black jacket he'd taken from the man in the stairwell at the Criminal Courts Building and slipped over the murdered deputy's uniform, he'd kept walking, trying to keep his composure and find a way to get off the street. Another half block and he'd seen the man who turned out to be Charlie Bailey, about Raymond's height and weight and dressed in a business suit. He was alone, unlocking a car in a quiet parking lot and starting to get in. Suddenly the black jacket was stuffed into a trash container and Raymond took on the persona of the uniform he wore, that of an L.A. County sheriff's deputy.

Using the same American accent he'd used all along, he'd approached the man with authority, explaining there had been a raft of car thefts in the area and asking to see his driver's license and proof of car ownership. The man had shown him a New Jersey driver's license, identifying him as Charles Bailey, and told him the car was rented. When Raymond asked to see the rental papers and Bailey opened the trunk to take out his briefcase, Raymond shot him in the back of the head, stuffed the body in the trunk, and closed it. Then, taking Bailey's briefcase and car keys, he locked the car and walked off, stopping only to retrieve the black jacket from the trash container and pull it back on, masking the uniform once more.

The briefcase had been a treasure. Inside was Charles Bailey's identity: cash, credit cards, cell phone, and the card key to suite number 1195 at the Westin Bonaventure, the large glass-towered hotel just up the street. Why Bailey had left his car in the parking lot rather than park it at the hotel there was no way to know, but it was an act that had cost the design consultant his life.

Twenty minutes later, Raymond was in the dead man's suite, had showered, treated the bullet burn on his neck with antiseptic cream he'd found among a bathroom arrangement of soaps and lotions, and put on a reasonably well fitting gray suit and blue dress shirt, loosely knotting a red-striped tie to hide the wound. It was then that he used Bailey's cell phone, dialing a number in Toronto that forwarded to a number in Brussels and then to a number in Zurich where a voice-mail recording advised him his party was not available but that he could leave a message and the call would be returned shortly. Speaking in French, Raymond said his name was Charles Bailey, asked for Jacques Bertrand, and gave Bailey's cell phone number. Then he hung up and waited.

Now, nearly an hour later, he still waited, pacing the floor and wondering why Bertrand hadn't called back and if he should have said who he was directly instead of using the Bailey name and number.

Bertrand and the Baroness had his cell phone number, and if he'd been able to use that number his call would have been returned immediately. But that phone had been demolished when he'd purposely thrown it out of the stolen car Donlan had been driving to make certain the police didn't get it and use it to trace calls to either Bertrand or the Baroness. A telephone call placed to Bertrand by a Charles Bailey could be written off as simply a wrong number if it were ever traced, but leaving his name with that number risked linking Bertrand with himself and a man who, sooner or later, would be found dead, and that was something he didn't dare do. Especially now, when the police would have discovered the charade with his hostage and the girl would have told them where he got out of the taxi. Very shortly they would secure the entire area and be going door to door looking for him. It made protecting who he was and what he was about more important than ever.

31

PARKER CENTER. 9:48 A.M.

"1915, Huey Lloyd. 1923, Jack 'the Finger' Hammel. 1928, James Henry Green."

John Barron was hunched over a table in Red's office as, one by one, McClatchy set a number of eight-by-ten black-and-white photographs in front of him. The photographs were official LAPD documentations. Cold, formal pictures of deceased felons, toe-tagged and laid out on morgue tables. Naked dead men with mortician's wax filling in the bullet holes where they had been shot.

"1933, Clyde Till, 1937, Harry Shoemaker. 1948, '57, '64, '72." Red read off the years as he turned over more of the grim photos. "1985, 1994, 2000, most recent—" Without comment McClatchy turned over the last, the morgue photo of Frank "Whitey" Donlan.

"All multiple killers who somehow or another the courts kept putting back on the street." Red gathered the photos and slid them back into the large brown accordion file he had taken them from. "You use the word 'murder' to describe what happened to any of these men and you're talking about taking a human life. The trouble is none of them were human. They were monsters the system kept letting go free. Creatures who had killed before and were going to kill again and again." Red crossed the room and dropped the file on his desk. "So there is the 'why,' John Barron. He wasn't going to get another chance to kill someone else."

Barron stared at him. There was the answer to Donlan's killing. Like the long line of others, his had been no murder, just a simple extermination of vermin.

"You might be afraid, John Barron, that somehow, in some way, someone will find out. But in a century of this kind of work, nobody's found out yet. You know why? They don't want to."

"They?"

"John Q. Public. These are situations they don't even want to think about, let alone know about. It's what they pay us to take care of."

Barron watched him for a long moment, staggered by his simple justification of cold-blooded murder. "That's what 'the go' means, isn't it?" he asked quietly. "Permission to carry out the execution. That's why there was never a question of taking Donlan off the train at one of the earlier stops. The LAPD had no jurisdiction there; you would have had to call in a local agency, and this 'go' would never have happened."

"True." Red nodded.

"Who gives it?" Barron could feel his anger rise. Abruptly he stood and crossed to the window to stand in the bright glare of the March L.A. sun, then turned back to face McClatchy. "The chief? The commissioner? The mayor? Or by now is it all a computerized bunch of X's and O's tallying up the score and choosing who lives and who doesn't?"

McClatchy half smiled, and suddenly Barron realized he had been purposely manipulated into revealing his emotions. The way he'd been manipulated by Raymond, too.

"This is an old witch of a city, John. Over time she's found a thousand different ways to survive, not all of them entirely legal, but necessary just the same. You were exposed to it the same way we all were. You're a member of the squad, you're there, it happens. It's the way it's been done from the beginning, for a hundred years." Red sat down on the edge of his desk. "Don't think you're the first to be upset by it. I was myself a long time ago. But that day we didn't immediately have another mass murderer out on the streets like we do now." Red's eyes narrowed.

"Before you go, let me give you something to think about. It's what I've said to every member of the squad the day after he experienced his first 'go.' When you joined the Five-Two you took an oath of commitment to it for life. It means you're in it for the long haul. Get used to it, and don't get so angry and self-righteous over one incident that you make a mistake and forget your commitment. If you continue to have a problem, keep in mind another part of your oath, to resolve any differences inside the squad. That's the way it's been done for a hundred years, and in that same hundred years no one has ever quit. Remember that. And remember you have a sister who depends on you for everything. I wouldn't want to think about what her mental state might be if you betrayed your oath to the men and tried to walk out."

Barron felt ice creep across his neck and slide down his spine. The commander had not only manipulated him into revealing his emotions, it was as if he had also read his mind. For the first time he understood why Red McClatchy had become a legend. Why he was so respected and so feared. He not only headed the squad, he protected it. Try to walk away and they would kill you.

"If I were you, Detective, I would go back to my desk and file the report on the Donlan shooting right now. Show us all you're a hundred percenter, a partner we can trust without question. That way we can put Mr. Donlan behind us and give our full concentration to this Raymond Oliver Thorne we've got out there."

For the briefest moment McClatchy said nothing, just stared

at Barron. When he spoke again his manner was softer. "Do you understand what I've said, Detective?"

Barron could feel the cold sweat bead up on his forehead. "Yes, sir." His voice was little more than a whisper.

"Good."

32

SUITE 1195, WESTIN BONAVENTURE HOTEL. 10:20 A.M.

They spoke in French.

"Where are you?"

"A hotel in Los Angeles."

"Los Angeles?"

"Yes."

"Are you hurt?" Her voice was calm and, for the moment, matter-of-fact. Raymond knew her call would have been routed through switching devices in at least four countries and would be all but impossible to trace.

"No," he said, and turned to look out the window and to the street in front of the hotel a dozen stories down. From his vantage point he could see three black-and-white police cars and two groups of uniformed officers standing on the sidewalk talking among themselves. "I'm sorry, Baroness, I did not mean to involve you. It was Bertrand I called."

"I know, my sweet, but I am the one you are talking to. What is this number you've given us? Who is Charles Bailey? Where is your phone? I've called and called but with no answer. You are in trouble. What is it?"

Raymond's call to Jacques Bertrand in Zurich some ninety minutes earlier had been made with the express hope that the Swiss lawyer would speak to him first and not inform her until afterward. Obviously, that had not been the case.

"Her" was Baroness Marga de Vienne, his legal guardian, the widow of the international financier Baron Edmond de Vienne and, as such, one of Europe's wealthiest, most prominent, and most powerful grandes dames. Normally, at this time of year, she would be at Château Dessaix, her seventeenth-century manor just outside Tournemire, the picturesque village in Auvergne in the Massif Central, the mountainous middle region of France. Instead she was in her suite at the Connaught Hotel in London, where it was nearly six-thirty in the evening. He could picture her, jeweled, and dressed as always in her trademark combination of delicate white and pale yellow, her thick dark hair woven into an intricate bun, preparing for the dinner party she would be attending at 10 Downing Street given by the British prime minister for visiting Russian dignitaries, Nikolai Nemov, the mayor of Moscow, and Marshal Igor Golovkin, Russian Federation minister of defense. It would be a gathering where the principal intrigue was certain to be the very hush-hush rumor that in an effort to give stability to a society widely perceived as chaotic, corrupt, and increasingly violent, Russia was giving strong consideration to returning the imperial family Romanov to the throne in the form of a constitutional monarchy. True or not, there was little reason to believe the Russians would be willing to discuss it even in those heavily guarded quarters. Still, they would be pressured to do so, and the diplomatic banter would make for an interesting evening. It was an event he had looked forward to attending with the Baroness, but now, and quite obviously, that was not possible.

"Baroness, a regrettable series of circumstances left me in a position where it was necessary to kill several people, policemen among them. The authorities are looking for me everywhere. You will no doubt see it on the international news if you haven't already. I called Bertrand for assistance. I have no passport and therefore no way out of the country.

"Even if I were to avoid the police, getting out of the country without a passport, let alone to England in so short a time, would be all but impossible. Have Bertrand arrange for a private jet to pick me up at a local civil aviation airport. Santa Monica is closest and best.

"With the plane I will need money and credit cards and a new passport in some other name and nationality. French or Italian, probably. It doesn't matter."

Below he could see two motorcycle units pass and then two

more black-and-whites. And then an LAPD helicopter crossed overhead.

"Today Peter Kitner was knighted at Buckingham Palace," the Baroness said abruptly, as if she had heard none of what he'd said.

"So I would imagine," he said coldly.

"Do not take that tone with me, my sweet. I know you are in trouble, but you need to understand that all the other clocks are still ticking and we cannot afford to lose any more time than we already have. When we last spoke while you were on the train from Chicago, you assured me you had the keys. Where are they now?"

Raymond could have hung up there. He wanted to. Throughout his life he had never once heard sympathy from her, only the reality of what was at hand. Even as a child, a cut or scrape or even a nightmare was something not to be fussed over but to be dealt with and resolved as quickly as possible so that it was no longer an issue. Life was filled with bumps, large and small, she had preached for as long as he could remember. This was no different. No matter what had happened he was unhurt, still on his own, still able to phone Europe from the relative safety of a private hotel room.

"My sweet, I asked you about the keys."

"I was forced to leave my bag on the train. I assume the police have them."

"What about Neuss?"

"Baroness, you do not understand what is happening here."

"It is you, my sweet, who do not understand."

Raymond understood exactly. Alfred Neuss would have a key to the safe deposit box. Alfred Neuss would know where it was. Without a key, without the contents of the box, and without Neuss dead they would have nothing at all. To her there were only two questions, and the rest be damned. Had he gotten the name and location of the bank, and had he taken care of Alfred Neuss?

His answer: "No."

"Warum?" Why, she demanded in German, suddenly changing languages on a whim in that maddening way she had of force-feeding him what she thought he ought to know. French,

German, English, Spanish, Russian, the language didn't matter. He was expected to understand what was being said around him always, even if he acted as if he didn't.

"*Madame la baronesse, vous ne m'écoutez pas!*" Baroness, you are not listening, he said angrily, holding to the French. "I am the subject of a massive hunt by the police. What good am I under arrest or shot dead?"

"That is not an answer." She cut to the quick as she always had.

"No," he agreed in a whisper; she was right, she was always right. "It is not."

"For how long, my sweet, have we talked about the significance of difficult times, so that you can learn to adapt and rise above them? You have not forgotten who you are."

"How could I? You are always there to remind me."

"Then understand how severely your schooling and cleverness and courage are being tested. In ten years, twenty, it will all seem like nothing, yet you will remember it heroically as an invaluable lesson in self-knowledge. In casting you into the fire, God is commanding you as He always has, to be great."

"Yes," Raymond whispered.

"Now, I will work on what you need. The plane is easy. The passport and getting it to the pilot who will deliver it will be harder, but both will arrive sometime tomorrow. In the meantime do what needs to be done with Neuss. Get his key and find where the bank is, and then kill him. Afterward overnight the key to Bertrand, who will then go to France and retrieve the pieces from the box. Do you understand?"

"Yes." Below Raymond could see another group of police on the sidewalk across the street. These were different from the patrol officers he had seen before. They wore helmets and flak jackets and carried automatic weapons. He edged back from the window as several looked up toward the hotel's higher floors. They were a SWAT team, and it looked as if they were preparing to enter the hotel.

"Baroness, special police have gathered directly across the street."

"I want you to put them out of your mind and listen to me, my sweet, listen to my voice," she said quietly and forcefully. "You know what I want to hear. Tell me, tell me in Russian."

"I—" He hesitated, his eyes on the street below. The SWAT team hadn't moved, its officers still where they had been before.

"Tell me," she commanded.

"*Vsay*," he began slowly. "*Vsay . . . ego . . . sudba . . . V rukah . . . Gospodnih.*"

"Again."

"*Vsay ego sudba V rukah Gospodnih,*" he repeated. This time his voice was stronger and had more conviction.

Vsay ego sudba V rukah Gospodnih. All his destiny is in God's hands. It was a common Russian saying, but she had personalized it to mean *him*. The destiny he was talking about was his own; God directed everything, and everything happened for a reason. Again God was testing him, commanding him to rise and find a way out, because surely there was one.

"*Vsay ego sudba V rukah Gospodnih,*" Raymond said once more, repeating the saying like a mantra for perhaps the ten thousandth time in his life, exactly the way she had taught it to him from childhood.

"Again," she whispered.

"*Vsay ego sudba V rukah Gospodnih!*" His concentration was no longer on the police but on what he was saying, and he spoke it like an oath, forceful and compelling, an allegiance to God and to himself.

"There, my sweet, you see? Trust in providence, your education, and your wits. Do that and the way will be opened for you. With the police, with Neuss, and then on Friday with our dearest—" She paused, and he could feel the decades of hatred pour out as she said his name. "Peter Kitner."

"Yes, Baroness."

"Tomorrow, my sweet, you will have a plane and safe passage out. By Friday the pieces will be in our possession and you will be with me in London."

"Yes, Baroness."

"Godspeed."

There was a click and the phone went dead. Raymond hung up slowly, her aura still with him. Once again he looked out the window. The police were still there, across the street where they had been. But they seemed smaller now. Like chessmen. Not so much to be feared as played.

33

Believe in himself and a way would be shown. The Baroness had been right. In no time it was.

It began with the simple reasoning that if the police had tracked him that far, the media would be on top of the story, too, and he turned on the room's television hoping to find a news broadcast that might give him some sense of what the authorities were doing.

Quickly and rudely, he got a great deal more than he expected. Almost every channel was showing video clips of the aftermath of the shootout at Criminal Courts. He saw the covered bodies of the sheriff's deputies, the bailiff, the female police officer, and the man he'd strangled in the stairwell in order to take his black jacket loaded into coroner's vans. Shaken and outraged police officers and equally shocked and irate civilians were interviewed. Aerial video coverage of the slow-speed police chase after the taxi was immediately followed by clips of the African-American teenager and her mother. Then came the live studio anchor people announcing the "citywide most-wanted and extremely dangerous" alert 5-2 Squad Commander Arnold McClatchy had put out for him. Next came his physical description and a full-screen close-up of his LAPD booking photograph. With it came a plea to the public asking for help and directing them to immediately call 911 if he were seen.

Raymond stood back trying to absorb the sheer magnitude of it. The Baroness had been right. God was testing him, commanding him to rise up and find a way out. Whatever that way was, one thing had become indelibly clear—he no longer had the luxury of trying to hide for an extra day waiting for the Baroness's privately chartered aircraft to pick him up at Santa Monica Airport. What he had to do was get to Neuss, get his safe deposit key and learn the location of the French bank the safe deposit box was in, and then kill Neuss, get out of Los Angeles, and be on his way to Europe as quickly as possible. Which meant sometime late today. Considering the size of the force mounted against him it was a huge, if not impossible, undertaking. But he had no choice; the future of everything they had planned for so long depended on it. How to do it was something else again.

Abruptly the television channel he was watching cut to a commercial. Trying to think of a way out and looking for more video coverage, he switched channels. Inadvertently he came upon the hotel's in-house channel displaying a schedule of the Westin Bonaventure's events and activities for the day. He was about to continue when he saw a notice for a welcoming reception for Universität Student Höchste, a tour group of German university students, that was under way in a downstairs function room at that very moment.

Ten minutes later he entered the room, with his hair slicked back and still wearing the murdered New Jersey consultant's suit and tie and carrying his briefcase. Inside it were Charlie Bailey's wallet and cell phone and one of the two 9 mm Berettas. The second Beretta was tucked into his waistband under his jacket.

He stopped just inside the doorway and looked around. There were probably forty or more university students and three or four well-dressed tour guides enjoying coffee and a simple buffet and chattering away in German. Their number nearly an even split between boys and girls, they looked to be anywhere from their late teens to mid-twenties. They seemed happy and carefree and were dressed like students anywhere—jeans, loose-fitting shirts, some leather, some with body jewelry, some with brightly colored hair.

Beyond the obvious—the closeness in age to himself and the fact that he spoke fluent German and could easily blend in—were two other things Raymond coveted, and knew they would all have: a passport and at least one current credit card that would not only complement the passport as identification but fund a transatlantic airline ticket. What he needed was to find one of them, male or female, he could impersonate.

The approach had to be casual, and it was, going first to the buffet table and taking a coffee cup and filling it from a large silver-plated urn, and then, cup and saucer in hand, walking toward the back of the room, acting for all the world like one of the tour guides and as if he belonged there.

Again, he stopped and looked around the room. As he did, a man in a dark suit with a brass hotel-employee name tag on his lapel came through the main door. With him was a helmeted, flak-jacketed SWAT team sergeant. Raymond turned easily and set the briefcase down, his left hand holding the cup and saucer, his right just inside his jacket, resting on the grip of the Beretta.

For a moment the two men stood surveying the room; then an older man, a tour guide, he imagined, left a small gathering of students and walked up to them. The three stood talking, with the guide occasionally gesturing toward the people in the room. Suddenly the SWAT sergeant stepped away and moved toward the buffet area, his eyes searching the crowd. Raymond took a sip of coffee and stayed where he was, doing nothing to draw attention. After a moment the policeman turned back and said something to the others. Then he and the hotel man left, and the guide returned to the students.

It was in the moment of relief afterward that Raymond saw him—a tall, slim young man in T-shirt, blue jeans, and jean jacket, standing off to the side, chatting with an attractive young woman. A backpack over one shoulder, his blond hair dyed purple. Even if he was younger, his build and facial configuration were close enough to Raymond's to be workable, especially if one considered the notoriously poor quality of passport photographs. The purple hair could be a problem—he would have to find a way to dye his own hair, and it might call attention to him later—but the young man was the closest match to himself in the room and time was of the essence, so he would find a way to work around it.

A moment more and then two, and the young man walked away from the girl and went to the centerpiece of the buffet, a table overflowing with sweet rolls, breads, and fresh fruit.

Raymond picked up his briefcase and did the same. Loading a plate with melon and grapes, he struck up a friendly conversation in German, telling the young man he was an actor from Munich staying at the hotel and was in L.A. to play the villain in an action movie opposite Brad Pitt. He had heard that a German group was attending a hotel function and, feeling particularly lonely and having the morning off, had decided to join them, if for nothing more than to chat about the homeland.

His target responded immediately with warmth and good humor. In a matter of moments Raymond realized he had struck gold. Not only was the young German free-spirited like the others, but he was smitten with Hollywood movies, confiding that he would like nothing more than to be an actor himself; moreover, by his own admission, he was homosexual and—clearly sizing up the well-dressed, deeply handsome Raymond—ever eager for adventure.

Raymond had to smile. He'd opened a trap and a rabbit bounded in. As quickly, he snapped it closed behind him. It was almost too easy.

Feigning his own homosexuality, Raymond led the young man, who now gave his name as Josef Speer from Stuttgart, to a corner table, where they sat down. While young Josef flirted, Raymond did an equally frivolous dance, most particularly coaxing Speer to show him his passport and driver's license—on the pretext that if he was ever going to consider becoming a movie or television actor he needed to be photogenic and, as unflattering as passport and driver's license photos usually were, they were often used by professional casting directors as a measure of how a person's face played before a camera in the worst situations. It was a lie, of course, but it worked, with the gullible Speer enthusiastically opening his backpack and pulling out both passport and wallet to proudly show off his photographic likenesses. The passport photo was of inferior quality, as Raymond had suspected, and with his hair colored purple, and the right attitude when he presented it, he was reasonably certain he could pass as Speer. The driver's license, while helpful, was less important. What he wanted was to make sure Speer had credit cards. And as the young German opened his wallet and handed him his driver's license, Raymond saw he had at least three; one, a Euro Master-Card, was all he would need.

Raymond lowered his voice and looked the young German in the eye, in a heartbeat changing from seduced to seducer. He found Josef very attractive sexually, he said, but he would never consider a rendezvous at a hotel where he was staying because it left him too vulnerable to blackmail. If they were going to have a "mutual exploration," as Raymond put it, better they do it somewhere away from the Bonaventure. Speer agreed, and within moments they were walking out of the function room and into the lobby.

As they entered it, Raymond briefly froze. The lobby was filled with anxious and noisy hotel guests. Beyond them, stationed at the exits, were a dozen uniformed police.

"What's going on?" Speer asked in German.

"No doubt they are looking for homosexuals." Raymond grinned lightly, trying to decide what to do next. Then he saw the hotel employee in the dark suit who had come into the room with the SWAT sergeant. With Speer at his side, Raymond approached the hotel employee, asking in a thick German accent what was happening. The police were looking for an escaped killer, he was told. A SWAT team was searching the hotel, evacuating people floor by floor. Raymond repeated the story to Speer in German and then told the hotel man they were on their way to a specially arranged tour of Universal City Studios and asked if it was safe and permissible for them to leave.

The man studied them for a moment and then produced some kind of two-way radio and spoke into it, saying he had two of the German tour group who had an appointment and wished to leave the building. A moment later the SWAT team sergeant pushed through the crowd and walked brusquely up to them. Raymond swallowed but that was all.

"They are part of the student group," the hotel man said. "They just came from the function room."

SWAT looked from one to the other carefully. Still Raymond held his ground. Then SWAT's radio crackled; he answered in some sort of police-speak and then looked to the hotel man.

"Alright, let them out the rear door," he said abruptly, then walked off.

"*Danke,*" Raymond said after him, then followed as the hotel man led them across the lobby and past a police guard to a rear door leading to a street already secured by the authorities.

"Thank you," Raymond said in a thick accent.

And then he and Josef Speer stepped into the bright California sunshine and walked unmolested toward Charlie Bailey's rental car parked two blocks away.

A car with the New Jersey consultant's body still in the trunk.

11:30 A.M.

34

Dr. Janet Flannery was probably sixty and easily ten pounds underweight. Her hair was a mixture of gray and black and was cut short, but not stylishly so. It was the same with her clothes, an off-the-rack beige pantsuit and a lighter beige blouse, both of which fit her reasonably well. The furnishings in her small office—a coffee table, a couch, and two overstuffed chairs—were equally plain. The idea, of course, was for everything to be serviceable but not stand out. Attention in a psychiatrist's office was to be on the patient, not the therapist or the surroundings.

"You want to make a change in your life and leave Los Angeles." Dr. Flannery folded her hands in her lap and looked at John Barron sitting on the couch across from her.

"Not just L.A. I want to leave California," Barron said over the hum of the small white-noise fan sitting on the floor behind him. The reason for it, he knew, was so that conversations between therapists and patients could not be overheard in the next office or in the waiting room outside. "I would like to do it as soon as possible." Barron pushed his fingertips together. Red McClatchy's session with him a short while before, as threatening and frightening and formidable as it had been, had only served to magnify the scope of his horror and strengthen his resolve to take Rebecca and get away as quickly as he could.

"I must remind you, Detective, that your sister is in a place she is used to and in surroundings where she's comfortable. Is there not some alternative for you?"

"No." Barron had prepared an explanation for this sudden emergency request that Rebecca immediately be prepared to leave St. Francis and go with him to a strange, new, distant place. "You heard about what happened on the Amtrak train yesterday."

Dr. Flannery nodded. "You were there."

"Yes, for all of it. I've been thinking for some time that I'd rather do something else with my life. Yesterday put me over the top. I'm going to leave the LAPD as soon as I can. But before I do anything or say anything to anyone I want a destination for Rebecca." Barron hesitated. He was trying to be careful and not reveal any more of himself than he already had. "As I said on the phone, it all needs to be strictly confidential, just between you and me. When Rebecca's ready, I'll inform my superiors."

Thirty minutes earlier, in an act of complete resolve, he had done what he had thought he never could do: file the Donlan report as Red had asked and with his signature at the bottom. Immediately afterward he'd left Parker Center, knowing that despite the terrible risk of officially collaborating in an LAPD cover-up of murder, filing and signing the report was a necessary action. He had to cover himself with the 5-2 while Rebecca was being prepared and he found a new place for her. But once she was ready and Dr. Flannery had found a site for her in some other state, he would pack as many of their personal belongings as he could into his Mustang and call his landlord to cancel the lease on his house. After that he would call in sick and take off, sending McClatchy a formal letter of resignation from somewhere on the road.

The idea was simply to vanish. He had enough money put away so they could live for the better part of a year while he looked for a job. He was still young; he would change their names and they would simply start over. It seemed reasonable, even doable. And he doubted Red or any of the others would spend the time or money trying to find and silence a man who was keeping silent anyway and whose sister could say nothing even if somehow she learned what had happened and wanted to. But until that time came, he knew, he had to play along and stay on the job and act as if he had taken Red's talk to heart and had every intention of fulfilling his oath and staying on the squad for the rest of his professional life.

Dr. Flannery studied him for a long moment in silence. "If those are your wishes, Detective," she said finally, "I will see what I can do."

"Do you have any idea how long it will take?"

"In her current state, I'm sorry, no. It will take some looking into."

"Okay." Barron nodded gratefully and stood. "Thank you," he said, realizing that as much as he wanted to get out, as much as he needed to get out, Rebecca's situation could not be resolved in a day or maybe even a week. It was something he had to accept.

He was turning for the door, his mind still fully on Rebecca and Dr. Flannery, when the sudden chirp of his cell phone startled him. "Excuse me," he said, and lifted the phone from his jacket.

"Barron," he answered by rote.

"What?" he asked sharply. Immediately his demeanor changed. "Where?"

35

MACARTHUR PARK. 12:40 P.M.

Barron's Mustang banged over the curb, and he drove across the grass to pull up beside Red's unmarked Ford. Behind him four black-and-white units had set up a perimeter, and beyond them uniformed officers were keeping back a growing crowd of onlookers.

Barron stepped quickly from the car and walked toward a dense grouping of bushes near the water.

As he neared he could see Red and two uniformed officers standing to the side talking to a male indigent in tattered clothes and a big rat's nest of hair. Then Barron was there, reaching the bushes just as Halliday pushed carefully out through them, pulling off surgical gloves.

"White male," Halliday said. "Purple hair. Shot three times in the face at close range. No clothes, no IDs. Nothing. Unless somebody calls in a missing person or we get a fast make from his prints, it's going to be a helluva long winter before we know who he is."

"Take a look yourself," Halliday told Barron.

Red left the uniforms and came toward them, and Barron went in where Halliday had been.

The victim lay on his side in the dirt, dressed only in his socks and underwear. Most of his head was gone, but there was enough left to see that his hair had been dyed purple. Whatever clothes he might have been wearing were missing.

"What is he, twenty-one, twenty-two?" Barron stepped out from the bushes as people from the Scientific Investigations Division arrived. "Clean, manicured nails. He wasn't a bum. Looks like somebody wanted his clothes."

"Any guess when?" Red was looking at Halliday.

"Thirty minutes, maybe an hour ago. What'd he say?" Halliday indicated the indigent, still talking to the uniforms.

"Not much. Said he went in there to take a leak and almost pissed on the body. Scared the bejesus out of him, and he started yelling."

The three detectives stepped back to give the Scientific Investigations people room to sift the area.

"All but naked, like the deputies in the Criminal Courts elevator." Red watched the SIU people. There was an anger and intensity about him Barron had never seen before.

"You're thinking Raymond," Halliday said as the first contingent of media arrived. As usual, Dan Ford was in the lead.

"Yeah, I'm thinking Raymond."

"Commander." Dan Ford was looking at Red. "We know a young man was killed here. Are you tying Raymond Thorne to the crime?"

"Tell you what, Dan—" McClatchy looked at Ford, then to the reporters as a group. "You and the other folks talk to Detective Barron. He can speak for the investigation as well as any of us."

Immediately McClatchy beckoned Halliday and the two walked off. Barron glanced after him. That was it, Red's way of telling him he was back in his good graces, whatever rift there had been between them gone with his filing of the Donlan report. Moreover, the rules were still intact. *Resolve any differences inside the squad.*

"Is Raymond the suspect here, John?" Ford asked. Behind him more reporters moved in. Video cameras were rolling, microphones shoved forward. Then Barron saw another unmarked car pull in, as Red and Halliday reached Red's car. The doors opened and Polchak and Valparaiso got out. There was a brief exchange, and then the two detectives started across the grass toward where the uniforms still talked with the rat-haired indigent and the bushes where the Scientific Investigations people were working the body.

"Who's the victim?" someone called out from the crowd.

Barron looked back to them.

"We don't know. Except it's a male, twenty-something, shot multiple times in the face," he said sharply and with a sudden rush of anger. "Yeah, Raymond Thorne is a suspect in this, probably *the* suspect."

"Victim been identified?" a reporter shouted.

"Did you hear what I said?" Barron's edge and anger was still there. Initially he thought his emotion was directed at Red—his simple way of patting him on the head and welcoming him back into the squad for what he had done—but standing in front of Dan Ford and the other reporters, the cameras and microphones taking in everything, he realized McClatchy was only a part of it. The real problem was him, because he cared. Cared about the cold-blooded murder of Donlan, the dead kid in the bushes, and the kid's mother and father and the awfulness they would carry in their hearts for the rest of their lives once his identity was learned and they were told. Because he cared about the people killed at Criminal Courts and their children and their families. And because he could still not, after all these years, get the murder of his own mother and father out of his mind. Moreover, there was something else. Something that suddenly came to him now as he stood in the heat and smog of midday looking out to this congregation of media and their focused electronic paraphernalia: This thing with Raymond was his fault. He had been the booking officer; he was the one who had stood there in Parker Center and let Raymond toy with him—as if Raymond had known all along what had happened to Donlan—and trick Barron into revealing his inner feelings, thereby proving to Raymond that his suspicions were fact. Barron should have understood there and then how canny and dangerous Raymond was and done something about it, at the very least warned the guards to be especially vigilant. He should have, but he hadn't. Instead he had exploded at Raymond's coyness, thereby giving the gunman all that he wanted to know.

Abruptly Barron looked to Dan Ford. "I want a favor, Dan. Put Raymond's picture on the *Times* front page. Big as you can make it. Can you do it?"

"I think so." Ford nodded.

Immediately Barron looked to the rest. "This is the second time today we are asking for the public's help in finding Raymond Thorne. We would like to continue with his picture on every newscast and have you continue to urge anyone who sees him, or even thinks they've seen him, to call nine-one-one immediately. Raymond Thorne is a vicious public enemy. He is armed and should be considered extremely dangerous."

Barron stopped as he saw the coroner's van move past the black-and-whites and drive over the grass toward the bushes where the dead boy was. Abruptly his attention swung back to the media people and to the video camera directly in front of him.

"I have a word for you, too, if you're watching, Raymond." Barron paused, and when he spoke next it was with the same quiet and mock concern Raymond had shown him the day before in Parker Center.

"I'd like to know how you're feeling, Raymond. Are you alright? You can call nine-one-one the same as anyone else. Just ask for me—you know my name, Detective John Barron, Five-Two Squad. I'll come and pick you up myself, anywhere you want. That way nobody else gets hurt." Barron hesitated once more, then went on just as quietly. "It would be easiest for everyone, Raymond. You most of all. There are nine million of us and only one of you. Do the math, Raymond. It's not hard to figure the odds."

Finished, Barron said, "That's all," and walked off to where Polchak and Valparaiso talked with the head of the Scientific Investigations Division. If he had done nothing else in his speech to the cameras and his plea for the public's assistance, he had just made the war with Raymond personal.

36

Raymond parked Charlie Bailey's car in the 200 block of South Spalding Drive within sight of Beverly Hills High School, took the second Beretta from Charlie's briefcase, and slipped it into Josef Speer's backpack as a backup to the Beretta in his waistband. Then he took the pack and got out, locked the car, and walked the short block to Gregory Way.

He nodded pleasantly to two women chatting on the street corner, then turned down Gregory, walking toward Linden Drive. No longer the businessman with slicked-back hair, but wearing Speer's jean jacket, T-shirt, and jeans, his backpack over his shoulder, and an L.A. Dodgers baseball cap pulled down over freshly colored purple hair, Raymond looked like any young man in his early to mid-twenties walking through this quiet neighborhood of manicured lawns and apartment buildings.

Reaching Linden Drive, he turned left and started looking for number 225, the apartment building where Alfred Neuss lived and where he would return for lunch at exactly 1:15. The same as he had six days a week, every week for the past twenty-seven years. A precise seven-minute walk from his exclusive jewelry store on Brighton Way. Raymond had bought further insurance against any last-minute change of habit a week earlier using the same strategy he had in San Francisco, Mexico City, and Chicago, simply by calling ahead and, using a fictitious name and inventing a credible story, making an appointment to meet his victim. Neuss had been no different. He had simply called and, in a midwestern accent, told him he was a Kentucky horse breeder named Will Tilden who was coming to town, had heard of the jeweler's fine reputation, and was interested in buying an expensive diamond necklace for his wife. Neuss had been all too happy to make an appointment, and they had, for the following

Monday at two o'clock, thereby giving Neuss every opportunity to follow his daily routine. The ice storm forcing Raymond to change his method of transportation had delayed things, but he'd called Neuss from the train and changed the appointment to Tuesday. That he had not shown up would no doubt have irritated Neuss, but there had been little he could do about it. Still, if Neuss had been in town on Monday and Tuesday and had kept a strict six-day workweek, week in and week out all these years, there was no reason to believe he would have done anything to change it now, or, for that matter, his daily habits.

If Neuss's sense of the clock was excessively phobic, Raymond's timing was impeccable and had been done with near-military precision. He had killed Josef Speer in MacArthur Park at 11:42 and taken his clothes and backpack. At 11:47 he had gone into the men's room of a service station on Ninth Street in Koreatown and changed from Bailey's business suit into Speer's jean outfit; he found the jacket sleeves a little long but, rolled back, good enough. At noon exactly he'd stuffed the consultant's suit and now useless credit cards and driver's license into a Dumpster at the side of the service station and gotten back into the car. By 12:10 he was passing a strip mall on Wilshire Boulevard just east of Beverly Hills when he saw what he was looking for—Snip & Shear, a hairstyling store-front. What got his attention was a big, hand-lettered sign in the window—WE COLOR HAIR ANY COLOR, 30 MIN. At 12:45 he walked out with his hair barbered in the style of Speer's and colored purple. At 12:48 he came out of a sporting goods store in the same mall with the L.A. Dodgers cap he now wore.

1:08 P.M.

Raymond stopped in front of 225 Linden Drive, a three-story apartment building with its entrance shaded by a large royal palm. He slipped a credit card from Josef Speer's wallet into the lock of the ornamental ironwork door at the entrance. There was a click as the lock slid open and then he was inside.

1:10 P.M.

He walked up the last steps to the Neuss apartment on the top floor. The covered patio outside was decorated with several large potted, shaped podocarpus trees and a diminutive white iron table and two matching white-iron chairs. Directly across was an elevator door. Both the elevator and the stairs opened onto the patio, so it made no difference which Neuss chose to use. The elevator was more likely. Neuss was sixty-three years old.

1:12 P.M.

Raymond slid the backpack from his shoulder and took out a small hand towel he had purchased from the proprietor of Snip & Shear. Next he took the Beretta from his waistband and wrapped the towel around it as a makeshift silencer. Then, shouldering the backpack once more, he stepped behind the palm trees and waited.

Lufthansa flight 453 left Los Angeles International Airport at 9:45 P.M. and arrived nonstop at Frankfurt, Germany, the next day at 5:30 P.M. One seat, coach class, reserved for Josef Speer. Raymond had made the reservation himself using Charlie Bailey's cell phone during the drive from MacArthur Park to Beverly Hills. Frankfurt was Germany's main international airport. It was an obvious destination for a German student returning home. Moreover, once he had Neuss's safe deposit key and the location of the bank, he could fly to whatever city it was in and the next morning, Friday, go to the bank, open the safe deposit box, take its contents, and take a short flight to London, landing at Gatwick Airport instead of Heathrow and passing through passport control as a member of the European Community with no close check of his papers at all.

So it made no difference if the police had his bag with his first class British Airways ticket to London/Heathrow. Even if they had alerted the London Metropolitan Police, the search for him would be concentrated at Heathrow, looking for him on a flight coming in from the United States. Once he was at

Gatwick and through the gates it was a simple thirty-minute train ride to Victoria Station and from there a few minutes by taxi to the Connaught Hotel and into the welcoming arms of the Baroness.

1:14 P.M.

Sixty seconds and the indecently punctual Neuss would be there. Five seconds after that and Raymond would give the Baroness the prize she had demanded.

1:15 P.M.

No one. Nothing.

Raymond took a breath. Maybe Neuss was caught at a traffic light and had to wait to cross. Or there had been a problem at the store. Or he had stopped to talk with someone.

1:16 P.M.

Still no one.

1:17 P.M.

Nothing.

1:20 P.M.

Where was he? What was he doing? An old friend unexpectedly in town and he had reluctantly accepted an invitation to lunch? An accident of some sort? The former, no. Neuss did not social-ize during working hours. An accident was always possible, but not likely because the jeweler was as neurotic about his own physical well-being as he was anal about promptness. He would look four times before crossing a street and drove a car the same way. There could be only one thing keeping Neuss. Business. It was always business. That meant for some reason he had remained at his store. The only solution was to go to the shop, somehow get him alone, and do what he had to do there.

37

PARKER CENTER. 1:25 P.M.

"Okay, he killed the kid for his clothes. Why the hell did he shoot him in the face like that?"

"Maybe he was nervous."

"And maybe it was some other reason."

"You're still assuming it was Raymond."

"Yeah, I'm still assuming it was Raymond. Aren't you?"

Barron stood with Halliday and Valparaiso at urinals in a men's room down the hall from the squad room, one talking over the other, each as frustrated as the next. Never mind they were wholly focused on the situation or that most of the department's nine thousand sworn officers were mobilized in some way or other trying to find Raymond. Not only had they not been able to apprehend him, they still had no idea who he was. From what they'd learned he might as well have been a ghost.

Specialists from U.S. State Department Passport Services had scanned the information strip on Raymond's passport using the TECS II system linking communications terminals in law enforcement facilities across the country with a master terminal at the U.S. Department of the Treasury (and thereby the Department of Justice). The finding, confirmed by the Immigration and Naturalization Service, was that the passport itself was valid and had been issued from the Los Angeles passport office at the Federal Building in Westwood two years earlier. According to the record, Raymond Oliver Thorne (birth name: Rakoczi Obuda Thokoly) had been born in Budapest, Hungary, in 1969 and had become a naturalized U.S. citizen in 1987. The trouble was the INS had no record of that naturalization, even though

Raymond would have been required to provide the passport office with a U.S. government-issued Certificate of Naturalization. Moreover, the address he had given to the passport agency turned out to be a private postal box rental company in Burbank, California, and the address he had given the rental-box company as a place of residence was nonexistent.

So, what they had was a seemingly valid passport with nothing to back it up. Still, the passport did provide a record of his latest activities, showing that he had come into Dallas, Texas, from Mexico City on Saturday, March 9, and that he had come into Mexico City from San Francisco on Friday, March 8.

Raymond's prints and ID had come back clean from the Chicago Police Department. But there was still the question of the dual murders in the tailor shop and a ballistics test and report on the Sturm Ruger found in Raymond's valise, which was being done. So what they had was a valid but not valid passport and a possible murder charge against Raymond in Chicago. As a follow-up to the Chicago incident, inquiries had been sent to police departments in Dallas, Mexico City, and San Francisco for possible Raymond Oliver Thorne activity in their cities on the dates he had been there. Barron himself had initiated two other inquiries. The first, through FBI Special Agent Pete Noonan, a longtime racquetball partner at the Hollywood YMCA where they both worked out, sought information from FBI data banks on nationwide fugitives that might match Raymond's description. The second was even broader, a request for similar information internationally, made through Interpol Washington. He provided both agencies with Raymond's booking photo and fingerprints. It was all well-intentioned, professional police work. The trouble was none of it helped the here and now. Raymond was still somewhere in L.A., and no one here could find him.

There was a loud *whoosh* as Barron flushed and went to the sink to wash his hands. Despite his emotional and very public challenge to Raymond and despite his own desperate and equally emotional need to quit the 5-2 and leave L.A., two other things raged inside him—his sense of how very important it was to get Raymond off the streets before he killed again, and then the secondary piece that went with it: the knowledge that if it was the 5-

2 and not some other part of the nine-thousand-strong LAPD who got Raymond, they would quickly take him aside and kill him. Once again he would be right there and part of it. And horrifying as it would be, there was something that was worse. Some part of him was beginning to feel that Raymond's actions had been so savage and brutal that making certain he never had the chance to kill again seemed almost justified, even the right thing to do. It was a feeling that terrified him because he could understand how easy it would be to become like the others and immune to it. It was something he couldn't think about. Wouldn't allow himself to even contemplate. Immediately he dried his hands and turned for the door, purposefully shifting his thoughts to the dead kid in the park. As he did, a piece of it suddenly came together.

"Delay! Delay, damn it!" He turned back to look at Halliday and Valparaiso. "Multiple face shots make him all but impossible to ID in a hurry. That's why Raymond did it and why he picked him. They're close enough in age and build, and the kid wasn't poor. Raymond would know he'd have some kind of ID, money, and probably credit cards. It wasn't just the clothes he was after, it was the rest of it. He's going to try and pass himself off as the victim."

Barron shoved out the door and into a fluorescent-lighted corridor. Halliday and Valparaiso were right behind him.

"We're looking for a guy with purple hair trying to get out of town and maybe out of the country as fast as he can! We find out who the kid was, we'll know where Raymond is the minute he puts down a driver's license or tries to use a credit card."

38

BEVERLY HILLS. 1:30 P.M.

Raymond walked quickly down fashionable Brighton Way, passing exclusive shop after exclusive shop on sidewalks so clean they might have been polished. A Rolls-Royce went by and then a stretch limousine with darkened windows. And then he was there. Alfred Neuss Jewelers. A gleaming black Mercedes was double-parked in front, a chauffeur in a black suit standing beside it.

He'd been right. Neuss was doing business.

Raymond adjusted the backpack. Then, feeling the solid press of the Beretta under his Levi's jacket, he opened the polished brass and mahogany door and went inside, fully prepared to explain why a young man in jeans with purple hair under an L.A. Dodgers cap would be entering so fashionable and prohibitively expensive a store.

His feet touched thick carpet, and the door closed behind him. He looked up expecting to see Neuss right in front of him waiting on the Mercedes customer. Instead he saw a very well dressed, very well coiffed, very matronly saleswoman. The customer was there, too, a young, sensual blonde in a short, revealing dress. He thought he'd seen her in the movies, but he wasn't sure. But that, like the story he'd invented as to why he was there, made no difference. Because the moment he asked for Alfred Neuss his entire plan disintegrated.

"Mr. Neuss," the saleswoman informed him with more arrogance than he'd ever encountered even among the super-rich friends of the Baroness, "is out of town."

"Out of town?" Raymond was stunned. That Neuss might be away was never a consideration. "When will he be back?"

"I don't know." She drew herself up to glare at him. "Mr. Neuss and his wife have gone to London."

London!

Raymond felt his feet on the pavement as the door to Neuss's shop closed behind him. He was numb, beside himself with his own folly. There had to be only one reason Neuss had gone to London, and that was that he had learned about the killings in Chicago, and maybe the others as well, and had gone not only for his own safety but to confer with Kitner. If that were the case, there was every reason to believe they would go to the safe deposit box and move the pieces. If that happened, everything he and the Baroness had planned would—

"Raymond."

Suddenly he heard a familiar voice say his name and froze

where he was. Next to where he stood was a specialty pizza store. The door was open, and a number of patrons were gathered around a large-screen TV. He stepped inside, stopping by the door. The people were watching a news broadcast. On the screen was a videotaped interview with John Barron. He was standing in MacArthur Park in front of the bushes where Raymond had killed Josef Speer.

"I'd like to know how you're feeling, Raymond. Are you alright?" Barron was looking directly at the camera and mocking him with the same feigned concern Raymond had used against him at Parker Center barely twenty-four hours earlier.

"You can call nine-one-one the same as anyone else. Just ask for me—you know my name, Detective John Barron, Five-Two Squad. I'll come and pick you up myself, anywhere you want. That way nobody else gets hurt."

Raymond moved closer, piqued at Barron's manner but equally surprised to find they had come on Speer's body so quickly and in the same breath realized who had done it.

Abruptly he felt a presence and looked to his left. A teenage girl was watching him. When she saw him look at her, she turned away and moved closer to the screen, seemingly drawn to the immediacy of what was happening.

Raymond looked back and saw Barron's picture vanish from the screen. In its place came his LAPD booking photo. He saw himself shown front view and then side view. Now the video cut back to Barron in the park. The mockery had vanished and he was deadly serious.

"There are nine million of us and only one of you. Do the math, Raymond. It's not hard to figure the odds."

Again Raymond's photo flashed on the screen. The teenage girl glanced back over her shoulder looking for him.

He was gone.

1:52 P.M.

39

Raymond crossed Wilshire Boulevard in a rush of emotion. Angry with himself for taking Alfred Neuss for granted, with Neuss for going to London, with the arrogance of John Barron. What made it more serious was the effectiveness of the Los Angeles police and their exceedingly rapid and relentless pursuit of him. It made it all the more imperative he get out of the country now, tonight, as he'd planned. It meant, too, that he had to inform the Baroness.

He stopped in the shade of a large overhanging palm and took Charles Bailey's cell phone from his backpack. Calling the Baroness with more bad news was the last thing he wanted, but he had no choice, she had to know. Clicking on, he started to punch in her number. Immediately he stopped. Two in the afternoon in Beverly Hills was ten at night in London, and the Baroness would still be at 10 Downing Street attending the dinner the British prime minister was giving for the mayor of Moscow and the Russian Federation minister of defense, and he couldn't call her there.

Immediately he clicked back on and punched in Jacques Bertrand's number in Zurich, where it was 11:00 P.M. If Bertrand was sleeping it was too bad. The call rang through and Bertrand came on the line, awake and alert.

"Il y'a un nouveau problème," Raymond said in French. *"Neuss est à Londres. Il est là maintenant."* We have a new problem. Neuss has gone to London. He's there now.

"London?" Bertrand asked.

"Yes, and he's probably with Kitner."

"Did you get the—?" Their conversation continued in French.

"No, I have neither the key nor the information." Abruptly Raymond left the shade of the tree and moved on, passing Neuss's apartment and retracing his steps on Linden Drive, looking like anyone else walking along and talking on a cell phone.

"My picture has been shown on television. The police are everywhere. I have a stolen passport and ticket on Lufthansa flight number 453 tonight for Frankfurt. You have put the machinery in gear for a private jet and new passport, yes?"

"Yes."

"Cancel it."

"Are you sure?"

"Yes. There's no use taking a risk of it later being found out. Not now."

"Are you sure?" Bertrand asked again.

"Yes, dammit. Tell the Baroness I'm sorry, but that is the way it has worked out. We will regroup and start from the beginning. I'm going to get rid of this cell phone so that in the event of my capture this call cannot be traced to you. Consequently there will be no way for either you or the Baroness to contact me. I will contact you when I reach Frankfurt."

Raymond clicked off and turned up Gregory Way toward Spalding Drive, where he'd left the car. His plan was to drive to one of the long-term parking terminals at LAX, leave the car there and take a shuttle into the airport itself, then trust in Fate that he could carry off the charade well enough to be ticketed, pass through the security check, and board Lufthansa flight 453 as Josef Speer without incident.

He reached Spalding and turned the corner, then stopped. Two Beverly Hills police cars were pulled over midblock, their light bars flashing. People stood in the street and on sidewalks watching as uniformed officers studied a parked car. His car. The one with the body of Charles Bailey in the trunk.

Nearby an elderly woman was engaged in an animated conversation with one of the policemen while struggling to hold on to the leash of a small dog dancing in circles and barking incessantly at the car. Immediately another policeman walked back to his patrol car, retrieved a tool of some kind, and went back to Bailey's car. Shoving the tool underneath the latch, he popped the trunk.

A collective cry went up from the crowd as they glimpsed the body in the trunk. The dog barked louder, tugging at its leash and nearly pulling the woman from her feet.

Raymond watched for a moment longer, then turned and walked quickly in the opposite direction, heading back toward Wilshire Boulevard.

2:15 P.M.
LOS ANGELES CITY MORGUE. SAME TIME.

John Barron stood behind Grammie Nomura, watching her as she sketched. Grammie was sixty-seven, Japanese-American, a great-grandmother, accomplished ballroom dancer, and painter of some of the most intriguingly original landscape canvasses he'd ever seen. She was also the top professional composite sketch artist for the LAPD and had been for twenty years. Over that time she'd done a thousand composite drawings of wanted felons and half that many more of the missing or dead, people the police were either looking for or trying to identify. Now she sat here over the mutilated body of the purple-haired murder victim trying to draw him as he might have looked a few hours earlier when he was still alive.

"Draw two, Grammie," Barron said as she worked on the sketch that would be broadcast over every local television station in Los Angeles as soon as she finished. "One as if he had purple hair, one as if he didn't. Maybe he'd only had it colored in the last few days." Barron watched a moment longer, then turned away to pace up and down and let her do her work.

Learning the victim's identity was the key. It was why he was here, pressing Grammie himself. As long as Raymond was free he called the shots, and Barron was determined to cut that freedom short as quickly as possible by cranking up the media blast at him while at the same time working to learn the victim's identity and then coming at him from the other direction, trying to nail him the minute he used the victim's identification.

McClatchy had taken Barron's theory of identity theft to heart as well and immediately sent an advisory to all police agencies in Southern California that their fugitive might be masquerading as a young man with purple hair trying to leave the area by any means he could. He'd followed up by ordering the doubling of police presence at the major departure points—airports, bus and rail terminals—and directing that Raymond's photograph be distributed to every hair salon, with the expectation that Raymond had already had his hair dyed to match the victim's, or would attempt to. Last, he'd sent a terse directive to every local police department from San Francisco to San Diego requesting they pull over and identify any white male between the ages of fifteen and fifty with purple hair. "You can apologize later" was his finishing sentence.

"Detective." Grammie Nomura was looking up over her shoulder at Barron. "This suspect you're after—I can see it in everything about you. The way you stand, the way you're walking back and forth and up and down wishing I would hurry up—"

"See what?"

"You want to get him yourself. You, personally."

"I only want to get him, I don't care who or how."

"Then take my advice and keep it that way and just do your job. You let him get into your bones, you'll get yourself killed."

"Yes, Grammie." Barron smiled.

"Don't take it lightly, Detective, I've seen it happen before, and I've been around here a whole lot longer than you have." She turned back to her sketch. "Here, come take a look."

Barron came up behind her. She was filling in the eyes, making them bright and passionate, little by little bringing the murdered boy back to life. Seeing him touched Barron in his gut and made him despise Raymond even more. Grammie's perception was right, but her warning was too late. He did want to get Raymond himself. It was already in his bones.

40

MACARTHUR PARK. 3:10 P.M.

Polchak was hunched in the shade of the overhang of brush trying to get some sense of the whole. Red squatted a few feet in front of him studying the ground where the victim had been; the body long taken away by the coroner, the Scientific Investigations people gone as well. Now it was just the two of them, the 5-2's most senior detectives feeling it out afterward the way they had for years. Old bloodhounds sniffing around trying to understand what had happened and how. And where the perpetrator might have gone afterward.

Red stood up and carefully crossed to the opposite side. "No broken bushes, no scuff marks in the dirt. The kid wasn't dragged in here, he came because he wanted to."

"Homosexual thing?"

"Maybe." Red continued to examine the ground. What he wanted most was some clue as to where Raymond had gone afterward. "Remember the cab? We think Raymond's in it, he's not. Maybe the kid thought Raymond was gay because he let him think so." Red looked over at Polchak.

"He gets on the Southwest Chief in Chicago. Maybe he killed those guys there, maybe he didn't. Maybe he's with Donlan, maybe not. But all that aside, he's on a train that's due in to L.A. at eight-forty on a Tuesday morning. Yet he's got a ticket to London on a Monday flight leaving LAX at five-forty. I think it's pretty safe to say he took the train because of the ice storm in Chicago or he would have been in town on Sunday. But forget the day, the point is he was very determined to come here, and with a gun in his bag. Why?"

Just then McClatchy's cell phone rang, and he pulled it from his jacket. "Which one?" he said to Polchak, then clicked on. "McClatchy."

"Hey, Red, it's G. R.," a cheerful voice came back. "Having a nice day?"

G. R. was Gabe Rotherberg, chief of detectives for the Beverly Hills Police Department.

"What do you think?"

"Maybe I can help," Rotherberg said.

"You're not telling me you got him?"

Polchak snapped around. What the hell was this?

"No, but I think I've got one of his victims."

3:50 P.M.

Raymond was standing, grasping the handrail and squeezed in among the crush of afternoon commuters taking the green-and-white number 6 Culver City bus south along Sepulveda Boulevard toward the main transit center at LAX.

Vsay ego sudba V rukah Gospodnih. All his destiny was in God's hands. Everything was for a reason. All he had to do was trust in it. And once again he had.

Walking deliberately away from the police on Spalding Drive, he'd reached Wilshire Boulevard just as a Metro bus was discharging passengers. Boldly he'd approached a plump middle-aged woman getting off and asked her if she knew the way to Santa Monica by bus. At first she'd been startled, but then she'd looked at him and brightened in that way so many women did, as if she wanted to wrap him up right there and take him home.

"Yes," she'd said. "Come, I'll show you."

Immediately she'd walked him across the broad expanse of intersection where Wilshire and Santa Monica boulevards crossed and told him to take the number 320 Metro bus to Santa Monica. How long they'd stood there waiting he barely remembered, but it seemed like only seconds before the bus arrived and he boarded, politely thanking her. He looked out the window as the bus pulled away and saw her watching it. Finally she turned and trudged off, going back the way she'd come, bent over, purse tucked under her arm, the way she'd been when he'd first seen her, the light that had flared up so brightly when she'd been with him extinguished.

Yet for all the help she'd been, Raymond knew she could as easily become a major hindrance, especially if she turned on the TV when she got home and saw his picture and called the police. That was why he'd asked directions to Santa Monica instead of LAX and then waited to ask someone on the bus where to transfer to a bus that would take him to the airport.

"Get off in Westwood, take the number six Culver City bus. Goes right to the Transit Center," a postal worker in the seat behind told him cheerfully. "A free shuttle will take you right into the airport itself. Easy as pie."

That was what he had done, getting off in Westwood and waiting on the street corner with a half-dozen others until the number 6 bus came. When it did he made sure he was the last to board it, carefully slipping Charles Bailey's cell phone under the bus's front wheel just as he got on, then standing beside the driver as the bus pulled away and hearing the faint crunch as the weight of the bus mashed it into the pavement.

Then he had taken his place to stand among the passengers. There, as on the previous bus and while standing on the street corner waiting for the current one—and despite the public broadcast of his LAPD photograph on television and John Barron's plea to the public to find him—in jeans, denim jacket, and backpack, L.A. Dodgers baseball cap pulled down and covering most of his dyed-purple hair, not one person paid him the slightest attention.

41

WESTIN BONAVENTURE HOTEL, SUITE 1195. 4:17 P.M.

Barron, Halliday, Valparaiso, and Lee moved carefully. Each wore surgical gloves, and each watched exactly where he stepped and what he touched. The suite was large—a main living room with couch, TV, and work desk. Beyond it was the open door to a bedroom. To the right, a short hallway lined with closets led to the bathroom. Behind them the hotel's manager and two assistants stood nervously in the open door, watching. It was bad enough the SWAT team had gone through the building like combat troops; now there was a very real possibility a hotel guest had been murdered. It was hardly the kind of publicity they needed.

"Why don't you wait outside," Barron said quietly, then ushered them into the hallway and closed the door.

The Bonaventure was perfect. A large upscale hotel, a five-minute walk at most from where Raymond had left the cab after escaping Criminal Courts. How he had encountered and killed the New Jersey consultant Charles Bailey and how Bailey's rental car had ended up in Beverly Hills was anybody's guess and the reason Red and Polchak had gone directly there.

The trouble was neither the killing in MacArthur Park nor the murder of Charles Bailey could be attributed clearly to Raymond. Yes, the modus operandi and the timing—both men shot in the head at close range, and both within hours of his escape from Criminal Courts—pointed directly to him. But as yet the police had no hard evidence, nothing that clearly and without question said "Raymond" and showed them the trail he had left.

Without that, the killer or killers of both men could have been anyone, and the police were left sifting through straws while Raymond slipped farther and farther from their grasp.

"I'll check down here." Barron went down the hallway, checking the closets first, then moving into the bathroom. Like every other room in the hotel, suite 1195 had been thoroughly searched by the SWAT teams, but they had been looking for a fugitive in hiding, not a man who wasn't there. An empty suite was an empty suite, and they'd moved on.

"I got the bedroom." Lee had come back from taking his eight-year-old to the dentist and very quickly came up to speed.

"Here." Barron's voice suddenly echoed from the bathroom. Halliday and Valparaiso went down the hallway fast, with Lee coming out of the bedroom on their heels.

When they came in Barron was on his knees pulling a plastic trash bag from a small storage cabinet under the sink.

"Looks like somebody tried to hide it," Barron said. Opening it carefully, he reached into it and lifted out a still-damp washcloth.

"Blood," he said. "Looks like the same somebody tried to rinse it out. Didn't work. A couple of used towels in here, too."

"Raymond?" Lee stood in the doorway, his massive frame filling it.

Halliday looked at Barron. "You shot him. Outside Criminal Courts."

"Just a burn."

"Well, a burn is enough to get a DNA."

"Why would he leave it here, not get rid of it someplace else, a trash can or something?"

"SWAT's going through the building like a Marine Corps invasion looking for you. What're you going to do, cover everything? You just do whatever you have to and get the hell out of there as fast as you can."

Barron put the washcloth back into the bag, then pushed past them into the main room and went to the door and opened it.

The hotel manager and his two-man crew were still there.

"What time was housekeeping here?"

"Early, sir, about eight." The manager looked past Barron to the others as they came up behind him. "Mr. Bailey saw the maid in the hall when he left and said it was alright to make up the room."

"They wouldn't have left towels and a damp washcloth crammed into the storage cabinet in the bathroom."

"Definitely not."

"And besides the SWAT personnel, no one else has been in here since."

"No, sir. Not that I know of."

Barron glanced around once more, then looked at Lee.

"What about the bedroom?"

"Come see."

Barron followed Lee into the bedroom with Halliday behind him. An open suitcase sat on a rack in a corner, a closet door was partially open, and the bed was rumpled but unopened, as if someone had lounged on top without pulling back the covers.

"Let's get a Scientific unit up here fast," Halliday said quickly, and turned to look at Valparaiso in the doorway. "Room cleaned and made up, then somebody comes in. Whoever it was used the bathroom and bedroom. We have Raymond's prints. If it was him, it won't take long to verify."

"Marty, Jimmy, anybody." Red's voice crackled sharply from their radios.

"Marty, Red." Valparaiso clicked on. "Go ahead."

"Beverly Hills PD is dusting the car, there's prints everywhere. Mr. Bailey was shot clean, close range in the back of the head like the deputies at Criminal Courts. More important, we got a double maybe here. Two calls just came in to the BHPD back to back. Young girl in a pizza shop says she's sure Raymond was in the store maybe an hour and a half ago. Another woman says she helped him onto the three-two-zero Metro bus to Santa Monica maybe twenty minutes after that. Santa Monica PD is going to cover the bus. You and Roosevelt go talk to the woman. Edna Barnes. B-A-R-N-E-S. Two-four-zero South Lasky Drive. BHPD is there now.

"Jimmy, you and John see the girl in the pizza shop. Alicia Clement, C-L-E-M-E-N-T, at the Roman Pizza Palace, nine-five-six-zero Brighton Way, she's there talking to the BHPD. Maybe it's not him, but the pizza shop and the Lasky Drive location are within blocks of each other and where the car was found. I'm assuming it is him. By now he'll be long off the bus, but he's on the west side and making mistakes. We're not there yet, gentlemen, but we're closing. Good luck, be careful."

4:40 P.M.

42

CULVER CITY BUS NUMBER 6. SAME TIME.

Raymond felt the bus slow and then stop. The doors opened, and a number of people got off and as many more got on. Then the driver closed the doors, and the bus moved off.

In less than ten minutes they would be at the LAX Transit Center, then on the shuttle into the airport itself. So far so good. He was just a passenger like everyone else. No one had so much as looked at him. Now he looked toward the front of the bus. When he did, his heart came up in his throat. Two uniformed and armed Transit Police had come on with the last passengers. They stood near the bus driver, one talking to her, the other looking back at the passengers.

Slowly, carefully, Raymond turned away only to find an elderly black man with white hair and a full white beard sitting across the aisle staring at him. Raymond had seen him standing earlier, so he must have taken the seat when one of the departing passengers vacated it. Tall and thin and dressed in a brightly colored pull-around reaching to his ankles, he looked like some sort of tribal prince, proud and exceedingly intelligent.

Raymond looked at him for a moment and turned away. Fifteen seconds later, he casually looked back. The man was still staring, and Raymond began to wonder if maybe he thought Raymond looked familiar and was trying to place him. If that were so, and he realized who Raymond was, it would make him very dangerous, especially with the Transit Police on board.

Again Raymond looked away, only this time he changed his grip on the rail beside him and slid his free hand under his jacket to take hold of the Beretta in his belt. Just then the bus began to slow and he saw the bright lights of the Transit Center, then felt the swing of the bus as it turned in. He looked back to the old man. He was still watching him.

It was unnerving enough even without the Transit Police, and Raymond knew he had to do something to break the man's train of thought before he came to a conclusion and acted on it. As a result he did the only thing he could think of. He smiled.

What came next was the longest moment of his life, a point in time where the elderly man did absolutely nothing but continue to stare. Raymond thought he would go crazy. Then, finally, and to his undying relief, the old gentleman smiled back. It was an immense, knowing smile, one that cut to the quick. A smile that said he knew exactly who Raymond was, but for reasons particular to himself had decided to keep it a secret. It was a gift from one stranger to another. One Raymond would cherish forever.

43

THE BARRON/HALLIDAY CAR, SANTA MONICA
FREEWAY. 5:10 P.M.

Halliday was pushing eighty, weaving in and out of freeway traffic, the red and yellow light bars flashing in the rear window.

"What do you think's going on with him?" Halliday asked. It was the first time he and Barron had been alone since that morning when Halliday had sent Barron hustling to Criminal Courts to make certain Raymond wasn't allowed out on bail.

"Three identical safe deposit keys to a box most likely in a bank somewhere in Europe. Raymond Oliver Thorne, born"—Halliday stumbled over the pronunciation—"Rakoczi Obuda Thokoly, Budapest, Hungary, in 1969, becomes a naturalized U.S. citizen in 1987. He's raising hell in L.A., but he's got all this London and Europe and Russian business. Who the hell is he and what the hell is he up to?"

London and Europe and Russia.

Other things had come to light after Raymond's murderous rampage began and the Scientific Investigations people started going back over the things found in his valise in earnest. Along with the Ruger automatic, the clips of ammunition, the passport, and the safe deposit keys—keys manufactured by a Belgian company that did business only in the European Community; and a company that could not (or perhaps would not) divulge to anyone, police agencies included, the location of safe deposit boxes that their safe deposit keys would unlock—had been a neatly folded change of clothes (sweater, shirt, socks, underwear, a shaving kit)—and a slim and inexpensive daily calendar. Inside it, four dates had been checked off and a simple handwritten notation made beneath each.

Monday, March 11. London.

Tuesday, March 12. London.

Wednesday, March 13. London, France, London.

Thursday, March 14. London. Beneath this was a short entry written in a foreign language and then, in English, *Meet I. M. Penrith's Bar, High Street. 8:00 P.M.*

Friday, March 15. 21 Uxbridge Street.

That had been all until:

Sunday, April 7. After the "7" was a handwritten forward slash followed by a single word written in the same language as the one under the March 14 date, a language quickly discovered to be Russian. Translated, the notation read: *April 7/Moscow.* The translated March 14 entry read: *Russian Embassy/London.*

What any of it meant or how it pertained to what Raymond was doing or had done, if anything, was impossible to tell. The only connecting factor was that he'd had a plane ticket leaving L.A. on March 11 that would have put him in London on March 12. What he had planned to do when he got there and whether any of the other dates had to do with why he came to L.A. or had been in Chicago was equally impossible to tell.

The FBI had been given access to the information to cross-check with their terrorist identification databases, and the London Metropolitan Police had been contacted. So far nothing untoward had come back. The dates were simply dates. London, France, and Moscow were nothing more than places, as was the Russian Embassy in London. The 21 Uxbridge Street address was also in London and within walking distance of the Russian Embassy, but it was a private residence, the ownership of which was being checked. Penrith's Bar on High Street was in London, too, but it was merely a city pub frequented by students, and who I.M. was was impossible to know. So aside from the Ruger, the passport, and possibly the safe deposit keys there seemed little else to be gleaned from what they had unless they got Raymond himself and asked him.

"We kill him, we'll never know," Barron said quietly.

"What?" Halliday's eyes were on the freeway in front of him.

"Raymond." Barron turned to look at Halliday directly. "The 'go' is on for him, right?"

Halliday changed lanes quickly. "Red showed you the photos, didn't he? Little speech about this 'old witch of a city,' the warning about your oath to the squad, threatening you not to try and walk away from it. We all got it."

Barron studied him, then looked away. Next to him, Halliday was the youngest of the squad. There was no way for Barron to know if Red had told him about every felon they'd taken down, so there was no way to know how many Halliday had been present for, or might have even done himself. What was clear, just in his manner and the way he talked about it, was that he had become immune to it. By now it was just part of the job.

"You want to talk about it?" Halliday slowed behind a Cadillac limousine, eased the wheel left, then pounced on the accelerator. The car veered into the breakdown lane and shot forward in a storm of freeway dust.

"About what?"

"About the 'go.' You got a problem with it, talk, get it out. That's the way it works, one player on the team talking to another about something that troubles him."

"It's okay, Jimmy. I'm fine." Barron looked away. The last thing he wanted was further justification for murder.

"John." Halliday looked over, warning written all over his face. "The legend is that no one has ever quit the squad. It's not true."

"What do you mean?"

Abruptly Halliday looked back, then goosed the siren and cut hard across four lanes of traffic to take the next off-ramp. At the bottom he slid to a stop behind a line of cars, then revved the siren again and swerved around them, taking a hard right through a red light and racing off, heading north on Robertson Boulevard toward Beverly Hills.

"May 1965, Detective Howard White," Halliday said. "August 1972, Detective Jake Twilly. December 1989, Detective Leroy Price. And those are just three I happen to know about."

"They quit?"

"Yeah, they quit. And they're all dead because of it, by and for the squad. All honored by the department as heroes afterward. That's why I said if you have a problem, talk it out. Don't be stupid and think you can act on your own. You'll end up with a bullet in your head."

"It's okay, Jimmy, don't worry," Barron said quietly. "Don't worry."

5:20 P.M.

44

LAX, LOS ANGELES INTERNATIONAL AIRPORT. 5:55 P.M.

The shuttle bus's doors closed, once more compressing the pungent smell of sea air and jet exhaust with the stale body odors of weary travelers as the driver pulled away from Tom Bradley International Terminal and into traffic inside the airport's inner loop.

Raymond stood midbus, as anonymous as anyone else, gripping the handrail and waiting patiently for the stops at Terminals 2 and 3 and then Tom Bradley International Terminal, where Lufthansa was located.

Increasingly, his nerves were on edge, knowing that with each passing minute more and more Angelenos would be seeing the television news broadcasts. What had Barron said?

"There are nine million of us and only one of you." How long would it be before one of them recognized him and pulled out a cell phone right there to call the police?

Lucky as he'd been, he had yet to reach the Lufthansa counter and the major hurdle of using Josef Speer's passport and credit card to purchase a ticket. And afterward, assuming he was successful, there were still more than three hours before his flight took off, which meant waiting in public all that time. The Baroness had assured him that if he had the wit and guile to survive, this would be an experience beyond value, and she was right. So far those tools had worked, and he knew if he stayed alert and did not fall prey to his own fears or the tenacity of the police, if he kept on just as he had, there was every reason to believe that by this time tomorrow he would be in London.

LAPD PARKING GARAGE, PARKER CENTER. 6:25 P.M.

John Barron went through the motions as if in a dream—unlocking the Mustang's door, sliding behind the wheel. He barely remembered the interview with the teenage girl at the pizza shop in Beverly Hills. At about 2 P.M. she had observed a man she thought looked like the police fugitive whose photograph she had seen on television, but she hadn't thought much about it and had gone home. Then she'd seen his picture on TV again and told her mother, who immediately called the Beverly Hills PD. They had interviewed her and taken her back to the pizza shop, where she described the circumstances and pointed to the spot where he had been standing. She told the same story again to Halliday and Barron when they arrived. The man had looked like Raymond. He had worn jeans and a blue-jean jacket. She couldn't tell if he'd had purple hair, because he was wearing a baseball cap. If the cap had had an identifying logo, she didn't remember.

The Beverly Hills woman Lee and Valparaiso had talked to had given a similar description of a young man she'd helped to find a bus to Santa Monica at a little past two. Right there was a bingo because the times of day coincided. It told them, too, he had gone west from Brighton Way to the corner of Wilshire and Santa Monica boulevards. The older woman had added to the teenager's description by saying he had been exceedingly handsome and was carrying a backpack.

That information in hand, Red had immediately ordered the investigation moved to the area between Beverly Hills and Santa Monica and brought in the L.A. Sheriff's Department and the Santa Monica PD. Brought in, maybe, but as everyone knew, Raymond belonged to the 5-2, and if he were found the media and the public would be kept far away until they got there and took charge.

Barron started the Mustang's engine, eased the car out of the parking space, and headed out of the garage. He was going home, as was Halliday, to get some rest while Red and the others stayed on the job, coordinating efforts from Parker Center.

Home? Rest? What did that mean?

For nearly five years he had thought he was in an honorable profession, and then came the seemingly dream promotion to the 5-2. Then, almost overnight, the dream wrenched into an unthinkable nightmare, all twisted and warped and turned upside down. The idea of standing by and watching while Raymond was killed sickened him. Yet if Raymond had so much as raised a weapon against any of them, Barron would have shot him in an instant with no second thought at all. And the fact was he had tried to bring him down in the parking lot outside Criminal Courts, but Raymond had spun away at the last second and he'd missed the kill shot. So if he could have done it right there in public, why was it any different just to get him somewhere alone and do the same thing?

Initially the answer had been easy. He was a cop, not a murderer. Red's warning had given him more reason than ever to quit the 5-2. And frightening as it had been, Halliday's warning had not deterred him. The problem was time. In going along with the squad, showing nothing, as he'd planned, until Dr. Flannery had found a place for him to take Rebecca, he was giving the 5-2 and himself every chance to catch Raymond. And when it happened he would be forced to be a part of his execution. Horrible enough in itself, but not as vile as the thought that had come over him that afternoon and continued to haunt him still—increasingly he was beginning to see how killing someone like Raymond could be *justified*. And once that premise was accepted the rest was easy. Just go along with it like the others did—impervious, immune, unaffected—believing it was for the good of everyone and the right thing to do.

"No, goddammit!" Barron spat out loud.

The whole thing was like some monstrous seductive drug and something he could not and would not be part of again. It was only a matter of time before they caught Raymond. Only a matter of time before they had him alone and one of them put a gun to his head and squeezed the trigger. That meant he had no choice but to go to St. Fràncis, collect Rebecca, and leave Los Angeles right then, right now, tonight.

45

6:30 P.M.

Barron felt the pound of his heart and the cold sweat on his forehead as he eased the Mustang out onto the street. A moment later he clicked on his radio, tuning it to the 5-2's secure channel 8. He wanted to know where they were and what they were doing.

He heard nothing. The channel was silent.

Abruptly he clicked to the main LAPD frequency, thinking maybe there was something there, but all he heard was the usual police chatter.

He turned down San Pedro Street and clicked back to channel 8. It was as silent as before.

Ahead he saw a man with crutches in the crosswalk. He slowed and stopped, waiting for him to pass. Sitting there the thought came to him that the squad should have done their homework better. Known more what kind of a person he really was before they brought him into it.

The man with crutches reached the curb. Barron touched the accelerator and the Mustang shot forward. At the end of the block he took a hard right toward the freeway and Pasadena, his decision made, Raymond erased from his thoughts.

Channel 8 was still silent, and he switched the radio to channel 10, the frequency Central Dispatch used to communicate with the 5-2. As he did the radio suddenly came to life.

"Commander McClatchy." Dispatch was trying to reach Red.

"McClatchy." Red's voice came back.

"German student tour group staying at the Westin Bonaventure. One of their people is missing. They just saw the composite sketch of the MacArthur Park victim on TV. They believe it's him. Male Caucasian, twenty-two years. Josef, with an *f*, last name Speer. S-P-E-E-R. His hair was dyed purple. He hasn't been seen since before noon."

"Copy. Thank you." Barron heard Red pause, then, "Marty, Roosevelt. Get the hell back to the Bonaventure."

"Copy." Valparaiso's voice came back.

"Christ!" Barron said out loud. Why the hell hadn't he thought to look for the victim in the hotel? Raymond had been there, it was a natural. His prey was right under his nose. He'd found him and used him to get past the police units and then took him to MacArthur Park. Immediately a second thought flashed. Raymond's notes were focused on Europe and Russia, and the kid was *German!*

Barron glanced at the dashboard clock.

6:37 P.M.

He picked up his cell phone.

46

"Dan Ford, hang on a minute," the one-eyed reporter said. He was bent over, fussing with the printer-connection plug on his laptop, a half-eaten tuna sandwich on the desk beside him, the telephone receiver tucked under one ear.

"It's me," Barron said sharply.

Ford stood up. "I've been trying to get you." His questions came rapid fire. "Where the hell are you? What's with your cell phone? What's going on with the Beverly Hills PD?"

"They found a body in a car, a New Jersey consultant. Looks like Raymond's work."

"You get an ID on him? How did Raymond get to Beverly Hills? Any more on the kid in the—?"

"Dan—I need your help. You in your office?"

"More or less." Minutes earlier Ford had just come huffing and sweating into his tiny cubicle of an office in the *Los Angeles Times* headquarters after several hours of covering the LAPD missing persons unit scouring the area around MacArthur Park trying to get an identification of the dead man.

"Let me find my chair." Ford walked around his desk holding the phone, lifting the cord over the piles of notes, books, and research materials that took up every inch of free space. "It's gonna rain, you know, and soon. I can feel it all through my body. My wife thinks I'm nuts." Dan Ford might have been twenty-six but any hint of rain gave him more sore joints, sore muscles, and sore bones than someone three times his age. It also gave him a throbbing ache behind his good eye.

"Dan, I didn't call for a weather report." Urgency punched through Barron's voice.

"What do you need?" Ford found his chair and sat down.

"Bring today's international airline schedules up on your screen. I want to know what flights are still to go out from LAX to Germany tonight, nonstop."

"Germany?"

"Yeah."

"Tonight?"

"Yes."

"Raymond?" Ford felt a rush. Barron knew something or was guessing something.

"Maybe, I don't know."

"Where in Germany?"

"Don't know that either. Try the three big ones, Berlin, Frankfurt, and Hamburg. Raymond had a ticket for London in his bag. It's only a puddle jump there from any one of those cities."

Ford swiveled his chair and pulled his laptop to him, clicking onto the *Times* in-house travel reference.

"Why Germany?"

"Serendipity."

"That's a no-answer, John. You don't tell me, I don't look it up."

"Dan, please—"

"Okay. Why nonstop?"

"I doubt he'd take a chance putting down at some other U.S. airport. He's too hot."

Barron's voice was strong. Maybe he was guessing about Raymond, maybe he wasn't, but whatever was going on—hunch, hard knowledge, or something Barron couldn't talk about—the electricity of it carried over to Ford as he watched the monitor in front of him waiting for the information to come up.

"Come on," Barron urged.

"I'm waiting."

"Jesus."

Suddenly the information popped up on Ford's screen. "Okay, here it is."

British Airways, Continental, Delta, Lufthansa, American, Air France, Virgin Atlantic, KLM, Northwest—Ford scanned the list. Any number of flights left Los Angeles that day for the three cities. But the only nonstops were to Frankfurt. The others had changes in London, Paris, and Amsterdam. It was now 6:53 P.M., and of the three nonstops that evening only one had yet to take off.

"You want a nonstop, John, you lucked out. There's only one still on the ground. Lufthansa, flight four-five-three. Leaves LAX for Frankfurt at nine-forty-five."

"That's it?"

"That's it."

"Lufthansa."

"Four-fifty-three."

"Thanks, Dan."

"John, where the hell are you? What's going on?"

Click.

Ford stared at the phone. "Dammit!"

47

"Etwas geht nicht?" Something wrong? Raymond asked in German, puzzled, smiling at the pert blond Lufthansa ticket agent across the counter from him. She was hanging on the phone waiting for some kind of reply.

"Your reservation is not on the computer." She continued their conversation in German.

"I made it myself, this afternoon. My seat was confirmed."

"Our computer was down for several hours."

She looked at her terminal, then typed something on the keyboard. Raymond looked to his right. There was only one other coach class ticket agent working. Behind him passengers were backing up. Twenty or more waited impatiently, a number with their eyes on him as if it were his fault the line was being held up.

"You do have seats?" Raymond tried not to show his growing concern.

"I'm sorry, the flight is full."

Raymond looked away. This was not something he'd even considered—what to do if—

"Thanks," she said suddenly in English and hung up the phone. "I apologize for the confusion, Mr. Speer, we do have your reservation. May I have your passport and a credit card, please?"

"Danke." Thank you. Raymond smiled carefully with relief, then took Speer's wallet from his jacket and handed her the dead man's passport and his Euro/MasterCard. To his left was the first class check-in, where a lone, well-dressed businessman railed at the Lufthansa attendant behind the counter. His seat was not the one he had reserved; he wanted accommodations made, and quickly. First class, where Raymond knew he should be, but wasn't.

He looked back. The ticket agent had his passport open and was looking at it; then she glanced at him, comparing his likeness to the photograph on the passport.

"Ah!" he said quickly and smiled.

Immediately he lifted his L.A. Dodgers cap to reveal his purple hair. "I was younger, you know, but—" He smiled again. "The hair is the same."

The ticket agent grinned and handed him the credit card receipt to sign. Effortlessly he scribbled Speer's signature—something he had practiced over and over on the Santa Monica bus—then handed the receipt back, and she returned his passport and the credit card.

"You have luggage to check?"

"No, I—" Raymond had rid himself of Josef Speer's backpack at the LAX Transit Center, slipping the second Beretta into his belt under his jacket at the small of his back and then stuffing the backpack into a trash receptacle just before he'd boarded the shuttle into the airport. The thing had become cumbersome and was an added burden he no longer wanted, but he'd forgotten about the obvious need for some kind of luggage. One did not travel six thousand miles without some kind of personal belongings. Quickly he covered it with a smile. "I have only a carry-on bag," he said, still speaking German, then nodded toward a fast food restaurant on the far side of the ticketing area, "I left it with a friend in the sandwich shop over there while I came to check in."

She smiled and handed him his ticket and boarding pass. "Gate One Twenty-Two. Boarding will begin at approximately nine-fifteen."

"Gute Reise," she added as he turned away. Gute Reise. Have a good trip.

"Danke," he said and walked off.

48

Barron drove west on the Santa Monica Freeway, the same highway he'd taken a little over two hours earlier with Halliday. Traffic crawled, jammed from downtown all the way to the beach. It made him wish to hell he had a police car instead of the Mustang, something with flashing lights and a siren.

Traffic still crept. Maybe he was crazy. Maybe this was nothing. The report said the German student group *believed* the composite sketch was their missing friend. So he had purple hair; thousands of people had purple hair. Why should he be struggling to get to the airport to intercept a possibly/probably/maybe missing Josef Speer when he should be collecting Rebecca and getting out of L.A? It made no sense, especially if his guess about the Frankfurt flight was wrong and there was no one at all named Speer when he got there.

Immediately he clicked on his cell phone and dialed information. Identifying himself as an LAPD homicide detective, he asked to be connected directly to Lufthansa Airlines at LAX. Forty seconds later he had a reservations supervisor on the phone.

"Flight four-five-three for Frankfurt tonight," he said distinctly. "Do you have a reservation for a Josef—with an *f*—Speer? S-P-E-E-R."

"One moment, sir." There was a long silence and then, "Yes, sir. Mr. Speer purchased a ticket nearly thirty minutes ago."

"Lufthansa is in which terminal?"

"Tom Bradley International Terminal, sir."

"Thank you." Barron clicked off.

Jesus, he was right. Suddenly another thought came. Maybe

it was Speer after all. Maybe he'd had a personal reason and just decided to go home without telling anyone. The trouble was—to locate him inside the terminal and verify his identity, he would need the cooperation of Lufthansa security. In asking for it he would have to say why, and because there was a possibility this Josef Speer might be Raymond, Lufthansa would alert the Airport Police Division, a situation that would bring McClatchy and the others, red light and siren, directly to the Lufthansa terminal. And they *had* red lights and sirens.

7:24 P.M.

A large delivery truck slowed to a stop in front of him. Barron stopped behind it and glanced in the mirror. An ocean of headlights stretched into the distance. The truck crept forward. So did he, only now he changed lanes, working toward the inside so that he could get off at the next exit ramp and take surface streets to the airport. Again, he glanced in the mirror. This time he saw not only the wash of headlights behind him but his own image, and for a moment he held there, looking into his eyes.

Never mind Red McClatchy and the 5-2. What he saw was a sworn police officer charged with enforcing the law and protecting the public. Yet he was a police officer so blinded by personal beliefs he had not seen the depth of Raymond's cunning or sensed his capability for cold-blooded butchery. As a result he'd taken no precaution at all against them. It was a flaw paid for with the lives of four policemen, one of them a woman, a man wearing a black jacket, a New Jersey consultant, and a purple-haired kid hardly out of his teens. The feeling of responsibility for those deaths and the guilt that went with it were gargantuan.

7:29 P.M.

He glanced at the radio on the seat beside him. All he had to do was pick it up and call Red, tell him what he had learned, then turn for Pasadena and let the squad deal with whoever Josef Speer was or wasn't. But he knew he couldn't, because if he did and it was Raymond, it would be as if he had ordered his murder himself.

7:32 P.M.

Barron left the freeway and took the La Brea off-ramp. His thoughts went to Rebecca, and he realized that in the name of his own conscience he could be killed himself, and not by the squad but by Raymond. He had life insurance, and Rebecca was his sole beneficiary, and he had seen to it that there was enough money in his policy to provide for her for the rest of her life if something happened to him. Except she would be alone. He was the only person she had left in the world. She fared well with the nuns and took care of herself because of him. Both Sister Reynoso and Dr. Flannery had told him so. He was the anchor to what little sanity she had; her silent, fragile existence held together because she loved him and depended on his being there. It was true that upon his death Dan Ford and his wife, Nadine, would become her legal guardians, but Dan Ford, as much as he was loved by both of them, was not her brother.

7:33 P.M.

Barron stopped behind a dozen cars at the traffic light at the top of the ramp and buried his head in his hands. "Christ," he said out loud, his sanity pushed to the point where he had to struggle just to think. Turn right when he reached the traffic light, collect Rebecca, and be five hundred miles away by daylight. Turn left and go after Raymond. If it *was* Raymond.

Ahead, the light changed and traffic eased forward. It was still green as Barron reached it. It was now he had to decide what to do. And he did. There was only one answer. Rebecca was his to care for. Their parents had already died a terrible and violent death; he would not subject her to that kind of horror again no matter what he felt he had to do for himself.

He tugged on the wheel and took a sharp right, accelerating for Pasadena. In an hour they would be out of L.A. heading north/south/east, it made no difference. In a week things would have calmed down; in a month they would be calmer still because by then Red would have realized he was no threat. And in time everything would be forgotten.

Then it came—the chilling, overpowering sense of truth.

Josef Speer *was* the dead kid in MacArthur Park, and it was Raymond who had purchased the Lufthansa ticket to Frankfurt. In that blinding moment all the momentous considerations of before vanished. Only one thing mattered. That he get to LAX before flight 453 took off.

49

GIFT SHOP, TOM BRADLEY INTERNATIONAL
TERMINAL 6, LAX. 7:50 P.M.

Raymond walked down the aisle doing his best to act like any other traveler looking for something in particular—in this case a piece of luggage he could carry onto the plane. The Lufthansa ticket agent had accepted his explanation of having a carry-on bag left in an airport sandwich shop. It was a detail, not much at all, but he had overlooked it and someone else might not, especially at the boarding gate with no carry-on luggage and no baggage receipt clipped to his ticket envelope.

Learn well from your mistakes; another directive from the Baroness, repeated like so many others since childhood. Annoying? Yes, but again her teachings were valid. The last thing he needed, especially with the high state of airport security, was a question to arise, any kink in the flow of airline procedure that might raise eyebrows and call attention to him.

At the end of the aisle he saw them—a dozen or more canvas shoulder bags hanging on a display rack. Selecting one in black, he picked it up and started toward the cashier. At almost the same time he realized he needed something to put in it. In quick order came a LOS ANGELES sweatshirt, an L.A. LAKERS T-shirt, a toothbrush, toothpaste; anything to give it bulk and be something that he might use en route.

Finished, he went to the checkout stand to wait behind several customers already in line. Then he froze. Not a foot away was a rack filled with the latest edition of *Los Angeles Times* newspapers. The booking photograph the police had taken of him at Parker Center filled the front page. Above it in bold letters were three words—"Cop Killer Fugitive." That he had been on television was bad enough, now the newspapers. Newspapers that would be available throughout the airport and might even be brought on board the aircraft.

Now he saw a subheadline and things grew worse—*May Have Purple Hair!* The police again. Fast, efficient. Correctly presuming he had taken Josef Speer's identity.

Abruptly he set his items on a side counter and retreated down another aisle and in rapid succession picked up several more things—a small hand mirror, a battery-powered electric razor, batteries for the razor.

The line was gone when he reached the cashier, and he set his items on the counter beside her, letting his hand slide under his jacket to take hold of one of the two Berettas in his belt as he did. If she recognized him and acknowledged it in any way, he would kill her right there and walk away, leaving the terminal building under cover of the horror and confusion that would follow. The same way he had planned to escape the police trap at Union Station and the Southwest Chief before Donlan changed everything.

He watched her carefully, waiting for her to look at him, but she didn't. Just watched the items as she rang them up. It was the same when he handed her Speer's Euro/MasterCard to pay for them. The same, too, when he signed the receipt, and when she put the items in a large plastic bag. Finally she handed him the bag and glanced at him. "Have a nice evening," she said by rote and turned to the person in line behind him.

"Thank you," he said and walked off.

He'd stood right there in front of her, his picture full on the front page of the *Times* inches from her sleeve, and she'd never even seen him. The only rationale he could give was that she was like the people on the buses. They saw hundreds of people every day, day in and day out for months, even years, on end, and by now not one looked any different than another.

8:00 P.M.

Barron turned hard off La Brea at Stocker. Three-quarters of a mile later he took a left onto La Cienega Boulevard, then looked for the La Tijera cut-across to Sepulveda a mile or more farther south. Altogether he had maybe four miles to go before the airport turnoff at Ninety-sixth Street. Suddenly several big, fat raindrops splattered across his windshield, the thing Dan Ford told him was coming though the weather people had forecast only a ten-percent possibility. He hoped Ford was wrong and the forecasters right.

Another hundred yards and the drops became a steady rain and then a heavy downpour. The traffic in front of him slowed to nothing. In no time the roadway was as backed up as the freeway he'd abandoned.

"Dammit!" he swore out loud. Again he wished for a light bar and siren. Those three miles could take forty minutes, even an hour if the rain continued the way it was. An hour to Ninety-sixth Street. Another ten minutes through the airport loop traffic to the International Terminal. Then identifying himself to Lufthansa security and collecting the Airport Police and afterward trying to locate Raymond without alerting him inside the terminal. It was too much time and risked putting him dangerously close to losing Raymond altogether.

Carry-on bag over his shoulder, Raymond entered a men's restroom twenty yards from the Lufthansa security checkpoint. He walked past a row of sinks and a half-dozen men standing at urinals. He entered a stall and closed the door, latching it.

Inside he took off Speer's jean jacket, unzipped the bag, and took out the mirror, electric razor, and batteries, then snapped the batteries into the razor. Seconds later he passed the razor over his head. A minute, then two and the last of the purple hair dropped into the toilet bowl. He flushed, put the mirror away, and pulled on the LOS ANGELES sweatshirt. Then, putting the jacket in the bag, he flushed the toilet once more, left the stall, and went to one of the sinks to shave. Two minutes' work with the razor and his face was cleanly shaven. A quick, casual glance around the room followed. No one was paying him the least attention. With the same casualness he looked back to the mirror in front of him, moved the razor to his head, and shaved his skull bare.

8:20 P.M.

Barron crept along La Cienega Boulevard, using the highway's inside shoulder to pass backed-up traffic. Fifty yards, a hundred. In front of him a car straddled both the shoulder and the traffic lane, giving him no room to pass. He pounded on his horn and flashed his lights, trying to get the driver to move. Nothing worked. He swore again. He was stuck where he was like everyone else. The rain came down harder. He could picture Raymond inside the terminal. He would be cool and extremely professional, simply waiting for flight time and trying to pass himself off as just another faceless passenger. But—and here was the rub—what if the ocean of media attention they had so strongly courted to get the public's help in finding Raymond turned against them? What if someone who had seen his picture on television or in the newspapers recognized him and pointed him out? They knew all too well what Raymond was capable of when he was cornered. What would he do if that happened in a packed airport terminal?

Barron looked to the radio beside him. Then abruptly past it to his cell phone. He hesitated for a heartbeat, then picked it up.

8:25 P.M.

"It may be Raymond Thorne trying to pass himself off as passenger Josef Speer." Barron's call was to Lufthansa security at LAX, his tone urgent and emphatic. "If it is Thorne, he will be trying to act like any other traveler. Thorne or Speer, assume he is armed and extremely dangerous. Just locate him and do nothing else. Don't give him any reason to think he's being watched until I get there and make the ID. Give me twenty minutes and have an agent meet me at the door. Repeat, give him no reason to believe he's being watched. We don't want a shootout in the terminal."

Barron gave his callback number, clicked off, and then hit a speed dial number to another cell phone. He heard it ring through and then a familiar voice.

"Dan Ford."

"It's John. I'm on the way to LAX, the Lufthansa terminal. There's a missing student from a German tour group named

Josef Speer, and a Josef Speer checked in for the Frankfurt flight. I think it might be Raymond."

"I had a hunch you had a hunch. I'm halfway to the airport now."

Barron half smiled. That was Dan; he could have guessed he would be. "I've got Lufthansa security looking for him. It might be a wild goose chase, it might not. Whatever it is let's keep it between us, just you and me until we know for sure."

"Hey, I love exclusives."

Barron ignored the joke. "When you get there, tell security you're with me, have them bring you to wherever I am. Tell them I said it was okay. I'll tell them myself when I get there. And Dan—" He paused. "You already know you're doing this at your own risk."

"So are you."

"I just want to remind you who we're dealing with. If it is Raymond, stay out of the way and just watch. I'm giving you the chance for a story, I don't want you dead."

"I don't want me dead either, John, or you. Be careful, huh? Be damned careful."

"Yeah. See you there." Barron clicked off. He hadn't wanted to involve Ford like that, but he had, because his call to Lufthansa security had included a proviso he didn't like but that had been necessary—that they bring in the Airport Police to back them up in case something happened. He'd done it because he'd had to, for the safety of the public if it was Raymond. But in doing it he knew it would only be minutes before Red learned what was going on, and when he did, he and the others would be on their way to LAX as if they'd been fired from a cannon. It was why Barron had included Ford. He wanted a major media witness right there in the middle of things to see what was going on.

Of course, that was assuming everything else worked, and that revolved around Barron's biggest gamble, time. McClatchy and the others were still somewhere in the city, and with the rain and traffic, even with red light and siren, it would take them time to get there. Enough time, he hoped and prayed, so that it would be all over—either student Speer would have been cleared and sent on his way, or Barron would have Raymond in handcuffs surrounded by Lufthansa security, airport cops, and probably federal police from the Transportation Security Administration, maybe even the FBI and, with luck, Dan Ford of the *Los Angeles Times*. In other words, the situation would be far too public with too many people from too many agencies for Red and the 5-2 to carry out "the go."

8:29 P.M.

"John."

Red's voice suddenly cracked from the radio on the seat beside him. Barron started. It had been barely four minutes since he'd spoken to the Lufthansa people.

"John. You there?"

Barron hesitated, then reached for the radio and clicked on.

"I'm here, Red."

"Where is here? What are you doing? What's going on?"

Red's voice was calm yet concerned, like a father talking to his son. It was the same voice he had used in his office when he had shown him the pictures of the men the squad had killed over the years and then not so gently reminded him of his own responsibility as a member of it, and the penalty he would pay if he went against it. Just the tone of it was enough to tell Barron that if Red heard anything in his voice that suggested he was doing this on his own to protect Raymond from the squad, Raymond would not be the only one who would end up dead.

"I'm stuck in traffic on La Tijera near LAX," he said as evenly as he could. "The missing Josef Speer bought a ticket on Lufthansa flight four-five-three to Frankfurt about seven o'-clock. It might be the kid, but it also might be Raymond. The flight leaves at nine-forty-five."

"Why didn't you contact me right away?" The calmness that had been in Red's voice was suddenly gone. In its place was harsh demand. "Why did you call the airline first?"

"It's only a guess, Red, that's why. It probably is just the kid, Speer. I alerted security to be on the safe side. They're just going to locate him and stay back until I get there and make the ID."

"We're on our way now. Wait for us. Don't approach him. Don't do anything until we get there. Copy me, John."

Suddenly the car just ahead of Barron inched forward, giving him a clear shot out of the logjam.

"I got a traffic break, Red, I'm moving out."

Barron dropped the radio on the seat beside him, his foot slammed the accelerator, and the Mustang shot up the inside shoulder.

50

LAX, TOM BRADLEY INTERNATIONAL TERMINAL 6, A STARBUCKS COFFEE KIOSK. 8:44 P.M.

One hour and one minute to takeoff.

Raymond stared at a clock behind the counter, then paid the cashier and took a cup of coffee and a croissant to a small table. Sitting down, he glanced at the few customers at tables around him, then took a sip of coffee and picked up the croissant. He ate not because he was hungry but because he'd had little nourishment since he'd been arrested and needed to eat. He also needed to keep a careful eye on the clock because timing was crucial. He could not pass through the metal detectors carrying the Berettas. They would have to be disposed of, but only at the last moment, after boarding had been announced and was under way. Then he would get rid of them, walk through the detectors and directly to the gate, and then board the plane.

8:53 P.M.

Raymond finished his coffee and dutifully got up to put the paper cup and the tissue from his croissant into a trash container, wondering, as he did, what the police had done about the safe deposit keys in his bag and if there was any way they could determine the location of the box they would open. At the same time, he wondered if they had tried to determine the meaning of the dates and places he had written in his address book. Or what the initials I. M. meant.

8:54 P.M.

Raymond left the kiosk and stepped out into the central corridor, looking down it toward the Lufthansa security checkpoint. Maybe a dozen people waited to pass through. No delays. Nothing unusual. He watched for a moment longer, then glanced back at the clock inside the Starbucks kiosk.

8:55 P.M.

9:05 P.M.

Barron peered through the downpour trying to see the roadway in the glare of oncoming headlights. Then he was at a major intersection. The traffic lights went from green to yellow. He accelerated, making it across just as yellow changed to red. In the same instant static crackled from his radio and he heard Red speak to dispatch:

"This is McClatchy. Request Airport Police delay boarding Lufthansa flight four-five-three."

9:08 P.M.

The rain eased just a little and Barron saw the Ninety-sixth Street sign. Downshifting, he heard the deep rumble of the Mustang's exhaust, then accelerated and turned for the airport.

"John." Red's voice came over his radio. "Where are you?"

"Coming up on the airport loop."

"We're just minutes behind you. I repeat what I said before. Don't go after him on your own. Wait for us. That's an order."

"Yes, sir." Barron clicked off. Dammit, they had come in faster than he thought. All he could do was try to stay ahead of them and hope Dan Ford was not far behind. Then he was at the loop and moving fast into the terminal area.

He passed a taxi and an airport shuttle bus on the inside, then cut in under the upper deck and out of the rain, passing what seemed like a block-long limousine.

He saw Terminal 2, Terminal 3, then the Tom Bradley International Terminal. Then he was there pulling up at the curb in a no-parking area. He jumped out, running.

"Hey, you! No parking!" A big, bald parking control cop was coming off the curb, yelling at him.

"Police officer! Emergency! Barron, Five-Two!" Barron was right up to him, tossing him the keys as he passed. "Take care of it for me, huh?"

In a blink he was across the sidewalk and into the building.

51

9:13 P.M.

Once more Raymond studied the flow of people passing through the metal detectors at the security checkpoint. Then he heard what he had been waiting for.

"Lufthansa flight four-five-three is ready for boarding at gate one twenty-two. Lufthansa flight four-five-three is ready for boarding at gate one twenty-two."

The aircraft was boarding; it was time.

9:14 P.M.

He crossed the corridor and entered the same men's restroom where he'd cut his hair and shaved his head. He was just turning the corner toward the urinal area when he suddenly stopped. A bright yellow sign was perched on the floor just inside the door-way. RESTROOM BEING CLEANED.

In the distance he heard another call for flight 453. Quickly he stepped forward and peered around the corner into the room. A lone maintenance man was entering a stall near the back with a mop. Directly in front of him, just past the yellow sign, was a large orange plastic bucket filled with detergent and murky water. Raymond glanced behind him and then toward the stall area. The maintenance man was still inside, his feet visible, the mop working back and forth across the floor.

Raymond looked behind him once more, then edged around the sign and slid the Beretta automatics from his belt. A quick glance toward the mop man working in the stall and he eased them into the bucket, watching for the briefest moment as they slipped out of sight. A heartbeat later, he turned and left.

9:16 P.M.

Barron took the stairs two at a time. Two dark-suited Lufthansa security people, a man and a woman, raced up behind him. Despite McClatchy's request, and despite having clear copies of the LAPD photos of Raymond, neither Lufthansa security nor plain-clothes Airport Police had been able to locate him among the large number of passengers. Nor had they been any more aggressive, for fear of alerting him. The best they could do was look for a man his size and age wearing blue jeans, a jean jacket, and a baseball cap—and maybe purple hair.

"Find the agent who sold Speer his ticket," Barron said as they reached the top of the stairs and started down the corridor toward the security checkpoint. "Have him or her meet us at the gate area."

9:18 P.M.

Raymond stood in line at the security checkpoint. As he reached the conveyor, he took off his shoes, the same as the other passen-gers were doing, then set the shoes and his black carry-on bag onto the conveyor belt and stepped through the metal detector.

9:19 P.M.

Raymond scooped his shoes and bag from the conveyor, then pulled on his shoes and walked off toward the departure gate. None of the security people had so much as blinked.

9:20 P.M.

Halliday cut quickly across the airport loop's traffic lanes and pulled up hard at the Bradley Terminal, parking nose-in between a taxi and a white Chevy SUV, the unmarked detective car's red and yellow lights still flashing in the rear window. A moment later he was inside the terminal, clipping his gold detective shield to his jacket pocket and lifting his radio.

"John, it's Jimmy, I just came in," he said as he crossed the main lobby, heading toward the escalator leading to the departure gates on the floor above.

9:21 P.M.

Emergency lights flashing, one, two, the McClatchy/Polchak car and the Valparaiso/Lee car pulled in next to Halliday's in the space just vacated by the white SUV. In a wave the four detectives were out, slamming car doors and clipping on badges as they headed inside.

9:22 P.M.

"We're here, Jimmy," Red's voice came over Halliday's radio.

"Upper deck, gate one twenty-two." Halliday was half walking, half running, as he talked to Red. With him were two uniformed LAPD Airport Police officers and a Lufthansa security agent. "So far we've got a big negative on locating Speer."

9:23 P.M.

Raymond stood in line behind twenty or more passengers waiting to board flight 453, the area around him brimming with a hundred or more others here for the same reason.

"Almost," he thought. "Almost."

Then he heard someone in front of him mutter about nothing happening, and he looked up to see the Lufthansa people at the jetway entrance talking among themselves. Suddenly they were letting no one pass. For some reason they'd held up the line. Behind him someone complained. As if in answer the public address system crackled.

"Your attention, please. Boarding for Lufthansa flight four-five-three to Frankfurt will be delayed."

A collective groan swept through the crowd, and Raymond felt a sudden uneasiness punch through him. He looked around and saw two tall, armed Airport Police standing not twenty feet away watching the crowd.

Christ, could this delay be because of him? Again he thought of the police and their cold, almost uncanny efficiency. How could they know? Was it possible they had determined Speer's identity and traced him here? No, that was crazy. Impossible. It had to be something else.

He glanced back down the corridor to see if there were more police. Instead he saw the young Lufthansa agent who had sold him his ticket pushing through travelers coming toward him. With her were two men in dark suits.

Jesus God—

He turned away, trying to think what to do next. Then he saw him and his heart shot to his throat. John Barron was moving intently through the crowd; a man and a woman in the same dark suits as the others were with him. All three were looking for someone.

Then he saw the others coming, too, their faces stamped in his memory for all time—the men from the parking garage. And if he had any doubts at all, there was no mistaking their leader, the one they referred to as Red, or Lee, the massive African-American who had visited him in jail to ask about the Ruger.

All around him people were groaning, complaining about the

delay, wondering what was going on. He kept tight in their midst, looking for a way out.

9:29 P.M.

"Any sign of him?" Red was pushing up to Barron. Lee was with him. So was the young Lufthansa ticket agent and the two airline security men with her.

"No, not yet. And we still don't know if it is Raymond. Could be the German kid after all. He could have just decided to go home."

Red's eyes found Barron's. "Right," he said quietly. It was a moment, that was all, but Barron knew Red wasn't happy he'd done this on his own.

Abruptly Red looked past him, his eyes moving over the crowd, and Barron knew he didn't believe it was the German kid any more than he did. Raymond was here, somewhere.

Red looked to the young Lufthansa ticket agent. "He spoke German?"

"Yes, fluently." She was looking at the crowd, the way Red had, the way they all were. "He was very good-looking, with purple-colored hair."

Red turned to Lee. "Cordon off the walkway behind us. We're going to take a hike through the crowd. Nobody gets out until we're through." Abruptly Red looked to Barron. "From here on in you're my partner. You understand?"

"Your partner?" Barron was thunderstruck. The squad didn't have partners; everyone was interchangeable with everyone else. Now suddenly he and Red were a team.

"Yes. And this time stay with me, don't be going off on your—"

Boom! Boom! Boom!

The roar of gunshots took away whatever McClatchy was going to say next.

"Get down!" Barron pushed the Lufthansa ticket agent to the floor as the detectives wheeled, guns drawn.

For a microsecond time stood still and nothing moved. Then Raymond broke, darting through the crowd and crossing the boarding area, heading for the jetway at a dead run.

52

"Dodgers cap! He's in the jetway!" So much for staying at Red's side. Barron was yelling as he ran through the confusion. The entire area was in a panic. People were running, shouting, shoving, and screaming, all trying to get out of there. Over everything hung the acrid smell of gunpowder.

Barron twisted past a priest racing the other way. At the same time, he caught sight of Lufthansa security people near the jetway. "Close off the aircraft from the inside!"

Red was coming behind him, fighting his way through the melee. Guns drawn, Polchak and Valparaiso, and Lee and Halliday, were doing the same, all closing on the jetway.

Behind them the priest was kneeling beside the two Airport Police officers who had been standing nearest Raymond—policemen he'd taken down with lightning speed and complete surprise, the same as he had the deputies in the elevator at Criminal Courts, deftly snatching the gun from the holster of the first and shooting him point-blank in the head as he reacted, then firing two quick shots into the face of the other as he attempted to counter. Then, gun still in hand, he dodged through the startled crowd and raced for the jetway leading to the plane. In that instant he and Barron locked eyes.

Barron pulled up sharply at the jetway's entrance. Beretta up, held in two hands military style, he peered carefully into the dimly lit tunnel. It was empty. Immediately he felt a presence behind him. He whirled hard. Red stood there. He was solemn, cold, unemotional.

"You understand, we get him, what's going to happen."

Barron stared at McClatchy for a nanosecond; then his eyes shot past him, looking for Dan Ford. If he was there he didn't see him. He looked back to Red, and he knew he had to forget about Ford.

"I understand," he said, then suddenly turned and twisted gun-first into the jetway.

In the faint light he could see the passageway veer to the left twenty feet ahead. How many times had he walked down one of these with no thought at all? Just follow the other passengers and get on the plane with no thought that someone was there, just past the turn of the passageway, waiting to end your life as you came around it.

"This is McClatchy." Red was still with him, talking hushed into his radio. "Patch me into Lufthansa security."

Barron inched toward the turn point, his heart pounding, his finger full on the Beretta's trigger. He was expecting Raymond to be right there as he came around the corner, and was prepared to fire the instant he saw him.

"McClatchy," Red said again. "Is the suspect on the aircraft?"

Barron counted to three and turned the corner.

"No!" he yelled suddenly and dashed forward. "He's outside!"

A door was open at the jetway's far end. Barron charged toward it, stopped as he reached it, then took a breath and went through it. He hit the top of the stairway outside just as Raymond tugged open a service door on the ground level and ran into the terminal building.

Barron took the jetway steps on the run. Behind him he could see Red come out through the door, barking orders into his radio.

At the bottom he crossed the tarmac, then pulled up quickly as he reached the door Raymond had gone through. Another breath and he eased it open to see a hallway brightly lit by overhead fluorescents. He moved forward. Just ahead, a door to the left. Another breath. He opened it and froze. It was an employee cafeteria. Several tables were turned over. A half dozen employees were on the floor. Hands clamped over their heads.

"Police! Where is he?" Barron yelled.

Suddenly Raymond stood up from behind an overturned table just in front of a far door.

Boom! Boom! Boom!

The slain airport cop's automatic danced in his hand.

Boom! Boom! Barron fired back and dove to the floor.

Rolling over, he came back up, ready to fire again. The door was open, Raymond was gone.

An instant later Barron was through it, charging into another hallway on the full run. Suddenly a door at the far end flew open and Halliday came through it, Beretta in hand.

"He didn't come this way!" Halliday yelled.

Barron saw a partially open door halfway down the corridor between them and ran toward it. He reached it first, pulled up hard, then went through it and into another hallway. Farther down he heard one gunshot, then a second.

"Christ!"

Now he was running full out. His lungs on fire, he slammed through a door at the far end. It was the baggage area. A baggage handler was dead on the floor in front of him; another was on his knees and bleeding ten feet away.

"There! He went up there!" The handler pointed toward the conveyor belt carrying luggage up into the terminal.

Shoving aside suitcases, bags, and boxes, Barron pulled himself onto the conveyor.

Boom! Ping!

Barron heard the shot and the ricochet. At the same time, he felt something whiz past his head. Then he was riding up. Twenty feet ahead he saw Raymond, crouched between baggage. By now he'd lost the L.A Dodgers cap, and Barron could see his head was shaved to the scalp.

Boom! Boom!

Barron fired. His first shot slammed off a large suitcase next to Raymond's head. The second missed entirely. Then he saw Raymond rise up on one knee to fire. Barron hit the floor expecting to hear a thundering gunshot. Instead he heard a metallic *Click!* Then came another and another. Something was wrong with Raymond's gun.

Barron moved up, twisting to the side, ready to fire. But it was too late. Raymond was gone. He could hear him scrambling up the conveyor, shoving aside luggage as he went.

The conveyor was narrow and made for luggage, not people, but if Raymond could ride it, Barron could. He shoved the Beretta in his belt, then ducked low and started up, pulling himself over two large golf bags. One second, two. He ducked again as the conveyor passed under some electrical conduit.

Abruptly it took a sharp left and he had to grab on to the golf bag to keep his balance. Suddenly Raymond was right there, dropping like a huge rat from the conveyor support structure overhead. In an instant he had Barron by the collar and was swinging the jammed automatic like a hammer.

Barron ducked away, then slammed a fist hard against Raymond's head. Barron heard him cry out, and he grabbed Raymond's shirt with his other hand, jerking him toward him to hit him again. As he did, Raymond swung the automatic once more. The move was fast and short and very hard. The blow caught Barron just in front of his ear, and for the briefest second everything went black. Then the conveyor belt gave way beneath them and both men tumbled downward, one after the other, with baggage in between. A second later they were on the luggage carousel. Barron's head cleared and he saw faces. People were screaming and yelling at him, but he didn't understand why or what. Then he realized he was on his back. His hand went for the Beretta in his belt. It wasn't there.

"Looking for this?"

Raymond stood above him, Barron's gun in his hand, inches from his face.

"*Dasvedanya.*" Good-bye, he said in Russian. Barron tried to turn away, somehow shield himself from the shot.

"Raymond!"

Barron heard the bark of Red's voice and saw Raymond whirl. There was the terrible roar of exchanged gunshots. Then Barron saw Raymond jump from the carousel and disappear from sight.

53

Dan Ford came through the door in lockstep with a black-suited Lufthansa security agent to see Raymond running right at him. For an instant their eyes met; then Raymond veered to the side, shoving an elderly man out of the way, and dashed through a sliding door. It took a moment for Ford to realize whom he had seen and what had happened. Then he became aware of screams and shouts coming from the baggage area behind him. He turned and ran toward it.

Red lay on the floor in a mass of blood. People milled around him in shock, too stunned and horrified to do anything but watch. Ford rushed forward just as Barron fought his way in from the opposite direction, pushing people aside, yelling for them to get back. Both men reached Red at the same time. Barron dropped beside him and tore open Red's jacket, shoving both hands hard into the middle of Red's chest, trying to stop the bleeding.

"Somebody call nine-one-one! Somebody call a fucking ambulance!" he screamed, then his eyes came up and he realized it was Dan Ford.

"Call a fucking ambulance!" he yelled at him. "Call a fucking ambulance!"

"He wouldn't wear a vest," Barron heard someone say, and he felt an arm try to pull him away. He wrenched free.

"John, forget it," the same voice said quietly. Barron looked up to see Roosevelt Lee standing beside him.

"Fuck you!" Barron screamed at Lee.

Then he saw Dan Ford talking forcefully with Halliday and Polchak and Valparaiso, pointing the way Raymond had gone. Suddenly the three cops bolted in that direction. Barron's eyes came back to Red, and he heard Lee's voice, soft with tears.

"It's too late, John."

Puzzlement came over Barron's face, and Lee took him by the arm, pulling him up, looking him in the face.

"It's too late, do you understand? The commander is dead."

The world floated. Sound did not exist. Everywhere faces stared. Barron saw Dan Ford come back and take off his blue blazer and cover Red's face with it. He saw Halliday and Polchak and Valparaiso come back, too, breathing heavily, their jackets wet from the rain. He saw huge Roosevelt Lee shake his head at them, his tears, rivulets now, running unhurried down his cheeks.

It was 9:47 P.M.

54

It was Halliday who sent him home. They'd need someone fresh in the office in the morning, he'd said; besides, he and Valparaiso were enough manpower to coordinate the hunt for Raymond from the airport. Lee and Polchak were already gone, traveling the longest miles of their life to the city's Mount Washington section and the plain, three-bedroom bungalow at 210 Ridgeview Lane to tell Gloria McClatchy her husband was dead.

"Drive."

"Where?"

"Anywhere. Just keep moving."

Dan Ford started the engine and drove John Barron's Mustang out of LAX, turning north toward Santa Monica. Red's blood was still on Barron's shirt and on his hands. He didn't seem to notice, just sat in the passenger seat of his own car and stared at nothing.

That a five-square-mile area around Los Angeles International Airport had been cordoned off within minutes after the incident and that literally hundreds of police, aided by helicopters and dogs, had begun combing the area for Raymond Oliver Thorne didn't seem to matter. Nor did the fact that every outgoing flight had been delayed until each passenger was carefully checked to make certain Raymond hadn't simply switched airlines in his attempt to escape.

What did matter was that Red McClatchy was dead. Maybe he could have simply shot Raymond on the luggage carousel without yelling his name. Or maybe people had been in the way and he couldn't have shot without endangering them. Or maybe he was afraid that if he didn't distract Raymond right then, in the next split second he would have killed Barron. But in the end, in those last horrible seconds there had been a brief, thundering exchange of gunfire, which meant Red had fired at Raymond. The trouble was, as good as Red was, Raymond had been better. Or faster or luckier, or all three. Whatever it had been, Red McClatchy was dead and John Barron wasn't.

Whatever had happened, Red had saved John Barron's life.

Red McClatchy, whom Barron respected, despised, and loved in the same breath. Who had made him his partner only minutes before the horror had taken place.

No matter what he had done, or what the 5-2 was about, it was impossible to think of him as mortal. He was a giant, a legend. Men like that didn't die on the floor of a busy airport terminal with all the lights on and two hundred people milling around trying to collect their luggage. They didn't die at all, they were enshrined. Maybe one day forty years into the future you'd hear he'd passed away after a long retirement. Even then, the obituaries written about him would be heroic and endless.

"He wore a flak jacket in the garage like the rest of us. But he never wore a vest. I didn't realize it." Barron continued to stare off, the rain lighter now, only fine mist in the headlights. "Maybe he believed his own myth. Maybe he thought nothing could kill him."

"Knowing Red, it was more like he just didn't like the damn things. They came from a period after his," Dan Ford said quietly and just kept driving. "Maybe that was reason enough in itself."

Barron didn't reply, and the talking stopped. In an hour they were away from the city lights, driving north into the hills on the Golden State Freeway toward the Tehachapi Mountains. By then the rain had stopped and the stars were out.

55

Thirty-five minutes after he'd left the airport Raymond was in the parking lot of the Disneyland Hotel looking up at the overhead monorail that brought guests to and from the hotel to the fabled park. For a moment he grinned in amusement—not because he had escaped a police trap by the skin of his teeth, or because he had managed to get out the same way he'd come in, by simply boarding the nearest bus at hand and riding out on it toward Disneyland even as the first sirens raced past going toward the International Terminal, the beginning of what he knew would be an enormous confluence of police that would descend within moments. He grinned because he remembered that in 1959 the then premier of the Soviet Union, Nikita Khrushchev, had asked to visit Disneyland and had been turned down by the U.S. government. It was a diplomatic faux pas that became an emotional and bitter international incident. What happened finally he didn't remember. It was the bizarre absurdity of it, to imagine what could have happened in the dark and harried chambers of Washington and Moscow as the thumbs of the cold war superpowers were edged ever closer to all-out nuclear confrontation by Mickey Mouse.

As quickly, his musing ceased. The intensity of the hunt for him, he knew, was already spiraling upward. They knew how he was dressed and that his head was shaved nearly bald. He needed a place to go where he could safely rest and regroup and try again to reach Jacques Bertrand in Zurich. This time it would not be about his arrival in Frankfurt but once again about a plane and a passport and getting him out of California as quickly as possible.

The headlights of another airport bus crossed him, and then the bus stopped. The doors opened and a group of French-Canadian tourists disembarked. Immediately he joined them and walked into the hotel lobby. Then he went to the gift shop. Once again he used Josef Speer's Euro/MasterCard, this time to buy a

Disneyland hat and a *Pirates of the Caribbean* windbreaker.

His appearance changed, if only a little, he once again used public transportation. He took the next bus back toward the city, going first to John Wayne Airport, then transferring to another bus that would take him to the only place he was reasonably certain he could spend the rest of the night undisturbed, the Beverly Hills apartment of Alfred Neuss.

An hour later he was there and thinking about a way to get in. He expected a wealthy American jeweler, even one who kept a modest apartment like Neuss, to have an electronic security system, every door and window wired against a break-in. He'd been trained to disable a dozen widely varying security systems simply by isolating the control wire to the place he wanted to gain entry, then splicing a loop into it and back-feeding the power to the monitoring station before making the cut, thereby maintaining a closed circuit and making the surveillance system appear intact when in fact it had been broken. And he'd been prepared to deal with whatever system Neuss had, but it wasn't necessary.

Alfred Neuss was not just excessively predictable, he was arrogant. The only thing protecting entry to his Linden Drive apartment was a front door lock that could easily have been picked by the most simpleminded burglar, and at twenty minutes past midnight Raymond did just that. By 12:45 he had showered, put on a clean pair of Alfred Neuss's pajamas, made himself a pumpernickel and Swiss cheese sandwich, and washed it down with a glass of the ice-cold Russian vodka Neuss kept in the freezer portion of his refrigerator.

At 1:00 A.M.—choosing not to use Neuss's telephone despite the complex way he switched numbers for fear that at some point the law enforcement experts could utilize a sophisticated trace-back—he was at Neuss's home computer in a small study across from the front entryway with Barron's Beretta on the table beside him. Within seconds he had pulled up the terminal emulator, dialed in the contact number in Buffalo, New York, and then, tel-neting into its host, logged on and sent a coded message to an e-mail address in Rome that would be electronically forwarded to another e-mail address in Marseilles, then sent on to Jacques Bertrand's e-mail address in Zurich. In it he told the Swiss attorney what had happened and asked for immediate assistance.

Afterward he poured himself a second glass of Russian

vodka, and then, precisely at 1:27 in the morning, Thursday, March 14, while nearly every police officer in Los Angeles County searched for him, Raymond Oliver Thorne climbed into Alfred Neuss's king-sized bed, pulled the covers around himself, and fell soundly asleep.

56

THURSDAY, MARCH 14. 4:15 A.M.

"Stemkowski. Jake, right?" John Barron leaned on the counter in the kitchen of his rented house in the Los Feliz section of the city, pencil in one hand, phone in the other.

"You have his home phone? I know it's six-fifteen in the morning. It's four-fifteen here," Barron said forcefully. A moment later he scratched out a phone number on a pad next to him. "Thank you," he said and hung up.

Ten minutes earlier an exhausted Jimmy Halliday had called with three pieces of information that had just come in. The first had been about two 9 mm Berettas found in a custodian's floor-washing bucket in a men's restroom at the Lufthansa terminal. Whatever fingerprints there might have been had been dissolved by the detergent in the bucket. But there was no doubt where the Berettas had come from—they had belonged to the sheriff's deputies Raymond had killed in the elevator at Criminal Courts.

The second piece of information concerned the ballistics test on the Sturm Ruger automatic found in Raymond's bag on the Southwest Chief. Matching tests proved without doubt it was the weapon used in the torture and murder of the two men in the tailor shop on Pearson Street in Chicago.

The third was that reports had just come in from the inquiries sent yesterday afternoon to the police departments in San Francisco, Mexico City, and Dallas—cities the magnetic strip on Raymond's passport had shown he had visited just before he went to Chicago, which was a period of little more than twenty-four hours from Friday, March 8, to Saturday, March 9. Unsurprisingly there had been murders in all three cities across that time frame. In both San Francisco and Mexico City, authorities reported finding the bodies of men who had been brutally tortured before they were slain. Afterward their faces had been wholly disfigured by point-blank gunshots. The victim in San Francisco had been dumped into San Francisco Bay, the one in Mexico City left at a vacant construction site. The motive behind the disfiguring and dispersal of the bodies appeared to be the delay of identification thereby giving the killer time to get away or time to pass before the bodies were discovered and their murders announced, or both. It was the same MO Raymond had used for Josef Speer. Halliday had ended the call by saying he was working with the San Francisco PD and Mexico City police to get more information on the murder victims there and asking Barron to do the same with Chicago.

Barron took a sip of hastily made instant coffee and dialed the number he had been given and waited as the call rang through. On the counter beside him rested a .45 caliber Colt Double Eagle automatic. It was his own gun, pulled from a locked drawer in his bedroom to replace the Beretta Raymond had taken from him at the airport.

"Stemkowski," a rugged, raspy voice came back as the phone was picked up.

"This is John Barron, LAPD, Five-Two Squad. Sorry to wake you, but we've got a real bad man on the loose out here."

"So I hear. What can I do?"

A real bad man. Barron was alone in his house dressed in sweatpants and a worn LAPD Academy T-shirt. He could have been stark naked standing in the middle of Sunset Boulevard at rush hour for all it mattered. He wanted as much information as Chicago PD homicide investigator Jake Stemkowski could give him on the men killed in the tailor shop.

"They were tailors," Stemkowski said. "Brothers, sixty-seven and sixty-five years old. Last name Azov. A-Z-O-V. They were Russian immigrants."

"Russian?"

Suddenly Barron flashed on the notes in Raymond's daily calendar. *Russian Embassy/London. April 7/Moscow.*

"That surprise you?"

"Maybe, I'm not sure," Barron said.

"Well, Russian, whatever, they had been U.S. citizens for forty years. We retrieved a file of Russian names covering half the states in the country. Thirty-four in the L.A. area alone."

"L.A.?"

"Yeah," Stemkowski grunted.

"They Jewish?"

"You thinking hate crime?"

"Maybe," Barron said.

"Maybe you're right, but they weren't Jewish. They were Russian Orthodox Christians."

"Get me the list."

"Soon as I can."

"Thanks," Barron said. "Go back to sleep."

"Nope, time to get up."

"Thanks again."

Barron hung up and stood there. In front of him was the .45 Colt Double Eagle. To the right, near the refrigerator, was the photograph of him and Rebecca taken at St. Francis with the caption "Brother and Sister of the Year" under it. He didn't know what to do about Rebecca now. Though it had been barely forty-eight hours, everything that had gone on before seemed to be in a distant past. The horror and revulsion he'd felt at Donlan's execution, at finding out what the squad did and had done for so long, at Red's warning and Halliday's, too, all seemed part of another life, lived when he was a much younger man. All that mattered now was that Red was dead and his killer was still out there. A man they knew almost nothing about but who would kill again and again until he was stopped. The sense of it filled him with rage. He could feel the pump of his heart and the blood rushing through him. His eyes left the photograph and swung back to the Colt automatic.

It was then he realized what had happened. He had become what he feared most. He had become one of them.

57

Raymond hunched over the computer screen in Alfred Neuss's small study. On it was a coded message from Jacques Bertrand in Zurich. Translated, it read:

Documents being prepared in Nassau, Bahamas. Aircraft arranged for. Confirmation to follow.

That was all. The Baroness had told him earlier that arranging for a passport to be prepared and delivered to the pilot who would bring it to him would take time. He had told Bertrand to cancel the entire thing after alerting him to the fact that he had abandoned the original plan and was on his way to Frankfurt. So they'd had to begin the process all over. It had been no one's fault, it just was. No, that was wrong, it was something else.

God was still testing him.

The thing John Barron looked at was pure white. Then he saw the hand, its fingertips covered with red, touch the white, making a big, scarlet circle. An eye was dropped into the middle of it, then a second eye. Then a quick triangular nose. And finally a mouth, downturned and sad, like the mask of tragedy.

"I'm okay," Barron mouthed. He tried to smile, then turned from where Rebecca stood finger painting at her easel in St. Francis's cramped little art room and went to an open window to look out at the sweeping green of the institution's carefully tended lawns.

The rain from the night before had given a God-cleansing

shower to the city, leaving Los Angeles clean and fresh and drying out in sparkling sunshine. But its purity and radiance only masked the truth of what Rebecca had drawn—too many people were dead and he was going to do something about it.

Barron started at a touch at his sleeve and turned. Rebecca stood beside him, wiping the last of the finger paint on a small terrycloth towel. Finished, she put the towel aside and took both his hands in hers and looked up at him. Her dark eyes reflected everything he felt—his anger and pain and loss. He knew she was trying to understand all of it and was upset and frustrated that she could not tell him so.

"It's alright," he whispered, and put his arms around her. "It's alright. It's alright."

PARKER CENTER. 8:30 A.M.

Dan Ford had positioned himself in the front row among the cameras and microphones as the mayor of Los Angeles read from a written statement. "Today the people of Los Angeles mourn the death of Commander Arnold McClatchy, the man everyone knew as Red. 'No hero, just a cop,' as he would say, who gave the supreme sacrifice so that a fellow officer might live—"

The last words caught in the mayor's throat and for a moment he paused. Then, collecting himself, he continued, saying the governor of California had ordered flags to be flown at half-staff over the state capitol in McClatchy's honor. Further, he said, following the commander's wishes there was to be no funeral, "just a simple gathering of friends at his house. You all know how Red hated things maudlin and liked to get them over quickly when they started to get that way." There was a brief smile but no one laughed. Then the mayor passed the microphone to Chief of Police Louis Harwood.

As quickly, the mood changed from somber to stern as Harwood said that at his orders, members of the 5-2 Squad would not be available to the media. Period. They were working to apprehend the fugitive Raymond Oliver Thorne. Period. Any questions the press might have were to be addressed through LAPD Media Relations Division. Period. End of session.

Local media people who covered the LAPD understood. The rest, who, by now, numbered nearly a hundred—with more on the way as the international press began to flood in—felt they were being kept from the center of a huge, ongoing drama. And they were, purposely. Apart from respecting the privacy and devastating sorrow of the men of the 5-2, the department itself, suffering its own grief and loss, was enraged at the treatment the media was giving the whole thing.

The killing of Red McClatchy not withstanding, five other peace officers and two civilians were dead and the killer was still on the loose. As a result the 5-2's legendary reputation as one of the finest law enforcement units in the country was starting to be portrayed to the public as, if not inept, then certainly ironic. Overnight, Raymond's actions had made the City of Angels the Wild West again. Instantly a cold-blooded killer had become a tabloid hero, a bold, daring outlaw someone had dubbed "Trigger Ray Thorne," whose headline exploits were being blazoned across the world. Seemingly without conscience or past, Raymond Oliver Thorne had become a twenty-first-century John Dillinger and Billy the Kid rolled into one. He was a young, super-handsome, fearless, and merciless gunman who shot his way out of impossible situations and outwitted the authorities at every turn. Better yet, he was still at large, and the longer he stayed that way the greater the already huge television ratings and gargantuan sales of daily newspapers.

That kind of circus was something the LAPD would not tolerate, especially now, when every reporter there wanted an interview with some member of the squad. The simplest solution, it was concluded, was to keep them incommunicado from the media. And that was what had been done.

The lone exception was Dan Ford. The department knew they could trust him not only to report the truth but to keep silent when he knew things that would make the tabloids salivate and intensify the circuslike atmosphere or interfere with the investigation. For instance, his knowledge of the ballistics test connecting Raymond to the murders in Chicago. Or the ongoing investigations into the torture-murders in San Francisco and Mexico City. Or, more personally, that at Halliday's phone call confirming the Chicago-murder association, John Barron had abruptly cast off his tragic pall and been immediately in touch with the Chicago PD and its homicide detective assigned to the Pearson Street murders. These were the kinds of things Dan Ford knew but kept to himself, and that was why the department let him in when the others were kept out.

58

BEVERLY HILLS. 8:45 A.M.

Raymond stared at the computer screen. It had been exactly four hours since he had received the e-mail from Jacques Bertrand. What was taking so long to confirm the rest he didn't know. He wanted to pick up the phone and call him, demanding to find out. But he couldn't.

All he could do was wait and trust this was not the day Neuss's maid or some other household help would show up and demand to know who he was and what he was doing there. Instead of worrying, he kept the Beretta at hand and put his full energy into a systematic search of the files in Neuss's computer and then of his apartment—examining every drawer, closet, cabinet, piece of furniture, even planter, inspecting literally every inch of the space, looking for another safe deposit key or information that would tell him the location of the safe deposit box. Everywhere he turned up nothing. The closest he had come was finding a false drawer in Neuss's wife's dressing table where she kept her jewels. The jewels were there. The key was not. The information was not.

In the end all he could do was put things back the way he found them and wait for Jacques Bertrand to confirm what he'd promised.

And hope no one watching television news or reading a morning newspaper had seen him walk down Linden Drive last night, or glimpsed him from an apartment window across the street.

ZURICH, SWITZERLAND. SAME TIME,
5:45 P.M. ZURICH TIME.

Baroness Marga de Vienne's attention was on the television so tastefully mounted into the mahogany bookshelves in Jacques Bertrand's elegant private fourth-floor office on the Lindenhof, a quiet square overlooking the Old Town and the River Limmat.

As beautiful at fifty-two as she had been at twenty, the Baroness—dressed in a dark, tailored, and very conservative traveling suit, her long hair turned up under a lambskin cloche hat hiding most of her features—was clearly uncomfortable. Rarely did she meet face-to-face with her attorney. Their business was done by secure telephone and encrypted e-mail, and most certainly when they did meet she did not come to him. But this was different. She had come to Zurich because things had changed markedly. What only days before had been a precisely timed, precision-drawn, but essentially very simple operation had turned into a nightmare of unforeseen happenstance. Raymond's very survival now depended as much on them as on him. What they would do now about Friday in London or April 7 in Moscow had to be fully reconsidered.

Whether Neuss and Kitner suspected who had committed the murders in the Americas there was no way to know. Even if they had seen his likeness on television it was doubtful that after all these years they would recognize him, especially when they would have remembered someone with dark hair and dark eyebrows, not the blond man with blond eyebrows and the cosmetic surgery to his nose that wholly changed his facial appearance. Still, it was clear that Neuss *had* gone to London on the spur of the moment, most probably because he was afraid that whoever had killed the others might well come after him next. Moreover, once in London he would confer with Kitner about what to do next, which might very well entail moving the pieces from wherever they were now to still another safe deposit box elsewhere and complicating matters all the more.

Yet troubling as that was, it was nowhere near as troubling as what they saw on Bertrand's television screen now: Raymond's photograph broadcast on a CNN special report, and with it, scenes videotaped the previous night at Los Angeles International Airport of the aftermath of his shoot-out with Los Angeles police and his killing of three of them—one, a most prominent and beloved detective—as he tried to board Lufthansa flight 453 to Frankfurt.

The abrupt ring of Bertrand's telephone interrupted the news story, and he picked up. As he did, the Baroness's gloved hand hit the mute key on the remote and the sound of the television faded.

"Yes," Bertrand said in French. "Yes, of course, notify me immediately." He hung up and looked at the Baroness. "It's done. The plane is in the air. The rest will be up to him."

"God is trying us all." The Baroness turned back to the television to see a tightly edited montage showing the massive scope of the police manhunt for Raymond as departments across California positioned themselves to apprehend him. As she watched, her thoughts turned inward and she wondered if he were strong enough to make it through.

Or if she should have pushed him even harder.

LOS ANGELES, PARKER CENTER. 9:05 A.M.

Barron walked quickly along an inner corridor talking on his cell phone to Jake Stemkowski in Chicago. Despite Chief Harwood's order, a phalanx of media had tried to corner him as he'd arrived and just as Stemkowski called. Uniforms had forced the media to retreat, and he'd taken a side door and come up a back elevator, pulling out the phone as soon as he knew he had clear reception.

"We put together the list of Russian names and addresses found in the murdered Azov brothers file," Stemkowski said. "I'm faxing the whole thing to you now. We'll keep on it and update you with anything new."

"Thanks," Barron replied.

"Sorry about your commander."

"Thank you."

Barron clicked off and opened the door to the 5-2 squad room. Polchak was there; so was Lee. They were standing at the window near his desk, as if they'd been waiting for him. He could tell they'd been drinking, but they weren't drunk.

"What is it?" He closed the door behind him.

Neither Polchak nor Lee said a word.

"Halliday and Valparaiso go home?"

"Just left," Polchak said tersely. He still wore the same suit he had at the airport, his eyes were heavy, and he had a stubble growth of beard. "You let that asshole take your gun. You fucked up bad. But then you know that."

Barron looked to Lee. Like Polchak, he wore the same clothes as the night before and had the same heavy eyes, the same stubble of beard. Neither of them had been home since they'd delivered the news to Red's widow. Clearly neither was in the best emotional state, but it made no difference. To them Red had been a god. Barron was a young, green fuckup who should have killed Raymond and didn't—and then had made things all the worse because Raymond had taken his gun from him and killed Red with it. Those things put together made what he saw in their faces unmistakable. They were blaming him for Red's death.

"I'm sorry," he said quietly.

"You armed?" Polchak's eyes were filled with a disgust that bordered on hatred.

"Why?" Barron was suddenly wary. Did they hate him enough to kill him here?

"Raymond took your gun," Lee said. "He killed Red with it."

"I know." Barron studied each man, then slowly opened his jacket. The .45 Colt rested in the holster at his waist. "I had it at home." Barron let the jacket swing closed.

"How you feel about me isn't important. The only thing that matters is getting Raymond off the street. Right?"

Polchak stood breathing, his eyes searching Barron's. Finally he grunted, "Yeah."

Barron looked to Lee. "Roosevelt?"

For a long moment Lee said nothing, just watched him as if he were deciding what to do next. For the first time Barron realized how big he was. Huge, as if he could crush him with one hand.

A hum from the fax machine broke the moment as Stemkowski's transmission came through from the Chicago PD. It was enough, and Lee nodded. "Right," he said. "You're right."

"Okay." Barron stared at both men and then went to retrieve the fax.

He tried to ignore them as he scanned the phone list Stemkowski had compiled from the address book of the murdered brothers. Azov, their family name, was Russian, as were most all the other names on the list, as Stemkowski had said. The majority of the addresses were scattered over Southern California, mostly in and around L.A. A handful were north in the San Francisco Bay area.

Barron read down the list once, then did it again. The first time he missed it completely. He nearly did the second time as well and was about to write the whole thing off as useless when something caught his eye and he looked back. A name two-thirds of the way down the page was not Russian, or at least didn't appear to be, but the street address was all too familiar. Abruptly he looked to Lee and Polchak.

"The Chicago murder victims had a friend in Beverly Hills. He has a business just a few doors down from the pizza shop where the girl said she saw Raymond and only a few blocks from where the Beverly Hills PD found the car with the consultant's body. The address is nine-five-two-zero Brighton Way. The friend's name is Alfred Neuss."

9:17 A.M.

59

BEVERLY HILLS. 10:10 A.M.

Once again Raymond checked the computer screen for Bertrand's follow-up message. There was still nothing. What had happened? Why no reply?

Had Bertrand simply no new information to pass on? Had there been a problem getting a plane and pilot? Or maybe there had been trouble getting the passport and a delay in getting it to the pilot. Had something else come up? God only knew.

Angrily Raymond turned from the screen. How long could he stay like this? By now the street outside was becoming busier. There were gardeners, repairmen, delivery people, people parking on the street and walking back the short distance to Wilshire Boulevard and the shops and offices nearby.

He looked back to the screen.

Still nothing.

He went into the hallway and then into the kitchen and then came back, his anxiety level rising with each passing minute. He knew the longer he stayed there the more his chances of being found amplified. As a precaution, he had looked for a way out if something happened before Bertrand got back to him. He'd found it in the form of keys to Alfred Neuss's dark blue, five-year-old Mercedes, which he'd discovered locked and parked in a carport in the alley at the back of the building. In an emergency it was a means of escape, but that was all. The real truth was he had no other place to go.

10:12 A.M.

Once more he turned back to check the computer, certain he would find nothing and curse Bertrand even more. But this time, and to his amazement, a message waited. Again it was coded. Decoded it read:

West Charter Air, Nassau, Bahamas. Gulfstream IV to pick up Mexican businessman, Jorge Luis Ventana, at Santa Monica Municipal Airport, 1300 hours, today. Necessary identification papers will be on board.

That was it, all he needed.

Abruptly, he went to the Web browser and clicked on Tools. Then he went to Internet Options. In the Temporary Internet Files section he clicked on Delete Files and then deleted Offline Content and clicked Clear History. Those actions combined with the labyrinth of multiple IP hosts he had used to contact Bertrand would make tracing either the sending or receiving of their correspondence all but impossible.

Next, he shut down the computer and went to Neuss's closet, where he took out the tan linen suit he had tried on earlier. The trousers were a little short and the waist too large, but with a tightened belt, the jacket would hide the excess material. From Neuss's bureau he pulled a starched white shirt and an expensive green-and-red-striped tie.

Within minutes he was dressed, knotting the tie and pulling on a straw Panama hat to cover his close-shaven head. Done, he picked up Barron's 9 mm Beretta from the bed and stuck it in his belt, then looked at himself in Alfred Neuss's full-length mirror. He looked more than presentable and smiled in satisfaction.

"Bueno," he said, and for the first time in as long as he could remember, he relaxed. There was no inspection of passports or other identification papers when one left a country on a private aircraft. Those would be needed when he landed, and he was certain they would be on board as Bertrand had promised. All he had to do was get to the airport in Santa Monica, and he already had the instrument of transportation, Alfred Neuss's Mercedes. *"Bueno,"* he said again. Finally things were going his way.

One last glance in the mirror, an adjustment of hat and tie, and he turned for the door. Suddenly he stopped, deciding it would be prudent to take one last look out the window. When he did, his entire being froze. A car was double-parked in the street outside, and John Barron was stepping from it. With him were two of the LAPD detectives who had been at the airport and in the garage when Donlan was shot. Accompanying them, leading them toward the building, was the arrogant saleswoman from Alfred Neuss's store.

10:19 A.M.

60

The four disappeared from sight below. Obviously the saleswoman had a key to Neuss's apartment or she would not be with them. That meant it was only a matter of minutes, even seconds, before they reached the front door. There was no time to replace things to try to cover up his being there. Hurriedly Raymond went into the bathroom and peered out the tiny window to the alley in the back, wondering if they had police stationed at the rear of the building. As far as he could tell, the answer was no.

In an instant Raymond was through the kitchen, out the back door, and down the stairs. At the bottom he slid the Beretta from his belt, then opened the door. A large municipal garbage collection truck blocked the alley partway down as two city workers collected trash from the apartment buildings. At the other end the alley was clear to the street. Beretta held to his side, Raymond opened the door and went directly to the carport. Coolly, he pushed the remote control button on the ignition key, disabling the alarm and unlocking the doors, and got in. A moment later the Mercedes came to life, and he backed out into the alley. The trash truck was closer now, but he still had room to maneuver.

He backed up as far as he could, then shoved the gearshift into DRIVE and touched the accelerator. The car jumped forward—immediately he slammed on the brake. A second garbage truck had come in from the other end, trapping him in between.

10:23 A.M.

Greta Adler was the woman who ran Alfred Neuss Jewelers when neither Neuss or his wife was there, and it was she who unlocked the front door to his apartment.

"Thank you," Barron said. "Now please wait out here." He glanced at Lee and Polchak, then pulled the Colt Double Eagle from the holster at his waist and went in. Lee and Polchak were right behind him.

Hallway. Small computer room. Living room. Bedroom. Kitchen. Doors opened, closets checked. There was no one there.

"Let's take a closer look." Lee went into the kitchen, Polchak the bedroom.

Barron holstered the Colt and went back to the front door. "Come in, Mrs. Adler," he said.

"Miss Adler." She corrected him as she came in.

Greta Adler had recognized Raymond's photograph the moment Barron had shown it to her at the store. He had been there yesterday afternoon, she told them.

"He said he was looking for Mr. Neuss and seemed amazed, even astonished, to learn he was not there but in London."

"Does Mr. Neuss know Raymond Thorne?" Barron asked.

"I don't think so."

"Had you ever seen Raymond Thorne before?"

"No."

"Ever hear Mr. or Mrs. Neuss use his name?"

"No."

"Did he give any reason for wanting to see Mr. Neuss?"

"I didn't give him the opportunity." Greta's eyes hardened. "The way he was dressed I wanted him out of the shop as quickly as possible, so I simply told him Mr. and Mrs. Neuss had gone to London. Which they had."

"Raymond's picture has been all over television and on the front page of the *L.A. Times*." Barron was incredulous. "You didn't see it?"

"I do not watch television." Greta's nose lifted toward the ceiling. "And I do not read the *Los Angeles Times*."

10:27 A.M.

Anxiety carved into his face, Beretta in hand, Raymond kept his eyes locked on the rear entrance to the apartment building, certain Barron and the others would crash through it at any moment. But there was nothing he could do. The trash trucks still had the Mercedes blocked between them, their drivers standing nose to nose arguing with each other in Spanish over money one owed the other.

10:28 A.M.

Lee suddenly came out of the kitchen looking at Greta Adler. "When did Mr. and Mrs. Neuss leave for London?"

"Tuesday evening."

"Do they have children, or would anyone else have stayed here?"

"The Neusses have no children, and no one else would have stayed here. They are not that kind of people."

"They travel a lot? Maybe they had a regular apartment sitter?"

"Mr. and Mrs. Neuss do not travel often, in fact hardly ever.

They would not have had an apartment sitter. And if they had I would have been the first to know about it."

Lee looked to Barron. "Someone's been here and not very long ago. There's water on the countertop, and a glass in the sink has fresh droplets on it."

Polchak came out of the bedroom. "It was Raymond."

"What?" Barron looked up; so did Lee.

"The same kind of jeans he was wearing in the airport when he shot Red are on the floor in the closet. Along with a Disneyland cap and jacket."

Lee looked at Polchak. "What makes you think they're Raymond's and don't belong to Neuss?"

"Mr. Neuss would be put over hot coals before he would wear blue jeans," Greta Adler snapped. "The same could be said for the Disneyland things."

"That doesn't mean they were Raymond's."

"They weren't," Polchak said. "I'll bet a year's pay they originally belonged to Josef Speer. Little tag says they were bought in a department store in Germany."

Raymond threw open the Mercedes door, slid the Beretta into his belt under his jacket, and walked up to the arguing men.

"Yo soy el doctór," he said hurriedly in Spanish. *"Esta es una emergencia. Por favor mueve tu troca."* I am a doctor. This is an emergency. Please move the truck.

They paid him no attention, just kept arguing.

"Emergencia, por favor," he said forcefully.

Finally the driver of the truck blocking the exit to the street looked at him. *"Sí,"* he said grudgingly. *"Sí."* With a hard glance at the man he'd been arguing with, he got in the truck and put it in reverse. A dozen steps and Raymond was back in the Mercedes, putting it in gear and impatiently edging it forward, waiting for the alley to clear.

Barron and Polchak came down the back stairs fast. Lee was behind them on the radio calling for Beverly Hills Police backup. Both men stopped at the bottom of the stairs and drew their guns. Barron looked at Polchak, Polchak nodded, and they burst through the door.

As quickly they stopped. The alley was empty except for two city trash trucks, nose to nose, their drivers standing in between, arguing.

61

12:05 P.M.

Trigger Ray Escapes Again! Internet newsgroups flashed to the world. Alfred Neuss's Mercedes had been found, and once more Beverly Hills was in a state of near-lockdown as uniformed police and plainclothes detectives, aided by dogs and helicopters, swarmed an area nearly three miles square.

The media were loving it. The homeowners, business community, and politicians had had enough. To all the result was the same—the Beverly Hills Police Department had just joined the LAPD and the 5-2 Squad as top candidates for "buffoons of the decade."

Standing in Alfred Neuss's front hallway watching the Beverly Hills PD's Scientific Investigations people going over the jeweler's apartment inch by inch, Barron didn't care what the media said or what the politicians thought. The police were not buffoons. The problem was that Raymond was incredibly bold and almost maniacally cunning. He had gone to Alfred Neuss's apartment because he knew no one was there. It was the one place he could count on for rest and refuge, and trust he would not be found. And if he had come to L.A. to encounter Neuss, possibly even to murder him, which they were all but certain he had, what better place to hide and wait than in the victim's own lair? Then they had surprised him and he'd fled, wearing Neuss's clothes and driving his car and leaving the major questions unchanged.

Who was Raymond Oliver Thorne? And what was he doing?

They had all heard him speak English with a perfect American accent, yet he had spoken fluent Spanish to the trash collectors and blurted *"Dasvedanya"* to Barron on the baggage ramp at the airport as he'd been about to kill him. *Dasvedanya* meant "good-bye" in Russian, which meant he knew at least one word, and perhaps many more, of Russian. A midlevel employee at the Bonaventure hotel had told them he'd heard him converse with Josef Speer in German. The Lufthansa ticket agent, too, had told them "Speer" had spoken fluent German.

Moreover, the men he had killed in Chicago had been Russian, and Alfred Neuss's name had been found in their address book among a listing of Russian-Americans. Questioned about it, Greta Adler had simply said she didn't know why his name had been listed as it had. As far as she knew his only dealings with the tailors had been that he had once used their services in Chicago and had the bill sent to his store. As for his own heritage, Mr. Neuss had never discussed it. So whatever his connection to Neuss or the men in Chicago might have been, so far none of it helped answer the question of who this multilingual gunman was. An international hitman? Russian mafia? Some kind of lone terrorist with unknown links to others? And still there was no way to know for certain that he hadn't somehow been involved with Donlan.

These were complications that not only angered but frustrated Barron, and opened up even more questions. Why had he killed the men in Chicago? What about the tortured, disfigured dead men in San Francisco and Mexico City? Investigators there had asked for ballistics tests from Raymond's Ruger automatic, which were in the process of being done and forwarded. Why had Raymond come to Los Angeles? What was the significance of the safe deposit keys? Was there any importance to the names, places, and dates he had marked in his calendar?

Monday, March 11. London.

Tuesday, March 12. London.

Wednesday, March 13. London, France, London.

Thursday, March 14. London. With the short entry written in Russian beneath it—*Russian Embassy/London*—and then, in English, *Meet I. M. Penrith's Bar, High Street. 8:00 P.M.*

Friday, March 15. 21 Uxbridge Street.

Sunday, April 7. With the forward slash after the "7" and the word that had also been written in Russian, the translated entry read *April 7/Moscow.*

And last, where and how did a wealthy, respected, longtime Beverly Hills jeweler like Alfred Neuss fit in?

They certainly didn't know, but maybe Neuss did. At that moment London Metropolitan Police were trying to locate him, and when they did he might well have an answer or at least shed some light on what was happening. Still, none of it helped in trying to determine where Raymond was now. Or what his plans were. Or who would be hurt, or even killed, when he struck next.

12:25 P.M.

Barron left the front hallway to walk through the kitchen and go back down to the alley where Polchak and Lee were working with Beverly Hills detectives. As he did, a sudden thought crossed his mind. Because of Greta Adler, Raymond knew where Neuss had gone. If he slipped them again and got out of L.A., the next they would hear of him would be in a call from Scotland Yard saying they'd found Alfred Neuss and he was dead.

62

12:35 P.M.

Raymond sat quietly in the backseat of a taxi as it turned off Olympic Boulevard and onto Bundy Drive, nearing Santa Monica Airport.

He had taken Alfred Neuss's Mercedes to drive to the airport himself but was barely out of the alley when he realized the woman from Neuss's store would know what kind of car Neuss had and what color it was. In no time they would find it missing from the carport and put out an alert. So any attempt to drive it more than a few blocks, let alone from Beverly Hills to Santa Monica through midday city traffic, would be the same as painting the doors in Day-Glo orange with the words WANTED FUGITIVE INSIDE.

For that reason he'd parked it a quarter of a mile from Neuss's apartment, locked it, and dropped the keys into a storm drain. Five minutes later, in Alfred Neuss's tan linen suit and Panama hat, he'd crossed Rodeo Drive and entered the elegant lobby of the Beverly Wilshire Hotel. Two minutes after that he stood at the rear motor entrance waiting as a doorman signaled a cab. Sixty seconds later he was in the backseat of a taxi as it drove off.

"Shutters at the Beach Hotel in Santa Monica," he told the driver in English but with a heavy French accent. "You know where it is?"

"Yes, sir," the driver said without looking at him. "I know where it is."

Twenty minutes later he got out of the taxi at the luxury seaside hotel in Santa Monica and went into the lobby. Five minutes later he came out a side door and got into a taxi at the curb.

"Santa Monica Airport," he said with a Spanish accent.

"*¿Habla usted español?*" the Hispanic taxi driver asked. Do you speak Spanish?

"*Sí,*" Raymond said. "*Sí.*"

12:40 P.M.

The cab swung in from Bundy Drive and turned down a narrow street to drive alongside a chain-link fence with private aircraft parked behind it. They passed one turnoff, and then the cab driver took the next, heading in toward the Santa Monica Airport terminal.

The cab slowed as they neared, and Raymond sat forward, looking toward the terminal and the planes parked on the tarmac beyond it. They seemed to be small, propeller-driven civilian aircraft, not a jet among them. Nor was there anything to indicate that even one of them might be a charter. He looked at his watch and wondered if the plane Jacques Bertrand sent was late or if there had been some miscommunication or even a mechanical problem with the plane itself.

In the distance a twin-engine Cessna took off. And then nothing. Where was his plane? Raymond felt his pulse rise and, with it, a trickle of sweat on his upper lip. What should he do, get out and wait? Call Bertrand in Zurich? What?

Calm down, he told himself. Calm down and wait.

They were nearing the terminal, and the cab driver swung wide around another taxi, then slowed, waiting for traffic to clear in front of him. It was then that Raymond saw it, a big silver Gulfstream jet with WEST CHARTER AIR stenciled in bold red and black letters across its fuselage. It was parked on the tarmac on the far side of the terminal with its passenger door open. Two uniformed pilots stood on the ground beside it chatting with a maintenance worker.

"Damn, more cops," the Hispanic taxi driver suddenly grumbled in Spanish, and Raymond looked to the front of the cab. Three blue-and-white Santa Monica police cars were parked directly in front of the terminal building, and uniformed police stood in the doorway. From a distance it was impossible to tell what they were doing.

"I'm getting sick of this," the taxi driver complained again. "I don't know who this guy is, but he's making life miserable. I hope to hell they catch him and soon, you know what I mean?" He turned to look over the seat at Raymond.

"Yes, I hope they catch him, too," Raymond said in Spanish. "This will be fine, I'll get out here."

"Okay." The driver pulled the cab to the curb and stopped fifty yards from the terminal.

"*Gracias.*" Raymond paid him with Josef Speer's American dollars and got out.

He waited for the taxi to pull away, then started toward the terminal, wondering if there was another way to the plane that did not involve passing the police, or if he dared try to bluff his way through them, playing the Mexican businessman he was supposed to be and speaking Spanish.

As he drew closer he could see two policemen sitting in the first patrol car. Four others were at the terminal door, and now he could see what they were doing. Meticulously checking the identification of everyone entering. It would be one thing if he already had the identification papers Bertrand had sent, which he knew were on the plane. But to try to explain who he was without them would draw too much attention. The police would ask questions, and they would have been supplied with copies of his photograph.

He glanced through the fence at the Gulfstream. The pilots were still chatting, still waiting, but there was no way he could get to them. He hesitated, then decided against it and turned and walked away, back toward the street, the way he had come in.

63

LOS ANGELES, 210 RIDGEVIEW LANE. 8:10 P.M.

Red's house was a plain, three-bedroom, one-story bungalow with what a real estate person would call a "partial city view" from the backyard. Tonight the view was more than partial. With a clear sky and the overhanging sycamore trees still winter-bare, the lights of L.A. reached like a galaxy almost to the horizon. It was more than magical. It drew the eye into them, and the viewer realized that somewhere out there was Raymond.

John Barron watched for a short while longer, then turned and walked past several people chatting quietly on the lawn and went back into the house. He was dressed somberly in a dark suit, the same as most everyone else there.

In the five or ten minutes he'd been outside, the parade of mourners had grown substantially, and more were filing in. One by one, they stopped to give condolences to Red's wife, Gloria, acknowledge with hugs his two grown daughters, and playfully embrace one or all of his three young grandchildren. Afterward they would move off to other parts of the house for a drink or something to eat and then to talk quietly among themselves.

Barron knew most of them by sight: Los Angeles mayor Bill Noonan; His Eminence Richard John Emery, Cardinal of Los Angeles; Police Chief Louis Harwood; Los Angeles County Sheriff Peter Black; District Attorney Richard Rojas; venerable Rabbi Jerome Mosesman; almost every member of the city council; the head football coaches from both UCLA and USC. There were more top LAPD brass, too, men Barron knew but couldn't name; several prominent sports and broadcast figures; an Oscar-winning actor and his wife; a half dozen veteran detectives, one in particular, the tall, craggy-faced Gene VerMeer, who he knew had been one of Red's oldest and closest friends; and then there were Lee and Polchak and Valparaiso and Halliday, all as soberly dressed as Barron and with women he'd never met but presumed were their wives.

Standing there, watching the slim, energetic Gloria McClatchy, a highly regarded public schoolteacher in her own right, bravely and graciously playing the role of hostess, Barron was swept by a crush of near-overwhelming emotion: grief, rage, loss, anger, and frustration about their inability to apprehend Raymond, combined with what was, by now, huge physical and mental exhaustion.

This was the first time he'd seen Halliday or Valparaiso since Red's death. He knew they'd talked to Polchak because he'd heard him on the radio advising them what had happened at Alfred Neuss's apartment. Both had been at the house when he'd arrived, but they'd been with Gloria and Red's daughters, and then other people had started coming and they'd broken away, and since then neither had sought him out or even so much as acknowledged him. So he had to assume that it wasn't just Polchak and Lee who blamed him for Red's death, but Valparaiso and Halliday as well and maybe Gene VerMeer and the other detectives.

And now as he watched them all—Lee and Halliday as they stood silently with their wives; VerMeer and the others talking quietly among themselves; seeing Polchak and Valparaiso go to a makeshift bar in the corner to stand alone with drinks in their hands, saying nothing, their women elsewhere—he began to realize the extent of their grief and knew that his emotions were dwarfed in comparison to theirs. Halliday, as young he was, had known, worked alongside, loved, and respected Red McClatchy for years. Lee and Valparaiso had been shoulder to shoulder with him for more than a decade. Polchak, longer than any of them. Each man knew risk of death came with the job, but that didn't make it any easier now. Nor did it help knowing Red had died to protect the newest and youngest of them. It helped even less that the murderer was still free and the media were rubbing their faces in it. But perhaps most troublesome of all, he knew they were holding themselves up to the light of the squad's long and proud history and felt they were unworthy.

It was enough! Abruptly Barron turned away and walked down a hallway toward the kitchen, not knowing what to do or say or even think. Halfway down, he stopped. Gloria McClatchy sat alone on a small plaid couch in a room that must have been Red's den, a single lamp turned on in the corner. In one hand she held an untouched cup of coffee; the other gently stroked an old black Labrador who sat at her feet, its head in her lap. She looked old and pale and very tired, as if everything she had had suddenly been whisked from her life.

This was the Gloria McClatchy who had taken both Barron's hands in hers when he'd arrived and, although they'd never met, had looked him in the eye and genuinely thanked him for coming. And for being a fir e policeman. And then told him how proud Red had been of him.

"Damn it to hell," he swore to himself and tears welled up in his eyes. Suddenly he was turning, going back into the living room and pushing through the crowd, dodging one familiar face and then another, trying to find the front door.

"Raymond!"

Red's thundering bellow shot through him as loudly as if he were there. A shout that had pulled the gunman's deadly attention away from Barron to him in what was the last command of his life.

"Raymond!"

He heard Red yell again and half expected to hear the roar of gunfire.

Then he was at the door and opening it and going outside.

Cool night air hit him a split second before a wall of light engulfed him in the glare of what seemed like the lights of a thousand television cameras. From the darkness beyond them came a thunderclap chorus of "John!" "John!" "John!" shouted by the mob of unseen reporters screaming for his attention and wanting him to make a statement.

He ignored them and quickly crossed the lawn at the far side of it, stepping around the yellow POLICE LINE tape that kept the media back. He thought he had seen Dan Ford, but he wasn't sure. In a moment he was away from them and in the dark and relative quiet of the suburban street walking toward where he'd parked the Mustang. He was almost to it when a voice called out from behind him.

"Where the hell you goin'?"

He turned. Polchak was coming toward him, passing under the glow of a streetlight. His jacket was off and his tie was gone, his shirt open partway down the front. He was sweating and breathing heavily, as if he had chased after Barron from the house.

Polchak stopped and rocked back on his heels. "I said, where you goin'?"

Barron stared at him. This morning in the squad room it was evident he'd been drinking, but he hadn't been drunk. Now he was.

"Home," Barron said quietly.

"No. We're goin' downtown for a drink. Just us. Just the squad."

"Len, I'm tired, huh? I need to sleep."

"Tired?" Polchak took a step forward, his eyes riveted on Barron. "What the hell did you do to get tired except lose him again?" Polchak moved closer still, and Barron could see his Beretta stuck into his waistband as if it had been a purposeful afterthought. "You know who I'm talkin' about—Raymond."

"I didn't lose him alone, Len. You were right there beside me."

Barron saw Polchak's nostrils flare in his square face and he came in a rush. Grabbing Barron by the jacket, he spun him around hard and slammed him headfirst into the Mustang.

"He took it for you, you little shit!" Polchak was screaming in rage.

Barron staggered and turned, putting up a hand. "I'm not going to fight you, Len."

The squat detective's left hand came out of nowhere in reply, hitting Barron somewhere between his mouth and nose, sending him reeling backward onto the street.

Polchak rushed forward, this time using his feet, kicking at Barron's head, his ribs, anyplace he could find. "That's for Red, you bastard fuck!"

"Len, stop it for Chrissake!" Barron twisted away on the ground and Polchak chased him like a wild man, kicking and kicking.

"Fuck you, you cock prick!" Polchak was lost, ferocious. "Here's some more, you little shit-bastard!"

Suddenly someone was on Polchak's back, trying to pull him away, "Stop it, Len! Jesus Christ! Stop it!"

Polchak wheeled, not even looking, throwing a hard right as he did.

"Aw! Shit! Jesus!" Dan Ford staggered backward, his glasses gone, both hands to his nose, blood gushing between his fingers.

"Get outta here, you fuck!" Polchak yelled.

"Len!" Suddenly Lee was right there, out of breath from running, his eyes darting between Polchak and Barron and Ford. "For Chrissake, no more."

"Fuck off!" Polchak yelled at Lee, his fists up, his chest thundering in and out.

Then Valparaiso stepped out of the darkness behind Lee. "Having fun, Len?"

Polchak suddenly ripped his belt from his pants and wound it around his fist. "I'll show you some fuckin' fun."

Then Halliday was there. "That's all, Len, back off." Halliday's Beretta automatic was pointed directly at Polchak.

Polchak glared at the Beretta, then looked to Halliday. "You pull a piece on me?"

"Your wife's waiting, Len. Go back to the house."

Polchak took a step forward, his eyes fixed on Halliday. "Go ahead, use it."

"Len, for Chrissake." Lee was staring at him. "Calm down."

Valparaiso grinned, as if the situation somehow tickled him. "Go ahead, Jimmy, shoot. Can't make him any uglier."

Barron got to his feet and went to Dan Ford. He was wearing a new blue blazer, the old one given up to cover Red's body at the airport. He found his glasses and gave them to him.

"Get out of here," he breathed, and pulled out a handkerchief and handed it to Ford.

Ford took the handkerchief and put it to his nose, but his attention was fully on Polchak and Halliday.

"I said get out of here. Now!" Barron's tone was brutal.

Ford looked to Barron, then suddenly turned and walked away into the darkness, toward the house and the gathered media.

It was an interchange Polchak had seen none of. The whole time, he was looking at Halliday. Now he took another step forward, ripping his dress shirt open, tearing it back.

"You got the balls, Jimmy, give it to me." Polchak touched the center of his chest. "Right here in the pump."

Abruptly Halliday holstered the Beretta. "It's been a long day, Len. Time to go home."

Polchak cocked his head. "What'sa matter? What's one more little death between friends?"

Suddenly he looked to the others standing in the harsh semicircle of light thrown by the streetlamp. "Nobody up to it? Then I'll do it myself."

Polchak reached for the Beretta in his waistband. It wasn't there. Puzzled, he staggered around looking for it.

"Looking for your gun, Len?"

Polchak looked back.

Barron held Polchak's Beretta loosely in his hand. Blood ran down from his nose but he ignored it. "It's yours. You want it, take it."

In a single motion Barron slid the automatic across the ground to see it stop halfway between him and Polchak. "Go ahead."

Polchak glared at Barron, his eyes shining in the dim light like some demented beast's. "Think I won't?"

"I don't think at all."

"I'm the only one here who's got what it takes." Polchak's eyes went to the others. "I can kill anything. Even myself. Watch."

Suddenly Polchak bent over and lunged for the gun. In the same instant Barron stepped forward and kicked a field goal. The full weight of it caught Polchak under the jaw, snapping his body upward. For a moment he hung in midair, struggling against gravity; then his legs buckled under him and he dropped to the ground.

Slowly Barron walked over and picked up Polchak's gun. He looked at it for a second, then handed it to Halliday. Every last bit of him twisted, wasted, gone.

Polchak lay on the ground in front of them, his eyes open, his breath coming in huge gasps.

"He alright?" Barron asked anyone who would answer.

"Yeah." Lee nodded.

"I'm going home."

64

Barron eased the Mustang past the big growth of bougainvillea bordering his driveway and into his carport, then shut off the engine. Everything hurt; it was agony just to pull off the seat belt and get out of the car. He climbed the long flight of back stairs one step at a time. Sleep, just to sleep, was all he wanted.

Key in the door, he stepped inside and into the kitchen. Just reaching up to turn on the light was an effort; so was the simple act of locking the door behind him. He took one slow deep breath and then another. Maybe Polchak's kicks had broken ribs or maybe they were only bruised, he didn't know.

He looked across to the dark rectangle of doorway that led to the rest of the house. It seemed years since he'd been home, even longer since he'd done anything even close to normal.

Slowly he took off his suit jacket and tossed it over a chair, then went to the sink to dampen a dish towel and blot the matted blood from his nose and mouth. Done, he glanced at the answering machine on the sideboard. A bright red number "3" glowed on its face.

He hit MESSAGE, the number shifted to "1," and he heard the voice of Pete Noonan, his friend at the FBI whom he'd asked to check FBI terrorist data banks for information on Raymond.

"John, Pete Noonan. I'm sorry to tell you we've got nothing at all on your friend Raymond Thorne. His prints are not on file in any data bank we have, national or international. And there's no other information on him at all. Whoever he is, he's not one of ours yet. We'll keep trying. You know where to reach me if you need anything else, day or night. Real sorry about Red."

Beep! The message finished and the number "2" appeared.

"John, it's Dan. I think my nose is broken, but I'm okay. I'll be home in an hour, call me."

Beep! Message over, the number "3" appeared.

Barron turned to hang up the towel.

"This is Raymond, John."

Barron's head came around like a pistol shot. The hair on the back of his neck stood straight up.

"I'm sorry you're not home." Raymond's voice was calm and very matter-of-fact, making him sound almost genteel. "We have something we need to work out tonight. I'll be calling again soon."

Beep!

Barron stared at the machine. His number was unlisted. How had Raymond gotten it?

Immediately he picked up the phone and punched up Halliday's cell phone. It rang four times before the recorded voice of the wireless operator came on saying the party was unavailable. Barron hung up and called Halliday's house. Again the phone rang, no one picked up and no answering machine came on. He was about to hang up and try one of the others, Valparaiso or Lee, when someone did pick up. It was a young boy's voice. "Hello?"

"This is John Barron. Is your daddy there?"

"He's with my mommy, my brother is throwing up."

"Would you ask him to come to the phone, please? Tell him it's important."

There was a sharp clunk as the child put the phone down. In the distance he could hear voices. Finally Halliday came on the line.

"Halliday."

"It's John. I'm sorry to bother you. Raymond called me."

"What?"

"Left word on my machine."

"What'd he say?"

"That he wanted to talk to me again tonight. That he'd call back."

"How'd he get your number?"

"No idea."

"You alone?"

"Yeah, why?"

"If he can get your number he can get your address."

Barron glanced around the room and again at the dark rectangle of door frame leading from the kitchen to the rest of the house. Absently he touched the Colt automatic in his belt holster.

"I'm okay."

"We'll put a trace on your phone. If he calls again, keep him on the line as long as you can. He'll put himself right in a corner. I'm going to send a surveillance unit, give you some protection in case he decides to show up."

"Right."

"He's smart, he may have done it to throw us off."

"Your kid alright?"

"Babysitter gave him pizza. I don't how much he ate, but it's all coming up. I've been holding him over the toilet for ten minutes."

"Go take care of him. Thanks."

"You okay?" There was genuine concern in Halliday's voice.

"Sore."

"Red was Polchak's best friend."

"I know."

"We'll see what the night brings. I'll leave both my radio and cell phone on. Get some sleep."

"Yeah. Thanks."

Barron hung up and stared at the phone; then his eyes went back to the answering machine. He was reaching for it, about to play Raymond's message again, when he heard it.

A sound, faint but distinct, had come from beyond the dark rectangle leading to the rest of the house. The building was old, built in the 1920s. It had been remodeled a number of times, but the floors were the original oak, and in places they creaked when they were stepped on.

Creak.

The sound came again, a little louder this time, as if someone were coming through the rooms toward the kitchen. Barron slid the Colt from his holster. A half second later he was across the room and next to the doorway, pressing back tight against the wall.

Gun up and ready, he held his breath and listened. Silence. He cocked his head. Still nothing. He was tired, beaten up by Polchak and his own emotions. His nerves were like raw wire. Maybe he was hearing things. Maybe he—

Creak!

No! Someone was there! Just on the far side of the door. Suddenly there was a movement in the doorway. Barron lashed out.

His hand found a wrist and he twisted it to him, shoving the automatic full in the face of—

"Rebecca!"

His heart pounding, Barron let go, and Rebecca shrank back in horror.

"Jesus God! I'm sorry, honey. I'm sorry."

Barron put the gun away and went to her, gently cradling her to him. "It's okay," he whispered. "It's okay. It's okay . . ." His voice trailed off as she looked up at him and smiled. Frightened as she had been, her black hair tucked behind her ears, in sweatshirt, jeans, and tennis shoes, she was as fragile and beautiful as ever.

She couldn't hear him, but he asked anyway because he knew she could read his lips, enough at least to answer a simple question.

"Are you alright?"

She nodded, studying his face.

"Why did you come?"

She pointed at him.

"Me?"

"How did you get here?"

"Bus," she mouthed.

"Does Sister Reynoso know? Dr. Flannery?"

She shook her head, then gently reached up to touch his face. He winced at her touch and turned to a mirror behind the kitchen table.

Polchak had done a good job. A big, ugly black-and-blue knot sat over his left eye. His nose was red and swollen; so was his upper lip. His right cheek looked more like a large grapefruit, the way it was yellowed and puffed up. He turned back to Rebecca and saw the big red "3" on his answering machine. What if Raymond called back now and he had to do something? Or if he suddenly showed up before the surveillance car arrived? It was no good; he had to do something about Rebecca.

11:02 P.M.

65

It had taken Barron a little more than an hour to drive Rebecca back to St. Francis, get her settled, and turn back for home. Now, for the second time in less than two hours, he turned the corner at the end of his street and drove down the hill past the darkened houses toward his own.

"Bus," Rebecca had mouthed when Barron had asked her how she'd gotten to his house. She had explained the rest, writing on the page of a notebook in the car as Barron had driven her back to St. Francis. She'd known that morning when he'd come to visit that something bad had happened and that he was very sad and very worried, and she had been concerned all day. In the end she wanted to make sure he was alright, and so without telling any-one, for fear they would stop her, she had simply walked out of St. Francis around 7:30 and taken the bus. She'd written down the address where she wanted to go, and the bus driver had helped her. It had been simple, one transfer and afterward a short ten-minute walk, and she'd arrived about an hour later.

Getting in had been easy because she had the key he'd given her when he'd moved in. It had been a gesture on his part to re-assure her about St. Francis and let her know there was always a place for her at his house.

When she got there and realized he wasn't home she decided to watch TV. After a while she got tired and fell asleep. When she woke the light was on in the kitchen. She hadn't meant to startle him; her whole purpose in coming was because he was her brother and she was concerned about him.

Ahead, two houses up from his bougainvillea-bordered driveway, Barron saw the surveillance car parked at the curb with its lights out. Slowing, he stopped beside it and rolled down his window. The man behind the wheel was Chuck Grimsley, a young detective he'd worked with briefly at Robbery-Homicide. With him was veteran detective Gene VerMeer, whom he had seen at Red's house earlier.

"Anything?" Barron asked.

"Not yet," Grimsley said quietly.

"Thanks for coming."

Gene VerMeer stared at him. "Our pleasure," he said coldly.

"Hello, Gene." Barron tried to keep it cordial. VerMeer, he knew, had been almost as close to Red as Polchak had been.

"What happened to you?" Grimsley was looking at Barron's bruised and swollen face.

"Looks bad, I know."

"Shame Halloween's over," VerMeer said, as if he wished he'd done the job on Barron himself.

Again Barron brushed it off. "I ran into a lamppost. I gotta sleep, guys. I'm going in. You here all night?"

"Unless the world blows up," Grimsley said.

"You never know." VerMeer glared at him, and then sat back.

Barron forced a smile and said, "Thanks again."

12:20 A.M.

Key in the door, Barron opened it, turned on the kitchen light, then locked the door behind him, the same as before. This time he went directly to the answering machine. The big red "3" still glowed. He had erased none of the messages and no new calls had come in. Wherever Raymond was, whatever he was doing, he had not called back. And whatever they had "to work out tonight," in Raymond's words, hadn't materialized.

With neither the strength nor the energy to sit up and wait for something that might never happen, Barron went straight to the bedroom.

Sliding the Colt automatic from its holster, he put it on the nightstand next to the clock, then took off his clothes and went into the bathroom. Looking at himself in the mirror, he marveled at Polchak's work a second time. His attack had been the kind cops were trained to handle, but the aggression didn't often come from other cops. Polchak had been distraught and he had been drunk, but that wasn't all. There was something more, and it was the reason Barron hadn't fought back. Polchak himself.

He didn't know if what had happened tonight was a result of Polchak's years in Homicide and dealing with the terribleness of death on so many levels for so long, the loss of Red, to whom he was probably closer than he was to his own wife or kids, just plain exhaustion, or some combination of it all—but the truth was, Polchak was crazy.

He had seen glimpses of it earlier—the almost gleeful way he handled the riot gun in the garage as they were about to go after Donlan; the eager way he had held the handcuffed Donlan in his grip when he knew Valparaiso was about to kill him; the coldness with which he removed the dead man's handcuff and placed the gun in that same hand; the hatred with which he had looked at Barron in the squad room that morning, blaming him for what had happened to Red. And then what had happened tonight.

It was why he hadn't fought back. He knew that if he did, just the act of it could push Polchak over, and the end result might well have been either one or both of them dead.

Barron brushed his teeth as best his body would allow, then shut out the light and went back into the bedroom.

He picked up the Colt from the bedside table, checked its magazine, then set it down and climbed into bed. Hand to the lamp, he shut out the light and lay back in the dark, purposefully putting the events of the day out of his mind and letting exhaustion overtake him.

He sighed as he pulled up the covers in the dark, then grimaced in pain as he rolled onto his side to nestle into his pillow like a child. Sleep was all that mattered. The last thing he saw was the glow of his digital clock.

12:34 A.M.

66

"NO!"

Barron's own cry yanked him from the deepest sleep of his life. He was soaked in sweat and staring into the dark. He'd seen Raymond in his dreams. He'd been right there in the bedroom watching him as he slept.

One deep breath and then two. And he realized it was okay. Instinctively he put his hand out to the nightstand to touch his gun. All he felt was the smoothness of lacquered wood. His hand moved again. Nothing. He sat up. He knew he'd put the Colt there. Where was it?

"Now I have both your guns."

Barron started, crying out once more.

"Stay exactly as you are. Don't move at all." Raymond was standing in the darkness on the far side of his bed, Barron's Colt in his hand and pointed directly at him.

"You were very tired, so I let you sleep. Two hours and a half isn't much but it's something. You should be grateful." Raymond talked quietly, easily.

"How did you get in?" Barron could just see him in the dark as he crossed at the foot of the bed to stand with his back to the wall near the window.

"Your sister left the door open."

"My sister?"

"Yes."

Suddenly Barron realized. "You've been here all the time."

"For a while, yes."

"The phone call?"

"You invited me to call you and I did. You weren't home. Then I decided if we were going to meet anyway, why not just come over?" Raymond moved again, only a foot or two, but enough for Barron to see that he'd stepped off the throw rug where he'd been standing and onto the hard wood of the floor. He wasn't about to lose his footing to a quick move by the policeman.

"What do you want?"

"Your help."

"Why would I help you?"

"Get dressed, please. Put on the kind of clothes you would wear to work. What you wore earlier will do." Raymond nodded toward the hard-backed chair where Barron had left the suit, shirt, and tie he'd worn to Red's.

"Mind if I turn on a light?"

"The lamp by your bedside, no other."

Barron turned on the lamp and got out of bed slowly. In the pale light he could see Raymond holding the Colt evenly. He wore an expensive tan linen suit with trousers that were too short and too big in the waist, a crisp white shirt that didn't quite fit either, and a green-and-red-striped tie. Barron's Beretta, the one Raymond had taken from him at LAX and used to kill Red, was prominent in the waistband, its grip and trigger housing protruding from behind the belt buckle.

"That suit wouldn't belong to Alfred Neuss?" Barron said as he dressed.

"Please finish putting on your clothes." Raymond pointed the Colt toward Barron's shoes on the floor.

Barron hesitated, then sat back down on the bed to slide on one sock and then the other. One shoe and then the next.

"How did you find me?" He was taking his time, trying to see a way to take Raymond down physically. But the gunman purposely kept his distance, his back against the wall, his feet solidly on the wooden floor, the Colt pointed at Barron's chest.

"America seems to have copy shops on almost every corner. They rent computers and Internet access time by the minute. For very little money one can collect and send electronic mail and, with a little knowledge, one can access the data banks of almost any institution, including those of the police. As for getting here, the taxi drivers in this city have very little interest in what their fares look like."

"I'll make a note of it." Barron finished tying his shoes, then stood. "Tell me something. The killings in L.A. I can understand, you were trying to avoid arrest. What about the men in Chicago, the Azov brothers?"

"I don't know what you're talking about."

"And Alfred Neuss." Barron kept it up. "You were going to kill him. You went to his store but he wasn't there. That must have been a surprise."

Raymond's eyes went to the clock.

3:12 A.M.

He looked back to Barron. The police had done as he assumed they might and connected his gun to the Chicago killings. What surprised him was how they had found out about Neuss. And since they had been to his store and had talked to the saleswoman they would know Neuss had gone to London. As a result they would have contacted the London Metropolitan Police, who would attempt to question the jeweler themselves. It was unfortunate enough that Neuss had gone to London. That he would be talking to the police made it all that much worse.

Again he looked to the clock.

3:14 A.M.

"You are about to receive a call on your cell phone."

"My cell phone?"

"You have a wiretap on your landline. You were hoping to trace where I was when I called you back."

Barron studied him. The idea that Raymond had slipped the entire dragnet and was somehow in his house and in his room astounded him. Now he even knew about the wiretap. He was one up on them at every turn and remained that way.

"Who's going to call?"

"A good friend of yours, a Mr. Dan Ford of the *Los Angeles Times*. At eleven-thirty I sent him an e-mail from you saying your sister had come to your home and you were taking her back to her residence and asking him to call your cell phone number at three-twenty exactly. He replied that he would."

"What makes you think he's my friend?"

"The same things that told me the young lady was your sister and that her name is Rebecca. Not only did I see her as she watched television and then slept on the couch, but you have photographs of both her and Mr. Ford in your kitchen. I have read Mr. Ford's articles about me in the paper. And I have seen him in your presence, twice. Once at the Los Angeles airport and once outside the parking garage following the murder of Frank Donlan."

So that was why Raymond had come. He'd seen Barron as a way out from the moment he'd gotten into the car after Donlan had been killed. That was why he'd pushed him to anger to make him reveal the truth, at Parker Center, after he'd been booked. Now he was trying to use it against him as a tool in his attempt to escape.

"Frank Donlan shot himself," Barron said flatly.

Raymond smiled a kind of catbird smile. "For a policeman you make the truth very obvious. It was there before. It's still there. It will always be there."

The clock clicked to 3:20. There was silence, and then Barron's cell phone chirped. Raymond smiled his smile again. "Why don't we ask Mr. Ford what he thinks happened to Mr. Donlan?"

The phone chirped once more.

"Pick it up and ask him to hold," Raymond said, "then give the phone to me."

Barron hesitated and Raymond raised the Colt. "The pistol is not to threaten you, John. Its purpose is to keep you from attacking me. The real danger to you is your own conscience."

The phone chirped for the third time. Raymond nodded toward it and Barron picked up.

"Danny," Barron said evenly. "Thanks for calling, I know it's late . . . Rebecca? She was worried about me. Somehow she took the bus and got here. Yeah, she's alright. I took her back to St. Francis. Yeah, I'm okay. You? . . . Good. Hang on a minute, huh?" Barron handed the phone to Raymond, who pressed it against his chest so that Ford couldn't hear.

"The plan is this, John. We are going to get into your car. I will be in the backseat out of sight in the event there are police waiting outside, which I would fully expect there to be, assigned to protect you in the event I followed up my telephone call with a visit. You will stop and tell them you couldn't sleep and are going to work. You will thank them and then drive off." Raymond paused. "Mr. Ford is my insurance that you will do it."

"Insurance for what?"

"For the truth about Frank Donlan." Raymond smiled once again. "You wouldn't want to put Mr. Ford in the position of having to investigate you personally, would you? Tell him you want him to meet you in thirty minutes. You have some very important information and you can discuss it only in person."

"Where?" Barron felt leaden. Raymond was fully in control of everything.

"The Mercury Air Center at Burbank's Bob Hope Airport. A chartered jet is coming for me. It's not as incredible as it sounds. Tell him." Abruptly Raymond handed him the phone.

Barron hesitated, then spoke into the phone.

"Danny—there's something we need to discuss and I can only do it one on one. Bob Hope Airport, the Mercury Air Center. Thirty minutes. Can you do it?" Barron nodded at Ford's reply. "Thanks, Danny."

Barron clicked off and looked to Raymond. "There will be police at the airport."

"I know. You and Mr. Ford are going to see me safely past them."

Two minutes later they went out the back door and down the stairs to the carport and the Mustang. As they were leaving Raymond had made one final demand and he wore it now, an adornment under the starched white shirt and linen suit jacket taken from Alfred Neuss's apartment. John Barron's bulletproof Kevlar vest.

67

3:33 A.M.

Barron backed the Mustang out of the carport, then drove down the driveway to stop at the overgrowth of bougainvillea at the street. Raymond was on the floor in the back directly behind him, and Barron was certain the Colt or the Beretta or both were in his hands.

Up the street to his left, he could see the Grimsley/VerMeer surveillance car. By now they would have seen his headlights and be wondering what was going on.

He accelerated toward them, then slowed and stopped.

"Couldn't sleep." He followed Raymond's instructions to the letter. "Too much on my mind, I'm going in to work. Why don't you guys sign off and go home?"

"Whatever you say." Grimsley yawned.

"Thanks again," Barron said, then put the Mustang in gear and drove off.

"Good," Raymond said from the backseat. "So far."

A minute later Barron turned onto Los Feliz Boulevard and then onto the Golden State Freeway, heading north toward Burbank Airport.

Raymond had said the real threat to Barron was not a gun but his own conscience. Then Raymond had protected himself even further, or at least said he had. The safeguard was in the form of delayed e-mails, to be automatically sent at a certain time to the district attorney of Los Angeles, the *Los Angeles Times*, the American Civil Liberties Union of Southern California, the Los Angeles office of the Federal Bureau of Investigation, CNN headquarters in Atlanta, and the governor of California.

The e-mails explained who he was and told what he believed had happened to Frank Donlan while he was in police custody, adding that he had been with Donlan for some time as a hostage and during that time the only gun he had seen had been the one used to kill the people on the train—a gun Donlan had ultimately thrown out to the police in the parking garage, before stepping out naked in surrender to show he was unarmed. These delayed e-mails, Raymond promised, he would recall later—"unsend," as he put it—once he was on the plane and safely away.

In Raymond's view he was simply sparing Barron the ordeal of being called before a grand jury trying to determine whether there was sufficient evidence to try him and the other detectives for the murder of Frank Donlan. And in that he was right, because no matter what the others said or did to protect themselves and the squad, under oath it would be impossible for Barron not to tell the truth. He knew it and Raymond knew it.

On the other hand, if Raymond did escape, what then? The man who had killed Red McClatchy, five law enforcement officers, a New Jersey consultant, and a kid from Germany in cold blood would be free to continue his murderous storm for whatever twisted reasons he had begun it in the first place. How many more innocent people would die before he was done? And would one of them be Alfred Neuss?

So Raymond had been right. It was a matter of conscience. That was why, minutes earlier in his telephone conversation with Dan Ford, he had called him Danny. The last time he'd done it they were nine years old and Ford had told him outright that he hated being called Danny and wanted to be called Dan. Barron had laughed and told him he was full of himself and called him Danny again. As a result Dan Ford had punched him squarely in the nose, sending him running home, crying for his mother. Ever since, he had wisely called Dan, Dan—until moments ago when he'd called him Danny, hoping Ford would realize Barron was in trouble and was trying to tell him so.

68

BOB HOPE AIRPORT. 3:55 A.M.

Raymond eased up in the backseat just enough to see them pass the western end of the airport's runway, then turn right along Sherman Way toward the Mercury Air terminal building, a freestanding modern structure across from the main terminal.

A light drizzle had begun to fall, and Barron reached up and flicked on the Mustang's windshield wipers. Through them Raymond could see a number of private aircraft parked behind the chain-link fence separating the tarmac from the street. All were dark.

The drizzle, the chain-link fence, and the rows of vapor lamps lighting the street and the taxiways brought an eeriness to the whole area, making the Mercury Air terminal and its commercial buildings farther down feel like part of an elite high-security complex guarded not by men but by technology.

"We're here." Barron's words were the first he'd spoken since they'd left the detectives in the surveillance car. He slowed, then turned the Mustang off the street and stopped in front of a steel gate. A call box was just to the side, and on it was a sign asking after-hours customers to contact the front desk by pressing the intercom button.

"What do you want me to do now?" Barron asked.

"Ring the bell, as it says. Tell them you are here to meet the West Charter Air Gulfstream due in at four o'clock."

Barron rolled down the window and pressed the button. A voice answered and Barron did as he had been directed. A moment later the gate slid back and he drove in.

Three cars were in the parking lot to the left as he swung in. They were wet, their windows covered with moisture. It meant they'd been there for some time, most likely all night. Barron drove on.

Five seconds more and they were nearing the terminal's main entrance. Beside it, to the right, were two Burbank police cars. Three uniformed officers stood inside the terminal doorway watching them approach.

"The police are here."

"Look for Mr. Ford."

"I don't see him. Maybe he didn't come."

"He will be here," Raymond said, with calm assurance. "Because you asked him."

Then Barron saw Dan Ford's dark green Jeep Liberty parked in front of a lighted gate leading out to the tarmac and the parked planes beyond it. A Burbank police car was parked to the left of it with two uniformed policemen inside.

Suddenly Barron's stomach turned. What if the "Danny" hadn't worked? What if Ford had been too tired or was too numbed from painkillers taken for his broken nose to have even noticed? What if he was here, naively, only because Barron had asked him to come, as Raymond said? If so, it added another level of horror because if something went wrong Raymond would have no hesitation whatsoever in killing Ford. He'd do it in an instant.

69

Barron was about to turn away and tell Raymond Ford wasn't there and probably wasn't coming when the Liberty's door opened and Ford stepped out. Blue blazer, khakis, horn-rimmed glasses resting over his bandaged nose, everything, except that now he wore a golf hat against the drizzle.

Raymond suddenly hunched forward, peering over the top of the seat. "Stop here."

Barron slowed and stopped a good twenty yards from where Ford stood at the entry gate.

"Call his cell phone. Tell him you are going to pick him up, and then drive out to the tarmac to meet an incoming flight. Tell him you will talk to the police."

Barron looked at the parked and darkened aircraft on the far side of the fence. There was no sign of a ground crew or mechanics. Not a person visible anywhere. The clock on the dashboard read nearly 4:10. Maybe there was no plane coming at all. Maybe Raymond was doing something else entirely.

"Your Gulfstream is late, Raymond. What happens if it doesn't come?"

"It will be here."

"How do you know?"

"Because there it is." Raymond nodded toward the runway as the landing lights of a plane appeared through the drizzle at the far end of the runway. Seconds later a Gulfstream IV touched down.

They could hear the shrill reverse of the jet engines as the pilot slowed, turned at the end of the runway, then taxied back toward the terminal, its lights cutting a sharp swath through misty darkness.

Raymond moved lower in the seat as the plane approached, the whine of its engines deafening, its lights illuminating the Mustang like million-watt torches. Then abruptly the lights swung off as the charter jet turned in and stopped on the far side of the gate. The pilot shut the engines down and the roar faded.

"Call Mr. Ford and do exactly as I have said."

"Alright." Barron picked up his cell phone and dialed.

They could see Dan Ford put a hand to his mouth and cough as he pulled the phone from his blazer and clicked on.

"Here, John." Ford coughed again.

"Danny—" Barron's voice hung in the air, again calling Ford the name he hated, trying to tell him something was wrong and give him the chance to get out of there.

"Remember the waiting e-mails, John. Tell him," Raymond said.

"I—" Barron hesitated.

"Tell him."

Barron felt the cold steel of the Colt touch his ear.

"Danny, you and I are going out to meet the Gulfstream that just came in. I'm going to pull up beside you. When I do, just open the door and get in. I'll talk to the uniforms."

Ford clicked off and motioned them forward.

"Go ahead," Raymond urged.

Barron didn't move. "You've got the e-mails in the pipeline, Raymond. Why do we need him?"

"So the policeman in you doesn't suddenly rise and make you say something to your friends when you ask them to open the gate."

Dan Ford waved them forward again. At the same time, the doors to the police car opened and both uniforms stepped out. They were looking at the Mustang, apparently wondering what the driver was doing, why it had been stopped for so long.

"Time to go, John," Raymond said quietly.

Barron hesitated a moment longer, then eased the Mustang forward.

Barron could see Dan Ford clearly in his headlights as he approached the gate. The reporter took a step toward them, then stopped and said something to the policemen, gesturing toward the car.

They were almost there, ten yards to go at most.

"When you reach the gate," Raymond instructed, "roll down your window just enough for the police to see you clearly. Tell them who you are and who Mr. Ford is. Tell them you are there to meet the Gulfstream that just landed. You can say that it has to do with the investigation of Raymond Oliver Thorne."

Barron slowed and stopped, watching the uniforms come in from the left and Dan Ford from the right. Ford was a step ahead of them, maybe two, head down against the rain.

Then Ford was there and opened the passenger door. At the same moment, the nearest uniform rushed the driver's door. Barron heard Raymond yell in alarm. In the same instant, his own door was jerked open. For the briefest moment he saw Halliday's face, and then came a thundering explosion and the brightest flash he'd ever seen.

70

4:20 A.M.

His ears ringing, half blinded, Barron felt hands drag him from the car. Somewhere, he thought he heard Raymond shouting. The rest was a dream.

Vaguely, he remembered seeing Lee pulling up in an unmarked car and an alert but obviously still hungover Polchak, dressed as Dan Ford, handcuffing a stunned Raymond and hustling him into the back of it. Then there was another car, and Halliday in the blue uniform of a patrol cop was helping him into the front passenger seat and asking if he was okay. Then came the sound of doors slamming, and the car he was in was moving off with Halliday at the wheel.

How much time passed, Barron wasn't sure, but little by little the ringing in his ears lessened and the searing afterglow from the flash-bang grenade diminished in his eyes. "Dan called you," he heard himself mumble.

"As soon as he got off the phone with you he called Marty at home." Halliday kept his eyes on the road. "You didn't give us a lot of time."

"I wasn't exactly making the schedule." Barron shook his head, trying to clear it, make his thoughts come together. "That was Dan's car. Where is he?"

"In the terminal probably talking to SWAT. We brought them

in for backup. If it was Raymond we weren't going to let him get away again."

"No." Barron looked off. It was still pitch-dark, and the two cars were traveling bumper to bumper through a quiet residential area just east of the airport.

Valparaiso had been the other uniform at the security gate. And in blue blazer, khakis, bandaged nose, horn-rimmed glasses, and rain hat, Polchak had looked enough like Dan Ford to pass for him in the dark and drizzle. Barron knew that was why he had coughed over the phone. If Barron had recognized his voice he might have reacted, and who knew what Raymond might have done then. In the end they'd done what the 5-2 had always done, taken a fast, wild, and decisive chance. And, despite all Raymond's intelligence and cunning, it had worked.

"Jimmy." Valparaiso's voice suddenly came over Halliday's radio.

Halliday picked up the radio from the seat beside him. "Go ahead, Marty."

"We're gonna stop for coffee."

"Right."

"Coffee?" Barron looked at Halliday.

"It's been a long day already." Halliday clicked off. "Besides, Raymond's not going anywhere."

STILL FRIDAY, MARCH 15. 4:35 A.M.

Jerry's 24-Hour Coffee Shack was on a corner in an industrial area near the Golden State Freeway close enough to the airport that the glow of its lights could still be seen. Halliday pulled in first, and Valparaiso stopped beside him. Then the two got out and went inside.

Barron watched them go and then looked at the other car. Raymond sat in the backseat locked between Lee and Polchak. It was the first time Barron had seen him since the grenade went off. He looked tired and still shocked, as if he weren't exactly sure where he was or what had happened. It was the first time he'd seen Polchak, too, since the incident outside Red's house. He turned back, not wanting to think about it. Inside the coffee shop he could see Halliday and Valparaiso at the counter, talking and waiting for the coffee.

Suddenly there was a rap on the window beside him, and he started. Polchak stood there, motioning for him to roll down the window. Barron hesitated, then cranked it down. The two men looked at each other.

"Sorry about what happened," Polchak said quietly. "I was drunk."

"I know. Forget it."

"I mean it. I apologized to Dan Ford, too, okay?" Polchak put out his hand. Barron looked at it and then took it. Maybe Polchak was no longer drunk, and maybe he was apologetic, but his eyes hadn't changed. Whatever had so troubled him before was still there.

"Good," Polchak said, looking up as Halliday and Valparaiso came back carrying cardboard trays holding coffee cups capped with plastic lids. Valparaiso had four of the containers, Halliday two.

Polchak looked at Valparaiso. "Ready?"

"Wait," Barron said. They needed to know. "Raymond knows what happened to Donlan."

"How?" Valparaiso's eyes hardened.

"He figured it out."

"You mean you told him," Polchak growled without thinking. Barron could see his fists tighten as he glared at him. The demons were back, full force.

"No, Len, I didn't tell him, he guessed. That was why he wanted Dan there, in case I started to say something to the uniforms at the gate. He was going to tell Ford."

"Dan Ford's not here now and he's not going to be." Halliday looked at Valparaiso. "Let's go, huh?"

"Wait," Barron said sharply. "There's more. Raymond sent out delayed e-mails, that he told me he'd 'unsend' once he got away safely. To the DA, the FBI, the ACLU, Dan Ford, a lot of others. According to him, he spelled out the whole thing. It's no proof, but it's enough to start people asking questions."

"John," Halliday said quietly. "He's a cop killer, nobody's going to believe him."

"What if they do?"

"So what?" Polchak sneered. "It's his word against ours." Suddenly he looked at Valparaiso. "Coffee's gettin' cold, Marty."

4:44 A.M.

The slam of car doors clapped across the early morning quiet and the vehicles moved off the way they had before, Halliday leading, Valparaiso close behind.

They turned out of the industrial area and drove past the Burbank Airport Hilton, then crossed over the tracks of the Metrolink commuter rail line. Halliday said nothing, just drove, the two coffee containers on the seat between them unopened and untouched.

It's his word against ours.

Barron could hear Polchak's words and see his sneer. But it wasn't "ours," it was "theirs." The airport heroics aside, he was no more a part of them now than he'd been since Donlan's murder. If Polchak had demons, if they all did, they were the 5-2's alone, entangled in the makeup and history of the squad. No matter what he had thought or felt after Red's death—that he had come close to becoming one of them—he knew again that he wasn't part of the 5-2 the way the others were. It was what he'd known all along. He was different from them and would always be. The barbs of his own conscience clung to him like talons.

A sudden shriek of tires and the sharp lean of the car as Halliday turned down a side street snapped Barron from his thoughts. Abruptly Halliday swung the car again, this time turning into a dimly lit alley of cheap automotive repair shops, and stopped in front of a darkened, ramshackle auto body paint shop. A second later Valparaiso pulled up behind them, and for an instant his headlights bathed them in a bright glare, then the lights went out. Instinctively Barron glanced around. The entire area was dark, run-down, and isolated. Aside from a lone streetlamp at the end of the alley the only lights he could see came from Jerry's 24-Hour Coffee Shack where they'd stopped, maybe a quarter of a mile away.

Barron heard the thump of car doors closing behind them, then saw Polchak and Lee take Raymond fast across the alley toward the auto body shop. Valparaiso, carrying something, stepped ahead of them and kicked open a door, and the four disappeared inside.

"You know beforehand this time, John." Halliday opened the car door. The interior lights went on, and Barron could see Halliday's jacket deliberately pulled back revealing the 9 mm Beretta automatic in the holster at his waist. "Let's go."

71

4:57 A.M.

Raymond was standing under a single fluorescent lamp as Barron and Halliday came in. His hands were cuffed in front of him with Polchak to his left and Lee to his right. Valparaiso was a few feet in front, standing near a workbench, his hand around the thing he'd been carrying—one of the coffee containers. In the dimness behind them an old Volkswagen Beetle loomed like a ghostly sculpture, its tires and windows papered over and taped in preparation for painting, its body primed an ethereal gray-white. All around, the floor, walls, equipment, doors, and windows were coated with layers of the same gray-white, a product of years of drifting paint molecules that, in its flatness, sucked up what little light there was. It felt like the inside of a tomb.

Halliday closed the door and he and Barron moved into the room. Barron saw Raymond's eyes follow him as he crossed behind Valparaiso. They were desperate, pleading, looking to him for help. What he had no way of knowing was Barron's situation. Even if he wanted to help him he couldn't. If he tried to intervene, he would be killed himself. All he could do was stay and watch.

But Raymond continued to stare at him. It was then Barron realized what was really going on. Raymond's look was not so much terror as insolence. He wasn't just asking for help, he was expecting it.

It was the wrong thing to do, because Barron was not only offended, he was suddenly, and very deeply, enraged.

Here was a man who had killed without mercy, heinously

slaughtering one person after another in cold blood. A man who, from the beginning, had taken Barron's deepest principles and twisted them for his own good. Who had stolen into his home and manipulated him into helping him escape. Who had carefully and purposefully involved Dan Ford because of his professional influence and his close friendship with Barron and would have killed him in the blink of an eye to serve his own interests. Now, here he was, moments from death, expecting Barron to step in and save him.

Barron had never felt such revulsion in his life, not even toward the murderers of his mother and father. Red had been right. Men like Raymond were not human beings, they were despicable monsters who would kill again and again. They were a disease that had to be eliminated. For people like them laws and courts were porous and indecisive and therefore not to be trusted with the public welfare. So it was up to men like Valparaiso and Polchak and the others to do what civilization could not. And good riddance. Raymond had misjudged him grievously because Barron no longer cared.

"You were the one who asked for coffee, Raymond." Valparaiso stepped forward, a coffee container in his hand. "Being nice guys we stopped for it. Even brought it out to the car for you. When we did, and even though you were still handcuffed, you took yours and threw it at Detective Barron." Abruptly Valparaiso flicked his wrist, splashing hot coffee over Barron's shirt and jacket. Barron started and jumped back.

Valparaiso put the coffee container down and moved closer still. "At the same time, you grabbed his Colt Double Eagle automatic, a personal firearm he carried to replace the Beretta you had taken from him at the Lufthansa terminal. The one you used to kill Commander McClatchy. This gun, Raymond."

Suddenly Valparaiso pulled Barron's Beretta from his waistband with his right hand and held it in front of Raymond. A heartbeat later he reached behind him with his left hand and lifted Barron's Colt from where it had been tucked into his waistband at the back of his belt. "Two-Gun Raymond." Valparaiso took a half step backward. "You probably don't remember, but Detective Polchak took both of these away from you just moments after he set off the stun grenade. You later saw him return the Colt to Detective Barron."

Barron watched, transfixed, as Valparaiso worked Raymond, giving him the details of the story that would become the official version of his death. It was akin to torture and Barron didn't care. Instead he found himself enjoying it. Suddenly Raymond turned and looked right at him.

"What about the e-mails, John? Kill me and no one can call them back."

Barron smiled coldly. "Nobody seems very concerned about them, Raymond. The real story is you. We already have your fingerprints. Any part of your body will give us a DNA sample. A sample we can match against the bloodstains on a washcloth we found in a dead man's suite at the Bonaventure Hotel. We're going to find out about the men in Chicago. About the people in San Francisco and Mexico City. About the Gulfstream and who sent it. About Alfred Neuss. What you had planned for Europe and Russia. We're going to find out who you are, Raymond. We're going to find out everything."

Raymond's eyes went around the room and then looked away. "*Vsay,*" he said under his breath. "*Vsay ego sudba V rukah Gospodnih.*" What hope he had held out that Barron would aid him was gone. All he had left was his own inner strength. If it was God's plan to have him die here, then so be it.

"*Vsay ego sudba V rukah Gospodnih,*" he repeated, strong and compelling, an allegiance to God and to himself, the way he had for the Baroness.

Slowly Valparaiso handed the Beretta to Lee. Then he stepped forward and shoved the Colt between Raymond's eyes and finished what he had to say.

"After you took Detective Barron's gun, you ran away and hid in here. When we tried to come in after you, you shot at us—" Abruptly Valparaiso stepped back and turned the automatic toward the paint shop's front door.

Boom! Boom!

Thundering .45 caliber gunshots rocked the building, and paint-coated windowpanes exploded into the alley, leaving jagged patterns of black from the night outside in the gray-white wall.

Valparaiso turned back, poking the Colt up under Raymond's chin. "We stayed outside and ordered you to come out with your hands up. You didn't. We called in again and gave you another chance. But all there was was silence. And then we heard—one last shot."

Barron watched Raymond carefully. His lips were moving, but no sound came. What was he doing? Praying to God? Asking for mercy before death?

"John."

Barron looked up. Abruptly Valparaiso turned and grabbed his hand and put the Colt into it.

"For Red," he whispered. "For Red."

Valparaiso's eyes held on Barron for the briefest moment, then went to Raymond. Barron followed his gaze and saw Polchak move in to put Raymond in the same iron grip he had Donlan.

Raymond fought against Polchak's hold, all the while staring open-mouthed at Barron. How could God allow this? How could the man he had chosen to save him instead become his executioner?

"Don't, John, please don't," Raymond whispered. "Please."

Barron looked to the automatic in his hand, felt the heft of the gun. He took a step forward. The others were silent, watching. Halliday. Polchak. Valparaiso. Lee.

Raymond's eyes shimmered in the fluorescent light. "This isn't you, John. Don't you understand? It's *them!*" Raymond's eyes darted to the detectives, then came back to Barron.

"Remember Donlan. How you felt afterward." Raymond's words were hurried, but the manipulation and insolence were long gone. He was pleading for his life. "If you believe in God in Heaven, put the gun down. Don't do it!"

"Do you believe in God, Raymond?"

Barron came closer. Anger, hatred, revenge. His emotions combined like the rush from some fantastic drug. The reference to Donlan meant nothing. The gun in his hand was everything. And then he was there right beside him, his face inches from Raymond's.

Click!

Mechanically he pulled back the hammer. The barrel of the Colt went to Raymond's temple. He could hear Raymond's breath go out of him as he struggled against Polchak and the handcuffs. Barron's finger tightened on the trigger and his eyes locked on Raymond's. And then . . .

He froze.

5:21 A.M.

72

"Kill'm, goddammit!"

"He's an animal. Pull the fuckin' trigger!"

"Shoot him, for Chrissakes."

Voices shouted behind him as Barron's face twisted in agony. Suddenly he turned away.

Boom! Boom! Boom!

Gunshots roared as he fired into a tattered, paint-splattered overstuffed chair.

"What the fuck's the matter with you?" Lee didn't understand.

Barron turned back, trembling, horrified at what he'd nearly done. "The matter, Roosevelt, is that somewhere this old 'witch of a city' suckered us. A man forgets about the law, he forgets about a lot of things—like who the hell he is." For a moment Barron stared at them all. His next words came in a whisper. "What you don't understand is—I'm not capable of murder."

Valparaiso moved forward and held out his hand. "Give it to me."

Barron stepped back. "No, I'm taking him in."

"Give him the gun, John." Lee crossed in front of Halliday.

Abruptly Barron swung the Colt, leveling it at Lee's enormous chest. "I'm taking him in, Roosevelt."

"Don't do it," Halliday warned.

Barron ignored him. "Everyone put his weapon over there."

He nodded toward a paint-splattered workbench near the door.

"You're all fucked up, John." Polchak moved out from behind Raymond.

Valparaiso inched forward. "You're gonna get yourself killed."

"You were the first one here, John." Lee paid no attention to the gun pointed at his chest. "Raymond had the Colt. By the time we caught up, you were already dead."

"Raymond buys it anyway." Polchak closed in a little more. "What about your sister, who's gonna look after her? You gotta think about these things, John."

Suddenly Barron swung the gun, jamming it into Polchak's crotch. "Another centimeter, you lose your brains."

"Jesus Christ!" Polchak jumped back.

"Guns on the workbench. Roosevelt, you first."

The Beretta still in his hand, Lee stayed where he was, and Barron could see him judging, wondering if he could bring the gun up to fire before Barron did. Or even if Barron would fire.

"It's not worth the chance something goes wrong, Roosevelt," Halliday said quietly. "Do what he says."

"The Beretta, Roosevelt. Use your left hand. Two fingers on the grip, that's all," Barron ordered.

"Alright." Slowly Lee raised his left hand and picked Barron's gun from his right hand in a two-finger grip, then walked to the workbench and set it down.

"You're next, Marty. Same way." Barron shifted the Colt toward Valparaiso.

For a moment Valparaiso did nothing, then slowly he lifted his automatic from his belt holster and put it on the workbench.

"Now back away," Barron said sharply. Valparaiso did, his eyes going to Polchak and then Halliday.

Cautiously Barron went to the workbench, picked up his Beretta, and stuck it in his belt.

"Now you, Jimmy. The same way, two fingers."

Halliday crossed to the bench, slid out his Beretta, and put it down.

"Move away," Barron said, and Halliday did. "Len."

For the longest moment Polchak did nothing. Then his eyes went to the floor and he shrugged. "This isn't good, John. Not good at all."

Barron saw Polchak move. In the same instant Lee turned to

the workbench, grabbing for his Beretta. Barron lunged, hitting Lee hard with his shoulder and driving him backward into Polchak.

Polchak went down with Lee on top of him.

Barron whirled with the Colt. There was a single thundering report. The work light over Raymond's head shattered and everything went black. Then Barron lashed out, found Raymond's handcuffs, and dragged him forward in the dark.

Boom! Boom! Boom!

Lee's muzzle flashes lit up the garage behind them. Glass shattered around them. Slugs ricocheted off wood and steel as Barron found the door.

Boom! Boom!

Lee fired toward the door.

"You're gonna hit me, you asshole!" Polchak screamed.

"Then get the fuck outta the way!"

Barron and Raymond came through the door fast. Outside the air was wet with drizzle, the sky just beginning to lighten on the horizon. Barron glanced at the unmarked cars, then realized he had no keys. The thought took almost too long.

"Look out!" Raymond yelled as Lee came through the door. Handcuffs and all, he grabbed Barron by the jacket and dragged him behind the second unmarked car.

Lee fired twice in the dark, his shots blowing out the car's rear window. Polchak was right behind him. Then Valparaiso and Halliday.

Lee came around the car fast, Beretta in two hands, ready to fire. Polchak came from the other side. No one.

"Where the f—?"

Then they saw the hole in the wooden fence just beyond the car.

73

Barron kept Raymond in front of him as they half scrambled, half fell down a short, steeply pitched hill. Then they were at the bottom and Barron pulled Raymond up in the dark. They could hear the others coming, crashing through the fence and starting down the hill. Then a powerful flashlight flicked on, and then a second.

"Stay with me, Raymond." Barron grabbed Raymond by the handcuffs and dragged him blindly forward. "You try to get away, I will kill you. I promise."

A flashlight beam swung past them, then came back.

Boom! Boom!

Two quick shots thundered behind them, the slugs tearing up the ground at their feet. Wildly, Barron tugged at Raymond's handcuffs, dragging him one way and then another in a zigzag pattern as they ran on, scrambling through weeds and over rough ground made slick by the light rain. Behind them flashlight beams cut the air and they could hear more shouting. Then Barron saw pieces of giant earth-moving equipment loom up in the dark and he dragged Raymond toward them.

Seconds later, soaked with sweat and rain and gasping for breath, they took cover behind a massive bulldozer. In the distance they heard the throaty rumble of a jet aircraft on takeoff. The sky lightened a little more and Barron looked around, trying to get his bearings. All he could see was mud and vague forms of the heavy equipment.

"Don't move," he whispered to Raymond, and pulled himself up into the bulldozer's cab. From there he could see the distant lights of Burbank Airport's main terminal and realized they were on the far side of a construction area on the south side of it. Behind him was an open area maybe thirty yards wide and then a steep embankment topped by a chain-link fence. Beyond it were the lights from the airport Metrolink station.

Hurriedly he jumped from the bulldozer, landing beside Raymond in the dark. He looked at his watch. It was approaching six in the morning. Just when the Metrolink commuter trains began running. He looked to Raymond.

"We're gonna take a train ride."

74

5:47 A.M.

They saw Polchak go past in the dim light and then stop. Barron knew Lee would be to his left or right, with either Valparaiso or Halliday coming up behind. The other would have taken one of the cars and be headed for the street on the far side of the construction zone between where they were and the Metrolink station. What they were doing was flushing them out the way hunting dogs would a game bird from a thicket.

If they didn't find them then, they would call in helicopter air support and black-and-white units and probably even dogs. Their story would be simple: Raymond had broken free and taken Barron prisoner. It meant the force against them would be massive, their capture all but certain.

How they would get them into their custody afterward he wasn't sure, but there was no doubt at all they would. And it would happen very quickly. In no time Raymond would be shot dead and Barron taken off, most probably to his own house, where they would give him a lethal combination of alcohol and pills and then either shoot him with his own gun or just leave him to die. Another tragic police suicide caused by family circumstance, the violent deaths of Red McClatchy and the other police officers, and intolerable pressures of the job.

"Move," he whispered, and then he and Raymond were up and running for the distant lights of the Metrolink station.

"There they are!"

Barron heard Valparaiso yell in the dimness behind them. That meant it was Halliday who would be in the car trying to cut them off as they attempted to reach the station.

Heart pounding, feet sliding on the slippery ground, one hand holding the Colt, the other tucked inside Raymond's handcuffs, Barron raced them across the construction area toward the station, praying they'd get there before Halliday or a bullet did.

Then they were at the far embankment and scrambling up it to the fence at the top. He could still hear them coming behind them, the police flashlights crisscrossing in the dark trying to find a target. Now they were at the fence and Barron literally picked Raymond up and threw him over it, then vaulted over himself.

"Car," Raymond said as Barron hit the ground beside him. A half mile away headlights turned the corner and accelerated toward them.

"Go!" Barron yelled, and they were up and running. Crossing the street and charging up the ramp to the Metrolink station.

6:02 A.M.

Halliday saw them cross the street in the distance. Ten seconds later he pulled the car to a stop and jumped out just as the others came over the fence.

"Station!" he yelled, and the four took off on the run for the ramp where Raymond and Barron had gone.

The light of day began to appear, as a pale streak on the horizon, as the detectives reached the top. Polchak and Halliday ran down the platform one way, Lee and Valparaiso the other. There was nothing. The platform was deserted.

"Too late."

Winded and wet, cold and grim, Valparaiso was looking down the tracks, watching the lights of a commuter train disappear in the distance.

75

6:08 A.M.

They were in the car behind the locomotive with a half-dozen early commuters. One, a young and very pregnant woman, looked as if she would deliver at any moment.

Suddenly Barron realized he had to secure Raymond to some part of the train to protect both himself and the passengers. Quickly he glanced down the car and saw a luggage rack bolted to the floor and ceiling near the front. If he had a key he could release Raymond's handcuffs and then lock him to it, but—in that instant Barron realized he was wearing the same pants and jacket he had worn the night before and that his own departmental handcuffs were in a small black leather pouch at the back of his belt.

"Come on!"

Abruptly he took Raymond through the passengers and shoved him up against the luggage rack. Then he shook out the handcuffs and snapped them over the cuffs Raymond already wore and locked him to it.

"Don't move, don't say a word," Barron hissed. Immediately he turned and held up his gold detective shield to the startled passengers.

"Police officer," he said, "I'm escorting a prisoner. Please go into the car behind this one."

The pregnant woman looked from Barron back toward Raymond. "Oh, my God," she said, wide-eyed and loud enough for everyone to hear. "It's Trigger Ray, the killer from the TV! The cop's got Trigger Ray!"

"Please," Barron urged. "Go to the car behind."

"I gotta tell my husband! Oh, my God!"

"Move, lady! Everybody get out of here and into the next car!" Barron herded them back and out the door into the vestibule between cars. He waited for the door to close, then took out his cell phone and started back toward Raymond.

6:10 A.M.

"What're you doing?" Raymond was looking at the phone as Barron reached him.

"Trying to keep you alive a little bit longer."

The faintest smile crossed Raymond's face. "Thank you," he said. It was the arrogance again, as if he were certain Barron was still afraid of him, and protecting him for that reason.

Suddenly Barron erupted. "If those people weren't out there in the other car," he whispered hoarsely, "I'd beat the living crap out of you. Fists, feet, anything. And I wouldn't give a rat's ass that you were handcuffed. Do you understand, Raymond? Tell me that you do."

Slowly Raymond nodded. "I understand."

"Good." Barron stepped back, then clicked on the cell phone, punched in a speed dial number, and waited. Then:

"Dan Ford."

"It's John. I have Raymond. We're on the Metrolink from Burbank Airport. Probably twenty minutes from Union Station. I want you to put out the word to as much media as you can as fast as you can. Full coverage when we get off the train. Local TV, national, tabloids, foreign TV, CNN. Everybody and anybody. Make it a fucking circus."

"What the hell are you doing on the train? Where's the squad? What—?"

"We're real short on time, Dan—full coverage, huh? The best you can do. The best."

Barron clicked off, glanced once more at Raymond, then looked back at the door to the next car. Commuter faces pressed against the glass staring in. In the center of them was the pregnant woman, her face round, her eyes wide and ogling madly, as if this were the most popular game show in the world and she wanted desperately to get on it.

"Christ." Barron swore out loud and walked quickly up the aisle to the door, taking off his jacket as he went and hanging it over the window so they couldn't see in.

He glanced back at Raymond handcuffed to the luggage rack and checked his guns. The Colt had two rounds left, and his Beretta, a full fifteen-shot clip. He prayed he'd have to use none of them. Prayed the squad had reached the platform too late to have seen the train pull out and were still searching the station and the area around it.

6:12 A.M.

76

6:14 A.M.

The train began to slow. Just ahead was Burbank Station and after that Glendale. These were quick commuter stops with barely more than five or six minutes between stations. Barron's first thought when they'd come on board had been to call Metrolink headquarters, identify himself, and ask them not to stop at all before they reached Union Station. But he knew that if he did, Metrolink officials would alert security and in a blink the squad would know where they were and exactly which train they were on.

Within minutes LAPD units would set up in Union Station and cordon off the entire area, and then the squad would arrive and take over. Once they were in control, no matter how large a media army Dan Ford had amassed, none of them would get anywhere near the action. It meant that all Barron could do was wait it out and hope the train got to Union Station before Lee and Polchak and the others figured it out and got 'here first.

6:15 A.M.

Barron felt the train slow and then slow even more. Then came the sharp clang of warning bells as the train moved at a crawl into Burbank Station. In the drizzle and faint light he could see probably twenty commuters waiting on the lighted center platform. He glanced at Raymond. The killer was watching him. Waiting for whatever was next. Barron wondered what was in his mind. That he was unarmed and shackled to the luggage rack meant little. As Barron well knew, he had slipped handcuffs before. That was how he had killed the deputies in the elevator at Criminal Courts.

And as always, he bided his time, watching, thinking, as he was now, waiting for the suitable moment to strike. Abruptly Barron's thoughts shifted to the new commuters. He'd have to do the same with them as he had with the pregnant woman and the others, identify himself as a police officer and order them into the car behind.

Through the window he could see them roll past the commuters to the far end of the platform. Then came the shriek of steel on steel as the engineer applied the brakes. There was a slight bump, the train stopped, and the passenger doors midcar slid open.

6:16 A.M.

Barron held the Colt beside him out of sight and moved back, watching carefully, half expecting to see Polchak or Valparaiso suddenly appear, leading the others in a rush. But all he saw was commuters loading onto the cars behind. Five seconds, ten. He glanced at Raymond, then past him and through the closed door to see the massive hulk of the locomotive just beyond. He looked back to the passenger doors. So far no one had tried to come in. Another five seconds and the doors slid closed. A whistle sounded from the locomotive, there was a whine of diesel engine, and the train moved off, little by little picking up speed. Barron let out a sigh of relief. Five minutes more and they would be at the Glendale stop. Then it was straight on to Union Station, a fourteen- or fifteen-minute ride. He tried to picture the rush of media Dan Ford would have unleashed. A horde of reporters, paparazzi, camera and sound crews, invading the station and battling for space on the platform to so very publicly capture the infamous Trigger Ray

Thorne as Barron brought him off the train. Then and only then would he be able to—

Suddenly dread shot through him. Why had no commuters attempted to board the car they were in?

"Damn!"

In an instant he was shoving the Colt into his belt and racing toward the rear of the car. He reached the door and ripped down the jacket he'd used to cover the window and keep the prying faces out.

"Oh, Christ!"

All he saw was train tracks. The passenger cars that had been there before no longer were. The brief moments they had been in the station had been time enough for someone to uncouple the cars. The train was now made up of only two components, their car and the engine.

6:18 A.M.

77

"What are they doing?" Raymond shouted at him as he walked back down the car.

"Shut up."

"Take off my handcuffs, John, please."

Barron ignored him.

"If we can get off the train before they see us, John, I can have the plane brought back to any airport. We can all go. You and me and your sister."

"My *sister?*" Barron reacted as if he'd been slapped.

"You wouldn't leave her behind."

"And you'd pull every string in existence to have me get you out of this."

"Think about it, John—you love her. You really couldn't leave without taking her with you. Could you?"

"Shut up!" Barron spat angrily. It was bad enough Raymond had violated him by coming into his house. But Rebecca? What the hell was he doing even *thinking* about her? Suddenly Barron remembered where he was and what was happening. He turned and looked out the window. They were rounding a bend. Ahead was Glendale Station. In seconds they would be there. He slid the Colt from his belt, and his other hand slid to the Beretta. His first thought when he'd seen that the train had been uncoupled from the other cars was to call Dan Ford and alert the media there had been a problem with the train. But it was no good. Even if Ford had gathered them, they would be at Union Station, and he knew this train would never get that far. Where it was going he didn't know either. Glendale Station was coming up fast, and after it there was a myriad of sidings and rail yards where the engine and its lone car could be diverted.

"Give one to me." Raymond was looking at the guns.

Barron looked at him.

"They'll kill us both."

A loud whine of diesel engine suddenly came from the locomotive. Instead of slowing, the train picked up speed. Barron grabbed a seat back to brace himself. Outside, in the gray-wet light of early morning he saw Glendale Station flash by. He expected to see a group of surprised commuters, instead of the blur of uniforms and a half-dozen black-and-whites in the parking lot. Then he saw Lee rushing up from the parking area, staring straight at the car as he came. For the briefest moment their eyes met, and Barron saw him raise his radio.

Then they were out of the station, the train racing forward like a runaway. He glimpsed the L.A. River and beyond it the headlights of cars jamming the Golden State Freeway.

Suddenly the train slowed and Barron had to grab on to a handrail to keep his balance. The train slowed more. He heard a distinct clunk-clunk as they passed over a series of switches, and then the train turned onto a spur line. He saw another spur line beside them and warehouses on either side. They rattled over more switches, and then what little daylight there was abruptly disappeared. For a few seconds they moved forward in the dark, and then the train gave a lurch and stopped. Seconds later the engine shut down and everything was silent.

"Where are we?" Raymond said in the dimness.

"I don't know."

6:31 A.M.

78

Barron slid the Colt into his belt and took out the Beretta, then moved down the car looking out the windows. From what he could see they were under a roof or some kind of enclosure for a massive, U-shaped warehouse that had raised platforms all around to accommodate the unloading of freight cars. High, closed overhead doors reached to the platform and were individually spotlighted and identified by large, brightly colored numbers painted in reds and yellows and blues. Spill from the lights flooded in through the car's windows, cutting its interior into areas of searing brightness and equally deep shadow.

Barron craned his neck. Outside he could see several freight cars on the spur line next to them. Other than that the area was dark. They had gone from night to early morning and back to what felt like night all in the space of barely twenty minutes.

Barron glanced back at Raymond, handcuffed at the far end of the car. Then motion outside caught his eye and he saw a tall man in a railroad uniform run from the locomotive and disappear from view. The train's engineer.

"Give me a chance, John. Take off the handcuffs." Raymond had seen the engineer, too.

"No."

Suddenly Barron remembered his police radio. It was in his jacket at the far end of the car. Ducking low he rushed for it, passing through the black-and-white chiaroscuro like a harlequin.

Then he was there, retrieving his jacket, slipping the radio from it and clicking on the squad's secure channel. Loud static crackled through the ear, then—

"John, you there?" Valparaiso's voice came over the radio. It was relaxed, even calm.

Barron felt the hair on his neck rise up. He looked outside. All he saw were the rows of brightly lit doorways. He crossed to the other side and saw nothing but the dark silhouettes of the freight cars and the hint of more lighted warehouse doors beyond them. Then he saw the headlights of a car turn in at the far end of the buildings and start down the uneven gravel between the tracks. A moment later the car stopped, the lights went out, and the car door opened. For the briefest moment he saw Lee's silhouette, and then he was gone in the darkness.

"John?" again Valparaiso's voice sounded over the radio. "You're in an enclosed warehouse. The uniforms have the entire area outside sealed off. We can do it hard or we can do it easy. You know how the patter goes. Give us Raymond and you can walk away, nothing will happen. Even if you felt you had to report it, it would still be four to one against. They'd just give you a little stress-related time off."

"He's lying." Raymond's voice suddenly came from the far end of the car.

Or had it?

It sounded closer, and Barron wondered if he'd slipped out of both sets of handcuffs and come partway down the car.

"Just Raymond, John. Why take you out when we don't need to?"

"It began on a train, John, it ends on a train," Raymond's voice came again.

Radio in one hand, Beretta in the other, Barron peered down the car. All he could see were the zebra stripes, jet black cut by bright light. Yet the voice had been closer. Raymond was coming toward him, he knew it.

6:36 A.M.

Gun in hand, Halliday slid from the shadows near a doorway with a red number "7" painted next to it and crossed the tracks to the front of the locomotive. To his left he could see Lee move up beside Valparaiso, and then the two of them go toward the Metrolink car's rear door.

Barron slid back in the dark, listening. He heard nothing and wondered if he was mistaken.

"Make it easy, huh, John?" Valparaiso's voice rattled through his radio again.

Barron's eyes were on the black-and-white lights and shadows in front of him. He was listening for Raymond even as he lifted the radio. "Marty," he said.

"I hear you, John."

"Good. Fuck you."

6:37 A.M.

Raymond heard Barron click off the radio. He was flat on the floor and out of the light spill, inching forward on his elbows and knees. He had purposely kept one of the handcuffs on, holding the free half in the same hand. A perfect garrote for Barron's throat when he got to him. He stopped and listened. Where was he? There was no sound, nothing.

Suddenly cold steel jabbed hard under his ear.

"You're missing the concept, Trigger Ray. I'm trying to keep from killing you."

Suddenly Barron squatted beside him. "Try something again and I'm going to let them have you."

Raymond felt a trickle of sweat by his ear where Barron's gun was. Abruptly Barron took hold of the free handcuff and pulled him close, shoving the Beretta hard under his chin.

"Who the hell are you?" Barron's eyes danced in the reflected light.

"You wouldn't guess in a lifetime." Raymond smiled arrogantly. "Not in two."

Suddenly Barron erupted in rage. He grabbed Raymond hard. Slammed his head against a handrail. Once. Twice. Three times. Blood ran from Raymond's nose and dripped onto his shirt. Then Barron pulled him up close, staring into his eyes.

"What is Europe about? And the dead men and Alfred Neuss and Russia? What are the safe deposit keys to?"

"I said you would never guess."

Barron pulled him closer still. "Try me," he said, his voice full of menace.

"The pieces, John. The pieces that will ensure the future."

"What pieces?"

Again came the arrogant smile. Only this time it came slowly and was more calculated. "That, you will have to find out for yourself."

"John—" Valparaiso's voice floated from the radio. "John?"

Abruptly Barron snapped the free handcuff back over Raymond's wrist. "Take that off again, I'll kill you."

Barron reached for his cell phone. At least he knew where they were and he still had Dan Ford. If they could hold on long enough, Ford might bring the media here—he flipped open the phone and hit the POWER button and waited for the phone to light up. It didn't. He tried it again. No luck. Maybe he hadn't charged it. Maybe he had forgotten to—

"Dammit," he swore under his breath. He tried it once more. Still nothing.

"It's dead, John." Raymond was staring at him.

"Alright, it's dead. We aren't. When I say move, we're going to the locomotive end of the car. We're going low and we're going fast. Okay?"

"Okay."

"Move."

79

6:48 A.M.

Someone in the media horde at Union Station had picked up the warehouse action on a police scanner. Immediately Dan Ford tried Barron on his cell phone, but he got nothing more than Barron's voice mail. A second try and the response was the same. A call to a confidant in Robbery-Homicide at Parker Center confirmed what had been picked up on the scanner. Raymond Thorne was holding John Barron hostage on a Metrolink train. The police had diverted it to an isolated warehouse district that was now cordoned off. The 5-2 Squad had been put in charge of the situation.

Normally, it would take about fifteen minutes by car from Union Station to the warehouse. Ford made it in nine, a full five minutes ahead of the rolling tidal wave of media he'd organized.

He parked his Jeep Liberty on the street and walked quickly through the drizzle, approaching the line of black-and-whites that had cordoned off the area. He was nearly to them when Chief Harwood suddenly appeared out of the mass of uniforms, a ranking lieutenant at his side. Harwood had his hands up to stop him.

"No one past the line, Dan. That includes you."

"John's in there?" Ford nodded toward the bleak row of warehouses behind them.

"Raymond Thorne has taken him hostage."

"I know, and the Five-Two's in command."

"There'll be a press briefing when we have more," Harwood said abruptly, then turned and walked back into the crowd of uniforms. His lieutenant glanced at Ford, then followed Harwood.

Dan Ford had been a reporter and around police and department brass far too long not to know a little about eye movement and body language, even in men trained not to show it. That Harwood himself was there and had come out to speak with him alone spoke volumes. What Harwood said might be the official word, but it was a lie. Ford knew full well Barron had Raymond in custody and had been bringing him to Union Station. And then suddenly the train was diverted off the main line and stopped out of sight behind warehouses with the 5-2 in charge and police keeping everyone a long way back, and with the chief of police himself coming out to tell the one reporter the police had been more open with than anyone else in the media that he couldn't go in because Barron had become a hostage.

Why? What was going on? What had happened?

He had seen the squad take Raymond into custody at Mercury Air Center and drive off with him about 4:20 A.M. Then, nearly two hours later, at about 6:10, Barron had called from the train saying he had Raymond in custody by himself and asking Ford to arrange for a media circus to meet them when the train arrived at Union Station. What had happened in the meantime? How and why did Barron come to have Raymond in custody by himself?

Suddenly Ford began to think that something had gone terribly wrong inside the squad. It made him think back to the way Barron had acted in the coffee shop the night Frank Donlan had shot himself. When he had asked him about it, Barron had given him an almost word-for-word version of the story Red had given to the media, that Donlan somehow had a gun hidden in his clothes and shot himself rather than be taken into custody. Maybe that was true, but maybe it wasn't. There had been rumors for years that the 5-2 had, on more than one occasion, extended the meaning of law enforcement and had themselves killed a suspect in custody. But the rumors had never been more than that, and no reporter that he knew of, least of all himself, had ever pursued it.

There was no way to know for certain, but still he had to ask himself—*what if the stories were true?* What if the squad had killed Frank Donlan and Barron had been there and hadn't known what to do about it? Barron certainly couldn't have told him. He could have told no one. The murder of Barron's parents had wholly traumatized him, turning him from a student of landscape architecture into a man obsessed with criminal law and victims' rights. If the squad had assassinated Donlan, it would have horrified him. If they intended on doing the same to Raymond, then—suddenly Ford wondered if that was why Barron had called him from his car on the way to LAX telling him about the Josef Speer/Raymond thing and clearing the way for him with Lufthansa security, because he was afraid the squad was going to kill Raymond at the airport and he wanted someone from the media present to disrupt their plan. And he'd called *before* he got to LAX, giving Ford a big lead on the story, and maybe even *before* the squad knew what was going on. What had he said? *Let's keep it between us, just you and me, until we know for sure.* Just you and me, meaning Barron and himself, not the rest of the media, who he knew would be kept back if the 5-2 was already there or nearly there.

But it was a situation that had never come because Raymond had killed Red, an action in itself that was enough reason to take Raymond down once they had him in custody. If that was what they had planned after they'd left Mercury Air Center and had taken him somewhere to do it, there was every chance Barron would have been horrified all over again and refused to let it happen. If that was so and somehow he had wrestled Raymond away from the squad and made it to the train—

It was the only line of reasoning that made sense and would have been the motive for Barron's wanting a media circus at Union Station when the train arrived because, like his thinking at LAX, he knew the squad wouldn't act with the whole world watching.

If Barron had done that, Harwood would have been the first to know about it. And if history had given the squad a free hand in doling out the law as they saw fit, the LAPD was not going to risk exposing that history now, not after the years of scandals and very public police misconduct. As a result, LAPD machinery had gone into high gear. Barron and his prisoner were isolated and out of sight, with the chief of police telling the world he had been taken hostage instead of telling the real truth—that he had been cornered by his own men because he had been trying to keep his prisoner alive.

Ford looked again at Harwood in the crowd of uniforms. Then he saw a familiar car pulling in. It was fifty yards away and moving toward the wall of black-and-whites in the drizzle. He ran toward it, his feet slipping on the wet ground. As he got closer he could see its rear window had been blown out. Then he saw Polchak at the wheel. Someone was in the front seat with him. He couldn't tell who it was.

"Len," he yelled, running harder. "Len!"

He saw Polchak glance over his shoulder. Then the phalanx of uniforms opened a path and Polchak drove through. As quickly, the way closed behind him and the uniforms turned toward Ford, the sergeant-in-charge motioning him back. Ford stopped and stood there in the light rain, his horn-rimmed glasses fogging over, his blue blazer heavy with wet, his spirit and hopes as broken as his nose throbbing under the bandages. It made no difference that he was surrounded by police, or that he knew a great many of them personally, or that he was the most respected police reporter in Los Angeles. John Barron was going to be killed.

And there was nothing he could do about it.

80

Barron and Raymond lay flat on the ground between the rails under the Metrolink car watching Lee and Valparaiso come toward them. Berettas in hand, the detectives were ten feet apart and looking up at the car as they came. Where Halliday was, or Polchak, Barron had no idea. Most likely they were somewhere back in the darkness waiting and watching.

What was clear, as Lee and Valparaiso approached, was that both men thought Barron and Raymond were still inside the car. They kept coming. Five paces more. And then six. And then seven. Now the detectives were midcar and all they could see were their legs from the thighs down. Barron could almost reach out and touch Lee's size-fourteen shoes.

"Now," Barron whispered, and he and Raymond rolled out from under the car on the opposite side from the detectives. In an instant they were on their feet and running for the cover of the freight cars on the second spur line twenty feet away.

Halliday saw them as he came around the nose of the locomotive. He swung his gun to fire, but too late, missing, and they slipped out of sight into the darkness under a Southern Pacific freight car, the fourth car down in a line of six.

Barron saw Halliday start toward them from the locomotive, then saw Lee climb over the coupling between the Metrolink car and the locomotive. A split second later Valparaiso came around the car's far end. They were a dozen yards apart and closing on them. Barron could see Lee lift his radio.

"You fucked with the wrong guys, John." Lee's voice came over Barron's radio.

"It's just us now." Valparaiso was speaking into his radio as they closed the distance, his eyes locked on the dark space under the car where Barron and Raymond had gone.

"The outside is sealed off. No more chances, John," Valparaiso continued, his voice crackling through Barron's radio. "Not even for you. We have to protect the squad."

Raymond suddenly looked to Barron, "Give me a gun," he whispered. "If you don't we are both going to die."

"Move back along the rails," Barron said quietly. "Slide under the car behind us."

Raymond glanced behind him, then back. They could see Halliday move left and out of sight. Valparaiso and Lee stayed where they were.

"Give me a gun," Raymond pressed again.

"Do as I say." Barron's eyes shifted hard to Raymond. "Now!"

"I'm here, Marty." Polchak's voice suddenly jumped from Barron's radio. Barron looked around. Polchak. Where was he? Where had he been?

"John." Now it was Valparaiso's voice over the radio, "Len's got a surprise. Kind of a going-away present."

A loud noise rattled behind them. Barron whirled to see the overhead door to warehouse number 19 fly open. Then Polchak stepped out into the light. He had the monstrous Striker 12 riot gun in one arm. Rebecca was in the other.

"Len, what the hell are you doing?" Halliday's shocked voice slapped through the radios.

"Let her go!" Suddenly Barron was pushing out from under the freight car and climbing up on the platform, moving toward Polchak in front of him.

"Let her go! Let her go!"

Barron's eyes were locked on Polchak, the Beretta tightening in his grip. "Let her go!" he screamed again.

Suddenly Valparaiso was running in from the left behind him, and Barron heard Raymond yell a warning. At the same time, Lee stepped from the shadows at the far end of the freight car and started toward him, his Beretta coming up to fire.

Barron saw him and jerked left, firing three quick rounds just as Lee's gun went off. The giant detective jolted to a stop where he was, tried to regain his balance, then toppled over to lie face first in the gravel, his Beretta sliding forward across it.

Barron steadied, then looked back to Polchak. Rebecca was frozen against him, confused and terrified.

"To your right!" Raymond screamed.

Barron whirled.

Valparaiso was feet away, the hammer already falling on his automatic.

Boom! Boom!—Boom! Boom!

The guns of both detectives fired at the same time.

Barron felt something thump into his thigh and slam him backward. In the same instant he saw Valparaiso grab his throat and start falling. Then Barron bounced hard off the freight car and went down, his own Beretta sent flying. He started to black out but fought against it. At the same time he saw Rebecca watching him in horror, straining to break from Polchak's grip. Polchak jerked her back, hefting the Striker 12. Barron tried to get up but couldn't. Suddenly Raymond pulled up over him, jerking the Colt from Barron's belt.

Barron started to yell at him, but Raymond was already swinging the Colt toward Polchak.

In the same instant Polchak let go with the Striker 12. The sound of a thousand thundering jackhammers filled the air. For a millisecond a look of disbelief crossed Raymond's face; then he crashed against the freight car and dropped to the pavement at the edge of the platform.

Barron saw him covered in blood trying to get up, then he lost his balance and twisted backward. For a heartbeat his eyes locked on Barron's, then he rolled sideways and fell from view onto the tracks below.

Barron swung back. Polchak was moving toward him, the Striker 12 pointed at his chest. Behind him Barron could see Rebecca, her hands to her ears, frozen in horror.

Barron's eyes went to his Beretta on the platform ten feet away and then to the Colt, half that distance, where Raymond had dropped it.

He could see Polchak grinning as he closed the distance. There was a loud clank of steel as he cocked the Striker. Then, from the corner of his eye, he saw Halliday move in, his Beretta up, ready to finish it as if the Striker wouldn't.

"Jesus Christ, Jimmy," Barron breathed.

"For Red, you fuck!" Polchak suddenly yelled, starting to squeeze the Striker's trigger.

It was then that Rebecca screamed. Wide-eyed in terror, she screamed and screamed and screamed. After years of silence it was a pent-up, primeval cry. Horror, terror, and fear erupting and roaring out as one. None of them had ever heard a sound like it, and she wouldn't stop. Or couldn't. The sound went on forever. Resounding off the buildings, the railcars, everything.

Polchak squinted, as if he were having trouble thinking, her wail throwing him wholly off balance mentally. Slowly he turned and stepped toward her, his eyes like saucers, the pupils in them shrinking to almost nothing. The Striker still filled his hands.

"STOPPPPP ITTTTT!" he screamed, his face sheer alabaster, his voice high-pitched and bizarre, more that of an animal than a man.

"STOPPPP ITTTTTT! STOPPPP ITTTTTT! STOPPP ITTTTT!"

Rebecca didn't stop. She kept screaming, shrieking.

Desperately Barron tried to get to the Beretta, but he could only push off with one leg. There was no feeling at all in the other.

"STOPPPP ITTTTT! STOPP ITTT!" Polchak advanced on Rebecca, still screaming in that awful, unworldly high pitch, holding the Striker pointed directly at Rebecca but with the stress making his hands shake and his aim waver.

"Len! Don't! Don't!" Barron was on his stomach now, pushing with his good leg toward the Beretta.

Another step and Polchak was right there, the riot gun fully in Rebecca's face.

"Len!"

This time the cry didn't come from Barron. It came from Halliday. Hearing it, Polchak stopped. Barron saw his chest heave and then Polchak whirled again, this time leveling the Striker at Halliday.

Boom! Boom! Boom! Boom!

Halliday's 9 mm slugs caught Polchak in the neck and right shoulder. The Striker started to slip. Polchak tightened his grip and tried to lift the riot gun, but he had no strength. All he could do was blast away at the concrete at his feet as he fell. There was a sickening thud as he hit the pavement. As if he hadn't so much fallen as dropped from a high place. His chest heaved one last time and he groaned once as life left him.

And then silence descended.

PART 2

EUROPE

1

John Barron heard the sharp whine of the engines, then felt the press of his body against his seat as British Airways flight 0282 hurtled down the runway at LAX bound for London. Seconds later the plane lifted off and there was the distinct clunk of the landing gear closing into the fuselage. Below, he could see the cityscape of Los Angeles vanish as the aircraft gained altitude. Then he saw the coastline and the deep blue of the Pacific and the string of white beaches reaching north to Malibu. And then the plane banked gently left and all he saw was sky. They were safely up and away.

Barron let out a breath in relief and turned to see Rebecca curled up on the seat beside him. A blanket pulled up over her, she was sound asleep. Yet, heavily sedated as she was, she looked surprisingly at peace, as if finally her life and his had turned in the right direction.

Barron glanced around. The eight other passengers in the first class cabin paid them no attention whatsoever. To them he was just another traveler with a companion sleeping beside him. How could any one of them know they were running for their lives?

"Would you care for a cocktail, Mr. Marten?"

"What?" Distracted and puzzled, John Barron looked up to see a male flight attendant standing in the aisle beside him.

"I asked if you'd care for a cocktail, Mr. Marten."

"Oh—yes, thank you. A vodka martini. A double."

"Ice?"

"Please."

"Thank you, Mr. Marten."

Barron sat back. He had to get used to people calling him Marten. The same as he would have to respond to being called by his first name, Nick or Nicholas. The same as Rebecca would have to get used to the name Rebecca Marten, or Ms. Marten, and react to it as if she had been doing so all her life.

The plane banked easily once again as they turned east. A moment later the flight attendant returned and placed his drink on the armrest beside him. Barron nodded a thanks and picked it up and tasted it. It was cool and dry and bitter all at the same time. He wondered when he'd last had a martini, if ever, and why he'd ordered it. On the other hand, he did know it was strong, and it was a strong drink he wanted now.

Today was exactly two weeks and two days since the terrible bloodbath in the rail yards. Sixteen days of pain and anxiety and fear. He took another sip of his drink and glanced at Rebecca asleep beside him. She was okay, so was he. He watched her for a moment longer, then looked out the window at the passing clouds and tried to put together what had happened in so blisteringly short a time.

He could still smell the stench of gunpowder and see Halliday on the rail platform screaming into his radio for ambulances. Still see Rebecca running wildly toward him from the fallen Polchak. Shrieking, crying, nearly hysterical, dropping to the concrete, to cradle him in her arms. In what seemed like slow motion he saw Police Chief Harwood and his entourage come down the platform just as the first rescue vehicles arrived. And, in the same slow motion, emergency medical technicians taking over. He saw horror contort Rebecca's face as she was pulled from him, and then she vanished, swallowed up in a sea of uniforms. He remembered his clothes being cut from him and morphine being shot into his arm. And glimpsing Halliday talking with Chief Harwood. And seeing EMT people slipping under the freight car to work on Raymond on the tracks below. Then Barron was being loaded onto a backboard and carried toward an ambulance past the prostrate figures of Lee and Valparaiso and Polchak. And he knew they were dead. As reality faded under the sway of the morphine he had one last glimpse of Chief Harwood surrounded by aides. There was no question they knew what had happened, and damage control had already begun.

Within the hour, world media were clamoring for details

about what was being called "The Great Metrolink Shootout" and demanding more on the identity of the man tabbed Trigger Ray Thorne. What they got instead was a terse LAPD news brief stating only that three detectives had been killed in a deadly crossfire with the suspect while trying to rescue one of their own, that Thorne himself had been seriously wounded, and that a concentrated internal investigation was in progress.

And then, for everyone, the whole thing spun suddenly and impossibly out of hand. With John Barron taken to Glendale Memorial Hospital for emergency treatment for multiple gunshot wounds—wounds that by the grace of God were all in soft tissue and not life-threatening. Raymond Oliver Thorne was rushed to County-USC Medical Center in far more serious condition.

And there, barely thirty hours later, following multiple surgeries, and without ever regaining consciousness, he died of a pulmonary embolism, a blood clot in the lungs. Then, in a mix-up at the county coroner's office that bordered on the comedic and added grievously to the embarrassment of the department, his body was inadvertently released to a private funeral home and within hours was cremated. Once again the LAPD shuddered while the world's press did cartwheels.

7:30 P.M.

Three hours into their flight. Supper over, the cabin lights were off; passengers were sipping after-dinner drinks and watching movies on their personal TV screens. Rebecca still slept. John Barron tried to do the same but sleep wouldn't come. Instead the memories of what had happened continued.

Early the same evening that Raymond had died and been cremated, Saturday, March 16, Dan Ford visited Barron in his hospital room. Clearly concerned for his best friend's life, there was something about him, about his manner, that told Barron he knew what had happened in the shoot-out and why, but he said nothing. Instead, he told of visiting Rebecca at St. Francis; she had been sedated and was resting when he came in, but had recognized him and taken his hand. And when he'd said he was on his way to visit her brother and asked if he could tell him she was okay, she'd squeezed his hand and nodded yes.

Then Ford had given him two pieces of news concerning Raymond. The first was about an interview the Metropolitan Police had had with Alfred Neuss in London.

"All he told them," Ford said, "was that he had come to London on business and had no idea who Raymond was or what he'd been after, and the only reason he could guess why his name was in the address book of the brothers Raymond allegedly murdered in Chicago was that they were tailors he'd once used when he was there and had had them send the bill to his shop in Beverly Hills."

Ford's second piece of information had to do with what LAPD investigators had learned in their attempt to find out who had contracted for the private jet sent to pick up Raymond at the Mercury Air Terminal in Burbank.

"West Charter Air sent a Gulfstream for Raymond not once, but twice. A day earlier, the same plane had gone to meet him at Santa Monica Airport, but he had never shown up. The aircraft had been contracted for by a man calling himself Aubrey Collinson, supposedly a Jamaican lawyer, who came into the company's Kingston office and paid for the charter in cash. Later, obviously knowing Raymond hadn't met the plane, he returned, apologized for the mix-up, and paid again, asking simply that this time his client be picked up at the Burbank airport instead of Santa Monica. The rest of the instructions remained the same.

"The pilots were to pick up a Mexican businessman named Jorge Luis Ventana and fly him to Guadalajara. Along with the instructions was a small package to be delivered to Ventana when they met him—a package the LAPD took as evidence from the Gulfstream at the Mercury Air Center. Inside, they found twenty thousand dollars in cash, a Mexican passport in the name of Jorge Luis Ventana, an Italian driver's license with a Rome address, and an Italian passport, both in the name of Carlo Pavani. All three bore Raymond's photograph. The address in Rome turned out to be a vacant lot. Both the Italian driver's license and passport were false, as was the Mexican passport. And so far inspectors from the Jamaica Constabulary Force have been unable to find anyone named Aubrey Collinson."

It had been then, with Ford's last words barely out of his

mouth, that the door to Barron's hospital room had opened and
LAPD Police Chief Louis Harwood, dressed in full uniform,
and accompanied by his deputy chief, came in. Harwood nodded a simple hello to Ford and then quietly asked if they could
be alone. Without a word Harwood's deputy chief walked Ford
to the door, saw him out, and closed it behind him.

It was a gesture that, under other circumstances, might have
suggested the need for intimacy, a police chief concerned about
the well-being of one of his officers wounded in the line of duty.
Instead, it was an act of menace and filled with foreboding.

Barron distinctly remembered Harwood crossing the room,
telling him he was happy to learn his wounds weren't serious,
and that Harwood had been informed Barron could be released
from the hospital as early as Monday. And then Harwood's eyes
became stone cold.

"As of an hour ago the case of Raymond Oliver Thorne was
officially closed. He had no allies, no ties to terrorist cells. He
was a single gunman acting alone."

"What do you mean acting alone? Somebody sent a chartered plane for him to two different airports and on two different days. You know that as well as I do," Barron, even in the
shape he was in, had protested directly, even angrily. "You've
got people dead here in L.A., in Chicago and San Francisco and
Mexico City. You've got safe deposit keys to a bank somewhere
in Europe. You've got—"

"The formal announcement," Harwood cut him off, "will be
made at the appropriate time."

Under ordinary circumstances Barron would have kept up his
protest, pointing to the specific references Raymond made in
his calendar to London, France, and April 7/Moscow. He would
have told Harwood what Raymond had said on the train about
"the pieces that would ensure the future" and then warned him
that even though Raymond was dead he was certain that what
he had begun wasn't, that there was something else perhaps
even more deadly still to come. But these were not ordinary circumstances, and he didn't. Besides, Harwood wasn't finished.

"As of an hour ago," Harwood continued in a monotone icier
than his glare, "the one-hundred-year-old Five-Two Squad was
officially dissolved. It no longer exists.

"As for its remaining members—Detective Halliday has been

given a three-month leave of absence, after which he will be assigned to a less stressful post at Valley Traffic Division.

"You, Detective Barron, will sign a nondisclosure agreement pledging never to divulge anything about the actions and operations of the Five-Two. Following that you will resign from the Los Angeles Police Department for medical reasons and be given a lump-sum medical disability payment of one hundred and twenty-five thousand dollars."

Abruptly Harwood looked to his deputy chief, who handed him a large manila envelope. Holding it, Harwood turned back to Barron.

"As you know, for her own safety, your sister was medicated with psychotropic drugs on-scene at the rail yards. I have been assured that the effect of those drugs in combination with her emotional state and her need to continue on the medication for some time will leave her with little, if any, memory of what happened there.

"As it stands the people at St. Francis believe she was taken to see you at the hospital because you had been wounded in the shootout with the fugitive and suffered a breakdown on the way. As a result she was taken to the nearest hospital. That's all the media and public know and ever will know. There will be no record in the official report that she was ever at the rail yards."

Abruptly Harwood handed the manila envelope to Barron. "Open it," he commanded, and Barron did.

Inside was a twisted, badly scorched California automobile license plate. It was from Barron's Mustang.

"Somebody torched your car in the parking lot of the Mercury Air Center where you left it yesterday morning."

"Torched," Barron said quietly, "as in 'deliberately set on fire'?"

"Yes, as in 'deliberately set on fire,' as in 'burned up.'" Slowly Harwood's eyes filled with hatred. So did his voice.

"You should know there are any number of rumors circulating through the department. Chief among them is that you were directly responsible for the deaths of Detectives Polchak and Lee and Valparaiso. And, ultimately, for the end of the squad.

"Whether it's true or not, once you leave the hospital you will be returning to a very unfavorable, even hostile, environment."

Harwood paused, and Barron could see the loathing in him grow even stronger. Then Harwood continued.

"There is the story of a note handed to the mayor of a small city in a war-torn South American country. It was given to him by a farmer but sent by a guerrilla commander. It read something like—'For the good of your health, you must leave the city. If you don't, you will become a target.'

"For the good of your health, Detective, I would take the same advice, and act on it as quickly as is humanly possible."

2

STILL BRITISH AIRWAYS FLIGHT 0282.
MONDAY, APRIL 1. 12:30 A.M.

Only one soul stirred in the darkened first class cabin. It was John Barron, wide awake and wired, as if he were pumped full of caffeine. As much as he tried to forget, memories still twisted.

It was as if it had just happened. The sharp click, the abrupt close of the door as Harwood and his deputy chief left. Harwood had not said another word. There'd been no need. Barron had been explicitly warned that his life was in danger. It meant he had no choice but to do what he had planned to do after the squad's murder of Frank Donlan. Take Rebecca and leave Los Angeles as quickly and with as little trail left behind as possible. He had stopped short of it before because of Raymond and because he felt it was his duty to do anything he could to help bring him in before he killed again. But now Raymond was dead and whatever else he had been involved in, whatever else had been set in motion and was yet to happen, was someone else's responsibility. He had to concentrate on one thing alone. Saving his life and Rebecca's.

The first time it had been a matter of working things out with Dr. Flannery, finding a destination, packing his car, collecting

Rebecca, and leaving. But then the shootout had taken place, and because of it her massive psychological breakthrough had happened. As a result of the intensive psychiatric care she would require to help her continue through it, to say nothing of his own physical condition, the idea of going anywhere and quickly seemed impossible. But there was no alternative. If the retribution Harwood promised came to be and he was killed, Rebecca would freak out again and very quickly slip away to nothing.

Wholly unnerved, he'd called Dr. Janet Flannery early the next morning, Sunday, March 17, and asked her to come to the hospital. She arrived just before noon and, at Barron's request, took him in a wheelchair to a large outdoor visitor seating area, where he asked about Rebecca's condition.

"She's made a huge advance," Dr. Flannery had said. "Enormous. She's speaking haltingly and responding to questions. But the period here is crucial and very difficult. She's medicated and very in and out. Hysterical one minute, withdrawn the next, and asking for you with every other breath. She's strong and exceptionally bright, but if we aren't very careful we could lose her and she could easily slip back to where she was before."

"Dr. Flannery," Barron had said quietly but emphatically, "I have to get Rebecca and myself out of Los Angeles as quickly as possible. Not to Oregon or Washington State or Colorado as we talked about before, but farther. Canada or maybe Europe. Wherever it is, whatever we choose, I have to know how soon she can travel that long and that far."

He remembered Dr. Flannery studying him and knowing she saw the same urgency and desperation she had seen before. Only this time it was stronger and far more desperate.

"If everything goes well, maybe two weeks at the earliest before she could be handed off for treatment elsewhere." Dr. Flannery studied him even more closely. "Detective, you have to understand Rebecca is on an entirely new plateau, one that needs intense management. Because of it, and because of what you want to do, I need to ask you why."

Barron hesitated for a long moment, unsure of what to say. Finally he realized he could not do what had to be done alone and asked if he could have a private session with her, he as the patient, she as the professional counselor.

"When?"

"Now."

She told him it was unorthodox and that it would be better if she were to arrange for him to see another therapist. But he pleaded with her, confiding there was real physical danger here and time was truly of the essence. She knew him and she knew everything about Rebecca; moreover, he trusted her.

Finally, she agreed, and wheeled him to a far corner of the area, away from the other patients and visitors. There, under the shade of an enormous sycamore tree, he told her about the squad, about the execution of Frank Donlan, about Raymond's killing of Red, his fight with Polchak and what happened at the auto body shop after they'd captured Raymond, and then what happened in the rail yards. He ended with the burning of his car and Chief Harwood's solemn warning.

"I have to change my identity and Rebecca's, and then we have to get as far from L.A. as we can, and as quickly as possible. The identity part I can handle. The rest I need help with—where we can go so that Rebecca can get the treatment she needs without people asking too many questions, and where the LAPD would not be likely to follow us. Someplace far away, where we can fit in and safely start a whole new life, maybe even another country."

Dr. Flannery said nothing, just studied him, and he knew she was measuring the reality of what needed to be done against the reality of what could be done.

"Obviously, Detective, if you change your identities, as you feel you must, the health insurance she now has will no longer be valid unless you want to risk leaving a paper trail."

"No, I can't do that. No paper trail."

"But you understand, wherever you go, her treatment will be expensive, at least initially, when she will need the most care."

"I have been given a kind of substantial 'severance package,' and I have a small savings account and some bond investments. We'll be alright for a while, until I can find work. Just—" Barron stopped in midsentence and waited for a male nurse escorting an elderly patient to walk past. Then, lowering his voice, he continued, "Just tell me what Rebecca's needs are."

"The key," Flannery said, "is finding a top post-traumatic stress treatment program, one that will expedite and help create what's called 'personality stability,' getting her to the point where she can comfortably function on her own. If you're thinking of Canada—"

"No," Barron interrupted suddenly, "Europe would be better."

Dr. Flannery nodded. "In that case three places come to mind, and each is excellent. The post-trauma treatment center at the University of Rome in Italy, the post-trauma treatment center at the University of Geneva in Switzerland, and the Balmore Clinic in London."

Barron felt his heart catch in his throat. He had suggested Canada or Europe because he knew there were Americans everywhere and felt they could find some community where they could fit in without drawing undue attention to themselves. They would also be far enough away to make it both impractical and difficult for the forces on the LAPD that Chief Harwood had warned him about to track them down, especially if they had new identities and left no trail for those people to follow.

But now he realized he had abruptly narrowed it to Europe for another reason. Raymond and what else he had been about pointed to Europe, and most directly to London. Wounded as he was, as concerned as he was for his safety and Rebecca's and her continued treatment, there was something inside him that would not let Raymond go. Raymond had been good, too good, too professional, too controlled in handling what he had had to deal with to be written off simply as a madman. Clearly he had had other goals and, as the chartered aircraft attested, he hadn't acted alone. Even without concrete evidence, Barron, as young as he was, was still a seasoned detective, and the sense that something more was to happen crawled inside him and stuck in his gut. That was why, when put on the spot, he had picked Europe over Canada. And by suggesting London as a potential site for Rebecca's rehabilitation, Dr. Flannery narrowed his focus even more.

London had been Raymond's immediate destination after he'd finished with whatever he had intended for Alfred Neuss in L.A., and Neuss's life had been spared simply because he had gone to London. It was a journey that had obviously surprised Raymond because he had clearly expected to find Neuss in Beverly Hills.

There were the other things, too, the "pieces," as Raymond had said: keys to a safe deposit box of Belgian manufacture whose company did business only within the European Union, which meant the box and whatever was in it was in a bank somewhere in continental Europe; and the three notations referencing London specifically: an address—21 Uxbridge Street, which the London Metropolitan Police had described as a well-kept private home near Kensington Gardens, which was owned by a Mr. Charles Dixon, a retired English stockbroker who lived most of the year in the South of France, and was within easy walking distance of the Russian Embassy; the reference to the embassy itself; and the reminder to meet someone called I. M. in Penrith's Bar on High Street, a person a Metropolitan Police investigator looking into it had been unable to identify.

That information was still fresh, barely two weeks old, and it meant whatever operation it centered on might very well be active and findable. The FBI had been checking possible terrorist links, and presumably they would have passed on whatever information they had to the CIA and probably even the State Department, but Barron knew he would never learn what they had found out or reported.

The most recent and intriguing information had come from Dan Ford, who had just learned of it and confided in him the day before they were to leave for London. Russian Ministry of Justice investigators had quietly arrived in L.A. the week after Raymond's death. Overseen by the FBI, they had been given access to LAPD files and talked to people at the Beverly Hills PD. Three days later they had left, saying that despite Raymond Thorne's actions, despite the fact that a chartered jet had been sent to pick him up at two different airports on two separate days with packages containing false passports and driver's licenses, despite the vanished "Aubrey Collinson" who had chartered the plane in Kingston, Jamaica, and despite the brief handwritten notes in his calendar, they had found no evidence of a threat to the Russian government or its people. When questioned, they had volunteered that there seemed to be no significance at all to Raymond's notation *April 7/Moscow*. To them April 7/Moscow was a date and place and nothing more.

The Russians had come, Barron thought, in the spirit of international cooperation in a time of increased terrorist activity, because the use of a chartered jet suggested that whatever threat there might have been was exceptionally well funded and could have global implications. But that trail had quickly turned cold, and as for Raymond himself, while what he had done had been brutal and murderous, neither he nor it fit the current profile of terrorists or terrorist organizations.

Yet the dismissal of his rampage as having no further implication or complication—by the Russians, by the FBI, and most especially by LAPD, which wanted to quickly bury what could easily turn into a major tarnishing of an already severely tarnished department if the truth of the Metrolink shootout were exposed—was, to John Barron, a grievous error because, to him, all those other things strongly suggested Raymond had been involved in something major and possibly catastrophic that hadn't ended with his death. Particularly ominous, no matter what the Russian investigators had said, was April 7, a date that was fast approaching. How could anyone know for certain whether Raymond's notation was personal, to remind him of someone or something in Moscow that day, or was a reference to a day and place for some act of terror like the hostage-taking Chechen rebel attack on the Melnikova Street theater or the suicide bombings at a Moscow rock festival—or something even more monstrous, like the train bombings in Madrid, or one designed to kill thousands, not unlike the horror that rained down on New York and Washington on the infamous September 11?

If the notation did refer to a terrorist attack, did that mean the official posture taken by all of the agencies, the LAPD and the Russians included, was merely a smoke screen to avoid terrifying the public? And if it was only a posture, did that mean that the FBI, the CIA, Interpol, and other international counterterrorist organizations were working with Russian security and secretly monitoring the situation worldwide, hoping to discover and then crush whatever Raymond and the people behind him had planned?

Or—

Was nothing planned? Was there no significance to any of it? Was everything as dead as Raymond himself?

Either way there was something else Barron had to keep strongly in mind—regardless of whatever else was going on, and the LAPD's public dismissal of anything Raymond might have been involved in, they might still be following up on Raymond's notes and other evidence themselves. If so, and if Barron did the same, he might very well cross paths with Chief Harwood's detectives. If that happened, it could cost him his life. But he also knew staying away was impossible. The burden of guilt he still carried for the deaths of the people Raymond had murdered in L.A. was enormous, and the idea that more people might die horrified him. So, no matter the risk, he had to go on until he was certain that the fire Raymond had begun was finally and utterly extinguished.

But he couldn't be certain. Not now. Not at all.

Deep inside him a voice struggled to get out, the same as it had from the moment he learned that Raymond was dead. Every time it rose up, he tried to push it away. But he couldn't. It kept coming back, urging him to keep on, to find the beast and make sure it was dead.

When he listened to the voice, as he did now, he realized that if he were ever to pick up the scent of the beast again, clearly there was only one place to start.

"London," Barron said to Dr. Flannery directly.

"The Balmore Clinic?"

"Yes. Would you be able to get Rebecca into a program there? And quickly?"

"I will do what I can," Dr. Flannery said.

And she had. And done it very well.

3

LONDON, YORK HOUSE, THE BALMORE CLINIC, MONDAY, APRIL 1. 1:45 P.M.

John Barron's, no, Nicholas Marten's (he had to force himself to remember who he had become) first impression of Clementine Simpson was less than startling. Tall and about his age, with neck-length auburn hair and wearing an oversized navy business suit, she gave the impression of being a reasonably attractive but rather dowdy hospital supervisor. What he would later learn was that she was not a supervisor at all but a member of the Balmore Foundation participating in one of her twice-yearly weeks as a clinic volunteer. It was in that capacity that she had accompanied Rebecca's new psychiatrist, Dr. Anne Maxwell-Scot—a short, rather heavyset, particularly astute woman Marten guessed to be somewhere in her early fifties— and two medical attendants to Heathrow Airport to meet Rebecca Marten and her brother when their British Airways flight from Los Angeles landed just before noon.

By then Rebecca had been awake for nearly an hour and, though still groggy from her medication, had had a light breakfast and seemed to understand where she was and why she and her brother were on the plane and going to London. The same calmness and understanding carried over during the ambulance ride from the airport and into London and to York House, the inpatient facility of the Balmore Clinic in Belsize Lane.

"If you have any questions at all, Mr. Marten, please don't hesitate to ask," Clementine Simpson said as she left Rebecca's small yet cheery third-floor room. "I shall be here for the remainder of the week."

And like that she was gone, and Nicholas Marten turned to the process of getting Rebecca settled. Afterward, he spent a few moments alone with Dr. Maxwell-Scot as she told him how well Rebecca seemed, certainly better than she had expected, and then explained what would happen next.

"As I'm sure you are aware, Mr. Marten, you are not only Rebecca's brother but her security blanket, and it is important you stay close by, at least for a few days. Yet it is equally important that Rebecca be weaned from that kind of crutch as quickly as possible. It is essential that she gain confidence and make advances on her own.

"Soon, perhaps as early as tomorrow, and aside from private two-a-day-meetings with me, Rebecca will be introduced to group therapy sessions where she and the other participants will work on putting on a play or designing a new building for the hospital. Tasks that require cooperation and prevent the participants from creating safe, singular hiding places where they could easily regress or become stranded. The whole idea is to socialize Rebecca and allow her to become more and more self-sufficient."

Marten listened carefully, trying to be certain that the practice at the Balmore, as Dr. Flannery had promised, was the same as it was elsewhere in the world of psychotherapy: A patient's personal records and psychiatric history were confidential and, if the family requested it—which he had—were available only to the patient's therapist. Dr. Flannery had assured him further that her explanation of the need for Rebecca to be admitted to the Balmore so promptly had been completely confidential and Marten was simply looking to make certain that was so.

Fifteen minutes with Dr. Maxwell-Scot had given him that reassurance and more. She had talked only about Rebecca's situation and about the program she and Dr. Flannery had designed for her and about how successful she thought it could be. It gave Marten a sense of trust and comfort that was enhanced by Dr. Maxwell-Scot's warm and personable nature. It was a feeling that seemed to flow throughout the Balmore. He had felt it with Ms. Simpson and everyone else from the moment they had been met at the gate at Heathrow and seen quickly through customs and passport control and to the waiting ambulance, and even during the admittance procedure once they reached the clinic.

"You look drawn from your journey and, I'm sure, your concern, Mr. Marten," Dr. Maxwell-Scot said finally. "I trust you are staying somewhere close by."

"Yes, the Holiday Inn in Hampstead."

"Good." She smiled. "Not far away. Why don't you get some rest yourself. Rebecca will be just fine here. Perhaps you will come back about six o'clock for a short visit before she has dinner."

"Alright," Nicholas Marten said gratefully, then added genuinely, "and thank you. Very much."

4

The Hampstead Holiday Inn was a short taxi ride from the Balmore Clinic, and Marten sat back trying to get a sense of a city he had known only through history and books and movies, and the thunder and rattle of British rock bands.

The taxi turned onto Haverstock Hill, and he became aware of the traffic coming toward him on the right instead of the left. He had not noticed it during the ambulance ride with Rebecca from Heathrow; that he did now made him realize he was truly somewhere else and that thanks to Dan Ford and Dr. Flannery everything in Los Angeles was closed tightly behind them.

Putting Marten up quietly at a friend's house in a citrus-farming area northwest of Los Angeles, Ford had settled the lease on Marten's rented house and taken care of his personal belongings, giving away almost everything and putting a few important items in storage under Ford's name. For her part, Dr. Flannery had not only arranged for Rebecca to come to the Balmore but dealt with the situation at St. Francis, informing Sister Reynoso only hours before they left L.A. for London that, at John Barron's request, she was transferring Rebecca to an institution out of state. Less than thirty minutes after her talk with Sister Reynoso, Dr. Flannery, in her own car, was driving Barron and Rebecca directly to the airport, where, because of Rebecca's condition, she and her brother were allowed to board the aircraft far in advance of the other passengers and hence were kept out of public view.

And so the major steps had been taken and they were safely here. It made it alright for Nicholas Marten to take a moment and sit back and watch the city go by. To take a moment and not think about why he chose the Balmore over the clinics in Rome and Geneva. To take a moment and not think about why he had come to London.

5

Marten checked into his hotel and unpacked. Immediately afterward he took a quick shower, changed into fresh jeans, a light sweater, and sport coat, and went down to the lobby, where he asked directions to Uxbridge Street. Twenty minutes later his taxi was turning off Notting Hill Gate onto Campden Hill Road and then down Uxbridge Street.

"What number, guv?" the cabbie asked.

"I'll get out here, thank you," Marten said.

"Right, sir."

The taxi pulled to the curb. Marten paid the driver and got out, and the cab drove away. And like that he stepped into Raymond's world. Or at least the piece of it he found noted on a slip of paper in Raymond's valise.

Number 21 Uxbridge Street was an elegant three-story private home separated from the street and sidewalk by a black six-foot-high ornamental iron fence. Just inside it were two enormous plane trees beginning to bud out, encouraged by a sunny and, according to the cabbie, exceptionally warm early spring afternoon.

As Marten approached he could see an iron gate leading to the house propped open by a painter's ladder. A drop cloth covered the ground beneath it, protecting the brick walkway, while a painter's bucket, half filled with black paint, hung from a rung on the ladder. Wherever the painter was, he wasn't in sight.

Marten stopped at the gate and looked up at the house. The front door was closed, and a garden walk led around the house to the left. Still no sign of the painter. He took a breath and pushed around the ladder and past the gate, walking down the pathway along the side of the house. Near the back he found three steps leading up to a partially open door. He glanced around once more. Still he saw no one. Quickly he climbed the steps, then stopped at the door to listen.

"Hello," he called out. There was no reply. Another breath and he went inside. Within minutes he had covered the house from the ground floor to the third and back down again and found nothing but a grandly furnished home with no sign of anyone currently living there. He was greatly disappointed, but in a way it was what he had expected, even without the grand tour he'd taken for himself. The home, as Marten remembered from the London Metropolitan Police report, belonged to a Mr. Charles Dixon, a retired stockbroker living in the South of France. Dixon, the report stated, had never heard of a Raymond Oliver Thorne, nor did he know anyone who looked like him. He occupied the house during the Christmas holidays and again through Wimbledon week at the end of June, and that was it. The rest of the year he spent in France and the house was vacant. And yet Raymond was to have been in London and ostensibly had gone to the same address in the middle of March. It made no sense, unless the house was rented out from time to time, but the Metropolitan Police had made no mention of that.

"Just who the bloody hell are you?"

Nicholas Marten stopped short. He was halfway out the door he'd come in and suddenly found himself face-to-face with a large white-haired man in overalls.

"You must be the painter."

"I am, but I asked who the bloody hell you are and what the Christ you're doing in here!"

"I was looking for Mr. Charles Dixon. The gate was open so I came in. I was told he might rent the house on occasion, and I—"

"I don't know who told you that or who you are." The painter looked him up and down carefully. "But Mr. Dixon never rents, ever. Is that clear to you, Mr.—"

"Ah—" Marten made up a name quickly. "Kaplan. George Kaplan."

"Well, Mr. Kaplan, now you know."

"Thank you. Sorry to have bothered you." With that Marten started to leave; then a thought struck him and he turned back.

"Do you happen to know if Mr. Dixon is a friend of a Mr. Aubrey Collinson of Kingston, Jamaica?"

"What?"

"Mr. Aubrey Collinson. His name came up with Mr. Dixon's. I believe he's a lawyer. He travels to London and elsewhere quite often by charter jet."

"I don't know what the bloody hell you want. But I never heard of an Aubrey Collinson, and if Mr. Dixon knows him that's his business." The painter took a menacing step toward him. "If you're not gone in the next five seconds I'm calling the police."

"Thank you again." Marten smiled, and then turned and left.

4:15 P.M.

Some five streets and twelve minutes later he stood in front of the imposing structure at number 13 Kensington Palace Gardens—the Embassy of the Russian Federation, London, W8 4QX, United Kingdom. There were guards at the gates and a few people in the small courtyard beyond and that was all.

Marten stood observing for a few moments, and then the guard gate opened and an armed soldier came toward him. Marten put up a hand and smiled. "Just looking, sorry," he said and walked quickly off, going away from the embassy and toward the green sprawl of Kensington Gardens. He had seen nothing at the house in Uxbridge Street that suggested it was anything more than it appeared, and the Russian Embassy was simply that, a foreign embassy within walking distance of the Uxbridge Street residence. So what did it mean, if anything at all? The only one who knew for certain was Raymond, and he was dead.

Besides, what did Marten think he was going to do even if he came across something? Alert the authorities? Then what? Try to explain what was going on and have them start wondering who he was? No, he couldn't. He had to leave it alone and he knew it. But how? Suddenly he was back to the push-pull of it.

Common sense told him to have nothing whatsoever to do with resuming, privately, his investigation of that larger something that Raymond had been involved in, and had been killed because of his involvement in. The voice inside him dragged him full force back into it. It was as if the investigation were a seducer and he were its slave or, more to the point, he were an addict who could focus on nothing but his habit. The voice was everything. Somehow he had to find a way to stop it.

6

THE HAMPSTEAD HOLIDAY INN. 9:00 P.M.

Nicholas Marten woke with a start in the darkness. He had no idea where he was or how long he'd been asleep. He sat up. Then he saw a light coming from a partially open door and realized it was the bathroom and that he must have pulled the door open himself. Then he remembered. He'd left the Russian Embassy and walked across Kensington Gardens to Bayswater Road and then taken a cab to the Balmore Clinic to visit Rebecca. She'd been happy to see him but was clearly worn-out from the long trip, so he hadn't stayed long. Promising to see her the following morning, he'd come back to the hotel, taken off his jacket, then curled up on the bed to watch television and must have simply fallen asleep.

Jet lag and the emotion of the trip itself had exhausted him, but he'd slept enough to take the edge off, and now he was up and alert and with no idea what to do. After a quick wash of his face, he combed his hair and went down to the lobby and then walked outside. The night was still warm and London was bright and alive. He crossed the street and walked down Haverstock Hill, a tourist out for a stroll, taking in the sounds and sights of a place he'd never been before.

"The pieces." Suddenly there was Raymond's voice again. It was low and sharp and urgent, as if it had been deliberately whispered in his ear. "The pieces," the voice repeated. "The pieces."

"No!" he said out loud and picked up his pace. He'd already had that battle today. He wouldn't have it again.

"The pieces," the whisper came once more. Marten walked faster still, as if he might actually be able to get away from it.

"The pieces," it came again. "The pieces."

Suddenly Marten stopped. All around him were bright lights and crowded sidewalks and steadily moving traffic. What he saw was not the same London of moments before, but the London of this afternoon, of Uxbridge Street and the Russian Embassy. It was then that he realized the whispered voice had not been Raymond's but his own, and had been all along. The squad no longer existed, but he did. He had come to London, brought Rebecca to London, for one reason. Because Raymond and whatever he had been involved with had led him there. The last thing he could do was walk away and forget it.

7

PENRITH'S BAR, HIGH STREET. 9:35 P.M.

Nicholas Marten came in and for a moment stood inside the door looking around. Penrith's was a classic dark-paneled English pub, noisy and elbow-to-elbow with patrons even on a Monday night. The bar itself was a kind of horseshoe in the center of the room with tables and booths on the sides and toward the back. Two bartenders stood in the horseshoe's center. One was dark-haired and muscular, the other, taller, with a medium build and close-cropped, dyed-blond, hair; both looked to be in their early thirties. By his actions the taller man, the blond, seemed to be in charge, and now and again he would step out of the action to move to the end of the bar to converse with someone Marten could not see clearly.

This was his man, Marten decided, and started through the

crowd toward him. As he did, he looked more closely at the patrons. Most, he thought, looked like university students, sprinkled here and there with professor types and the occasional businessman or woman. Hardly the kind of people a killer like Raymond might hang out with. On the other hand, he had to remember how chameleonlike Raymond had been, in dress, style, even language, and that it had been a student group he had picked Josef Speer from. It meant that someone like Raymond, someone trained like him, with his kind of confidence and mentality, could fit in anywhere.

The crowd grew thicker and noisier as he approached the bar. Through the din and constant shifting of bodies Marten could see the blond bartender near the back, still in conversation. He squeezed past two young men, and around a young woman eyeing them. Then Marten was there, not ten feet from where the bartender stood. Suddenly he stopped short. The barman was talking with two middle-aged men dressed in slacks and sport coats. One he didn't know; the other, the one nearer to him, he knew all too well—the rough and dogged veteran LAPD Robbery-Homicide detective Gene VerMeer; one of the two detectives stationed outside his house when he had driven a concealed Raymond away to Burbank Airport. VerMeer had been one of Red McClatchy's closest friends and a drinking buddy of Roosevelt Lee and Len Polchak and Marty Valparaiso. A cop he knew had been purposely kept out of the 5-2 Squad because he was too violent and unstable, as if that were possible. A cop he knew, too, who blamed him for Red's death and hated him because of it. Of anyone on the LAPD, VerMeer was the last man he wanted to run into and in all probability the first who would want to see him go down. Preferably in pieces.

"Christ!" Marten breathed and immediately turned away. VerMeer had to be there for one of two reasons. Either he was following up on the same information Marten had—Raymond's notation to meet someone with the initials I. M. at Penrith's Bar—or he had learned Marten's identity, found out where he had gone, and come to London thinking he might cross paths with Marten if he stayed on Raymond's trail. If that were the case VerMeer could well be asking the bartender not only about Raymond and I. M. but about Marten, too.

"It's Mr. Marten, isn't it?" A loud female voice with an English accent resonated over the din. Marten's heart came up in his throat and he turned to see Clementine Simpson coming toward him.

"Clem Simpson," she said with a broad smile as she reached him, "Balmore Clinic. From this afternoon."

"Yes, of course." Marten glanced over his shoulder. VerMeer and the man with him were still talking with the blond bartender.

"How on earth do you happen to be here?" Clem asked, and Marten moved her away and through the crowd.

"I—needed a little bit of a distraction," he said quickly, "and someone I met on the plane suggested this might be a good place to sample the London atmosphere."

"I'm sure you could use a distraction." Clem smiled sympathetically. "I'm here celebrating a friend's birthday. Would you care to join us?"

"I—" Marten glanced back. VerMeer and the other man were turning from the bartender and starting through the crowd, coming toward them.

"That would be nice, thank you," Marten said quickly and followed Clementine Simpson across the room toward a far table where a half-dozen professor types were gathered.

"Do you come here often?"

"When I'm in the city, yes. I have friends who have been gathering here for years. It's what makes a good neighborhood pub."

Marten took a chance and looked back. VerMeer had stopped and was staring in his direction; then the other man touched his sleeve and nodded toward the door. VerMeer watched a moment longer, then suddenly turned and followed the man out.

"Ms. Simpson." Marten put a hand lightly on her arm.

"Clem." She smiled.

"If you don't mind," he forced a grin, "Clem—I need to use the facilities."

"Of course. Our table is just over here."

Marten nodded and turned back, his eyes on the front door. There was no sign of VerMeer or the man with him. He glanced at the bar. There was a lull in business and the blond bartender was alone washing glasses. The other barman was nowhere in sight.

Marten wondered if VerMeer had asked the bartender about him, maybe even described him and given him a number to call if he saw him. Again, Marten looked to the front door. All he saw was patrons. He looked back to the bartender, hesitated for a moment, then decided to take the chance. Crossing to the bar, he walked to the end of it and ordered a draft beer. Twenty seconds later the bartender set a foaming glass on the bar in front of him.

"I'm looking for someone who is supposed to be a regular here." Marten slid a twenty-pound note next to his glass. "A tip on an Internet chat room said he, or she, has great deals on apartment rentals. Whoever it is signs off with the initials I. M. I don't know what their name is, maybe just I. M. or 'Im,' or if it's a nickname or just short for something else."

The barman looked at him carefully, as if he were trying to place him. Suddenly Marten was certain VerMeer had given him Marten's description and the bartender was trying to decide if Marten was the man. Marten didn't flinch, just waited. Then abruptly the barman leaned forward.

"Let me let you in on something, mate. A few minutes ago a police detective from Los Angeles asked me the same question about an I. M. A Scotland Yard inspector was with him, only neither of them said anything about a chat room or apartment rentals." He glanced deliberately at the twenty-pound note near Marten's sleeve and lowered his voice.

"Whatever you're up to is your business, but I'll tell you what I told the two of them. Man, woman, or a little of each, or just plain can't tell, I've been behind this bar six nights a week for eleven years and in all that time I never once heard anyone or anything, for that matter, referred to as 'Im' or 'I. M.' or 'Eye-mmm!' or with a bloody nickname that might fit like 'Iron Mike' or 'Izzy Murphy' or 'Irene Mary.' And if anyone else here knew, I would know because it's my business to know because I'm also the owner. Understand?"

Marten nodded. "Yes."

"Alright, then." The barman reached out, took the twenty, and slid it into his apron. All the while his eyes stayed on Marten's.

"Mr. Marten." Clementine Simpson was at his sleeve. "Are you joining us?"

"I—" Marten looked at her and smiled. "I'm sorry, I got caught up in conversation."

Quickly Marten picked up his beer glass, nodded to the bartender, and walked away with her. In total innocence she had just given the bartender his name.

"Clem," he said, "if you don't mind, I suddenly feel jet lag catching up with me. Another time, if that's all right."

"Of course, Mr. Marten. Will I see you at the clinic tomorrow?"

"I'll be there in the morning."

"So will I. Good night."

Marten nodded a good night, then started for the door. He was tired and he had learned nothing. Moreover, he had exposed himself by talking with the bartender, and now the man even had his name.

"Damn," he swore under his breath.

Discouraged, angry with himself, he was nearly at the front door when he saw a group of young people crowded around a table in a small room off to the side. Tacked to the wall behind them was a large red and white banner that read RUSSIAN SOCIETY GROUP.

Marten felt the sudden pound of his heart. There it was. The Russian thing again. A glance back toward the bar. The bartender was busy, not watching at all. Quickly Marten went into the room and walked up to the table. There were ten people in all, six men and four women, and they were all speaking Russian.

"Excuse me," he said politely, "does anyone speak English?"

The response was a huge laugh.

"What do you want to know, mate?" A slight young man in thick glasses grinned broadly.

"I'm looking for someone called I. M. or," he stole the bartender's pronunciation, "Eyemmm, or with the initials or nickname I. M."

Ten heads looked around the table at each other, and a moment later the same ten heads looked back. All had the same blank expression.

"Sorry, guv," a black-haired man said.

Marten glanced at the hand-printed RUSSIAN SOCIETY GROUP sign tacked up on the wall behind them.

"If you don't mind my asking, what does your group do?"

"We get together every couple of weeks to talk about the ins and outs of our homeland. Politics, social stuff, things like that," the slim man in thick glasses said.

"What he really means is we're all homesick," a chubby blond girl said with a grin, and everyone laughed.

Marten smiled and studied them for a half beat longer. "What is going on in your homeland that might be worthy of discussion?" he asked casually. He was trying to get them to bring up April 7 on the off-chance they would know. "Something coming up the rest of the world might want to know about?"

The black-haired man grinned. "You mean besides the separatist movement, corruption, and the Russian mafia?"

"Yes."

"Nothing, unless you want to believe the rumors that Parliament might vote to reinstate the monarchy and bring back the tsar." The black-haired man grinned again. "Then we could be just like the Brits, give the people someone special to rally 'round. Not a bad idea if whoever he is is a decent fellow, because it would help take their minds off all the other crap that's going on. But that, like every other big change that's supposed to come back home, is nothing more than street drivel because it never happens. Still," he shrugged, "that's why we get together, so we can talk about those kinds of things and take the edge off being"—he glanced at the chubby blond girl—"homesick."

They all laughed but Marten. Clearly they weren't going to bring it up, so he did himself.

"Might I ask one thing more?" he said. "Does the date April 7 mean anything special to Russians, particularly people who live in Moscow? Is it some kind of local holiday? Does something unusual happen?"

The chubby blond girl grinned again. "I'm from Moscow, and as far as I know April 7 means April 7." She looked around the table and giggled.

"She's right, mate." The slim man in thick glasses smiled in agreement. "April 7 is April 7." Abruptly he leaned forward and became more serious. "Why?"

"Nothing." Marten shrugged it off. It was the same answer the inspectors from the Russian Ministry of Justice had given when they were in L.A. "Someone suggested it was a holiday. I had never heard of it. I guess I misunderstood. Thanks, thanks very much."

Marten turned to leave.

"But why the questions?" the young man asked again.

"Thanks again," Marten said.

And then he was out of the room and gone.

8

THE HAMPSTEAD HOLIDAY INN. STILL MONDAY, APRIL 1. 11:35 P.M.

Nicholas Marten lay back against his pillow in the dark listening to the traffic pass outside. It was quieter than it had been when he'd gone out and quieter still than when he'd come back from Penrith's Bar thirty minutes earlier. But it was there nonetheless, a steady hum, reminding him the city was very much awake.

The house on Uxbridge Street. Aubrey Collinson/the chartered jet. A chartered plane sent not once, but twice, and a huge expense for someone. *The Russian Embassy. Penrith's Bar and I.M., the Russian Society Group. April 7 in Russia/Moscow is just that, a date, April 7, nothing else. No new information at all. I learned nothing.* He had picked up a small journal in the hotel gift shop that afternoon when he'd checked in and made his first notes just before he went to bed.

Maybe he had learned nothing—the afterthought to ask the painter about Aubrey Collinson had been nothing more than a shot in the dark—but the clues, like the city, were there just the same. The same as Gene VerMeer had been there. He knew there was every chance the LAPD detective had already received a call from the blond barman telling him a man bearing the description he had given him earlier had come into the bar asking about an I.M. He had been an American and his name had been Marten. Or Martin, as he probably heard it.

If it was true and the bartender had made the call, there was no question VerMeer would already be doing something about it, using his connections with Scotland Yard to scour every hotel in London for an American with the last name of Martin. How long would it be before they called this hotel and found there was an American named Marten registered there? VerMeer wouldn't give a damn about the spelling, and it would only be a matter of time before there was a loud knock on his door.

Marten turned away and tried to forget what had happened. He probably shouldn't have gone to Penrith's Bar at all. Even if VerMeer hadn't been looking for him, he had still been there inquiring about I. M. That fact alone meant the LAPD was still involved and hadn't closed the Raymond file as completely as their public posture suggested. He had worried before that if they were still on the case he might cross paths with them, and he had. It was only by sheer luck that VerMeer hadn't seen him, and it meant he had to really think about what he was doing. He and Rebecca were safely in London and blessed with the beginnings of a new life. He had to realize he simply did not have the luxury, if that was the word, of indulging his seducer and letting the unconscious addict inside him drag him back into the game. For his sake and hers, he had to promise himself to get Raymond and everything he had been about out of his mind. In that, he prayed VerMeer had never asked the blond bartender about him and that the bartender had never heard Clementine Simpson speak his name.

He glanced at the bedside clock.

11:59 P.M.

An emergency vehicle passed outside, its siren blaring, then quickly fading. Again came the sound of traffic and now a loud discussion from people passing in the hallway outside his room. Did London never sleep?

A moment passed and then two. For some reason he thought of the real Nicholas Marten. And the memory that went with it.

Ten days earlier, Friday, March 22—the same day as the massive police funeral for 5-2 Squad detectives Polchak, Lee, and Valparaiso—using a cane to help support a still very painful right leg, Marten, then John Barron, had boarded a flight from Los Angeles to Boston. From there he took a commuter flight to Montpelier, Vermont, where he spent the night.

Early the next morning he drove a rental car to the tiny village of Coles Corner, where he met Hiram Ott, the jovial, bear-sized publisher and editor of the *Lyndonville Observer,* a local newspaper serving rural north-central Vermont.

"His name was Nicholas Marten," Hiram Ott said as he led Barron across an open, grassy field scattered with patches of melting snow, "Marten with an *e*, not Martin with an *i*. He was born the same month and year as you, but I guess you already know that."

"Yes." John Barron nodded, leaning on his cane as he picked his way over the uneven turf.

His meeting with Hiram Ott had been the work of Dan Ford, who, within days of the Metrolink shootout, had been promoted (or, as he put it, because of his close relationship with John Barron, expediently removed from the area) to a position as staff writer at the *Los Angeles Times* Washington bureau. He and his wife, Nadine, quickly found themselves living in a three-room apartment on the banks of the Potomac, and the outgoing French-born Nadine, very much at home in a city far more like her native Paris than Los Angeles, quickly found a job teaching French in an adult education program while her husband covered inside-the-beltway politics.

Yet for all the disruption and hubbub of change that kept Ford in a whirl eighteen hours a day, no one had taken away his Rolodex or his connections as a reporter or as an active alumnus of Northwestern University's Medill School of Journalism.

For John Barron to disappear in the way he needed to, he had to wholly become someone else. Simple enough in a simpler time. In days past he could have picked a half-dozen streets in L.A. alone where for a few hundred dollars he could have a new identity in a matter of minutes—complete with birth certificate, Social Security card, and California driver's license. But these were not simple times and authorities everywhere, from national security agencies to local police to financial institutions, were building huge databases to crack down on false identities. So his change had to be as real as was currently possible. He had to find someone about the same age with a legitimate birth certificate and Social Security number—but more, someone who had recently died and whose death certificate had not yet been filed. He knew finding such a thing and quickly was not just a near impossibility, it was crazy. But Dan Ford didn't think so. Such large obstacles only raised the level of his game. Immediately Ford sent out a massive e-mailing—a curious appeal, as he put it. He was looking to do a story with a political twist. It concerned people who were recently deceased but for one reason or another remained alive legally with their names on a current voting register. In other words, he was looking to do a story on voter fraud.

Enter directly Hiram Ott with a midnight reply to Ford's e-mail. Had Dan Ford ever heard of a Nicholas Marten? No. Of course not. Few people had. And those who might would remember a Ned Marten, because that was what he had called himself.

The illegitimate son of a Canadian trucker and a Vermont widow, Nicholas Marten had run off to join a traveling rock group as a drummer when he was fourteen, and that was the last he'd been heard of. It was only a dozen years later when he learned he had pancreatic cancer and only weeks to live that he came home to Coles Corner to see his mother. There he learned that both parents were dead, his mother buried in the family plot on her hundred-acre farm. Alone and broke, he'd turned for help to the only person he knew, family friend and lifelong bachelor Hiram Ott. Ott brought Nicholas into his home and set about trying to find some kind of hospice where he could live out his final days under medical care. It wasn't necessary. Nicholas died in Ott's guest room two days later. As official keeper of county records, among other things, Ott made out a death certificate and had Marten buried next to his mother in the family plot.

But for some reason he'd never gotten around to filing the certificate. It had been in a box in his office for more than a month when fellow Northwestern alumnus Dan Ford's e-mail arrived. When Ford called to reply, Hiram Ott had been told the truth—Ford had a very close friend whose life depended on a new identity. Ford followed up by asking if this was a situation that Ott could feel comfortable with. For anyone else it would have been a definite no. But there were other things at play here. First, Hiram Ott had a rambunctious, mischievous personality. Second, few people in Coles Corner remembered that Edna Mayfield had had a child out of wedlock twenty-six years earlier, fewer still that a young man named Ned Marten had come to town and died, and only Hy Ott himself knew that the death certificate had never been formally filed. Third was that on the afternoon of his death Nicholas Marten had told Ott that he was ashamed he'd done nothing with his life and wished somehow he could still make some kind of contribution that might help someone else. The final thing was the kicker. While at Northwestern, Ford had gotten Hy Ott out of an extremely sticky and potentially bone-shattering situation involving Ott and the girlfriend of a particularly large and mean-spirited varsity football player. It was one of those things where a favor done was a favor owed until it was repaid, and now Hy Ott was repaying it—walking John Barron across a meadow in Coles Corner on an early spring day to view Nicholas Marten's final unmarked resting place among the new-fallen leaves in the tiny family graveyard.

For Barron's part, he'd come in gratitude, wanting to thank Hiram Ott personally for what he had done and because he'd wanted to know who he was becoming, where his namesake had lived as a boy, and what the land and town and people were like. There were other reasons, too. Guilt and reverence, and, perhaps more pointedly, self-protection, in the event he was ever questioned about his past. He tried not to show it, but he knew Hiram Ott could see the conflict and emotion and uncertainty in him; this was not something one did every day. And he knew it was why the burly newspaperman had suddenly put his arms around him and given him a great hug, and then stepped back and said, "It's between you and me and Dan Ford and God. No one else will ever know. Besides, Nicholas would have liked it. So don't think. Just accept it as his gift."

John Barron had hesitated, moved and still unsure, then finally he smiled. "Okay," he said, "okay."

"In that case"—Hiram Ott's grin suddenly became wide as a river and he put out his hand—"Let me be the first to call you—Nicholas Marten."

1:15 A.M.

Nicholas Marten rolled over and looked across the darkened room to the main door. It was closed, the chain lock in place. As it had been all along. Maybe the bartender had done nothing at all. Maybe Gene VerMeer had never asked about him.

1:30 A.M.

Outside, finally, London was quiet.

9

YORK HOUSE, THE BALMORE CLINIC. NEXT DAY,
TUESDAY, APRIL 2. 11:30 A.M.

Marten made his way across a lobby crowded with people he assumed were therapists, patients, staff, and patients' family members like he was. A dozen steps and he turned down a less busy hallway and started toward the exit doors at the far end. He'd spent the last two hours with Rebecca and afterward chatted briefly with Dr. Maxwell-Scot, who had told him how well and how quickly his sister was acclimating, so much so that she was starting her in group therapy that afternoon. Once again Rebecca had told him that if he was okay, she would be okay. It was an ongoing thing with her, designed, he knew, as much to help him as to reassure her. And he had done his part by saying he was fine and was enjoying his time catching up on sleep and seeing London. Laughingly he told her how he'd gone out to explore London the night before and had run into Clementine

Simpson in a pub. She liked Clementine Simpson and thought it was wonderful that he had met her, and he agreed it was. It kept it all fun and airy and light. He had said nothing of the rest, especially of his near-encounter with Gene VerMeer, nor why he had gone to the pub in the first place. Nor had he told her of calling Dan Ford in Washington as soon as he'd come back to the hotel and telling him he had seen VerMeer in London and asking if Ford could get a rundown on how deeply the LAPD was still involved with the Raymond investigation.

Nor had he said anything about Ford's return call earlier that morning telling him VerMeer had requested to come to London on his own and was due back in L.A. later that day. Nor had he mentioned Ford's warning that VerMeer's request to come on his own probably meant his real reason for going to London, maybe with LAPD approval, had been to look for John Barron, on the hunch he might still be working the Raymond trail as well. Nor had he told her of what else Ford had said, that he thought it would be in Nicholas Marten's best interest to lie low and to stay completely away from whatever he thought Raymond might have been involved with.

It was a thought that still lingered as Marten reached the exit doors and pushed through them and turned up the sidewalk, heading for his hotel, his focus on the future and what he would do to secure it once Rebecca was able to leave the clinic. Then he saw a poster announcing a special ballet to be performed at the Balmore auditorium this coming Sunday, April 7.

April 7!

There it was again!

Immediately he heard his own inner voice. This time it was not about the "pieces" but rather a single exclamation—"April 7/Moscow!"

With it came the stark realization that with everything he had been doing he had lost track of time and April 7 was this coming Sunday! Suddenly it didn't matter what the Russian investigators in L.A. or the Russian students at Penrith's Bar had said. To Marten it was not just a date or a day like any other, it was something very real because Raymond had written it down. If it was nothing, why had he written it? What had he, or whoever he had been affiliated with, planned to have happen on that day in Moscow?

And what if the official posture taken by all the security agencies dismissing Raymond's actions as being part of a larger conspiracy had not been a smoke screen for further top-level investigation at all but, in truth, a final dismissal of everything he had been about? That April 7/Moscow was simply another of the brief jottings of a deceased madman and meaningless to anyone but him?

What then?

Would they just hand it over to some fifth-level bureaucrat and forget it? The answer was most probably yes, because they had nothing else to go on. The trouble was none of them had known Raymond the way he had. None of them had ever looked in his eyes, or watched how he moved, or seen the supreme arrogance in him. In Raymond's own words, there were still the "pieces." And what if those "pieces" were set to detonate in Moscow this coming Sunday?

Stop it! He suddenly told himself. Stop thinking about it. Get Raymond out of your mind! Remember Dan Ford's warning you to stay away from it all and lie low. Think about Rebecca and your own life, the same as you did last night. There's nothing you can do, so just stay away from it.

Marten took a deep breath and kept walking. He reached the street corner and waited for the light to change. Suddenly the memory of I. M. came roaring back and with it April 7/Moscow all over again.

Maybe April 7 was just an ordinary date and too vague to have any particular meaning. I. M. was equally vague, but it was something more than a date, or safe deposit keys, or a house, or an embassy, or a charter aircraft no one could find anything more about, because I. M. almost certainly was a person. And obviously VerMeer, whatever his true reason for being in London, had thought enough of it, too, to ask Penrith's bartender about it.

Today was Tuesday. It meant there was still time. If somehow he could find out who this I. M. was and get to him or her he might also find out what was to happen in Moscow on Sunday and, in turn, stop it. Promise to himself or not, it was something he had to do because he was afraid no one else would.

Abruptly he turned from the street corner and went back to the Balmore. He might have had no luck with the Penrith's bartender or with the Russian students, but there was someone else who just might be able to help.

The Balmore Foundation office where Clementine Simpson worked was small and, at the moment, silent, as the half-dozen people who crowded the workspace sat staring impatiently at their darkened computer screens. Obviously the computers were down and they were waiting for them to come back up.

"Mr. Marten." Clementine Simpson stood up when she saw him. "How nice of you to drop by."

"I was with my sister and just leaving when I realized what time it was. I thought maybe you might be free for lunch."

"Well"—she smiled and glanced at the still-dark computer screens, then back to Marten—"why not?"

10

SPANIARDS INN, SPANIARDS ROAD,
HAMPSTEAD. 12:20 P.M.

"This was a favorite watering hole of Lord Byron and Shelley, as well as the infamous 1700s highwayman Dick Turpin, who stopped by for a drink between coach robberies, or so the story goes," Clementine Simpson said as they sat down at a corner table in the sixteenth-century tavern to look out at a garden dappled with sunlight. "And that is the first and last of my historical commentary."

"Thanks." Marten smiled.

Clem Simpson was dressed as she had been the day before, in the same kind of dowdy, dark navy, oversized business suit. This time she had added a crisp white blouse buttoned up to the throat and small, gold hoop earrings that hung just inside the curl of her auburn hair. In her own way, and even though she seemed to work hard to hide it, she was quite attractive.

A waiter who looked as if he'd been there since Dick Turpin's time brought menus, and when he asked if they'd like drinks, without a second thought she ordered a glass of Châteauneuf-du-Pape.

"It's a very nice Rhône, Mr. Marten," she said.

"Nicholas."

"Nicholas." She smiled.

Nicholas Marten never drank at lunch, but for some reason he looked to the waiter and heard himself say, "That would be fine."

The waiter nodded. Marten watched him walk off and then quietly, and in an offhand way, as if he were just curious, got to the reason he had invited her to lunch.

"Last night, when I was leaving Penrith's Bar, I passed a small side room near the door. A group of Russian students were sitting near a sign that read 'Russian Society Group.' I asked them about it and they said it was a get-together of young Russians to talk about what was going on at home. Before, you said you went to Penrith's rather often when you were in the city. I wondered if you knew anything about it?"

"The Russian Society Group?"

"Yes."

The waiter brought the Châteauneuf-du-Pape and two glasses. Pouring a taste, he set the glass before Clementine Simpson. She picked it up, tasted it, and nodded her approval. The waiter then amply filled both glasses, set the bottle on the table, and left.

Clementine fingered her glass and looked at Marten. "I am sorry to disappoint you, Nicholas, but I don't know anything about a Russian Society Group. I've seen their sign up on the wall, but I have no idea who they are or what they do. But that doesn't mean anything. There are any number of Russians living in London, and the area around Penrith's is a very popular Russian neighborhood. I would imagine there are all kinds of committees and societies there." She lifted her glass and took a long sip of the wine. "Is that the reason you invited me to lunch?"

Whatever concern Marten might have had earlier about how much information Dr. Flannery had passed on to Dr. Maxwell-Scot about Rebecca and himself, and who at the Balmore might know about it, was put to rest, at least in Clementine Simpson's case. From her manner and the way she reacted to his question, he was certain she had no idea who he was or why he would be asking that kind of question. Still, he had known that once he asked it she might very well ask why, and in her own way she had. He had an answer ready. It was a lie, of course, but he knew it would work.

"I told you last night I was at Penrith's because someone I met on the plane suggested it might be a good place to sample London atmosphere. The someone," he lifted his own glass and took a sip, "was a very attractive young Russian woman. I went there hoping to bump into her. She wasn't there, but I saw the Russian sign and—"

"Bumped into it instead of her."

"Yes."

"You had been on a long flight. Add to that the emotion of taking care of your sister and to that pile on jet lag, and still you had the fortitude to venture out halfway across London." Drink in hand, Clementine sat back and smiled wryly. "She must have been very attractive."

"She was." Marten hadn't expected the wit or the deliberateness of her response. It made him wonder what else to expect. She might dress like someone's dowdy aunt, but she hardly acted like one. "I never even got her name. She just called herself I. M."

"Her initials?"

"I guess, or a nickname. You said your friends had been gathering at Penrith's for years." Marten pressed her carefully. "I wonder if any of them might have connections in the Russian community."

"Who might help you track down this young lady."

"Yes."

Clementine studied him for a heartbeat, then again came the wry smile. "You really were smitten."

"I would just like to find her." Marten knew getting Clementine Simpson involved was a long shot at best, but she was his last concrete connection to Penrith's and the steady group of people who frequented it. His hope was that through her or them, someone just might know, or have heard of, I. M., assuming the initials referred to a person. If so, that person would be defined immediately, as in, "Well, we know an I. M., but it hardly fits your picture of a lovely young lady. The I. M. we know is not a she but a he, is fifty years old, and weighs two hundred and thirty pounds."

If that happened, he would have a description and a beginning, and take it from there, somehow press her to find out who this person was and where he or she could be found.

"Blonde?" Clementine asked with a raised eyebrow.

Suddenly Marten needed to describe her. He needed a description, any description. "No, auburn brown and neck length, kind of like"—he paused—"yours."

Clementine Simpson stared at him, then took another sip of her wine and reached into her purse for her cell phone. A moment later she was talking to a woman named Sofia and asking her help in locating a "hot, young Russian bimbo" (her words exactly) with neck-length reddish brown hair and the initials or nickname I. M. Then she thanked Sofia, hung up, and looked at Marten.

"I told you last night we were at Penrith's celebrating a friend's birthday. It was Sofia's. She just turned eighty. She came here from Moscow forty-five years ago and has been a godmother to almost every Russian immigrant to London ever since. If anyone can track down your little cutie, she can." Abruptly she took another sip of wine, then picked up her menu and very deliberately studied it.

Despite the urgency of the clock ticking toward Sunday, Marten had to let himself grin at Clem's near-schoolgirl attitude toward a woman who didn't exist. He took a sip of wine and watched her for a moment longer, then picked up his own menu.

Short of going house to house through the neighborhood around Penrith's banging on doors asking for someone named I. M., he had done what he could. Never mind it was a huge neighborhood and there were thousands of doors, there was also the very real probability Gene VerMeer, through the Metropolitan Police, had done or would be doing the same, and all he needed was to stumble across their path and find himself suddenly singled out and being questioned. So all he could do now was hold his breath and pray that the ubiquitous Sofia would come up with something. That left only lunch and making small talk with Clementine Simpson.

———

What happened over the next hour and a half Marten didn't clearly remember. They ordered from the menu. The waiter poured more wine. Somewhere along the line Clementine told him again, as she had the night before, to call her Clem.

At some point, as they finished lunch and the waiter was taking away the plates and silverware, Marten clearly remembered Clem reaching up and undoing the top button of her blouse. Just the top button, nothing more, but for some reason it was the sexiest thing he had ever seen a woman do. And maybe that, and of course the Châteauneuf, was what led to the rest. In what seemed like no time their conversation turned to sex. In talking about it Clem Simpson made two pronouncements that, to him, should be ranked with history's greatest moments of sheer erotica. The first was said with a great Cheshire Cat–like smile—"I just like to lie back and let the man do all the work." The second, which came shortly afterward, concerned the size of her breasts—"I really am huge, you know."

It was a dialogue that washed away any further thought of I. M. and was followed by her shamelessly propositioning him. It was done with a tilt of her head, a look in her eye, and one simple question—"What are you doing tonight?"

His reaction was even more direct, calling her hand and cutting to the chase with his own twist of her phrase—"What are you doing right now?"

It was a question whose answer led unswervingly and within minutes to his room at the Hampstead Holiday Inn.

11

3:52 P.M.

They were, for the moment at least, no longer soaked with sweat. The shower had taken care of most of it, but they had made love there, too—after having already done it three times in the span of some forty minutes on the king-sized Holiday Inn bed. Now they lay naked in the semidimness of drawn shades looking alternately at the ceiling and at each other and he gently played with this or that part of her—a nipple at the moment (Clem's breasts were huge, as she had said—her brassiere had four snap-hooks, and he could barely hold one bosom in both hands clasped together). What he liked best, or at least second best, was the areolas around her nipples. They were not only large, but little bumps rose all over them when he touched his tongue to them. The result, of course, only served to stimulate him once more and give rise to another erection, the size and pulse of which amazed him, the thing the cops called a "blueveiner." But beyond all that—and it was difficult to discern what was lust and passion and genuine affection shared by them both—what he found was a human being the likes of whom he'd never before encountered. Smart and caring and feisty and funny and, at times, certifiably crude. As in the shower, where they played and laughed and lathered each other, and where she slid down on her knees to take the length of his penis in her mouth and nearly brought him to climax, then suddenly stood in the steamy downpour and turned around with her ass toward him, breathing, "Doggie me, Nicholas, oh do doggie me."

Which, of course, he did.

Now, as he lay next to her, the sheets still damp from the wet of their bodies, he wondered if she had really believed what he had told her when they first began to undress and he had warned her about the healing wounds covering his thigh and shoulder and upper arm. It was an answer he had prepared before he left for London, knowing an eye might be raised if he went to a gym or needed to see a doctor, or in the event he somehow got lucky and ended up like this, in bed with an attractive woman.

After college, his story went, he had wanted to go to law school but because of Rebecca needed to find a steady job. He had a friend in the television business and went to work as a reader for a small production company. Later he became an associate producer and was on the set of an action show when a stunt went wrong and a gas canister exploded, hitting him with flying pieces of shrapnel and hospitalizing him for several days. The resulting, and rather substantial, insurance settlement enabled him to bring Rebecca to the Balmore, something he had long wanted to do but could not because he could not afford to walk away from his job.

"So what will you do now?" Clem rolled over and looked at him, as if she, too, were thinking about what he had said. "Finally go to law school?"

"No." He smiled with relief. She had believed him, or at least seemed to. "It's something I"—he chose his words carefully—"lost interest in."

"Then what will you do?"

"I don't know."

Abruptly she rose on an elbow and looked at him directly.

"What were your dreams before you had to take responsibility for Rebecca? What would you like to have done with your life?"

"Dreams?"

"Yes." There was a great sparkle in her eyes.

"What makes you think I had dreams?"

"Everybody has dreams."

Nicholas Marten looked at her. Looked at the way she was waiting for him to answer, as if she genuinely cared what was inside him.

"What were your dreams, Nicholas?" she asked again and smiled quietly. "Tell me."

"You mean—what to do with my life?"

"Yes."

12

"Gardens," he said.

Clementine Simpson, wholly naked in Nicholas Marten's room at the Hampstead Holiday Inn at four o'clock in the afternoon, looked at him curiously.

"Gardens?"

"Since I was a kid I was fascinated by formal gardens. I have no idea why. I collected books on them. I was drawn to places like Versailles, the Paris Tuileries, gardens in Italy and Spain. The spiritual magic," he smiled wistfully, "of Oriental designs, especially places like Ryotan-ji, the Zen temple in Hikone, Japan, or Katsura Rikyu, in Kyoto. Yesterday, I walked through Kensington Gardens here in London. Amazing."

"Katsura Rikyu?" Clem asked, with sudden caution to her voice.

"Yes, why?"

"Tell me more."

"Why?"

"Just tell me."

Marten shrugged. "I started in college at Cal Poly in San Luis Obispo—that's on the California coast between L.A. and San Francisco—to study landscape architecture and—" He stopped, realizing he couldn't tell her about the murder of his parents and why he suddenly transferred to UCLA, because that would lead to what had happened later. Quickly he picked up and went on. "Rebecca had been living with me in an apartment near the campus. When she became ill we decided the best place for her was in Los Angeles, so I transferred to UCLA to be near her. My major was English because, then, it was the easiest course to get into. But in my junior and senior years I managed to take elective courses at the School of Arts and Architecture." He smiled, covering the transition and hoping she wouldn't ask questions. At the same time he realized he was smiling, too, at the fond memory of his studies. "Courses with names like 'Elements of Urban Design' or 'Theories of Landscape Architecture.'" He lay back and looked at the ceiling. "You asked me what I would have done. There it is. Learn to design and build those kinds of formal gardens."

Suddenly Clem was hunched over him, looming down, her great breasts touching his chest. "You're fucking having me on," she said, playfully indignant, but with an edge that said she was more than a little piqued.

"What?"

"You're fucking having me on, you know all about me."

Marten pulled back, as if in sharing his fondest dreams he had said the wrong thing. "I've barely known you a day and a half. How could I know all about you?"

"You fucking do."

"No, I fucking don't."

"Then how do you know that's what I do?"

"What's what you do?"

"That."

"What?"

"Gardens."

"Huh?"

"The clinic is part of my yearly volunteer work. My full-time occupation is as a professor of town and country planning at the University of Manchester in northern England. I'm in the business of educating people to become, among other things, landscape architects."

Marten stared at her. "Now you're having me on."

"I am not." Suddenly Clementine Simpson got up from the bed and went into the bathroom. When she came back she had a towel wrapped around her.

"UCLA. The University of California at Los Angeles?"

"Yes."

"And you have a bachelor's degree in English with elective courses in landscape architecture?"

"Yes," Marten grinned, "why?"

"Do you want to do it?"

"Make love again?" Marten laughed and tugged at her towel, trying to make it come undone. "If you're up for it, I am."

Instantly she pulled back, pulling the towel tightly around her. "I am talking about the university. Do you want to go to Manchester and study landscape design?"

"You're kidding."

"Manchester is three hours by train from London. You could go to the university and still visit with Rebecca as often as you like."

Marten stared at her in silence. Continuing his education, especially in an area that would follow his childhood dream, was something that had never, ever crossed his mind.

"I am returning to Manchester this Saturday." Clem pulled open the towel, then immediately closed it again, tightening it. "Come with me. Visit the university. Meet some of the students. See what you think."

"You're going Saturday. . . ."

"Yes. Saturday."

13

Nicholas Marten and Clem Simpson arrived by train at Manchester Piccadilly Station at twelve minutes past four, exactly thirty-one minutes behind schedule and in a pouring rain.

By four-thirty he had checked into a room at the Portland Thistle Hotel on Portland Street, and fifteen minutes later they were standing under Clem's broad umbrella walking under the stone arch of a Gothic building with the words UNIVERSITY OF MANCHESTER emblazoned above it.

By then—in fact, by the end of the first hour on the train—he'd received two distinctly separate pieces of information.

The first had been in a call from Clem's maternal Russian detective Sofia reporting that not only had the Russian neighborhood surrounding Penrith's Bar been thoroughly canvassed for a person called, initialed, or nicknamed I. M., so had the entire Russian émigré population of the eight-hundred-square-mile city of London, and, surprising to almost all, not one single person with either the initials, nickname, or description she had been given had turned up. For fun they had even suggested that Marten's young woman might have been putting him on and that I. M. really stood for something else—a place or thing—or was an acronym for some organization. Nothing turned up. So, in other words, if there were any Russian-affiliated I. M.'s in that part of England, no one who might know them, or of them, did. That, of course, left open the possibility that whoever Raymond had been going to meet was not a local Russian but one who might have been coming from somewhere else. That, or I. M. was not Russian at all. Either way, his last-ditch hope for uncovering I. M. was gone, unless he was prepared to scour the entire planet looking for him or her or it.

The second piece of business had come, to his utter amazement, when he'd learned that Clementine Simpson was not simply Clem, or Ms. Clementine Simpson, or, for that matter, even Professor Simpson, she was Lady Clementine Simpson, the only child of Sir Robert Rhodes Simpson, Earl of Prestbury, member of the House of Lords, a Knight of the Garter, the highest order of English chivalry, and a leading member of the University of Manchester's Court, the school's supreme governing authority. It meant Lady Clem—Marten's traveling companion, newly appointed career advisor, proud and dutiful member of the Balmore Foundation, and "Doggie me" lover—was something she had yet to confide in him: a titled member of British aristocracy!

The revelation had come out of the blue when the ticket taker stopped beside their seats in the first class car and said, "Welcome aboard, Lady Clementine, nice to see you again. And how is your father, Lord Prestbury?"

The two chatted briefly, and then the man moved on to continue his ticket taking. He'd barely gone when a very well dressed matronly woman, making her way down the aisle, also recognized Clem and stopped to ask very nearly the same thing. How was she? How was Lord Prestbury?

Marten had politely ignored both conversations, but when the woman had gone, he'd looked at Clem, raised an eyebrow, and said "*Lady* Simpson?" It was then, and reluctantly, that Clem explained the whole thing—how she was born to wealth and title, how her mother had died when she was twelve and how, from that point on, she and her father had more or less raised each other, and how, as both child and adult, she had hated both the title and the impudence of the upper class and tried to be as little a part of it as possible. Yet, it was a feat that was far from painless, considering her father was an eminent member of British nobility—as well as an exceedingly respected, powerful, headstrong force in both the government and the private sector, where he sat on the boards of any number of large corporations—who expected his only child to fully represent it when occasion called. That was far too often as far as she was concerned and made all the more difficult because "he is damnably proud of his heritage, his prominence, and his Queen and Country patriotism!" It was a bearing and attitude that drove her nuts.

"I can understand how it might." Marten smiled lightly.

"No, Mr. Marten," her dander fully up, her eyes flush with anger, "without having lived it, you cannot even begin to understand it!"

With that she abruptly turned and dragged a large dog-eared paperback—*David Copperfield* by Charles Dickens—from her purse. Opening it with a final flash of anger, she purposefully immersed herself in reading. It was the kind of emotional "end of conversation" she had used with him at Spaniards Inn when he'd asked for help in finding I. M., or his bimbo, as she'd curtly put it, and then forcefully turned to her menu.

Marten watched her for a moment and then looked out at the passing English countryside. Clem, or Lady Clem, was unlike any other woman he had ever known. Wholly open with her emotions—at least with him—she was learned, funny, brusque, vulgar, angry, and engaging, not to mention encouraging and even nurturing. Being more than a little disgusted with the whole idea of belonging to the upper class and to the manor born, had been, if nothing else, in character and amusing. The trouble was that it, like Clem, the trip to Manchester itself, and the days leading up to it, was plagued by something else—two unfinished pieces of business: the chartered jet, and April 7/Moscow.

Wednesday morning he had called Dan Ford in Washington asking if there was any further information on Aubrey Collinson, the man who had twice chartered planes for Raymond in Kingston, Jamaica, and provided the package with the false documents to be given to him upon arrival in California. Again Ford had warned him to stay out of it, but Marten pressed him, and Ford told him the CIA and the Russian Ministry of Justice had sent investigators to both Kingston and Nassau, where the flights had originated. From statements made later, both agencies reported the same dead end as before. The plane's pilot had simply been given the document package by his supervisor and asked to deliver it to the party he was to pick up. There was nothing unusual in that. Nor was there anything particularly unusual about the man calling himself Aubrey Collinson—a man the Kingston West Charter Air manager remembered as being about fifty, speaking with a British accent, and wearing dark glasses and a well-cut suit—paying cash for the fare. That he had come back and done it a second time when his man had missed the original flight in Santa Monica, asking that the plane be sent back, this time to a different airport, might have raised eyebrows but hadn't. Kingston and Nassau were a world all their own, peopled in part by the very rich—some of whom had made their fortunes legitimately and an equal, if not greater, number who had not, but almost all of whom preferred to keep their personal business private and used third parties to conduct their transactions, often paying for their flights in U.S. dollars. It was a world where staying in business meant not asking too many questions and made uncovering anyone who didn't want to be uncovered—especially by police, journalists, or agents of foreign governments—all but impossible.

And so, warned again by Ford to stay away from the Raymond thing completely, and as much as he hated to do so, Nicholas Marten had put Aubrey Collinson and the chartered flights into the same category with the other dying clues and did his best to forget about it.

April 7/Moscow was different and, Dan Ford or not, something he could not put aside because it had yet to happen. Thursday and Friday, Marten had been able to think of almost nothing else. This morning, when he had wakened and then met Clem and boarded the train for Manchester, had been worse because April 7/Moscow was now tomorrow! As much as he tried to keep it from his mind, every turn of the wheels over the tracks raised his level of anxiety, and with it came the throb of his own inner voice unleashed like some Elizabethan arrow that made him wish he'd never been an English major. What horrid thing lies on the morrow? It asked over and over.

What horrid thing?

What horrid thing?

Comes the morrow.

April 7.

April 7.

What horrid thing comes tomorrow?

———

Suddenly Nicholas Marten glanced at Clem. She was still reading. Silent. Absorbed in her book. She didn't know. How could she know? And even if he dared reveal himself and told her who he was, how could he even begin to explain his fear when the best he could give was the tale of a vague entry in a calendar and with it a date and a place?

He looked back at the rolling countryside dappled by clouds and sun and knew all he could do was get on with the business at hand.

And hold his breath.

And wait.

And watch.

14

STILL MANCHESTER. STILL SATURDAY,
APRIL 6. 9:40 P.M.

His jacket collar turned up against a fine rain, Nicholas Marten walked alone along the city streets, turning down one and then another without purpose. What he wanted was a sense and a feel of the city around him—and to keep moving and try to keep Moscow and tomorrow out of his mind. He remembered a war movie where a German U-boat captain told a subordinate, "Never think. You pay a penalty for thinking. You can never rest." The captain had been right.

Minutes earlier he had put Lady Clem into a cab, sending her home to her flat on Palatine Road. Manchester might be a good-sized city, she'd said, insisting she go home and not to his hotel room as he wanted, but she and her father were very well known and it would not do for rumors to start flying that she had been seen accompanying a man to his hotel, especially when that man might very well end up at the university and possibly at some point even under her tutelage. One thing the university did not tolerate was cohabitation between faculty and students, unless they were married, which, of course, she and Nicholas Marten were not. So a peck on the cheek good night and into the taxi she went and then, just like that, he was alone.

Walking down Oxford Road, he passed the university buildings and kept on, through areas called Hulme, Knot Mill, and Castlefield, stopping finally to stand on a bridge over the River Irwell and look down it toward where it became the Manchester Ship Canal. A great waterway, which, he had been told, ran some thirty-six miles west to Liverpool and the Irish Sea.

What he had seen so far was a large, modern city built around this center or that, driven strongly by commerce and at the same time filled to brimming with a sense of the arts, of opera, live theater, pop music, and pop culture. It was a city where electric trams and double-decker buses passed every few minutes. New construction popped up in some part of almost every street and alleyway, and lovingly restored stone buildings and brick-and-mortar textile mills from the city's illustrious past when Manchester was a gemstone of the industrial revolution, were carefully preserved in between.

What Marten saw and felt as he stood in the rain and looked from the bridge was a world centuries distant from the slick, ultra-fast, and ruthless sun-pounded streets of L.A.

It was a distinction made all the more personal a short while earlier at dinner when he and Clem had entertained three university landscape design students Clem had arranged for him to meet. The three, two men and a woman, were Marten's age or a little younger, and each had the same enthusiasm for the school, the courses they took, the professors they had, and the careers they were looking forward to. One in particular had been unwaveringly certain that a student who was smart and developed the proper connections could, within a few years of graduation, do very well indeed. Or, as it was put, become "almost rich."

It had been a valuable experience and made Marten feel that he shared something in common with these people and that he might actually succeed if he came there. But it had been a throwaway remark from one of the men as he sipped an after-dinner brandy that brought everything home.

"The winters here are freezing," he said, "there's hardly any summer, and it's almost always raining. Why in God's name would anyone want to leave Southern California to come here?"

Why?

It was as if a bright light had suddenly shone down from the heavens. Nothing any of them said could have resonated stronger. The idea of following a lifelong dream and becoming an accomplished landscape designer aside, for all intents, Nicholas Marten was little more than a man on the run for his life, with a counterfeit identity and a violent past he didn't want known, who had to get out of the mainstream and stay there. What better place than a large industrial city in the north of England? It was rainy, dreary, and cold. The man was right. Who in Southern California would be likely to come looking for him there? The answer was no one. And that more than anything else was what sold him.

So the idea was right and the place was right. What made it doable was Rebecca's progress. Not only did she like the Balmore and her bright, portly psychiatrist, Dr. Maxwell-Scot, she had adjusted to both with remarkable ease and enthusiasm. And yesterday, when he had taken Clem and gone to visit her to tell her where he was going and why, and to explain he would be away overnight, Rebecca had simply looked at him and then Clem and smiled, saying she thought what he was considering was wonderful and reminding him of what they had talked of before—that if she knew in her heart he was alright, it would make it that much easier for her to be alright.

It was an attitude echoed by Dr. Maxwell-Scot when Marten first discussed the idea of his going to Manchester and leaving Rebecca in London.

"The more independent Rebecca becomes," Maxwell-Scot had said, "the faster and better chance for a full recovery. Besides, in an emergency you would only be a train or very short plane ride away. So yes, I think if the university situation works out, it would be more than alright, it would be very good for you both."

Soaked through from the rain, Marten turned from the bridge and started back toward his hotel. In his mind, if things worked out and he was accepted into the university program, it was a done deal. Very shortly, the city and streets where he walked now would become his home.

15

SUNDAY, APRIL 7. 6:02 A.M. IN MANCHESTER.
9:02 A.M. IN MOSCOW.

Today was—April 7/Moscow.

Marten stood in boxer shorts and a T-shirt in front of the television in his room, anxiously clicking back and forth between channels—BBC1, BBC2, ITV1, Sky, CNN. What he saw was nothing more than typical Sunday morning fluff. Weather, a smattering of sports, human interest filler—a store selling car-sized bagels, a couple married at a horse race, a dog stuck in a toilet—intermixed with talking-head, political discussion shows about the state of the world and church services. If Moscow was under attack it was not being reported. In fact, neither Moscow nor Russia was mentioned at all. As far as the major television outlets were concerned, nothing immediately newsworthy seemed to be happening anywhere in the world.

7:30 A.M.

Marten was showered, shaved, and dressed and back in front of the TV. Still nothing had happened.

9:30 A.M.

Still nothing.

10:30 A.M.

Nothing. Nil. Zilch.

LONDON. SAME DAY, SUNDAY APRIL 7. 6:15 P.M.

Marten had toured the university with Clem once more, had a rather formal lunch with two of her professor-colleagues, and then taken the 1:30 train for London, which had arrived at Euston Station at a little past 5:30. From there he'd taken a cab back to the Hampstead Holiday Inn and, once in his room, immediately turned on the television. Ten minutes of switching channels and still there was no news from or about Moscow.

A quick change of clothes and he went to the Balmore, where a cheery-eyed Rebecca eagerly pressed him for news of his trip to Manchester and what had happened there. When he told her of the city and the people he had met and the rather certain assurances Clem had made that he would be accepted into the graduate program, she was overjoyed. And when he told her about who Clem was and who her father was and their social position, she became all bubbly and giggly and very schoolgirlish. To learn that Clem was actually titled and could be called Lady Clementine made her seem like royalty. "It's the kind of life," she said wistfully, "people like us can only dream about."

Shortly afterward Rebecca was called to dinner and Marten left. Then, as he had in Manchester, he walked and walked and walked. This time he paid little attention to the city at all. His thoughts were on himself and Rebecca and Clem and what the future might be. With them came the logistics of it all and how long he could afford to pay for Rebecca's care and his schooling before he had to find work.

"The pieces."

Suddenly the sound of his own inner voice startled him and he stopped in the early twilight to look around, unsettled by the voice and unsure where he was. As quickly, he realized where his journey had brought him. To the house at 21 Uxbridge Street.

"The pieces," the voice said again.

Instinctively he pulled back out of sight behind a large plane tree. Even though Gene VerMeer had gone back to L.A., he might have asked Scotland Yard detectives to keep the house and grounds under surveillance and, among other things, given his description as someone he would very much like to talk to.

Yet, looking up and down the street, he saw no one, not even

a parked car, and the house itself was dark. It, along with the
safe deposit keys, the Russian Embassy, Penrith's Bar, I. M., the
charter jet, and April 7/Moscow, had turned out to be a dead
end. Like a pricked balloon, nothing but spent air.

Marten watched a moment longer, then abruptly turned and
walked away. The voice had been the push-pull again, some
part of him trying to keep the whole thing alive.

"Raymond is dead," he pushed back at the voice, "and whatever he had been about is dead with him. Three strikes and you're
out, Mr. Marten. Accept it and get on with your damn life. Clem is
leading you in that direction. Go with her and forget the other. Because, like it or not, the truth of it is, whatever the 'pieces' might
have been, there are none left to ponder. Zero. Zilch. None."

16

The following day, Monday, April 8, Nicholas Marten formally
applied for admission to the graduate program at the School of
Planning and Landscape at the University of Manchester. With a
letter of recommendation from—and, he was certain, the personal intervention of—Lady Clementine Simpson, on Thursday,
April 25, he was accepted. On Saturday, April 27, he arrived in
Manchester by train and, with Clem's help, on Monday, April 29,
found a small, furnished converted top-floor loft on Water Street
overlooking the River Irwell. That same day he signed a rental
agreement and moved in. On Tuesday, April 30, he began classes.

It had all been done rapid-fire, with ease and without incident
as if in some way Heaven had greased the boards and sent him
sprawling headlong into a new life. As the weeks progressed
and he settled in, he continued to make short entries into the
journal he had begun when he first arrived in London. Most
were exceptionally brief and variations of the same, "no pieces,
no voices, no sense of Raymond at all."

On May 21, little more than seven weeks after they had come
to England, Rebecca's psychiatrist, Dr. Maxwell-Scot, was
transferred to a new rehabilitation facility called Jura, which the

Balmore Clinic had recently taken over in Neuchâtel, Switzerland.

A huge, sprawling manor on the shores of Lake Neuchâtel, Jura was an experimental program designed to take no more than twenty patients at a time and built on a concept of combining accelerated psychotherapy sessions with rigorous outdoor activities. It was a situation Dr. Maxwell-Scot thought would be excellent for Rebecca, and she recommended that Rebecca accompany her to Switzerland. At Rebecca's enthusiastic urging, Marten had agreed.

The second week of June, Marten made his first visit to Jura. Although Dr. Maxwell-Scot warned him of his sister's still-substantial fragility and suggested that even the most casual reminder of the past could trigger her darkest memories and cause her to slip back into the awful state she had been in before, he found Rebecca, while somewhat unsure and still experiencing up-and-down mood swings, more enthusiastic, independent and stronger than he'd seen her since her breakthrough. Moreover, any reservations he might have had about the physical characteristics of Jura itself—he'd pictured an austere, almost asylumlike institution—were immediately put to rest. Jura was an extremely well managed magnificent estate surrounded by acres of vineyards with manicured grounds running a good half mile to the shores of Lake Neuchâtel. Rebecca had a large private room overlooking both the grounds and the lake, with a breathtaking view of the Alps across the water. It was as if Rebecca, come to be healed, had been plunked down in the middle of some hugely grand, impossibly expensive spa.

Seeing Jura firsthand, Marten worried privately to Dr. Maxwell-Scot, as he had earlier, about the cost of it, and was told again what had been explained to him before: Jura was an experimental extension of the clinic, and Rebecca's expenses, like those of all the patients there, were fully covered by the foundation.

"It is part of the stipulation of the grant by the benefactor who provided the facility," Maxwell-Scot had said, "that treatment here be at no cost to any of the patients or their families."

"Who is the benefactor?" he had asked directly, and Dr. Maxwell-Scot had said she didn't know. The foundation was large, and grants often came from wealthy individuals who, for one reason or another—many quietly had family there—preferred to remain anonymous. It was something Marten understood and could accept, and he told Maxwell-Scot so, saying it was a gift that he and Rebecca fully and gratefully appreciated.

At the end of June, Marten went to Paris to visit Dan and Nadine Ford to celebrate Ford's promotion to the *Los Angeles Times* Paris bureau—a promotion heavily, yet good-naturedly, lobbied for by Nadine to the wife of the *Times*'s chief Washington correspondent, a woman to whom she had been giving French lessons almost from the first day of their arrival in Washington—and to camp out for a long weekend at their tiny new Left Bank apartment on the rue Dauphine.

The first evening, Marten and Dan Ford took a walk along the Seine, where Marten asked Ford if there was anything new in the LAPD's take on Raymond and if they were still engaged in a follow-up investigation. Ford's reply was that as far as his friends at the *Los Angeles Times* knew the whole Raymond thing had been put to bed. "By the LAPD, the FBI, the CIA, Interpol, even the Russians. Not even a glow in the ashes," he said. VerMeer was back on his regular shift at Robbery-Homicide, and Alfred Neuss was doing business as usual in Beverly Hills and sticking to his story that he had no idea whatsoever what Raymond Thorne had wanted with him.

Finally Marten had asked if he knew how Halliday was doing, and all Ford could tell him was that Halliday was still working out of Valley Traffic Division, which meant he was still employed but his job now was little more than handing out traffic tickets. In essence he'd been demoted and put out to pasture. A big fall for an elite 5-2 detective, and to a place from which there was no recovery, at least not for him. And Halliday was still in his early thirties.

Afterward they stopped in a brasserie for a glass of wine, and at a quiet table Ford told Marten there was something he needed to know.

"Gene VerMeer's got his own Web site. It's cute. It's called 'Knuckles and Knuckles dot com.'"

"So?"

"I bet he's asked for information on John Barron a half-dozen times in the last couple of months."

"You mean he did come to London looking for me?"

"I can't put myself in his head, Nick." Ford had long ago programmed the name Nick Marten into his mind and Nadine's. To them Nick Marten was Nick Marten and always had been. "But he's a brutal, malicious bastard who's taken it upon himself to avenge the squad. He wants to find you, Nick, and if he does he'll kill you as fast as he said hello."

"Why are you telling me now?"

"Because he's got the Web site and because he's got a lot of cronies in sympathy with him. And because I don't want you to forget it."

"I won't forget it."

"Good."

Ford fixed Marten with a stare. He had been warned and that was enough. Abruptly he grinned and shifted gears, boyishly ragging Marten on his bohemian lifestyle as a university student and especially gibing him about his ongoing clandestine affair with one of his professors, the not-so-demure Lady Clem.

Early the following day Marten, Ford, and Nadine had boarded a train at the Gare de Lyon and taken a long day trip to Geneva and then Neuchâtel to visit Rebecca at Jura. It was a short but joyous and loving reunion that reestablished Rebecca's relationship with Dan and Nadine Ford, and one that allowed them all to marvel at how enormously their lives had changed in so little time.

In mid-July Nicholas Marten went to visit Rebecca again, this time taking Clem, as a member of the foundation, with him. What he found was a Rebecca even more remarkable than before. For the first time she looked like the beautiful twenty-four-year-old she was. Gone were the hesitancies and up-and-down moods of before. She seemed bright and healthy and athletic, and, as Dr. Maxwell-Scot had first discovered in London and encouraged here, was developing a skill, one she had great aptitude for and wholly enjoyed, learning to read and speak other languages.

Playfully she teased her brother with a smattering of French and Italian and even a little Spanish. Marten was not only thrilled with her sharpness and mental agility, he was tickled.

And like his visit to her with Dan and Nadine Ford, it was warm and happy and fun all at the same time.

In mid-August Clem returned to Jura on foundation business and was surprised to find Rebecca down by the lake and on her own visiting with a Swiss family.

Gerard Rothfels was general manager of European operations for an international pipeline design and maintenance firm based at the corporation's Swiss headquarters in Lausanne. He had recently moved his family—wife Nicole and their young children, Patrick, Christine, and Colette—from Lausanne to Neuchâtel, less than a half hour's drive away, because he wanted to distance himself and his family from the surroundings of his work.

Rebecca had met the Rothfels several weeks earlier on the beach and almost immediately she and the children had fallen in love. Within days, and even though they knew she was a patient at Jura, Rebecca—with the approval of Dr. Maxwell-Scot—was invited to their magnificent lakefront home. Very soon she was going there several times a week, playing with the children and taking meals with them. Gradually but increasingly, and under the watchful eye of their mother, the children were entrusted to her care. It was the first time Rebecca had had any true responsibility since the death of her parents, and she reveled in it. It was a situation greatly applauded by Dr. Maxwell-Scot, and one reported in full to Marten by Lady Clem on her return to Manchester.

By early September Marten had gone to Jura again and had been invited to the Rothfels home, where Rebecca was spending more and more time and where, Gerard Rothfels confided, she was beginning to feel increasingly like family. He hoped that at some point she might move in with them to take care of the children as a kind of full-time au pair.

And with Jura close by, and Rebecca able to continue her sessions with Dr. Maxwell-Scot, by the end of September she had. It was a move that not only underscored the enormous strides she had made and gave her a huge boost of confidence, but came with an additional benefit. In their determination to give their children a complete education, the Rothfels employed private tutors several days a week to give the children lessons in piano and foreign languages, and Rebecca was invited to partake of both. The result was an introduction to the discipline of classical music and a marked elevation of her language skills.

For Nicholas and Rebecca the change over barely half a year had been extraordinary. In both, there had been growth and healing and independence. For Marten had come the further delight that, while his relationship with Lady Clem out of necessity remained secret from anyone but Rebecca, Clem had become not only his best friend but Rebecca's as well. It made for an almost familylike comfort that was warm and loving and a feeling he could only remember from years before when he and Rebecca had been children.

Little by little the horror of the past was fading and wholly new lives, safe and happy, were taking root. In much the same way John Barron had given way to Nicholas Marten, the life of the homicide detective had morphed into that of a graduate student in search of green and order and tranquil beauty.

17

THE UNIVERSITY OF MANCHESTER, WHITWORTH HALL.
SUNDAY, DECEMBER 1. 4:10 P.M.

Winter howls and "the pieces" still lie dormant, Marten wrote in his journal. *Eight months and no sign of Raymond's purpose whatsoever.*

Nicholas Marten had come to England on April first, and now, nearly three-quarters of a year into British society, he still did not know how to hold a teacup properly. Yet today he was expected not only to hold it but to carry it, and the saucer beneath it, around a large room, stopping to sip from it every now and then as he was introduced to this person and that.

For a foreigner the formality of an English four o'clock tea and the inevitable proper small talk that went with it was difficult enough, but add to it a place as official and venerable as Whitworth Hall and pack it with several hundred supercilious guests invited to make acquaintance with the incoming chancellor of the university—among them the vice-chancellor; members of the Court, the university's supreme governing authority; any number of university directors, deans of faculty, and professors; and local political power brokers such as the Bishop of Manchester and the city's Honorable Lord Mayor— and the idea became more than uncomfortable, it bordered on the horrifying, especially for a man who wanted nothing of the public limelight whatsoever.

Under other circumstances Marten might have been less concerned about his lack of refinement, Tetley savoir faire, or even public presence and simply kept in the background and passed the time as best he could. But this was different. He was there because Clem had invited him and because, as he had just learned, her father would be there. How conveniently she had devised their meeting.

Meeting her father was something he had successfully avoided for those same eight months—made easier in a way because most of the old man's time was spent in London, and dodging him when he did come to Manchester was done under the pretext of being crushed with university work or the coincidence of an already planned trip out of the city, say to Paris to visit Dan and the now-pregnant Nadine Ford.

It wasn't so much that Marten wanted to avoid the man, it just seemed the wisest thing to do. Social standing aside, or his reputation as a fiery, abrupt, demanding man who spoke his mind, expected you to speak yours, and then immediately demolished you once you had done it—there was something else, the nature of their relationship. Or, more particularly, the secret nature of their relationship. They had been lovers since that day in London and yet, with the exception of Rebecca and Dan and Nadine Ford, no one knew and no one could know. As Clem had said before, copulation between students and professors was strictly forbidden, so it had to be done in secret, and for eight months it was. Naturally, meeting any parent under those circumstances would be somewhat awkward, especially when it was the first time and particularly when the parent, not to mention the rest of the university-at-large, was unaware of what was going on.

What pushed it past difficult was her father's position as a ranking member of the university Court. That Robert Rhodes Simpson, Earl of Prestbury, was a member of the House of Lords and a Knight of the Garter didn't help either.

"Afternoon, sir." Marten nodded at a familiar face and, balancing his teacup on its saucer, moved on across the great stone cathedrallike hall that was filling by the moment with suits darker and more sober than his and with people of much higher ranking than the lowly graduate student he was. Another sip of tea. It was cold now, and the milk in it nearly made him gag. He was a coffee man, hot and strong and black, as he'd always been. He looked around. Still no sight of them. Suddenly he wondered why he was even there, his stomach in knots, putting himself through all this. He swore he didn't know.

Well, yes he did.

She'd blackmailed him into it at a quarter to midnight three days earlier during one of her usual and impressive performances of oral sex. Suddenly she'd stopped and looked up when he was all sweaty and quaking with exhilaration and invited him there. The manner of her gaze and the tone of her voice—while holding his penis in one hand like a bulging Popsicle and keeping her mouth breathing only inches away—made it perfectly clear that if he didn't agree to come to tea at Whitworth Hall Sunday afternoon, he wouldn't be coming at all. Considering her timing, it was hardly a decision to be fussed over, and he'd immediately agreed. It had been a teasingly wicked thing to do, but it was also the kind of bawdy humor that was built into her and one of the reasons he loved her. Besides, it had seemed innocent enough at the time; he assumed she simply hadn't wanted to spend a long two or three hours alone in the company of academics. He hadn't known then about her father.

"Good afternoon." He nodded to another familiar face, then looked past him, scanning the ocean of dark suits holding teacups and munching little cakes and cucumber sandwiches, looking to see if Clem and her father had arrived.

Not yet. Not that he could see. If they were there, they were elsewhere in the building perhaps with father holding court with the Lord Mayor or the bishop or vice-chancellor. It was a moment in which he realized he still had time to escape. An excuse could be made up later. All he had to do was put down the teacup and saucer and find an exit door as quickly as possible. That it was raining cats and dogs outside, or that it had been raining in Manchester almost every day since he'd been there, didn't matter. He'd had no raincoat then, he had no raincoat now. All he wanted was out. Father could be met at some time in the distant future.

There it was, a side table. Carefully, he set down the cup and saucer, then turned, looking for a way out.

"Nicholas!"

His heart caught in his throat. It was too late. They had come in through a side door and were making their way toward him through the crowd. There was no mistaking "Father." He was in his early sixties, tall and very fit, and very tweedy in his perfectly tailored London-cut suit, just as Nicholas had seen him on television and in the newspapers, and in the photograph she kept on her dressing table. A powerful man of immense aristocratic bearing, he had sharply chiseled features, coal black eyes, and dazzling curly gray hair that matched perfectly his great bushy eyebrows.

"Okay," he said to himself, "deep breath, take it easy, make the best of it."

He saw the sparkle in her eye as they reached him and knew right away she thought the whole thing was sheer, devilish, if dangerous, fun.

"Father, I would like you to meet—"

Father didn't let her finish.

"So, you are Mr. Marten."

"Yes, sir."

"And you are a graduate student."

"Yes, sir."

"School of Planning and Landscape."

"Yes, sir."

"American."

"Yes, sir."

"How do you find my daughter as an educator?"

"Challenging, sir. But very helpful."

"I understand that from time to time you employ her as a personal tutor."

"Yes, sir."

"Why?"

"I need it."

"You need it. What is 'it'?" The old man's glare cut him in half, as if he knew everything.

"It—tutoring. There are things, terms, processes, manners of approach that as a foreigner I don't quite understand. Especially as they apply to European sociology and the psychology of landscape."

"You know how I am called?"

"Yes, sir. Lord Prestbury."

"Well, you are learning some of our ways." Suddenly his black eyes shifted to his daughter. "Clementine, will you please leave us." His order was both abrupt and unexpected.

"I—" Lady Clem glanced at Marten, surprise and apology written all over her. Quickly she looked back to her father. "Of course," she said. Her eyes darted to Marten once more, then she turned and was gone.

"Mr. Marten." Robert Rhodes Simpson, Earl of Prestbury, Knight of the Garter, fixed his eyes on those of Nicholas Marten. He crooked a finger. "Come with me."

18

"Whiskey. Two glasses. And the bottle," Lord Prestbury said to a plumpish, red-faced young man in a starched white jacket standing behind a heavy oak bar in what was a very secretive tavern somewhere in the bowels of the Whitworth Hall complex. So secretive that at the moment, the three were the only ones there.

Moments later Lord Prestbury and Nicholas Marten sat down at a small table toward the back, the two glasses and a bottle of Lord Prestbury's private-label single-malt scotch between them.

To Marten there was no question as to why they were here. Lord Prestbury knew about his relationship with his daughter, was sickened by it, and was determined to end it right then and there, probably by threatening to have Nicholas expelled from the university if he put up a fight. It was easy to understand. Nicholas Marten had no title, no blue-blooded family, and no money, and, worst of all, he was an American.

"I have only just met you, Mr. Marten,"

Lady Clem's father poured three fingers of whiskey in each glass, then looked up and let his eyes bore into the young man across from him.

"I have been accused of being abrupt. That is because I say what is on my mind. It's the way I am and I don't know if I would correct it if I could." Lord Prestbury suddenly picked up his glass, drained half the whiskey with one swallow, then set the glass down and once again let his eyes cut into Marten's.

"That said, I wish to ask you a direct and personal question."

Just then the great oak door they'd entered through opened and two other members of Court entered. They nodded toward Prestbury and then went to the bar. Prestbury waited for them to engage the barman, then looked to Marten and lowered his voice.

"Are you porking my daughter?"

Jesus Christ! Marten's eyes went to the glass in front of him. Abrupt and to the point was right. The old man knew. Now he was demanding confirmation.

"I—"

"Mr. Marten, a man knows if he is porking or not. And to whom he is slipping the old nail. The answer is simple. Yes or no?"

"I—" Marten's fingers circled his glass and he picked it up and drained it.

"You have known her for eight months. She is why you are at university. Correct?"

"Yes, but—"

Lord Prestbury stared, then refilled both their glasses.

"My God, man, I know the story. You met her at the Balmore, where you had brought your sister for treatment. You had been hurt in an industrial accident and were pondering what to do with the rest of your life. Landscape design was a lifelong dream and, at Clementine's urging, you decided to pursue it."

"She told you this?" Marten was astounded. He had no idea Lady Clem had told her father anything about him except that he was one of her students.

"No, sir, I made it up. Of course she told me." Suddenly Lord Prestbury's hand shot across the table and grabbed Marten's, his coal-black eyes boring into him once more.

"I am not here to cause you trouble, Mr. Marten. I am gravely concerned about my daughter. I know I don't see her often. Certainly not often enough. But she is nearing thirty years old. She dresses like a dowdy matron from an era even before mine. I know the rules of the university, far better than you, I'm sure. No bedding between teacher and student. Good rule. Necessary rule. But by God, she talks about you as if you were her best friend in the world. And that is what I am worried about. And why I must know, between gentlemen, if you are pumping her or not."

"No, sir—" Nicholas Marten lied. He had no intention of falling into one of the old man's infamous traps. Pleading for a truthful answer and then slamming him with his own admission.

"No?"

"No."

"Oh, Jesus, man." The Earl of Prestbury let go of Marten's hand and sat back. As quickly he leaned forward again.

"For the sake of God, why not?" he said in a harsh whisper. "Is she that unattractive?"

"She's extremely attractive."

"Then what is wrong? By now she should have been a mother twice over at least." Lord Prestbury picked up his glass and took another strong pull at the whiskey.

"Alright," he said with sudden resolve, "if it's not you, do you know of some chap who *is* boffing her?"

"No, sir, I don't. And with all respect, I find it very difficult to continue this conversation. If you will please excuse me—" Marten started to get up.

"Sit down, sir!"

The two members of Court looked over from where they stood at the bar. Slowly Nicholas Marten sat back down. Then, his eyes fearfully on Lord Prestbury, he picked up his glass and took a large sip of the scotch.

"You don't understand, Mr. Marten." Lord Prestbury was clearly upset. "As I have said, I don't spend much time with my daughter, but in all her years at Manchester she has only twice brought a man home. And not the same man either. My wife is thirteen years dead. Lady Clementine is my only child. I am becoming deathly afraid that as a single parent—Order of the Garter, House of Lords, noble rank and proud and ancient lineage bloody aside, I have raised—" the Earl of Prestbury leaned even closer and whispered, "a Leslie."

"A what?"

"A Leslie."

"I don't understand." Marten took another pull of the scotch and held it, waiting for whatever was next.

"A lesbian."

Marten reacted suddenly, swallowing the whiskey he held in his mouth. The rush of straight scotch nearly choked him and he coughed loudly, bringing them the sharp attention of the two men at the bar. Lord Prestbury ignored it all, only stared at Marten.

"I pray you, sir, tell me she is not," he said fearfully.

Nicholas Marten's response, whatever it might have been, never came, because at that same moment every bell in the entire Whitworth Hall fire alarm system erupted.

19

Marten lay in the dark watching Lady Clem as she slept—nude, the way she always did when they were together—her body rising and falling ever so gracefully as she breathed; her grand mane of chestnut hair in a gentle tumble to her jawline; her skin milky white; her breasts, large and firm, with the big areolas around the nipples he so particularly liked. The only child of the Earl of Prestbury might dress and act like a plain and dowdy matron, but that was for England and the university and for self-protection. Beneath the dark folds of the conservative dresses she wore almost as a uniform was the figure of an exceptionally well endowed and beautiful woman who, even at the age of twenty-seven, could well have been any magazine's centerfold.

Lord Prestbury had no cause for concern about his daughter's sexual orientation, although she would have been no less striking as a lesbian. She was bright and sexy and handsome, and at the moment held the innocent expression of a child, as if she were soundly asleep with a stuffed animal cuddled in her arms.

Innocent?

Lady Clementine Simpson, daughter of the Earl of Prestbury, was absolutely mischievous, wildly profane, and wholly without remorse when necessity called. Barely six hours earlier they had stood with her father and God knew how many highly prominent others beneath hastily grabbed umbrellas in a bone-chilling rain outside Whitworth Hall watching as dozens of firemen from the Greater Manchester Fire Service, sirens blaring, arrived full-bore at the scene. With police holding onlookers back, the firefighters rushed forward donning masks and breathing apparatus and bravely entered the treasured building expecting to encounter a cauldron of flame and choking smoke. What they found instead was little more than the silent remains of a rapidly abandoned afternoon tea. Someone, it seemed, had chosen the occasion of greeting the university's new chancellor to sound a false alarm.

Someone?

Lady Clem!

It was something she never would have admitted to anyone but him. Even then it was done with no more than a fleeting wink as the first firefighters rushed past—the smallest gesture in an attempt to redeem herself, snatching him from God only knew what horror her father was bestowing on him in the basement tavern by using the most practical tool at hand.

A "Leslie," Lord Prestbury had called her, terrified she might have somehow turned gay. A father's fear that he had lost touch with his only child, and she had become something he could neither understand nor accept.

A "Leslie"? Hardly. And the balls of her, coming right back to his top-floor loft on Water Street overlooking the River Irwell the same night as the false alarm fiasco, immediately after sitting straight-faced through dinner with her father and the Bishop of Manchester and the Lord Mayor, where the principal topic of discussion was the terrorist act of the false alarm.

Then, while slowly undressing, or rather performing a strip-tease in front of him, insisting he tell her what it was that her father had been so eager to discuss in the secretive Whitworth Hall tavern. And when he did, using her father's genteel terminology for it, her reaction had been to say simply, "Poor Daddy. Wonderful father. House of Lords. But so much of life he doesn't quite get."

The words barely from her mouth, she slid naked in front of him, stripped off his clothes, and made a party of the rest of the night. Laughing, teasing, working him into bed and onto his back. Then, with his sizable erection pointed squarely at the ceiling, she climbed astride him and with her eyes closed, back arched, her great breasts heaving, began thrusting and pumping, losing herself in the overflow of joy and love and mischief and passion. All the while chanting over and over so loudly he was certain people passing in the street four stories down would hear, "Fuck me! Fuck me! Fuck me!"

Jesus. And she was a professor, the daughter of a Knight of the Garter. Upper class, titled, and wealthy beyond reason.

Marten smiled again. This was what life had become. Now, at age twenty-seven, he was working toward a master's degree in planning and landscape and literally flirting with nobility.

At the same time and little by little the dark heartbeat of Raymond diminished. What had ever become of his threatened e-mails was anybody's guess. Either they had been a desperate bluff and never existed in the first place, or they had been sent on a delayed basis as he'd promised and were simply lost, stuck floating for eternity somewhere in cyberspace. Either way it didn't matter, because they never materialized. At least they hadn't in the weeks and months since, and each turn of the calendar made it easier to forget about them and to believe they had never existed.

In a way it was hard to believe any of it had ever existed. Los

Angeles and all that had been was a dream somewhere in a distant past. Here in the cold rain of Manchester he had become a man who found joy in every passing day, who was increasingly involved with his studies, with his secret life with Clem, and with the peace and wholeness of a brand-new life.

20

MANCHESTER. MONDAY, JANUARY 13.

The psychological impact of preserving and maintaining urban parks in an increasingly fast-paced, global, and Ethernet-driven society cannot be too strongly stated. Whether we realize it or not, these great tracts of sweeping landscapes . . .

Marten stopped and pushed back from his keyboard. He was alone in his flat working on his term paper, a study of the psychological and functional importance of sustaining urban parks in Europe in the twenty-first century. It was a work he estimated would be some eighty to one hundred pages long and take some three months to complete. Although it wasn't due until early April, he knew it would be a struggle, especially since he had already been at it for more than a month and so far had written just twenty pages.

It was now three-thirty in the afternoon and a cold rain was spitting against the dormer window, as it had been doing since seven this morning when he'd first gone to work. His mind numb from concentration, he got up and navigated around the piles of books and research papers scattering the floor to go into the kitchen to make a fresh pot of coffee.

As he waited for it to brew, he glanced through the daily newspaper, the *Guardian*. Drained, his thoughts still on his writing, he was doing little more than skimming pages when a short article caught his eye. It was an Associated Press article headlined NEW POLICE CHIEF FOR LOS ANGELES and went on to briefly relate that the mayor of L.A. had appointed a new, highly regarded, highly credentialed chief to run the department. The new man had been selected from outside the organiz-ation and given the mandate to set a long-tarnished police agency on its feet.

"Good luck," Marten thought but in the next instant hoped it was possible. Obviously, with all that had happened, the mayor and city council had seen, at least politically, the need for a change. But even if the new man was good and the rank and file respected him, it would take a long time to shake out the old at-titudes and traditions, especially with veteran detectives like Gene VerMeer. Still, it had been done, and maybe with time change for the better would come.

Standing there in the kitchen, listening to the patter of rain against the window, Marten felt a warmth and comfort he hadn't felt in as long as he could remember. The mind-numbing trauma of Raymond and whatever he had been about had slowly faded into a distant memory, and now, with Chief Har-wood gone, a new era was beginning at the LAPD. Mercifully, it seemed, that part of his life was finally over.

Marten turned the page and was about to close the paper and go back to work when another short article caught his attention. It was a Reuters news service piece from Paris. The unclothed body of a middle-aged man had been found in a public park. The vic-tim had been shot a number of times in the face at close range, de-stroying his features and making identification all but impossible.

Marten felt the breath go out of him and the hair stand up on the back of his neck. It was Los Angeles and MacArthur Park and the body of the German student, Josef Speer, and the murder vic-tims found in Chicago, San Francisco, and Mexico City all over again. In the next instant a single word flashed through his mind.

Raymond.

But it was impossible.

Shaken, Marten put the *Guardian* away, poured his coffee, and went back to his work.

Raymond.

No. Not possible. Not after all this time.

His first thought was to call Dan Ford in Paris and see what he knew and if he had more details. But then he decided no, it was crazy. He was doing it to himself again and he had to stop it. It was simply a murder and nothing else, and Ford would tell him the same thing.

At seven-thirty he stopped, collected his raincoat and umbrella, and took a brisk ten-minute walk to Sinclair's Oyster Bar in Shambles Square for a pint of ale and a plate of fish and chips. At eight-forty-five he was back at work, and at eleven he wearily turned out the light and went to bed; mentally exhausted, five more pages completed.

11:20 P.M.

Lights from passing cars below created haphazard, dancing patterns across the dark of the ceiling above his bed while the incessant rain on the roof and windowpane provided the images with a kind of comforting soundtrack. Taken with his weariness, it was like some gentle drug, and he relaxed and let his thoughts go to Lady Clem as if she were there beside him instead of in Amsterdam, where she had gone for a weeklong seminar.

Fleetingly, he thought of Rebecca, safe and happy in the Rothfels home in Switzerland.

11:30 P.M.

Sleep began to overtake him, and his thoughts drifted to Jimmy Halliday and how he was managing at Valley Traffic Division. Halliday, who, in the final seconds in the rail yards, had so heroically saved Rebecca's life and his by facing Polchak's murderous machine gun himself and stopping him the only way he could, by killing him. He tried to picture Halliday's face, remembering what he had looked like and wondering if he had changed, but the image faded, replaced by the warm grin of Dan Ford, snuggled comfortably with Nadine in their tiny apartment in Paris proudly awaiting the birth of their first child.

Paris.

Again he saw the short article in the *Guardian*. The unclothed body of a man found dead in a public park. Shot numerous times in the face. Immediate identification all but impossible.

Raymond.

It was absurd. There had been no raised pulse, no whispered inner voice, no sense of doom. Raymond was dead.

Walking back in the rain from dinner, he'd thought again that maybe he should call Ford in Paris and talk about it. Again he'd decided against it. It was his own disquiet and he knew it. What had happened was nothing but coincidence, and the idea that it could be anything else was preposterous.

"NO!"

His own cry startled him from a deep sleep. He was soaked in sweat and staring into the dark. He'd seen Raymond in his dreams. He'd been right there in the bedroom, watching him as he slept.

Instinctively he reached out to the nightstand to touch his gun. All he felt was the smoothness of lacquered wood. His hand moved again. Nothing. He sat up. He knew he'd put the Colt there. Where was it?

"Now I have both your guns."

Raymond's voice rocked through him, and he looked up expecting to see the killer standing at the foot of his bed staring at him in the dark with John Barron's Double Eagle Colt in his hand and dressed in the ill-fitting suit he'd taken from the Beverly Hills jeweler, Alfred Neuss.

A hard sheet of rain suddenly hammered against the window and he realized where he was. Raymond was not there. Nor was Lady Clem. Nor was anyone else but him. It had been a nightmare—a replay of what had happened in L.A. when he'd dreamed Raymond was in his room and he'd wakened to find out the dream was real and Raymond was right there at the foot of his bed.

Slowly he got up and walked to the dormer window to look out. It was still dark, but from the streetlamps below he could see that the wind-driven rain was beginning to mix with snow and turning the icy dark of the River Irwell almost deadly black against the dim gray around it. He took a deep breath and ran a hand through his hair, then looked at his clock.

It was just past six. He was up, he might as well shower and get to work. He had a term paper to think about, not the haunting of his own past. For the first time he realized how true and simple that was.

Quickly he stripped off the boxer shorts he had slept in and started for the bathroom and a hot shower, his enthusiasm for his term paper and his life in Manchester recharged. Then his telephone rang and he froze where he was.

It rang again. Who was it? No one would call at this hour unless it was a wrong number or an emergency. It rang again and he crossed the room, naked, and picked up.

"This is Nicholas."

The person on the other end hesitated; then he heard the familiar voice. "It's Dan. I know it's early."

A chill slid down Marten's spine. "The man shot in the park."

"How did you know?"

"I saw a clip in the paper."

"The French police have discovered his identity."

"Who—?"

"Alfred Neuss."

21

BRITISH AIRWAYS FLIGHT 1604,
MANCHESTER TO PARIS.
TUESDAY, JANUARY 14. 10:35 A.M.

Puffy clouds intermixed with sunshine gave Marten glimpses of the English Channel as they passed over it. Ahead he could see the shoreline of the Normandy coast, and then they were past it and over the huge checkerboard that was French farmland.

For ten months he had been waiting for something to happen and nothing had, and he had all but let it go. And then this. With the confirmation that the disfigured body was Alfred Neuss, a wave of fear, anxiety, and exhilaration had rushed through him. In one way he felt exonerated because he had not been crazy but right all along. But he was equally disturbed because there was no way to know what was going on: the reason for the murder, why it had come all these months later, how it fit into the scheme of what had happened before, who Raymond had been involved with, and, most frightening of all, what the whole was about, what was yet to happen.

His decision to go to Paris had been made on the spot in the middle of Dan Ford's call. On the practical side it had been easy because for the next week he had no classes, just the occasional meeting with a supervisor; Lady Clem was one of them, and she was in Amsterdam. Instead he had planned his calendar to focus on his term paper, and right now that could wait. The only other consideration was cost. His settlement with the LAPD had allowed him and Rebecca to come to England, with enough for her to go to the Balmore and for him to pay his rent in Manchester and his not inconsiderable university tuition. Rebecca's luck in going to Jura had saved substantial expense, and his only real outlay for her now was clothing. Her sundries and spending money were taken care of by the small salary she earned working for the Rothfels. What remained of his compensation he had put aside, drawing out only what he needed for expenses and to dutifully pay off the monthly balances on the two credit cards he kept.

Still, it was a long way until he graduated and could look for a job, and he had to watch what he spent. Flying to Paris was costly, but so was the Eurostar, the Chunnel train, and the plane was faster; besides, it would be the bulk of his expense because for the short time he was there he would sleep on the couch in Dan Ford's living room. On the other hand, if he had classes back to back and no money at all, he still would have gone. The pull of Raymond and what he had been about was far too strong.

22

Dan Ford was waiting for him as he cleared immigration at Roissy–Charles de Gaulle airport, and together they drove into the city in Ford's small, white, two-door Citroën.

"A couple of teenagers found Neuss's body in the Parc Monceau under some bushes near the Metro station." Dan Ford shifted gears and accelerated onto Autoroute A1, heading into

Paris. "Neuss's wife asked the hotel people to check on him when she hadn't been able to get in touch with him. They were the ones who called the police. Things came together pretty quickly after that.

"Neuss was here on business. The hotel where he was staying is near the park. He'd flown from L.A. to Paris, taken a connecting flight to Marseilles and then a cab to Monte Carlo, then come back to Paris. He bought a quarter of a million dollars' worth of diamonds in Monte Carlo. They're missing."

"The police have anything solid?"

"Only that Neuss had been tortured before he was killed."

"Tortured?"

Ford nodded.

"How?" Immediately Marten thought of the Azov brothers in Chicago and the men murdered in San Francisco and Mexico City. All had been tortured before they were killed.

Raymond! Again the name shot through him. But he knew it was crazy and so he said nothing.

"The police didn't give specifics. If they have anything more they're not talking about it, but I doubt it. Philippe Lenard, the chief inspector assigned to the case, knew I'd covered the LAPD, and when I told him I'd been involved with the Neuss story earlier he asked if he could call on me with questions. I think if the method of torture meant anything, or if he had something else, he'd tell me because he'd want my input."

Ford changed lanes and slowed behind traffic. Marten hadn't seen him since early fall, when he and Nadine had suddenly arrived in Manchester to surprise him and announce her pregnancy. Now, nearly five months later, approaching fatherhood seemed to have affected him little. He still wore the rumpled blue blazer over khaki trousers and horn-rimmed glasses, still looked at the world and his place in it with the same one-eyed fire and intensity he always had. Moreover, it seemed to make little difference where he was on the planet—California, Washington, D.C., Paris, each fit his soul like a slipper.

"LAPD know about Neuss?" Marten asked.

Ford nodded. "Guys from Robbery-Homicide talked to his wife and to the detectives at London Metropolitan Police who interviewed him there before. And then to Lenard, here in Paris."

"Robbery-Homicide, you mean VerMeer?"

Ford looked at him. "I don't know if it was VerMeer."

"What happened?"

"Neuss's wife said she had no idea who it could have been or if it might have had to do with what happened before. Her feeling was that it was just a robbery gone bad. All London Metro had was the transcript of the conversation they'd had with Neuss last year, and the same story he told all along, and that his wife corroborated—that he had gone to London on business and that he had no idea who Raymond was or why he'd been in his shop or his apartment and that the only way his name was in the phone book of the brothers Raymond killed in Chicago was because they were tailors he used one time when he was there and had them bill his store in Beverly Hills."

"Those guys were Russian. Anybody get hold of the Russian investigators who came to L.A. after Raymond died? With Neuss murdered they might have some new take on the whole thing."

"I don't know. If they have, neither Lenard nor his men have said anything about it."

Dan Ford slowed the Citroën as they crossed the Porte de la Chappelle interchange and came into the north of Paris. "You want to go to the park, see where they found Neuss's body?"

"Yes," Marten said.

"What do you think you're going to find that the Paris police haven't?"

"I don't know, except the Paris police weren't at MacArthur Park when we found Josef Speer."

"That's just the point." Ford turned to look at Marten directly. "I called you about Neuss because I knew once you learned who it was and how he'd been found, you'd come running anyway." Abruptly Ford downshifted, turned right, and accelerated once more.

"This is Paris, Nick, not L.A., and it was Alfred Neuss, not Josef Speer. And there were diamonds involved. The police see it as a murder-theft, nothing more. The MO was a coincidence. That's why the LAPD guys are still there and not here."

"Maybe it's a coincidence, maybe it isn't."

Ford touched the brake and slowed to a stop behind a line of traffic. "What do you think you're going to do about it either

way? You're not a cop anymore. You have no authority anywhere. You start probing and twisting, trying to find something,
and people are going to start asking who you are and what
you're doing.

"Neuss's murder is bringing the whole thing back. The media's perked to sell tickets, the tabloids will create a story where
there isn't one. Raymond was on TV worldwide. So were you.
And people remember. You may have changed your name but
not your face. What if somebody starts putting things together,
guesses who you are? They get your name and find out where
you live."

The traffic in front of them moved off, and Ford eased the
Citroën forward. "What if that information gets back to the
wrong guys on the LAPD who still want to know about John
Barron—what happened to him, where he went, where his sis-
ter went? I warned you before about Gene VerMeer's Web site.
Now there's a new one innocuously called 'Copperchatter.'
Ever hear of it?"

"No."

"It's cops talking shop to each other around the world. And
in cop vernacular and with cop humor and cop vindictiveness. I
bet you the name John Barron comes up twice a month, egged
on by VerMeer and kept in play by people who remember Red
and Len Polchak and Roosevelt Lee and Valparaiso and Jimmy
Halliday. They're willing to pay money to find you, telling people you left something important behind in L.A. and they want
to return it to you."

Marten looked away.

Ford kept on. "You start making noise, Nick, and you're putting your life and everything you've built in jeopardy. You're
exposing Rebecca, too, if somebody wants to take it that far."

Marten turned back. "What the hell do you want me to do?"

"Turn around and go back to Manchester. I'm on top of this.
If something breaks, you'll know right away."

Ford stopped at a crosswalk for a red light. Pedestrians bundled against the January cold swarmed past in either direction,
and for a moment the boyhood friends sat in silence.

"Nick, please, do what I ask, go back to Manchester," Ford
said finally.

Marten stared at him. "What's the rest of it?"

"Rest of what?"

"Whatever it is you're not telling me. I could see it the minute you picked me up at the airport. You know something, what is it?"

"Nothing."

"I'm a big fan of nothing, try me."

"Alright." The light changed and Ford moved the Citroën off. "When you read about the body in the park, what was your first thought?"

"Raymond."

"It was automatic. Cut right through your gut."

"Yes."

"But we know Raymond's dead and has been for a long time."

"Go on." Marten studied Ford, waiting for the next.

"When I first heard about the body in the park, nude and disfigured, before I knew it was Alfred Neuss—for the hell of it I had one of the *Times* staff reporters in L.A. do a little legwork."

"And?"

"This morning, while you were on your way here, the information came back. Raymond's file is missing from the L.A. County coroner's office. It was deleted from the database. His fingerprints, photographs, everything—gone. Same thing with his LAPD records at Parker Center. The same with his file at the Department of Justice in Sacramento. The same with the report the Beverly Hills PD made after they went over Neuss's apartment. The same with Chicago PD. And perhaps most interesting of all, the FBI database was hacked into—all the Raymond files and related evidence were completely deleted. They're checking now with Interpol Washington and the department files in San Francisco and Mexico City where Raymond's booking photo and copies of his fingerprints were. If the hackers got into everything else, what do you suppose they're going to find?"

"When did this happen?"

"No way to tell." Ford glanced at Marten, then back to the road. "There's more. There were three people from the coroner's office who were fired or transferred because of the cremation fiasco—two men and a woman. The men died three weeks apart and the woman vanished, all less than four months after the incident. The woman supposedly went to live with a sister in New Orleans, but there is no sister in New Orleans. Just an uncle who can't remember the last time he heard from her."

Marten felt as if someone had just touched an icy hand to the back of his neck. This was the thing he had felt when he'd first read about the dead man in the park but had talked himself out of even bringing up ever since. "You're suggesting Raymond might still be alive."

"I'm not suggesting anything. But we know somebody sent a plane for him, twice. It means he wasn't working alone and whoever was helping him obviously had money, a lot of it."

Marten stared off. It was more of what he'd known all along. More of what had been so rudely dismissed by Chief Harwood in his resolute determination to end the Raymond story and protect the truth about what had happened to the squad. Abruptly Marten looked back. "What about the doctor who pronounced him dead at the hospital?"

"Felix Norman. He's no longer on staff. I have a couple of people looking into it now."

"Jesus Christ." Marten looked off and then quickly back. "Does the LAPD know?"

"I don't think so, or if they do they didn't make anything of it. The two deaths were apparently from natural causes. There was never a missing person report on the woman, and who goes back into old files and databases for information on a case that's been officially closed and no one wants anything to do with?"

Ahead, they could see the round edifice of Barrière Monceau, one of the myriad of tollhouses built around the old city in the late 1700s and one of the few still standing. Just beyond it was the sprawling winter drab of a city park.

"That it? The place where they found Neuss's body?"

"Parc Monceau. Yes."

Ford saw the fire rise up in Marten's eyes as they drew closer. Felt the electricity as he sat up straighter, unconsciously studying the streets, the surrounding neighborhood, the various approaches to the park. Looking for a way a killer might have come and gone. It was the cop inside him coming back to life. The very thing Ford had been afraid of.

"Nick," he warned, "stay out of it. We don't know anything.

Let me work this through with my guys in L.A. Give the Paris police a chance to come up with something here."

"Why don't we just take a walk in the park and see what we see."

Three minutes later Ford pulled the Citroen into a parking space on the rue de Thann diagonally across from the park. It was just twelve-thirty when they got out and crossed the Boulevard de Courcelles in bright January sunshine, entered Parc Monceau, the Duc de Chartres's elegant eighteenth-century innovation, through ornate iron gates near the Monceau Metro station, and started down the path toward the area where Neuss had been discovered.

They were twenty yards down it when they saw three uniformed policemen standing outside a thick planting of evergreens towered over by a massive, winter-barren chestnut tree. Closer in and near the evergreens, two men in plainclothes stood together chatting. Clearly they were detectives. One was short and sturdily built and gestured here and there as if he were explaining things; the other nodded in response and seemed to be asking questions. He was younger and much taller than the first man and was by no means French.

Jimmy Halliday.

23

"Get out of here," Ford said the instant he saw him. Marten hesitated.

"Now!" Ford said, and Marten turned and headed back in the other direction with Ford behind him. VerMeer he might have expected, but Halliday? What was he doing here?

"That's exactly what I was talking about, only suddenly we're a little closer to home." Ford caught up with him and they went back out through the gates by the Metro station.

"How long's he been in Paris?"

"I don't know. I haven't seen him before and, as I said, the LAPD's been keeping their distance. He must have just come in."

"The detective with him, is he the one running the investigation?"

Ford nodded. "Inspector Philippe Lenard, Paris Prefecture of Police."

"Give me the car keys. I'll wait there. Halliday knows you. Go back and see what you can find out."

"He'll ask about you."

"No, he'll ask about John Barron." Marten grinned just a little. "You haven't seen him since you were in L.A."

Marten got into the Citroën and waited. Halliday. No matter their official posture, he should have expected the LAPD would send somebody. And Halliday, wherever he was currently assigned, knew more about the Neuss situation than anyone else on the force, so he was a natural. He might even have asked to come. It made Marten wonder if Neuss's murder had sent the LAPD scrambling for information the same way Ford had put the *L.A. Times* on it—and if so, if they had come up with the same missing elements and, as a result, the same unnerving supposition: that somehow Raymond had been spirited away from the hospital alive, leaving a death certificate and a cremated body in his wake. And now, with his records gone, his possible accomplices either dead or vanished, and no one with any real knowledge of his true identity, he had suitably recovered and picked up from where he had been so rudely interrupted before.

NEUCHÂTEL, SWITZERLAND. SAME TIME.

Rebecca had first seen him when he was one of several guests who came to tour Jura in mid-July. Several weeks later she met him at a luncheon at the Rothfels home. He knew she was a patient at Jura and showed great interest in the new program there. They spent an hour or more talking and then playing with the Rothfels children, and in the end she knew he was in love with her. Even so it had been more than a month before he held her hand and another month after that before he kissed her.

Those first months before he made any physical contact had been agony for her as well. The look in his eyes told her how he felt, and her feelings quickly escalated until they matched his or were even stronger. The most fleeting thought of him made her tingle, and the moments when they were alone together overpowered any experience she'd ever had, even if it was no more than a stroll by the lake where they watched the breeze ripple the surface and listened to the twitter of birds. To her, Alexander Cabrera was the most beautiful man she had ever known, or could have imagined knowing. That he was thirty-four and ten years older than she made no difference whatsoever. Nor did the fact that he was a highly educated, exceedingly successful businessman who just happened to be Gerard Rothfels's employer.

An Argentinean, Cabrera owned and operated Cabrera WorldWide, a company that designed, installed, and operated high-capacity pipeline delivery systems and served industries from agriculture to petroleum exploration and production in more than thirty countries. His corporate headquarters remained in Buenos Aires, but his large European center of operations was in Lausanne, where he spent parts of every month while still retaining a small office in Paris in the permanent suite he kept at the Hotel Ritz.

Highly respectful of her personal situation as well as her position as an employee of his European manager, and wanting to disrupt neither his Lausanne office with undue gossip nor the household of which she had become an integral part, Alexander had insisted they see one another discreetly.

For four wondrous and loving months their relationship had been just that, discreet—when he was in Lausanne on business, or when he could persuade the Rothfels into giving up their nanny for a night or two or three. He would spirit her suddenly away to Rome or Paris or Madrid. Even then their relationship was guarded—separate hotels, a private car to pick her up and whisk her away to wherever he was, and then later to take her back again. Moreover, in all the time they had known each other, never once had they slept together. That, he promised, was for their wedding night and not before. And there would be a wedding night. He'd pledged that, too, the first time he kissed her.

This particular afternoon, warmly dressed against the January cold, Rebecca sat on a bench beside a frozen pond on the rolling grounds of the Rothfels home on the shores of Lake Neuchâtel and watched her charges—Patrick, three, Christine, five, and Colette, six—as they took ice-skating lessons. In twenty minutes they would finish and go into the house for hot chocolate. Afterward she would take Patrick off to play while Christine and Colette were given piano lessons and then schooled in Italian by the tutor who came at three every Tuesday and Thursday. At four on Wednesdays and Fridays another tutor came to teach them Russian, and after that spent an hour with Rebecca instructing her in the same. By now she was increasingly comfortable with French, Italian, and Spanish and was quickly approaching the same ease with Russian. German had been a problem for her and still was, the guttural sounds nearly impossible for her to manage correctly.

What made today special and at the same time very difficult was that Alexander was coming to Switzerland for a business dinner that evening following a ten-day trip home to Buenos Aires. The difficulty was that the dinner was in St. Moritz, and St. Moritz was on the opposite side of the country from where she was in Neuchâtel. Moreover, he was due to return to Paris immediately afterward. Although they talked on the phone at least once every day, they had not seen each other in weeks and she longed to go to St. Moritz, if only to be with him for a short while. But because of his position as head of the company, his pressing schedule, and his own very dignified and proper view of their relationship, she knew it was not possible. And she had to accept it. Just as she accepted the secrecy of their relationship. When the time came for them to marry, he told her, the world would know. Until then their life had to remain theirs alone, theirs and the only others who knew—Rothfels and his wife, Nicole, and the burly Jean-Pierre Rodin, Alexander's French bodyguard who went everywhere with him and took care of everything.

Well, in truth, there was one other person who did know—Lady Clem, who had met Alexander for the first time when she visited Rebecca at the Rothfels' in September and learned of his interest in Jura. She met him again in London during a Balmore fund-raising event at the Albert Hall, where he presented the foundation with a large and very generous gift earmarked especially for Jura. They met a third time when she visited Rebecca in Neuchâtel several months later. By then he and Rebecca were clearly involved with each other, and Rebecca took Clem aside to confirm it and to impress upon her the importance of keeping it secret, even from her brother, who was staunchly protective of her and would view her emotional maturity as delicate at best. After everything he'd been through with her, he might well react emotionally, if not irrationally, himself if he were to find out about the depth of her involvement with a man as worldly as Alexander Cabrera—a man, she was certain, he would see as using her as little more than a toy, which wasn't so at all. Besides, it was what Alexander wanted, at least for now.

"Not only that," Rebecca told Clem with a girlish grin, "if Nicholas can have a clandestine relationship with you, there is no reason I can't have the same kind of thing with Alexander. We'll just make a game of it." She grinned again. " 'Keep Away from Nicholas.' Alright?"

Clem laughed. "Alright," she impishly agreed. Then, in a hooked-finger ritual between them, she promised to say nothing to Nicholas until Rebecca gave her permission to do so. As a result, even months later, Nicholas Marten still knew nothing of the conspiracy against him or of the love of his sister's life.

24

PARIS, L'ECLUSE MADELEINE WINE BAR,
PLACE DE LA MADELEINE. SAME DAY,
TUESDAY, JANUARY 14. 2:30 P.M.

Dan Ford dialed a number, then handed Halliday his cell phone and picked up a glass of Bordeaux, waiting as Halliday changed his airline reservations so he could stay in Paris a few days longer than originally planned.

They'd come here by taxi from the Parc Monceau twenty minutes earlier. Halliday had wanted a drink and Ford wanted to get him away from the park, and L'Ecluse, tucked away near the Place Madeleine in the bustle of the inner city, was far enough from the park and any route Marten might take to leave it.

Ford had purposely walked Halliday out of the park at the Metro exit and across the Boulevard de Courcelles in plain sight, then waited there as he hailed a cab. He knew Marten was just down the street in the Citroën and hoped he would see what was going on and simply take the car and go to Ford's apartment on the Left Bank. Whether Marten had or not, or whether he had seen them at all, there was no way to tell. For all he knew Marten could still be sitting there, waiting.

"Sorry, I'm on hold." Halliday indicated the phone and then picked up his glass of brandy and took a solid pull from it.

"It's alright," Ford said. Halliday looked as if he'd aged a decade in the ten-odd months since he last saw him. He was thin, his face gaunt and lined, and the blue eyes, once so penetrating, now seemed drained and weary. His wrinkled gray slacks and light blue sports jacket looked as worn as he did.

Clearly tired and jet-lagged, he had arrived from Los Angeles that morning and gone directly to Inspector Lenard's office at the Prefecture of Police, and shortly afterward had accompanied Lenard to the murder scene in the park.

What was interesting was that Halliday was no longer a member of the LAPD but a private investigator hired by Neuss's insurance company to find out what had happened to the missing quarter million dollars in diamonds. Normally police had little to do with private investigators, but Halliday had been an LAPD detective involved with Neuss before, and because of it Lenard had no trouble welcoming him, the same as he had Dan Ford.

Halliday's initial plan had been to spend two or three days in Paris sifting through whatever evidence the French police had and then, having made the personal connection with Lenard and knowing he would be kept informed, go home. But things had changed unexpectedly soon after Ford joined them in the park when Lenard received a call informing him that Fabien Curtay, one of the world's wealthiest diamond merchants, had been murdered a few hours earlier in his luxury apartment in Monte Carlo by a hooded intruder who had broken in and shot Curtay and a bodyguard to death.

There had been no need for Lenard to fill in either Ford or Halliday as to the significance. It had been Fabien Curtay whom Alfred Neuss visited in Monaco and from whom he had purchased the now-missing diamonds.

Lenard had left immediately for a flight to Monte Carlo, and that was when Halliday asked Ford if there was some place they could go for a drink and where he could make a call to change his flight reservation. The real reason, of course, was that he wanted to talk, so there was little for Ford to do but go with him.

On the way Halliday had said little, speaking briefly of Neuss and the killing of Curtay, and then making small talk, telling Ford he was glad to see him and envious that his career had sent him to a place like Paris. Not once did he bring up John Barron, where he was, or what had happened to him. Raymond he had mentioned only in passing and in the past tense, giving no hint at all to suggest he might have the same information Ford did.

It made Ford wonder why Halliday had come to Paris at all, except that he was working as a private investigator on a specific job for an insurance company. Unless—it was all a carefully orchestrated means to renew his past relationship with Ford and through him find John Barron. No matter how he appeared now, he had once been a first-rate detective whose skills at control and manipulation had been honed razor-sharp under Red McClatchy in the 5-2. It was something Ford had to remember so he could make sure he gave nothing away.

"Thank you," Halliday said, then clicked off the cell phone and handed it back to Ford. "All set."

Halliday picked up his glass and sat back. "I'm divorced, Dan. My wife has the kids. It's been what—?" he stopped to think. "Almost seven months now."

"I'm sorry."

Halliday looked at his glass and swirled the liquor around inside it, then finished it and signaled the waiter for another.

"The squad was disbanded."

"I know."

"A hundred years of it and Barron and I are the only ones left. Just John and me. The last of the Five-Two."

There it was, Halliday's way of bringing up Barron. Ford

wasn't sure how he would take it further, but he didn't have to wait long because Halliday followed up in the next breath.

"Where is he?"

"Barron?"

"Yeah."

"I don't know."

"Come on, Dan."

"I don't, Jimmy."

Halliday's drink came and he took half of it in one pull, then put the glass down and looked at Ford.

"I know he had a tough time with some of the guys on the LAPD. I wanted to talk to him about it. I couldn't get a phone number or address. I tried to get him through his sister at St. Francis. She wasn't there anymore. They wouldn't tell me what happened to her or where she went." Halliday's hand tightened around his glass. "I tried to reach you, too. I don't remember just when. You'd already been transferred to Washington. I tried you there."

"I never got the message."

"No?"

"No."

Halliday looked across the room and then back. "John and I need to talk, Dan. I want to find him."

Ford wasn't about to be pushed. "I haven't seen him since L.A. I wish I could help you, I can't. I'm sorry."

Halliday held Ford's gaze for a long time and then looked off again.

Ford took a swallow of Bordeaux. There was no doubt Halliday knew he was lying, and before, he would have called him on it, but now he just sat there, glass in hand, blankly watching the bar thin out as Parisians drifted away after the lunch hour.

Ford didn't know what to think. Maybe Halliday was simply beaten down—the huge emotional blow of the 5-2 disaster followed by the demeaning assignment to Valley Traffic Division; and then, after everything, his divorce and losing his kids. Maybe all he wanted with Barron was camaraderie. To sit and talk things over with the only other member of the squad still alive. On the other hand, maybe he blamed Barron for everything and that was why he had come. Maybe he'd even manufactured the insurance company business. Neuss's murder and the fact Dan Ford was in the same city were a perfect excuse.

"I need to get some sleep, Dan." Halliday suddenly stood. "What do we owe here?"

"I'll take care of it, Jimmy."

"Thanks." Halliday finished what was left of his drink, then set the glass on the table and leaned close to Ford.

"I want to talk to John. Tonight, tomorrow at the latest. I'm at the Hôtel Eiffel Cambronne. You let him know, huh? Tell him it has to do with Raymond."

"Raymond?"

"Just tell him, huh? Tell him I need his help." Halliday stared at Dan Ford a moment longer, then abruptly turned and started for the door.

Ford stood quickly, dropped two twenty-euro notes on the table, and followed Halliday across the room and out into the stark afternoon sunshine.

25

Neither Dan Ford nor Jimmy Halliday had noticed the bearded, heavyset man sitting alone at a table by the door as they passed. Nor did they see him come out onto the sidewalk behind them to stand innocently nearby listening as Ford put Halliday into a cab and gave the driver the name of his hotel. Nor had Ford known he was being watched as he walked quickly toward the Place de la Madeleine Metro station afterward, taking his cell phone from his jacket as he went.

Nor had they been aware of him earlier as he sat on a bench feeding pigeons in the Parc Monceau, observing as they examined the crime scene with Lenard until the Paris detective received a phone call and abruptly left. They had not been aware, either, that he had followed them out of the park and watched as they got into a cab and then followed it in a cab of his own to L'Ecluse Madeleine.

The bearded man spent another ten seconds on the sidewalk in front of L'Ecluse, looking as if he were trying to make up his mind what to do next and making certain it did not appear as if he had deliberately followed the Americans out. Finally he turned and walked off down the block, vanishing in the throng of pedestrians crowding the Place de la Madeleine.

His name was Yuri Ryleev Kovalenko. At forty-one, he was a homicide investigator for the Russian Ministry of Justice and in Paris at the request of the French government to assist in the investigation of the murder of Alfred Neuss. Officially he was a member of the French homicide investigation team, but he had no police powers and was answerable to the senior investigating officer, Philippe Lenard, a man who showed him every professional courtesy but kept him at arm's length, including him when he chose to and at other times feeding him only the information Lenard was willing to share.

Lenard's attitude was understandable on two counts. The first was that the crime had happened in his city and his agency was expected to solve it. The second was that the French appeal for a Russian investigator had been initiated by the Russian government through their Foreign Office, with the French invitation coming as a diplomatic courtesy to avoid making the case appear as if it had some kind of international significance; instead, it would be seen as a simple request for input on the murder of a former Russian citizen. In effect Lenard had been handed a political situation in the form of a Russian detective and told to make him full party to his investigation with no more explanation than that. All of this made for somewhat strained relations between them and was one reason why Kovalenko had not yet been introduced to the *Los Angeles Times* reporter Dan Ford, or been invited when Lenard had taken Halliday to study the murder scene in the Parc Monceau.

Not invited, perhaps, but there was no rule preventing a visitor to the city from putting on dark glasses and sitting on a park bench to feed the pigeons and casually observe what was going on around him.

Doing so had given him the opportunity to learn something about Halliday on his own. And he had. He knew what he looked like, that he enjoyed or needed to drink, and the name of the hotel where he was staying. Moreover, there had been a bonus to his diligence: When Dan Ford first arrived at the Parc Monceau, a second man had been with him, and upon seeing the police, Ford had immediately spoken to that man and then had turned and walked away. Kovalenko wondered who this second man was, and why the journalist had so quickly turned him back when they'd seen the police. Given that he was accompanying Ford, it was safe to assume he had been interested in the crime, yet clearly Ford had not wanted him to be seen. But by whom—Lenard or Halliday, or both?

What was interesting was that the entire circumstance—Lenard's exclusion of him from the meeting with Halliday, a former LAPD detective who had earlier covered the Neuss situation in Los Angeles; the appearance of Ford, a newspaper reporter who had also covered the Neuss story in Los Angeles; and the unusual behavior of the man who had accompanied Ford to the park—gave further credence to Kovalenko's belief that the killing of Alfred Neuss was more than the murder/robbery it appeared and was an extension of what had taken place in the Americas nearly a year before. Which was the reason he had come to Paris in the first place.

Known to very few—the Russian Ministry of Justice, and now the Paris Prefecture of Police—was the fact that Alfred Neuss was a former Russian citizen. So were the Azov brothers, the Chicago tailors shot to death by the infamous Raymond Oliver Thorne a short time before he boarded the train for Los Angeles. In addition, two other men of Russian descent had been murdered in the Americas in the days immediately preceding Thorne's visit to Chicago, one a bank manager in San Francisco, the other a well-known sculptor in Mexico City. San Francisco and Mexico City—cities, verified by entry data on the magnetic strip on Thorne's passport, that he had visited on the dates the murders there had taken place. Four former Russian citizens killed within days of each other. The fifth, whom Thorne had been trying to get to when he was killed himself, was Alfred Neuss. That the Beverly Hills jeweler had been in London at the time no doubt saved his life. The problem was, the alleged perpetrator of most of these crimes, Raymond Oliver Thorne, was dead, his body cremated, his true identity and the motive for his crimes never known.

Because of that, Russian investigators had been sent to North America by Moscow to work with local law enforcement agencies to determine if the killings were part of an organized conspiracy against former citizens. With federal approval the LAPD had allowed the Russian investigators access to the contents of Raymond's bag recovered from the Southwest Chief. After close examination, those contents—the safe deposit keys, Raymond's handwritten references to London, the house on Uxbridge Street, the Russian Embassy, Penrith's Bar, and I. M., and the separate entry, April 7/Moscow—were as much a mystery to them as to anyone else. And while the Ruger automatic had proved to be the weapon used to kill the Azov brothers in Chicago, it was not the weapon used in the murders in either San Francisco or Mexico City. So if Raymond Thorne had committed those crimes, there was no direct evidence to tie him to them. His death and cremation and lack of any further information had ended everything, and the case and subsequent paperwork had been filed away in a block-long Moscow storeroom overflowing with the files on other unresolved murder cases. And then Alfred Neuss was viciously slain in Paris by a person or persons unknown and the file was reopened and the investigation handed to Kovalenko.

If someone asked him directly, he would have said he guessed that the murder and robbery of Neuss and the killings in the Americas earlier were *razborka,* a violent settling of some kind of accounts. Why, or for what reason, he had no idea. Moreover, there was no hard evidence now, nor had there been before, to suggest he was right.

Nonetheless Neuss's murder had brought renewed interest—not only from the Russian Ministry of Justice and the Paris Prefecture of Police, but from a retired LAPD homicide detective and a *Los Angeles Times* reporter, both of whom had covered the Neuss story earlier.

In Russia, foreign journalists and their friends and activities were almost always under suspicion because they were presumed to be an element of their country's intelligence community, and in Kovalenko's mind there was no reason it should be any different here in Paris. What Ford and Halliday had discussed at L'Ecluse was not possible to know. Equally mysterious was the identity of Ford's friend in the park and why he had acted as he had.

There was no reason to believe that the Russian investigators sent to the Americas earlier had been deprived of information. On the other hand, since approval for them to examine evidence and confer with local law enforcement had come through Washington, it was not out of the question to suppose they had not been told everything. Taken as a whole, and considering Russian experience with foreign journalists and Ford's actions in the park, the combination piqued Kovalenko's interest, and he told himself Ford might be a key man, one around whom things swirled. And therefore one to be watched, and carefully.

26

DAN AND NADINE FORD'S APARTMENT
ON THE RUE DAUPHINE.
STILL TUESDAY, JANUARY 14. 8:40 P.M.

"Halliday didn't bring up Raymond for no reason. He didn't ask for my help for no reason." Nicholas Marten leaned in across the dinner table in the Fords' compact dining room.

Marten had seen Ford and Halliday cross together from the Parc Monceau and wait for the taxi as Ford had hoped, realizing the maneuver was a signal for him to take the Citroën and get out of there. And he had, managing his way across the city and driving in circles until he finally found Ford's address on the rue Dauphine and surprising Ford's wife, the pert Nadine, only a little because she had known he was coming. Although she was beginning to feel the effects of her pregnancy, she'd welcomed him right away, making him a sandwich and pouring him a glass of wine and entertaining him until her husband came home, doing it all with warmth and cheer because he was Dan Ford's best friend in the world.

And now those two best friends in the world sat arguing at

the dinner table in the Fords' small first-floor apartment. Marten was determined to call Halliday and find out what he knew about Raymond. Ford wanted him to get out of Paris right then and stay out until Halliday left.

Maybe Marten would have listened if he hadn't seen Halliday in the Parc Monceau walking the Neuss murder scene with Lenard the way Halliday had walked the Josef Speer murder scene in MacArthur Park in L.A. with Red, himself, and the others. It was an image he couldn't shake, nor could he get rid of the sea of memories that came with it. Memories that made him realize how enormous the guilt still was—not just for the innocent people who died because of his misjudgment about the kind of man Raymond was, but also, self-defense or not, for his own shooting to death of Roosevelt Lee and Marty Valparaiso in the rail yards. The stark recollection of it was so clear at this moment the acrid stench of gunpowder might as well have hung above the chair where he sat.

Halliday's presence had brought it all back and somehow he had to address it, finally and once and for all. Talk it through. And out. Cry. Scream. Rage. Whatever it took, in some way, any way, to put it behind him. It was why he had to talk with Jimmy Halliday. He was the only person on earth who would understand, because he had been right there when it happened.

"What if the reason he brought up Raymond and asked for help was nothing but bait?" Dan Ford put down his coffee cup and sat back from the table. "Give you a taste of something strong enough to tempt you to tip your hand and call him."

"You think he's got it in for me?"

"How do you know he wasn't the one who started the whole LAPD thing against you in the first place? And even if he wasn't, since then he's lost his friends, his self-respect, his job, and his family. Maybe he knows what we've found out about Raymond. Maybe he's found out even more and wants to tell you about it. Then again, what if he holds you responsible for all of it and wants to even the score? You want to take that chance?"

Marten studied him, then looked away. Ford was only trying to protect him, he knew, the same as he had earlier on the ride in from the airport and then when they'd seen Halliday in the park. And he might have been right to do it, but there was one thing he was wrong about. No matter how far down Halliday was, he would never have been the one who turned against Marten. Dan Ford might have guessed what had gone on in the rail yards, but he had never pressed Marten to talk about it and Marten never had. So there was no way for him to know what Halliday had done there.

So, yes, maybe Ford was right by trying to keep him from Halliday, but alongside his own emotions, the weight of his own guilt and remorse and just wanting to talk with him, there was the possibility that what Ford had suggested was true—that Halliday had learned something and wanted to tell him about it. Both those things overrode Ford's common sense. He turned back.

"I want to see Halliday. I want to go to his hotel. Now, tonight."

"See him?" Ford was incredulous. "As in face-to-face?"

"Yes."

Nadine Ford put her hand on her husband's. She understood only a little of what had been said, but she knew the argument had suddenly gone in another direction. She saw the way they looked at each other and she felt the emotion of it and it frightened her.

"*C'est bien,*" Ford told her gently in French, smiling and patting her belly. "*C'est bien.*" It's okay.

Marten had to smile. Nadine had begun teaching Dan to speak French when they were still in L.A. Obviously she'd been a good tutor, because his ability with the language was a chief reason for his posting to the Paris bureau, and by now it seemed to fit him with the comfort of an old sweater.

Ford's cell phone chirped in the kitchen and he got up to answer it.

"Dan Ford," Marten heard him say. Then, "*Comment? Où?*" What? Where? Ford's voice was suddenly filled with surprise and alarm. Marten and Nadine looked toward the kitchen. They could see Ford standing there, the phone in his hand, listening.

"*Oui, merci,*" he said finally and clicked off. A moment later he came back into the room.

"That was Inspector Lenard just back from Monaco. Halliday was found dead in his hotel room."

"What?"

"He was murdered."

27

Dan Ford pulled the Citroën into a parking space a half block down the street from the hotel. From where they sat they could see uniformed police and a number of emergency vehicles at the hotel entrance. Among them was Lenard's unmarked maroon Peugeot.

"Nick," Ford warned quietly, "right now nobody knows who you are. If the LAPD hasn't been informed yet, they will be soon enough. You go in there, Lenard will want to know who you are and why you're there. You'll be asking for all kinds of trouble."

Marten smiled. "Use your charm. Just tell him I'm a friend from the States."

"You're determined to get yourself killed, aren't you?"

"Dan, Jimmy Halliday was a friend and a partner. Maybe I can get some sense of what happened. Maybe better than the French police. At least I can try." Suddenly Marten paused. "He would have done the same for me."

Lenard was there when they came in. Another detective was with him. A small tech crew worked both the bedroom and the bathroom just off it. A police photographer took pictures wherever he was asked.

Halliday's body was on the bed. He wore a white T-shirt and boxer shorts. The T-shirt and the bedding around his upper torso were soaked in blood. The curious thing was the way his head was twisted back on the pillow. Another step and they could see why. His throat had been cut, nearly through to the spine.

"*Qui est-ce*?" Who is he? Lenard was looking at Marten.

"Nicholas Marten, *un ami américain*," Ford said. An American friend. "*D'accord?*" Okay?

Lenard studied Marten for a moment, then nodded. "As long as he doesn't get in the way or touch anything," he said in English.

Ford nodded gratefully. "Any idea who did it or how it happened?"

"There is blood on the carpet by the door. I would think perhaps he was resting or in the toilet and someone came. He went to answer the door and whoever it was cut him the moment he opened it, then carried him to the bed. It was done very quickly, the murder weapon very sharp, a razor, I would think, or some kind of attack knife."

"What was it, robbery?" Ford asked.

"At first glance, it doesn't seem so. His wallet appears untouched. His luggage was not yet unpacked."

Marten took a careful step toward the bed, trying to get a better look at Halliday. As he did so a bearded man in a baggy suit stepped from the bathroom.

He was about forty, a little overweight, and had big brown dog-eyes that almost made him look sleepy.

"This is Inspector Kovalenko, Russian Ministry of Justice," Lenard said to Ford. "He's helping us with the Alfred Neuss murder. Neuss was a former Russian citizen."

"I knew Russian investigators were in L.A. following up shortly after the Raymond Thorne incident," Ford said with a brief glance at Marten. Here was the answer to Marten's wondering if anyone had been in touch with the Russians. "I didn't know that Neuss was Russian." He looked to Kovalenko. "I'm Dan Ford, *Los Angeles Times.*"

"I know who you are, Mr. Ford," Kovalenko said in heavily accented English. "I understand Detective Halliday was a friend of yours. My deepest condolences," he said genuinely.

"Thank you."

Kovalenko's eyes went to Marten. "And you are a friend of Mr. Ford."

"Yes, Nicholas Marten."

"How do you do, Mr. Marten?"

Kovalenko nodded slightly. This was the man in the park who had so quickly turned away when he had seen the police; and here he was walking straight into their midst with no hesitation whatsoever.

Ford looked to Lenard. "Who found him?"

"A housekeeper came to turn down the bed. There was no answer when she knocked, so she let herself in with her passkey. She saw him and immediately called the manager. It was then about seven-twenty."

The police photographer moved in to photograph the bed from a different angle, and Marten stepped back. It gave him a chance to look at Halliday more carefully. His face was more lined than he'd remembered. And he was thin, too thin really. And there was something more. For somebody still in his early thirties, he seemed almost old. Whatever he looked like now, or had before he was killed, he was still the man who had been instrumental in getting him into the squad in the first place, who had been with him through the Donlan crises and through all the horror and bloodshed with Raymond. And finally, the man who, in the most crucial moment of his life, had come over to his side and saved Rebecca and himself from the crazed Len Polchak.

Suddenly an enormous wave of anger and loss washed over Marten. Without thinking, he looked to Lenard.

"The housekeeper. Did she call the manager or go get him?"

Dan Ford shook his head, warning him off.

"You mean did she call from here or from somewhere else?" It was too late, Lenard was already involved.

"Yes."

"As you might suspect, she was horrified. She ran from the room and used a house telephone at the end of the hallway near the elevators." Lenard glanced at Ford. "I believe your friend is suggesting the murderer might have still been somewhere here, perhaps in the bathroom or closet, and then left when the housekeeper went for help." He looked back to Marten. "Yes?"

"I only asked what happened."

Ford swore under his breath. It wasn't just Lenard who had Marten's attention. Kovalenko did, too. He didn't give it time to go any further.

"I know Halliday's wife." He stepped between Marten and Lenard. "Would you like me to make the call?"

"If you wish."

At their exchange, Marten stepped back and looked around the room. Halliday's suitcase was open on a luggage rack at the foot of the bed and filled to the top with his clothes. Even his shaving kit was there, tucked to the side. It looked as if he had barely opened it before whatever happened, happened.

"Nick, let's go, let these guys do their work." Dan Ford was standing by the door, and Marten could tell he wanted him out of there and quickly.

"Do you know of any reason someone would have wanted to kill him?" Lenard asked Ford as Marten reached them.

"No. None."

"Perhaps you will come and see me in the morning. Maybe together we can shed some light on this."

"Of course," Ford said, and he and Marten turned for the door.

"Mr. Ford." Kovalenko stood blocking it. "You knew Detective Halliday when you were working in Los Angeles, correct?"

"Yes."

"I believe he was a member of the legendary Five-Two Squad, yes?"

"Yes, he was." Dan Ford was cool and matter-of-fact.

"The reputation of the Five-Two is very well known to policemen around the world. Russia is no exception. Its late commander, Arnold McClatchy, I have a picture of him in my office. He was a hero, yes? Like Gary Cooper in *High Noon*."

"You know a lot about America," Ford said.

"No, just a little." Kovalenko smiled slightly, then looked to Marten. "Were you acquainted with Detective Halliday as well, Mr. Marten?"

Marten hesitated. He'd known that by staying in Paris and getting involved in Neuss's murder, then wanting to meet Halliday, and finally going to the murder scene where the French police were, he was taking on more and more risk, as Ford kept reminding him. That risk-taking had led to his questioning Lenard the way he had, and unfortunately the Russian detective had picked up on it. Bearded and pudgy with his big brown eyes, Kovalenko looked soft and professorial, but that was a cover. In truth he was sharp and highly perceptive. Moreover, he'd done his homework. He knew about the 5-2 and he knew about Red. Whether he actually had a photograph of him was beside the point. What Kovalenko was doing was looking for a recognition factor, some indication that either Marten or Dan Ford knew more about what happened here than they were letting on.

Or, Marten suddenly thought, maybe the question was really about Neuss and what Ford and Marten might know that Kovalenko, the French police, and the Russian investigators who had gone to L.A. earlier did not.

Whatever it was, and whatever Kovalenko was trying to find out, Marten knew he had to be careful. If he said the wrong thing or gave any hint at all of familiarity with the case, it would only make the Russian push harder, and that was the last thing he wanted.

"Yes, I knew him, but not well," he said evenly. "What little there was came mostly from Dan's stories about him."

"I see." Kovalenko smiled pleasantly and eased up a little but not completely. "You are in Paris visiting Mr. Ford, are you not?"

"Yes."

"May I ask where you are staying?"

"At my apartment," Ford answered for him.

"Thank you." Kovalenko smiled again.

"My office at nine tomorrow morning," Lenard said to Ford.

"Nine, yes. *Au revoir.*" Ford nodded and then hustled Marten out the door.

28

"Why did you have to start with the questions?" Ford sounded like Marten's father, an older brother, a wife, and a boss all rolled into one, ripping him under his breath as they walked fast down the hallway and toward the elevators. Uniformed police were everywhere, cordoning off the entire area around Halliday's room. "Lenard might have let it go for now, but tomorrow morning he's going to be asking me who the hell you are and what you were up to."

"Alright, so I said something."

"Nick," Ford warned him, "just keep your mouth shut."

They reached the end of the corridor and turned toward the bank of elevators.

"Ask one of these cops to point out the house phone the housekeeper used," Marten said abruptly. "I want to see where it is."

"For God's sake, stay out of this."

"Dan, Jimmy Halliday had his throat cut."

Ford stopped, took a breath, and went up to the closest uniform. He told him in French that Inspector Lenard had spoken of a house telephone the hotel housekeeper used to call the manager and asked him where it was.

"*Là-bas.*" Over there.

The uniform pointed to a simple white hotel house telephone mounted on the wall across from them. Marten glanced at it, then back down the hallway the way they had come. The phone was eighty, maybe a hundred feet from the open door to Halliday's room. A housekeeper, horrified and rushing toward it, would have had her back to the door the whole way, giving anyone in the room more than enough time to go to the fire stairs at the opposite end unseen.

"*Merci,*" Ford said, and turned Marten back toward the elevators.

As they reached them, the doors to the nearest elevator opened and two ambulance attendants came out pushing a gurney with a silvery gray body bag folded on top. They passed without a glance and turned down the corridor toward Halliday's room.

"Dammit," Marten said out loud. "Damn it to hell."

29

Both men stared at the floor as the doors closed and the elevator started down.

"I don't understand how somebody with Halliday's training and experience could let himself be taken out like that," Ford said quietly.

Marten tried to replay what happened. "You're in a seemingly safe hotel, depressed, jet-lagged, a little drunk, and maybe taking a nap, and somebody knocks on the door. You have no reason to expect trouble, so you answer it. Or if not, you at least ask who it is. The person outside replies innocently enough and in

French, like hotel staff. What's to even think about? So you open it. And whoever's there knows exactly what they are going to do the moment you do. The instant slice of a razor or knife across your throat." Marten's eyes glistened in anger as he thought about it. The ease, the simplicity of it.

"It was a deliberate murder, Dan. So the question is why? What did the perpetrator think Halliday knew or did or was going to do that he had to be killed for it? And Neuss was Russian? We never knew that. Did you?"

"No." Ford shook his head. "Obviously the Russian investigators who came to L.A. kept it to themselves. I tell you something else," Ford said, "Fabien Curtay, the Monaco diamond merchant, was a Russian expatriate, too."

"What?"

"I didn't make the connection until Lenard talked about Neuss. Curtay was one of the world's top diamond traders. Neuss was a wealthy Beverly Hills jeweler. Both were Russian. So were the Azov brothers Raymond allegedly killed in Chicago."

"You're thinking diamond traffic, the Russian mafia?" Marten said. "That's what this is all about? What Raymond was about? What was supposed to have gone on in London? And maybe what Halliday was onto and why he was killed?"

"It would explain the plane sent for Raymond, what happened to his files, even the circumstances of the cremation and what happened to the people involved with it afterward. It would also explain the Russian investigators in L.A. afterward and what Kovalenko is doing in Paris."

Marten nodded. "I agree he's here for more than a murder investigation, but I have yet to see anyone send a private jet to rescue a hit man. The idea might fit with the Chicago killings and with Neuss and with Fabien Curtay, but add Raymond and it doesn't feel right.

"I was in too many rooms with him. I watched his face, heard him talk, saw how he moved. He was well educated and fluent in at least three languages, and maybe a fourth, which was Russian. He might have been a highly trained killer, but he was more aristocrat than hired gun."

Marten half shrugged. "Maybe Halliday was playing it as Russian mafia, and maybe Lenard and Kovalenko are, too.

Maybe they'll find something in that line, but I doubt it. I was there with Raymond, Dan." Marten paused. "It's something else."

It was just after ten when Ford steered the Citroën away from the hotel. The clear skies of earlier had become overcast during dinner, and now a light rain was falling. Through it Marten could see the grand spectacle of the Eiffel Tower disappear into low-hanging clouds two-thirds of the way up. Then they were past it and crossing the Seine on the Pont d'Iéna and moving onto the Rive Droite, the Right Bank, where the Arc de Triomphe was and the Parc Monceau and L'Ecluse Madeleine. Minutes afterward they were traveling along the Avenue de New York and heading back along the river toward the Quai des Tuileries and the Louvre. The whole time neither man said a word. Finally Dan Ford spoke.

"You're the last of them, you know that."

"The last of who?"

"The squad. Halliday said that this afternoon. A hundred years and you and he were the only ones left. Now there's only you."

"I'm hardly the guy they would want to stand up for it, or who even wants to remember he was a part of it." Marten looked off and for a long moment was silent. "Halliday was a good guy," he said finally.

"That's why his murder makes it all the worse. You thought all this was dead, but we can both see it's not." Ford slowed the Citroën behind a taxi and looked over at Marten, his glass eye behind the black horn-rims revealing nothing, the other, the good eye, deeply troubled and full of concern. "What if I told you to get out of here now and go back to Manchester, like I did before? That I would handle it and let you know what was going on?" Ford looked back to the traffic in front of him. "You wouldn't do it."

"No."

"Not for me, not for Rebecca, not for Lady Clem. Not even for yourself as Nick Marten, student of landscape architecture, somebody who is safe and sane and finally doing something he's wanted to do all his life."

"No."

"No, of course not. Instead you're going after this with all you have and for as long as it takes until you get it or it gets you. And if lovable Raymond is somehow still alive, you won't know until it's too late. Because by then you'll already be in the cave and then—suddenly there he is."

Marten stared at Ford and then abruptly looked away. Ahead were the lights of Notre Dame. To the right was the long dark ribbon that was the Seine. Across it, through the rain, were the lights of the Rive Gauche, the Left Bank, where they were headed and where Dan Ford lived.

"You're going to do it anyway. Maybe this will help," Ford said and slid something from inside his blue blazer and gave it to Marten.

"What is it?" Marten turned over an old, overstuffed, dog-eared, daily calendar, its leather covers and bulging contents held together by a thick rubber band.

"Halliday's appointment book. I took it off the night table while you were playing detective with Lenard. Halliday said he wanted to talk to you. Maybe he still will."

The slightest hint of a grin crossed Marten's face. "You are a thief."

"It's what happens when somebody knows somebody else better than he ought to."

30

The sound of a door opening and closing woke Nicholas Marten from a deep sleep. It was dark, and for the moment he had no idea where he was. Had someone come in or gone out? Or had he dreamt it? He pressed the button on his digital watch and for the briefest second the face glowed in the dark.

2:12 A.M.

He sat up and listened.
Nothing.

Gentle spill from a streetlamp outside the window gave just enough illumination for him to remember where he was—on the couch in Dan Ford's living room. He listened again, but there was nothing. Then he heard the distant slam of a car door and a moment later an engine start up. Quickly he threw back the blankets and went to the window. Twenty yards down he saw Ford's white Citroën pull away from the tight parking space Ford had squeezed into when they had come back from the Hotel Eiffel Cambronne.

He looked at his watch again.

2:16 A.M.

No, not 2:16. It was 3:16. His watch was still on Manchester time; Paris was an hour later.

Seconds later he pulled on the robe Ford had lent him and walked the short distance to Dan and Nadine's bedroom.

"Nadine?"

There was a long silence, and then the door opened and a sleepy Nadine Ford stood there. She wore a long white night-dress, and her right hand rested on her very pregnant belly.

"Did Dan go out?"

"It is not a problem, Nicholas," she said quietly and a little awkwardly in English. "He got a telephone call, and then put on his clothes and went."

"Was it the police?"

"No, not the police. It was a call he had been waiting for, something he was working on, he didn't tell me."

"So you don't know where he went."

"No." Nadine smiled. "He is alright, don't worry."

"I'm sure," Marten said. L.A. or Paris, married or not, nothing had changed. It was how Dan Ford worked and always had—a tip, an informant, the hint of a story, and he was gone. He was usually working on a dozen articles at once, and time of day or where he had to go to get information made no difference. It was why he was Dan Ford and as good as he was.

"Go back to bed," Nadine said. "I will see you in the morning."

She smiled and closed the door, and Marten padded back down the hallway to the couch. He didn't like the idea of Ford going out alone. Too much was still going on with too many questions still unanswered. He supposed he could call Ford's cell phone and ask him to come back and pick him up. On the other hand, if Ford had thought he was in danger, he would have taken Marten with him to begin with. Moreover, Nadine had not been alarmed, not the way she had been earlier at the dinner table when they were talking about Halliday. After all, Ford was a correspondent for a major newspaper and this was his job. French cooking or a dinner party or whatever, insiders had information that could lead to an important story or just frothy gossip, and either was news, and that was Dan Ford's business. So, if Nadine had seen this as everyday business and was not concerned, why should he be?

Marten glanced out the window once again, then went back to the couch and pulled the blankets up around him. The street outside was quiet; Nadine was asleep and unconcerned about her husband. Yet something troubled him. It was as much a feeling as anything—that Ford was going somewhere he shouldn't and wasn't aware of it.

Marten rolled over and scrunched up his pillow, trying to get comfortable and to shake the unease he felt inside. Purposely he let his thoughts go to Halliday's battered, overstuffed appointment book crammed with loose pages, which contained last year's calendar inserts as well as this year's (it was only mid-January, the year had barely started). Its pages were filled with Halliday's small, hard-to-read reverse-slash handwriting Marten remembered from L.A. It was a book that seemed more of a personal journal with appointments and accompanying notes concerning himself and his children than a revelation about the squad or Raymond. And at first glance, it appeared to hold no significant information at all.

Slowly the thoughts of Halliday's book faded to visions of Lady Clem, the scent of her, the sensuous feel of her body against his, her smile and her droll, if sometimes raunchy, humor. He grinned at the memory of his terrifying conversation with Lord Prestbury in the secretive tavern in the bowels of Whitworth Hall in the moments before she'd rescued him by pulling the fire alarm.

Clem.

Abruptly his smile faded, pushed aside by the echo of what

Dan Ford had said. *If lovable Raymond is somehow still alive, you won't know until it's too late. Because by then you'll already be in the cave and then—suddenly there he is.*

Raymond.

The disquiet in him grew stronger.

Like a whispered voice it told him that Neuss was dead because of Raymond. So was Fabien Curtay. So was Jimmy Halliday. And now Dan Ford was somewhere out there alone in the rain and dark.

Suddenly he heard himself speak out loud. "The pieces," he said, "the pieces."

Quickly Marten got up. Fumbling to find his cell phone in the faint light, he dialed Ford's number. The call rang through but there was no answer. Finally a recorded voice came on speaking French. He didn't understand the language, but he knew what was being said—the caller was either away from the phone or out of the calling area, please try again later. Marten hung up and redialed. Again it rang through; again he got the same message.

His mind racing, his first thought was to call Lenard, but then he realized he had no idea where Ford had gone; even if he did reach the French policeman, what would he tell him? Slowly he clicked off and stood there in the dark. Dan Ford was on his own and there was nothing he could do about it.

31

3:40 A.M.

Yuri Kovalenko switched on the rented Opel's cruise control, purposely staying a half mile behind Ford's white Citroën as the reporter drove southeast along the Seine, passing the Gare d'Austerlitz and continuing on through Ivry-sur-Seine, still following the river.

Kovalenko had no idea where Ford was going, but he was surprised that his friend was not with him. But then he had been equally surprised to see Marten walk into the hotel room in the midst of the police.

From their brief encounter at the murder scene it had been hard to get a grip on who Marten was or why he was there. Or what his relationship was with Ford, or had been with Halliday. The one thing he had learned was that from the bold way Marten had questioned Lenard, it was not the inspector he had turned away from in the park, it had been Halliday. So at least that question was answered.

In the morning, when Ford came to Lenard's office, Kovalenko would learn more, and when he did—when he had Marten's full name, his employment, and the address where he lived—he would begin a thorough background check. In doing so, he would find answers, or at least the beginnings of answers, to some of these uncertainties. To Kovalenko, Nicholas Marten was more than simply the reporter's *"un ami américain,"* an American friend.

Ahead, the Citroën's taillights suddenly brightened as Ford touched the brakes; then Kovalenko saw him change lanes and accelerate again, crossing the Seine at Alfortville and taking the N6 Autoroute south toward Montgeron.

Kovalenko shifted the position of his hands on the Opel's steering wheel. He was not a man who slept well when he was in the middle of a murder investigation, and the fact that there was now a second murder only added to his suspicion that Ford probably knew more than he was telling. Marten's staying at the reporter's apartment only added to the intrigue and was why Kovalenko had decided on the surveillance long after everyone else had gone home and to bed. He had no idea what he hoped to gain from it, nor had he brought it up to Lenard, because there was no point in trying to make it official. It was simply an undertaking he thought prudent.

He'd found a parking space just down and across from Ford's residence at ten minutes past midnight and snuggled the Opel into it. Then, on the chance that even at this hour some pertinent information might be exchanged, he took a small Kalinin-7 micropak from his briefcase, put on its headset, and fixed its tiny parabolic antenna on Ford's front window. A call on Ford's landline phone would be impossible to intercept without a physical wiretap. But Kovalenko had seen Ford with a cell phone twice, giving it to Halliday to use in L'Ecluse and then later on the street when Ford left, so there was every chance that was the device he used primarily. If a call came in on it, the Kalinin-7 would pick up the conversation almost as clearly as if Kovalenko were on the line himself.

At twelve-fifteen Kovalenko had settled in to listen and watch and wait. Once, about two-thirty, he thought about calling his wife, Tatyana, in Moscow but realized she would still be sleeping. At that point he must have dozed off because at five minutes past three a steady beep through his headset woke him, alerting him to an incoming call. The phone rang three times before someone clicked on. "Dan Ford," he heard the journalist answer sleepily.

Next came a male voice speaking French. "This is Jean-Luc," the voice said. "I have the map. Can you meet me at four-thirty?"

"Yes," Ford said in French, then immediately clicked off, and the Kalinin-7 went silent.

Seven minutes later the front door to Ford's apartment building opened and the reporter stepped out into the rain and walked to his car. Kovalenko wondered who this Jean-Luc was and what map he was talking about. Whoever he was and whatever the map was, it was obviously important enough for Ford to get out of bed at that hour, dress, and drive off alone in the rain.

THE N6 AUTOROUTE.

The Opel's windshield wipers beat gently back and forth, the wet roadway ahead pitch-black except for the distant Citroën's taillights. Kovalenko looked at his watch.

4:16 A.M.

It was 6:16 in the morning Moscow time. Tatyana would be up and beginning the lengthy process of getting their three children ready for school. They were eleven, nine, and seven, and each was more independent than the other. He often wondered how they could be the children of employees of the Ministry of Justice and of RTR, the state-owned television network, where his wife was a production assistant. Yuri and Tatyana Kovalenko lived their lives following orders. Much of the time their children did not, especially when those orders came from their parents.

4:27 A.M.

Again he saw the Citroën's brake lights flare up. They had just passed a forested area about fifteen minutes south of Montgeron, and Ford was slowing.

Now he turned, taking an off-ramp and leaving the N6.

Kovalenko slowed as well, then shut off his headlights and took the same exit. In the rain and dark it was difficult to see anything, and he was afraid he might go off the tarmac and into a ditch, but his car and Ford's had been the only two on the highway and he didn't dare risk letting Ford think he was being followed.

Straining to see, he reached the bottom of the ramp and stopped. Then he saw the Citroën moving away in the distance as Ford accelerated west. Immediately Kovalenko clicked the Opel's headlights back on and sped after him. A mile later he slowed, holding his speed.

One minute passed, then two. Suddenly Ford turned right onto a secondary road, moving north along the forested banks of the rural Seine.

Kovalenko followed, watching as the Opel's headlights illuminated thick woods on either side of the road with occasional breaks to his left, which suggested some sort of access to the river. Abruptly the trees to his right gave way to a golf course and a turnoff for the village of Soisy-sur-Seine.

4:37 A.M.

The Citroën's brake lights shone in the distance, and Kovalenko slowed once again. Ford slowed even more, then suddenly swung the Citroën left, off the highway and toward the river.

Kovalenko continued at speed. Twenty seconds later he was

at Ford's turnoff point and moving past it. Through the dark and rain he saw Ford bring the Citroën to a stop beside another car and abruptly shut off the lights.

Kovalenko drove on. A quarter mile later the road veered sharply right through a thick stand of conifers. Again he switched off his headlights, then made a sharp U-turn and came back.

Slowing, he rolled to a stop fifty yards from where Ford had turned off the highway, and stared into the dark, trying to see the parked cars. It was impossible. In the blackness, he opened the Opel's glove compartment, took out a pair of binoculars, and scanned the area where the Citroën had stopped. There was nothing but the same pervasive black he had seen with the naked eye.

32

Kovalenko put down the binoculars and ran his hand over the Makarov automatic in his belt holster, cursing himself for not bringing a night-vision scope.

Once again, he tried the binoculars. If there was movement near the parked cars, he couldn't see it. He waited. Sixty seconds, ninety, then three full minutes. Finally he dropped the binoculars on the seat, turned up his collar, and stepped out into the rain.

For a moment he did nothing but listen. All he could hear was the sound of the rain and the deep-throated wash of the river rushing past in the distance. Slowly he lifted the Makarov and moved forward.

Forty paces and the ground under his feet went from roadside mud to the crushed gravel of the turnoff. He stopped and peered into the black, listening again. It was the same as before, the drum of the rain with the muted roar of the river behind it. He went forward another twenty paces and stopped. He didn't understand; he was nearly to the river's edge and there was nothing.

Nervously he shifted the Makarov from one hand to the

other and moved to the river's edge. Black water rushed past
fifteen feet below. He turned back. Where were the cars? Had
he misjudged, had they been parked farther down than he
thought? At that moment he saw the gleam of headlights as a
large truck rounded the bend in the highway. For an instant its
lights swept the area and then it was past, vanishing in the distance.

"Shto?" What? Kovalenko said out loud in Russian. Brief as it
had been, the truck's headlights had illuminated the entire area
and there was nothing there. Ford's white Citroën and the other
car were gone. But how? It had taken him less than thirty seconds
to drive past, make a U-turn, and come back. Even in the dark and
rain, the place where he'd stopped had a clear view of the area
where he now stood. If the two cars had driven off, they would either have had to come past him or go the other way; in the other
direction the road was straight for at least two miles, and they
would not have driven that far at night and in this weather with
their lights off. So where were they? Automobiles did not just vanish. There was no explanation. None at all.

Unless.

Kovalenko turned and looked back toward the river.

33

VIRY-CHÂTILLON, FRANCE. WEDNESDAY, JANUARY 15.
BRIGHT SUN AND COLD AFTER THE RAIN. 11:30 A.M.

People lined the banks on either side of the river watching in silence as the tow truck's winch cable tightened and a white two-
door Citroën, its windows open, was slowly pulled from the
water and up onto the embankment. There was no need to wonder whether someone was inside. Police divers had already confirmed it.

Nicholas Marten moved closer, standing just behind Lenard
and Kovalenko as the divers pulled open the driver's door.

Muddy water poured out; then a collective gasp went up as the closest people saw what was inside.

"Oh, God," Marten breathed.

Lenard went down the embankment alone and studied the situation; then he stepped back and waved for his tech people, and they and the commander of the Viry-Châtillon police, whose patrol officers had found the car hung up on a rock outcropping in the river below, went down to the Citroën. Kovalenko followed.

Lenard watched a moment longer and then climbed back up, looking to Marten as he came. "I'm sorry you had to see that. I should have kept you back."

Marten half nodded. Below he could see Kovalenko squat down and study the corpse. Several seconds later he stood and came up beside them, the cold breeze off the water whipping his hair. Marten could tell from his expression and that of Lenard that they, like him, had never seen anything like what was in the car. Dan Ford had been all but butchered with some kind of razor-sharp weapon.

"If it's any comfort," Kovalenko said quietly in his heavy Russian accent, "brutal as it was, it seems to have been done very quickly. As it was with Detective Halliday, the throat was sliced straight across and almost to the spinal column. I would think the other wounds came afterward. If there was a struggle, it would have been brief and beforehand, so perhaps he didn't suffer." Kovalenko looked to Lenard as the divers moved away and the tech people began their work.

"It looks as if it was done inside the vehicle and then the perpetrator opened the windows and rolled the car into the river hoping it would sink," Kovalenko said. "The current picked it up and took it downriver until it became tangled in the rocks and stopped here."

Lenard's radio suddenly crackled, and he turned away to answer it.

"Brought it down from where?" Marten looked at Kovalenko.

"The Citroën went into the river a number of miles upstream, near Soisy-sur-Seine. I know because I followed Mr. Ford there from his apartment."

"You followed him?"

"Yes"

"Why? He was a reporter."

"I'm afraid that is my business, Mr. Marten."

"Was it your business to let that happen?" Marten's eyes swung angrily to the Citroën, then back to Kovalenko. "If you were there, why didn't you stop it?"

"The circumstance was beyond my control."

"Was it?"

"Yes."

Lenard clicked off his radio and looked to Kovalenko. "They've found the other car at the pullout where you were. The current took it only a short distance before it became lodged between boulders at the bottom."

34

Lenard drove the maroon Peugeot south under puffy white clouds and through the bucolic countryside that bordered the rural Seine. Kovalenko rode beside him; Marten was in the back. All three were silent, as they had been on the drive from Paris, the only sound the hum of the motor and the tires over the road.

Earlier, in Paris, they had asked Marten if he wished to come with them to view the recovery of the car. The real purpose then had been for him to identify Ford's body and spare Nadine the awful task. He wasn't sure why they had brought him with them now when they could as easily have had a patrol car take him back to Paris.

Marten looked out at the passing countryside, sickened and numbed, trying to piece together what had happened. When Ford had still not returned home at eight that morning, Marten had tried his cell phone without success. By nine he had called Lenard's office to see if perhaps Ford had gone directly there for his appointment with Lenard and Kovalenko. It was then he'd been told that both detectives were on their way to Ford's apartment on the rue Dauphine. Marten knew instantly what it meant and tried to prepare Nadine. Her reaction was to calmly call her brother and sister, both of whom lived within blocks of each other, and ask them to come over. In the brief, tension-filled moments before the police arrived, Marten had had the presence of mind to take Halliday's appointment book and give it to Nadine to hide away. She'd done it just as the front doorbell chimed.

Several police cars, a diver's van, and a large tow truck were at the scene when Lenard pulled in and stopped. The three got out and crossed the gravel to the top of a rocky ledge that stood two or three times a man's height above the swift flow of the river.

The tow truck had backed up to the edge of the bank and had its lift arm out over the water, its heavy cable attached to something beneath the water's surface. Lenard looked at two divers below him in the water. One of them gave him the thumbs-up and he nodded. The diver signaled the tow truck. A motor revved, its winch turned, and the cable tightened.

"Monsieur Marten." Lenard watched the top of an automobile become visible in the water below. "Does the name Jean-Luc mean anything to you?"

"No. Should it?"

The truck's motor grew louder as the cable fought against the weight of the car and the pull of the river.

Lenard took his eyes from it to look at Marten directly. "Dan Ford was coming here to meet someone named Jean-Luc. Do you know who he is?"

"No."

"Did he ever talk about a map?"

"Not to me."

Lenard held Marten's gaze a moment longer, then turned back just as the top of a gray Toyota sedan broke the surface. The truck's motor revved higher, and the car was lifted into the air. When it was high enough to clear the riverbank the lift arm swung landward, bringing the dripping Toyota over the gravel. Lenard nodded and immediately the car was lowered to the ground. Like Ford's Citroën's, the Toyota's windows were open, allowing the water to quickly fill it and sink it below the surface.

Lenard moved away from Marten, and he and Kovalenko approached the car together. Kovalenko reached it first, and Marten saw his face twist up as he looked into it. His expression revealed everything. Whoever was inside had suffered the same fate as Dan Ford.

35

"What is your full name, Mr. Marten?" Kovalenko had opened a small spiral notebook and was turned in the front seat, looking at Marten as Lenard drove them away from the scene and back toward Paris.

"Nicholas Marten, M-A-R-T-E-N."

"Middle name or initial?"

"None."

"Where do you live?"

"Manchester, England. I'm a graduate student at the university."

"Place of birth?" Kovalenko was talking easily, his big dog-eyes gently inquisitive.

"United States."

Suddenly the vision of Dan Ford's body in the river-soaked Citroën blocked out everything else. A wave of almost unbearable guilt swept over him as he remembered the infamous homemade rocket-launcher explosion that had caused Dan, at age ten, to lose his right eye and wondered, if he'd had his full sight, if he might have seen his assailant sooner and had a chance to save himself.

"What city?" he heard Kovalenko ask.

Abruptly Marten's thoughts shifted to the present. "Montpelier, Vermont," he said flatly, Nicholas Marten's history programmed into him.

"Mr. Ford was from Los Angeles. How did you happen to know him?"

"I went to California one summer when I was a teenager. I met him and we became friends." No hesitation here either. Marten had already thought it through. No need to mention Rebecca, or any other part of his life in L.A. Just keep it simple. He was Nicholas Marten from Vermont, nothing more.

"That was when you met Detective Halliday?"

"That was later. I went back after Dan had become a police beat writer." Marten looked directly at Kovalenko as he said it, giving the Russian nothing that could raise doubt. At the same time, three names rattled through him as if they'd been stamped out by a machine. Neuss. Halliday. Ford. And then one last name, the one that connected them all.

Raymond.

It had to be Raymond. But that was crazy. Raymond was dead. Or was he? And if he wasn't, who was next on his list? Him? Maybe even Rebecca? Even though Chief Harwood had expunged any record of her being at the firefight, she had been there nonetheless, and whether she remembered it or not, she had seen him, and Raymond knew it.

Suddenly he thought maybe he should tell Lenard and Kovalenko who he was and what he knew. But the minute he did they would be in touch with the LAPD, telling them John Barron was in Paris and asking them to reexamine the circumstances surrounding Raymond Thorne's supposed death and cremation. If that happened it would only be a matter of time before Gene VerMeer or the others still looking for him would descend on Paris like vultures. The late Raymond Thorne would be of little interest. It was John Barron they would be looking for.

So, no, Marten could say nothing. If Raymond was alive, Marten as "Marten" was the one who had to find out and then do something about it.

Dan Ford had been sadly prophetic when he told him this was "his war"—*and you are going after it until you get it or it gets you and everything else be damned."*

It was never more true.

"What is your age?" Kovalenko was talking to him again and at the same time scribbling something in his notebook.

"Twenty-seven."

Kovalenko looked up. "Twenty-seven?"

"Yes."

"What did you do in the years before you came to Manchester?"

Anger suddenly touched Marten. He wasn't on trial here and he'd had enough. "I'm not sure I understand why you're asking me these questions."

"Mr. Ford was murdered, Mr. Marten." Lenard was looking at him in the mirror. "You were his friend and one of the last people to see him alive. Sometimes the most trifling information becomes helpful."

It was a solid, standard answer and there was no getting around it. Marten had no choice but to try to keep his reply as vague and simple as he could.

"I traveled around, tried different things. I was a carpenter, a bartender, I tried my hand at writing. I wasn't sure what I wanted to do."

"And when you finally decided you chose a university in England. Had you ever been there before?"

"No."

Kovalenko was correct in implying that suddenly leaving America for college in the north of England was out of the ordinary. His question needed a response both detectives would believe and without a second thought. So he told the truth.

"I met a girl. She happened to be a teacher at Manchester. I followed."

"Ah." Kovalenko half grinned and again put it down in his notebook.

It was clear now why they had wanted him along, especially as they went to retrieve the second car. Identifying the body had been one thing, but seeing Ford's savaged body had been a shock for them all, and they knew Marten, as Ford's close friend, would be even more shaken than they, and they had counted on it. It was why Lenard had asked him about Jean-Luc and why Kovalenko was pressing him now, trying to make him reveal something under emotional duress he might not have otherwise. It was a course of action Marten should have been prepared for because as a homicide detective he'd done the same thing any number of times. But he hadn't been. He was out of training and had only started actively investigating again when he arrived in Paris yesterday. He'd had little time to prepare for everything. Not being ready for police questioning in a homicide investigation, even though the necessity had never been apparent, was a lapse he knew could trip him up. Kovalenko's questions also made him wonder what they were after. Yes, he had made the mistake of questioning Lenard too boldly in Halliday's hotel room, but that wasn't enough for this kind of questioning, and he knew there had to be some other reason. In the next instant he found out what it was, and it caught him wholly off guard.

"Why did you turn away in Parc Monceau when you saw Detective Halliday?" Kovalenko's soft manner and warm, doggy-eyed look had vanished. "Yesterday you came into Parc Monceau with Mr. Ford. When you saw Detective Halliday with Inspector Lenard, you immediately turned and walked away."

It wasn't just the Russian bearing down. Lenard was staring in the mirror, watching him, too, as if this were a plan between them. Let the Russian question him while Lenard watched for a reaction.

"I owed him money and had for a long time." Marten gave them something believable, as he had before. "It wasn't much, but I was embarrassed. I hadn't expected to see him there."

"How did you come to owe him money," Kovalenko pushed back, "when, as you said, you barely knew him?"

"Baseball."

"What?"

"American baseball. Halliday and Dan and I had lunch one day in L.A., we were talking baseball. We bet on a Dodgers game and I lost. I never paid him and I never saw him again until yesterday in the park, but it always bothered me. I left hoping he wouldn't see me."

"How much did you owe him?"

"Two hundred dollars."

Lenard looked back to the highway and Kovalenko's severity faded.

"Thank you, Mr. Marten," he said, then scribbled something on a notebook page and tore it off, handing it to Marten.

"That is the number of my cell phone. If you should think of anything you feel might help us, please call me." Kovalenko turned back, made a few more notations in his book, then closed it and for the rest of the time was quiet.

36

Lenard brought them back into Paris at the Porte d'Orleans, turning onto the Boulevard Raspail and passing Montparnasse Cemetery in the heart of the Left Bank, going toward Ford's apartment on the rue Dauphine. Suddenly he turned onto the rue Huysmans, drove halfway down the block, then pulled over and stopped.

"Number twenty-seven, apartment B." Lenard turned to look over his shoulder at Marten. "It is the apartment of Armand Drouin, the brother of Dan Ford's wife. It is where she is and where your personal things have been taken."

"I don't understand."

"The law allows us to take over a crime scene for investigation, and we are treating the Ford apartment as a crime scene."

"I see." Immediately Marten thought of Halliday's appointment book. Even hidden away it would be found. They were already wary of him. Even if they thought Dan had taken it they would try to blame him. And if they dusted it for fingerprints and then took his, they would have him right away. What would he say then?

"When will you be returning to England?"

"I'm not sure. I want to be here for Dan's funeral."

"If you don't mind, I would like a telephone number in Manchester where I can reach you if we have further questions."

Marten hesitated, then gave Lenard his number. It would have been foolish not to. The detective could get it in a moment if he chose. Besides, he would need every ounce of their good graces once they found Halliday's book and came asking about it.

He was pushing open the door, his mind already jumping ahead to Nadine and her brother's apartment and the mountain of emotion he knew he would find inside, when Lenard called him back.

"One last thing, Monsieur Marten. Two Americans you knew personally have been brutally murdered within a very short period of time. We don't know who did it, or why, or what is going on, but I would warn you to take extra precaution in everything. I would not want it to be you who is next pulled from the Seine."

"Neither would I."

Marten stepped out and closed the door, standing for a moment to watch as Lenard drove off. Then he turned for the apartment. As he did, he stepped directly into the path of a man walking a large Doberman. He let out a startled cry and took an awkward step back. In the very same instant the dog's ears went flat and with a horrifying snarl it lunged for Marten's throat. Marten cried out again and threw up an arm to protect himself. Immediately the man jerked on the Doberman's leash, pulling the animal back.

"Pardon," he said quickly and moved the dog past and on down the sidewalk.

His heart pounding, Marten stood frozen where he was, staring after them. For the first time since he'd left L.A. he realized he was genuinely afraid. The Doberman had only added to it. But it hadn't been the dog's fault. The animal had simply sensed the fear, and its attack had been instinctive.

The feeling itself had begun while he was still in Manchester and had first seen the article about the dead man in the park. His first reaction then was *Raymond!* But he knew Raymond was dead and he'd tried to push it away, say it wasn't so, that it was someone else who had committed the crime. Then Dan Ford had called to tell him the victim was Alfred Neuss, and again came the awful feeling that Raymond was still alive. It was a sensation made worse by Ford's revelation that all of Raymond's medical and law enforcement records had been expunged. Now Ford and Jimmy Halliday and the man in the Toyota were, like Neuss, heinously dead. And Lenard had warned him he could be next.

Raymond.

Just the idea of it chilled him to the core. He had no proof whatsoever, but inside he knew there was no question, either. It was no longer "the pieces" alone, or trying to understand what Raymond had been about, or what he'd set in motion. It was now all of those things—and Raymond himself. He was not dead at all, but alive and somewhere here in Paris.

37

Kovalenko wore two sweaters and sat huddled over his laptop in his cold and tiny fifth-floor room of the seventeenth-century Hôtel Saint Orange on the rue de Normandie in the city's Marais district. Today was Wednesday and he had been in Paris since Monday. Barely three days and he was certain he would freeze to death—in this archaic, run-down excuse for a hotel. The slightest breeze made the windows rattle mercilessly. The flooring was warped and the boards creaked loudly almost anywhere he stepped. The drawers in the lone dresser were a game of either in or out because they stuck both ways and made the simplest act of opening or closing them a wrestling match. The bath, in the *salle de bains* at the far end of the hallway, gave lukewarm water for two minutes at best before it turned ice cold. Then there was the heat. What little there was came on for less than a half hour at a time and then the furnace shut down for two or three hours more before it came on again. Finally, there were bedbugs.

Complaints to the management had been futile, and he'd had no better luck with his superior at the Ministry of Justice in Moscow when he'd called asking for permission to change hotels and was told the hotel had been selected and nothing could be done about it. Moreover, he was in Paris, not Moscow; he should count his blessings and stop complaining. End of conversation, end of telephone call. He might be in Paris, but at least in Moscow he had heat.

So the best he could do was forget his surroundings and get on with the business at hand. That was what he had done the moment he'd come in—laptop in one hand and a paper bag with a ham and cheese baguette, a container of mineral water, and a bottle of Russian vodka, all purchased in a small neighborhood market, in the other.

His first order of business was with Nicholas Marten, who was still a mystery and whom he didn't trust. He might have been a friend of Ford and known Halliday briefly, but Kovalenko didn't like his seemingly offhand yet pat answers to questions. They were definitive but vague at the same time, all except for the girl he had said he had met and followed to Manchester, where he now lived. He might be a graduate student, he might not, but there was certainly more to him than what appeared. And maybe the girl, too.

Kovalenko opened his laptop and turned it on. Three clicks of the pointer later he had the number he wanted. Readying his notepad, he picked up his cell phone and dialed.

A switchboard operator at Greater Manchester Police headquarters put him through to an Inspector Blackthorne. After he identified himself, he asked for help in verifying that a Nicholas Marten from Vermont, U.S.A., was indeed a graduate student at the University of Manchester, England.

Blackthorne took his number and said he'd see what he could do. Twenty minutes later he called back with confirmation. Nicholas Marten was indeed a registered graduate student, had been at the university since April.

Kovalenko thanked Blackthorne and hung up, satisfied but not quite. He made a notation in his notebook: *Marten in graduate school. Where did he do his undergraduate work?* And then a second: *Find out who the girl is and what her current relationship is with Marten.*

That done, he took a bite of his sandwich, washed it down with a solid two fingers of vodka, and turned back to his laptop to write out his report for the day, hoping that in doing so he might get some sense of what had happened.

Aside from the still-troubling sense about Marten, foremost in his mind were the murders of Dan Ford and the man in the other car, and the troubling questions surrounding them. Putting aside his own considerable feelings of guilt at having been unable to prevent at least the killing of Dan Ford, a number of other things remained in the forefront—the absolute butchery of the victims, the short time span between when he'd seen Ford pull into the turnout and when he had been murdered, and how the cars had been moved into the river.

Those questions were worrying enough, but they raised others. Had there been a lone perpetrator, or had he had accomplices, and by what means had he or they come there and left? For the moment Kovalenko was assuming the crimes had been committed by a male; few women had either the strength or mind-set for that kind of horrific attack. Then, too, there was the man called Jean-Luc, now confirmed to have been the body in the Toyota.

What was it he had said to Ford over the telephone? *This is Jean-Luc. I have the map. Can you meet me at four-thirty?*

Map?

What kind of map, and of what? Where was it now, and had it been the reason both men were dead?

Kovalenko took another sip of vodka and chased it down with mineral water, his thoughts shifting from the murders to something else. His surveillance of Dan Ford had had a secondary effect he hadn't reckoned on—a closer relationship with Philippe Lenard. The French policeman had kept him at a distance since his arrival, bringing him closer to the investigation only after Halliday's death. Even then Kovalenko had been content to stay in the Frenchman's shadow and work on his own. But the sudden vanishing of the cars at the river had changed things entirely, and he'd called Lenard right away, waking him in the early morning hours to report what had happened. He'd expected to be reprimanded for acting without authority but instead had been thanked for his vigilance, and Lenard had come to the scene immediately.

For whatever reason, personal frustration or pressure from above, solving the murders of Alfred Neuss and Fabien Curtay had suddenly become a Lenard priority, and who eventually took credit or became the hero seemed to make little difference. It was helpful because it brought Kovalenko closer to the heart of the investigation, but it was also complicated because his assignment reached beyond the obvious and the murders at hand, and was something the French knew nothing of. Strictly Russian, it involved the future of the Motherland herself and was known only to himself and his superiors inside the special section of the Russian Ministry of Justice to which he was attached. So working too closely with Lenard created the risk that Lenard or one of his people would sense Kovalenko was doing something else. Still, that was the way things had turned out, and he would simply have to be careful and handle it as best he could.

A sudden gust of icy wind rattled the building and made Kovalenko feel even colder than he was. Another sip of vodka, another bite of sandwich, and he shifted from his current document to the Internet to check his e-mail.

There were a half dozen, and most were personal and from Moscow: his wife; his eleven-year-old son; his eight-year-old daughter; his next-door neighbor, with whom he was still arguing over a shared storage locker in the building's basement; his immediate superior wondering where his daily report was; and then last—the one he had been hoping for.

It was from Monaco and the Monte Carlo office of Captain Alain LeMaire of the Carabiniers du Prince, Monaco's security police. LeMaire and Kovalenko had met three years earlier when both had taken an information-exchange course at Interpol headquarters in Lyon, France. Ten months later they were reunited when LeMaire assisted in freezing Russian mob-related accounts at a major Monte Carlo bank in the midst of an international Russian money-laundering scandal. And it was LeMaire whom Kovalenko had called when he'd first learned of Fabien Curtay's murder, to ask for assistance. With any luck this was it and LeMaire had found something.

His message was encrypted, but it took Kovalenko only seconds to decode.

Re: F. Curtay. Large personal safe at his residence found compromised. Curtay kept a precise inventory of the safe's contents and dates deposited. Many items are of great value but only two are missing: (1) small reel of Super 8 movie film; (2) antique Spanish knife, a switchblade called a Navaja, in horn and brass, circa 1900. Next to each item were the initials A. N.—perhaps Alfred Neuss? The date of deposit was 01.09. The day Neuss arrived in Monte Carlo. They were old friends— 40 years—so perhaps Curtay was keeping them for him. No other details.

Kovalenko shut down the laptop and closed it. He had no way of knowing whether Lenard had the same information or if he would share it with him if he did. But politics aside, the logic of what might have happened played out right away. They all knew that Neuss's journey had taken him from L.A. to Paris, and then to Marseilles before he went to Monte Carlo. Did that mean he had picked up the knife and 8 mm film in Marseilles and transferred them to Curtay's private safe in Monte Carlo? Did that mean, too, that the diamond transaction had been merely a cover to give the appearance of business as usual?

Neuss had been found dead on Friday the tenth, and Curtay had been murdered in Monaco early on Monday the thirteenth, making it reasonable to believe that the disfiguring of Neuss was done with one and possibly a second purpose—the first, to give the assailant time to get to Monte Carlo and size up the situation there before he attacked Curtay, and before Neuss's identity was known and Curtay put on guard; the second, to cover up deliberate torture done to make Neuss reveal the whereabouts of the knife and the film. If so, the same thinking might apply to the other Russian victims—those tortured and then murdered in San Francisco, Mexico City, and Chicago. What if the killer had come to each victim expecting to find not only the safe deposit keys but the location of the box they would open? Suppose the victims had the keys but no idea of the location of the safe deposit box itself, but their assailant thought they did and tortured them hoping to find out.

Abruptly Kovalenko's thoughts shifted back to Beverly Hills and the idea that the reason Raymond Thorne had gone to Neuss's residence was not simply to murder Neuss but to learn the location of the knife and film. That would have been the reason for his plane ticket to England, particularly if he knew they were hidden somewhere in Europe—perhaps in a bank, which would in turn explain the safe deposit keys found in his bag on the train in L.A.

Detective Halliday, Dan Ford, and Jean-Luc had all been killed with some kind of razor-sharp instrument. Was it possible the murder weapon was the retrieved knife? If so, why? Was it just handy, or did the instrument itself hold some special significance? If it did, and because of the depraved manner in which all three were slain, did its use suggest ritual killing? If the answer to that was yes, did it mean the killer was not yet done?

38

Whether it had been pure instinct or sheer chutzpah, somehow, despite her emotional state of shock, made all the worse by the knowledge that the unborn child inside of her would never see its father, and under the eyes of the police Lenard had sent to seize and lock down the Ford apartment, Nadine Ford had managed not only to pack her clothes and Nicholas Marten's into two suitcases, but at the same time smuggle out a little contraband—Halliday's appointment book and a large accordion file holding Dan Ford's current working notes. It had been a bold and courageous maneuver that somehow went off without the slightest hitch. Now, tucked away in a small study in Nadine's brother's apartment, Marten, half drunk and emotionally drained by the awfulness of the day, had both the accordion file and Halliday's appointment book open in front of him.

In the rooms beyond, among the vases of flowers and tables spilling over with food and bottles of wine, were Nadine, her brother, Armand, her sister, their spouses, and her father and mother. There were also friends. And friends. And more friends, including the two women who ran the *L.A. Times* Paris bureau and who had been Dan Ford's assistants. That so many people could fit into one small apartment seemed a mathematical impossibility but it didn't matter; they were there anyway, hugging, crying, talking, some even managing a laugh at some recollection.

Earlier, when Marten had started for the study to get away from the mourners and to try to do something with purpose, he had walked past a small bedroom. The door had been open and he had seen Nadine sitting alone on the bed absently stroking a large tawny cat that had one paw playing gently against her big belly as if trying to comfort her. It was the same portrait he had seen at Red's house after Red had been killed—the rooms filled with mourners and Red's wife alone in the study, the heavy head of Red's black Labrador in her lap as she held a cup of coffee and stared off at nothing.

Marten had to leave right then, get out of the apartment and out into fresh air, just to walk and be alone before he suffocated on his own grief. The crisp air helped, and despite Lenard's warning he let down his guard and just walked, maybe in some way hoping Raymond was there watching, even following him. With luck he would reveal himself and then, one way or another, it would be over. But nothing had happened and forty-five minutes later he came back, went directly to the study, closed the door, and went to work, deliberately trying to find some key that would lead him to Raymond. If it was Raymond.

Now, scanning Halliday's book, trying to keep the ragtag jumble of loose pages in order, he tried again, as he had the night before, to decipher Halliday's tiny backhand scrawl and find something he could use. But it was as impossible now as it had been then. Page after page crammed with half sentences, one-word notes, names, dates, places. As before, the few he could read were personal and about Halliday's family, and Marten felt they were none of his business and he shouldn't be reading them at all. Yet, as increasingly frustrated and uncomfortable as he was, he kept on.

Fifteen minutes later he'd had enough and was about to put it down and turn instead to Ford's accordion file when a name popped out at him—*Felix Norman*. Felix Norman, the doctor who had signed Raymond's death certificate in Los Angeles. On the next page Halliday had written another name, *Dr. Hermann Gray, plastic surgeon, Bel Air, age 48. Abruptly retired, sold home, and left country*. In parentheses alongside Gray's name was *Puerto Quepos, Costa Rica, then Rosario, Argentina, name changed to James Patrick Odett—ALC/hunting accident.*

And next to that, written in pencil and erased and then printed over again as if for some reason Halliday had been angry at himself was *1/26—VARIG, 8837.*

1/26—a date, maybe. And Varig was, or could be, an airline. And 8837, was, or could be, a flight number.

Immediately Marten swiveled in his chair and booted up Armand's computer. When it was up and running he went to the Varig Web site and typed 8837 in the search box. A second later he had it—flight 8837, Los Angeles to Buenos Aires, Argentina.

Marten looked back to Halliday's stuffed, unwieldy journal. Maybe he hadn't gone through it carefully enough. His concentration had been on what was written on the pages. Maybe there was something else, something he had missed.

Picking it up, he turned it over and carefully opened the back cover. There were a number of loose pages and beneath them an awkward bulge where the cardboard backing to the day/date calendar was fitted into the cover's leather sleeve. He slid the pages out and turned over the first of them. What he found were photographs of Halliday's children and eleven hundred dollars' worth of traveler's checks. Next were Halliday's passport and two folded pieces of paper. Marten looked at one and then the other. They were faxed electronic airline tickets. The first was Halliday's round-trip LA–PARIS United Airlines ticket; the second was a Varig ticket—round-trip from L.A. to Buenos Aires that left on January 26 and had an open return.

"Christ," he breathed. Halliday had been planning to go to Argentina, maybe even before Neuss's murder or maybe because of it. And it was to have been no vacation. Written in pencil across the top of the Varig ticket was the name *James Patrick Odett*, and in parentheses beside it, *Dr. Hermann Gray* and again the *ALC*.

Marten felt his heart skip a beat. Was Argentina where Raymond had been taken at the same time he was supposedly being cremated in L.A.? And had Dr. Gray, the plastic surgeon, been recruited to oversee his physical rebuilding? The ALC and the "hunting accident" note he didn't understand, unless for some reason Halliday had transposed the letters and what he really meant was ACL, for an anterior cruciate ligament knee injury, suggesting that someone, Raymond or maybe the doctor himself, had badly hurt his knee in a hunting accident. It made no difference. The real question was—had Halliday been killed because he'd found out about Dr. Gray and Argentina and was going there himself to continue his investigation?

Suddenly another thought came and it chilled. If Neuss and Halliday and Dan Ford and this Jean-Luc had all been killed by the same person and that person was Raymond—and if Dr. Gray, as a plastic surgeon, had done his job properly—they would have no idea what he looked like. He could be anyone. Cabdriver, florist, waiter. Anyone who could get close to you without your giving him a second thought. Raymond was smart and very inventive. Just look at the variety of costumes he had used in L.A. From salesman to skinhead to dressing up in Alfred Neuss's own clothes.

"Nicholas."

The door behind Marten suddenly opened and a pale and drawn Nadine came in. Someone was behind her. Marten stood.

"Rebecca," he said, wholly surprised, and then his sister eased past Nadine and came into the room.

39

Her long black hair turned up in an elegant bun, dressed in a long dark skirt and matching jacket, in the swirl of heartache and sorrow, Rebecca was poised and beautiful. Away from the Rothfels family and on her own, it was remarkable to see how far she'd come from the fragile invalid she'd been for so long.

"*Merci*, Nadine," she said quietly, hugging the woman who had come with Dan to visit her so often when she had been in St. Francis and then again when she was at Jura. Rebecca went on, telling her in French what Nadine already knew, that Dan had been like a second brother to her for most of her life, and then, so gently, expressing her deepest sympathy for her terrible loss. Then Nadine's father appeared, and, saying they had family business and apologizing, he took his daughter from the room.

"I called you in Switzerland this afternoon." Marten closed the door behind them. "You weren't there. I left word. How did you—?"

"Get here so quickly? I was away from the house with the children. I got your message when I came back. Mrs. Rothfels saw I was upset, and when I told her what had happened she spoke to her husband. The corporate jet was bringing a client here anyway, and Mr. Rothfels insisted I go along. His driver met the plane. When we got to Dan's apartment the police sent us here."

"I wish you hadn't come."

"Why? You and Dan are the only family I have, why wouldn't I come?"

"Rebecca, Jimmy Halliday was in Paris investigating the murder of Alfred Neuss. He was murdered in his hotel room last night."

"Jimmy Halliday, from the squad?"

Marten nodded. "So far it's been kept quiet."

"Oh, God, and then Dan—"

"And another person, someone the police think Dan was on his way to meet. And now the police have warned me to beware."

"They don't know who you are."

"No. But that's not the point."

"What is?"

Marten hesitated. For all Rebecca appeared to be now, healthy and adjusted and sophisticated, somewhere in her was that which Dan Ford had referred to and which Marten feared—the idea that her psychotherapy had been successful only to a degree and that the smallest reminder of the past could trigger memories that could send her reeling into the state she had been in before.

On the other hand, she couldn't live in a vacuum, and he had to think she was strong enough for him to take the risk of preparing her for what he was certain they would all find out soon enough.

"Rebecca, there is the possibility Raymond is still alive and that he may be the one responsible for what happened to Dan and Jimmy Halliday and the others."

"Raymond? The Raymond from Los Angeles?"

"Yes."

Marten could see her jolt in reaction. In the long transition from illness to health, she'd learned a great deal about what had happened in L.A. She knew about Raymond's escape from the Criminal Courts Building, his cold-blooded murder of any number of police officers, Red McClatchy among them, and that Nicholas himself had nearly been killed trying to bring him to justice. More than once, and despite the emotion of her breakthrough and the haze of psychotropic medications given to her immediately afterward, she had been encouraged by Dr. Flannery to relive her terrifying experience in the rail yards. He knew it had been very difficult for her, and that what little memory she had of it at all was all crazed and fearsome and filled with gunfire and blood and horror. But there was no doubt she understood that Raymond had been at the center of everything. And like the rest of the world, she thought he was dead.

"He was cremated. How could he still be alive?"

"I don't know. After Neuss was murdered Dan started working on it. Jimmy Halliday was on it, too, only he started some time ago."

"And you think it was Raymond who killed both of them?"

"I don't know. I can't even say for certain he's alive. But Alfred Neuss is dead, so are Jimmy and Dan—all people who were involved with him in L.A. Even if you don't remember it clearly, you were there in the rail yards. You saw him and he saw you. If he is here in Paris, I don't want you anywhere around." Marten hesitated; this was something he didn't want to think about but had to. "There's something else," he said. "If it is Raymond, there's every chance he will have had cosmetic surgery, so we won't know what he looks like."

Suddenly there was fear in Rebecca's eyes. "Nicholas, you were the one trying to bring him in. He would know you better than anyone. If he knows you are in Paris—"

"Rebecca, let me make sure you are okay, then I can worry about me."

"What do you want me to do?"

"I assume that if Mr. Rothfels sent you here by private jet, he also arranged a hotel room."

"Yes, at the Crillon."

"The Crillon?"

"Yes." Rebecca blushed and smiled. The Hôtel de Crillon was one of the most luxurious and expensive in Paris. "It's nice to have a wealthy boss."

"I'm sure it is." Marten smiled, and then it faded. "I'm going to ask Nadine's brother to take you to the hotel. When you get there, I want you to go to your room and lock the door and don't answer it for anyone. I'll book you on a flight to Geneva early tomorrow morning. Have the concierge arrange for a hotel car to take you to the airport. Make sure the concierge knows the driver personally, and ask him to call the airline and arrange to have that driver stay with you until you board the plane. In the meantime I will have called the Rothfels to have someone they know meet your flight and get you safely to Neuchâtel."

"You're frightened, aren't you?"

"Yes, for both of us."

Rebecca was a mix of emotions as Nicholas left to find Nadine's brother. If Dan Ford had died in an accident or of some dread disease, they would still have been devastated, but the way it had happened, so quickly and horribly and out of nowhere, was unfathomable. Unfathomable, too, was the idea of Raymond still alive and inflicting such terror so many months later and fifty-six hundred miles from where it started.

Yet, frightening and overwhelming as it all was, there was something apart from it that she wanted desperately to share with her brother. It was about her and the love and light of her life, Alexander Cabrera, and how central they had become in each other's lives. Secretive as their relationship had been, and despite the conspiratorial pact of silence Lady Clem shared with her, she felt the time drawing closer to when Alexander would fulfill his promise and ask her to marry him, and she wanted Nicholas to know beforehand.

In the past the secrecy of their relationship had been fun, a rambunctious game of keep-away where big brother didn't know what little sister was doing—but now as the bond between her and Alexander tightened and worked its way toward the inevitable, she felt as if she were deliberately hiding something from Nicholas, and it made her increasingly uncomfortable.

Tonight had been a perfect example. She had not told him the entire truth about Gerard Rothfels' insistence she come on the corporate plane from Switzerland. It was true Rothfels had made the arrangements, but it had been at Alexander's order. And it had not been a company driver who had met her at Orly Airport when she'd arrived but rather Alexander's driver and bodyguard, Jean-Pierre Rodin. Her hope had been that Alexander might have come to the airport himself so that she could have coaxed him to come with her, and meet her brother even under the heartbreaking circumstances, but he had been in Italy on business, and Jean-Pierre had said he would not arrive in Paris until later this evening, so it was a matter of simple logistics and, for now, out of the question.

· And then there was Raymond and whether to tell Alexander about him. To do so would bring up why there was reason for concern, and while both Alexander and Clem knew about her breakdown, neither knew the real truth of it, nor what had happened to shock her out of it.

The story she had told them had been concocted by Nicholas and her psychiatrist, Dr. Flannery, before they left L.A. In it, she had said she and Nicholas had grown up in a small town in Vermont. When she was fifteen her parents died within two months of each other and she went to California to live with Nicholas, who was in college there. Shortly after arriving she had gone to the beach with Nicholas and some friends. A while later she and a friend wandered off down the beach, where they saw a young boy caught in a strong riptide being dragged out to sea and screaming for help. Sending her friend to get the lifeguards, Rebecca swam out through heavy swells toward him. Reaching him, she struggled in the big waves for what seemed hours trying to keep both their heads above water until lifeguards arrived. It was only when they did that she learned the boy was already dead. Later she was told he had probably drowned even before she got to him. Suddenly she realized she had been holding on to a corpse for the whole time. The thought of it, coming so soon after the tragic loss of her parents, galvanized her, and almost instantly she suffered a massive psychological collapse—one that lasted for years until she finally began to come out of it and her brother had her transferred to the Balmore for specialized treatment under Dr. Maxwell-Scot.

So now, if she brought up Raymond she could hardly tell them about what had happened at the rail yards and instead would have to put the onus on Nicholas. She would have to tell Alexander that her brother had not only known Dan Ford when he was a police reporter in Los Angeles but, through him, had known Detective Halliday as well, and that both men had been heavily involved in investigating Raymond there.

Now Ford and Halliday were dead in Paris, and if their killer was indeed the same Raymond, thought to be dead but wasn't, there was every reason to believe he might come after Nicholas as well. And then, in turn, come after her for fear Nicholas had said something to her.

So Rebecca's question to herself was, why alarm Alexander when Nicholas had said he was not by any means certain the killer was Raymond, or if Raymond was even alive? In thinking about it she decided it was simply best to say nothing about Raymond period and let it go at that.

Yet, even as she made the decision, she knew she had to be fully aware of her brother's warning and do exactly as he said once she reached the hotel.

40

STILL 27 RUE HUYSMANS, THE APARTMENT OF ARMAND DROUIN. 10:45 P.M.

The front door to the apartment house opened and Nicholas and Rebecca came out, accompanied by Armand, Nadine's twenty-four-year-old brother, and another man, a friend of Armand's and a soldier in the French army.

Armand was a professional bicycle racer, young and head-strong and generous. His car was right outside. The Crillon at this time of night was a ten-minute drive, it was a pleasure for him to take her there. He led her quickly across the street to his green Nissan, climbing in behind the wheel, while his friend got into the back.

Marten glanced cautiously around and opened the passenger door for Rebecca. "What's your room number at the Crillon?"

"Why?"

"Because I'll call you as soon as I have the flight information. I want you out of Paris first thing in the morning."

"Room four-twelve." She looked at him and he could feel the worry in her. He tried to soften it.

"I said before there's no proof this is Raymond at all. The fact is he probably is dead and what's gone on here is just coincidence, done by a crazy who has no idea in the world who we are and who couldn't care less. Okay?"

"Yes." Rebecca smiled and kissed him on the cheek.

Abruptly Marten looked to Armand. "Thank you, Armand, thank you."

"She is in safe hands, *mon ami*. We will make sure she gets to her room, and I will speak to the concierge myself about a car for her in the morning. We have had enough tears for one day."

"For any day." Nicholas closed the door and stepped back as Armand started the Nissan, then made a sharp U-turn and drove off. At the far end of the street he turned onto the Boulevard Raspail and the Nissan disappeared from view.

41

Raymond sat in the rear seat of a darkened black Mercedes parked three doors down. He had seen the four come out of the apartment and cross the street to the green Nissan, and then watched as three of them got in and the car drove off. Now he saw Nicholas Marten step from the shadowed sidewalk to cross under a streetlamp alone and go back into the apartment at number 27 rue Huysmans.

It had been ten months since he'd last seen him and seven since he'd tracked him to Manchester, or rather since the Baroness had. In that time he'd learned everything about him; his change of name, where he lived, what he was doing with his life. He even knew about Lord Prestbury and Marten's secret affair with Prestbury's daughter, Lady Clementine Simpson. He knew, too, about Switzerland and Rebecca, where she lived and for whom she worked.

But for all Raymond had learned about Marten, for all those months, he'd purposely pushed him from his mind, done his best not to think about him at all.

Now, having seen him alive and in the flesh and crossing the street with his sister, he was reminded how dangerous a man he was.

Marten was either inhumanly cunning, bulldog-determined, or just plain lucky, or some combination of all three. Like some ancient hound, he was on Raymond's heels seemingly at every turn; the same as he had been in Los Angeles after his escape from jail, and then suddenly appearing out of the rain at Los Angeles International Airport to prevent him from escaping on the Lufthansa flight to Germany, and then once more, coming out of nowhere to arrive at Alfred Neuss's residence in Beverly Hills while Raymond was there, and then, even after he had been terminated from the police force, sequestering Rebecca in London to, he was certain, follow up on the handwritten notations they would have found in his bag on the Southwest Chief, and now here he was in Paris.

Some of it, he knew, was his own doing—knowing Marten was only an hour or two away in Manchester but going ahead and killing Neuss anyway. But with Neuss in Paris and the close timing of things, he'd had no choice; besides, the irony of doing it in the Parc Monceau had been delicious, especially when Neuss realized who he was and that he was going to die.

Still, seeing Marten cross his path so very few feet in front of him tantalized. More than anything, Raymond wanted to get out of the car right then, follow Marten into the building, and kill him, cruelly and savagely, the way he had Neuss and Halliday and Dan Ford and Jean-Luc Vabres, but he knew he couldn't, not just yet, and certainly not tonight. Tonight was for something else. So he had to pull back his feelings and put his thoughts and energy to what was at hand.

Lightly fingering a long, gaily wrapped rectangular package, he mused a moment longer, then looked to his driver.

"L'Hôtel Crillon," he said. "L'Hôtel Crillon."

42

Raymond's black Mercedes turned onto the Place de la Concorde and stopped across from the hotel. The green Nissan was in front, parked in the passenger-loading zone.

Raymond brushed back his hair, then ran a hand over his carefully trimmed beard and waited.

11:08 P.M.

A taxi pulled up and several well-dressed people got out and entered through the hotel's large revolving door.

11:10 P.M.

A middle-aged couple in evening clothes came out through the door. A chauffeured car pulled up and a uniformed majordomo opened the door. The couple got in and the car drove off. The revolving door turned again and Armand and his friend came through it and went directly to the Nissan. Several seconds passed, then its lights came on and the car squealed off past them, its headlights illuminating Raymond briefly as it went by. Another moment and Raymond opened the door and stepped out into the crisp air, the gaily wrapped package under his arm.

Neatly bearded, poised, his hair jet-black and combed stylishly back, and wearing a tailored double-breasted charcoal suit, he looked for all the world like a successful young executive on his way to enjoy some late-evening intimacy with an attractive young lady. This was precisely what he had in mind, though the intimacy would be more far-reaching than most.

He brushed back his hair once again, then looked across at

the Crillon, elegantly lit against the night sky, and started toward it.

At two weeks past his thirty-fourth birthday, and for the first time in what seemed an exceedingly long time, he felt truly alive. Even more energetic than he had been early this morning when he'd met and killed Jean-Luc and then Dan Ford at the river in the dark and the pouring rain. The minor limp he walked with seemed trivial, as did the lingering aches that were the result of the multiple surgeries and physical rehabilitations he had endured for what felt like an eternity but what—thanks primarily to the Kevlar vest he had taken from John Barron and was wearing in the confrontation in the rail yards—had been barely four months. In the meantime the Baroness had delicately maneuvered the major players into the position they had been in before, and now things were moving swiftly forward and they were operating with the same kind of self-contained and precisely timed schematic they had used then. Only this time Neuss was dead and the "pieces" were in their possession. It was a twin deed they were certain Sir Peter Kitner would suspect they had been responsible for, but could do nothing about. Nonetheless he would fear greatly for himself and his family. But it was a fear he could share with no one. It would become worse as the days progressed because he would have no more idea what they were planning now than he had before, when Neuss had so hastily fled to London. As a result there was nothing he could do but extend the guard around himself and his family and move forward toward what was to be the crowning moment of his life. And by doing that he would step fully into their trap.

Another twenty paces and Raymond reached the Crillon's revolving front door. The majordomo nodded as he went by and pushed through it. Inside, the grand lobby was alive with a bubbly congregation of hotel guests and Parisians out for the evening. He stopped briefly and scanned the room, then started toward the concierge desk toward the rear.

He was halfway there when the bright lights of television cameras drew his attention and he saw a small gathering of people surrounding two businessmen being interviewed by the media. As he neared he couldn't believe what he saw. There he was—the regal, white-haired, global-media industrialist and billionaire—Sir Peter Kitner himself. With him was his thirty-year-old son, Michael, president of his empire and heir apparent to it.

Then he saw the third man, standing to Kitner's immediate right. He was Dr. Geoffrey Higgs, a former Royal Air Force flight surgeon and Kitner's personal physician, bodyguard, and chief of intelligence. Exceptionally fit, with a protruding jaw and buzz haircut, Higgs had a tiny earphone in his left ear with an even smaller microphone clipped to the lapel of his suit coat. Wherever Kitner went, so did Higgs and the corps of unseen security people he was electronically connected to.

Raymond should have kept going, but he didn't. Instead, he stepped into the relative dark behind the gathered reporters and the glare of television lights as Kitner was being questioned about the high-level board meeting he and his son had just attended. Was it true, the French media wanted to know, that his U.S.-based company MediaCorp was attempting a takeover of the French television network TV5?

Raymond could feel the rise in his pulse as he watched Kitner play around with the question.

"Everything is for sale, is it not?" Kitner asked in French. "Even MediaCorp. It is simply a matter of price."

This was the Peter Kitner Raymond had known about all of his adult life. Best-selling books had been written about him. He was the subject of endless articles in magazines and newspapers and had been interviewed over and over again on television. But this was the first time Raymond had seen him in person in years, and the suddenness of it came as a total surprise.

Yet there he was, standing in the darkness only feet away, and Raymond knew full well he could step forward and kill him in a blink. But to do that would defeat everything he and the Baroness had so carefully planned for years as they watched the clock of history slowly tick to the exact right moment. It had done so once before, nearly a year earlier, and then had come the debacle in Los Angeles. Yet, with his recovery and the Baroness's grand manipulation of the key players, that moment was once again at hand. So, as much as he might savor it, killing Peter Kitner was the last thing to do now. On the other hand, it was impossible for him to simply turn and walk away without at least giving the great man something to think about.

"Sir Peter," Raymond abruptly called out in French from behind the reporters, "is the TV5 takeover the announcement you will make at the World Economic Forum in Davos this weekend?"

"What?" Kitner was obviously taken by surprise and tried to peer beyond the lights to see who had spoken.

"Is there not some major announcement involving you personally to be made at Davos, Sir Peter?"

"Who said that?" Kitner stepped forward, shielding his eyes from the lights, looking for the speaker. Media people turned, looking, too.

"Who said that? Turn off those damn lights." Angrily Kitner pushed through the gathering, trying to find the man who had spoken. Michael was moving with him. So was Higgs, snapping orders into the microphone on his lapel as he went. At the far side they stopped and looked around. Whoever had spoken had disappeared among the guests crowding the lobby.

"*Et Davos,* Sir Peter?" What about Davos, Sir Peter?

"Sir Peter, *quelle est la nature de votre annonce?*" Sir Peter, what is the nature of your announcement?

"Sir Peter." "Sir Peter." "Sir Peter."

Raymond heard shouts from the French media behind him as he continued toward the concierge desk. Seconds later, several men in dark suits entered from an adjacent doorway and moved protectively toward Kitner. Bodyguards called in by Higgs.

Raymond smiled confidently. A seed had been planted and the media had picked up on it. Kitner's style and assurance, he knew, would quickly swat the troublesome media away, and soon his surprise and anger would fade. After that, curiosity would rise as to who the questioner had been and how, and just how much, he knew about what was to happen in Davos. Then, at some point later, Kitner would realize who it had been and what had happened. When he did, fear and suspicion would quickly supersede everything else. Which was precisely what Raymond had intended.

Ahead were the elevators. He tucked the package under his arm and looked at his watch.

11:20 P.M.

He stopped at the elevators, then pressed the button and looked around. A well-dressed elderly couple chatted nearby, but other than that he was alone.

An elevator door opened, and three people came out. The elderly couple made no move toward it, and Raymond stepped inside. A moment later, the door closed, and he pressed the button for the fourth floor. Another moment and the elevator rose. Again he looked at his watch.

11:24 P.M.

He took a breath and shifted the package from one hand to the other. Rebecca would be alone, relaxing in her room, her brother safely across the Seine in the apartment on the rue Huysmans, her draining emotional activity of the day, done. Perhaps she had even changed clothes.

Perhaps not.

Considering what was yet to come, what she wore would make little difference.

43

Geoffrey Higgs and three of the dark-suited bodyguards led Peter and Michael Kitner through the Crillon's side entrance and out onto the rue Boissy d'Anglais where Kitner's limousine waited. One of the bodyguards opened the door and all three got in, Higgs last. Immediately the driver moved away, picking up speed and crossing the Place de la Concorde, then turning up

the Champs Elysées toward Kitner's Paris residence on the Avenue Victor Hugo.

"I want to find out who that was and what he knows." Kitner
was looking directly at Higgs.

"Yes, sir."

"From now on we will have a separate area for the media.
Michael will give you an approved list. Credentials will be
checked. No one else will be permitted."

"Yes, sir."

Michael Kitner looked to his father. "If he was a reporter
we'll find out who he was."

Peter Kitner said nothing. He was visibly upset and coldly
distant.

"How could he know about Davos?"

"I don't know," Kitner snapped. Briefly he let his eyes go to
Higgs, then turned to stare out at the crowds that even at this
hour and in the January cold lined the Champs Elysées.

I don't know, Kitner said to himself. *I don't know.*

Telephone to his ear, Nicholas Marten hunched over the desk in
Armand's tiny office waiting as his call rang through.

"Come on, Rebecca," he urged, "pick up."

This was the sixth time he'd called. The first three had been
to Rebecca's cell phone and he'd had no answer. Anxious and
frustrated, he'd given it another ten minutes and tried again.
Still there'd been no response. Finally he hung up and called
the Crillon directly, giving her room number and asking to be
connected. The results were the same.

"Come on," he breathed and glanced down at the notes
scratched on the desktop pad in front of him.

*Air France flight 1542 leaves Paris Charles de Gaulle, Termi-
nal 2F, at 7:00 A.M.,* arrives Geneva 8:05 A.M., Terminal M.

"Dammit, Rebecca, pick up."

Marten could feel the anxiety rise with each unanswered
ring. He'd already wakened Armand, getting the same information he'd received when Nadine's brother first came home. Yes,
he had seen Rebecca to her room at the Crillon. Yes, she had
closed the door as he left. Yes, he heard her lock it. That was all

he knew. Did Marten want him to drive him back to the hotel to double-check? No, it was alright, Marten had told him, just some mix-up, nothing to worry about. With that Armand had nodded gratefully and gone back to bed.

Two more rings and a French-accented male voice came on:

"I'm sorry, sir, your party is not answering."

"Do you know if Ms. Marten might have left her room?"

"No, sir."

"Would you please check with the front desk to see if perhaps she went out and left word where she was going?"

"I am sorry, sir, we are not permitted to give that information."

"I'm her brother!"

"I apologize, sir."

"What time do you have?"

"Just midnight, sir."

"Please try the room again."

"Yes, sir."

Just midnight, the same time as Armand's desktop clock. Rebecca had arrived at the hotel at eleven, exactly an hour earlier.

The call went through once more, ringing a dozen agonizing times before the male voice came back on.

"I'm sorry, sir, still no answer. Would you like to leave a message?"

"Yes, tell Ms. Marten her brother called and to please call me back as soon as she gets the message." Marten gave the operator Armand's phone number and hung up.

He looked back to the clock.

12:03 A.M.

It was now Thursday, January 16.

Where the hell was she?

44

Rebecca sat in a red velvet chair, her mouth open, barely able to breathe. All around her was elegant eighteenth-century rococo decor—chairs and couches covered with red silk fabric, polished wood-paneled walls, floor-to-ceiling windows outlined by rich floral draperies. In the far corner was a Steinway grand piano, its top open, ready to be played, and everything was gently lighted by a mixture of extraordinarily tasteful and ornate table lamps and wall sconces.

Through the doorway to her left was a private dining room, and past it, glass doors opening onto a broad terrace, and beyond that, nighttime Paris. The doors a way to escape, if she had the courage. But she knew she didn't and wouldn't, not now or ever.

"Take a long and deep breath and everything will be alright."

Raymond stood an arm's length away, his eyes glistening as he looked down at her. He had surprised her in her room and brought her quickly down a flight of fire stairs and into one of the Crillon's most expensive suites. Other than Adolf Sibony, the night concierge, no one knew he was there. Nor had anyone seen them come, nor had word been left where she might have gone. On top of it all were his orders to Sibony that he was not to be disturbed.

"Is it so very difficult for you to say something?"

"I—" Rebecca was trembling, her eyes filled with tears.

Raymond came closer. He hesitated and then touched her. Felt her quiver as he ran the back of his hand along her cheek and down the nape of her neck to her throat.

"You began to speak," he whispered. "What were you going to say?"

"I—" Suddenly she pulled away from him and straightened up in the chair. As quickly her eyes went to his.

"Yes," she said definitively through her tears. Then a glorious smile escaped her and she stood. "Yes. Yes. Yes. A thousand times, yes. I love you, I always have and always will. Yes, I will marry you, my wonderful *señor*—my wonderful Alexander Luis Cabrera."

Raymond looked at her in silence. This was the grandest moment of his life and one he'd known would come, from the first time he'd seen her asleep in front of the television the night he had invaded John Barron's house in Los Angeles. This was God's doing. It was his *sudba*, his destiny, and why he was certain he had been forced into John Barron's life. Not an hour or a day had passed without his thinking of her. It had been the thought, the visualization, and the fantasies of her that had seen him through the surgeries and the months of recovery.

With her long dark hair and piercing eyes, the regal stretch of her neck and high, delicate cheekbones, just the idea of her haunted him. Rebecca was the living image of Princess Isabella Maria Josepha Zenaide, grandniece of King Ludwig III of Bavaria, who, at age twenty-four, had been murdered by Communist revolutionaries in Munich in November of 1918. Her portrait hung, among others, in the private library of the Baroness's seventeenth-century country manor in the Massif Central of France, and Raymond had been captivated by it since he was a child, the fascination becoming only stronger as he grew into manhood. Regal, beautiful, unforgettable, she had been Rebecca's age when she died. And now, in his mind and fantasy, she lived again, reborn as John Barron's sister.

He'd breathlessly described her to the Baroness when she joined him at his bedside at his ranch in Argentina after his first surgeries. Rebecca was truly his *sudba*, his destiny, he told her. The woman he had to make his wife.

It was the manner in which he talked about her—over and over for months as the Baroness supervised his long recovery and laborious rehabilitation from his physical and cosmetic surgeries—that made her realize the effect Rebecca had had on this man to whom she was legal guardian. There was a light in his eyes she had never before seen, and she knew that if Rebecca was truly as he described, and, depending on her mental state, if she could be made healthy and then molded in the right way, she could supply a critical part missing from both their futures.

In little time she had Rebecca traced to St. Francis sanctuary in Los Angeles and learned of her care under Dr. Flannery. Within hours Dr. Flannery's personal computer had been hacked into and Rebecca's files accessed. As a result, the Baroness had learned where Rebecca had gone and the name of the therapist she had been transferred to. In no time Dr. Maxwell-Scot's computer files at the Balmore had been compromised, and the Baroness learned of Rebecca's condition and her very promising prognosis. She also learned the name of the guarantor of Rebecca's fees: her brother, Nicholas Marten, living first in London at the Hampstead Holiday Inn and then, later, at 221 Water Street, Manchester, England.

That Rebecca was already in Europe simplified things greatly. Lausanne, Switzerland, was the European headquarters of Alexander's corporation, and Switzerland was an ideal location for him to be introduced to Rebecca and to begin to develop a relationship.

Immediately the expertise of Maître Jacques Bertrand, the Baroness's Zurich-based attorney, came into play. Within the month realtors found an elegant and private health spa in Neuchâtel, a short drive from Lausanne. An offer was made to buy it. The owners said it was not for sale. A second offer was made, also rejected. A third was not. The price was outrageous.

Forty-eight hours after the sale closed, Joseph Cumberland, Esq., a prominent London lawyer, arranged a meeting with Eugenia Applegate, head of the Balmore Foundation. At the meeting, he told her of a client who was a great admirer of the clinic's work who had recently purchased a spa on the shore of Lake Neuchâtel, Switzerland. The client, who wished to remain anonymous, was prepared to donate the building and grounds to the foundation. Additionally, a private grant would be made available for the operation of the institution and to cover patient fees. The hope was that the setting, away from the bustle and noise and distractions of London, would enable therapists to develop a concentrated program that, with immediate access to the outdoors and therefore physical activities like boating and hiking, might help accelerate their patients' healing process and thereby considerably shorten the therapy period.

The number of patients was to be limited to the number of private rooms available, twenty, and they would be overseen by a staff chosen by the foundation. Further, as the donor had done due diligence and carefully monitored the clinic's operation over the past several months, it was strongly suggested that the staff initially include some of the present Balmore psychotherapists, Doctors Alistair James, Marcella Turnbull, and Anne Maxwell-Scot, taking with them, of course, their most current patients.

And then came the last. Because of the donor's tax situation, the transfer of title and beginning of operation of the facility had to be done within thirty days. Whether that was feasible was, of course, something for the foundation to decide.

For the Balmore, for the foundation, the gift was enormous. Thirty-six hours later, the buildings and grounds had been toured by foundation board members, Balmore attorneys consulted, and the proposition accepted. Two days after that, the papers were exchanged. On Sunday, May 19, beating the deadline by two days, the facility was staffed, repainted, given the name "Jura," for the nearby Jura mountains, and opened. On Tuesday, May 21, it was fully operational with Doctors James, Turnbull, and Maxwell-Scot and their primary patients ensconced there, Rebecca foremost among them.

It was a feat made possible only by extraordinary wealth and outrageous chutzpah, both of which the Baroness possessed in abundance. Still, she was not quite done. In the next month, and at Alexander's request, Gerard Rothfels and his family relocated from Lausanne to Neuchâtel, and soon after, Alexander Cabrera was introduced into Rebecca's life.

And little more than seven months after they had first seen each other at Jura, and from her own heart, she had agreed to become his wife.

"What beautiful children we will have," he whispered, and pulled her to him. "What beautiful, beautiful children."

"Yes." Rebecca laughed and cried and tried to brush away tears all at the same time. "What beautiful, beautiful children."

The whole thing was astounding. And Alexander knew it.

45

Rebecca watched Alexander get up from the couch and cross the room to answer the ring of his cell phone.

Champagne glass in hand, and a little bit drunk for the first time in her life, she wondered how many times she'd seen him do that. They were deeply in love and had just become engaged to be married. This should have been a quiet and very personal interlude in their lives, but still he'd answered his phone. He was always busy, always working. Calls came in from around the world at almost any hour and he took them all. Everything done quickly and with intensity—yet at the same time he displayed an extreme gentleness, especially toward her. They were traits very similar to those of her brother, and for a moment she thought how remarkably alike they were and wondered if, once they met, they might not become lifelong friends. The thought made her realize she had no choice but to tell Alexander of her past, especially now when she had agreed to become his wife.

"I will be down in five minutes." Alexander clicked off the phone and turned to face her.

"That was Jean-Pierre waiting in the car outside. It seems your brother has come to the hotel looking for you."

"My brother?"

"No doubt he tried to reach you and couldn't. He will have the front desk try your room. If you aren't there he will cause a fuss and they will send someone to look for you."

The same feeling rose in Alexander as had nearly two hours earlier when he'd seen Marten outside the apartment on rue Huysmans. This was why he had to be killed. To let him live even a day longer was courting the time when he would no longer be that half step behind but right on top of him and at his throat. But, even with the increasing risk, he couldn't kill Marten now. Davos was quickly approaching, and moreover, the death of her beloved brother now would send Rebecca reeling, most likely to the point of collapse. That was something he would not let happen.

"Will you meet him?" Rebecca was suddenly on her feet and coming toward him, joyous and smiling. "Now, tonight, so that we can tell him."

"No, not tonight."

"Why?" She stopped, her head cocked to one side, hurt.

Alexander stared at her in silence. There would be no meeting with Marten, no taking the chance that somehow Marten might recognize him, until it was time to kill him.

"Rebecca." Alexander went to her and gently took her hands in his. "Only you and I know what has happened between us tonight. For any number of reasons it is essential we keep our joy to ourselves for a few days more. Then we shall make an announcement and have a grand celebration in Switzerland, to which we will most certainly invite your brother. And when we meet, I will embrace him fully and with deepest affection and love and goodwill.

"But for tonight, my darling, go to your room. When your brother calls, tell him you were exhausted and fell asleep in the bath and did not hear the phone. Invite him to come up, and in the meantime pull on a robe and put your hair up in a towel as if you had just come from the bath."

"You want me to lie to him even now?"

Alexander smiled. "No more than you've done all along. It was always a game, was it not? And one you played very well."

"Yes, but—"

"Then let it still be a game, at least for a short while longer. You have trusted me so far, trust me now. Soon you will understand why. What the future holds for us both, my darling, you could never, in your wildest fantasy, begin to imagine."

46

Nicholas Marten rolled over on the sofa in Armand's study. Still wired and on edge, he replayed once more what had happened in the last hours.

Intensely concerned for Rebecca's safety but not wanting to wake an exhausted Armand or Nadine or frighten an already emotionally spent household, he'd simply left the apartment on his own, gone out onto the street, and hailed a taxi.

At twelve-thirty he'd reached the Crillon. Unshaven, and dressed in jeans, old running shoes, and a sweatshirt, he'd entered the lobby and gone directly to the front desk, where his single-minded demands to the clerk brought him the swift attention of hotel security and then the night concierge. At length, and having finally reached Rebecca by phone, he'd gone to her room in the company of security personnel. At their knock, she'd opened the door wearing a stylish Crillon bathrobe, her hair wrapped in a rich Crillon terry towel. Embarrassed, she'd kissed him and told him the same thing she had when he'd called from the lobby— she'd taken a hot bath and fallen asleep in it. When he'd said that was unlike her, and asked about the smell of liquor on her breath, she'd simply said the day had been long and very emotional, and the hotel had provided a complimentary bottle of Tattinger champagne, some of which she'd drunk before taking her bath, which was probably the reason she'd fallen asleep.

The thought of it made him smile. How far she'd come. She was a woman now, and beautiful, who spoke several languages and in many ways was far more sophisticated than he ever would be. Yet, because illness had stolen such a massive piece of her adolescence, she was in many ways still a child, naive and inexperienced in the realities of life and love. There were times, as her healing had progressed and he'd visited her in Neuchâtel, that he'd probed, lightly asking her about her personal life and male friends. Her response had been simply to flash a teasing smile and say something like "I have friends." And each time he'd left it at that. Inside, wishing her well, wishing her all the happiness that could be, and letting her find her own way.

God, how he loved her.

47

3:20 A.M.

Creak!

Marten sat up at a sound just outside the door. He listened.

Nothing.

Abruptly he threw back the blankets in the dark and went to the door and listened again.

Still nothing.

Maybe he'd fallen asleep and had been dreaming or—Armand's study was just off the entrance hall, and maybe someone from one of the apartments above had come in and gone upstairs—or maybe he was just on edge.

3:30 A.M.

He was wide awake. For the first time he thought of Clem. He should have called her long before this and at least told her what had been going on. But he hadn't, the sweep of emotion and motion had been too great. Now, wherever she was, still in Amsterdam or back in Manchester—at this stage he could hardly be expected to remember her personal itinerary—it was too late. What he would do was track her down and call her first thing in the morning.

3:35 A.M.

Raymond. The idea that he might be, or was, alive and in Paris never left his mind.

3:40 A.M.

Click.

He turned on a small halogen lamp on Armand's desk, sat down, pulled open Dan Ford's accordion file, and found the section headlined DECEMBER. It had been the murder of Alfred Neuss that triggered Ford's probe of Raymond's "cremation," but Neuss had been killed only days ago, so what he might find in the December file he had no idea, unless Ford had still wondered about Raymond's actions in L.A. and had been quietly investigating on his own. Perhaps there was even a reference to the man called Jean-Luc, a person of whom neither Nadine nor Armand had ever heard Ford speak. This confirmed what Marten had earlier believed, that Jean-Luc was some sort of acquaintance, the kind every reporter courted and depended on for leads. And since Ford had gone off willingly in the middle of the night, it seemed obvious that whatever he was meeting Jean-Luc to discuss was relatively harmless. Or so he'd thought.

4:10 A.M.

So far nothing except a deeper appreciation for Dan and the exhaustive work that made him the kind of reporter he'd been. There were handwritten notes and clippings from newspapers all over Europe, ideas and working outlines for stories five months into the new year and on subjects from garden exhibits to local and world politics to medicine, sports, business, society, and the entertainment world.

4:40 A.M.

Marten turned one page, then another. Then he came across a computer printout article from the *London Times*. The story was about a knighthood bestowed by the Queen on world media mogul Peter Kitner nearly a year earlier.

Puzzled, Marten put the sheet aside. This was a long-past event. Why was it in the current December folder? He turned the next page and found out. In front of him was a formal menu for a dinner to be held at a private home. Printed on expensive off-white card stock with raised dark gold lettering, it announced what seemed to be a ceremonial dinner that was to take place in Paris on January 16.

> Carte Commémorative
> En l'honneur de la
> Famille Splendide Romanov
> Paris, France — 16 Janvier
> 151 Avenue Georges V

Marten's French was all but negligible, but it wasn't hard to understand what he was reading—a commemorative menu in honor of the "splendid" Romanov family for a dinner taking place in Paris at 151 Avenue Georges V on January 16, and almost every item on it was *Russian*.

Suddenly he realized today was January 16. The dinner was tonight! Slowly, almost mesmerized, he turned the menu over. Written in Ford's hand at the top were the words *Kitner to attend* and then at the bottom, in the same handwriting, *Jean-Luc Vabres—Menu #1*.

A commemorative dinner for what he assumed was the fabled Romanov family. The royal imperial family of Russia. Russia! There it was again. And Peter Kitner was to attend.

Again Marten looked to the Kitner knighthood clipping.

"Christ," Marten swore under his breath. Kitner had been knighted in London on Wednesday, March 13, of last year. That was the day after Neuss had left Beverly Hills to go to London, which meant, because of the length of the flight and the time difference, March 13 was the day Neuss would have arrived in London. Was it possible he had gone there to see Kitner? Neuss had told the London Metropolitan Police he had come to London on business. It made Marten wonder what kind of business and if the investigators had asked the details of it. If they had, he hadn't seen it in their report, and he certainly couldn't call them now and ask to speak with one of the original investigators. Marten clenched his fist in frustration and looked off, trying to decide what to do. Suddenly he thought of someone he could call. Someone who might very well know.

Abruptly he looked at the clock. It was nearly quarter to five Thursday morning in Paris, which meant it was about quarter to eight Wednesday evening in Beverly Hills. Marten reached into his jacket for his cell phone. One pocket and then the other, and then the inside pocket. The phone wasn't there. What had happened to it, where he had lost it or left it, he didn't know, but it made no difference because it was gone. Immediately his eyes went to the phone on Armand's desk. He didn't want to use it for fear his call might later be traced back. But at this time of day, and with the time pressure of the Romanov dinner tonight, he had no other choice.

Quickly he picked up the receiver, punched zero, and asked for AT&T. Twenty seconds later he was put through to Los Angeles directory information and asked for the home telephone number of Alfred Neuss in Beverly Hills. It was a nonlisted number, he was told. Marten grimaced and hung up. There was a special number police and other emergency services personnel in L.A. used to access the nonlisted directory. He knew because he'd employed it many times himself when he'd been on the LAPD. All he could hope now was that it still worked and that neither the system nor the number had been changed.

Once again he picked up the receiver, dialed zero, and asked for AT&T. A moment later he had a line and punched in the number. It rang through and then a male voice came on and, to his relief, confirmed he had reached the target he wanted. He took a breath, then identified himself as Detective VerMeer of LAPD Robbery-Homicide, saying he was involved with an important investigation overseas and was calling from Paris. Within seconds he had Alfred Neuss's home number. Immediately he hung up, then clicked back on and went through the AT&T procedure again. An instant later he punched in the number and waited, concerned that, because of the publicity after Neuss's murder, all he would get was some kind of voice mail, but to his surprise a woman answered.

"Mrs. Neuss, please," he said.

"Who's calling?"

"Detective Gene VerMeer, Los Angeles Police Department, Robbery-Homicide Division."

"I am Mrs. Neuss, Detective. Haven't we spoken before?" Marten heard hesitation in her voice.

"Yes, of course, Mrs. Neuss," he covered quickly. "I'm calling from France, the connection's not so great. I'm in Paris following up on your husband's murder with the local police."

Marten ran the receiver over his shirt to simulate bad-connection static. He didn't know if it worked and shrugged it off with a self-deprecating, it-was-worth-a-try half grin. "Mrs. Neuss—are you there?"

"Go ahead, Detective."

"We're starting from the day your husband landed in Paris and are working backward." Suddenly Marten remembered what Dan Ford had told him on the way in from the airport. It was something that had seemed inconsequential in light of what else was going on at the time and maybe still was, but here was a chance to ask it before he got on with the rest.

"Mr. Neuss flew from L.A. to Paris and then took a connecting flight to Marseilles before he went on to Monaco."

"I didn't know about Marseilles until your people told me. It was probably just a convenient connection."

"Are you sure?"

"Detective, I said I didn't know about it. I hardly asked for his itinerary. I was not that kind of wife."

Marten hesitated. Maybe she was right. Maybe the stop in Marseilles was only a convenient connection.

"Let me go a little further backward in time." Now Marten got to his main point. "I believe you and he were in London last year. March thirteenth to be exact."

"Yes."

"Your husband told the London Metropolitan Police that he had gone there on business."

"Yes."

"Do you know what business it was exactly? Whom he met with?"

"No, I'm sorry. We were there for only a few days. He went out in the morning and I didn't see him again until evening. I don't know what he did during the day. He didn't discuss that kind of thing with me."

"What did you do in the meantime?"

"I shopped, Detective."

"Every day?"

"Yes."

"One more question, Mrs. Neuss. Was your husband a friend of Peter Kitner?"

Marten heard the smallest expulsion of air, as if she had been caught off guard by the question.

"Mrs. Neuss," he pressed her, "I asked if your husband was a friend of—"

"You are the second person who has asked that."

Marten suddenly perked up. "Who was the first?"

"A Mr. Ford of the *Los Angeles Times* called my husband sometime before Christmas."

"Mrs. Neuss, Mr. Ford was just found murdered, here in France."

"Oh—" Marten heard her strong reaction. "I'm so sorry."

"Mrs. Neuss," Marten pressed her again, "did your husband know Peter Kitner?"

"No, he didn't," she answered quickly. "And he told that to Mr. Ford."

"You're certain?"

"Yes, I'm certain."

"Thank you, Mrs. Neuss."

Marten hung up, his question answered. Mrs. Neuss had been lying when she said her husband did not know Peter Kitner. That Ford had already asked Neuss the same question was hardly unexpected because, for whatever reason, he was interested in Kitner and had thought there might have been some sort of connection between the two. Why he had waited so long to try to find out was hard to judge unless he had only come across the Kitner piece just before Christmas and the coincidence of the March 13 dates had come to him then. It made him wonder if Ford had tried to call Kitner and ask him about

Neuss—and if he should do the same. Unfortunately, the likelihood of getting a man like Kitner on the phone and then having him answer personal questions was next to nil, even for a reporter, or a cop unless he had some kind of very substantive suspicion that Kitner had committed a crime. Moreover, if he tried, he risked Kitner's people trying to find out who he was. So, at least for now, he put that idea aside.

Still, putting Ford's call to Neuss in perspective, it had been made long after the hubbub of Raymond Thorne and his interest in the Beverly Hills jeweler had died down. So, if there was a connection between Neuss and Kitner, especially considering the March 13 date, by then both Neusses would have had a pat "no, Alfred Neuss does not know Peter Kitner" as a response, especially if they were trying to hide the fact that the men knew each other and had met in London and were trying to keep it quiet. And Ford, with nothing more concrete than a coincidence of dates, had simply accepted it and gone on about his business.

Since then, Neuss had been murdered, and police and reporters would have had questions flying at his wife from every direction. And Mrs. Neuss, still distraught over losing her husband and with her nerves still on edge, even if no one else had asked her about her husband and Peter Kitner, had been caught off guard by Marten's question and inadvertently given herself away. Nick Marten (or rather John Barron) had been a homicide detective too long not to have heard the little gasp of air and recognized it as surprise. So the answer was yes, Alfred Neuss had known Peter Kitner. More to the point, had they been close enough for Neuss to have visited Kitner in London last March? If so, why? And why then? And about what? And why had both Neuss and his wife denied it?

Now Halliday was dead in Paris and Dan Ford had been killed because he'd gone to meet Jean-Luc Vabres, whoever he was. Suddenly Marten wondered why Ford had made the note about Kitner attending the Romanov dinner and why, after Neuss had been murdered and everything pointed to some kind of Russian connection, he had not so much as mentioned the dinner to him. Maybe the answer was that Ford suspected something but had no proof and wanted to keep Marten out of it. Or maybe, like everything else—from the house on Uxbridge Street to I. M. and Penrith's bar to April 7/Moscow and even to the chartered jet—there was nothing to grasp, and he simply saw the Romanov family dinner as nothing more than another society affair that the public liked to read about. After all, that was his job, too.

The trouble was that Marten now knew there had been some kind of relationship between Alfred Neuss and Sir Peter Kitner. What it was and whether it had to do with the Romanov family, at this point there was no way to know.

Suddenly two thoughts came in rapid succession. The first—what was the dinner commemorating?

Second—if menu #1 had been given a number, did it mean there was a menu #2? If there was, what was that occasion? Where was it to be held and when? And if there was a menu #2, was that what Ford had gone to see Jean-Luc about? But why in the middle of the night and to such a remote location? On the other hand, it made no sense, because Lenard had asked about a map. He glanced back at the menu.

Carte Commémorative.

Carte? What was that?

Next to the lamp on the far side of Armand's desk was a small pile of books. All were in French except one—a French-English dictionary. Quickly he picked it up and opened it to the *C*'s. On the sixth page he found *carte*—it meant (*marine, du ciel*) chart; (*de fichier, d'abonnement, etc., à jouer*) card; (*au restaurant*) menu; (*de géographie*) map!

Map!

Maybe Kovalenko had misinterpreted the French to mean "map" when the meaning that really applied was "menu."

Marten put down the dictionary and went through the rest of the entire Ford file looking for more on a second menu, Kitner, the Romanovs, or Jean-Luc Vabres, but he found nothing until he came to a nine-by-twelve envelope marked KITNER in pencil. He opened it to find a series of reprints of articles about Peter Kitner gleaned from various newspaper databases around the world. Most carried photographs of the tall, distinguished, white-haired Kitner and were in English, though several were in other languages—German, Italian, Japanese, and French. A quick read told him they were mostly gloss-overs about Kitner, his family, his British knighthood, the building of his media empire from his roots as the son of a moderately successful Swiss watchmaker. As far as he could tell there was nothing at all to indicate why he would be attending a Romanov family dinner other than the fact that he was Sir Peter Kitner and probably on the A-list of a thousand social events held around the world at any one time. As for the hoped-for second menu, or even a reference to it, or another reference to Jean-Luc Vabres, there was nothing.

Finally Marten put the clippings back and closed the file. Weary, discouraged he hadn't found more, he was getting up, finally ready for bed, when his eyes wandered to Halliday's appointment book and he suddenly wondered if there was something else in that unruly mass of paper and notes he had missed. Maybe Halliday had come upon a Romanov or Kitner, too.

He opened the book and went through it again, this time looking for any reference to Kitner, the Romanovs, Jean-Luc Vabres, or a menu.

5:20 A.M.

Wholly exhausted and finding nothing, he reached the book's last page. The only pieces still untouched on this go-round were the loose pages stuffed into the back, which he'd begun to look through earlier. With a deep sigh and a final effort, he pulled them out again. He saw the same photographs of Halliday's children and traveler's checks he'd seen before, then Halliday's electronic airline tickets and passport. For no particular reason he opened the passport. Halliday's photograph stared out at him. He looked at it for a moment, started to close it, then didn't. Something drew him to Halliday's eyes. It was almost as if the murdered detective were reaching out to him from the other side trying to tell him to look further. But where? He'd seen everything, there was nothing else. Slowly Marten closed the passport, put it with the papers, and then started to put the papers back into the pocket. It was then he again saw the awkward bulge where the cardboard backing of the day/date calendar had been slipped into the cover's leather sleeve. Thinking the bulge was just a crease in the cardboard, he tried to flatten it so the papers would fit more easily into the pocket. It wouldn't flatten.

"Dammit," he swore, too tired to fight it any longer. Then he realized the bulge was not a crease in the cardboard but something else. He pulled the cardboard sleeve out entirely and eased open the leather pocket. Inside, he saw a small, dog-eared packet of three-by-five cards held together with a rubber band. Quickly, he took the packet out and slid the elastic from it. When he did the cards fell open. Between them was a single computer disk.

Marten felt his heart skip a beat. He took a deep breath, and then a second, and booted up Armand's computer. Sliding in the disk, he clicked it on. The lone file on it was titled "Nonsense" and he felt the air go out of him. "Nonsense," some kind of computer game or a joke file someone had passed on to Halliday that he had stuck inside the cover of his book and forgotten about.

Disheartened, he clicked on the file anyway. A millisecond later its contents came up on the screen and the disappointment vanished.

"My God," he breathed. "Nonsense" was a copy of Raymond's missing LAPD booking file. On it were clear pictures of his mugshots and his fingerprints. As far as Marten knew, these were the only copies of his fingerprints still in existence.

5:50 A.M.

Abruptly Marten popped the file from the computer and shut it down. Then, sliding the disk back between the cards, he closed them with the rubber band and put them back in Halliday's appointment book, securing it with the big elastics. The question was what to do now. He had to sleep, at least for a while, but he also had to protect the information. Then he remembered the courtyard outside Armand's ground-floor dining room.

He stood quickly and gathered Halliday's appointment book and Ford's accordion file; then, carefully opening the door, he went out into the darkened hallway.

48

Seconds later Marten entered the dining room and looked out through French double doors to the small courtyard separating Armand's apartment building from the next. It wasn't much, but it was something, especially if the police—with Kovalenko distrusting him anyway, and having gone over Dan Ford's apartment inch by inch with a tech squad—had any suspicion at all that something was wrong or missing or not as it should be and came around asking questions, maybe even bringing some French version of a search warrant.

He was an American living in England, caught up in a series of ugly murders in France, where he had known two of the victims personally. If the police found the Ford and Halliday materials in his possession, Lenard would not only arrest him on the spot for concealing evidence but might be angry enough to send his photograph and fingerprints to Interpol to see if he had outstanding warrants against him in other countries. And who knew if his "friends" on the LAPD hadn't posted a Code Yellow/Missing Person "wanted" notice with Interpol on the off chance someone might identify him? Then what? Everything would be found out—who he was, where he was, about Rebecca, everything. Even Hiram Ott in Vermont could be exposed and prosecuted for illegally passing the identity of a dead person on to someone else.

And then it would be as he'd feared earlier. In very short order Gene VerMeer or some other messenger or messengers would be sent to execute the payback by those in the LAPD who still believed he was responsible for the deaths of Polchak and Lee and Valparaiso and for destroying the squad. It was something he couldn't let happen. On the other hand, it still remained "his war." What he'd found in Dan Ford's files and on Halliday's computer disk brought that war closer than ever.

———

Armand's wife kept her petite kitchen tidy and well organized, and it took Marten almost no time to find what he was looking for, a box of dark vinyl trash bags. He took one, put Halliday's appointment book and Ford's accordion file into it, twisted it closed, sealed it with a plastic tie, and went back into the dining room. There, he turned on a small lamp, unlocked the glass doors, and stepped out into the frigid early morning air. In the dim spill of the lamp he could see the courtyard was roughly ten by twenty feet with a six-foot-high wall at the back connecting the apartment buildings on either side. The wall itself was a scramble of winter-dead vines with a few evergreen shrubs in front of it and a large brick fountain, unused in winter, near the top.

Five steps and Marten was at the wall and pulling himself up. By now his eyes were becoming accustomed to the dark and he could see a narrow alley on the far side of the wall and several refuse cans on the ground immediately below. Twisting around, he peered into the fountain. Save for a collection of fallen leaves at the bottom, it was empty. Quickly he shoved the garbage bag inside and covered it over with the leaves. Then he turned and jumped to the ground.

The sky was still dark as he went back inside and locked the courtyard door. Three minutes later he was on the couch in Armand's study, blanket pulled up, his head eased into the pillow. Maybe he had bought himself insurance against the police, maybe not. Maybe they wouldn't come at all and he had just been overly cautious. At least he had the peace of mind of knowing Dan's files and Halliday's book were hidden away in a place not easily found and where he could retrieve them later from the alley side if he had to. He took a breath and rolled over. All he wanted now was sleep.

49

It was still dark when three men and two women stepped from the train in a group of departing passengers and crossed toward a dark gray Alfa Romeo sedan parked in the railway station lot. They were dressed plainly and spoke Spanish and looked very much like middle-class Spaniards entering France. The first two men were older and carried the women's bags as well as their own. The third was twenty-two, slight, and boyish, and carried his own luggage. The women were his mother and grandmother. The other men were bodyguards.

As they reached the car, one of the bodyguards stepped back to survey what was going on around them. The other loaded the luggage into the trunk. Two minutes later the Alfa turned out of the parking lot. Five minutes after that, it accelerated onto the A63 motorway heading away from the Spanish border toward the French coastal resort of Biarritz, the bodyguards in the front seats, the women and younger man in the back.

Octavio, the man driving, dark-haired and with a narrow scar across his lower lip, adjusted the rearview mirror. A quarter mile behind he could see a black four-door Saab following them. He knew the Saab would still be there when they turned east off the A63 and still with them when they turned north and passed through Toulouse on the A20 toward Paris. Two cars, four bodyguards protecting the three who had come in so quietly from Spain—Grand Duchess Catherine Mikhailovna of the Russian imperial family Romanov in exile; her mother, Grand Duchess Maria Kurakina, widow of Grand Duke Vladimir, a cousin of Tsar Nicholas II; and her twenty-two-year-old son, Grand Duke Sergei Petrovich Romanov, the man recognized by royal houses around the world as the legitimate heir to the throne of Russia, who, if the monarchy were to be restored, would become the first Tsar of Russia since Nicholas Alexandrovich Romanov, Tsar Nicholas II, was murdered with his wife and five children at the beginning of the Russian Revolution in 1918.

Grand Duchess Catherine glanced briefly at her son and turned to look back at the trailing Saab and then out at the dark of the passing countryside. In little more than twelve hours they would be in Paris and at a formal and very secretive gathering of the Romanov family at a private home on the Avenue Georges V. It was a gathering called for by one of the highest envoys of the Russian Orthodox Church, requesting that the family select the legitimate successor to the Russian throne, and was, for all intents, a clear signal that Russia was, in some way, prepared to reestablish the monarchy, most likely in the form of a constitutional monarchy where the Tsar would be little more than a figurehead. Still it was a day for which the Romanov family had held its collective breath—and had fought over, often desperately and angrily, casting aside one pretender to the throne after another—for nearly a century. With the gathering, everyone knew, would come the final battle, the choosing of a successor the entire family would agree on: the one Romanov who was the true heir in accordance with the fundamental laws of the Russian throne, which were that the crown must pass from the last Emperor to his eldest son, and from his eldest son to his eldest grandson, and on down.

In the long, Byzantine line of split families and family branches, Grand Duchess Catherine was certain there was only one true heir, and that was her son, Grand Duke Sergei Petrovich Romanov. She had taken great pains to make sure that when the time came, as it seemingly had now, there would be no question about it.

Since the fall of the Soviet Union, she, her mother, and Grand Duke Sergei had made yearly trips to Russia from their home in Madrid, developing friendships with key political, religious, and military leaders and all the while courting the media at every turn. It had been a shrewd and carefully orchestrated maneuver to create the lasting and very public impression that Sergei and Sergei alone was the legitimate heir to the throne.

If her ploy had been shameless and audacious, it had also split the family from the outset, because, while many supported Grand Duke Sergei in the complex labyrinth of claimants and pretenders to the throne, there were others who staked equal claim. Most notable was Prince Dimitrii Vladimir Romanov, who at seventy-seven, was the great-great-grandson of Emperor Nicholas I and a distant cousin of Nicholas II and who, as head of the Romanov family, was considered by many as the true heir. That his Parisian home on the Avenue Georges V was the setting for tonight's gathering made things all the more difficult if Grand Duke Sergei's supporters suddenly had a change of heart and sided with Prince Dimitrii instead.

Catherine let her gaze fall on her mother dozing in the seat between them and then looked to her son, who had the passenger lamp on and was absorbed with a game of solitaire on his laptop.

"When will we arrive in Paris?" she suddenly asked Octavio, the driver, in Spanish.

"Barring difficulty, about five this afternoon, Grand Duchess." Octavio glanced at her in the mirror; then she saw his eyes shift off to something in the distance behind them, and she knew he was looking to make certain the black Saab was still behind them.

Outside, the first streaks of the dawn on the horizon were bleak and gave the promise of a cold winter day. In the distance she could see the lights of the city of Toulouse, in the fifth century the capital of the Visigoths, now a high-tech center and home to giant aircraft makers Airbus and Aerospatiale.

Toulouse.

Suddenly a wave of melancholy passed through her. Twenty-three years earlier to the month, and five years before the death of her husband, Hans Friedrich Hohenzollern of Germany, Grand Duke Sergei had been conceived there, in a suite at the Grand Hôtel de l'Opéra.

Once again she saw Octavio glance in the mirror.

"Is there a problem?" she asked quickly. This time there was an edge to her voice.

"No, Grand Duchess."

She looked over her shoulder. The Saab was still there with two cars in between. She turned back, clicked on her own passenger light, and took a crossword puzzle from her purse to pass the time and help ease the worry that increased inside her by the mile. It was the reason for the bodyguards and the wearisome means of travel—an overnight train ride from Madrid to San Sebastian, the short commuter train to Hendaye, followed by a ten-hour trip by car to Paris—when a flight from Madrid to Paris took little more than two hours.

They were traveling in this exhausting and laborious manner because, despite the relative secrecy of the meeting tonight, any number of people knew of it, and the brutal murders of four Russian expatriates in the Americas a year earlier still resonated. Each victim had been a prominent Romanov—a fact known to few outside the family, but learned and carefully protected by the Russian investigators who had come to the scene for fear a political football would be made of it, both at home and abroad—and among Grand Duke Sergei's most vocal and outspoken supporters. Furthermore, the killings had come at a time when the rumors of a reinstatement of the monarchy were nearly as loud as they were now. A family gathering had even been arranged to discuss it but, in light of the murders, had been abruptly canceled.

At the time she had protested to the Russian government, suggesting the murders had been committed to silence family voices loyal to the Grand Duke, but no proof had ever been found. Instead the slayings were laid to the madman Raymond Oliver Thorne, who had been in each of the cities at the time of the crimes and who had died at the hands of the Los Angeles police. At about the same time, the talk supporting a reinstated monarchy quieted, and for a long time nothing happened.

Then, in just the last days, had come the murders of prominent Russian expatriates Fabien Curtay in Monaco and Alfred Neuss in Paris. Although neither had been a member of the royal family—and their political support of either candidate was not known—the killings unnerved all the Romanovs, especially when one considered Neuss had been a known target of Thorne before and the family gathering to which they were going was in the same city where he had been murdered.

"Your Highness." Octavio grinned and nodded toward a large overhead highway sign: PARIS. "We are getting closer."

"Yes, thank you." Grand Duchess Catherine Mikhailovna

tried not to think about what lay ahead and instead turned to the crossword puzzle in her lap. One question answered easily, and then two. The next nearly took her breath away in its irony.

It was 24 Across, asking for a nine-letter word for "Tsar-to-be." She smiled and swiftly, and in pen, wrote the answer.

T-S-A-R-E-V-I-C-H.

50

PARIS. 7:50 A.M.

Somewhere far off Nicholas Marten heard a doorbell ring. It rang once and then twice. Then rang again with the same impatient one, two. Finally the chimes stopped, and he thought he heard voices but wasn't sure. A moment later there was a knock on his door and Armand came in wearing a T-shirt and jockey shorts and wiping shaving cream from his face.

"I think you'd better come."

"What is it?"

"The police."

"What?" Marten was suddenly alert.

"And a woman."

"Woman?"

"Yes."

"Who is she?"

"I don't know."

Abruptly Marten threw back the blanket, pulled on his jeans and sweatshirt, and followed Armand out of the room. How long had he slept? An hour, two at most? He'd been right about the police. But who was the woman? Certainly not Rebecca. Armand would have said so. Then they were at the door and he saw her and his jaw dropped.

"Clem!"

"Nicholas, what the fuck is going on?"

Lady Clementine Simpson pushed toward him, half dragging a uniformed policewoman with her. Her navy business suit rumpled, her hair disheveled, she was exasperated, exhausted, and clearly infuriated.

Then he saw Lenard waiting in the hallway behind her, a large manila envelope tucked under his arm. With him was another Parisian detective Marten knew as Roget, two uniformed officers, and—Kovalenko.

"This man," Lady Clem turned to glare at Lenard, "and the one with the beard, he's Russian, met me at the airport and took me into a back room and started questioning me! They've been asking me questions ever since." She looked back to Marten.

"How the hell did they know I was coming? Or even who I was? I'll tell you how. One of them called the university and managed to find out what no one but a very select few have found out in eight months! And you know very well what I am talking about."

"Clem, calm down."

"I have calmed down. You should have seen me before."

Lenard stepped forward. "It would be better if we talked inside."

Nadine came out of her bedroom as Armand led them back into the apartment and down a narrow hallway toward the living room. The confines had no effect on Lady Clem. She was all wound up and still roaring mad.

"They tried to contact me in Amsterdam, but I'd already left to come here because I had seen the story about Dan on the news and couldn't reach you or Rebecca. Or Nadine—the police were at her apartment. I left word, but"—she glared back at Lenard—"no one seems to have paid much attention until I landed in Paris!" She looked back to Marten. "The hotel in Amsterdam advised them what flight I was on. How is that for good business practice?"

"They are the police."

Again Clem looked over her shoulder at Lenard. "I don't care who they are."

Again she swung back to Marten. "I was worried. I tried to call you a dozen times at least. Do you never answer your cell phone or at least check your voice mail?"

"Clem, a lot's been going on. Somewhere I lost the phone. I never got around to checking my voice mail either."

Clem glared at him for the briefest moment, then abruptly dropped her voice. "They wanted to know about you and Dan. And a man named Halliday. Do you know a man named Halliday?"

"Yes."

"They also wanted to know about an Alfred Neuss."

"Clem, both Halliday and Alfred Neuss were murdered in Paris."

51

Marten and Lady Clem and Nadine Ford sat on a couch in front of a large antique coffee table. Armand was in an armchair at one end of it, and the detective Roget sat on a straight-back chair at the other. The two uniforms took up positions outside the living room door, while the policewoman stood just inside it.

Marten could see Lenard holding the manila envelope and talking with Kovalenko in the hallway. They chatted a moment longer and then came in, with Lenard pulling up a chair directly across from Marten and putting the envelope on the coffee table between them. Kovalenko stepped back to cross his arms over his chest and lean against the window casing, watching them.

"I don't know what you're doing, why you involved Lady Clementine, or why you're here," Marten said, looking directly at Lenard, "but in the future, if you have a question that has to do with me, I would appreciate it if you came to me first, before you start involving other people."

"We are dealing with murder, Monsieur Marten," Lenard said flatly.

Marten kept his eyes on Lenard. "I'll say again, Inspector. In the future, if you have a question that has to do with me, I would appreciate it if you came to me first."

Lenard ignored his comment. "I would ask you to look at some photographs." He fingered the manila envelope and looked to Nadine and Lady Clem. "You may wish to turn away, *mesdames*. They are rather graphic."

"And I'm rather fine the way I am." Clem had lost none of her fire.

"As you wish." Lenard glanced at Marten and opened the envelope, then one by one placed a series of photographs in front of him. They were crime scene photos taken in Halliday's room at the Hôtel Eiffel Cambronne. Each photo had a date and time code in the lower right-hand corner.

The first was a wide shot of the room with Halliday's body on the bed. The second, of Halliday's opened luggage. There was another angle of Halliday on the bed. And still another and then another. Then Lenard selected three of the photographs.

"In each we see the dead man, the bed, and the nightstand behind it. All taken from a slightly different angle. Is there anything you find noticeably different from one to another?"

"No." Marten shrugged. He knew what was coming, but he wasn't about to show it.

"The first pictures were taken as you and Dan Ford arrived. The last was taken some twenty seconds after you left."

"What's the point?"

"In the first pictures you will see an old and rather substantial daily calendar or appointment book on the nightstand. In the last it is no longer there. Where is it?"

"Why are you asking me?"

"Because either you or Dan Ford took it. And it wasn't in Monsieur Ford's car or anywhere in his apartment."

"I didn't take it. Maybe somebody else did. There were other people in the room." Marten looked to Kovalenko. "Did you ask the Russian?"

"The Russian did not take it," Kovalenko said without emotion, and Marten watched him for a moment longer. There was something in the way he stood leaning against the window casing with his arms crossed over his chest watching them. It reminded him of the feeling he'd had when they'd first met at the Halliday murder scene. Kovalenko looked soft, even academic, but he was far from either and was now, as he had been then, digging for something more. Maybe even more than he'd told the French police. What that was or what he thought Marten knew that he wasn't revealing wasn't possible to know.

What was clear was that it had been Kovalenko who learned about his relationship with Clem, tracked her down in Amsterdam and learned she was on her way to Paris, and then persuaded Lenard to apprehend and question her under whatever French law applied and then bring her here. It was the same thing they had done to him when they'd brought him to the murder scenes at the river and questioned him afterward. They wanted to see how she would react and then how he would react to her presence and the way she had been treated. If it seemed extreme, it was, and it meant whatever Kovalenko was after was larger than a few murders. And obviously he didn't care what buttons he pushed or on what level, because he certainly would have known who Clem was and who her father was.

"You packed two pieces of luggage when you left your apartment to come here." Lenard was suddenly looking at Nadine. "What did you put in them?"

Marten started. This was what he'd been afraid of. Nadine was in no emotional state to be interrogated. There was no way to know how she would react or what she would say. In one way he half expected her to tell Lenard exactly what she'd done. In another, he realized she had been strong enough to do what she had done in the first place and therefore was prepared to be questioned by the police in the event it came to that.

"Clothes," she said impassively.

"What else?" Lenard pressed her.

"Just clothes and toiletries. I packed mine and put Monsieur Marten's into his own suitcase, as I believe you asked me to do when you so hurriedly took over my house."

Marten smiled to himself. She was good. Maybe she'd learned that self-assurance from Dan, or maybe that was what Dan had seen in her to begin with. He knew then she had done this for Dan, and for Marten, too, because of their friendship and because he would have wanted her to.

Abruptly Lenard stood up. "I would like to have my people look through the apartment."

"This is not my apartment," Nadine said. "The permission is not mine to give."

"It's not mine either, but if it's alright with Armand, go ahead," Marten said. "We have nothing to hide." He saw Nadine glance at him in alarm, but he didn't respond.

"Help yourselves," Armand said.

Lenard nodded at Roget and the detective got up and left the room. The two uniforms went with him.

Marten had done what he had to immediately take away any suspicion and trusted Lenard's men would do their search quickly and confine it to the apartment itself and not venture out into the freezing cold of the courtyard. The trouble was Nadine didn't know the materials were hidden away. She'd done well and she was strong, but her glance at Marten had revealed her anxiety. Lenard was still in the room; so was Kovalenko. The longer the search took, the more nervous she would become and they would see it. He needed to do something to ease the tension and at the same time learn something.

"Maybe while your men are tearing things apart you could tell us something about what you found when you went over the cars," he said to Lenard. "After all, I was there at your invitation."

Lenard stared at him for a brief moment, then nodded. "The body in the second car was indeed the man called Jean-Luc."

"Who is he?"

"A salesman for a printing company. It's as much as we know so far."

"That's all? You found nothing else?"

"Perhaps it would not be inappropriate, Inspector," Kovalenko said from where he leaned against the window casing, "for us to share our information with Mr. Marten or Mrs. Ford."

"As you wish," Lenard acquiesced.

Kovalenko looked to Nadine. "Your husband did not struggle long, but he did manage to do so long enough to force his assailant to press his hand against the window glass on the driver's side. A few moments later the killer rolled the window down so that the river water would fill the car and sink it. In doing so he inadvertently helped preserve his own evidence by taking the glass out of the rush of water."

"You're saying you have a fingerprint?" Marten worked deliberately not to reveal the jolt of excitement that shot through him.

"Yes," Lenard said.

Marten glanced down the hall. Lenard's men were still there. He could see two in the kitchen, another entering the bathroom, another still standing in the door of the den where he had gone over the files and slept. How long were they going to take?

Marten looked back and saw Lenard glance at Kovalenko. The Russian nodded, and Lenard turned to Marten.

"Monsieur, I could put you under arrest for suspicion of removing evidence from a crime scene. Instead, and for your own well-being in the face of what is going on, I will politely ask you to leave France."

"What?" Marten was completely taken aback.

Abruptly Lenard stood. "The next Chunnel train leaves for London in forty-five minutes. I will have my men take you to it and see you on board. To make certain you arrive safely we have asked the London Metropolitan Police to meet the train and after that the Greater Manchester Police to advise us upon your arrival there."

Marten glanced at Kovalenko, who pushed away from the window and walked out of the room. So that was what Kovalenko's nod to Lenard had been about. The Russian had learned all he could and had no more need of Marten, so he gave Lenard his blessing to get rid of him.

"I've done nothing," Marten protested. The swift arrival of Lenard and Kovalenko had proven his instincts right, and hiding the files away outside of the apartment had been a prudent move, but Lenard's action was wholly unanticipated. The police were still there and being extremely methodical. If Lenard's men escorted him to the train right then and they kept on the way they were, eventually they would go out into the courtyard. Once they did, and found the files, they would be in touch with the London police, who would put him under arrest the moment he stepped off the train and send him straight back to Paris.

"Monsieur Marten, perhaps you would prefer to wait in a jail cell while your protest is discussed with the examining magistrate."

Marten didn't know what to do. His best bet was to find a

way to stay there and hope Lenard's men found nothing. At least he could retrieve the files right then. It was true that if he left and they found nothing, he might find a way to have Nadine or Armand recover them and ship them to him in Manchester, but that would take time, and there was every chance they would still be watched.

Moreover, what was going on was happening here in Paris, not Manchester. Lenard himself had said the murdered Jean-Luc was a salesman for a printing company. That substantiated the fact that he had delivered the first menu to Dan Ford, which meant there was every chance, as he had thought before, there was a second menu, and that second menu was what Ford had gone to get from Jean-Luc when he was murdered. And tonight in Paris was the occasion of the first menu—the Romanov dinner, which Peter Kitner was to attend.

Better to try to stay and hope they don't find the files, Marten thought. If they do, whether I'm here or in England, they'll lock me up anyway. If they don't and I'm in Manchester, too much time will pass. More than that, Lenard will make certain a warning is sent to French Immigration—meaning trying to get back into the country once I'm out will be very difficult.

"Inspector, please." Marten took the only avenue he had left, Lenard's mercy. "Dan Ford was my closest friend. His wife and family have made arrangements to have him buried here in Paris. I would very much like to be permitted to stay until then."

"I'm sorry." Lenard was abrupt and final. "My men will help you gather your belongings and see you to the train." He looked to Lady Clem.

"With all respect to you, madame, and to your father, I would suggest you accompany your friend on the train and afterward make certain he does not attempt to return to France. I would hate to see how the tabloid press would react should they learn of our investigation." He hesitated, then half smiled. "I can already imagine the headlines and what a clamor, warranted or not, they would cause. To say nothing of the exposure of what"—he glanced at Marten—"seems to be a rather confidential relationship."

52

Inspector Roget and two of Lenard's uniforms escorted Nicholas Marten and Lady Clem through the crowd of waiting passengers and down the platform alongside the Eurostar, the high-speed Paris-to-London Chunnel train.

Marten walked as if he were in handcuffs and a straitjacket, helpless to do anything but what he was told. At the same time he kept a careful eye on Clem, who was ready to explode but so far had managed to keep silent, no matter her rage. Probably because she knew what Lenard had threatened about the British tabloids was true. Their livelihood was built on just this kind of stuff, and they would have a field day with it. And Clem well knew that her father would be more than embarrassed, he would be enraged—demanding to know what the damn hell had gone on. When he found out, he might very well demand a public apology from the French government, which would enliven the tabloid coverage a hundredfold and make a mess out of their life in Manchester, to the point where, because of university rules, either Lady Clem would have to resign or he would be forced to leave the school, or both. Moreover, the paparazzi would instantly be on their doorstep, and their photographs would be plastered everywhere, even across the U.S. tabloids. And for Marten that brought the risk that someone on the LAPD would see them. So if things were bad, they threatened to get a great deal worse if Clem exploded. Thankfully, she hadn't. Quite obviously Lenard had known exactly what buttons to push that would keep Clem and the entire affair silent.

That aside, the two most important pieces of information— Raymond's LAPD files found on the computer disk inside Halliday's appointment book and the clear fingerprint that Dan

Ford had somehow forced his killer to leave against the Peugeot's window glass even as he was being murdered—had been left behind; one, in the green trash bag hidden in Armand's courtyard fountain; the other, in the investigative files of the Paris police. Together they would have revealed a definitive truth: that either the fingerprints matched and Dan Ford's killer had, without doubt, been Raymond; or that they didn't and the present madman was someone else entirely. But it was something he would never know without revealing the materials to the police—and that was something he couldn't do. If he did, the materials would immediately be confiscated and he would be thrown in jail himself for, as Lenard said, "removing evidence from a crime scene." Right away he would be wholly out of the picture, trapped in the machinery of French jurisprudence, and most likely waiting for someone from the LAPD to arrive to question him further. So instead, the files, at least when he had left the apartment, remained hidden and he was on his way out of the country.

Suddenly Roget stopped beside car number 5922.

"We are here." Abruptly he turned to Marten. "Your passport, please."

"My passport?"

"*Oui.*"

Sixty seconds later Marten and Lady Clem were seated in standard class seats, with Roget and the two uniforms in the aisle in front of them discussing the situation in French with the train's ticket collector and one of its security guards. Finally Roget handed the ticket collector Marten's passport and told Marten his passport would be returned to him when the train reached London. Then he wished him a pointed *bon voyage,* looked at Lady Clem, and left, along with the uniforms.

Afterward the security guard and ticket collector fixed them with a stare and then they, too, turned and walked off, glancing back as they reached the end of the car before walking through the sliding door into the car beyond.

"What was it?" Lady Clem looked at Marten.

"What was what?"

"The whole time the police were showing you the photographs and afterward when you were arguing with them, something was going on between you and Nadine."

"No."

"Oh, yes, there was." Clem looked up at the boarding passengers, then back to Marten. "Nicholas, this train, apart from most others traveling to and around the U.K., is on time. It will leave at exactly ten-nineteen, which means you have"—Lady Clem looked at her watch—"about thirty-five seconds before the doors close and it begins to move."

"I don't know what in the world you're talking about."

Clem leaned in and lowered her voice, her British accent increasingly clipped. "Inspector Lenard came to Armand's apartment looking for the late Mr. Halliday's address book. Obviously whatever is in it is important or you, or Nadine, wouldn't have hidden it away."

"What makes you think—"

"Twenty-five seconds."

"Clem, if I had given it to them"—Marten was whispering—"at this moment Nadine and I would both be in a French jail, and you might very well be with us."

"Nicholas, maybe Inspector Lenard has found the book and maybe he hasn't. But I know you are a very bright man and would have hidden it well. So I think it's best to assume he hasn't and make one last try to retrieve it before he does. Twenty seconds."

"I—"

"Nicholas, stand up and get off the train. If the ticket taker or security man comes I'll say you're in the loo. When we get to London I'll tell the Metropolitan Police you suffer terribly from claustrophobia and couldn't possibly survive a thirty-mile ride through a tunnel a hundred and fifty feet beneath the English Channel without having a seizure. You had no choice but to get off the train before it left, promising me, cross your heart, you would take the next flight to Manchester and inform Inspector Lenard the moment you got there."

"How could I fly to Manchester? I don't have a passport!"

"Nicholas, get off the fucking train!"

53

Peter Kitner watched the black Citroen sedan pass through the gates and start up the driveway toward his extensive four-story home on the Avenue Victor Hugo. In it would be Dr. Geoffrey Higgs, his personal bodyguard and chief of intelligence. By now Higgs would know whether his greatest fear was true—that the man who had spoken to him from the darkness behind the media lights at the Hôtel Crillon was who he had finally admitted to himself it might be.

"How could he know about Davos?" His son, Michael, had pressed him in the limousine as they'd left the Crillon. And he'd snapped, "I don't know."

The trouble was he did know. And had known even then but had refused to acknowledge it, even to himself. But finally he had, and had asked Higgs to find out what he could and as quickly as possible, most especially if the questioner had planned to attend the forum at Davos himself.

Alfred Neuss and Fabien Curtay were dead, and the Spanish knife and the reel of 8 mm film Neuss had protected for so long were gone, taken by Curtay's killer. Other than Neuss and Curtay and himself, only two others knew the knife and film existed, the two people who he was certain had them now—the Baroness Marga de Vienne and the man to whom she had been legal guardian for most of his life, Alexander Luis Cabrera. And it was Cabrera, he was certain, who had spoken from behind the lights.

Michael's words echoed again. *How could he know about Davos?*

Kitner sat down behind his massive glass-and-stainless-steel desk. Maybe it was a guess, he thought. Maybe Cabrera just assumed he would be attending the World Economic Forum in Switzerland, which he had not done in years, and wanted to toy with him by getting the media fired up. It had to be that, because there was no way he could know. Even the Baroness with her extensive reach and connections could not know. What was to really happen in Davos was all too secret.

There was a sharp knock at the door and then it opened and Taylor Barrie, Kitner's fifty-year-old executive secretary, stepped inside.

"Dr. Higgs, sir."

"Thank you."

Higgs entered and Barrie left, closing the door behind him.

"Well?"

"You had raised concern that Alexander Cabrera would be attending the economic forum at Davos," Higgs said quietly.

"Yes."

"He is not on any of the guest panels, nor has he registered to attend any discussion groups. However, a mountain château outside of the city has been rented by a Zurich-based attorney named Jacques Bertrand."

"Go on."

"Bertrand is a middle-aged bachelor who shares a small Zurich apartment with an elderly aunt."

"So?"

"The château he has rented is called Villa Enkratzer. Taken literally it means Villa Skyscraper. It has sixty rooms and an underground garage for twenty cars."

"How does that bring us to Cabrera?"

"Helilink, a private helicopter firm based in Zurich—"

"I know Helilink. What about it?"

"The firm has been hired to provide twin-engine helicopter service from Zurich to the château in Davos, Saturday, two days from now. The booking was made by the private secretary of a Gerard Rothfels. Rothfels is in charge of Cabrera's European operation."

"I see." Kitner turned slowly in his chair, then stood and walked to the window behind him to look down at his formal garden, stick-bare on this January day.

So his fears had not only been confirmed, they'd become infinitely darker. Yes, it had been Cabrera who'd taunted him at the Crillon about Davos. But his purpose had been more than to taunt. Cabrera was telling Kitner that he knew what was to happen there. Now Higgs had confirmed Cabrera would be there when it did.

That left little doubt the Baroness would be there, too.

What had originally been conceived by a Swiss professor of business administration as a kind of annual weeklong think tank for top European business executives to discuss international trade in the isolated Swiss alpine resort of Davos had evolved into a colossal coming-together of world political and business leaders to, in essence, work out the future on a world scale. This year would be no different except that Russian president Pavel Gitinov was to make a major announcement about the future of the new Russia in an increasingly electronic and global world. And Kitner, with his huge media reach and expertise, was to be a key player in what that future would bring.

That was what troubled him, and deeply.

Cabrera knew of the announcement, and that was information that would only have come from the Baroness herself. How she knew was another subject altogether because it was secret—a decision reached only days earlier at a meeting between Kitner, President Gitinov, and top Russian leaders at a private villa on the Black Sea. But the how of it made little difference. The fact was, she knew, and Cabrera knew, and both would be in Davos when the announcement was made.

Abruptly Kitner turned to Higgs. "Where is Michael?"

"In Munich, sir. And then Rome tomorrow. Later in the day he will join you and your wife and daughters in Davos."

"Do they have the usual security?"

"Yes, sir."

"Double it."

"Yes, sir."

"Thank you, Higgs."

Higgs nodded sharply, then turned and left.

Kitner watched him go, then went to his desk and sat down, his thoughts wholly on the Baroness and Cabrera.

What in God's name were they doing? The Baroness had nearly as much money and influence as he did. Cabrera had become a very successful businessman. That Neuss and Curtay were dead and the knife and film were the only things taken from Curtay's safe made him assume the Baroness was not only responsible for their deaths but had both items in her possession. If that was true, both of them were safe. So why the taunting at the hotel, and why were they coming to Davos—what else did they want?

It was something he had to find out and quickly, before the forum at Davos even began. Immediately he pressed a button on his intercom. Seconds later the door opened and Taylor Barrie entered.

"Yes, sir."

"I want you to arrange a private meeting for tomorrow morning, somewhere away from Paris. It is to be between me, Alexander Cabrera, and the Baroness Marga de Vienne. No one else is to be present. None of their people, none of mine."

"You will want Michael to be there."

"No, I do not want Michael to be there. Or even to know about it," Kitner said harshly.

"What about Higgs and me, sir?"

"No one. Is that clear?"

"Yes, sir. No one, sir," Barrie said quickly and then turned and left, closing the door behind him. It was the first time in his ten-year employment he'd seen Kitner filled with such grave intensity.

54

THE PARIS METRO. STILL THURSDAY, JANUARY 16.
11:05 A.M.

Nick Marten held on to a handrail in the swaying subway car praying he had taken the right Metro line from the railway station. Apart from the sweater, jeans, sports jacket, and running shoes he wore, all he had was his wallet with his English driver's license, Manchester University student ID, a photograph of Rebecca taken at Jura, two credit cards, and about three hundred dollars in euros. Enough for an enjoyable student week in Paris perhaps, but hardly enough for a man already in trouble with the police and now in the country illegally. Yet that part of it was something he couldn't think of. His job, first and foremost, was to get to the rue Huysmans, find the alley behind Armand's apartment, and then find the wall behind his courtyard. And then hope to God Lenard's men had left without finding the trash bag.

If they had, it was a simple matter of scaling the wall and retrieving the hidden trash bag from the fountain. It was a process that should take no more than ten seconds, fifteen at most if he had trouble climbing the wall. Simple enough if he had taken the proper Metro line and could find the rue Huysmans. Beyond that were two major obstacles. First, what to do if Lenard's men were still there. Second, what to do if they weren't and he was successful in retrieving the bag containing the files. What then? Where would he go? Or stay? And, after that, and most difficult of all, how to get a copy of the fingerprint Dan Ford's killer had left from the Paris police? But for now he had to address the first of his problems—finding the alley and retrieving the trash bag.

BOULEVARD RASPAIL. 11:27 A.M.

Marten emerged from the Metro station in bright sunlight and stopped to get his bearings.

Down and across the boulevard he could see the imposing buildings of what appeared to be a university. He walked toward them until he could make out an identifying sign—COLLÈGE STANISLAS. His heart jumped. Lenard had driven past it when they had come in from the Seine and dropped him off at Armand's apartment. Another twenty feet and he saw a familiar street to his right. Rue Huysmans.

He walked quickly down it, part of him alert for the police, another looking for a walkway that would lead to the alley behind. He passed one building and then two and then saw a narrow opening between buildings. He turned down it and a moment later was in the alley.

He started forward cautiously. A blue car was parked to the side halfway to the end, and beyond it, a delivery truck. No one seemed to be in either. He picked up his pace, looking for a courtyard wall separating buildings with trash cans stored against it. A dozen paces more and he saw them. Instinctively, he stopped and looked back at the alley behind him. There was no one, not even a dog.

Three steps and he was climbing on the cans, then pulling himself up the wall. At the top he stopped and peered over. As quickly his eyes went wide and he jumped back. It was a cold January day, and yet a completely naked young couple was making love on a courtyard bench. He recognized neither of them. Who were they? How long would they be there? At the same moment he saw something from the corner of his eye. A police car had turned into the alley and was slowly coming toward him.

He started and looked around. There was no place to go. Nor could he simply turn and walk away without drawing attention to himself. What to do? Then he saw several cardboard boxes stored against the wall in the shadows behind him. Pulling back, he ducked behind them and knelt down, trying to get out of sight. Five seconds passed, then ten. Where was the police car? Had the uniforms seen him and stopped? Were they already out, guns drawn, approaching him? Then the car's front bumper passed and then the entire car rolled slowly by. He let out a breath and counted slowly to twenty and then eased forward and looked down the alley. The car was gone. He glanced in the other direction. Nothing but the blue car and delivery truck beyond it. Then he saw several more trash cans stored against another wall. They were the ones he remembered seeing before. That was Armand's wall.

Boldly he went forward. Five seconds later he was at the wall, once again using the trash cans to climb up. He hesitated at the top as he had before and carefully peered over. He recognized Armand's courtyard immediately. Hurriedly, he scanned the apartment windows for signs of movement inside. He could see none. Taking the chance, he eased up and looked down into the fountain nestled in the winter-dead ivy covering the wall. He could see the trash bag covered with a layer of leaves, just as he had left it. One last glance at the apartment and he reached down. His fingers grasped the cold plastic. In a split second he had the bag up and out and was back over the wall. His feet touched the trash cans and he stepped down into the alley. Just as he did, the driver's door of the blue car opened. A man stepped out.

Kovalenko.

55

"Three freshly broken twigs in the ivy stalks," Kovalenko said as he drove them quickly off, turning down the Boulevard Raspail and then onto the rue de Vaugirard. "Lenard's men came into the courtyard, looked around for a moment or two, then went right back into the building. City people, I think. Not like a Russian brought up with the beauty and hardships of life in the country, or Americans who like to watch western movies. Do you like westerns, Mr. Marten?"

Nick Marten didn't know what to say or think. Kovalenko had simply shown himself and asked politely if Marten would get into the blue car, which, considering his lack of alternatives, he had. Now Kovalenko was obviously delivering him to the French police.

"You found the bag and saw what was in it," he said unhappily.

Kovalenko nodded. "Yes."

"Why didn't you give it to Lenard?"

"For the simple reason I found it and Lenard did not."

"Then why did you leave it there, why not just take it?"

"Because I knew that at some point the person responsible for hiding it would want to retrieve it. And now I have both the person and the evidence." Kovalenko turned onto the Boulevard Saint-Michel and slowed for traffic. "What did you find or think you might find in Detective Halliday's appointment book that was so important you risked arrest, not once, but as we have seen, twice? Evidence that might incriminate you?"

Marten was startled. "You don't think I killed Halliday?"

"You turned away when you saw him in Parc Monceau."

"I told you why. I owed him money."

"Who is to corroborate that?"

"I didn't kill him."

"Nor did you take his appointment book." Kovalenko looked at Marten directly, then turned back to the traffic in front of him.

"Let's assume for the moment that you did not kill him. Either you or Mr. Ford exhibited not inconsiderable bravado by snatching a piece of evidence from under the noses of the police at a murder scene. Which means you either knew, or believed, that what was in it had considerable value. Correct? And then, of course, there is the other piece that was in the bag, the accordion file. Where did that come from and what is its value?"

Marten looked up. They were crossing the Seine on the Pont Saint-Michel. Directly ahead were the headquarters of the Paris Prefecture of Police.

"What good does it do to put me in jail?"

Kovalenko didn't reply. In a moment they were at police headquarters. Marten expected the Russian to slow and turn in, but he didn't. He kept on going, driving along Boulevard de Sebastopol and venturing deeper into the city's Right Bank.

"Where are we going?"

Kovalenko remained silent.

"What do you want from me?"

"My reading of English, Mr. Marten, especially handwritten English, with all its uses of slang and shortcuts, is not the best." Kovalenko took his eyes from the road to look at Marten. "So, what do I want from you? I want you to take me on a journey through the appointment book and the other file as well."

127 AVENUE HOCHE. 12:55 P.M.

Flashlight on, electric power off.

One screw at the top and then a second and then two more on the bottom and Alexander lifted the cover from the main electric panel. Two more screws and he loosened a large 220-volt circuit breaker. Being careful not to disturb the wires connecting it, he lifted it free.

Next he opened a canvas workbag and took out a miniature

timer with heavy-gauge wire-connectors at either end. Cautiously, he removed a connecting wire from the circuit breaker and attached it to one end of the timer, then did the same with a similar wire at the other end of the circuit breaker, in effect giving the timer control over the entire breaker. He put the breaker back in the panel and screwed it tight, then replaced the panel cover and the original four screws he had taken out.

Flashlight off, electric power restored.

Five seconds later he walked up the stairs from the basement, opened a service door, and went out into the alley. Parked outside was a rented Ford van. He got into it and drove off. The blue overalls and blond wig he wore, and the fake electrician's license in his pocket, had been unnecessary. The door had been unlocked; no one had seen him come or go. Nor had he given anyone time to complain that the lights were out. The entire procedure from beginning to end had taken less than five minutes.

At precisely 3:17 tomorrow morning, Friday, January 17, the timer would go off, sending an arc of electricity through the entire panel and plunging the building into darkness. Within seconds an intense electrical fire, driven by a phosphorus pellet inside the timer, would erupt inside the panel. The building was wood framed and old, as was the wiring. As with many memorable buildings in Paris, the landlord's money had been spent on plaster and cosmetics, not safety. Within minutes the fire would spread throughout the structure, and by the time the first alarm had sounded the building would be a roaring inferno. Without electricity its elevators would be useless and the interior stairway, pitch-black. The building had seven floors, with two large apartments to each floor. Only those residents on the bottommost floors would survive. Those higher up would have very little chance to escape. Those at the very top, the penthouse, would have no chance at all. It was the top-floor penthouse at the front he cared most about. It had been rented by Grand Duchess Catherine Mikhailovna for herself, her mother, Grand Duchess Maria Kurakina, and her son, twenty-two-year-old Grand Duke Sergei Petrovich Romanov, the man most suspected would, if Russia allowed, become her next Tsar. Alexander's work had assured he would not.

56

Nick Marten stood by the window in Kovalenko's cold, ramshackle hotel room listening to the click of the keys as the Russian detective worked his laptop, writing a report on the events of the day that needed to be forwarded to Moscow immediately. On the bed behind the small desk where Kovalenko worked were Halliday's appointment book and Dan Ford's large accordion file. Neither had been opened.

Watching Kovalenko work—big, bearded, bearish, his belly pushing solidly against the blue sweater he wore beneath his suit jacket, a large automatic just visible in a waist holster—Marten again had the sense that he was far from the easygoing, professorial man he appeared. It was what he had felt the first time they'd met in the hotel room with Lenard's men all around and Halliday's body on the bed and then again in Armand's apartment.

As good a detective as Lenard was, Kovalenko was better; shrewder, more independent, more persistent. He had proven it over and over: his unauthorized stakeout of Dan Ford's apartment, his early-morning pursuit of Ford into the countryside, his deliberate questioning of Marten on the way back from the river murder scenes; his apparent orchestration of the whole intimidating thing with Clem; his exacting search of Armand's courtyard when Lenard's men had turned away, and his subsequent discovery of the hidden trash bag. Then, instead of giving it over to the French police, he staked out the area and waited for someone to retrieve it—someone he was certain would come from the alley side and not from the apartment. Chiefly, Marten himself. How long the Russian had been prepared to wait, Marten had no idea, but it was the kind of canny, forceful behavior Red McClatchy would have loved.

His intensity and diligence aside, the question was, why? What was he up to? Again came the sense that Kovalenko's presence in Paris had to do with more than the murder of Alfred Neuss, something he was not acknowledging, even to the French police, and that he was working wholly on his own agenda. Put that together with what he might have learned from the Russian investigators who had been in L.A. shortly after Raymond had been killed and the knowledge that Halliday had been part of the original LAPD investigation team and it made perfect sense to think that Kovalenko had clearly tied the past to the present, meaning he believed what happened before in L.A. had everything to do with what was going on now in Paris.

"Vodka, Mr. Marten?" Kovalenko abruptly shut down his laptop and got up, crossing the frigid room toward a relic of a night table where a bottle of Russian vodka sat, two-thirds empty.

"No, thanks."

"Then I will drink for both of us." Kovalenko poured a double shot of the colorless liquid into a small glass, lifted it in toast to Marten, and downed it.

"Explain to me what is there," he said, gesturing with his glass toward the bed, Halliday's appointment book and Dan Ford's accordion file beside it.

"What do you mean?"

"What you found in Detective Halliday's book and the other piece."

"Nothing."

"No? Mr. Marten, you should remember I am not entirely convinced you are not Mr. Halliday's killer. Nor, for that matter, is Inspector Lenard. If you wish me to include the French police, I will."

"Alright," Marten said brusquely and went over and poured himself a double shot of vodka. Downing it in one swallow, he held the empty glass and looked at Kovalenko. There was no point in keeping quiet now. All the information was there on the bed. It was only a matter of time before Kovalenko uncovered it.

"Do you know the name Raymond Oliver Thorne?"

"Of course. He was looking for Alfred Neuss in Los Angeles. He was shot in a battle with the police and later died. His body was cremated."

"Maybe not."

"What do you mean?"

"I mean Dan Ford didn't think so. He discovered that Thorne's police records were missing from the numerous official files they were in. Moreover, the people involved with Thorne's death certificate and his cremation are either dead or missing. Apparently Halliday had the same opinion, because he was following a prominent California plastic surgeon who suddenly retired and moved to Costa Rica within days of Thorne's death. Later the same man showed up in Argentina with his name changed. What that means, I don't know. But it was enough to make Halliday buy himself a plane ticket to Buenos Aires. He had planned to go there right after he was finished here in Paris. It's in there." Marten nodded toward the appointment book on the bed. "His notes on it, his ticket, too."

"Why were you keeping this information from Inspector Lenard?"

It was a good question and Marten didn't know how to answer it, or at least answer without revealing who he was. Or telling what had happened with Raymond in L.A. and why the men of the squad were dead.

Suddenly it occurred to him how he could avoid a direct answer and at the same time get the thing he needed most but had no access to—a copy of the fingerprint the police had lifted from Dan Ford's car. It was chancy, because if Kovalenko turned against him he could lose everything and in a blink end up in the custody of the Paris police. Still, it was an opportunity he hadn't expected, and whatever the risk he would be foolish not to at least try.

"What if I told you Dan Ford suspected it was Raymond Thorne who killed Alfred Neuss?"

"Thorne?"

"Yes. And maybe Halliday and Dan himself. As you know, all three of them were involved when Thorne was in L.A."

A spark Marten hadn't seen before suddenly showed in Kovalenko's eyes. It told him he was on the right track, and he kept on.

"Neuss is murdered in Paris. Halliday comes to follow up. And Ford is already here as the *Los Angeles Times* correspondent. None of them recognized Raymond because he'd had cosmetic surgery, but he knew them all and they were getting too close to whatever he was doing."

"That means you are accepting that Neuss was his primary target, Mr. Marten." Kovalenko picked up the vodka as if it were part of his arm, poured what was left into his glass and then Marten's, and handed Marten the glass. "Did Ford have a theory about what this Raymond Thorne might have wanted from Neuss, before, in Los Angeles, or now, in Paris? Or why he might have killed him?"

"If he did, he didn't tell me."

"So." Kovalenko took a long pull of vodka. "What we have amounts to a faceless suspect, with no known motive for killing Neuss and no known motive for killing Ford or Halliday other than the fact that they had both seen him in his previous incarnation. Furthermore, as far as anyone knows he's dead. Cremated. It doesn't make much sense."

Marten took a sip from his drink. If he was going to give Kovalenko the rest, this was the time. *Trust the Russian*, he said to himself. *Trust he has his own agenda and won't turn you over to Lenard.*

"If it was Raymond who left the fingerprint in Dan's car, I can prove it beyond question."

"How?"

Marten lifted his glass and drained it. "Halliday made a computer copy of Raymond Thorne's LAPD booking record. When? I don't know, but Raymond's photograph and fingerprints are on it."

"A computer copy. You mean a disk?"

"Yes."

Kovalenko stared at him in disbelief. "You found it in his appointment book."

"Yes."

57

A clerk put the bottle of vodka into a bag along with a large piece of Gruyère, a hand-wrapped package of thinly sliced salami, and a large loaf of bread. Also a toothbrush, a tube of toothpaste, a packet of razors, and a small aerosol can of shaving cream.

"*Merci.*" Marten paid the bill and then left the small neighborhood store, turning up the rue de Normandie and walking toward Kovalenko's hotel. In the last hours a chill wind had come up, pushing a wall of dark clouds and bringing with them a spit of snow. Marten's hands were cold and he could see his breath. It felt like Manchester in the north of England, not Paris.

Kovalenko had sent him out to replenish supplies and get the toiletries he needed for the night—and, he was sure, give him time to look through Halliday's appointment book and Ford's accordion file to see what he could uncover for himself without Marten's help. Both men knew Marten could simply have walked away, passport or not, and disappeared into the vastness of the city, with Kovalenko none the wiser until it was too late.

To guard against such a thing, the Russian had given him a little information as he'd opened the door to leave, to wit: The Paris police were looking for him. The Eurostar had arrived in London three and a half hours earlier without him, and the Metropolitan Police had notified Lenard within minutes. Furious, Lenard had called Kovalenko right away, not just to inform him but to vent, telling him he had taken Marten's behavior as a personal affront and had put out a citywide alert to arrest him.

Kovalenko had simply said it was something he felt Marten

should know and take to heart when he went shopping. And then, like that, he had sent him out.

In a way Kovalenko hadn't had much choice. Moments before Marten left, Kovalenko had requested that Lenard send a duplicate of Dan Ford's murder file to his hotel room right away. A complete file, he had emphasized, one that included a clear photocopy of the fingerprint lifted from his car. So it was obvious Marten couldn't very well be in the room when Lenard or his people came to deliver the file.

It was equally obvious, Marten thought as he walked, head down against the wind and thick flakes of blowing snow, that he had to be very aware of police looking for him.

He came into the decaying lobby of the Hôtel Saint Orange warily, shaking snow from his head and shoulders. Across it, a short, emaciated woman with stringy gray hair and a black sweater stood behind the desk chatting on the phone.

He saw her eye him as he walked past, then turn away as he reached the elevator and pushed the button. Nearly a minute passed before it arrived and he saw her look at him again. Then the door opened, and he got in and pressed the button for Kovalenko's floor.

A moment more and the door slid closed and the elevator started up. It creaked and whimpered as it rose, and Marten relaxed. Alone in the elevator, for the moment at least, he was out of the public eye. It gave him a second to think. Beyond the obvious—Kovalenko, the pressure from the French police—something else troubled him and had since morning, and he wished he had had the presence of mind to talk to Lady Clem about it. It was the increasing sense that Rebecca hadn't told him the whole truth when he finally confronted her at the Crillon the night before, that her story about drinking a glass of champagne and falling asleep in the bath had been just that, a story, and, in fact, she had been doing something else. What it was she couldn't or wouldn't talk about—if she had been with a boyfriend, or a lover, maybe even a married man—didn't matter. This was no time for her to be blithely fooling around, not if it *was* Raymond who was out there, and somehow he had to make her understand she just couldn't take life as she had before. She had to be very seriously aware of where she was and whom she was around. She had to—

The loud thud as the elevator jerked to a stop cut Marten's thoughts. The door slid open and he peered into the hallway. It was empty. Cautiously he stepped out and started toward Kovalenko's room.

Suddenly he was unsure. He had seen no police vehicles outside, and he wondered if Lenard's messenger had not yet come, or perhaps had come and gone. Or—what if he or she had used an unmarked car and was in the room with Kovalenko now?

He went to the door and listened.

Nothing.

He waited a moment longer and then knocked. There was no response. He hadn't been gone that long, and Kovalenko had not said anything about going out. He knocked again. Still nothing. Finally, he tried the knob. The door was unlocked.

"Kovalenko," he said cautiously.

There was no reply and he eased the door open. The room was empty. Kovalenko's laptop was on the bed, his suit jacket next to it. Marten went in and closed the door behind him, setting his bundle on a side table. Where was Kovalenko? Had the police come or not?

He took another step and then he saw it, a manila envelope with the seal of the Paris Prefecture of Police sticking out from beneath the Russian detective's jacket. Breathlessly he picked it up and opened it. Inside was a thick file folder. And inside it, on top of maybe fifty carefully typed pages and a dozen crime scene photographs, was an eight-by-ten enlargement of a fingerprint. Beneath it were the words *empreinte digitale, main droite, numéro trois, troisième doigt* (fingerprint, right hand, number three, middle finger), and stamped beneath that was *Pièce à conviction #7* (Exhibit #7).

"You'll want this," Kovalenko's voice crackled behind him. Marten whirled. Kovalenko stood in the doorway, a computer disk in his hand.

Marten looked past him. He was alone.

"Where were you?"

"Taking a piss." Kovalenko came in and closed the door.

58

"Did you look at it?" Marten indicated the disk.

"Did I compare the two? Yes."

"And?"

"See for yourself."

Kovalenko crossed to the bed, loaded the disk in the laptop, and stood back as Raymond's LAPD fingerprint sheet came up on the screen. He clicked to the right hand, then to the number three middle finger and hit the "maximize" cube. And the screen filled with a single, exceptionally clear fingerprint.

Marten could feel his pulse rise in anticipation as he held the eight-by-ten enlargement up beside it. Slowly a chill settled over his shoulders and eased down his spine as, one after the other, each whorl, loop, and arch matched perfectly.

"Jesus God," he breathed and looked to Kovalenko.

The Russian was watching him closely. "It would seem Raymond Oliver Thorne has emerged from his own ashes and landed in Paris," Kovalenko said quietly. "I think it would be safe to assume it was he who killed Dan Ford and also the man he went to meet, the printer's representative, Jean-Luc—"

"Vabres."

"What?" Kovalenko's response was sharp.

Abruptly Marten twisted from the screen and looked directly at Kovalenko. "Vabres was the printer rep's surname."

"How did you know? Neither Lenard nor I divulged it to you or anyone else."

"I found it in Dan's notes."

Marten clicked off the laptop. The deep, almost animal fear Raymond had aroused in him, as some unstoppable, untouchable, unknowable, netherworld creature, was oddly calmed with the certainty that he was alive. It was an assurance that gave Marten courage to go the next step with Kovalenko.

"The French word *carte* can mean map or chart, but it can also mean menu. You were looking for a map, but it turned out to be a menu Dan Ford was going to pick up from Vabres when he was killed."

"I have learned the meanings of the word, Mr. Marten. Vabres's company does not print maps, and it had not printed a menu in more than two years. Nor was there a map or a menu in either Ford's car or in Vabres's Toyota."

"Of course not, Raymond took it." Marten got up and crossed the room. "Somehow he learned Vabres had it and was going to give it to Dan. He not only wanted it, he didn't want either of them talking about it afterward. So he killed them."

"Where did Vabres get this 'menu' if his company did not print it? And why did he call Mr. Ford at three in the morning and ask him to drive far out into the countryside to give it to him?"

"That's what I wondered when I found the menu in Dan's accordion file. What was the urgency?" Marten looked at the floor, then ran a hand through his hair and looked back. "Maybe we're thinking behind the game. What if Vabres had already alerted Dan to the menu's existence and told him what the occasion was? If it was important enough, if the event was more than a simple social affair, Dan would have wanted to see it for himself, for verification if nothing else. And what if he told Vabres to call him any time of day or night once he had it and he would meet him? Then Vabres got it and realized how important it was and began to worry if maybe it was none of his business, if he should be passing that kind of information to the press. The thought kept him awake. Then finally, in the middle of the night he decided yes, that Dan should have it. And he called him right then to meet him. Who knows, maybe they had arranged the place beforehand or had met there before—"

Kovalenko watched him for a long time before he spoke; when he did it was quietly. "That is a very believable scenario, Mr. Marten. Especially if it was, as you suggest, a menu for an event Raymond didn't want made public or even talked about between two men."

"Kovalenko," Marten said, walking toward him, "it wasn't the first menu but the second."

"I don't understand."

"I'll show you."

Marten opened Ford's accordion file and took out the Kitner envelope, then slid the menu from it and handed it to Kovalenko.

"This is the first. Vabres had given it to Dan earlier. I don't know what Dan was after, or thought he was after, or if it had anything at all to do with the second menu and why he was killed. It centers around prominent Russians. Maybe you can give it some meaning."

Kovalenko looked at it. The crisp, expensive off-white card stock, the raised dark gold lettering.

> *Carte Commémorative*
> *En l'honneur de la*
> *Famille Splendide Romanov*
> *Paris, France — 16 Janvier*
> *151 Avenue Georges V*

Marten saw him register surprise when he looked at it, but Kovalenko didn't acknowledge it.

"It seems to be a harmless gathering of members of the Romanov family," Kovalenko said simply.

"Harmless until people started getting killed and we discovered Raymond is alive and somewhere out there on the streets." Marten moved closer, looking Kovalenko directly in the eye.

"Raymond sliced my best friend to pieces. You are a Russian policeman investigating the murder of Alfred Neuss, a former Russian citizen. He bought diamonds in Monaco from Fabien Curtay, also murdered, also a former Russian citizen. A year ago your own investigators were in America and Mexico following up on the murders of former Russians Raymond allegedly murdered there. The Romanovs are one of the most celebrated families in Russian history. What's the connection, Inspector—between the Romanovs and Neuss and the others?"

Kovalenko shrugged. "I don't know if there is one."

"You don't?"

"No."

"What the hell is it, a bunch of coincidences?" Marten was getting angry. The Russian was giving him nothing. "If it is, is it a coincidence that two menus are involved?"

"Mr. Marten, we don't know for certain there is a second menu. That is your conjecture. For all we know Mr. Ford could have been after a map, as I first said."

Marten jabbed his finger at the Romanov menu. "Then why did he give this one a number?"

"A number?"

"Turn it over. Look at the bottom."

Kovalenko did. Written by hand at the bottom were the words *Jean-Luc Vabres—Menu #1.*

"That's Dan's handwriting."

Marten saw Kovalenko's eyes travel up the back of the menu to the top, saw him fix on something there. Then he handed the menu back with a shrug. "A numbering method for his own filing system, perhaps."

"There was something else. It was written in the same hand at the top of the card. I saw you look at it. What did it say?"

Kovalenko hesitated.

"Tell me, what did it say?"

"Kitner to attend." Kovalenko showed no expression at all, just said the words.

"You told me earlier your reading of English was not the best. I wanted to make certain you understood what was there."

"I understood, Mr. Marten."

"He's referring to Sir Peter Kitner, the chairman of Media-Corp."

"How can you be certain? I'm sure there are many Kitners in the world."

"Maybe these will explain." Marten spilled the contents of the Kitner envelope in front of Kovalenko—the newspaper clippings Ford had collected of stories about Sir Peter Kitner.

Basing the next on his telephone conversation with Alfred Neuss's wife and taking the chance Kovalenko would assume the information had come from Dan Ford's notes, he said authoritatively, "Peter Kitner was a friend of Alfred Neuss. Neuss arrived in London on the same day as Kitner's knighthood ceremony. The same day Raymond was trying to find him in L.A."

Abruptly Marten walked away, then turned and looked back. "I'm asking you, where does Kitner fit into this?"

Kovalenko smiled faintly. "You seem to know a great deal, Mr. Marten."

"Only a little—it's what you said when Dan asked you what you knew about America. Only a little? No, you know a lot more. You were surprised when you saw the menu. You were even more surprised when you saw Kitner's name. Okay, I've told you what I know, now it's your turn."

"Mr. Marten, you are in France illegally. There is no reason for me to tell you anything at all."

"Maybe there isn't, except that I have the feeling you would just as soon keep this between you and me. If not, you would have called Lenard the minute you picked me up." Marten came back across the room. "I told you before, Inspector, Raymond sliced my best friend to pieces. I want to make sure something is done about it. If you won't help, I'll take the chance and go to Lenard myself. I'm sure he'd find all this rather interesting. Especially when he wonders why you brought me here without informing him, even more so when he finds you have Halliday's appointment book and Ford's file."

Kovalenko looked at Marten in silence. Finally he spoke, and when he did his voice was quiet, even gentle. "I think your friendship with Mr. Ford was very important to you."

"It was."

Kovalenko nodded slightly, then crossed to take out the bottle of vodka Marten had brought back from the store. Pouring some in a glass, he held it for a moment, then looked to Marten. "It is possible, Mr. Marten, that Peter Kitner may have been still another target of Raymond Thorne."

"Kitner?"

"Yes."

"Why?"

"I said it is possible, not probable. Peter Kitner is a very prominent man who was, as you say, a friend of Alfred Neuss." Kovalenko took a pull at his vodka. "It's simply one theory among many we've entertained."

The sharp chirp of Kovalenko's cell phone stopped the conversation, and he put down his glass to answer it.

"*Da*," he said as he clicked on, then, phone in hand, turned away and continued his conversation in Russian.

Marten put the menu and clippings back in Ford's accordion file. Both Ford and Halliday had thought Raymond was still alive, and they had been right. And for some reason Dan had pursued the Kitner angle. How he had come to it there was no way to know, but now Kovalenko himself had included Kitner when he said he might have been still another of Raymond's targets—and in the process all but confirming that Marten had been right when he guessed Neuss and Kitner were friends. Still, it didn't explain what was going on or why Neuss and Curtay and others killed in the United States and Mexico had been involved. Yet Marten knew that somehow it was interwoven and included April 7/Moscow and the safe deposit keys and the other notations in Raymond's calendar, particularly those that pertained to London. But those were things he couldn't discuss with Kovalenko because of who Marten was and what he was trying to keep secret. Even if he said he had learned them from Dan Ford, the Russian was still suspicious of him, and bringing up those kinds of details would only increase his mistrust. It was something Marten couldn't do, particularly when all of it rested on the assumption that it was Raymond who had murdered Neuss and Curtay and not someone else. But who else, now that they knew he was alive and in Paris?

Even so, the question remained *why*—why had he done it, and what had he expected to gain from it? Moreover, where did the *second menu* fit in? What "menued" event was yet to come that was so secret that Raymond had had to massacre—and that was the only word for it—Dan Ford and Jean-Luc Vabres to keep anyone from finding out about it?

Marten glanced at Kovalenko across the room gesturing and chattering away in Russian. Alright, Raymond was here, but how to find him, how to even know what he looked like? Suddenly he thought of the trail Halliday had followed to Argentina. If somehow they could find the plastic surgeon who had done the cosmetic work on Raymond, maybe Kovalenko could arrange for the Argentine police to get some sort of court order that, with luck, would force the physician to reveal the name his patient had used while under his care, and perhaps even a photograph of him as he looked now. If so, they would have a name and a face. Additionally, if Raymond had come to France legally and by air with an Argentine passport, he would have had to pass through passport control, and that would give them an airport and a date when he had arrived.

Marten went to the bed and opened Halliday's appointment book. He turned one page and then another and then another—and then he found what he was looking for.

Dr. Hermann Gray, plastic surgeon, Bel Air, age 48. Abruptly retired, sold home, and left country.

In parentheses alongside Gray's name was *Puerto Quepos, Costa Rica, then Rosario, Argentina, name changed to James Patrick Odett—ALC/hunting accident.*

ALC—who or what was that? Before, he had thought that maybe Halliday had transposed the letters and really meant ACL—anterior cruciate ligament, a severe knee injury one might suffer in a sporting accident. Now he wasn't so sure.

Suddenly he felt a presence and looked up. Kovalenko was no longer on the phone but was standing at the foot of the bed staring at him. "Something puzzles you—"

"Do the initials ALC mean anything to you?"

Again Marten saw the look of surprise register on Kovalenko's face. "It depends," he said.

"On what?"

"On the context in which they are used."

"They're in Halliday's notes tracing Raymond and his plastic surgeon to Argentina."

"A surgeon by the name of James Patrick Odett?"

"So, you *did* go through Halliday's book."

"Yes, but only to find the disk."

"Then how did you know about Odett?"

"The day Detective Halliday was murdered, Dr. Odett died in a fire in a rented office building in Rosario, Argentina. The entire building burned to the ground. Seven other people died as well. Everything inside the building was destroyed."

"Patient records, X-rays—"

"Everything wiped away, Mr. Marten."

"Just like all the other medical and law enforcement databases."

Kovalenko nodded. "The information came to me from my office in Moscow. I received it on my return from the Halliday murder scene and shortly before I went to stake out Mr. Ford's apartment." Kovalenko's gaze wandered off as if he were working through some kind of thought process, as if something were troubling him.

Marten had the sense that part of Kovalenko's information was new and he found that discomforting. The rest was how much, if anything, to tell Marten. Finally the gaze came back. His eyes were disturbed yet filled with a sincerity, or maybe it was a vulnerability, Marten hadn't seen before, and he knew the Russian had decided to include him.

"You would like to know how and why I would have that information? For the same reason I told you it depended on what context in which the initials ALC were used. James Patrick Odett was a plastic surgeon who treated one patient exclusively. His name is Alexander Luis Cabrera. He was shot and very seriously wounded in a hunting accident in the Andes when his gun blew up in his face as he fired at a deer."

"When"—Marten paused as if he already knew the answer—"did it happen?"

"In March of last year."

"March?"

"Yes."

"Who was with him?"

"No one. His lone shooting companion was farther down the trail." Kovalenko's manner suddenly hardened. It wasn't that he had said too much, it was more that he didn't want to believe it.

"I know what you are thinking, Mr. Marten, that this was a made-up incident. That the accident wasn't an accident at all. And that it didn't happen in the Andes but in Los Angeles, in a gun battle with the police. But the fact is, it is not so. There are records from emergency medical people who rescued him by helicopter, hospital records of his stay there. Records of the physicians who treated him."

"Those records could be false."

"Perhaps, except that Alexander Cabrera is a very prominent and legitimate Argentine businessman and the accident was well publicized in his country."

"Then why was Halliday onto him? Why did he put it in here?" Marten pushed Halliday's appointment book toward Kovalenko.

"It is not an answer I have." Kovalenko smiled. "But I will tell you, Alexander Cabrera is not only prominent, he is exceedingly successful. He owns a global pipeline company with offices around the world. He keeps offices and permanent suites in five-star hotels in a dozen major cities, including one here in Paris at the Hôtel Ritz."

"Cabrera is here in Paris?"

"I'm not aware of his current whereabouts; I merely said he keeps a suite here. Don't try to make coincidences when there are none, Mr. Marten. I hardly think a man like Cabrera is likely to be your infamous Raymond Thorne."

"Halliday did."

"Did he? Or was it just a notation, something to ask Dr. Odett about?"

"Obviously it is something we will never know, because both men are dead."

Marten looked at Kovalenko in silence, then went to the window and looked out. For a long moment he simply stood there rubbing his hands together against the cold and staring at the whirling snow outside.

"Why do you know about Alexander Cabrera at all?" he said finally.

"He is the eldest son of Sir Peter Kitner."

"What?" Marten was astounded.

"Alexander Cabrera is the product of an earlier marriage."

"Is this common knowledge?"

"No. In fact I think very few people are aware of it. I would doubt his own family knows."

"But you do."

Kovalenko nodded.

"Why?"

"Let's just say that I do."

There it was, confirmation that Kovalenko did have some other agenda. Marten decided to take it as far as the Russian would let him. "So now we're back to Kitner."

Kovalenko found his glass and picked it up. "Would you like a drink, Mr. Marten?"

"I would like you to tell me what is going on with Peter Kitner. Why he is attending the Romanov dinner tonight."

"Because, Mr. Marten—Sir Peter Kitner *is* a Romanov."

59

The front penthouse apartment at number 127 Avenue Hoche was large, newly decorated, and freshly painted. It had two master suites and a private maid's quarters. From the windows, even in the snow, one could see the lighted Arc de Triomphe two blocks away and the heavy rush hour traffic swirling around it.

Grand Duchess Catherine Mikhailovna and her mother, Grand Duchess Maria, would share one of the suites. Catherine's son, Grand Duke Sergei Petrovich Romanov, would take the other. The maid's quarters, into which two single beds had been moved, would be used by their four bodyguards, two of whom would be on duty at all times. It was the way Grand Duchess Catherine had planned it and the way it would be until they left two days from now. By then, she was certain, crowds would line the avenue outside hoping for a glimpse of her son, the newly chosen Tsarevich, the first Tsar of Russia in nearly a century.

"Like Moscow," her mother, Grand Duchess Maria, said as she looked out of the living room window at the falling snow.

"Yes, like Moscow," Catherine said. Despite the long trip, both women were fresh, elegantly dressed, and eager for the night to begin. Immediately there was a knock at the door.

"Come in." She turned as the door opened, expecting to see her son enter, dressed and ready for the short drive to the house on the L'Avenue Georges V. Instead it was Octavio, their scar-faced bodyguard.

"We have swept the building and it is secure, Your Highness. There are two doors to the alley in the rear; both are locked. Though one was not, it is now. The front entrance has a door-man posted twenty-four hours. His employer knows we have arrived. No one will be permitted to the penthouse without authorization from us."

"Very good, Octavio."

"The car is ready when you are, Your Highness."

"Thank—"

Grand Duchess Catherine Mikhailovna stopped midsentence. She was looking past Octavio to where her son stood in the doorway, the light from the hall behind touching his shoulders and bathing him in gold. Dressed in a dark, well-fitted suit over a starched white shirt with a deep burgundy silk tie tied four-in-hand, his hair parted on the side and then combed slightly back, he was as handsome as she had ever seen him. More than that was a presence and bearing that overrode his physical beauty. It was cultured, self-assured, and royal—if she'd had any doubt earlier as she'd watched him playing computer games in the car during the long ride to Paris looking like any twenty-two-year-old, with tousled hair and wearing blue jeans and an oversized sweater, there was none now. The boy that had been was gone. In his place was a highly educated, mature man, fully prepared to become a national leader.

"Are you ready, Mother, Grandmother?" he said.

"Yes, we are ready," Catherine said and smiled, and for the first time called him by the name she was certain the entire world would use by this time tomorrow. "Yes, we are ready—Tsarevich."

60

Peter Kitner put one arm and then the other into the starched formal shirt. Ordinarily he would have had his French valet to help him, but because of the snow the valet had been unable to get there. Instead, it was his private secretary, Taylor Barrie, who helped him dress, handing him now the silk-lined trousers to his black tuxedo, then turning to find the appropriate bow tie in the mahogany drawer to which formal ties were assigned.

Of all nights for Barrie to be pressed into service as Kitner's valet, this was the worst. The mogul was filled with fury, most of it directed at Barrie, and, from Kitner's point of view, for good reason—Barrie had been unable to arrange the private meeting he had requested with Alexander Cabrera and the Baroness Marga de Vienne. The site had not been a problem, a secluded villa near Versailles had been quickly found and arrangements made for its use tomorrow morning. The difficulty had been in reaching either Cabrera or the Baroness. The best Barrie had been able to do was leave word, and he had, anywhere he could—for Cabrera at the Ritz, at his head office in Buenos Aires, and at his European headquarters in Lausanne, and for the Baroness at her home in Auvergne and at her apartment in Zurich. In all cases he'd been curtly told the parties were traveling and simply not available. It was a response he knew Kitner would take personally. Sir Peter Kitner had the ear of kings, presidents, and the crème de la crème of business leaders around the world, and none ever, even in times of emergency, refused his phone call, let alone being "simply not available."

"Tie," Kitner said, abruptly securing the top button of his trousers.

"Yes, sir." Barrie handed him the selected tie, half expecting him to reject it. Instead he took it and glared at him.

"I'll finish dressing myself. Tell Higgs I want the car in five minutes."

"Yes, sir." Taylor Barrie nodded crisply and left the room, grateful to have been dismissed.

Kitner turned to the mirror. One angry loop of his tie, and a second, then he stopped. The fault was not Barrie's at all. It was him Cabrera and the Baroness had refused, not his secretary. Barrie had only been doing his job. Suddenly Kitner realized he was staring at himself in the mirror. Abruptly he turned away.

Alfred Neuss was dead; so was Fabien Curtay. The knife and the 8 mm film were gone. How long ago had it been since the incident in the Parc Monceau? Twenty years? He had been one of a half-dozen adults supervising a children's birthday party and taking home movies when Kitner and his wife Luisa's ten-year-old son, Paul, had run off into some trees to retrieve a soccer ball. Camera running, Neuss had followed, getting there just as fourteen-year-old Alexander came from nowhere to plunge the huge Spanish switchblade into Paul's chest. Instantly Neuss had grabbed Alexander's hand, spinning him around. The camera still running, Alexander struggled to get away but couldn't. Suddenly he let go of the knife, then pushed away and ran off. But it was too late, Paul was on the ground dying, blood everywhere, his heart destroyed.

The trouble was Alexander had left Neuss with both the murder weapon and the murder itself, captured on Super 8 film. Neuss told the police what happened—a young man had been behind the trees and had stabbed Paul Kitner to death and then run off—but that was all he told them. Not once did he mention that he had known who the assailant was or that he had the entire incident on film or that he was in possession of the murder weapon.

He'd said nothing about any of it because Peter Kitner was his dearest friend and had been for years, and because he was one of the very few who knew Kitner's true identity.

He'd said nothing because the decision as to what to do about the knife and the filmed evidence was not his to make, but Kitner's.

It was why, a day after Paul's funeral, Kitner had called both the Baroness and Alexander to a meeting at a suite in the Hotel Sacher in Vienna. There, not wanting Alexander's existence known to his family, nor wishing to put them through the ordeal and scandal of seeing one son on trial for the murder of another, he presented the evidence and offered a written pact. In trade for Kitner's silence, Alexander would leave Europe immediately and go to South America, where he would take a new name and a new life and where Kitner would provide money for his housing and education. In return Alexander would sign a document renouncing, forever, any claim to the family name and promising never to reveal his true heritage under penalty of having the evidence turned over to the police. In other words, in exchange for his freedom, he was being banished from Europe and disowned by his family in the cruelest sense of the word— his father was wholly denying his existence.

Kitner had the knife, the film, and, in Neuss, the eyewitness, and because of it Alexander had little choice but to comply. And the Baroness had been forced to sign the pact along with him, because Kitner knew that she had been the true architect of the deed and had driven him to it.

As the handsome, Russian-born Swedish wife of the French philanthropist Baron Edmond de Vienne and as Alexander's legal guardian, the Baroness was one of Europe's grandes dames; her path often crossed with Kitner's own, and they kept a cordial and businesslike relationship. But beneath that carefully styled facade was a deeply disturbed yet highly ambitious woman, who had been summarily spurned by Kitner and his family and had spent the rest of her life obsessed with settling the score.

Had he been wiser, he might have had some sense of what the future held years before, shortly after they met and were in the early stages of a youthful romance. It came in the form of a story she told him on a cold blustery day when they were walking hand in hand along the Seine. It was a story she said she had never told anyone and concerned a close friend from Stockholm who, when she was fifteen, had been visiting Italy on a school field trip. One day in Naples her friend became separated from her schoolmates and their chaperones. In trying to find her way back to the hotel where they were staying, she was confronted by a young street tough who showed a large knife and swore he would kill her if she didn't come with him. He took her to a dingy apartment where he put the knife to her throat and demanded she have sex with him. Terrified, she did what he demanded. As he lay recovering from his own ecstasy, she picked up the knife and stabbed him in the belly and then cut his throat. But it wasn't enough, and she bent down and cut off his penis and threw it across the floor. Afterward she went into the bathroom and carefully cleaned herself, then dressed and left. Thirty minutes later she had found her way back to the hotel and was reunited with her school friends, never telling any of them what had happened. It was more than a year before she finally confided in the Baroness.

At the time Kitner thought the tale slightly bizarre, if not simply made up, and passed it off as the machinations of a twenty-year-old trying to impress him with her knowledge of life's experiences. Yet the one thing that struck him, whether the story was true or not, was the mutilation of the man's body. He could understand her friend retaliating against a man who had raped her, even to the point of killing him. The mutilation was something else. Killing wasn't enough; she'd had to do more. Why, or what drove her to it, there was no way to know. But clearly there was something inside this woman that, when triggered, compelled her to exact a revenge that was not just brutal but savage.

The moment he saw the film of Paul's murder in the park he remembered her story and knew it had not been made up, nor had there been any friend. The Baroness had been talking about herself. In a blink she had gone from victim to murderess to butcher. It made the killing of his beloved young son by a teenaged half-brother he didn't even know he had far more than a simple act of murder, perhaps even with the same knife. It was a cold-blooded unveiling of the truth about what had really happened in Naples, done to let him know without doubt who and what he was dealing with; an unforgiving, murderous former lover, fully determined to destroy not only his heart but his soul.

Biblical, Shakespearean, ancient Greek all in one, the Baroness had become a sadistic, self-appointed goddess of darkness. Too old and prominent to any longer commit the act herself, in Alexander she had fashioned a new messenger, instilling her own twisted hatred of Kitner in him from infancy. Kitner should have killed her himself—and his own mother, were she alive, probably would have—but, as forceful as he was, that kind of thing was beyond him, and so instead he made a pact to keep the Baroness's personal assassin from his door. For a long time it had worked. And then they had both come back.

Kitner's eyes crept to his image in the mirror. He suddenly looked old and fearful and vulnerable, as if all at once he had lost control of everything in his life. How darkly like the Baroness to have had Alfred Neuss murdered in the Parc Monceau. The same stage where Paul had been slain. And with Neuss, the lone eyewitness to Paul's murder, dead, and the murder weapon and film undoubtedly in Alexander's possession, the pact he'd made with them was useless.

Kitner would be in Davos with his wife and children. The Baroness would be there, too, and so would Alexander, and there was nothing he could do about it. They knew of the announcement, and knowing that, they would know its substance. What if the Hell-Goddess sent her messenger again, Spanish switchblade in hand, to surprise himself or Michael or his wife or one of his daughters?

The thought chilled him to the quick.

A telephone was on a wall mount at his elbow. Immediately he snatched it up. "Get me Higgs."

"Yes, sir," Barrie's voice came back, and Kitner could hear him punch a speed dial number on his keyboard. A moment later his security chief came on.

"Higgs, sir."

"I want to know where Alexander Cabrera and the Baroness de Vienne are right now. When you find them, put them under surveillance immediately. Use as many men as you need. I want to know where they go, who they meet, and what they do. I want to know exactly where they are twenty-four hours a day until you hear differently."

"It will take a little time, sir."

"Then don't waste it." Kitner hung up. For the first time since Paul had been murdered he felt panicked and unsure. If he was being crazy or paranoid, so be it. He was dealing with a madwoman.

61

HÔTEL SAINT ORANGE. SAME TIME, 6:45 P.M.

"Tell me about Kitner." Nick Marten leaned across Kovalenko's small desk, intent on the Russian. "He's a Romanov but doesn't use the name. He has a son who lives in Argentina who has a Spanish surname."

Kovalenko poured a thimbleful more vodka into his glass and let it sit there untouched. "Kitner divorced Cabrera's mother before the boy was born and within the year remarried his present wife, Luisa, a cousin of King Juan Carlos of Spain. Fourteen months later Cabrera's mother drowned in a boating accident in Italy and—"

"His mother, who was she?"

"A university student when Kitner knew her. In any case, after her death her sister became the boy's legal guardian. Soon afterward the sister married a titled and very wealthy French philanthropist. Later, when Cabrera was a young teenager, she moved him to a ranch she owned in Argentina. He took the Cabrera name himself, supposedly after the founder of the city of Córdoba."

"Why Argentina?"

"I don't know."

"Is Cabrera aware Kitner is his father?"

"I don't know that either."

"Does he know he's a Romanov?"

"Same answer."

Marten stared at Kovalenko for a moment, then indicated the Russian's laptop. "Large hard drive. Lots of memory?"

"What do you mean?"

"If, as you said, it was Kitner who was Raymond's intended victim, you probably have a file on him in your database. True?"

"Yes."

"And it probably contains all kinds of information, maybe even photographs of Kitner and his family. And since Cabrera is a member of that family, you just might have a photograph of him. If we believe Halliday's notes, we can suppose he's had cosmetic surgery. Maybe it was severe, maybe not. I know we have a photograph of Raymond; if you have one of Cabrera"—Marten smiled just a little—"we bring them up side by side and see if they match."

"You seem fixated on the idea that Alexander Cabrera and Raymond Thorne are one and the same."

"And you seem just as convinced they're not. Even if they look as different as day and night, at least I would get some idea of what Cabrera looks like. It's a simple question, Inspector. Do you have a photograph of Alexander Cabrera or don't you?"

62

The streets of Paris were all but abandoned and nearly impassable in the heavy snow when Octavio turned the Alfa Romeo down the Avenue Georges V and began looking for the house at number fifty-one.

In the seat behind him Grand Duchess Catherine glanced at her son, then at her mother between them, and then looked out to the snow-choked streets. This would be the last time they would travel like this—faceless, in a nondescript car, almost as if they were fugitives.

In two hours, three at most—if family members supporting Prince Dimitrii raised too loud a voice over the supporters of her son and forced her to present the letters of support she had from the president of Russia, the mayor of St. Petersburg, and the mayor of Moscow, the letter with its accompanying pages containing signatures of three hundred of the four hundred and fifty members of the State Duma, and, the coup de grâce, the personal letter from His Holiness Gregor II, the Most Holy Patriarch of the Russian Orthodox Church—she would still triumph, and Grand Duke Sergei would become Tsarevich and, storm or no storm, they would be leaving the house at 151 Avenue Georges V not in the backseat of this everyday automobile driven by a scar-faced thug but in a flurry of limousines and under the guard of the Federalnaya Slujba Ohrani, the FSO, or Security for the President of Russia.

"We are almost there, Your Highness." Octavio slowed the car. Ahead, through the snow, they could see bright lights and street barricades and the policemen manning them.

Absently, Grand Duchess Catherine touched her neck and then looked at her hands. She wished she had felt safe enough to bring the diamond rings, the ruby and emerald necklace and earrings, the gold and diamond bracelets that should be worn for an occasion like this. She wished, too, that her overcoat had been elegant fur instead of the wool traveling coat she had been forced to wear under the circumstances—mink or sable or ermine, the kind of coat that befitted the most royal of the royal Romanov family. A coat and magnificent jewels suitable for the personage she was about to become and how she would be called from then on. No longer a simple Grand Duchess but Tsaritsa, mother of the Tsar of All Russia.

63

HÔTEL SAINT ORANGE. SAME TIME.

Nick Marten hunched over Kovalenko as the Russian brought the LAPD booking photograph of Raymond up on the laptop's screen. "Now bring up Cabrera," he urged.

There was a click, Raymond's face vanished, and the Russian detective brought up a digital photograph. It showed a tall, slim, neatly bearded, dark-haired young man in a business suit getting into a limousine outside a modern office building.

"Alexander Cabrera. Taken at his company headquarters in Buenos Aires three weeks ago."

Click.

A second photograph: Cabrera again, this time in overalls and hard hat looking at blueprints spread out on the hood of a pickup truck somewhere in the desert.

"Six weeks ago in Shaybah oil field in Saudi Arabia. His company is preparing to build a six-hundred-kilometer pipeline. The construction contract is just under a billion dollars U.S."

Click.

A third photo: Cabrera yet again, now wearing a heavy coat and smiling and surrounded by several winter-dressed, grinning oil-field workers with a huge oil refinery in the background.

"December third of last year at a LUKoil refinery in the Baltic, working on plans to link the Lithuanian oil sector with Russian oil fields."

"Now split the window," Marten said, "and bring up Raymond next to Cabrera."

Kovalenko did.

Cabrera had the same physical build as Raymond, but little else was familiar. The nose, ears, and facial structure were completely different. That he wore a beard made it all the more difficult.

"Hardly twin brothers," Kovalenko said.

"He was worked on by a plastic surgeon. There's no way to know if it was simply to reconstruct broken facial bones or to purposely make him look different."

Kovalenko clicked off the machine. "What else?"

"I don't know."

Frustrated, Marten walked away. Suddenly he turned back. "Do you have photos of him from before his 'accident'?"

"One. Taken on a tennis court at his ranch several weeks earlier."

"Put it up."

Kovalenko turned the machine back on and clicked through several files until he found what he wanted.

"Here, see for yourself."

Click.

Marten stared at the screen. What he saw was a relatively distant shot of Cabrera in tennis gear as he left the court, racket in hand. Again, he saw what he had before, a man with the same physical build as Raymond but little else. Instead of the blond hair and blond eyebrows he remembered when they had first taken Raymond into custody, he saw a man with dark hair and dark eyebrows and a much larger nose that made his facial appearance entirely different.

"That's all. The only shot you have from before?"

"Yes."

"What about in Moscow?"

"I doubt it."

"Why?"

"We were lucky to get this. It was the only shot taken by a freelance cameraman before he was thrown off the property. Cabrera is a highly private person. No media photos, no stories about him. He doesn't like it and has a bodyguard who keeps people away."

"You aren't the media. As you just proved, if you wanted photos you could get them."

"Mr. Marten, then it wasn't important."

"What wasn't?"

Kovalenko hesitated. "Nothing."

Marten crossed to Kovalenko. "*What* wasn't important?"

"It's Russian business."

"It has to do with Kitner, doesn't it?"

Kovalenko said nothing; instead he reached for his vodka. Marten picked up the glass and moved it away.

"What the hell are you doing?" Kovalenko demanded.

"I can still see what was left of Dan Ford when his car was pulled from the river. I don't like what I see. I want an answer." Marten stared at the Russian detective.

Outside the wind howled and the snow came down harder. Kovalenko blew on his hands. "Run-down Paris hotel, Russian winter."

"Answer me."

Deliberately Kovalenko reached for the glass Marten had taken away. This time Marten let him. The Russian picked it up, swallowed what was in it, and stood.

"Do you know of the Ipatiev house, Mr. Marten?"

"No."

Kovalenko walked to the table where the vodka was and poured more into his glass, then did the same with the glass Marten had used earlier and handed it to him.

"The Ipatiev house is, or rather was before they bulldozed it, a large home in the city of Ekaterinburg in the Ural Mountains many miles southeast of Moscow. The distance doesn't matter. It is the house that is important because it was where the last Tsar of Russia, Nicholas the Second, and his wife, their children, and servants, were held as hostages by Bolsheviks during the Communist revolution. On July 17, 1918, they were rousted from bed in the middle of the night, taken to the cellar, and shot to death.

"After the shootings the bodies were loaded on a truck and driven over heavily rutted roads into the forest and the designated burial site, an area of abandoned mines in a tract called the Four Brothers. The trouble was it had been raining all week and the truck kept getting bogged down in the rutted roads, so finally they put the bodies on sleds and dragged them to the selected mine shaft. Then in the predawn light they stripped the bodies and burned the clothes to destroy any possibility of identification if somehow the corpses were later discovered.

"Remember, this is central Russia torn apart by revolution in 1918. Corpses were hardly unusual, and investigations into killings were rare if done at all.

"In the meantime other high-ranking members of the imperial Romanov family had been murdered. But others escaped, helped in large part by European monarchies. So you had the clear line of succession to the throne severed by the murders at the Ipatiev house and the others in the imperial line, or what is called the Russian dynasty, scattered all over Europe and eventually the world. Ever since, one or another of them has stepped forward with some kind of evidence trying to claim the crown for himself.

"Today the surviving Romanovs break down into four main branches. Each descends from Emperor Nicholas the First, the great-great-grandfather of Tsar Nicholas who was killed at the Ipatiev house. It is the surviving members of those four branches who are meeting tonight at the house at one-fifty-one Avenue Georges V."

"Why?"

"To select the next Tsar of Russia."

Marten didn't get it. "What are you talking about? There is no Tsar of Russia."

Kovalenko took a sip of vodka. "The Russian parliament has secretly voted to reinstitute the imperial crown in the form of a constitutional monarchy. The president of Russia will make the announcement on Saturday at the World Economic Forum in Davos, Switzerland. The new Tsar will be a figurehead with no ruling power. His sole and primary purpose will be to rally the spirit and the pride of the Russian people and unite them in a time of national rebuilding. Maybe even," he grinned, "do a little public relations work around the world. You know, be a kind of global super-salesman for Russian goods and services, even help build up the tourist industry."

Marten didn't understand any more now than he did before. The idea that Russia would actually vote to return the monarchy in any capacity was staggering, yet he still saw no relationship between that and what was going on here.

Kovalenko took another pull at his drink. "It might help if I told you the people we believe were murdered by Raymond Thorne in the Americas before he went on his rampage in Los Angeles had more in common than the fact that they were Russian."

"They were Romanovs?"

"Not just Romanovs, Mr. Marten, but very influential members of the family, even the Chicago tailors."

Marten was incredulous. "That's what this is all about? A power play inside the Romanov family to see who becomes Tsar?"

Kovalenko nodded slowly. "Perhaps, yes."

64

THE HOUSE AT 151 AVENUE GEORGES V. 7:30 P.M.

Diminutive, animated, and rocking lightly back and forth on his heels as he talked, there was no mistaking the elegantly dressed Nikolai Nemov, the exceedingly outspoken, highly influential, and enormously popular mayor of Moscow, and Grand Duchess Catherine caught her breath when she saw him. He was standing in the middle of the grand home's marble-floored parlor holding court over a group of formally dressed Romanovs who represented all four branches of the family.

Nikki, as Mayor Nemov was known to his friends, was one of Catherine's most coveted prizes, a personal friendship molded carefully and gradually over the years to the point where they now chatted on the phone about nothing, the way friends do, at least once a week and often more. That he had come here was a complete surprise, and she knew he had done so for her and for her son, Grand Duke Sergei. And because he had, she knew it was already over and the war was won. Yes, there would still be fighting, but it would be for naught; by the sheer weight of Romanov factions surrounding Nemov, and the singular preeminence of the men within the factions, she knew her long battle was over and the rightful decision had been made. The imperial Romanov crown would soon rest on the head of her son. To her, Grand Duke Sergei was already Tsarevich of All Russia.

Peter Kitner rode alone in the passenger section of his limousine as the car neared the Arc de Triomphe, his driver moving the vehicle slowly in the blowing snow, guiding it warily through the deserted streets in what was an almost postcardlike still life of Paris. Up front, Kitner could see Higgs beside the driver talking on his cell phone, but security glass separated the front from the back, so he could not hear what was being said. The snow and glass insulated everything, making him feel like a prisoner in a silent cell.

65

"Why has Kitner kept it a secret that he is a Romanov?" Marten pressed Kovalenko. Outside, the wind and swirling snow rattled against the windows, making the room feel even colder than it already was.

"That is a question for him, not me." Kovalenko was distracted by an e-mail that had just come up on his screen, and he was replying to it in Russian.

"Who inside the family knows?"

"Few, if any, I think." Kovalenko tried to concentrate on what he was doing. "Why don't we talk about the blizzard?"

"Because I want to talk about Peter Kitner." Marten moved closer to look over Kovalenko's shoulder. All he saw was a screen filled with Cyrillic Russian.

"Does he have enough influence to cast the winning vote for the Tsar, is that why he's going to the dinner? Then call in that favor to expand his business in Russia when the Tsar is in place?"

"I am a homicide investigator. You are asking me about power and politics, which are not my domain."

"Who is Raymond working for? How does he fit into this 'war of the Romanovs'?"

Kovalenko finished his e-mail and sent it, then shut down the machine and looked up at Marten.

"You might be interested in an e-mail I just received from my office in Moscow. It was a forwarded Interpol communiqué from the National Central Bureau in Zurich. Some children were ice-skating on a pond when they came upon the body of a man in a wooded area nearby."

Marten felt a cautionary flag go up. "And?"

"His throat had been cut, the head nearly severed from the body. It happened at about three this afternoon. The police think he was killed several hours earlier. An autopsy has yet to be done."

"Do you have a Paris telephone directory?" Marten asked abruptly.

"Yes." Puzzled, Kovalenko went to the bedside table and forced open a warped drawer, then took out a Paris phone book and gave it to Marten.

"It started snowing heavily at what time?" Marten began turning pages.

Kovalenko shrugged. "The middle of the afternoon. Why?"

"By the looks of what's going on outside I would expect that by now the airports are closed and train and highway travel has been slowed to nothing."

"Probably, but what does the weather have to do with a man found dead in Zurich?"

Marten saw what he was looking for. He picked up the telephone and dialed.

Kovalenko's eyebrows came together in bewilderment. "Who are you calling?"

"The Hôtel Ritz."

Marten paused as the phone rang through and someone answered.

"Alexander Cabrera, please." There was a long moment as he waited, then, "I see. . . . Do you know if he is in the city? . . . Yes, the storm, I know . . . No, no word. I'll call back later."

Marten hung up.

"He's not there. That's the only information they'll give out. But they did ring his room, which makes me think that at some point today he was there."

"What are you suggesting?"

"That if he did the killing in Zurich, he can't get back to Paris because of the snow. Which means he might still be in Switzerland."

66

NEUCHÂTEL, SWITZERLAND. SAME TIME.

The snowstorm bringing Paris to its knees had not yet crossed into Switzerland and the night was bitter cold and star-bright with a sliver of a moon bathing Lake Neuchâtel and the countryside around it with faint silver light.

"Watch." Alexander smiled and blew out a breath of air. The vapor hung there, frozen in the air like a puff in a children's cartoon.

Rebecca giggled and did the same, her breath floating out to hang like Alexander's before simply vanishing into nothing.

"Poof." He laughed, and then took her hand and they walked on as they had been, along the frozen edge of the lake, both dressed in long mink coats with mink hats and mink gloves.

Some distance behind strolled Gerard and Nicole Rothfels. With them was the Baroness, at fifty-six, sleek and alert, like the others enjoying the predinner walk and the bracing air, and all the while watching Alexander and his future bride. The beautiful girl-woman who was the love of his life and for whom she had bought Jura and then given it away.

The girl-woman whom she had known for nearly five months now and whom she adored and who adored her, who was exceptionally bright and eager, and whose learning of languages she had carefully orchestrated and quietly overseen herself. By now Rebecca's French and Italian and Spanish and Russian were nearly fluent and were becoming almost second nature, enabling her, like the Baroness and Alexander, to switch between them at will.

The Baroness's education of Rebecca had not stopped with languages. On any number of occasions she had brought Rebecca to her apartment in Zurich, where, like a wealthy aunt, she took her shopping and dining, and carried on supplemental schooling—the instruction in style and personal presence, what clothes to wear and when, and how to wear them; the fashion of her hair and makeup, its selection, color, application; how to walk and carry herself; the learning of to whom one spoke, and how and when. The Baroness encouraged Rebecca to smile more without losing the fragile vulnerability that made her so attractive to men of any age; encouraged her to read, and then read more, the classics especially, and in more than one language. She schooled her, herself, in the intimacies of romance, in the ways to be with a man, socially and in private, how to care for him, pamper him, scold him—and how to make love to him, though she knew Rebecca was still a virgin. As the Baroness saw the romance between Rebecca and Alexander progress, she constantly assured Rebecca that when her wedding night came she would be unafraid and natural, pleasuring her husband and herself beyond measure, as the Baroness had pleasured herself and her husband on her own wedding night.

The teaching, the lessons, had been done over a period of scarcely five months, a period in which she had seen Rebecca fall ever more deeply in love with Alexander. The end result had been nothing short of extraordinary; in such a short time Rebecca had been transformed from little more than an unsure girlish American babysitter into a beautiful, poised, and self-confident young woman, one with the requisite underpinnings of a blue-blooded European aristocrat.

There was a muffled chirp as Nicole Rothfels's cell phone rang inside her pocket.

"*Oui? Ah, merci,*" she answered, and clicked off.

"Monsieur Alexander," she called, "if you please, dinner will be on the table in ten minutes."

"Go back to the house." Alexander grinned. "We will be there in fifteen."

Nicole Rothfels smiled and glanced at the Baroness.

"Love has its own clock," the Baroness said quietly, her breath, like that of the others, like Alexander's, a puff in the frigid air. Then she and Nicole and Gerard Rothfels turned and walked back toward the warmth of the lighted house in the distance.

Alexander watched the Baroness's strong step lead them swiftly away in the moonlight.

"Baroness," he'd called her since he'd first learned to speak.

"My sweet," she'd called him for as long as he could remember, their lives steadfastly intertwined for most of a lifetime. Yet, as much as he cared for her, the truth of it was, in all of his life there was only one human being he'd ever truly loved.

Rebecca.

67

7:50 P.M.

"Yes, yes—spell the name for me, in English, please." Kovalenko was hunched over, his cell phone in one hand, scribbling into his spiral notebook with the other. Lenard was on the other end of the line giving him information on the Zurich murder.

Marten stood back waiting, unsure what Kovalenko would do. So far Kovalenko had made no mention to Lenard of Marten, Halliday's computer disk, or that they had matched the fingerprint found in Dan Ford's car to Raymond Oliver Thorne. From what Marten could tell their conversation focused solely on the body found in Zurich and whatever else the French policeman had learned about the circumstances surrounding it.

"So maybe it's our man and we got lucky, or maybe not, eh? Maybe just another lunatic with a knife or a razor." Kovalenko glanced at Marten, then looked back to the phone and the notes he was making.

Marten knew Kovalenko had gathered just about all the information he could from him, so why not just turn Marten over to the French police? Legally and professionally it was what should be done, and it would remove any suspicion Lenard might have that Kovalenko had taken Halliday's appointment book from his hotel room himself, as Marten had jokingly suggested, if the whole thing came out later. Yet, and there was a big *yet*, Kovalenko had still not mentioned either Marten or the fingerprints, and that puzzled him.

"I will go to Zurich myself," Kovalenko said abruptly. "I want to see the body and where it was found. . . . Yes, the weather, I know. The airports are closed and the trains are barely running. But it's important I get there quickly. If he is our man and has moved his business to Switzerland, we have to stay on top of him. . . . How? I will drive. We Russians are used to snow and treacherous roads. Can you get me a good four-wheel drive snow car?"

Suddenly Kovalenko straightened from his hunched-over position and looked at Marten.

"By the way, Philippe, our friend Mr. Marten is in Paris. In fact he's here with me now."

Marten started. Kovalenko was giving him to Lenard after all. It meant he could forget about finding Raymond and instead try to keep the French police from finding out who *he* was.

"It seems he is still very upset over the murder of his friend. He went back to the apartment on rue Huysmans and stumbled across Detective Halliday's appointment book. . . . Yes, the book, that's right. . . . Someone seems to have left it in the courtyard. . . . I know your men searched it, perhaps you should ask *them* how they missed it. At any rate, I'd given Marten the number of my cell phone sometime before, he called me, and I picked him up. He's been telling me stories about what Dan Ford knew of the investigations in Los Angeles ever since. There may be more to learn, so I'm taking him with me."

"What?" Marten blurted.

Kovalenko covered the phone. "Shut up!" He fixed Marten with an icy stare, then turned back to the phone.

"I would appreciate it if you called off your dogs. I'll give Halliday's book to whoever brings the car. . . . What is in it? Tiny handwriting and a lot of notes. My reading of English scrawl is not so good, but there doesn't seem much there to help us. Have a look yourself, you may be better at it than I am. Can you get me a car quickly? . . . Good. I'll report from Switzerland."

Kovalenko hung up and his eyes went to Marten. "The dead man was a close friend and longtime business associate of Jean-Luc Vabres. More than that, he owned a small printing company in Zurich."

Marten caught his breath. "There is your *second* menu."

"Yes, I know. It's why we are going to Zurich tonight." Kovalenko looked to the materials on the bed.

"How do you know Lenard will not just throw me in jail?"

"Because I am a guest of the French government, not the Paris police. I have requested you come with me, and he will say nothing because he understands the politics of it.

"Now, open Halliday's appointment book and take out the page with the references to Argentina and the plastic surgeon, Dr. Odett, and the envelopes with the computer disk and Halliday's airline ticket to Buenos Aires and give them to me. Then get your coat and take a piss. It's going to be a long, snowy night."

Peter Kitner's driver eased the limousine guardedly down the Avenue Georges V, using the streetlamps on either side of the road as guide markers in the swirl of blowing snow.

The near-whiteout conditions made it almost impossible to see more than a few yards in any direction, and Kitner himself was becoming alarmed. What if they had taken a wrong turn? Somewhere close by was the Seine. What if they suddenly crashed through an unseen barrier and plunged into the water? The streets were empty. No one would see them. The limousine was hugely heavy, armored last summer at Higgs's insistence. It would sink to the bottom like granite and might never be found. To his family, to the world, Sir Peter Kitner would simply have vanished.

"Sir Peter," Higgs's voice suddenly came over the limousine's internal speaker system.

Kitner looked up. Higgs was peering at him through the security glass.

"Yes, Higgs."

"Cabrera and the Baroness are in Switzerland. Neuchâtel. They are dining at the home of Cabrera's manager of European operations, Gerard Rothfels."

"That's confirmed?"

"Yes, sir."

"Have your people stay on top of them."

"Yes, sir."

Suddenly Kitner felt enormous relief. At least he knew where they were.

"We're here, sir," Higgs's voice came again.

Suddenly the car was slowing and Kitner saw bright lights and a phalanx of French police behind street barricades. They stopped, two policemen came forward, and Higgs put down his window and identified Kitner.

A policeman peered into the car, then stepped back in the snow and saluted crisply. A barricade was moved aside and the limousine crept slowly forward through the gates and onto the grounds of the Romanov house at 151 Avenue Georges V.

68

NEUCHÂTEL, SWITZERLAND. SAME TIME.

The Baroness saw the candlelit dinner table in a blur, the people and activity there barely existent—Alexander across from her, Gerard Rothfels at one end, his wife Nicole at the other, Rebecca to her immediate right, the brief disruption as the Rothfels children came in in their pajamas to say good night. Her thoughts were elsewhere, for some unknown reason dipping back and touching people and events that had carried her to this point in her life.

Born in Moscow, she had been brought to Sweden from Russia by her mother as a young girl. Both her mother and father were of the Russian aristocracy, and their families, through guile, sacrifice, and love of the Motherland, had managed to live through Lenin's reign and then under Stalin's punishing iron rule through the Second World War and after it, when the dictator tightened his grip even more. The shadow of the secret police was everywhere. Neighbor turned in neighbor for the most minor offenses. People who complained loudly enough simply vanished. Then Stalin died, but the Communist noose continued to tighten against dissenters. Angry and fed up, the Baroness's father rebelled, raising his voice against the totalitarian regime. As a result, when the Baroness was five, he was arrested for subversion, tried, and sentenced to ten years at hard labor in one of the dreaded gulag work camps, the so-called corrective labor institutions. Stamped forever in her mind was the sight of him being led away in shackles toward the train that would take him to the gulag. Suddenly he twisted away from his guards and looked back at her and her mother. He smiled broadly and blew her a kiss, and in his eyes she could see not fear but pride and a fierce love—for her, for her mother, and for Russia. That same night her mother, suitcase in hand, woke her from sleep. In moments she was dressed and they were out of their apartment and into a car. She remembered boarding a train and later a ship for Sweden.

The next years of her childhood were spent in Stockholm, where her mother found work as a seamstress and she went to an international school and had friends who spoke Swedish, Russian, French, and English. Her mother made a ten-year calendar, and at the end of every day they crossed the date off. It meant they were a day closer to the time when her father would be freed and come to join them. Every day she and her mother wrote him notes of love and encouragement and mailed them, with no idea whether or not he ever received them.

Once, when she was seven, they received a short handwritten note from him that he'd somehow managed to have smuggled out. He did not mention their letters to him, but he told them he loved them dearly and was bearing up and counting the days until his release. He also confessed that he'd killed a man, another prisoner, in a fight because the man had stolen his comb and he had tried to get it back. No one cared about prisoners' lives, so nothing happened to him. Outside the gulag a battle to the death over a hair comb seemed insane, but inside the story was entirely different. Combs, all but impossible to come by, were greatly treasured because to be able to keep one's hair and beard neat was the one thing that allowed a prisoner to keep what little self-respect he still had, and inside the gulag self-respect was everything because that was all there was left. So for dignity a man had stolen her father's comb. And for dignity her father had killed him.

The note was short but terribly moving because it was the first communication they had had from him since he had been taken away. Yet for all the force and emotion of it, there was a single part that struck the Baroness more profoundly than anything else in her entire life because she loved him so terribly and because she felt as if he were talking to her directly, sharing some very deep part of himself and giving her a guideline for her own life.

My dearest loved ones, he wrote, *never let anyone take away your dignity. Never, for any reason. It is the one thing that in the darkest night keeps alive the fire of the soul. Our own and Russia's. Protect it with every breath you have and strike back with purpose if you can. Make them never able to touch you again.*

His words touched her to the quick, and she read them over and over for months until they were locked in her heart. Then one day she suddenly stopped midparagraph and calculated that she would be exactly fifteen years and sixty-one days old when he was freed. Far off as it was, it gave her hope and a rush of joy because she knew there would be a day when at last he would stand beside her and she could take his hand and look up at him and tell him how much she loved him.

It was a day that would never come. Two weeks after her ninth birthday they were informed by a telegram forwarded by mail from relatives still inside the Soviet Union that he had frozen to death in the most horrid labor camp of all, Kolyma in northeastern Siberia. Later they learned he had died still filled with fierce anger toward the soviet system and love for his wife and daughter and for the soul of the Russia that had been. They knew that because a guard, a good man under terrible circumstances, had, at his own peril, sent them a letter telling them so.

"God chose your father to help keep the sacred voice of the Motherland alive. It was his destiny from birth," her mother told her steadfastly. "Now that same destiny has been passed to us."

Even at this moment, sitting at the dinner table in Neuchâtel as Alexander conversed with Gerard Rothfels and Rebecca chatted with his wife, she could hear the echo of her mother's words and see her father smile and blow her a kiss as he was being led to the train that would take him to his death in the gulag.

The things that were inherently his—the fiery defiance, the ferocious pride, the strength and courage and conviction, the command that they protect their own dignity and that of the revered soul of Russia with everything they had—she had taken as her own. It was why, even as a teenager, she had done what she had to her attacker those many years ago in Naples, so cruelly and finally and with such cold dispassion. Her father's words were woven deeply into the fabric of her psyche. *Make them never able to touch you again.*

It was his spirit she had instilled in Alexander from the beginning and had nurtured through every day of his life since. It was what had enabled them to deal with Peter Kitner as they had before. And as they were still doing now.

69

8:20 P.M.

The car was a white, unmarked Mercedes ML500 SUV, and it carried Kovalenko and Marten slowly but surefootedly out of Paris in what the French were already calling the blizzard of the century.

"I used to smoke cigarettes. I wish I still did." Kovalenko eased up on the gas and let the Mercedes bump over a fresh berm made by a snowplow. "This would be a good trip for smoking. Of course I might be dead soon after we got there."

Marten heard Kovalenko's chatter distantly, his thoughts still on the moments before they left. Lenard had brought them the car himself, as quickly as he'd promised, and stood there in the cold and whirling snow outside the Hôtel Saint Orange while Kovalenko gave him Halliday's appointment book and loaded his small, bulky suitcase, which held, among his personal belongings, Dan Ford's accordion file, into the backseat. All the while Lenard had done little more than stare at Marten, his look speaking volumes. If it had not been for the urgent bravado of Kovalenko's manner, his anxiousness to get to Zurich as quickly as possible, his insistence that Marten go with him, and, as he said, the politics of it, there was little doubt Lenard would have taken him into custody on the spot. On the other hand, he had Halliday's book and was getting rid of an overly aggressive Russian and an irksome American he neither liked nor trusted but whom he had no real cause to hold. In the end he'd simply told Kovalenko he was looking forward to his report from Zurich and warned him to drive carefully in the storm and not to wreck the car. It was brand-new and the only SUV they had.

The ML was an SUV Kovalenko liked and increasingly trusted. Pleased by the way it held the road in the snow, he began to pick up speed as they crossed the Seine at Maisons-Alfort and took the deserted N19 motorway, heading south and then east toward the Swiss border.

For a time neither man spoke. Instead they listened to the howl of the storm and the steady beat of the windshield wipers as they battled the snow. Finally Marten pulled against his seat belt and looked at Kovalenko. "Politics or no politics, you could have turned me over to Lenard. Why didn't you?"

"It is a long drive, Mr. Marten," Kovalenko said, keeping his eyes on the roadway, "and I am beginning to enjoy your company. Besides, being here is better than being in a French jail. Yes?"

"That's hardly an answer."

"No, it is a truth." Kovalenko looked at Marten and then back to the highway.

Again, silence took over and Marten relaxed, watching the SUV's headlights cut a stark beam through what seemed little

more than a gray-white, endless tunnel of falling snow interrupted every once in a while by the vague form of a lighted
highway sign.

Seconds passed, then minutes, and Marten looked over to
study Kovalenko—his bearded face lighted by the glow from
the instrument panel, the bulk of his figure, the bulge under his
jacket where his automatic was. He was a career cop with a
wife and children in Moscow. He was like Halliday had been,
and Roosevelt Lee and Marty Valparaiso and Polchak and Red,
professional policemen with families to support. And like them,
he worked homicide.

Yet, as Marten had felt before, there was something different
about him. It was his other agenda. When he'd asked him if Kitner had the influence to cast the winning vote for the Tsar and
therefore increase his business in Russia, he'd said he was a cop
and that power and politics were not his domain. But then he'd
said Lenard would not arrest him because of the politics of it.
So politics of some sort *were* his domain.

"Russian business," he had said when Marten asked if he had
photographs of Cabrera *before* his hunting accident. His answer
had been no, and the reason was that it hadn't been important
then. What was important *now?* What had changed? *What*
"Russian business"? Maybe he didn't want to talk about it, but
in bringing him along Kovalenko had made the "Russian business" Marten's business, too.

"Why are you keeping Lenard in the dark?" Marten suddenly broke the silence. "Why did you say nothing about Cabrera or the fingerprints? Or about Raymond or Kitner?"

Kovalenko said nothing, just kept his attention on the road in
front of them.

"Let me guess why." Marten pushed harder. "It's because
somewhere inside you're afraid Alexander Cabrera and Raymond Thorne *are* one and the same person and you don't want
anyone else to find out. That's why you made me take out the
disk and the pages with any reference to Argentina. You left
Halliday's book because you had to, and you hope Lenard
never finds out the rest. That's why you brought me with you, so
Lenard couldn't start asking me questions. You and I are the
only ones who know, and you want to keep it that way."

"You would make a good psychoanalyst, or"—Kovalenko glanced over at Marten—"a detective, Mr. Marten." He turned back to the road and gripped the wheel more tightly as the snow came down harder. "But you are not a detective, are you? You are a graduate student at Manchester University. I checked up on you. It's how we managed to find Lady Clementine Simpson."

We or *you?* Marten wanted to ask, but he didn't because he already knew the answer. "I'd appreciate it if you stayed away from her," he said coldly. That Kovalenko and Lenard had done what they had done with Clem still rankled him strongly.

Kovalenko grinned in response. "An attractive young woman is not the point, Mr. Marten. The question is, you are a graduate student, where did you do your undergraduate work? Was it Manchester as well?"

For a moment Marten kept still. Kovalenko was smart and he had done his homework, and if Marten wasn't careful he was going to get caught. When he had applied to Manchester he had simply called UCLA as John Barron and asked for a copy of his transcripts. When he got them he had the pages scanned onto a disk, loaded it into his computer, then changed the name from John Barron to Nicholas Marten, printed them out, and sent them in. No one had ever questioned the pages, and until now the subject hadn't come up.

"UCLA," he said. "That was when I hung out with Dan Ford and met Halliday."

"UCLA, that would be the University of California at Los Angeles."

"Yes."

"You didn't mention it before."

"It didn't seem important."

Kovalenko's eyes went to Marten's and held there for the briefest instant, probing. But Marten gave him nothing and he looked back to the road.

"I will trade you one truth for another, Mr. Marten. It has to do with Peter Kitner. Perhaps afterward you will understand what you perceive as my concern about Alexander Cabrera and why it would not have been wise for me to leave you with Inspector Lenard."

70

Grand Duchess Catherine Mikhailovna touched her hair and smiled confidently as she waited for the official photographer to compose his shot. On her left arm was her son, Grand Duke Sergei; on her right, the silver-haired, mustachioed, and very regal seventy-seven-year-old Prince Dimitrii Vladimir Romanov, in whose grand home this night was being celebrated and who was the primary rival for the crown.

Behind the young photographer she could see her mother, Grand Duchess Maria Kurakina, and beyond her the faces of the other Romanovs gathered in Prince Dimitrii's high-ceilinged living room—thirty-three aging, elegantly dressed, defiantly proud men and women from a dozen different countries and representing all four branches of the family. None had let the weather interfere with their travel, nor would she have expected them to. They were preeminent in the imperial family and Russian to their souls; strong, noble, and steadfastly loyal to their God-given heritage as the true guardians of the Motherland.

After nearly a century, and spread across the globe in exile, they or the generation before them had watched as the Communists ruled under the hammer and sickle of Lenin and the iron fist of Stalin; seen the horrors of World War II as invading Nazi armies trampled their land and slaughtered millions of their countrymen; watched in fear and dismay in the decades following as a nuclear-arsenal-driven cold war became entangled with brutal KGB reprisals at home and in Eastern Europe; and then watched in total astonishment as almost overnight the Soviet Union crumbled and then vanished, leaving in its wake little more than a corrupt, chaotic, and deeply depressed nation.

Yet now, finally, mercifully, and after everything, a new day was dawning and a democratic Russian government was graciously, properly, and wisely—knowing that the real purpose of monarchies is to provide a sense of continuity and a rock of loyalty on which a nation can be built and sustained—inviting the imperial family's return, giving back three hundred years of Romanov rule to the people. To those present the significance was overwhelming. It was as if the history of Russia had been taken away, held hostage, and now was being given back.

Because of it, the members of the four houses of Romanov gathered there had fully accepted that the long battle of competitors for and pretenders to the throne was over. It had simply been reduced to the two men who stood on either arm of Grand Duchess Catherine Mikhailovna—her son, the young, eager Grand Duke Sergei Petrovich Romanov, and the family's regal elder statesman, Prince Dimitrii Vladimir Romanov. Which of them would assume the throne would be decided by an open show of hands in a vote that would immediately follow dinner. Or in Catherine's terms, it was now down to one hour, two at best.

Suddenly the photographer's strobe light fired a series of blinding flashes. With them came the loud clawing sound of film advancing through the motorized camera as the photographer took a dozen pictures or more. Then it was over and the photographer stepped back. The Grand Duchess Catherine relaxed her pose and squeezed her son's hand with assurance.

"May I escort you to dinner, Grand Duchess?" Prince Dimitrii's baritone voice resonated beside her. Instead of turning away after the photographs were taken and leaving his competitor to his mother, the elder Romanov had remained by her side.

"Of course, Your Imperial Highness." Catherine smiled graciously in return, well aware of her audience and purposely demonstrating that she could be every bit as congenial and charming as the opposition.

Regally she took his arm, and in step they crossed to the marble-floored central hallway and turned down it toward gilded doors at the far end, where white-tied and white-gloved servants waited.

Grand Duke Sergei and Catherine's mother, Grand Duchess Maria, followed, and after them came the thirty-three other Romanovs.

As they reached the end of the hallway, the servants pulled open the doors, and they entered a large, ornate dining room with rich, hand-carved paneling that rose upward twenty feet to the ceiling. A long and highly polished antique table ran down the room's center in front of them, while high-backed chairs upholstered in red and gold silk lined either side of it. The place settings were of gold and silver, with crystal glassware and bone-white china and white lace napkins in between. More white-tied servers waited to one side.

It was all formal and flamboyant and theatrical, and exceedingly impressive, yet there was one final piece that overshone everything. Mounted on the wall at the far end of the room was a massive twelve-foot-high golden double eagle, its wingspread nearly as wide as its height. One great talon grasped the imperial scepter, while the other held the imperial orb. High above the eagle's twin heads, at the apex of a great arch above them, sat a majestic, jeweled imperial crown. What they gazed upon was the great Romanov crest, and to a person they gasped as they saw it. Some clearly bowed their heads before it. Few were able to take their eyes off it even after they were seated.

Grand Duchess Catherine was no less moved by it until she drew closer and saw something else. Four chairs had been placed on a raised dais just beneath the crest at the far end of the dining table, yet everyone present was already seated. In that moment a deep disquiet swept over her.

A dais and four chairs.

What were they for?

And for whom?

71

Kovalenko slowed the Mercedes behind a train of snowplows working to keep the N19 open. Dropping back, he held his speed as blowing snow and wind rocked the car. All around it was night, the only illumination the SUV's powerful headlights and the red-glowing taillamps of the snowplows.

"You have heard the story of Anastasia, Mr. Marten."

"It was a movie, a play, I'm not sure. What are you getting at?"

"Anastasia was the youngest of Tsar Nicholas's daughters put in front of the firing squad with the rest of the family in the Ipatiev house." Kovalenko slowed the ML, his eyes on the increasingly treacherous road in front of them.

"Eleven people were taken down into a small room in the cellar by a revolutionary named Yurovsky—Tsar Nicholas, his wife Alexandra, his daughters, Tatiana, Olga, Marie, and Anastasia, and his son, a hemophiliac named Alexei, the Tsarevich, next in line for the imperial throne. The others were the family doctor and Nicholas's valet, a cook, and a maid.

"They thought they were being taken there for their own safety because of the revolution and because there was shooting in the streets. Eleven other men followed them into the little room. Yurovsky looked at the Tsar and said something like 'The shooting is because your royal relatives are trying to find you and free you, therefore the Soviet of Workers' Deputies has decided to execute you.'

"At that moment the Tsar yelled, 'What?' and quickly turned to face his son, Alexei, perhaps in order to protect him. At that same moment, Yurovsky shot Tsar Nicholas and killed him. In the next instant hell broke loose as the eleven other men began shooting, carrying out the execution of the family. The trouble was, it was a very small room with eleven to be executed and twelve men shooting and behind them another five to seven guards who were armed but not part of the firing squad. The sound of the guns and the confusion of screaming people and falling bodies were bad enough, but in 1918 a lot of those guns were using black powder cartridges. Seconds after the shooting began, seeing anything was almost impossible.

"I told you before that after the shootings the bodies were loaded on a truck and driven over rutted roads into the forest to a prechosen burial site."

Kovalenko glanced at Marten and then back, peering past the windshield wipers and through the heavy snow, trying to see the road.

"Go on," Marten urged.

Kovalenko concentrated on the road for several moments more, then they hit a pocket where the snow let up a little and he relaxed. "Because Alexei was a hemophiliac and because of the pressure of the revolution, two sailors of the imperial navy had been assigned to look after the children—a kind of combination bodyguard and nanny. At some point the sailors had a confrontation with Alexei's tutor, who thought their presence hindered Alexei's intellectual development. Finally one had had enough and left. The other, a man named Nagorny, stayed with them until they were detained at the Ipatiev house. Then the revolutionaries had him taken to Ekaterinburg prison. Supposedly he was killed there, but he wasn't. He escaped and later came back and found a way to join Yurovsky's men. He was one of the guards standing behind the firing squad.

"After the shooting stopped, in the dark, blinding smoke and chaos of the murder scene, while the others were loading the bodies onto the truck, Nagorny found one of the children still alive. It was Alexei, and he picked him up, carried him out. In the dark and confusion of all those men trying to get the bodies the hell out of there and onto the truck, how could one man and one body be missed? Nagorny got him away. First to a nearby house and then to another truck. Alexei had been wounded once in the leg and in the shoulder. Nagorny knew well of his hemophilia and how to use pressure to stop the bleeding, which he did successfully.

"Much later when the pieces of what happened began to come together and the bodies, including one thought to be Tsarevich Alexei, were found in the mine shaft, naked, burned, and soaked in acid to try and hide their identity, it was determined there were nine bodies, not eleven. Eventually they realized the two that were missing were Anastasia and Alexei."

"You mean Anastasia survived as well, and that was what her story was about?" Marten said.

Kovalenko nodded. "A woman named Anna Anderson was thought for years to have been Anastasia. Finally the DNA process came along and scientists were able to verify that the bodies recovered were indeed those of the imperial family, but the process also proved that Anna Anderson was not Anastasia. So what really happened to Anastasia? Who knows? We probably never will."

Suddenly Marten realized Anastasia wasn't who Kovalenko was talking about at all. "But you do know what happened to Alexei."

Kovalenko turned to Marten. "Nagorny got him out. By truck and then by railway to the Volga River. After that by boat to the port of Rostov and after that by steamer across the Black Sea to Istanbul, which was then Constantinople. There he was met by an emissary from a close and very well-off friend of the Tsar who had escaped the revolution and gone to Switzerland early in 1918. The emissary carried false papers for both Alexei and Nagorny, and together all three boarded the Orient Express for Vienna. Afterward, they vanished from sight."

Snow had begun falling again, and Kovalenko turned his attention back to the highway in front of them. "No one knows what happened to Nagorny, but—do you understand what I'm telling you, Mr. Marten?"

"The direct male descendant of the Tsar was still alive."

"For fear of Communist reprisal he never revealed his identity but grew to prominence in the jewelry business in Switzerland. He had one child, a son, who went on to gain immense wealth and far greater prominence."

"Peter Kitner," Marten breathed.

"The only true bloodline successor to the Russian throne. And a fact that will be revealed to the Romanov family tonight."

72

Grand Duchess Catherine sat mouth agape as she heard the evidence presented.

Three of the four chairs on the dais and beneath the great Romanov crest were filled with men she had been certain were her staunchest allies—Nikolai Nemov, the mayor of Moscow; Marshal Igor Golovkin, Russian Federation minister of defense and probably the most powerful officer in the Russian military; and the last, the man many felt was the most revered person in all Russia, bearded and berobed, His Holiness Gregor II, the Most Holy Patriarch of the Russian Orthodox Church. Taken together, the triumvirate was, without doubt, the most dominant political machine in Russia, more commanding even than the president of the country, Pavel Gitinov. And that power and influence was what she had counted on.

But now all that had vanished—her future, her son's future, her mother's, a dream burst by the man who sat in the fourth chair, Sir Peter Kitner, né Petr Mikhail Romanov, the irrefutable heir to the imperial throne.

It was all there in the lengthy but fully understandable explanation provided by Prince Dimitrii and in the assembled documents and photographs, copies of which were projected on a large screen put up to the right of the dais. A number of the photographs were faded black-and-white pictures taken by the Russian sailor Nagorny as he helped the young Tsarevich Alexei flee from Russia to Switzerland after the Ipatiev massacre. Others were of Alexei and the young Petr as he grew up in the family home in Mies, outside Geneva. Still others were technical and showed DNA chartings, the laboratories where they were done, and the technicians who had produced them.

But the photographs, charts, and documents only served to underscore the unassailable truth of the evidence presented. Bone samples had been taken from the remains of Tsar Nicholas in the crypt in St. Petersburg and a DNA analysis done. Those results were then compared with DNA samples taken from the remains of the supposed Tsarevich Alexei, Kitner's father, buried in a suburb of Geneva. The DNA sequences and the repetition of those sequences matched those of Tsar Nicholas without question. To make absolutely certain that what they had found was not some bizarre coincidence, they chose a contemporary DNA for comparison. Princess Victoria, the older sister of Empress Alexandra, Tsar Nicholas's wife and mother of Alexei, had had a daughter who became Princess Alice of Greece. Of Princess Alice's children, her lone son, Prince Philip, Duke of Edinburgh and husband of Elizabeth II, Queen of Great Britain, was an ideal, living candidate for a DNA comparison with his grand-aunt, the Empress Alexandra. Again bone samples were taken from the crypt in St. Petersburg, this time from the Empress Alexandra, and matched with samples provided by Prince Philip. Again the DNA sequences and repetitions matched perfectly. Then all four samples were compared with samples provided by Peter Kitner. Again a precise match.

Taken together, this evidence erased any question at all that Tsarevich Alexei Romanov had survived the execution of his family at the Ipatiev house or that Peter Kitner was not only his son but, from Swiss birth records and interviews with people who had known the family, his only child. The line from then to now was clear, simple, unmistaken, and unmistakable—Petr Mikhail Romanov Kitner was the true head of the house of Romanov, and as such was the man who would become Tsarevich.

Catherine's only recourse was to play the Anastasia card and protest that the DNA testing proved nothing and that Kitner was as much a pretender as Anna Anderson had been, but she knew it would be a futile gesture and only bring embarrassment to her, her mother, and her son. Besides, the triumvirate had not made the journey from Moscow for nothing. They had seen the material long before this, had their own people question the experts who had made the analyses, had the DNA procedures repeated by three additional and wholly separate laboratories, and afterward made up their minds. Further, Pavel Gitinov, the president of Russia, had asked Kitner to meet with him at his vacation residence on the Black Sea; and there, in the presence of the triumvirate and the leaders of both the Federation Council and the Duma, Russia's upper and lower houses of parliament, had personally asked him to return to Russia as titular monarch, and as such become a practical, emotional, and promotional force to help unite a nation filled with social and economic uncertainty and to shape a new Russia into the global power it once had been.

Slowly, Grand Duchess Catherine Mikhailovna rose to her feet, her eyes locked on Peter Kitner as she did so. Seeing her, Grand Duke Sergei rose as well. So, too, did his grandmother, Grand Duchess Maria Kurakina.

"Petr Mikhail Romanov." Catherine's strong voice echoed across the cavernous room. Heads turned to stare as she raised a golden goblet emblazoned with the Romanov crest toward him. "The family of Grand Duke Sergei Petrovich Romanov proudly salutes you and humbly acknowledges you as Tsarevich of All Russia."

With that the others stood, goblets raised in salutation. Prince Dimitrii stood as well. So did Nikolai Nemov, mayor of Moscow, Marshal Igor Golovkin of the Russian Federation Ministry of Defense, and Gregor II, the Most Holy Patriarch of Moscow and All Russia.

Then Sir Petr Mikhail Romanov Kitner rose, his white hair like a royal mane, his dark eyes gleaming. Raising his hands, he waited, staring out at the royal salutations. Finally and simply, he dropped his head in formal acceptance of his mantle.

73

Kovalenko saw the abandoned car too late. He swung the wheel hard, swerving wildly to avoid the car, and sending the ML500 spinning across the snow-slicked highway like a top. A split second later it hit a snow berm on the far side, went up on two wheels, then came back down to smash backward through the berm and slide tobogganlike down a long embankment, where it came to a stop, its engine running, its headlights still on, in the deep snow on the edge of a rock outcropping.

"Kovalenko!" Marten tugged against his seat harness and

looked toward Kovalenko's motionless form behind the wheel. For a long second there was silence, and then slowly the Russian turned and looked at him.

"I am alright. You?"

"Okay."

"Where the hell are we?"

Marten's right hand found the door handle and he pushed it open. He felt the car rock slightly as snow and freezing air rushed in. Gently he eased over and peered out. From the light of the open door he could just make out the dark chasm directly under the door and hear the rush of distant water below them. Leaning out a little more, he felt the car tip in his direction. Immediately he stopped.

"What is it?" Kovalenko demanded.

All Marten could see was the top of a snow-covered ledge and below that, pitch black. Slowly he eased back and closed the door.

"We're on the edge of a precipice."

"A what?"

"A precipice; a cliff. I'd be surprised if we have more than two wheels on solid ground."

Kovalenko leaned over to look and the car rocked with him.

"Don't do that!"

Kovalenko froze where he was.

Marten stared at him. "I don't know how far down it is and I don't want to find out."

"Nor do I. Nor would Lenard. He wants his car back in one piece."

"What time is it?"

Carefully Kovalenko squinted at the dashboard clock. "Just midnight."

Marten took a deep breath. "It's snowing like hell and it's midnight and we're way off the road in the middle of nowhere. A sneeze could put us over the side and that would be that. We'd either drown or freeze to death or burn up if this thing catches on fire.

"Even if we got through on your cell phone there's no way we could tell anybody where we are because we don't know. And even if we did and could, I doubt anybody could get here before daylight. And that would be if we were lucky."

"So what do we do?"

"We've got two wheels over the side, which hopefully means we still have two wheels on solid ground. Maybe we can just drive out of here."

"What do you mean 'maybe'?"

"You have a better idea?"

Marten could see Kovalenko considering alternatives, then as quickly deciding there were none.

"At least it would be helpful," Kovalenko said with authority, "if we had less weight on the passenger side."

"Right."

"And you can't very well get out on your side because you would plunge into the depths and maybe take the vehicle with you."

"Right."

"Therefore I will get out on my side. As I do, you will slide over and take the wheel and make the attempt to, as you say, drive out of here."

"And you get to stand safely back and see what happens. Is that it?"

"Mr. Marten, if the car does go over we do not need two inside it when one will do."

"But the one inside it won't be you, it will be me, Kovalenko."

"If it is any consolation, if you do go over I will no doubt freeze to death anyway."

With that Kovalenko unhooked his seat belt and pushed the driver's door open. A gust of wind pushed it back, but he put his shoulder against it and shoved it open again.

"Okay, I'm going. Move with me."

Kovalenko began to slide out from behind the wheel. As he did, Marten eased delicately over the center console, putting as much of his weight on the driver's side as he could. Suddenly the ML creaked and started to tip toward the ravine. Kovalenko moved back quickly, putting all of his weight on the edge of the seat. The car stopped.

"Mother of Christ—" Kovalenko breathed.

"Stay where you are," Marten said. "I'm coming the rest of the way over."

One hand on the driver's seat, then moving down on his elbow with as much of his body weight as he could, Marten lifted off the console and slid onto the seat, swinging his legs one by one under the wheel.

Marten looked up. Kovalenko's nose was inches from his own. A sudden gust of wind slammed the door into Kovalenko from behind, throwing him full into Marten. Their noses smacked hard and the car tilted toward the ravine.

Then Marten shoved Kovalenko away and out into the snow and leaned as far over as he could toward him. The move was enough; the ML righted.

"Get up and close the door," Marten said.

"What?"

"Get up and close the door. Gently."

Kovalenko rose like a ghost from the snow. "You're certain?"

"Yes."

Marten watched Kovalenko push the door closed and then step back. Slowly Marten looked out the windshield past the beating wipers. In front of him the headlights shone on nothing but white. It was impossible to tell whether what he was looking at went up or down or straight. All he knew was he did not want to turn right.

Taking a breath, he glanced out at Kovalenko staring in at him. Kovalenko's collar was up, his hair and beard covered with snow.

Marten looked back. His hand went to the gearshift and moved it into DRIVE, then ever so gently he touched his foot to the accelerator. There was a soft whir as the engine's rpms picked up and he felt the wheels start to turn. For a moment nothing happened. Then came the slightest lurch as the tires caught and the ML inched forward. Two feet, and then three and then the wheels started to spin in the deep snow. He eased off and the SUV rolled back. Instantly he touched the brake. The car slid and then stopped.

"Easy," he breathed, "easy."

Again the accelerator. Again the SUV inched forward. Again the wheels turned and then caught. Again they began to spin. Then Marten saw Kovalenko move forward and disappear behind the car. He looked in the mirror and saw the Russian throw his shoulder against the ML's rear door.

Marten's foot touched the accelerator and he opened the window a little.

"Now!" he yelled and eased the accelerator down. The wheels spun. Kovalenko strained with everything he had. Finally Marten felt the wheels take hold, and the car moved forward. This time it kept going. Then he was moving faster, going straight uphill through foot-deep snow. Again he glanced in the mirror. Kovalenko was behind him, running in the track the ML had made. Five seconds. Another five. The SUV was actually accelerating. Then Marten saw the big snow berm in the headlights. From this angle it was at least as high as the car, maybe higher. How solid it was or if it wasn't a berm at all but a stone wall covered with snow was impossible to tell, but he couldn't stop now and risk sliding backward. All he could do was hit the berm as hard and fast as he could and hope he broke through to the other side.

A half beat and he shoved the accelerator to the floor. The ML rocketed forward. Two seconds, three. The berm was right there and he hit it flush. For an instant everything went dark. Then he was through it and onto the roadway.

A deep breath and he lowered the driver's window all the way. In the outside mirror he could see Kovalenko running up the hill and through the tank-sized break in the berm behind him. His chest heaving, breath streaming from his nostrils, his entire being enveloped in snow, he was yelling in victory and pumping his fists in the air. In the red glow of the taillights he looked like a great dancing bear.

74

PARIS. SAME TIME, FRIDAY, JANUARY 17. 12:40 A.M.

Tsarevich Peter Kitner Romanov covered his ears against the deafening roar as the twin-rotor Russian Kamov-32 attack helicopter took off from a secured corner of Orly Airport in heavy wind and blinding snow.

Across from him sat Colonel Stefan Murzin of the Federalnaya Slujba Ohrani, the FSO, his personal bodyguard and one of ten Russian presidential security agents who had rushed him from the house at 151 Avenue Georges V and into the third of four identical limousines waiting outside the servants' entrance. The cars had left at once, driving through blowing snow past the French police and then bumper to bumper across the Seine and through nine miles of deserted, snowy streets to a cordoned-off area of a storm-closed Orly Airport.

Two Kamov-32s had been waiting, engines fired up, their rotors slowly churning. The moment Kitner's limousine stopped, its doors were pulled open and Colonel Murzin guided the Tsarevich and four heavily armed FSO agents to the first helicopter. In seconds they were on board, the doors closing, the rotors picking up speed, with the square-jawed, black-eyed Murzin personally strapping the Tsarevich into his seat. Then Murzin strapped himself in, and seconds later both helicopters were airborne.

Murzin sat back. "Are you comfortable, Tsarevich?"

"Yes, thank you." Kitner nodded, and looked at the faces of the other men protecting him. He had had personal bodyguards for years, but none were like these. Each was a former member of the elite Russian Special Purpose Forces, the *spetsialnoe naznachenie,* or Spetsnaz. They were all like Murzin; young, muscular, and extremely fit, their hair razor-cut to the scalp. From the instant Kitner had been named Tsarevich and bowed his head to the others in formal acceptance, he had become their property. In a flash Higgs was pushed into the background, his only job now to inform the top MediaCorp executives who needed to know that their chairman had been called away for "personal reasons," but that he was well and would return within a few days. At the same time, the remaining Romanov family members were sworn to secrecy. Requiring the same of the personnel working the dinner—waiters, chefs, beverage servers—was not necessary; they were all FSO agents.

For the Tsarevich's personal safety and because of the stunning historical magnitude of what was about to be revealed— that Alexei Romanov had indeed survived the Ipatiev massacre and that Peter Kitner, chairman of one of the few privately owned multinational media companies in the world, was his son, coupled with Moscow's near-incredible decision to reinstitute the imperial throne—made it essential that the information be kept secret until security elements were in place for the formal announcement to be made by the Russian president at the Davos forum. As a result, only Kitner's immediate family, Higgs, and his private secretary, Taylor Barrie, had been informed.

Moreover, the swift changeover to state security was not Kitner's alone. In the same moment that he had become Tsarevich and had been spirited away from the house on the Avenue Georges V, the FSO had taken over the protection of his son, Michael, in Munich on MediaCorp business; Kitner's wife, Luisa, still in Trieste; and their daughters, Lydia and Marie, in London, and Victoria, in New York. All of them would travel to Davos tomorrow under FSO guard.

Whether Kitner had been right or wrong in his fear that the Baroness was plotting physical harm against any of them, the presence of this highly trained security force resolved the question. He was isolated now and, as Tsar, would be for the rest of his life. The freedom he had given up, he had given up willingly—for his father, for his country, for his birthright. Finally, who he was was no longer secret. His father's great fear of a Communist reprisal against them had been resolved by time and history. The same, he knew, could be said about the Baroness and Alexander.

75

PARIS, THE PENTHOUSE APARTMENT AT NUMBER 127
AVENUE HOCHE. FRIDAY, JANUARY 17. 3:14 A.M.

Grand Duchess Catherine Mikhailovna lay awake in the dim glow of a bedside nightlight, her eyes absently focused on the digital bedside clock, which she had watched click past seemingly every minute since she had gone to bed just after one-thirty. How many times in those nearly two hours had she replayed the entire evening in her mind? Never mind the feelings of deep betrayal by her "close friends" the mayor of Moscow and the Patriarch of the Church. What troubled her most deeply was why, with the exception of Prince Dimitrii, none of them, not one other single Romanov, had known about Peter Kitner, or the truth about the escape of Alexei from the Impatiev house. Secrecy she could understand, the protection of the life of the true Tsarevich, but there seemed no reason to withhold the information from all the Romanovs except Dimitrii—not just about Kitner's existence, the truth of who he was and who his father had been, but about the decisions made in the Russian parliament and by the president of Russia that had so colossally affected the entire family.

Click.

3:15 A.M.

She thought of her son's reaction at the introduction of Peter Kitner and the announcement of who he was. She remembered that despite all his years in preparation and with the full expectation that he would become Tsar, he had not wavered at all. Not so much as blinked. He would not sit on the throne of Russia, but he would honor and obey the man who would. It was his privilege and duty to do so. At that moment she knew that, at age twenty-two, Grand Duke Sergei Petrovich Romanov was more Russian than any of them.

3:16 A.M.

She heard her mother roll over in the bed behind her. A strong gust of wind rattled the windows, and heavy snow spat against the glass.

They should have told her, the mayor if no one else. But he hadn't. Why had he said nothing and led her on? Suddenly it came to her there was someone else involved. Someone to whom both the mayor and the Patriarch had more loyalty than to her. But who?

Click.

3:17 A.M.

Suddenly everything went dark.

"What happened?" Her mother sat up in bed.

"It's nothing, Mother," Grand Duchess Catherine Mikhailovna said. "The power went off. Go back to sleep."

76

BASEL, SWITZERLAND. STILL FRIDAY, JANUARY 17.
6:05 A.M.

"We will want access to his files and business records, this morning if possible. . . . Yes, alright. Very good, thank you." Kovalenko clicked off his cell phone and looked to Marten.

"A Chief Inspector Beelr of the Zurich Kantonspolizei will meet us at the University Hospital morgue within the hour. The police already have permission to search the victim's personal property at both his home and his place of business."

Kovalenko's eyes were red and puffy, and stubble was beginning to show on his throat at the base of his beard where he normally shaved it. Both men were tired from the long drive, a journey made even more exhausting by the hazardous conditions. But the storm had eased as they crossed from France into Switzerland, and by now the snow had dwindled to little more than flurries in the throw of the ML500's headlamps.

Marten glanced at the SUV's navigation screen and then took the A3 expressway toward Zurich.

"The victim's name is Hans Lossberg. Age forty-one, three children. The same as me," Kovalenko said wearily and looked off toward the still-dark eastern sky. "Have you ever been in a morgue before, Mr. Marten?"

Marten hesitated. Kovalenko was probing again. Finally, he found a way to say it. "Once, in L.A., Dan Ford took me there."

"Then you know what to expect."

"Yes."

Marten kept his eyes on the road. Early as it was, commuter traffic was building and he had to watch his speed on the snow-slicked highway. Still, he couldn't help but be bothered by what Kovalenko was doing. He had obviously talked to the Russian investigators who had been in L.A. He knew about Red and Halliday and the squad. Marten wondered if somehow he suspected who he was, and that was why he kept pushing at him. Like just now about the morgue and the innuendoes about being a detective, and then the business with his university education and where he had begun it. And before, in Paris, when he watched him as he compared Raymond's fingerprint with the one the French police had taken from Dan Ford's car, knowing it took someone with considerable knowledge to understand what he was looking at. And again when he had made the conjecture about Dan Ford and why Vabres might have delivered the menu to him in the middle of the night the way he had, and Kovalenko had just stared at him in silence before he said anything.

He was also sure the reason Kovalenko had insisted on getting out of the car after they had gone off the road was not because he was afraid the ML would go over the side but because he wanted Marten behind the wheel, to see how well he handled an automobile in a difficult situation, if he had training and experience above and beyond what would be considered normal driving.

But even if he did suspect that Marten was not just the university-student-friend-of-Dan-Ford he said he was, and was waiting for him to give himself away, what did he hope to gain from it? Unless he had friends on the LAPD, which Marten strongly doubted.

Whatever the reason, Marten couldn't let it get in the way. He was convinced that with every passing moment he was getting closer to Raymond, and Kovalenko was the only ally he had. Moreover, with Kovalenko's opening doors in pursuit of his own agenda, he was sweeping Marten with him. They had begun a dialogue in which they shared information, and, after their experience in the snow and getting the car back on the highway, even started a friendship of sorts. It was something Marten didn't dare let go of, even if it meant exposing himself further. Slowing some against the icy roadway, he glanced at the Russian and let himself think out loud.

"Last year, in L.A., Raymond used a gun to break out of jail and murder a number of innocent people, some of them policemen. He used a gun in Chicago when he killed the Azov brothers. A gun was used to murder the Romanovs in the U.S. and Mexico. Neuss was killed with a gun in Paris, and Fabien Curtay was shot to death in Monaco. So why is Raymond—and we know it is Raymond—suddenly using a razor or knife? And not just using it, but handling it like some kind of crazed zealot. Butchering his victims."

"I had thought before we might be looking at some kind of ritual killing," Kovalenko said, "and maybe it is."

"Or maybe it's not," Marten said. "Maybe he's starting to lose it. Ritual is controlled. The only thing we've seen controlled here is the first cut, as if he had it planned out. After that it's all emotion and lots of it. Love, hate. One or the other, some of each. All very passionate, as if he couldn't hold himself back. Or didn't want to."

For a long moment Kovalenko said nothing, then finally did. "A large vintage knife, a Spanish switchblade called a Navaja, was taken from Fabien Curtay's private safe in Monaco. Something else was taken, too, a small reel of eight-millimeter motion picture film."

"Film?"

"Yes."

"Not video?"

"No, film."

"Of what?"

"Who knows?"

The sky was still winter-dark as the A3 became the A1 and they could see the lights of Zurich in the distance.

"Tell me more about Kitner," Marten said. "Anything that comes to mind. His family maybe, not Cabrera, but the one he talks about."

"He has a son who will one day take over his firm," Kovalenko said with a sigh. He was getting tired and it showed. "And a daughter who is an executive who also works for the company. Two other daughters are married, one to a doctor, the other to an artist. His wife, as I already told you, is Spanish royalty, a cousin of King Juan Carlos."

"Royalty marries royalty."

"Yes."

Marten felt the weariness, too. He put a hand to his face and felt the growth of his own stubble beard. They both needed to shave and clean up and rest, but they couldn't, not yet. "How long has his wife known who he is?"

"Maybe from the day they met, maybe only when he agreed to become Tsar. I couldn't say. I don't know how those kind of people talk to each other, what they say or don't, and I probably never will. It's a perch in life I'm not likely to reach."

"What else, personally? How did he know Alfred Neuss?"

"They grew up together in Switzerland. Neuss's father worked for Kitner's, that's why he ended up in the jewelry business."

Marten looked over and saw the Russian watching him, the way he had before. Watching his hands on the wheel. His feet as they alternately touched the brake pedal and the accelerator.

"What else?" Marten asked.

"Kitner had a son who was murdered when he was ten years old," Kovalenko said almost reluctantly. "It happened twenty-some years ago. Kitner's name wasn't as important as it is now, so it wasn't in the headlines; still, it was tabloid news. Some young criminal stabbed him while he was attending a children's birthday party in Paris."

"Paris?"

"In Parc Monceau. The same park where the body of Alfred Neuss was found."

"This is fact?" Marten was incredulous.

"It is fact. And before you again begin making scenarios, let me tell you that so far there is nothing at all to connect the crimes other than the fact that Neuss and Kitner were friends and the piece of real estate was the same."

"What happened afterward?"

"As far as I know the killer was never caught."

"You said Kitner's son was stabbed. What if the knife taken from Curtay's safe was the murder weapon?"

"You are guessing."

"Yes, but then there was the film taken along with the knife."

"What about it?" Kovalenko didn't understand.

"The murder was committed some twenty years ago, before video came into common use. Before that people used movie cameras. Children's birthday parties were a main event for home movies, and most of them were shot on eight-millimeter film. What if someone was taking movies of the birthday party and inadvertently filmed the murder itself, and that film was what was taken from the safe? What if Neuss and Kitner had both the murder weapon and a filmed record of the murder and had hidden them away, and Cabrera knew about it?"

My God! Marten suddenly thought. What if the knife and film were the "pieces"? The things Raymond had been after the whole time. If they were, they would have been the reason for the safe deposit keys. Keys to a safe deposit box that held the knife and the film. A safe deposit box that might have been in a bank in Marseilles, where Neuss had stopped before he went to see Curtay in Monaco. How the rest of it played, he didn't know—except that it was possible that the people murdered in the Americas had been given the keys for safekeeping in the event something happened to Kitner but were never told what they were for or to. Kitner knew Cabrera had murdered his son but didn't want it to come out, so he sent him away to Argentina and kept the knife and film of the murder as insurance he would never return.

So if the knife and film were indeed the "pieces"—how had Raymond put it? *The pieces that would ensure the future.* What future, what had he been talking about? And why had Cabrera committed the murder in the first place?

Abruptly Marten looked to Kovalenko. "Follow the thinking. Twenty years ago Alexander Cabrera would have been how old, thirteen, fourteen? What if he was your young criminal?"

"You are suggesting he would kill his own brother." Again Kovalenko sounded reluctant.

"You're the one who said he might be trying to kill his father."

"No, Mr. Marten. I said that Peter Kitner might have been the target of Raymond Thorne, not of Alexander Cabrera." Kovalenko fixed Marten with a stare, then looked off.

"What is it, Inspector?"

Kovalenko didn't reply, just kept looking off.

"I'll tell you what it is. It's the same as it was before," Marten pressed him. "You know in the pit of your stomach Raymond and Cabrera *are* the same person. But for some reason you don't want to admit it to yourself."

"You are right, Mr. Marten." Abruptly Kovalenko turned back. "Forget for the moment about Kitner's murdered son and suppose, as you say, Alexander Cabrera and Raymond Thorne are one and the same. And suppose it was Kitner and not Alfred Neuss or the others who was his primary target all along. In that situation, we do have a son trying to murder his father."

"It's happened before."

"Yes, it's happened before. But the trouble here is that very soon this particular father is to become the next Tsar of Russia. Suddenly that changes everything, taking it out of the category of attempted familial homicide and making it a very touchy matter for state security, one that must be kept entirely classified until it is proven one way or the other. Which is the real reason why we could not tell Lenard and why I could not leave you behind to discuss it. I sincerely hope you can appreciate my position, Mr. Marten. That's why we drove all night through a raging blizzard—for proof that this Hans Lossberg was killed by the same person who executed Dan Ford. Perhaps with luck, we will even get another fingerprint."

"Why don't you just get a writ of some kind that will force Cabrera to give you his fingerprints?"

"At this time yesterday we possibly could have. But yesterday morning I did not know of the existence of the LAPD file containing the fingerprints of Raymond Oliver Thorne."

"Yesterday, today, what's the difference?"

Kovalenko smiled faintly. "The difference is that today Cabrera has officially become a member of the imperial family. It is one of the difficulties with having a monarchy. The police do not ask a king or a tsar or a member of his family for his fingerprints. At least not without irrefutable evidence that a crime has been committed. And it is why, if I am to be the one who accuses him, there must be no doubt whatsoever that he is the right man."

77

Hans Lossberg. Age forty-one, married with three children. The same, as Kovalenko had said, as him. Only he wasn't the same as Kovalenko. He was dead, butchered with a razor-sharp instrument. The same way Dan Ford and Jean-Luc Vabres had been killed. Maybe with even more reckless passion. And no, the perpetrator had not left fingerprints. Fingerprints or not, the lone glance between Marten and Kovalenko said everything— Raymond had been in Zurich.

"Could we see Herr Lossberg's place of business?" Kovalenko asked as the young, friendly Inspector Heinrich Beelr of the Zurich Kantonspolizei was giving them details of the crime. When it had happened and where.

Fifteen minutes later they were in the sizable back room of Grossmünster Presse, an industrial printing firm on Zahringerstrasse, poring through drawers of artwork looking for the paste-up for a recently printed menu or one about to be printed. What kind of menu it might be, they had no idea, except that it might be in Russian or have something to do with the Romanov family.

An hour later they were still there with nothing to show for their labor. Making the situation more difficult was the steadfast assertion by Bertha Rissmak, the printing shop's large and decidedly severe fifty-three-year-old manager, that they were looking for something that didn't exist. While the late Hans Lossberg had been Grossmünster Presse's owner, he was also the company's only salesman and had been for the last fifteen years. And as far as Bertha Rissmak knew, in those same fifteen years Grossmünster Presse had not once printed a menu. Their specialty was business forms—inventory lists, letterheads, cards, shipping labels, and the like, nothing else. Compounding the problem was that Lossberg had literally handled all of the thousands of accounts himself and had his own filing system—fifteen four-drawer filing cases of it. Making things even more difficult was the fact that many of the accounts had been dormant for years and the files neither discarded nor updated. More frustrating still was that they were not categorized by date or subject but were simply in alphabetical order. It was a needle-in-a-haystack game, only they had no idea which haystack or even if there was anything to find at all. Still, they had no choice but to pore through every piece of artwork, look at every order and invoice. It was a tedious process that was taking up invaluable time, especially if Raymond had more on his agenda.

Then, twenty more minutes into it, Marten suddenly remembered what Kovalenko had told him about Cabrera's background; he had been raised in Argentina by the sister of his deceased mother, a European of great wealth. If she was European, why would she raise her sister's son in South America even if she could afford to?

Abruptly he crossed to where Kovalenko was hunched over a file case. "Cabrera's aunt, who is she?" he said quietly.

Kovalenko looked up, then, with a glance at Inspector Beelr studiously going through a stack of files behind him, took Marten by the arm and led him to a corner of the room where they could talk.

So far all the Zurich police knew was that Kovalenko was following up on murders of expatriate Russians that had taken place in France and Monaco. He had introduced Marten as a material witness and explained what they were looking for, but had said little else. In particular, he had said nothing whatsoever about Alexander Cabrera.

"Do not bring up Cabrera," he said quietly but directly. "I don't want Beelr asking about him and then having it get back to Lenard. Do you understand?"

"Who is his aunt?" Marten ignored him.

"Baroness Marga de Vienne, a prominent and exceptionally influential European socialite."

"And wealthy, you said."

"More than wealthy."

"That would explain the charter jet sent to help Raymond escape from L.A. It would also explain how he managed to have a death certificate filed, got out of the hospital and probably onto an air ambulance, and had a John Doe taken from the morgue and burned up in his name at the crematorium. But it doesn't explain Argentina, and why he was raised there."

Abruptly both men looked up.

Beelr was coming toward them accompanied by a middle-aged man with a short haircut who was wearing a printer's apron.

"Excuse my interruption. This is Helmut Vaudois. He was a close friend of Hans Lossberg and had known him for some time. It seems that before Lossberg took over the firm he was a printer himself. From time to time he enjoyed doing work on the side, especially if the order was small. So it is possible Lossberg took on this menu job outside of the company."

"Would he have done it here?"

"No," Vaudois said, "he had a small printing system at his apartment."

78

257 ZÜRICHBERGSTRASSE. 10:15 A.M.

Maxine Lossberg greeted them at the door of the small apartment a block and a half from the Zurich Zoo. Her hair obviously quickly put up, a housecoat pulled around her, Hans Lossberg's forty-year-old wife was still clearly in shock and disbelief. It was only the presence of Lossberg's friend Helmut Vaudois that comforted her at all, and she took his hand and held it the whole time they were there.

Carefully and sympathetically, Inspector Beelr explained they had come looking for information that might help find her husband's killer. Did she happen to know if her husband had recently done any printing work on his own? he asked. A private order perhaps, or a favor to a friend?

"Ja," she said and led them down a narrow hallway to a back

room where Lossberg had an old-fashioned printing press and racks of type, and which smelled of ink.

Hurriedly she looked through his file drawers and was surprised to find nothing.

"Hans always kept a copy of whatever he printed," she said in German.

Beelr translated, then asked her, "What was it that he printed?"

"Ein Speisekarte."

"A menu," Beelr translated quickly.

Marten and Kovalenko exchanged glances.

"Who did he print it for?" Kovalenko asked.

Beelr translated. Again she replied in German. Again Beelr translated.

"A business acquaintance, she doesn't know who. All she knows is that there were exactly two hundred menus to be printed. No more, no less, and then the proofs destroyed and type disassembled. She remembers that because her husband told her."

"Ask her if she knows when the print order was made."

Once more Beelr translated. Once more she replied in German and Beelr translated.

"She doesn't remember exactly when the order was placed, but her husband did a proof some time last week and then did the printing itself last Monday night. She wanted him to go out to a movie, but he refused because he had the print order. He was very busy, and the order had to be done quickly."

Marten and Kovalenko exchanged glances. Ford and Vabres were murdered early Wednesday morning. Vabres could easily have picked the menu up from Lossberg on Tuesday.

"What was on the menu?" Kovalenko pressed.

Again Beelr asked; again Maxine Lossberg replied. She didn't know. A man had come to the apartment Sunday, and she had seen him briefly as Lossberg took him into the back room, probably to show him the proof. After that she had never seen him again.

"Kovalenko." Marten touched Kovalenko's sleeve and motioned him out of the room.

"Show her," he said when they were out of earshot.

"Show her what?"

"The photos of Cabrera. If it was him, she'll tell us immediately. It would be enough for you to request his fingerprints."

Kovalenko hesitated.

"Are you afraid to find out?"

Maxine Lossberg sat at the kitchen table as Kovalenko opened his laptop, then sat down beside her and pulled up the Russian Ministry of Justice photo file on Alexander Cabrera.

Marten stood behind them, looking over Kovalenko's left shoulder, while Beelr and Helmut Vaudois looked over his right.

There was a click and Marten saw the photo of Cabrera getting into a limousine outside his company headquarters in Buenos Aires.

Kovalenko looked to Maxine Lossberg.

"I can't tell," she said in German.

Another click and Marten saw the photo of Cabrera in overalls and hard hat looking at blueprints spread out on the hood of a pickup truck somewhere in the desert.

Maxine shook her head. *"Nein."*

Click.

Another photo came up. One Marten had never seen before. It was taken outside a hotel in Rome. Cabrera stood beside a car, talking on a cell phone. To his immediate right, a chauffeur held open the car's rear door. A very attractive young woman with dark hair was sitting in the backseat, apparently waiting for Cabrera.

Suddenly Marten froze at what he saw.

"Nein." Maxine Lossberg stood up. That was not the man whom she had seen with her husband.

"Kovalenko," Marten said abruptly, "enhance that."

"What?"

"That photo, enhance it. Bring up the woman in the backseat."

"Why?"

"Just do it!"

Kovalenko looked over his shoulder at Marten, wholly puzzled. Beelr stared, too; so did Maxine Lossberg and Helmut Vadois. It was Marten's tone. Astonishment, rage, fear all in one.

Kovalenko turned back.

Click. He enhanced the photo; the woman became clearer.

"Again," Marten demanded.

Click.

The woman's face filled the screen. It was a profile. But there was no doubt who it was. No doubt at all.

Rebecca.

79

"Jesus God!" Marten grabbed Kovalenko by his jacket and dragged him out of the room and down the hallway.

"Why the hell didn't you show me that before, when we were in Paris?"

"What the hell are you talking about? I asked you if you wanted to see more, you said no."

"How did I know you had *that?*"

Now they had reached the living room. Marten shoved Kovalenko inside, slammed the door, and pushed him against it.

"You stupid bastard. You follow Cabrera everywhere. But you don't know who he's with?"

"Let go of me," Kovalenko said coldly.

Marten hesitated and then stepped back. He was white, trembling with rage.

Kovalenko stared at him, perplexed. "What is it, the girl?"

"She is my sister."

"Your sister?"

"How many more photos do you have of Cabrera with her in them?"

"None here. Perhaps a half-dozen more on the master file in Moscow. We never learned her name or where she lives; he's kept her quite protected. The hotels she stays in, he always takes care of the room. She meets him often. To us it was of little importance."

"How long has this been going on?"

"We have only been covering him for a few months, since we learned about Kitner. What happened before that I don't know." Kovalenko hesitated. "You had no idea she was seeing someone?"

"None." Marten crossed the room and then turned back. "I need your cell phone."

"What are you going to do?"

"Call her, find out where she is, make sure she's alright."

"Okay." Kovalenko reached into his jacket and took out his cell phone, then handed it to Marten. "Don't tip your hand, don't tell her why you are calling. Just find out where she is and make certain she's safe. We'll decide what to do afterward."

Marten nodded, then lifted the phone and dialed. It rang four times and then a recording came on in French telling him the customer he was trying to reach was away from the phone or out of the area. He hung up and dialed a second number. It rang twice and then someone picked up.

"Rothfels résidence," a female voice said with a French accent.

"Rebecca, please. This is her brother."

"She is not here, monsieur."

"Where is she?"

"With the Monsieur and Madame Rothfels and their children. They are spending the weekend in Davos."

"Davos?" Marten glanced at Kovalenko, then turned back to the phone. "Do you have a cell phone number for Mr. Rothfels?"

"I am not permitted to give it out, I'm sorry."

"It is *very* important that I reach my sister."

"I apologize, monsieur. It is the rule. I would lose my job."

Marten looked to Kovalenko. "What's your cell number?"

Kovalenko told him, and Marten turned back to the phone.

"I'm going to give you my number," he said to the woman on the other end of the line. "Please call Mr. Rothfels and ask him to have Rebecca get in touch with me right away. Can you do that?"

"Yes, sir."

"Thank you."

Marten gave her the number, had her repeat it, thanked her again, and hung up. He was still stunned. The idea that Rebecca was having an affair with Cabrera shocked him beyond anything he could imagine. No matter how she looked or dressed, or the languages she had learned to speak so fluently, or her sophistication in public, to him she was still a child barely recovered from a terrible illness. Yes, at some point she had to experience life and men. But Cabrera? How had they met? The chances of them even passing on the street were between nil and none, yet somehow they had.

"Curious how things work," Kovalenko said quietly. "The information was available all along and neither of us could have guessed. Curious, too, that it is Davos where your sister is."

"You think Cabrera could be with her?"

"Davos, Mr. Marten, is where Kitner will be, where the announcement is to be made."

"And if he's after Kitner—" Marten paused; there was no need to fill in the blanks. "How far is it to Davos from here?"

"If we have no more snow, two hours by car."

"I guess we're going."

"I guess we are."

80

DAVOS, SWITZERLAND, VILLA ENKRATZER—
LITERALLY VILLA SKYSCRAPER. STILL FRIDAY,
JANUARY 17. 10:50 A.M.

Tsarevich Peter Kitner Mikhail Romanov woke from a deep sleep, much deeper, he thought, than normal, almost as if he had been drugged. But the day before had been long and emotional, and he laid it to that.

Sitting up, he looked around. A light curtain was drawn over a large window at the far end of the room, but there was enough light to see that the accommodation was large, filled with antique furniture, and in every other way comfortable and well appointed. Unlike most hotel rooms, it had a high ceiling with large open beams, and he wondered what kind of place this was. Then he remembered Colonel Murzin telling him as they rode in the limousine convoy across Paris toward the waiting helicopters that they were going to a privately owned villa in the hills above Davos. It was safe, literally a mountain fortress, built in 1912 for a German arms manufacturer with entry through guardhouse gates and then up a winding five-mile forested drive to the château itself. It was where he was to be taken and where, later in the day, his family would be brought to join him—and where that same night he would dine with Pavel Gitinov, the president of Russia, to discuss the protocol for the pronouncement Gitinov would make in front of the political and business leaders gathered at the World Economic Forum.

Kitner threw back the covers and got up, his head still heavy from sleep. He was about to enter the bathroom for his toilet when there was a sharp knock on the door and Colonel Murzin came in dressed in a business suit.

"Good morning, Tsarevich. I regret to tell you I have bad news."

"What is it?"

"Grand Duchess Catherine, her mother, and her son, Grand Duke Sergei, along with their bodyguards—there was a fire in their leased apartment in Paris. They were trapped on the top floor."

"And—"

"They are dead, sir, all of them. I'm sorry."

Kitner was stunned, and for a moment he said nothing, then looked directly at Murzin. "Does President Gitinov know?"

"Yes, sir."

"Thank you."

"Would you like some help dressing, sir?"

"No, thank you."

"You are expected in twenty minutes, sir."

"Expected? Where, and for what?"

"A meeting, sir. Downstairs in the library."

"What meeting?" Kitner was completely puzzled.

"I believe you requested it, sir."

"I requested—?"

"A private meeting between you and the Baroness de Vienne and Alexander Cabrera."

"They are here? In this building?" Kitner felt as if a blade had suddenly been run through him.

"The château was taken for the weekend by the Baroness, sir."

"I want to telephone my office right away."

"I'm afraid that's not possible, sir."

"Why not?" Dread rose in Kitner, but he tried not to show it.

"It's an order, sir. The Tsarevich is to make no contact outside of the residence until the formal announcement is made tomorrow."

"Who gave this order?" Kitner's dread suddenly turned to disbelief and then outrage.

"President Gitinov, sir."

81

"Clem, it's Nicholas. It's very important. Call me at this number as soon as you can." Marten gave Lady Clem Kovalenko's cell phone number and clicked off.

The highway distance from Zurich to Davos was just over ninety miles and under ordinary circumstances should take, as Kovalenko had said, about two hours. But these were not ordinary circumstances, and the weather had little to do with it. The World Economic Forum increasingly drew sometimes-violent mobs of antiglobalization dissidents, mostly young and idealistic, protesting global economic tyranny by the rich and powerful countries, and the corporations that allegedly funded them. As a result highways, railway lines, and even mountain footpaths were blocked by hordes of Swiss police.

Zurich Kantonspolizei Inspector Beelr had given Kovalenko a pass but had warned that he couldn't guarantee it would work in what was bound to be a very difficult and hostile situation. Still Kovalenko had taken it and thanked him and both Maxine Lossberg and Helmut Vaudois for their cooperation. Then they were gone, with Marten at the wheel of the ML500.

It was just past eleven when they left Zurich, and the weather had cleared to puffy clouds with a bright sun drying out the roadway. The snow-covered Alps shimmered postcardlike in the distance.

Kovalenko looked over at Marten and saw his attention fixed almost trancelike on the roadway ahead, and he knew he was thinking of his sister and how and why she had ever come to be with Alexander Cabrera. It was a bizarre twist of coincidence that made Kovalenko begin to think about the idea of *sudba,* or fate. It was a concept carved deeply into the Russian character, but he'd always taken it with a grain of salt, a folk-myth from another time to be believed or not, if it was convenient. Yet here he was wholly entwined with an American he'd first seen only days ago in a Parisian park abruptly turn away from a police investigation, an act that immediately put him under a cloud of suspicion. In no time at all they'd been brought to the point where they were now, riding in the same car, hundreds of miles from Paris, rocketing toward a common destination with this man's sister as much the focus of their attention as their prime murder suspect, Alexander Cabrera. If that was not fate, what was it?

The sudden chirp of his cell phone broke Kovalenko's thoughts, and he saw Nicholas Marten suddenly look over as he plucked it from his jacket and clicked on.

"Da," he said in Russian.

Marten watched him anxiously, sure it was Rebecca or Lady Clem and waiting for him to hand him the phone. He didn't. Instead, he continued his conversation in Russian. Once, Marten heard him say the word "Zurich," and later "Davos" and then "Tsarevich," but those were the only words he understood. Finally, Kovalenko hung up. It was a long moment before he looked to Marten.

"I have been transferred to another assignment," he said.

"Transferred?" Marten was incredulous.

"I have been ordered back to Moscow."

"When?"

"Immediately."

"Why?"

"Why is not a question one asks. You do as you are instructed."

Kovalenko's cell phone chirped again. He hesitated, then answered.

"*Da*," he said once more, then "Yes," in English and handed the phone to Marten. "For you."

DAVOS, HOTEL STEIGENBERGER BELVÉDÈRE.
SAME TIME.

"Nicholas, it's Clem, can you hear me?"

Her hair in curlers, Lady Clementine Simpson was in the luxury hotel's salon, being worked on by two women at once, receiving a pedicure and a manicure. Her cell phone was on the countertop in front of her, and she was connected to it by an earpiece/microphone.

"Yes," Marten said.

"Where are you?"

"On the road from Zurich, on the way to Davos."

"Davos? That's where I am. At the Steigenberger Belvédère. Father is participating in the forum." Abruptly she lowered her voice. "How did you get out of Paris?"

"Clem, is Rebecca there?" Marten ignored her question.

"Yes, but I haven't seen her."

"Can you get in touch with her?"

"I'm having dinner with her tonight."

"No," Marten pressed her. "Before then. Right away, as quickly as possible."

"Nicholas, I can hear in your voice something's wrong, what is it?"

"Rebecca has been seeing a man named Alexander Cabrera."

Lady Clem gave a big sigh, and looked off. "Oh, dear," she said.

"'Oh, dear'? What does that mean?"

A sharp crackle of static suddenly came across the line and the signal broke up.

"Clem, are you there?" Marten said urgently.

As quickly the line cleared.

"Yes, Nicholas."

"I tried Rebecca's cell number, there's no answer. Do you have a cell phone number for the Rothfels?"

"No."

"Clem, Cabrera might be with the Rothfels."

"Of course he is with the Rothfels, he is Gerard Rothfels's employer. They've taken a villa here for the weekend."

"His employer?" Marten was stunned. So that was how Cabrera and Rebecca had met. He knew Rothfels ran the European offices of some sort of international industrial firm from offices in Lausanne, but he'd never thought to ask who employed him. "Clem, listen to me, Cabrera is not who Rebecca thinks he is."

"What do you mean?"

"He—" Marten hesitated, trying to find the right words—"He may have had something to do with the murder of Dan Ford. And with the murder of another man yesterday, in Zurich."

"Nicholas that's absurd."

"It's not, believe me."

Suddenly Clem looked to the women attending her. "Ladies, would you mind leaving for a few moments? My conversation is a bit personal."

"Clem, what the hell are you doing?"

"Being polite. I don't discuss family matters in front of strangers if it is at all possible."

Clem's attendants smiled respectfully and moved away, leaving her alone.

"*What* family matters?"

"Nicholas, I shouldn't be telling you this because Rebecca was going to surprise you, but, under the circumstances, there is something you should know. Rebecca has not only been seeing Alexander Cabrera, she is going to marry him."

"*Marry* him?"

Again the line crackled with static and again the signal started to break up.

"Clem? Clem!" Marten pressed her. "Can you hear me?"

There was more static. This time the line went dead.

82

The door opened and Colonel Murzin brought Tsarevich Peter Kitner Mikhail Romanov into Villa Enkratzer's library.

The Baroness sat on a leather sofa in front of a heavy oak coffee table in the center of the room. Alexander Cabrera stood farther away, near a large stone fireplace, staring out a large window that had a sweeping view of the Davos Valley. It was the first time Kitner had seen Cabrera in years, but even with the cosmetic surgery he would have recognized him anywhere, if by nothing more than the sheer arrogance of his being.

"*Spasiba,* Colonel," the Baroness said in Russian. Thank you, Colonel.

Murzin nodded and left, closing the door behind him.

"*Dobra-ye utro, Tsarevich.*" Good morning, Tsarevich.

"*Dobra-ye utro,*" he replied cautiously.

The Baroness wore a pale-yellow and white tailored silk pantsuit—her colors, he knew, but an odd choice of dress in the Alps in the dead of winter. She wore diamond earrings and an emerald necklace. Gold bracelets were at either wrist. Her black hair was turned up in a bun at the back of her head in a style that was almost Oriental, and her green eyes sparkled—not the sensual, enticing green he remembered from so long ago, but more those of a serpent, sharp, piercing, and treacherous.

"What do you want with me?"

"It was you who asked to meet with us, Tsarevich."

Kitner glanced at Alexander by the window. He hadn't moved. He just stood staring out as he had from the beginning. Kitner looked back to the Baroness. "I ask again—what do you want with me?"

"There is something for you to sign."

"Sign?"

"It is similar to the agreement you had us put our signature to all those many years ago."

"It was an agreement you have broken."

"Time and circumstance have changed, Tsarevich."

"Sit down, Father." Suddenly Alexander turned from the window and came toward him. His eyes were black as night, and they held the same menace as those of the Baroness.

"How is it the FSO do your bidding when I am Tsarevich?"

"Sit down, Father," Alexander said again, this time indicating a large leather chair next to the coffee table.

Kitner hesitated, then finally crossed and sat down at the table. On it was a slim, leather-bound stationery binder. Next to it was a longish rectangular box, wrapped in brightly colored gift paper. The same gaily wrapped parcel Alexander had carried into the Hôtel Crillon in Paris.

"Open the package, Father," Alexander said quietly.

"What is it?"

"Open it."

Slowly Kitner reached forward, picked it up, and for a moment held it without opening it. His mind raced. How to reach Higgs and call for help? How to warn his family to flee their FSO guards? How to escape from here? Which door, corridor, staircase?

He didn't know how this could have happened as it had, or how they had gained control of Murzin and his men. Suddenly he thought perhaps his guards were not FSO at all but paid mercenaries.

"Open it, Tsarevich," the Baroness urged in a tone that was soft and seductive and that he had not heard in more than thirty years.

"No."

"Shall I do it, Father?" Alexander took a step closer.

"No, I will." hands trembling, Sir Peter Kitner Mikhail Romanov, knight of the British Empire, Tsarevich of All Russia, pulled open the ribbon and then the bright paper wrapping. Inside was a long red velvet box.

"Go ahead, Father," Alexander urged. "See what is inside."

Kitner looked up. "I know what is inside."

"Then open it."

Kitner let out a breath and opened the box. Inside it, lying in a cradle of white silk, was a long antique knife, a Spanish

Navaja switchblade, its handle made of horn and intricate inlaid brass.

"Pick it up."

Kitner looked to Alexander and then to the Baroness. "No."

"Pick it up, Sir Peter." The Baroness's command was a clear warning. "Or should I ask Alexander?"

Kitner hesitated, then slowly reached toward the knife. His hand closed around it and he lifted it out.

"Touch the button, Father," Alexander commanded. Kitner did. There was a flash of steel and the blade leapt out. It was polished and wide and narrowed quickly to a near-needle point at the tip. Its cutting edge was a good eight inches long and had been honed to razor sharpness.

It was the knife Alexander had used to kill his son, Paul, when he'd been a child of ten. Kitner had never seen it in person, let alone held it. Not even when, so many years ago, Alfred Neuss had wanted to show it to him. It was too real, too awful. The most he'd ever seen of it was when Neuss had made him watch the film and he'd witnessed the murder with his own eyes.

Now that same killing tool, stolen from the slain Fabien Curtay, was in his hands. Suddenly his entire being overflowed with hate and loathing. Knife in his hand, its blade extended, he looked up savagely at the man who had murdered Paul— the man who was his other son, Alexander, who had been little more than a child himself when he'd done it.

"If you wanted to kill me, Father"—Alexander suddenly stepped in and lifted the weapon from Kitner's grasp—"you should have done it long ago."

"He didn't because he couldn't, my sweet." The Baroness smiled cruelly. "He had neither the strength, nor the courage, nor the stomach for it. Hardly a man to be Tsar."

Kitner stared at her. "It is the same knife you used all those years ago on the man in Naples."

"No, Father, it is not," Alexander said definitively, making it entirely clear that he and the Baroness had no secrets between them. "The Baroness wanted something more elegant. More appropriately—"

"Royal," the Baroness finished for him, and then her eyes

went to the leather-bound binder on the table. "Open it, Tsarevich, and read it. And when you have, sign it."

"What is it?"

"Your abdication."

"Abdication?" Kitner was astounded.

"Yes."

"To whom am I to abdicate?"

"To whom would you think?" The Baroness's eyes went to Alexander.

"What?" Kitner's voice resonated with fury.

"Your firstborn son, and after you, direct successor to the throne."

83

"Never!" Kitner suddenly stood. His temples bulged and sweat glistened on his forehead. He looked from the Baroness to Alexander. "I will see you both in hell first!"

"You know the FSO are guarding your wife and children." Alexander closed the knife and put it back in the box. "The FSO will do as they are ordered. The Tsarevich must be protected, even from his own family."

Kitner turned to the Baroness. This was a nightmare beyond imagination. "You have reached Gitinov."

The Baroness gave the slightest nod of her head.

"How?"

"It is merely a game of chess, Tsarevich."

Alexander sat down on the arm of the Baroness's chair. The lighting in the room and the manner in which they sat made them, together, nearly a portrait.

"Colonel Murzin has informed you of the tragic death of Grand Duchess Catherine," Alexander said quietly, "and that of her mother and Grand Duke Sergei. An early-morning fire in her leased apartment in Paris."

"You," Kitner breathed. The hellish violence went on without end.

"Grand Duke Sergei was the only other possible challenger to the throne. Unless you count Prince Dimitrii. But he doesn't matter. In agreeing with the triumvirate and presenting you as the true Tsarevich, he took himself forever out of the picture."

"There was no need to kill them."

The Baroness smiled. "With Alexander announced as Tsarevich, Grand Duchess Catherine would have become exceedingly distressed. She was a strong, willful, and arrogant person, but still she was admired in Russia. She would have brought up Anastasia, claiming you, and therefore we, were nothing more than claimants to the throne. And for all the proof presented, the populace might well have agreed with her. That possibility no longer exists."

Abruptly Kitner stood. "I will not abdicate."

"I'm afraid you will, Petr Mikhail Romanov." Once again the Baroness's tone was soft and seductive. "For the sake of your family and for the sake of Russia."

From outside the window came the slamming of car doors. Alexander turned at the sound of them, and Kitner could see the tiny headset tucked into his ear. Someone was talking to him and he was listening. He listened a moment longer, then turned back.

"Our first guests, Father. Perhaps you would like to see who they are. Please." Alexander stood and indicated the window.

Slowly, as if in a dream, Kitner got up and made his way to it. Outside he saw three black limousines in the snow-covered motor court. Murzin's men, dressed in dark suits with black overcoats, stood alongside them, their heads turned toward the entry drive. Then another limousine came into view. Behind it was an armored car, a Russian flag flying from its front bumper. The limousine circled the motor court, then stopped directly below them. Immediately Murzin's men went to it and opened the doors. For a moment nothing happened, and then one man got out—Nikolai Nemov, the mayor of Moscow; and then a second, Marshal Igor Golovkin, Russian Federation minister of defense; and then came the last, a tall man, bearded and berobed, Gregor II, the Most Holy Patriarch of the Russian Orthodox Church.

"It's not just President Gitinov, Father. They expect you to sign the abdication. It's why they are here."

Kitner was numb beyond reason, barely able to think. His wife, his son, and his daughters were in the custody of Murzin's troops. Higgs and any help he might have provided were far out of the picture. The knife and the film were no longer his. What he had left was nothing.

"You are not strong enough to be Tsar," the Baroness said. "Alexander is."

"Is that why you had him kill my son, to prove it?"

"One cannot lead a nation and fear to have blood on his hands. You would not want to force him to prove it once again."

For a moment Kitner stood staring at her; her face, her dress, the jewels she wore, the eerie calmness with which she threatened death. What drove her was revenge, dark and cruel—the way, as a teenager, she had taken brutal and depraved revenge on the man in Naples who had raped her—and nothing more. He realized now that she had been planning this for decades, gambling on the course of history and preparing for that one future day when Alexander, *her* Alexander, could, if things were done correctly, become Tsar of Russia. That, for her, would be the sweetest revenge of all.

It was why in the end, despite all of Grand Duchess Catherine's efforts, every manipulation, every glad hand, every friendship she'd forged, she had simply not had enough information nor been ruthless enough to compete with the Baroness. And because of it, she, her mother, and her adored son were dead.

Suddenly Kitner felt his own immense helplessness. He was prisoner, hostage, and victim, all in one. Moreover, it had been his own doing. Afraid to make Alexander's existence known to his family, afraid to put one son on trial for the murder of another, afraid for the lives of his other children, it was he who had made the pact that set them free. As a result his wife and children were hostage to Murzin's soldiers, and his family would learn of Alexander anyway and very publicly, along with the rest of the world.

His son Paul, Alfred Neuss, Fabien Curtay, Grand Duchess Catherine, her son and mother, those killed in the Americas, how many others were dead because of him? Again he thought of Murzin's soldiers holding his family. What orders had been given them? That any of his loved ones would be harmed or even killed was an idea he couldn't bear. He looked to Alexander and then to the Baroness. Both had the same savage eyes. Both wore the expression of cold and assured victory. If he had any doubts before, they vanished now. He knew they were capable of anything.

Slowly he turned and sat down to read the article of abdication. When he had finished, and slower still, he signed it.

84

That Rebecca would marry Alexander Cabrera was unthinkable. But so was America's seeming invulnerability before the World Trade Center and Pentagon disasters. After that, the entire world knew that anything was possible.

His foot nearly to the floor, the ML500 flying over bare pavement, Marten turned fast off the A13 exit for Landquart/Davos. In the last miles he'd tried Lady Clem's cell phone a half-dozen times but reached nothing more than the recording saying she was either away from the phone or out of the area.

"Take it easy," Kovalenko said. "Cabrera may not be who you think he is."

"You said that before."

"I'm saying it again."

Marten took his eyes from the road to look at Kovalenko. "Is that why you're still here instead of ordering me to take you back to Zurich to shuffle off to Moscow? Because Cabrera might *not* be Raymond?"

"Look out!"

Marten looked back to the road. Directly in front of them was a long line of stopped traffic. Marten jammed on the brakes, bringing the ML to a screeching stop inches from the rear bumper of a black Nissan sedan.

"What is this?" he said at the backup of vehicles.

"Either free speech or Black Bloc demonstrators, a collection of anarchists," Kovalenko said as suddenly a mass of antiglobalization protestors came running through the traffic toward them. They were mostly young and ragtag; many carried anti–World Economic Forum signs, and others wore large, grotesque masks resembling the faces of world political and business leaders, or black balaclavas to hide their identity.

Behind them came a rush of Swiss police in full riot gear. Almost on cue, the protesters turned and threw a fusillade of rocks. Marten saw the police duck behind plastic shields. An instant later, four policemen stepped forward. They were dressed in black, with the word POLIZEI stenciled on their hats and flak jackets, and carried small, short-barreled rifles.

"Tear gas!" Marten yelled and glanced in the outside mirror. A large truck was right behind them with more vehicles backed up behind it. Others had pulled to the outside lane hoping to pass and now completely blocked the road.

"Clear the area! Clear the area!" A police bullhorn blasted from nowhere. The order came in English, then in German, French, and Italian.

Marten looked to Kovalenko. "Bring up a local map on the GPS screen."

Now the protestors were surrounding the ML, using it as a shield while they threw more rocks and screamed at the police.

Seconds later there were four rapid-fire booms as the police fired the tear gas, the canisters bursting around the ML and filling the close vicinity with choking white smoke.

Immediately Marten cut off the air intake, put the ML in gear, and threw the wheel to the right. Leaning on the horn, he moved out of traffic and onto the right shoulder. Coughing, gagging, shouting, protesters pounded on the car. Then the ML was clear. Marten touched the accelerator and the SUV shot forward along the roadway's inside shoulder, moving fast toward the police.

"We're going to need Beelr's pass," he said to Kovalenko, "and all your influence as a cop."

Ahead, several of the black-uniformed Police broke toward them, waving their arms for them to stop. One of them raised a bullhorn.

"White SUV! Stop where you are!" The bullhorn blared the message again in German, French, and Italian.

Marten kept on. Looking for a way out. Then he saw it. A side road, little more than a path down from the shoulder and out across a frozen field. Swinging wide, he took it. The ML bumped off the highway and accelerated across the open track, a wide, grassy meadow dusted with light snow.

"Across this there appears to be a secondary road." Kovalenko was looking at a map glowing on the GPS screen on the dashboard. "It circumvents the town, crosses a bridge, and then picks up the main road again on the far side."

"I see it! Hang on!" Marten slowed a little for a ditch. The ML hit it, banged hard over it, then came up high on the far side. Suddenly they saw a narrow canal right in front of them. Instinctively, Marten accelerated, then touched the brakes and swung the wheel left, sending the SUV into a controlled four-wheel drift. The car touched the edge of the canal, hung there for an instant, then came back, and Marten accelerated forward.

"There's the bridge," Kovalenko yelled.

"I see it!"

The bridge, old and low, made of wood with iron girders, was a hundred yards ahead. Marten's foot pressed down on the accelerator. Five seconds, ten. They hit the planking at eighty miles an hour and in a blink were across it. Suddenly there was a tremendous roar. A shadow passed overhead. An instant later they saw a Swiss army helicopter. It dipped to near ground level, flew ahead, and then abruptly turned and came back to settle on the road directly in front of them.

Marten jammed on the brakes and the ML came to a stop no more than twenty yards away. Immediately the helicopter doors slid open and a dozen Swiss army commandos carrying automatic weapons jumped out and ran toward them. At that moment, Kovalenko's cell phone rang.

"Shto tyepyer?" What now?

"Answer it," Marten demanded.

Kovalenko clicked on. *"Da,"* he said and then looked to Marten.

"For you."

"Who is it?"

Kovalenko shrugged. "A man."

Quickly Kovalenko handed the phone to Marten. The commandos were nearly on top of them. Marten clicked on.

"Yes," he said, puzzled.

"Good afternoon, Mr. Marten." The voice was gentle and had a French accent. "My name is Alexander Cabrera."

85

Marten covered the phone and looked to Kovalenko, unbelieving. "It's Cabrera."

"I suggest you talk to him." Kovalenko fixed Marten with a hard stare, then, purposefully leaving his Makarov automatic on the floor, opened the door and stepped out to meet the commandos, raising his hands as he did.

VILLA ENKRATZER. SAME TIME.

Cell phone in hand, Alexander Cabrera stood at the window of a small study a floor above the library where his father had abdicated the Russian throne. Directly beneath him he could see snow removal crews clearing the snow that had fallen overnight so the guests could stroll at their leisure over the villa's network of spectacular wooded hiking trails.

"I telephoned you, Mr. Marten, because I understand you have been trying to reach Rebecca."

"Yes. I would like to speak with her, please," Marten said with measured calm, trying to ignore the Swiss army commando just outside his window with his finger on the trigger of a submachine gun. To his left, he could see Kovalenko surrounded by commandos, his hands still in the air, talking directly to their officer-in-charge. Now Marten saw him gesture to get permission to reach inside his coat. The officer nodded and Kovalenko carefully reached into his breast pocket and took out the pass Kantonspolizei Inspector Beelr had given them as they'd left Zurich.

"I'm afraid she is outside with the Rothfels children, Mr. Marten," Cabrera said as politely as could be.

Immediately Marten turned his full attention to Cabrera's voice and speech pattern. He listened for anything recognizable, but there was nothing. He needed to make Cabrera talk further, say more.

"I'm on my way to Davos now. I would very much like to see Rebecca when I get there. Maybe you could—"

"May I call you Nicholas, Mr. Marten?"

"Alright."

Alexander turned from the window and crossed to a large desk. At the moment the Baroness was downstairs in a private dining room enjoying lunch with the mayor of Moscow, the Russian Federation minister of defense, and Gregor II, the Most Holy Patriarch of the Russian Orthodox Church—explaining in detail how gracious Peter Kitner had been in signing his abdication for the good of Russia and how eager he would be to join them later that evening when Pavel Gitinov, the president of Russia, would arrive for dinner.

"I believe Lady Clementine Simpson—how do you say, 'spilled the beans,' and you know Rebecca and I plan to wed."

"Yes."

"I didn't mean to create a scandal, Nicholas, or seem rude in keeping secrets, but our relationship has been kept quiet from nearly everyone for many rather complicated reasons."

Marten heard nothing familiar at all in the way Cabrera talked. Maybe he *was* crazy. Maybe Kovalenko was right, Cabrera was not Raymond at all.

"Why don't you come to the villa, Nicholas? You can not only see Rebecca but it will give us the opportunity to meet. Come for dinner and plan to spend the night, please. We will be having some very interesting guests."

Marten saw Kovalenko nod to the Swiss army commander and then the two shook hands, the commandos lowered their weapons, and Kovalenko started back toward the car.

"The château is called Villa Enkratzer. Anyone in Davos can give you directions. Come to the guardhouse. I will leave word for you to be admitted. I am very much looking forward to meeting you."

"Me, too."

"Good. I will see you this evening, then."

There was a click as Cabrera hung up. And that was it, no good-bye, nothing more at all. Simply a polite invitation to dinner and to spend the night. It was the last thing Marten had expected.

86

STILL FRIDAY, JANUARY 17. 4:10 P.M.

The long shadows of afternoon slid across the Davos Valley as Marten turned the ML onto the Promenade, Davos's main street, and slowed behind a long line of taxis and limousines. Men and women in business suits and overcoats crowded the sidewalks, talking to each other or on cell phones and seemingly unmindful of the snow underfoot or the patrolling police or the soldiers wearing berets and carrying submachine guns. Little seemed safe anywhere anymore, even for the richest and most powerful people in the world, sequestered in a fortified village in the middle of the Swiss Alps. Still, they had accepted armed patrols as a way of life, and if there was danger here they chose to ignore it.

"Seven kilometers out of town and then turn right at a pyramid-shaped sculptured rock with the name 'Enkratzer' chiseled into it," a Davos policeman told them. "You can't miss it, the rock is thirty meters high. Besides, there are two armored cars full of commandos stationed at the entryway."

"How are you going to explain me?" Kovalenko asked as Marten navigated through the traffic. The Russian might have been ordered back to Moscow, but he had said nothing more about it and neither had Marten.

"I am Cabrera's guest, you are my traveling companion. It would be impolite not to admit us both."

Kovalenko smiled faintly and looked off. Within minutes they were out of the bustling village and into the deep shadows of a conifer forest, and then as quickly into the postcard beauty of the sprawling winter farmland that made up the Davos Valley. Rimming it high above on either side were snow-covered Rhaetian Alps with names like Pischa, Jakobshorn, Parsenn, and Schatzalp/Strela.

4:40 P.M.

Runoff from melting snow was beginning to harden on the roadway. Soon it would freeze solid and become treacherous and nearly invisible black ice.

Marten eased off the accelerator and felt the tires take a surer grip on the road, then glanced at Kovalenko. He was quiet and still looking off, and Marten knew he was troubled. By deliberately not returning to Moscow as he had been ordered, he had put himself in a difficult situation, one that became even harder as time wore on. The question was, why was he doing it? In his heart did he really believe that Cabrera *was* Raymond and not the contrary as he had said more than once? Or was he just not sure, and refused to get this close and not find out? Or—did it have to do with his own agenda? And if it did, was he working for, or with someone else? Someone important enough to risk turning his back on orders from his own department?

Suddenly something else came to mind. Why Marten hadn't thought of it before, he didn't know.

"London," he said sharply and looked to Kovalenko. "Was the announcement of who Kitner was and that he was to become Tsar to have been made in London the day or the day after he had been knighted?"

"No. It was far too important to have been tacked onto the coattails of that. The announcement was to have been made several weeks later."

"Several weeks?"

"Yes."

Marten stared at him. "April 7."

"Yes."

"In Moscow."

"That information was highly privileged. How did you know?" Kovalenko was astonished.

"Halliday's book," Marten lied, covering himself quickly.

"He had the date and the place, but there was a big question mark after it, as if he didn't know what it meant or what it was about."

"How did Halliday come to have it at all?"

"I don't know," Marten lied again and turned back, his eyes searching the road ahead for the turnoff to Villa Enkratzer. Then another thought came. Cabrera had rented the Davos villa just prior to the announcement. Had he planned the same for London? But not a villa, an elegant private home—at *21 Uxbridge Street* and close to the *Russian Embassy*. Furthermore, Raymond had noted in his calendar just beneath the *March 14, London* entry—*Russian Embassy/London*. Did that mean the presentation to the Romanov family was to have taken place there and on that day?

Abruptly Marten looked to Kovalenko. Once again he lied. "There were two more dates in Halliday's book. They were noted 'London'— March fourteenth and fifteenth. If the public announcement about Kitner was not to have been made then but three weeks later, when was he to be presented to the—"

"Romanov family?" Kovalenko finished the sentence for him.

"Yes."

"March fourteenth. At a formal dinner at the Russian Embassy in London."

Oh, Jesus! There it was! At least part of it. Raymond's notation about the Russian Embassy.

Marten looked away and then back. "And then the dinner was abruptly canceled."

"Yes."

"Who canceled it?"

"Kitner himself."

"When?"

"I believe it was on March thirteenth. The day of his knighthood ceremony."

"Did he give a reason?"

"I was not told. I don't know that anyone was. It was simply his decision to put it off until a later date."

"Maybe the reason was that Alexander Cabrera was still on the run from the police in Los Angeles as Raymond Oliver Thorne. Thorne wasn't brought down until March fifteenth. Kitner runs a huge global news operation. He may well have known about the killings in Mexico and San Francisco and Chicago and learned who the victims were even before the police confirmed them. Those murders might have been what sent Neuss running to London. Not just to save his life if he was next on Raymond's list but for him and Kitner to figure out what to do to stay ahead of Cabrera. Who, I should point out, as Kitner's eldest son is next in line for the throne."

"You're suggesting Cabrera thought he could become Tsar?"

"He thought it then and he thinks it now," Marten said. "All he has to do is wait until the family is informed who Kitner is and then, sometime before the public announcement is made, leak the word to the press. Suddenly the world knows who Kitner is and what he is about to become."

Kovalenko looked at him coldly. "And then Kitner is killed and, as his eldest son, Cabrera is automatically next in line for the throne and the process is already under way."

"Yes," Marten picked up the reasoning, "and within days, maybe hours, the handsome, successful, but reclusive Alexander Cabrera reveals who he is and travels to Moscow to mourn openly for his dead father, declaring at the same time that if the people want him, he is willing to serve in his father's place."

"And since the government has already agreed to the return of the monarchy, there seems very little reason to think they wouldn't go along. Which is something Cabrera and the Baroness have been counting on from the beginning." Kovalenko smiled thinly. "Is that what you're thinking?"

Marten nodded. "It should have happened a year ago, and it might have if Cabrera hadn't nearly been killed by the Los Angeles police."

For a long moment Kovalenko was quiet. Finally he spoke. "The problem with what you postulate, Mr. Marten, is that you are telling it from Cabrera's point of view. I remind you it was Peter Kitner, not Alexander Cabrera, who canceled the Romanov family meeting and postponed his own ascension to the throne."

"Until when?"

"Until now. This weekend at Davos. And with it the presentation made to the Romanov family yesterday in Paris."

"Kovalenko, who selected the dates? Kitner? Or was that a decision that came from inside the government?"

"I don't know. Why?"

"Because it seems neatly calculated to have given Cabrera enough time to find a way to expunge his records, both the hard evidence files and the databases, recover from the wounds sustained in his 'hunting accident' and the cosmetic facial surgery that followed—cosmetic surgery that might have been necessary or that might have been elective, so that anyone who had seen him as Raymond Thorne would not recognize him—and then get back to running his business so that nothing seemed out of the ordinary."

"You're suggesting someone was able to delay the entire process until Cabrera was ready."

"That's what I'm suggesting."

"Mr. Marten, to do that someone would have to have enormous influence inside Russia, enough to control both houses of parliament. It's not possible."

"No?"

"No."

"Not unless that person"—Marten carefully underscored each word—"was a hugely rich, impeccably credentialed, highly sophisticated, and very socially prominent person who personally knew—and, in one way or another, held influence over—the most important people at the highest levels of Russian business or politics, or both. And therefore had the money, the power, and the guile to manipulate them."

"The Baroness."

"You tell me."

87

VILLA ENKRATZER. 5:00 P.M.

Rebecca watched in the mirror as her lady's maid helped her dress. This was a night of nobility, elegance, and romance, and Alexander himself had chosen what she would wear—a Parisian-designer floor-length purple silk and velvet Chinese sheath dress with lace cutouts and sleeves that took the fabric to her wrists. She smiled as the lady's maid did the final clasp at the back of her neck and stepped back as she turned her profile to the mirror. The dress trimmed her slender figure all the more and gave her the look she knew Alexander wanted—that of a beautiful, exquisite doll.

Now she pulled her hair back, fastening it with a clip of South Sea pearls and then added elongated South Sea pearl and diamond earrings, finishing it all with a small emerald neck-lace. Standing back, she thought she had never looked so lovely—as lovely as she was certain the evening would be. Within the hour, dinner guests would begin to arrive from Davos. Among them would be Lord Prestbury and his daughter, Rebecca's closest female friend in the world, Lady Clementine Simpson, whose jaw she knew would drop to the floor when she saw the dress. Rebecca would enjoy the moment, of course, but considering the grandness of the evening the dress and Lady Clem's reaction to it were hardly that important.

What was important, more important than any of it, would be the arrival of Nicholas, invited as promised by Alexander. That Lady Clem had already told him their wedding plans didn't matter. What did was that he and Alexander would fi-nally meet and all the secrecy would be a thing of the past.

The abrupt ring of the telephone startled her. In the seconds it took for her lady's maid to answer, a thought crossed her mind—why had Alexander not told her earlier that Nicholas had called trying to reach her? She had learned of it from her maid, who had answered the phone when Gerard Rothfels had called, thinking Rebecca was in her room when in fact she was outdoors with Rothfels's wife and children. The curious thing was that Alexander had been in the room at the time deciding on her dress for the evening. Instead of relaying the message and letting her speak to Nicholas; he had taken Nicholas's num-ber and gone into the library, where he had called him himself. At the time she had thought little of it, except to wonder what business was bringing Nicholas to Davos, and so had let it go, thinking that Alexander was extremely busy and had simply wanted to surprise her, which he certainly had. Now it seemed strange and disturbed her, but she didn't quite know why.

"*Mademoiselle,*" the maid said as she hung up the phone, "*Monsieur Alexander désire que vous déscendiez à la biblio-thèque.*" Monsieur Alexander requests your presence in the li-brary.

Still troubled by her thoughts, Rebecca didn't respond.

"Mademoiselle?" The maid cocked her head as if perhaps her mistress hadn't understood.

Then Rebecca let it pass and smiled.

"Merci," she said. *"Merci."*

88

5:10 P.M.

The red glow of the setting sun outlined the westernmost mountain peaks as Marten slowed the ML in the twilight darkness, its headlight beams clearly illuminating a massive pyramidal rock sculpture with the name VILLA ENKRATZER chiseled into it in large, bold letters. Directly to the right of it was a driveway entrance. Ten meters inside it was a stone guardhouse. An armored car with a white equilateral cross on a red field—the flag of Switzerland—blocked the driveway entrance itself. A second armored car with the same markings was parked beneath the trees to the left.

Slowing more, Marten eased the ML to a stop in front of the first armored car. Immediately its doors opened and two commandos in fatigues stepped out. One carried a submachine gun; the other, taller than the first, had a pistol at his waist.

Marten lowered the window as the two approached. "My name is Nicholas Marten. I am a guest of Alexander Cabrera."

The tall commando looked at Marten and then to Kovalenko.

"His name is Kovalenko," Marten said. "He's my traveling companion."

Immediately the commando stepped back and went to the guardhouse. There was a brief conversation with someone inside, a telephone call was made, and then he came back.

"Go ahead, Mr. Marten. Drive carefully. The roadway to the villa is steep and winding and quite icy." Stepping back, he saluted. The armored car backed up, clearing the entrance, and Marten drove forward.

"How beautiful you look." Alexander took Rebecca's hand and kissed it as she came into the library. The room was dark and cozy with a high ceiling and comfortable leather furniture and lined floor to ceiling with leather-bound books. A log fire burned crisply in the marble fireplace. Across from it was a heavy oak coffee table and beyond it a leather sofa where the Baroness relaxed.

"You are absolutely stunning, my darling," she said as Rebecca neared, then patted a place on the sofa beside her. "Sit down beside me. We have something to tell you."

Rebecca looked from the Baroness to Alexander. Both were beautifully dressed, Alexander in a finely cut black tuxedo with a white ruffled shirt beneath and a smart bow tie of black velvet. The Baroness, as always, wore pale yellow and white. This time it was a long yellow oriental-style tunic with matching yellow shoes and white stockings. A small ermine stole was thrown over her shoulders and accented the ruby and diamond necklace at her throat.

"What do you have to tell me?" Rebecca smiled girlishly as she sat down beside the Baroness and looked again to Alexander.

"You begin, Baroness." Alexander moved to stand by the fireplace.

Slowly the Baroness took Rebecca's hands in hers and looked into her eyes.

"You have known Alexander for less than a year, but you know one another very well indeed. I know he has told you about the death of his mother and father in Italy when he was very young and how I raised him on my estate in Argentina. You know about his hunting accident and his long recovery. You know, too, he is Russian by birth."

"Yes." Rebecca nodded.

"What you don't know is that he is European nobility. Not just nobility, but great nobility, which is the reason he was raised far away from its influence in South America and not Europe. It was his father's insistence that he learn about life and not be coddled. It is also why he was not told until he was old enough to understand who his father really was and that he, unlike his mother, was still alive."

Rebecca looked to Alexander. "Your father is alive?"

Alexander smiled gently. "He is Peter Kitner."

"*Sir* Peter Kitner, the man who owns the media empire?" Rebecca was genuinely surprised.

"Yes. And all these years he has protected me from the knowledge of who he is and who I am. As the Baroness said, it was for my own good and so that I would neither be spoiled nor influenced in my youth."

"Peter Kitner," the Baroness continued, "is more than a successful businessman, he is the head of the imperial Romanov family and therefore heir to the throne of Russia. As his first-born son, Alexander is next in the line of succession."

Rebecca was puzzled. "I don't understand."

"Russia is about to establish a constitutional monarchy and return the imperial family to the throne. It will be announced at the Davos conference tomorrow by the president of Russia." The Baroness smiled. "Sir Peter Kitner is here at the villa."

"Here?"

"Yes, he's resting."

Again Rebecca looked to Alexander. "I still don't—"

"The Baroness is not finished, my love."

Rebecca turned back to the Baroness.

"Tonight the first Tsar of Russia in nearly a century will be introduced to our dinner guests."

Rebecca swung back to Alexander. She was wide-eyed, stunned and thrilled all at once. "Your father is to become Tsar of Russia?"

"No," Alexander said, "I am."

"You?"

"He has formally abdicated to me."

"Alexander." Tears welled in Rebecca's eyes. She understood, she didn't understand. It was too vast, too far from everything she knew, even for the person she was now.

"And you, my darling, upon your marriage . . ."—slowly the Baroness lifted Rebecca's hands and kissed them lovingly as a mother might kiss the hands of a treasured child, and all the while looking into her eyes— "will become Tsarina."

89

Seen through the trees as Marten made the final turn approaching it, Villa Enkratzer seemed, and was, massive. Brightly lit against the night sky, the vast, five-story stone and wood structure looked as much like a fortress as it did a grand residence, or, in this case, a hidden alpine embassy.

Flags of fifty nations snapping in a brisk wind flew from flagpoles in the center of the entry drive as the ML came in. As Marten swung around he could see six black limousines backed into parking spaces to the left of the main door, and now a quick glance in the mirror revealed headlights from more coming up the drive behind them. It seemed hardly the milieu for Raymond to be operating in. But then it wasn't Raymond, was it? The man here was Alexander Cabrera.

On one level it was as simple as that. International businessman introduces himself to the brother of the betrothed. But on another and infinitely more dangerous level was the idea that Cabrera and Raymond were one and the same. If that was true, both he and Rebecca were in grave danger, because what he had done was walk into a very carefully baited trap.

"Hosts," a dozen men in dark tuxedos and white gloves, waited at the entry as Marten pulled up. Immediately the doors were opened and he and Kovalenko were greeted as if they were royalty themselves and shown into the villa, while behind them the ML was driven away.

Inside, another white-gloved, tuxedo-clad host welcomed them as they entered the villa's imposing two-story-high lobby, its floor and walls of polished black slate. Across, on the far side, huge logs crackled in a mammoth stone fireplace, while high above flags of the twenty-three Swiss cantons hung from a legion of heavy oak rafters. To the left and right Gothic arches opened onto long hallways, the entrances to which were guarded on either side by gleaming suits of ancient armor.

"This way, messieurs," their host said and led them down the left hallway. Partway down, he turned them right and down still another corridor and then another and past a series of what appeared to be guestroom doors. Halfway down, he stopped at one of the doors and opened it with an electronic key.

"Your room, messieurs. Evening clothes have been laid out. There is a bath with a steam shower, and toiletries have been provided. There is a full bar in the cabinet. Dinner is at eight. Should you be in need of anything"—he nodded toward a multi-line telephone on an antique desk— "simply dial the operator." With that he bowed and left, closing the door behind him. It was five-forty-two exactly.

"Evening clothes?" Kovalenko crossed to the large double beds, where tuxedos, dress shirts, shoes, and ties had been laid out.

"Cabrera might have known you were coming," Kovalenko said. "He knew nothing about me. Yet dress clothes, seemingly correctly sized, have been laid out for two."

"The information could have been passed from the Swiss army commando who let us in."

"Perhaps." Kovalenko went to the door and locked it, then slipped the Makarov automatic from his waistband, checked the magazine, and put the gun away.

"You should know that while we were in Zurich I put Detective Halliday's computer disk and airline ticket into an envelope addressed to my wife in Moscow. I told Inspector Beelr that in the press of our ongoing investigation I had neglected to send an anniversary note and asked him to mail it for me. They are safer there than they would be with us now."

Marten stared at him. "What you really mean, Yuri, is now you have all the cards."

"Mr. Marten, we have to trust each other." Kovalenko glanced at the laid-out dinner clothes. "I suggest we prepare for the evening and in the process decide what to do about Cabrera and how to—"

A sudden knock at the door cut Kovalenko off, and both men looked up.

"Cabrera?" Kovalenko mouthed.

"Just a minute," Marten called out, then looked to Kovalenko and dropped his voice. "I need to find my sister and make sure she's alright. What I want you to do is get Cabrera's fingerprints on a hard surface, a glass, a pen, even a postcard, anything small we can take with us without its being seen and where the prints will be clear and not smudged."

"Perhaps a dinner menu." Kovalenko half smiled.

The knock came again and Marten crossed to the door and opened it.

A trim, extremely fit man with his hair shaved to the scalp stood in the doorway. He was formally dressed, like the other hosts, but that was where the comparison stopped. The way in which he held himself and the intensity of his presence was stamped with one label—authority.

"Good evening, gentlemen," he said with a Russian accent. "I am Colonel Murzin of the Federalnaya Slujba Ohrani. I am in charge of security."

90

6:20 P.M.

Where Kovalenko had gone, Nicholas Marten didn't know. Murzin had simply said that he wanted to confer with Kovalenko alone and that Marten should prepare for the evening as he normally would. The moment had been delicate and uncomfortable, but then Kovalenko had nodded his approval and gone off with Murzin, and Marten had done as he had been directed.

Shower. Shave. Look in the mirror. And hear Kovalenko's words, *Decide what to do about Cabrera. And how to*—he added the "go about it." The rest of Kovalenko's sentence that had been lost at Murzin's knock.

Rebecca was somewhere in this building. Where, exactly, would be difficult to ascertain without Cabrera's cooperation. Suddenly Marten realized he had never spoken to her, only been told by Cabrera that she was here. Perhaps she wasn't here at all.

Bath towel around him, Marten went into the bedroom and picked up the telephone.

"Oui, monsieur," a male voice answered.

"This is Nicholas Marten."

"Yes, sir."

"My sister, Rebecca, is here with the Rothfels. Would you please connect me to her room?"

"One moment, please."

Marten waited, expecting to be patched through, hoping the phone wouldn't ring and ring as it had at the Crillon in Paris when he'd finally had to go there and convince the concierge who he was and then be taken to her room. Suddenly it occurred to him that that was why the delay, why Rebecca had been dressed in a robe with her hair up and a little bit drunk. She hadn't been in the bath at all—she'd been with Cabrera. He might have a suite at the Ritz, but he'd been there in the Crillon all the time.

"Good evening, Nicholas." Alexander Cabrera's soft, French-accented voice came through the phone. "How happy I am that you have joined us. Would you please come up to the library? I will send someone to escort you."

"Where is Rebecca?"

"She will be here when you arrive."

"I'm not quite dressed."

"Should we say ten minutes, then?"

"Yes, ten minutes."

"Good."

Cabrera hung up and the line went dead.

Everything he'd said had been as it had before, calm, extremely polite and accommodating, and spoken with the same gentle tone and accent. What was going on? Was Alexander Cabrera Raymond Oliver Thorne, or wasn't he?

91

Kovalenko took a sip of vodka and set the glass down. He was in a room similar to the room he'd been in with Marten, the only difference being that before he'd been on the first floor and now he was on the second. Murzin had said little, simply asked him his name and where he lived and walked him to the room. Afterward he'd poured him a glass of vodka and asked him to wait. Then he'd left, and that had been more than ten minutes ago.

Clearly Murzin *was* FSO. How many more were here he had no way of knowing, but he suspected the black-tied "hosts" were agents and more of them would be among the serving staff, perhaps even among the guests, though he doubted few, if any, were of Murzin's rank or shared his trait of character. Murzin was old-school Spetsnaz, and that troubled Kovalenko because it meant Murzin was not only a first-rate commando but a professional killer whose first and only job was to follow orders. If he was here, something extremely noteworthy was about to happen.

Though Kovalenko had said nothing to Marten, he had seen one presidential limousine parked to the side as they'd arrived. President Gitinov was to make the public announcement regarding Peter Kitner tomorrow at the forum. So, considering the setting, the armored cars at the entrance, the limousines, and the hosts, to say nothing of Murzin, there was every reason to believe Gitinov would be among the guests here tonight. That being the case, he could have arrived and the presidential limousine was his. But it was highly unlikely he would have come in one car alone. It was Gitinov's method to travel in a caravan of three or four limousines, all the same make and with the same markings, so a sharpshooter or terrorist would not know in which car he rode. A more likely scenario would be for him to simply arrive by helicopter. It was safer and far more dramatic.

That left the question of who had come in the limousine. The answer to that, especially with the presence of a man like Murzin, was that it had been used by a Russian statesman, or statesmen, of equal power. Currently there was no single man who equaled Gitinov's influence. Instead there was a triumvirate, and he knew them by heart: Nikolai Nemov, the mayor of Moscow; Marshal Igor Golovkin, Russian Federation minister of defense; and Gregor II, the Most Holy Patriarch of the Russian Orthodox Church. And if they were here and Gitinov was coming—

Suddenly the door opened and Murzin came in. With him were two others, dressed in evening clothes but with the same scalp-short hair. One of them closed the door.

"You are Yuri Ryleev Kovalenko of the Russian Ministry of Justice," Murzin said quietly.

"Yes."

"You were to have returned to Moscow earlier today."

"Yes."

"You did not go."

"No."

"Why?"

"I was traveling with Mr. Marten. His sister is engaged to Alexander Cabrera. He asked me to continue with him. It would have been rude not to."

Murzin studied him carefully. "It would have been more prudent to follow orders, Inspector." Abruptly Murzin looked to the men who had come in with him. One of them opened the door, and Murzin looked back to Kovalenko.

"Come with us, please."

92

Nicholas Marten's host was a step ahead of him as they turned a corner and started down a stone-walled corridor toward a closed, intricately carved, antique door at the far end. The walkway was carpeted and the walls washed with light from lamps recessed into the ceiling at regular intervals. It was ancient and designer-modern at the same time, but to Marten it felt as if he were being willingly led toward some medieval dungeon. He couldn't help but wish Kovalenko were with him and at the same time wondered where he was and why he hadn't returned to the room.

The tuxedo provided for Marten, which had seemed comfortable and perfectly sized when he'd put it on, suddenly felt tight and stiff. He reached up to loosen the bow tie at his throat, as if that simple gesture in itself would help. It didn't. It only made him realize his palms were wet and that he was sweating.

"Relax," he told himself, "relax. You don't know anything yet."

"Here we are, monsieur." The host reached the door and knocked.

"*Oui*," a voice said from inside.

"Monsieur Marten," the host said.

There was a moment and then the door opened. Alexander Cabrera stood there, resplendent in a tailored black tuxedo and white ruffled shirt, a black velvet bow tie at his throat.

"Welcome, Nicholas." He smiled. "Please come in."

Slowly Marten entered Villa Enkratzer's library with its walls of books and well-worn leather furniture. Across the room, flames crackled from fresh logs in a marble fireplace, filling the room with the distinct smell of oak. Seated on the couch across from the fireplace was a handsome, extremely dignified woman, probably in her late forties or early fifties.

Her black hair was in a low bun at the back and she wore a long yellow tunic with an eemine stole over her shoulders. Her necklace was layered with alternating strands of small diamonds and rubies, while clusters of tiny diamonds hung like sparkling wisps from her ears.

Marten heard Cabrera close the door behind him. "This is the Baroness de Vienne, Nicholas. She is my beloved guardian."

"What a pleasure it is to meet you, Monsieur Marten." Like Cabrera's, the Baroness's English was accented with French. She raised her hand and Marten leaned over and took it.

"The pleasure is mine, Baroness," Marten said politely. The Baroness was younger, gentler, and far more handsome than he had imagined. She was gracious, welcoming, as if she were truly glad to meet him. Yet, as he let go of her hand and stepped back, her eyes stayed on his. The feeling was unsettling, as if she were purposefully reading him, searching for any flaw or weakness she could find.

Marten looked to Cabrera. "Where is Rebecca?"

"She will be here momentarily. Would you care for a drink?"

"Mineral water if you have it."

"Of course."

Marten watched Cabrera cross to a small bar in the corner of the room. He looked as he had in Kovalenko's photographs. Tall, slim, neatly trimmed black beard and hair. The last time he'd seen Raymond—as they faced Polchak and Lee and Valparaiso, and even Halliday before he'd come over to Marten's side, in the awful Metrolink shootout in L.A.—Raymond had been all but bald in his attempt to take on the identity of the murdered Josef Speer. But the hair wasn't the only difference. The face was wholly dissimilar, its structure more pronounced, the jawline, as much as he could distinguish it under the beard, even the nose. And his eyes. Before they had been a blue-green, now they were as black as night. Contact lenses, maybe, but the eyes aside, if he was Raymond the plastic surgeon had done a brilliant job in wholly changing his appearance.

"You are looking at me curiously, Nicholas." Cabrera came toward him carrying a crystal glass filled with mineral water.

"I was trying to get the measure of the man who is going to marry my sister."

"And how do I compute?" Cabrera smiled easily and handed Marten the glass.

"I'd like Rebecca to tell me. You seem to have won her heart."

"Why don't I ring for her and let you ask her yourself." Cabrera crossed to a small side table and pressed a button.

There was a moment and then a door on the far side of the room opened and Rebecca came in. He caught his breath. She was not only alive and healthy but, in the dazzling evening dress she wore, extraordinarily beautiful.

"Nicholas," she blurted when she saw him. Suddenly she was across the room, hugging him, holding him, her eyes filled with tears but laughing all the while.

"I so wanted this to be a surprise."

Marten stepped back to look at her and was suddenly aware of her emerald necklace and pearl and diamond earrings. "It *is* a surprise, Rebecca. You don't have to worry about that."

"Alexander"—suddenly she twisted away and went to Cabrera—"tell him. Tell him, please."

"I think first, you both should meet my father." Again Cabrera pressed the button. This time he spoke into a small microphone beside it. "Please," he said, then looked back. "He was resting. He will be here momentarily."

"Your father is Sir Peter Kitner," Marten said carefully. "He is to become Tsar of Russia."

"You are well informed, Nicholas." Cabrera smiled easily. "I should be surprised, but I'm not, considering you are Rebecca's brother. Yet, things have changed. It is what Rebecca wanted me to tell you." The smile faded. "My father will not become Tsar. He has relinquished the throne in favor of me."

"You?"

"Yes."

"I see," Marten said quietly. There it was, just as he had told Kovalenko. Only it wasn't quite the way he'd seen it. Cabrera hadn't had to kill Kitner to become Tsar, merely terrify him into abdicating. That way there were no politics involved at all. He would have to prove nothing. With the stroke of Kitner's pen, Cabrera had simply become Tsar.

An abrupt knock at the door broke Marten's thoughts.

"*Oui*," Cabrera said.

The door opened and Sir Peter Kitner entered. He was dressed formally and accompanied not by a host as Marten had been but by Colonel Murzin.

"Good evening, Tsarevich," Murzin said to Cabrera, and then looked at Marten. "Monsieur Kovalenko wishes me to convey his regrets. Circumstance has called him back to Moscow."

Marten nodded without remark. Kovalenko was gone. The how or why of it was not something he could ask. The simple fact was that from here on in, he was on his own.

"Father," Cabrera said, as he escorted Kitner into the room, "I want you to meet the woman I love and will soon marry."

Kitner didn't react at all, merely half bowed as he reached Rebecca. She looked at him for a moment, then put her arms around him and embraced him the way she had Marten. Again joyous tears filled her eyes, and she stepped back, taking his hands in hers and telling him in fluent Russian how wonderful it was to meet him and to have him here. It was all pure and genuine and from her heart.

"This is my brother," she said, turning toward Marten.

"Nicholas Marten, sir." Marten extended his hand.

"How do you do?" Kitner said in English, then slowly took Marten's hand. His grip was barely discernible and he let go almost as soon as the two had made contact. Kitner's eyes, his entire manner, seemed somewhere else, as if he were aware of what was going on but at the same time unaware. It was difficult to tell whether he was simply tired or under the influence of some kind of drug. Whatever it was, his demeanor was listless and unfocused, hardly what one would expect in a man who oversaw a global media empire and who had become Tsar of Russia, before abdicating to Cabrera.

"There, my love, you see?" Cabrera put his arm gently around Rebecca. "Our entire family is together. You and me, the Baroness, my father, and your brother."

"Yes." She smiled. "Yes."

"Tsarevich," Murzin suddenly interceded, touching his watch.

Cabrera nodded and smiled warmly. "Rebecca, it is time to greet our guests. Baroness, Father, Nicholas, please come with us."

93

The grand ballroom of Villa Enkratzer was sixty meters long and nearly that wide. Its polished marble floor was checkerboard black and white. Its ceiling, high and arched, was adorned with gloriously painted heavenly frescoes from the eighteenth century; its centerpiece, Zeus, enthroned on a flying eagle and presiding over a congregation of the gods.

A twenty-piece orchestra in white tie and tails played near French doors toward the back, while the hundred or more elegantly dressed guests of the Baroness Marga de Vienne and Alexander Cabrera sat at linen-covered tables around the perimeter or danced center stage on the ballroom floor itself.

"Nicholas!" Lady Clem left her father on the dance floor the moment she saw Marten come in and started toward him. It made no difference that Marten was part of Alexander Cabrera's entourage making a formal and dramatic entrance into the room. Everyone present knew what had happened, that Sir Peter Kitner Mikhail Romanov had abdicated the throne and that tomorrow Cabrera, né Alexander Nikolaevich Romanov, would be formally introduced to the world as Tsarevich of All Russia.

"Clementine!" Lord Prestbury tried to call her back, admonishing her under his breath.

There was no need. As soon as they saw the Tsarevich enter, the orchestra stopped playing; at the same instant, people stopped where they were and a hush fell over the room. And then, as it had for Peter Kitner barely twenty-four hours earlier, loud and sustained applause burst forth in a rousing salute to Cabrera.

———

Marten hardly knew Lady Clem was in his arms, or that they were on the ballroom floor dancing to a Strauss waltz.

Across the room he could see Rebecca glowing with happiness and dancing with a pocket-sized, jovial Russian who had been introduced to him as Nikolai Nemov, the mayor of Moscow. Beyond them Rebecca's employers, the Rothfels, danced in each other's arms as if they were newlyweds. Farther away, he could see Lord Prestbury sitting regally at a linen-covered table sipping champagne and engrossed in conversation with the Baroness and a surprisingly animated Gregor II, Patriarch of the Russian Orthodox Church.

It was like a dream that made no sense, and Marten struggled for some kind of mental foothold. Making it more impossible was that only moments before Lady Clem had told him she and her father had known the Baroness for years and, in fact, it had been the Baroness who had arranged for Rebecca's employment at the Rothfels' residence in Neuchâtel. Moreover, with a mischievous look the equal of the one following the pulling of the fire alarm at Manchester's Whitworth Hall, she fully admitted being as guilty as Rebecca in keeping Rebecca's relationship with Cabrera a secret, and then, in a well-practiced, highly superior British manner, answering Marten's question as to why before he even asked it.

"Because, Nicholas, we all know how disturbingly overprotective a brother you are. And not only that." She moved closer. "If you and I could have a clandestine affair, why not Rebecca? It's quite sensible, really. Furthermore," she said, looking into his eyes, "as for your absurd comment about the Tsarevich. I asked Rebecca if she knew where Alexander had been yesterday on the off chance he just might have been in Zurich. Her answer was very clear. He had been with her at the Rothfels' home in Neuchâtel."

Marten might have asked if Cabrera had been in Neuchâtel all day, or if he had arrived in the afternoon, plenty of time to have come from the murder scene in Zurich, but he hadn't. And afterward he had let it all go and simply let the evening unfold.

He had a glass of champagne and then another and for the first time in what seemed months began to relax. He felt the warmth of Lady Clem as they danced, and the press of her breasts against his chest—hidden as always in the folds of a dark, deliberately oversized evening dress—began to arouse him. Even his previous certainties seemed to fade. No matter that Kitner had signed away his throne; under the circumstances, with Kovalenko gone and Rebecca so close by, it seemed foolish for him to consider any of it, let alone pursue it.

It was all crazy, as if he had stepped into a parallel universe. But he hadn't, and if he didn't believe it, all he had to do was glance at Rebecca and see the wonder and love in her eyes when she looked at Cabrera. The same was true of Cabrera when he looked at her. Whatever else Cabrera might be, there was no mistaking the look of the total, unselfish, uncompromising love he had for Marten's sister. To see it so openly revealed like that was both moving and truly remarkable.

Earlier, when Nicholas and Rebecca had danced, she had told him she was studying to become a member of the Russian Orthodox Church, and she'd laughed, telling him how much she was enjoying learning the rites and the names of the saints and how normal and right it felt, as if it were all some integral part of her being.

That one day in the next months she would not only become Cabrera's wife but Tsarina of Russia boggled the mind. Lord Prestbury had even joked about it, telling Marten that soon Marten would be a member of the Russian royal family and therefore both Lord Prestbury and Lady Clementine would have to treat him with a great deal more deference than they were used to.

Marten couldn't get over what had happened to Rebecca. Not a year removed from the mute, terrified girl confined to a Catholic sanitarium in Los Angeles to this. How could it have come to be?

He pulled Clem closer as they danced, and then he heard Cabrera's voice.

"Lady Clementine—"

Marten turned. Cabrera stood next to them on the dance floor. "I wonder if I might engage Nicholas privately for a few moments. There is something I would very much like to discuss with him."

"Of course, Tsarevich." Lady Clem smiled and, curtsying knowingly in the royal manner, stepped away. "I will be with Father, Nicholas," she said, and he watched her walk away across the dance floor.

"Some crisp alpine air, Nicholas? It's rather close in here." Cabrera indicated an open French door behind them.

Marten hesitated and looked Cabrera in the eye. "Alright," he said finally.

Cabrera led the way, acknowledging the appreciative smiles and nods of the guests as they went.

Neither Cabrera nor Marten was dressed for the cold, but they simply went out unadorned, in the tuxedos they wore. The lone difference was that in one hand, Cabrera carried a slim, gaily wrapped, rectangular package.

94

9:05 P.M.

"This way, I think, Nicholas. There is a lighted walkway that gives a nice view of the villa, especially at night."

Their breath hung in the air as Cabrera led them across a snow-crusted terrace outside the ballroom and toward a pathway leading into the woods on the far side of it. Relaxed and a little bit drunk, Marten stayed with Cabrera step for step as they reached the walkway and started along it. In moments, the cold air began to invigorate, and Marten felt his senses sharpening. For some reason he glanced over his shoulder.

Murzin was following them, keeping his distance, but there just the same.

"There were rumors that some of the demonstrators had come into this part of the valley," Cabrera said at Marten's glance, and smiled his easy smile. "I'm sure there's nothing to worry about. The colonel is just being cautious."

Ahead of them the pathway narrowed between two large conifers and Cabrera slowed, ushering Marten ahead. "Please," he said. Marten went first and then Cabrera.

"There is something I want to share with you about Rebecca." Cabrera caught up and they walked side by side. "I think you will find it remarkable."

Now the trail turned and Marten could see the pathway ahead start upward, away from the villa. Again he looked back.

Murzin was still there, coming up the path behind them.

"His presence is unnecessary," Cabrera said suddenly. "I would rather have the colonel back at the villa than traipsing through empty woods protecting us. Excuse me just a moment."

Cabrera turned and walked back to meet Murzin as he came up, the brightly wrapped package still in his hand.

Marten blew on his hands in the cold and looked up. A light wind whispered through the treetops, and he could see a full moon begin to rise over the ridge to his left. There was a ring around it and behind it an advance of clouds. Snow wasn't far off.

He looked back and saw Murzin and Cabrera talking. Then Murzin nodded and turned for the villa. At the same time, Cabrera came back up the trail toward him. In that moment a voice stabbed through him. "Never mind how Cabrera looks. Who he knows. How he walks. Talks. Who he is. What he will become. Or anything else. He *is Raymond!*"

"I'm sorry, Nicholas." Cabrera was almost to him, the snow crunching sharply under his feet.

Marten's mind danced forward and back at the same time. Kitner had abdicated the Russian throne to Cabrera there at the villa. If all this had been planned before, to take place in London after Kitner's knighthood ceremony and his presentation as Tsarevitch the following day to the Romanov hierarchy at the Russian Embassy, it seemed inevitable that the house on Uxbridge Street was to have been used the day after that, the Friday, March 15, Raymond had noted in his calendar, for the same reason—as a place to bring Kitner to his knees and force him to abdicate.

"You know people in London, yes?" Marten asked casually as Cabrera reached him.

"Lord Prestbury is from the Baroness's circle."

"You must know others?"

"Some, why?"

Marten took a chance. "I recently met a retired British stockbroker. He spends most of the year in the South of France, but he has a large home near Kensington Gardens. His name is Dixon, Charles Dixon. He lives on Uxbridge Street."

"I'm sorry, I don't know him." He gestured forward, up the trail, "May we go on? I would like to tell you about Rebecca."

"What about her?" Marten said as they moved on. Cabrera had given no perceptible reaction whatsoever to either the name Charles Dixon or the designation Uxbridge Street. Nor had he anywhere displayed Raymond's mannerisms. Was he that good or was Marten just plain wrong?

"She is not the person you think she is."

"What do you mean?" Marten turned to look at Cabrera. Was he Raymond or wasn't he? If he had Halliday's disk and could get Cabrera's fingerprints, he could prove it one way or the other. But the disk was gone, in the mail to Kovalenko's wife in Moscow.

"Rebecca is your sister legally but not by birth because you were both adopted. I know because she told me. The more we became involved with one another, for both political and business reasons I felt it necessary to have her past looked into. I love her very much, but in love mistakes are easy to make. It may sound unkind or even cold, but I wanted to make certain of her before I proposed marriage. I trust you can understand that, Nicholas."

"Yes, I can understand."

They were walking side by side, step for step on the pathway. For the first time Marten saw that Cabrera walked with a slight limp. Again, uncertainty charged through him. Could Cabrera's leg have been damaged in the shootout? The answer was yes, of course. On the other hand there was no way to know. He had not seen Raymond's medical records because he had been in the hospital himself when everything had taken place, and of course those records no longer existed. Besides, a limp could have been a result of his hunting accident or caused by anything, a pulled muscle and twisted ankle, even something in his shoe. For all he knew Cabrera had been born with it.

Now the trail turned again. Below them Marten could see the brightly lit villa. The sight of it was comforting and made him relax and think maybe he was wrong and his emotions were playing tricks on him. How badly did he want Cabrera to be his prey? For Dan Ford, for Halliday, for Red, for all the others murdered? Did he want it badly enough to create something that was not there? And in doing so, chance sending Rebecca reeling back to the state she'd been in for all those years?

"In the course of my investigation I learned something of the adoption process," Cabrera continued. "In the time period in which you were both adopted the adoption procedures were closed. Meaning neither the children nor their adoptive parents knew who the birth parents were."

Marten had no idea what Cabrera was getting at. Whatever it was, he knew what he was talking about, because neither Marten nor Rebecca knew who their real parents had been. Nor had their adoptive parents known; they had discussed it with them any number of times.

"Money and persistence can open many doors, Nicholas," Cabrera went on. "You and Rebecca were both adopted from the same organization. A now-closed home for unwed mothers called the House of Sarah in Los Angeles." Abruptly Cabrera turned to look at him. "The city where you both grew up."

Marten felt his heart come up in his throat.

"I learned a great deal, Nicholas, not only about Rebecca, but about you as well." Cabrera smiled his easy, unthreatening smile. "Your real name is John Barron and not Nicholas Marten."

Marten said nothing as they turned a bend in the trail and once again the villa disappeared from view.

"But who you are and why you changed your name and hers is not important. What is important is what was discovered on my journey into Rebecca's past. Strangely, I was not surprised by what was found."

Cabrera shifted the gift-wrapped package from one hand to the other, and Marten wondered what it was and why he had brought it. He wondered, too, where the pathway led. It was becoming increasingly steep, and the lights illuminating it fewer and farther between. In the darkness the only saving grace was the bright of the cloud-scattered moon lifting over the mountaintops that little by little began to reveal the vast forest around them.

Perhaps he'd been foolish to come with Cabrera at all, but even if he was Raymond, Marten doubted he would take the chance and reveal himself and especially do anything that would frighten Rebecca or change her perception of him. Except that if he was Raymond, he was capable of anything.

Cabrera was keeping a half step ahead of Marten, in effect leading him. "As I said, your sister is not who you suppose her to be, that is, a baby given up for adoption by a frightened teenager who was pregnant." Cabrera looked at Marten directly. "Rebecca is a princess and was born to one of the noblest families in Europe."

"What?" Marten was stunned.

"Her name at birth was Alexandra Elisabeth Gabrielle Christian. She is a direct descendant of Christian the Ninth, King of Denmark. Her great-grandparents were George the First, King of Greece, and his wife Olga, daughter of Grand Duke Constantine, the son of Nicholas the First of Russia."

"I don't understand."

"You shouldn't be expected to, it's too outrageous. Nonetheless, it is true. There is even a DNA match that proves it beyond doubt."

Marten was completely thrown off. Any idea that Cabrera might be Raymond was overridden by the absurdity of what he was hearing.

"I can appreciate how you must feel, but it's all documented, Nicholas. The papers are in my office in Lausanne. You are welcome to see them at any time."

"How—?"

"Did someone like that come up for adoption to—I don't know quite how to say it—a middle-class American family like yours?"

"That's good enough."

"Her grandparents fled the Nazis in World War Two. They first went to England and then to New York, where like many royal families around the world, my own, for instance, they changed their names and did away with titles to protect themselves. In time their daughter, whose name was Marie Gabrielle, married Jean Félix Christian, hereditary Prince of Denmark, and moved back to Europe. They had one child, a girl born in Copenhagen, who, as an infant, was kidnapped on the Spanish island of Majorca to be held for ransom. But then the people who did it became frightened and gave her to a black market organization that sold children around the world. A person there took her to a family in California, but the transaction didn't work out and she was taken in by a home for unwed mothers. She was, of course—"

"Rebecca."

"Yes."

"What about her birth parents? What did they do?"

"No trace of her was ever found, and in time they had her declared legally dead."

"My God—" Marten said and looked away; then he looked back. "Does she know?"

"Not yet."

The trail grew steeper, and somewhere Marten heard the wild rush of water. Now Cabrera was still the half step ahead of him leading the way. In the moonlight, his breath came like steam from his nostrils and, even with the cold, perspiration stood out on his forehead. Again he shifted the package in his hands.

"Why are you telling me first?"

"Out of respect. Because your adoptive parents are dead and you are head of the household. And because I wish your blessing on our marriage." Cabrera slowed the pace and turned to look at Marten. "Do I have that blessing, Nicholas?"

Oh, God, Marten thought—to have it be brought to this.

"Do I?"

Nicholas Marten stared at Cabrera. Think of Rebecca and how much she loves him, nothing else. Nothing else at all. At least not now. Not until you know for certain who he is—or isn't.

"Yes," he said, finally. "Yes, you have my blessing."

"Thank you, Nicholas. Now you see why it was so important for you and me to be alone." Cabrera smiled. It was an inward smile, private. Of relief or satisfaction. Or both. "You understand Rebecca will not only become my wife, but Tsarina of Russia."

"Yes." Marten looked around. There were no more pathway lights illuminating the trail. The roar of rushing water was louder. Much louder. He looked ahead and saw they were approaching a wooden footbridge. Beneath it was wildly rushing black water, and upstream beyond it, the source of the din, a towering, thundering waterfall.

"What beautiful children we will have, Rebecca and I." Slowly, almost absently, Cabrera began to open the package in his hands. "Beautiful, noble children who, and whose children after them, will rule Russia for the next three hundred years, as the Romanovs ruled Russia for three hundred years before the Communists tried to stop us."

Abruptly Cabrera turned and the package wrapping fell away to the snowy trail at their feet. Marten saw a box in Cabrera's hands where the paper had been. Now the box, too, fell away. There was a loud *Click* and a flash of blade in the moonlight. And in a single motion Cabrera stepped toward him.

95

Marten saw it in a microsecond. Halliday's body on the hotelroom bed in Paris, his throat cut wide open. In the same spit of time he heard Lenard's voice say something like *Whoever it was cut him the moment he opened the door.* In the next, Marten twisted away, the blade of Cabrera's knife just nicking his cheek.

The quickness of Marten's move and Cabrera's miss momentarily threw Cabrera off balance and Marten countered, slamming his left fist into Cabrera's kidney, then throwing a right that caught him under the jaw. Cabrera let out a grunt and reeled back against the footbridge's wooden hand railing. Reeled back, but didn't drop the knife. The knife was what Marten went for. He was too late. Cabrera simply shifted it to his other hand and let Marten come. Again Marten twisted away. Again Cabrera's blade flashed in the moonlight. This time the razor-sharp knife caught Marten just above the elbow, slicing cleanly through the tuxedo jacket and the shirt beneath and drawing blood.

"Not quite!" Marten screamed at him and backed away. Marten was cut but the wound wasn't deep enough. Cabrera had been going for the brachial artery. But to reach that he needed to get at least a half inch down into the flesh, and he hadn't.

"No, not quite, Nicholas." Cabrera grinned and his eyes shone wildly. Suddenly his look was no longer that of Cabrera or even of Raymond, but that of a madman.

He came toward Marten again. Slowly. Shifting the knife from one hand to the other and back again.

"The wrist, Nicholas. The radial artery. I only need to cut a quarter inch there. In thirty seconds you will lose consciousness. Death will come in about two minutes. Or would you like it faster? The neck, the carotid artery. I'll have to cut a little deeper. But after that it's only about five seconds until you black out, twelve more until death comes."

Marten moved backward across the bridge as Cabrera advanced, his shoes slipping on the icy planking beneath his feet. The thunder of the falls dominated everything, drowning Marten's senses.

"How are you going to tell Rebecca, Tsarevich? Who are you going to say killed her brother?"

Cabrera's grin became wider. "The demonstrators, Nicholas. The rumors that some of them had come into this part of the valley turned out to be true."

"Why? Why?" Marten said, using anything he could to delay Cabrera and give himself time to think.

Cabrera kept coming. "Why kill you? Why did I kill the others?" The smile lessened, but the madness in his eyes remained. "For my mother."

"Your mother is dead."

"No, she is not. The Baroness is my mother."

"The Baroness?"

"Yes."

For the smallest instant Cabrera faltered. It was the opening Marten had been waiting for and he rushed. Shoving Cabrera's knife hand aside, he picked him up bodily and slammed him into the bridge's railing. Once. Twice. Three times. Each time he heard him grunt and felt the wind go out of him. Cabrera slumped forward, stunned, and his head went to his chest. In the same instant Marten grabbed him by the hair, lifting the head and throwing his right jab at his face.

Cabrera grinned arrogantly and simply moved his head aside, letting the force of Marten's missed blow carry him forward against the rail. A split second later Marten felt a devastating thump as Cabrera's blade sliced into his side. He cried out and at the same time grabbed Cabrera's shirt by the collar, dragging him around. The shirt tore open to the waist and Cabrera tried to strike again with the switchblade. But he couldn't. Marten jerked him close. For an instant they stared into each other's eyes. Then Marten slammed his forehead against Cabrera's in a vicious head butt.

There was a thundering crack and Cabrera staggered back, his head bleeding, to fall against the bridge railing. Marten started for him once more, but suddenly his legs weakened and he froze where he was. Never had he felt colder in his life. He looked down and saw his shirt soaked with blood. Then he felt himself falling, his feet slipping out from under him on the icy planking, and he realized Cabrera had hold of his leg and was tugging him forward toward him. He tried to pull free but couldn't. Now Cabrera was on his knees, one hand tugging him forward, the other raising the knife.

"No!" Marten yelled, and with all the effort he had left he kicked up, sending the switchblade flying across the bridge. But Cabrera hadn't let go of Marten. He still held him by one hand and was dragging him forward to the edge.

Marten heard the roar of the falls and saw the wash of black water beneath him. He tried to struggle back but it was no good. He was being pulled over the side and there was nothing he could do about it.

Then he was in the air and dropping. A second, an hour, a lifetime later he plunged into icy water. And then he was beneath the surface and gone, torn away by the raging current.

"*Dasvedanya,*" Cabrera had whispered as Marten slid past, his black eyes shining death in the moonlight.

"*Dasvedanya.*" It was what he had said on the luggage carousel in Los Angeles International Airport when he was about to kill John Barron with his own gun.

"Raymond!" a voice had suddenly jolted from nowhere. Not *a* voice. Red McClatchy's voice.

Those seconds or hours or days before he hit the water, Nicholas Marten prayed for that voice again. The cry that would save his life once more. But it never came.

How could it?

Red was already dead.

PART 3

RUSSIA

1

The rumors were true. Black Bloc anarchist demonstrators had come into the valley. Cabrera and Nicholas Marten had encountered them on a trail bridge above the villa. Their faces hidden behind balaclavas, heavy scarves, and ski masks, they'd said nothing, simply attacked. Both Cabrera and Marten had been punched and kicked. Cabrera's shirt had been nearly ripped from him. Both men had fought back furiously. Marten went after one who had pulled a knife. As he did, another grabbed Marten and held him. Cabrera tried to go to his aid but he was hit and thrown to the ground. At the same time, the one with the knife cut Marten savagely, and the one holding him pushed Marten off the bridge. He fell into the fast-flowing mountain river and disappeared. It was then that Cabrera made his break. Fighting off a ski-masked attacker, he rushed back down the trail yelling for help.

Murzin and a dozen FSO agents had come running. But by then clouds had covered the moon and it was beginning to snow, and the demonstrators had retreated back up the trail in the dark and disappeared into the forest. Murzin's men found their tracks, but Cabrera called them back to help search for Marten.

Led by Cabrera himself, in snow boots with only a parka pulled over his tuxedo, it was a search that lasted into the next day and was hampered by high winds and blowing and drifting snow. Kantonspolizei and Swiss army commandos joined in almost immediately, and mountain search and rescue teams arrived within the hour. Together they combed the treacherous corridor of the river that crisscrossed the mountain and rushed downhill through a series of waterfalls, some as much as sixty feet high, for seventeen miles. For a time they had even used the helicopter President Gitinov had arrived in only moments before Cabrera raised the alarm, but the ferocity of the storm and the rough terrain made flying exceedingly dangerous and the search had been left to men on foot. And in the end they had come up with nothing. Whatever had happened to Marten— whether he had been caught between rocks under the water, or had been washed into some subterranean cave, or had crawled out somewhere and was buried so deeply in the snow that even the search and rescue teams' avalanche dogs could not find him—one thing was certain. No one who had been brutally cut with a knife and was dressed in nothing more than a tuxedo could have survived the night in that kind of environment. If the knife wounds or the violent wash of water sweeping him over rocks and waterfalls had not killed him, hypothermia would have. Finally, there was nothing to do but call off the search.

2

Whether it was Rebecca's growing maturity or the presence of Cabrera, Lady Clem, and the Baroness, she took the news of the attack on her brother and his subsequent disappearance with surprising calm. Her main concern was the well-being of Alexander and the safety of the people looking for Nicholas. Several times she had gone down to the stream dressed in winter mountain gear to encourage them and help in the search. Her strength, they would realize, came from what she had said from the beginning, and what she seemed to truly believe—that somehow Nicholas had survived and was somewhere still alive. How, or where that somewhere might be, did not enter the equation.

The fact that daylight came and there was still no trace of him only strengthened her resolve. He might not be found to-day or tomorrow or in a week, she said, but he was alive and at some point would be found, of that there was no question whatsoever. Nothing any of them could say or do would make her think otherwise.

Lady Clem was a different story altogether.

That her father was present, waiting like the others for word during the long rescue attempt, was irrelevant. Lady Clem refused to acknowledge the personal horror and dread she felt, or admit, even to herself, the closeness of her relationship with Marten. Instead, her emotions were directed at the demonstrators who had perpetrated this monstrous act.

And when Swiss army commandos and Kantonskriminalpolizei tracked the demonstrators down, rousting them from their mountain tents in the hills high above the villa just before dawn, and brought them down to the villa to be loaded into vans for transport to the Davos Kantonspolizei compound, Lady Clem went straight to where they were. There were nine of them, six men and three women. Hearing them protest and deny everything, she went ballistic, threatening to have each prosecuted under every law imaginable. Even as cooler heads intervened and a police commander tried to lead her away and back to the villa, she suddenly pulled free and gave them one final salvo. "You have not only murdered Mr. Marten, you have left his sister wholly alone in the world. It is an act, I promise you, that will not go unpunished!"

3

The "act," as Lady Clem called it, was one Alexander Cabrera had set up with meticulous care and forethought. Although the battle with Marten had been far more difficult than he had anticipated, overall, it had worked, and worked well.

The idea of utilizing the demonstrators was something conceived much earlier as a relatively simple and inexpensive insurance policy to cover Marten's death. A telephone call to a European radical antiglobalization activist collective had put the plan in motion. Identifying himself as a member of a well-known group called the Radical Activist Network of Trainers, he told the collective of the high-level gathering of politicians and businessmen to be held at Villa Enkratzer. Describing the building and telling them where it was located, he detailed who would be there, how the villa could be reached from a little-known mountain fire road, and where, in the forests above it, it would be easy to set up a camp from which activists could make a surprise demonstration from the mountainside, joining a protest that would be trying to reach the villa from the main road on the morning of Saturday the eighteenth—the day after his nighttime rendezvous with Marten on the villa trail. In other words, the demonstrators would be camped and on-scene, but would not have expected to come down to the villa until the following day.

Authorities had planned for thirty thousand protesters trying to get into Davos, so he had little or no doubt that at least a handful of the most dedicated would take his bait. And he had been right. A follow-up call a week later saying he had heard about the protest and wanted to join those packing in had confirmed it. A small group was already going in, he was told. They needed no one else.

He'd made certain they were there himself when he, Rebecca, the Baroness, and the Rothfels had come in by helicopter from Neuchâtel earlier in the day and he'd had the pilot approach the villa's helipad from over the mountains instead of Davos Valley as was usually done. He counted five mountain tents, hidden among the trees, when they passed over. A glimpse was all he'd had, but it was all he needed to know his ruse had worked and his scapegoats were in place.

He'd made the tracks in the snow leading up toward their encampment himself, in the freezing but exhilarating moments after Marten had gone over the side and he'd recovered the knife. He'd turned back only when the storm became so intense he knew the falling snow would cover the tracks anyway. Then, with his blood pumping and unmindful of the cold, he'd rushed for the villa to sound the alarm.

His bravura all-night performance leading the search party immediately afterward had been done primarily to showcase his heroics as a people's Tsarevich but also to demonstrate his horror and dismay at what happened and to show his deep caring for Nicholas Marten. His only fear, of course, was that Marten might be found alive, but he knew the chances of that were next to none. He'd cut him badly, and the furious course of icy water over miles of rock and steep waterfalls combined with the storm and subfreezing conditions made survival an impossibility.

What he'd done last, in daylight and in the warmth of the villa, still dressed in his boots and a parka over his tattered tuxedo, was consult with the four most important men in his life, men who, with numerous others, had remained at the villa and kept vigil throughout the night—President Gitinov, His Holiness Gregor II, Mayor Nemov, and Marshal Golovkin. "Because of what has happened," he told them, "and because Nicholas Marten was the brother of the woman who is to become the next Tsarina of Russia, I ask that we postpone announcing the return of the monarchy until a more appropriate time and in a more appropriate place."

There was no question at all that it was the right and proper thing to do, and to a man they agreed. It was a moment underscored when the fifty-two-year-old President Gitinov had surprisingly taken him aside to personally extend his sympathy and to tell him he fully understood.

"It is best for you and it is best for Russia," Gitinov had said genuinely and with sympathy.

Alexander knew it was a gesture that was not easy for a man who had approved the return of the monarchy chiefly because of the combined political strength of the others there with them—the Most Holy Patriarch of the Russian Orthodox Church, the mayor of Moscow, and the Russian Federation minister of defense. Although each was hugely authoritative in his own right, when it came to national politics they thought and acted as one, and when they chose to raise or become involved with a state issue, their influence on the members of both houses of the Russian parliament was enormous.

The idea of a return of the monarchy had churned dinnertable arguments across Russia almost from the day Alexander's great-grandfather, Tsar Nicholas, had been murdered. But it had never been more than that until the triumvirate, through their own individual and collective experiences, had realized that Russia, reestablished as a state since the collapse of the Soviet Union, was still deeply troubled. Governed by a bloated bureaucracy, the young democracy was weighed down by an economy that, despite shedding much debt and showing solid gains in its oil and grain industries, was generally weak and unreliable. Further, it was protected by a vastly underpaid, rusting, and disheartened military and, as significantly, was, in virtually every corner of the country, rife with poverty, violence, and corruption. These were huge, complex problems they didn't believe the current government was successfully addressing with concrete plans. In examining the situation further, the triumvirate concluded that if Russia was to be a truly strong, economically progressive, and influential country it needed a very public and emotionally stabilizing force that would give the people an immediate and powerful sense of unity, pride, and self. They saw the answer in the reinstatement of the imperial family to the Russian throne in the form of a constitutional monarchy—a figurehead government that, like that in England, was essentially powerless to rule but, like England's, one that would be filled with pomp, circumstance, ceremony, and goodwill that could quickly and emotionally excite the public, and around which they could rally a new and enduring national spirit. Once their arguments for such a return had been organized and formally presented to parliament, they had fiercely pressed its members to see the measure through to passage.

For Gitinov the idea was impossible. He saw the triumvirate as hostile to his administration, and their influence as a dark and ever-hovering threat to his own power base. So to him, the idea of a return of the monarchy was little more than a political maneuver to further their own ends. Moreover, it was dangerous, because he knew that their backing a royal head of state, figurehead or not, could, at some point, begin to undermine his own authority—even theirs if the monarch became too influential. It was an issue made all the more worrisome when he learned Kitner was to abdicate in favor of his eldest son, because it meant that he would be competing for the public mind not only with a crowned head but with one who was young, handsome, and exceedingly charismatic, and who had an extraordinarily beautiful bride-to-be marching beside him. They looked like movie stars and would be perched on a pedestal by the world media for years as Russia's Kennedyesque supercouple. Worse yet, Alexander was true royalty, a direct descendant of the three-hundred-year Romanov dynasty, whom even the oldest of the old and poorest of the poor would revere as the beating heart of the Russian soul.

Gitinov knew he could have used his own considerable power and influence to turn the vote against the triumvirate and in the end most likely would have prevailed. By then, though, the idea that the parliament was considering returning the imperial family to the throne had become public knowledge and had received a groundswell of approval. To turn the vote against it would take enormous effort and would make it seem that he was afraid a return of the monarchy would weaken his power, and that was something he couldn't afford to have happen. So instead of fighting it he had acquiesced, even meeting with the triumvirate at His Holiness Patriarch Gregor II's residence at Peredelkino near Moscow to openly and enthusiastically champion the idea.

It was all politics; why he had consented, and why he had come to Davos, and why, too, he had gone out of his way to personally offer Alexander his sympathy for what had happened on the mountain. Alexander knew it but he had shown nothing, responding only with a respectful, heartfelt thank-you and a grateful handshake.

Then, his duties over, Alexander Nikolaevich Romanov, Tsarevich of Russia, had simply left and gone to bed. Wholly exhausted and utterly victorious.

4

MOSCOW. SUNDAY, JANUARY 19. 7:05 A.M.

The sound of the telephone woke Kovalenko from a restless sleep. Immediately he picked it up from the bedside table and hunched over it, trying not to wake his wife.

"*Da,*" he said.

"It is Philippe Lenard, Inspector. Sorry to wake you so early on Sunday," the Parisian policeman said. "I understand you have been taken off the case."

"Yes. Your car is being returned to you by the FSO."

"I know, thank you."

Kovalenko cocked his head. Lenard's speech was flat, his words just lying there. Something was wrong.

"You were traveling most of yesterday, is that right?"

"Yes. Zurich to Paris to Moscow. I should have called you during my layover in Paris. Sorry. What is it? Why are you calling me?"

"From the sound of your voice I have to assume you haven't heard."

"Heard what?"

"About Nicholas Marten."

"What about him?"

"He's dead."

"What?"

"He was attacked by a band of radical protesters in Davos on Friday night."

"Jesus God." Kovalenko ran a hand through his hair and got out of bed.

"What is it?" His wife rolled over, peering at him from her pillow.

"Nothing, Tatyana, go back to sleep." He turned back to the phone. "Let me call you in thirty minutes, Philippe. . . . Your cell phone, yes." Kovalenko hung up and stared off.

"What is it?" Tatyana asked again.

"A man I know, an American, was killed late Friday in Switzerland. I'm not quite sure what to do about it."

"He was a friend?"

"Yes, he was a friend."

"I'm sorry. But if he's dead, what can you do about it?"

Kovalenko looked off. Outside he could hear a truck pass, its driver shifting gears awkwardly.

Abruptly he looked back to Tatyana. "I had an envelope mailed to you from Zurich on"—Kovalenko had to stop and think, the days all ran together—"Friday. It hasn't arrived."

"That was the day before yesterday, so no, of course not. Why?"

"Nothing, it's not important." Kovalenko tugged at an ear and crossed the room, then turned back. "Tatyana, I realize I've just come home, but I must go to the ministry."

"When?"

"Now."

"What about the kids? They haven't seen you in—"

"Tatyana—right now."

5

Kovalenko had not called Lenard back in the thirty minutes he'd promised. The only call he'd made was to his immediate superior, fifty-two-year-old Irina Malikova, mother of five and the Ministry of Justice chief investigator. He needed to talk to her, and in the security of her ministry office, as soon as possible.

What he would tell her was the thing that he had been reluctant to present to anyone because of its sheer volatility and his lack of absolute proof. Now he felt he had no choice but to reveal it because it was critical to national security. What he would tell her was that Alexander Cabrera, next in the line of succession for the imperial throne, was, in all probability, the madman Raymond Oliver Thorne, the man responsible for the murders of the Romanovs in the Americas the year before, for the murder of Fabien Curtay in Monaco, and for the murders of Alfred Neuss, James Halliday, a former LAPD homicide detective, *Los Angeles Times* Paris correspondent Dan Ford, and two others, one outside Paris and one in Zurich—and, he was certain, for the death of Nicholas Marten at Villa Enkratzer in Davos.

What the gray-haired, blue-eyed Irina Malikova would tell him, in her third-floor, interior, windowless office in the faceless, utilitarian building at number 4a Ulitsa Vorontzovo Pole was, to the outside world, highly classified, but something those at Villa Enkratzer already knew.

"Señor Cabrera is not the *next* in line to become Tsar," Irina Malikova said. "He already *is* Tsarevich. Sir Peter Kitner Mikhail Romanov formally abdicated in favor of his son yesterday."

"What?"

"Yes."

Kovalenko was astounded. Nearly everything Marten had surmised had come true.

"So, Inspector, it should be more than apparent that the first Tsarevich of All Russia since the revolution cannot also be a common criminal. A mass murderer."

"The problem, Madame Chief Inspector, is that I am all but certain he is. And with his fingerprints, I can remove any doubt whatsoever."

"How?"

"I have a computer disk. It belonged to the former Los Angeles Police Department homicide detective murdered in Paris. It contains the original LAPD booking sheet on Raymond Thorne—it has his photograph and fingerprints. We need only Cabrera's fingerprints to know conclusively."

"Thorne is dead." Irina Malikova said with finality.

"No," Kovalenko pushed back, "I have every reason to believe he is Cabrera. His appearance has been changed by cosmetic surgery, but not his fingerprints."

Malikova hesitated, studying him. "Who else knows about the disk?" she asked finally.

"Marten and I were the only ones."

"You're certain?"

"Yes."

"There are no copies."

"None that I know of."

"Where is this disk now?"

"In the mail to me, sent from Zurich last Friday."

"When you get it, bring it to me right away. Day or night. I don't care. And—this is most important—you are to tell no one about it. No one."

Irina Malikova fixed Kovalenko with a stare, as if to underscore the extreme weight of her order; then her manner softened and she smiled. "Now, go home and be with your family. You have been too long away from them."

That was the end of it, and Malikova turned away to bring up a file on the computer screen on her desk. Kovalenko wasn't quite finished.

"If I may ask you, Madame Chief Inspector," he said quietly, "why was I removed from the investigation?"

Irina Malikova hesitated, and then she turned back. "It came from above."

"From whom?"

"The participation of Ministry of Justice personnel in cases outside of the country is to cease immediately. That was the wording, Inspector. There was no explanation."

Kovalenko smiled faintly. "There never is." Abruptly he stood. "I'm looking forward to time with my wife and children. When I have the disk I will notify you."

With that, Kovalenko left her office and walked down the long corridor past the cubicle-like rooms populated here and there with the few investigators working the Sunday shift. Afterward he took the elevator to the ground floor and flashed his identity card at a face behind a glass partition. A buzzer sounded and the door in front of him opened. A moment later he stepped out into a gray Moscow day. It was cold and spitting snow, the way it had been when two of Murzin's men had driven him from Villa Enkratzer and put him on the train to Zurich, leaving Marten alone to deal with Alexander Cabrera.

It wasn't until now, leaving the ministry and walking along the dull, overcast, wintry Moscow streets, that he realized how hard the news had hit him. Nicholas Marten was dead. It didn't seem possible, but it was. "Was he a friend?" Tatyana had asked, and without thinking, he'd said yes. And it was true. He'd hardly known him, but for some reason he felt closer to Marten than to people he'd known for years. Suddenly he felt a lump rise up in his throat. "And then that's it," he said bitterly and out loud. "And then that's it."

Everything that had been a man's life. Gone with his final breath. Just like that.

6

Against Rebecca's wishes, a private memorial service was held for her brother at St. Peter's House in the university precinct on Oxford Road.

Under a ceiling of umbrellas held against a cold rain by Colonel Murzin's FSO detail, Alexander led Rebecca, the Baroness, and Lady Clementine from a dark gray Rolls-Royce and up a flight of steps and into the building.

Lord Prestbury, the chancellor and vice-chancellor of the university, several of Nicholas's professors, and a handful of his friends were all who attended. The service lasted little more than twenty minutes and then it was over. People stood, solemnly paid Rebecca their deepest respects and condolences, and left.

"I really wish you hadn't done it," Rebecca said on the way back to the airport.

Alexander took her hand and looked at her gently and lovingly. "My darling, I know how difficult it is for you, but it's best to have closure on these horrible things as quickly as possible. Otherwise they will continue to eat at your heart and only beget greater sadness."

"My brother is not dead." Rebecca's eyes went to Lady Clem and then to the Baroness. "You don't believe he is either, do you?"

"I know how you feel in your heart." No matter the grief and pain and loss Lady Clem felt inwardly, outside she remained composed and dignified and at the same time respectful of her close friend. "I wish we could all wake from the same nightmare and find it isn't true, that none of it happened. But I'm afraid we shan't." Lady Clem smiled gently.

"Reality is not the same as what we might wish," the

Baroness said in the same quiet tone. "I'm afraid we have no choice but to accept the truth."

Rebecca sat up straight and her eyes flashed defiance. "The truth is, Nicholas is not dead. And no matter what either of you does or says, I will not change my mind. One day, a door will open and there he'll be. You will see, all of you."

7

The Baroness watched Rebecca, sitting across the cabin from her quietly reading, and then looked to Alexander, standing in the aisle farther down, chatting with Colonel Murzin. Finally she turned to look out the window as the chartered Tupolev jetliner broke through the clouds. Moments later they cleared the weather front and she could see the English coastline as they moved out over the North Sea heading east toward Moscow.

Rebecca had said little since her adamant defense of her brother's survival in the car, and Alexander had wisely decided to leave her alone. Her recovery from months of psychotherapy had left her not only healthy but strong-willed and exceedingly independent. The sense of it brought the Baroness back to a moment earlier when they had dropped Lady Clementine at her university office on their way to the airport and Rebecca had gotten out of the car in the rain to earnestly hug her good-bye. Witnessing it she felt a sudden pang of concern, even portent, that their relationship was too close and that at some future point it might cause trouble for her or Alexander. But it was a notion she shook off as groundless and only anxiety provoking, and she refused to think more about it.

Below she could see the roll of whitecaps on the gray sea and in the distance the coast of Denmark. Soon they would be across it and approaching the southern tip of Sweden. The thought of the land where she had grown up triggered memories, and she drifted back to the long journey she had begun at nineteen when her mother died and she left Stockholm for Paris to study at the Sorbonne. It was there she met Peter Kitner, and they instantly fell madly and passionately in love. It was a relationship so natural and so emotionally and physically charged that even the smallest part of an hour spent apart was agonizing. Theirs was a love like no other. They were certain it had been predestined and would last for all eternity. Because of it they told each other things that were deep and guarded and very personal. She told him about her father and their flight from Russia and his death in the gulag. Later she told him what had happened in Naples when she was fifteen, although she carefully couched it by saying the young woman who had been abducted and then raped and who had then killed and mutilated the man who had done it had been not she but a "close friend" and that the friend had never been caught.

And even though she'd told the truth without revealing herself, it was still the closest she'd ever come to sharing her murderous secret with anyone. Not long afterward Kitner shared his own secret with her, telling her who his father was and who his family had been and swearing her forever to silence because they were afraid of Communist reprisals and he had been strictly forbidden by his parents to ever speak of it.

It was an unveiling that shocked her to the core and literally took her breath away. If there had been any question at all before, there no longer was. Their coming together was indeed God's doing and their true destiny. She was born of Russian aristocracy and he was heir to the Russian throne. The sacred soul of the Motherland, the grave mantle of his ancestors and the thing her father had died for, lived in them both and was theirs to preserve. She believed it and he believed it. Very soon afterward she became pregnant with Alexander and, overjoyed, Kitner married her. After Kitner's father and himself, their child would be the legitimate heir to the crown of Russia. In what seemed a blink, their future and what they truly believed was Russia's, had been sealed. One day in their lifetime the Communist system would crumble, and finally and rightfully the monarchy would be restored, and they would sit at its head. Her husband and herself and their child.

And then, and as swiftly, it all came apart.

Told of their marriage and her pregnancy, Kitner's parents erupted in anger and outrage. His mother called her a whore and a user and, born of Russian aristocracy or not, hardly of the ancestry to be mother of a direct heir to the throne. Kitner was summarily ordered from their apartment and forbidden ever to see her again. The following day their marriage was annulled, and a lawyer representing the family presented her with a substantial check and directed her never to try to contact the family, use their name, or divulge who they were. Still they weren't through. Their final demand was cruelest of all—that she abort the child inside her.

Wildly, adamantly, vociferously, she refused. One day passed, and then two, and nothing happened. But on the third a steely, dark-eyed man came to the door. He told her an abortion had been arranged and that she was to come with him right then. Again she vehemently refused and tried to slam the door in his face. Instead she was slapped hard across the face and told to get her things. Minutes later they drove away in his car. To her it was Naples all over again. Rape, abortion against her will, the violation was the same. Her abductor's greatest mistake had been in letting her get her things. In her purse was the knife she had used in Naples and kept for just such a moment. A few moments later they stopped for a traffic light. The man grinned thinly and told her that where they were going was in the next block and that it would soon be over.

For him it was. Before the light could change, she slid the knife from her purse and in a single motion pulled it straight across his throat. A millisecond later she threw open the car door and ran, certain she would be caught any moment and sent to prison for the rest of her life. Collecting her things, she fled from Paris that same day, taking the train to Nice in the South of France. There she rented a nondescript apartment and lived on the money provided by Kitner's family. Six months later she gave birth to Alexander. All the while, she was waiting for the police who never came. Looking back, all she could think was that there had been no witnesses to her crime and that Kitner's family, fearing exposure, never notified the authorities of her, or their, connection to the murdered man. Still she had lived all those months on edge, working consciously to control her fear of the police and to calm the fury about what had been done to her. Then, with a healthy infant Alexander in her arms, she carefully turned her thoughts to what she would do next.

The deliberate and hateful actions of Peter Kitner's family had been one thing. In a way she could understand and even accept them as the same kind of perverse, cruel, and arrogant human behavior that had sent her father to the gulag and thrust the brutal rapist on her in Naples.

What she could not understand, nor would she ever accept, had been the conduct of Peter Kitner himself. The man who had sworn he loved her beyond life itself, who had fathered her child and married her, who shared the same dream for Russia as she—when ordered from her life by his mother and father, he had done just that, removed himself from her life.

Never once had he stood up and declared his love for her. Never once had he defended her or their relationship. Never once had he committed any action whatsoever on her behalf or on behalf of their unborn child. Never once had he said a word of kindness or comfort to her. What he had done instead was to simply cross the room and walk out, never once so much as looking at her. Her father, on the other hand, had looked back and smiled and blown her a kiss as he was being led to the train that would take him to the gulag.

Her father was proud and loving and defiant. To her he was the soul of Russia. Peter Kitner was direct heir to the Russian throne, yet he had simply done as he had been told to protect the imperial lineage, and later done it again by marrying into the royal family of Spain and raising a family of suitable imperial order.

That was a part of it she might have been willing to understand, but that he had walked out without ever so much as looking at her, without ever giving her even that much, was something she would never forgive him for and for which she had sworn he would one day pay dearly.

And he had. With the life of his son. With the crown of Russia. And he would continue to pay.

With what was still to come.

8

The motorcade was a block long. Horns blared. Sirens shrieked. Tons of tiny pieces of colored paper rained down from apartment and office buildings, where, despite the bitter cold, hundreds of people cheered from wide-open windows, while thousands more lined the streets below them.

The focus of their attention was the figures standing in the large wide-open sunroof of a black Mercedes limousine surrounded by eight black Volgas.

Alexander, in a tailored gray business suit, smiled exuberantly, waving to the wildly appreciative crowd as they passed. Beside him stood Rebecca, in a full-length designer mink coat and mink pillbox hat. She was smiling, beautiful, and glamorous. To the middle-aged and elderly they looked like a young Jack and Jackie Kennedy. To the young, like rock stars.

And that was the whole idea.

Less than forty-eight hours earlier Alexander Cabrera Nikolaevich Romanov had been officially named Tsarevich by President Gitinov in a very public introduction of him to both houses of parliament in Moscow. The response by members of the Duma, the lower house, and the Federal Council, the upper, was immediate—a thunderous standing ovation by everyone there, save fifty or so hard-line Communists who had shown their clear disapproval by simply walking out.

Alexander's acceptance speech had been no less rousing and emotional than the applause as he paid careful homage to his grandfather Alexei Romanov, son of Tsar Nicholas, and his father, Tsarevich Petr Mikhail Romanov Kitner, who had carefully protected the story of Alexei's escape from the Ipatiev-house massacre and therefore preserved the true line of succession until the time was right for the return of the monarchy. He then thanked President Gitinov and the members of parliament, Nikolai Nemov, the mayor of Moscow, Marshal Golovkin, Russian Federation minister of defense, and most profoundly Gregor II, the Most Holy Patriarch of the Russian Orthodox Church—all of whom were present—for having the grace and wisdom to return the heart and soul of Russian history to her people. He ended by speaking of his father one more time, praising him for seeing Russia not as a weakened country, old, corrupt, and decaying, but as a young and vibrant nation; troubled, yes, but free from the horrors of Stalin, Communism, and the cold war and fully ready to blossom from their ashes. It was the youth of Russia that would lead the way, he said, and that was why his father so unselfishly had stepped aside in favor of a Romanov more their own age who would stand at their forefront. Together they would lead Russia into a prosperous, healthy, and noble tomorrow.

His speech, televised live across the country's eleven time zones and by Russian-language stations around the world, lasted only thirty-two minutes and ended with a second thunderous standing ovation that continued for fifteen minutes more. When it was over Alexander Cabrera Nikolaevich Romanov had become not just Tsarevich of Russia but a national hero.

Twenty-four hours later, with cameras from nearly every news organization in existence jamming the Kremlin's gilded hall that was once the throne room of the Tsars, he introduced the beautiful Alexandra Elisabeth Gabrielle Christian as his bride-to-be and the woman who, upon his coronation, would become Tsarina of Russia. "I would have called her Alexandra, but she prefers her given name, Rebecca," he joked warmly as he put his arm around her. "I think so as not to confuse me."

It brought down the house. Overnight, and as if from nowhere, a Russian Camelot was born and the nation and the world went crazy.

"Wave, my darling!" Alexander shouted above the crowd, throwing off the blizzard of confetti that fell around them.

"It is alright?" Rebecca replied in Russian.

"Alright? They want you to, my darling." He looked at her, his eyes filled with love, his smile larger than ever. "They want you to. Wave, wave! They wait for neither our marriage nor my coronation. To them you are already their Tsarina!"

9

Images came and went.

Some were starkly clear, as if they were occurring in present time. Others were vague, as in a dream. Others still had all the dread and horror of nightmares.

Clearest of all was coming back from the edge of death when he saw himself on the floor-bed they had made for him in the tiny cabin. His eyes closed, his complexion ghostly white, his body covered with a tattered blanket, he lay perfectly still with no sign of life at all. Then, so effortlessly that it might have been an effect in a movie, he began to drift upward and away from himself. Higher he went, as if the room had no ceiling, the building no roof, and then he saw the door open and the young mother come in. She carried a hot drink in a tin cup, and she knelt down beside him and lifted his head, then opened his lips and forced the liquid inside. Warmth such as he'd never experienced surged through him, and suddenly he was no longer drifting away but looking into her gentle eyes.

"More," she said, or something like it, because she spoke a language he didn't understand. But whatever she had said didn't matter because she pressed the tin cup to his lips again and this time made him drink on his own. And he did. The taste was bitter but good and he drank it all. Then he relaxed and put his head back down, and he saw her pull the blanket up around him and smile kindly as he fell asleep.

In his sleep he remembered.

Swirling black water racing him downstream in the darkness, hurtling him viciously against ice and rocks and debris, and all the while trying to grab at sticks, logs, stones, anything at hand to stop himself as he flew past in a ride that seemed never to end.

And then suddenly feeling everything stop and finding himself in a still eddy away from the rush and roar of water. It was overgrown with winter-naked brush and fallen trees. He grasped one, a birch, he thought, and pulled himself up and into the snow. It was there he realized the storm had caught up. The wind screamed and snow blew almost horizontally. But in moments in between, because the storm had not gathered full course, the wind stopped and the full moon shone. It was there, soaking wet and in the freezing cold, he saw the patch of red in the snow beneath where he lay. And he remembered the flash of the knife and the deep cut Raymond had made in his side, above his waist, just beneath his ribs.

Oh, yes, it had been Raymond. In the fight on the footbridge Marten had torn open Cabrera's shirt, ripping it to the navel. For an instant he had seen the scar at his throat where John Barron's bullet had grazed Raymond in the exchange of gunfire during his bloody escape from the Criminal Courts Building in Los Angeles.

He might call himself Alexander Cabrera, or even Romanov, or Tsarevich, but whatever he called himself, there was no doubt whatsoever that he was Raymond.

The cabin where he was was little more than a shack some three miles downstream from the pathway bridge above Villa Enkratzer. The seven- or eight-year-old girl who, gathering firewood with her father, had found him in blinding snow at dawn, huddled in the protection of a great fallen fir, was one of four who had helped him. The others were her father, her mother, and her younger brother, who was five, maybe, or six. They spoke very little English, a half-dozen words at best, and he had no understanding of their language at all.

From what he could piece together—as he went from waking to dreams to hallucinations and back to waking in a fever caused by an infection developed from the knife wounds—

they were a family of refugees, possibly from Albania. They were very poor and were waiting in the cabin for what the father called "a hauler" to come. They had tea and herbs and very little food, but what they had they crushed in the tin cup and added boiling water and shared with him.

At some point there had been a loud argument between husband and wife when he was overcome with shivering and the wife was demanding the husband forget their own situation and go for a doctor. The husband had refused, huddling his children in his arms as if to say one man was not worth losing everything else for.

Later had come a sharp knock on the cabin door, but he had heard it from a distance as the family—fires put out, all traces of their presence expertly wiped away, as had been their everyday practice—hid away in the woods with Marten, while Swiss army commandos searched the cabin and left.

Much later, maybe days after the first, there was another sharp knock on the door, but this time it was heard from inside and came in the middle of the night. And he remembered the father so cautiously opening the door to find their "hauler" was finally there.

He remembered clearly the father trying to get his family out of there to go with the "hauler" and the wife and children refusing to leave without Marten. And the father finally relenting. And Marten, half walking, half stumbling, moving with the family a mile or more through the snow and darkness. And there, on the edge of an icy country road, being loaded, with the twenty others already there, into the back of a waiting truck.

After that had come the rattle and bounce of the truck over rough roads. He remembered the numbing pain of his wounds, from the knife cut in his side and the lesser one on his arm, and those that came as the result of the brutal ride down the river. Two broken ribs, maybe more, and a severely bruised shoulder.

He remembered sleeping and waking and seeing drained and gaunt faces staring at him. And then sleeping again, and waking, for what seemed like days. Once in a while the truck would stop in woods or fields hidden by trees. The father would help him out with the others and Marten would urinate or defecate or do nothing at all. Like the rest of them. Later the daughter or mother or son would give him something to drink and eat, and he would fall back asleep. How he managed to get through it, or in reality, how any of them did—he didn't know.

Finally there was no more movement and someone helped him out of the truck and up a long and narrow flight of stairs. He remembered a bed, and crawling into the indescribable luxury of it.

Much later he woke to sunshine in a large and entirely unfamiliar apartment. The boy and girl helped him up to a window to look out on a brilliantly clear late winter day. Outside he saw a large shipping canal with seagoing boats and people and traffic on the streets alongside it.

"Rotterdam," the girl said in English. "Rotterdam."

"What day is this?" he asked.

The girl looked at him blankly. So did the boy.

"Day. You know. Sunday, Monday, Tuesday."

"Rotterdam," the girl said again. "Rotterdam."

10

Marten had little more than a moment to reflect on what had happened to him and where he had been brought, let alone think of what to do next, when the door behind him opened and two men wearing balaclavas came in. One walked quickly past and pulled the curtains over the window. The other shooed the children out of the room to someone who waited in the hallway.

"Who are you?" Marten asked.

"Come," the throaty voice of the first balaclava answered, and suddenly the second balaclava was pulling a scarf over Marten's eyes and tying it tightly, then quickly binding his hands behind him with some kind of strap.

"Come," the first balaclava said again, and Marten was led out of the room and up one steep flight of stairs and then another. His ribs, his wounds, the effort made everything hurt. He could see nothing.

Next was a short walk down a hallway.

"Sit," the throaty voice said with a heavy accent Marten couldn't place. A heartbeat later he heard the sound of a door being closed.

"Sit," the voice commanded a second time. Slowly he lowered himself until he felt the hardness of a chair beneath him.

"You are American," the throaty voice said, and Marten could smell tobacco on his breath.

"Yes."

"Your name is Nicholas Marten."

"Yes."

"What is your profession?"

"Student."

What felt like an open hand suddenly hit him hard across the face. He recoiled and nearly fell off the chair. A strong hand pulled him back and he groaned out loud as pain shot through the wound in his side.

"What is your profession?" The voice repeated.

Marten had no idea who these people were or what they wanted, but he knew he had better keep his composure and not try to fight back, at least not now. "You know my name, so you must have my wallet," he said quietly. "You will already have looked at my papers and will know I am a student of landscape design at the University of Manchester in England."

"You work for the CIA."

"That's not true," Marten said evenly. He was trying to get some sense of who they were. From the questions they were asking and the way they were going about it he sensed they were either terrorists or drug smugglers, or maybe some combination of both. Whoever they were, they seemed to think that he was a prize, a large fish that had somehow been caught up in their net.

"Why were you in Davos?"

"I—" Marten hesitated, not sure what to say, then decided to tell the truth. "I was invited to a dinner party."

"What kind of dinner party?"

"Just a dinner party."

"It was not 'just a dinner party,' Mr. Marten." The voice suddenly filled with anger. "It was an event to announce the reinstatement of the Tsar of Russia. The Russian president himself attended. There was an envelope in your clothing. Inside it was a very formal card confirming the proclamation. A "souvenir" I think you would call it."

"Envelope?"

"Yes."

For the briefest instant Marten remembered an elegantly dressed maître d' in the villa's ballroom handing him a small plastic-covered packet, which he had simply put in his jacket pocket without looking at shortly before he'd gone out on the trail with Alexander. It had to have been an official remembrance of the affair given to all guests and, like his wallet, must have survived his trip down the mountain river.

"You say you are a student, yet you are invited to this kind of gathering?"

"Yes."

"Why?"

The last thing Marten wanted to tell them about was Rebecca. God only knew what they would do if they discovered he was the brother of the woman who was to become wife to the new Tsar; that would make him a pawn of the highest order salable to any of a dozen terrorist organizations in the world to use in any way they wanted. What he needed was a plausible answer and quickly.

"I was a guest of a professor friend from the university. Her father is a prominent member of the British parliament who was also a guest."

"What is his name?"

Marten hesitated. He hated to give them any information at all, especially naming Clem or her father. On the other hand, it probably wouldn't take a great deal of checking to get the list of the dinner guests that night. For all he knew, it, like most things, would be available on somebody's Web site or perhaps by now even in the press, which might well have been how they knew the Russian president had been there.

"His name is Sir Robert Rhodes Simpson. He is a member of the House of Lords."

For a moment there was no response; then he heard the click of a lighter and heard his man inhale. His interrogator had just lighted a cigarette. A half second later the raspy voice continued, "You were correct when you said we recovered your wallet. In it is a photograph of an attractive young lady pictured in front of a lake. Who is she?"

Marten started. It was Rebecca. The photo was a snapshot he taken shortly after her arrival at Jura. It showed her in health and full of hope and joy. He had liked it enormously and kept it tucked in the back of his wallet.

"I asked you who she is."

Marten swore to himself. He damned the photo. Damned himself for keeping it. Now they had something to tie him to Rebecca. But he couldn't let them find out what the connection was. "A girlfriend."

A vicious slap to the side of his head knocked Marten off the chair and onto the floor. Searing pain shot through the wound in his side. He cried out as rough hands dragged him up and shoved him back onto the chair. A moment later there was a hard tug at his eyes as someone tightened his blindfold.

"Who is she?" the voice repeated.

"I told you, a girlfriend."

"No, she is a fellow asset."

"Asset?" Marten was suddenly puzzled. *Asset* was military or espionage nomenclature. What did he mean? Where was he going with this?

"If you were a guest as you say, then why were you cut with a knife and thrown into the mountain river to die? You work for the CIA and someone found out, the Russians maybe. The trouble for you is"—the voice suddenly became quieter and more threatening—"that you lived."

So that was it. They thought he was an American intelligence operative who had penetrated the inner circle of top-level Russian politics and were guessing that in some way Rebecca was a collaborator.

"I ask you once again, Mr. Marten—who is the girl? What is her name?"

"Her name is Rebecca," Marten said matter-of-factly. He had given them that much and it was all he was going to give. "I do not work for the CIA or any other organization. I am a student at the University of Manchester. I was invited to the dinner in Davos by a professor friend whose father is Sir Robert Rhodes Simpson. I went for a walk in the snow and slipped and fell from a mountain bridge into a fast-running stream and was swept away by the current. My cut came from a sharp rock or stick that was submerged in the water. At some point I dragged myself out of the water and passed out. That was where someone of the family I was with found me, the girl, I think." Marten paused, then finished. "You can believe what you want, but what I've said is the truth."

For a long moment there was silence. Marten could hear rustling as several men changed positions in the room. Then Marten felt his interrogator lean forward. The smell of tobacco on his breath became stronger as he did.

"Please ask yourself this, Mr. Marten," the throaty voice said evenly. "Is continuing to tell falsehoods worth my life? Am I willing to die for these lies I am telling?"

Again there was silence, and Marten had no idea what they were going to do next. Then suddenly the strap binding his hands was pulled from his wrists. He heard the retreat of footsteps and the sound of a door being opened and then closed and locked behind him. Immediately he untied the scarf that blindfolded him. It made little difference; the place where they had brought him was as dark as night.

He got up uncertainly and tried to find the door. His hands moved over one wall and then another, and then another. Finally he felt the door's wood panels. His hands fumbled until he found the knob. It turned but did not open. He pulled hard; nothing happened. He felt across for the hinges and found them, but they were secured tightly. He would need a hammer and chisel or screwdriver to remove them.

He went back across the room, nearly fell over the chair, then sat down. He was in a large closet or inner storeroom of some kind. Occasionally he could hear sounds of the city, a horn or a siren, but that was all. What he had was a chair and darkness and nothing else but the clothes he wore—the same clothes he had worn when he left the ballroom of Villa Enkratzer, the tuxedo Alexander Cabrera had provided, now torn and wrinkled. He reached up and touched his face. What he felt was more than stubble. A full beard had begun to grow.

11

There was a sound and the door opened. He thought he saw three men silhouetted in the dim light of the hallway outside.

"Come." It was the same raspy, accented voice as before.

"What day is this? What month?" Marten demanded, trying at least to get that much.

"Keep quiet!"

Suddenly two men came forward, took hold of him, and led him to the door. For an instant he glimpsed two more balaclava-covered heads waiting in the hallway outside. Again came the blindfold. Then he was taken forward. Then there were the stairs again. This time going down. Three flights. And along a hallway and then a door. Suddenly cold fresh air hit him and he breathed it in deeply.

"Urinate," a voice commanded, "urinate." Hands pushed him against a wall. He fumbled with his fly and took out his penis. He was glad. Before, he had thought he would burst, had pounded on the door and yelled for someone to take him to a toilet, but no one had come, and he had nearly done it on the floor of the room. It was then that the door had opened and they had come in to take him to where he was now, and where he gratefully relieved himself.

The instant he finished and was zipped up, strong arms led him over cobblestones. Then the same arms lifted him, and he felt more hands take him from there. He heard the sound of an overhead door being rolled down. Suddenly whatever he was in lurched forward and he nearly lost his balance. Once again his wrists were bound and then hands took him and forced him facedown on the floor. The smell was musty, and he knew he was in the back of a truck and on a carpet of some kind. There was another lurch as the vehicle picked up speed. Suddenly he felt the carpet pulled up against his shoulders, and then he was rolled over, and then over again, and again.

"My God," he thought, "they're rolling me inside a carpet."

Then the rolling stopped. Everything was silent except for the sound of the truck as the driver shifted once more, and then they were on a smooth road traveling at highway speed.

12

MOSCOW. THURSDAY, JANUARY 30. 6:20 P.M.

Thirteen days after Zurich Kantonspolizei Inspector Beelr had mailed it, the envelope arrived and was waiting on the side table in the hallway when Kovalenko came in.

"Papa." His daughter, nine-year-old Yelena, ran down the hallway. "Guess what I did in school, Papa?"

"I don't know, what did you do?" Kovalenko picked up the envelope.

"Guess."

"Guess what? You do a hundred things."

"Guess anyway."

"You did a painting."

"How did you know?"

"I guessed."

"What's it about?"

"I don't know." He turned the envelope over in his hands, unsure what to do with it. Chief Inspector Irina Malikova had told him to bring the disk directly to her the moment he got it, day or night. Why, when barely a heartbeat earlier she had told him "it should be more than apparent the first Tsarevich of All Russia since the revolution cannot also be a common criminal. A murderer." So once she had the disk, what did she intend to do with it?

On the other hand—with Alexander Cabrera, and Marten's sister, a sister by adoption, the media was reminded, suddenly found to be a member of European royalty, the toast not only of Russia but the world—what would *he* do with it? He had been ordered to turn the disk over the minute he got it. Who knew if he was being watched by his own department to make certain he did, or if the Postal Security Service had been instructed to look for mail coming to him from Europe and report it immediately upon delivery. So what was his alternative? Take a chance and make a copy of the disk, then work on his own to get the Tsarevich's fingerprints so that he could prove to the world their beloved Alexander Romanov was really the crazed killer Raymond Oliver Thorne?

Maybe, just maybe, if Marten were alive, he might have made a copy and risked losing his job or even serving time in prison so they could have done something together. But maybe was not a viable concept because Marten was dead and he had been called back to Moscow, which essentially took him off the case. Chief Inspector Malikova was waiting for him to deliver the goods when he got them. Now he held them in his hand.

"Papa," Yelena asked impatiently, "what are you doing?"

"Thinking."

"About my picture?"

"Yes."

"Well, what is it?"

"A horse."

"No, a person."

"I suppose you want me to guess what person too."

"No, silly," Yelena giggled, then took him by the hand and led him down the hallway to the kitchen. Tatyana was standing at the stove, her back to him. Sons Oleg and Konstantin were already at the table, waiting to eat. Yelena picked a drawing from a side table and held it behind her back, grinning impishly at her father. "It's a portrait. Somebody you know."

"Your Mamma."

"No."

"Oleg."

"No."

"Konstantin."

"No."

"Yelena, I cannot guess everyone in the world."

"Try one more time."

"Just tell me who."

"You!" With a beaming cry Yelena held up a perfect carica-
ture of Kovalenko. Big eyes in a wide face covered with a big
beard, over a big belly.

"Is that what I look like?"

"Yes, Papa. I love you."

Kovalenko grinned and for the moment let the idea of the
disk and everything that went with it go out of his mind.

"I love you, too, Yelena." Bending down, he picked up his
daughter and put his head against hers, as if she and nothing
else were all that mattered in the world.

13

MINISTRY OF JUSTICE. 9:30 P.M.

Click.

Raymond Oliver Thorne's LAPD booking photograph appeared on Chief Inspector Irina Malikova's seventeen-inch computer screen. Two photographs, full front, and then profile.

Her hand touched the mouse.

Click.

Raymond Oliver Thorne's fingerprints. Clear, perfectly
readable.

Malikova looked at Kovalenko. "There are no other copies?"

"As I said before, there are none that I know of. The hard
files and numerous data banks containing Thorne's records are
gone, either simply stolen or hacked into and deleted. The same
way people who helped Thorne escape from the L.A. hospital
or were involved in transferring a 'John Doe' body from the
morgue to the crematorium in his place have either vanished or
are dead. The plastic surgeon who went to Argentina to rebuild
Cabrera's face and body after his 'hunting accident' is also
dead, caught in a building fire that not only killed him but destroyed all of his records."

"And these?" Irina Malikova looked at the rest of the contents of the envelope Kovalenko had brought: a plane ticket in the name of James Halliday from Los Angeles to Buenos Aires—and a page torn from Halliday's appointment book noting the trail of a plastic surgeon named Hermann Gray whom Halliday had followed from Los Angeles to Costa Rica to Argentina.

"I thought you should have everything," Kovalenko said quietly. He had told Marten he had given Inspector Beelr an envelope with the computer disk and Halliday's airline ticket in it to mail to his wife. He had said nothing about including a page from Halliday's book. There had been no reason.

"No one else knows of these?"

"No."

"Not the French?"

"No."

"The FSO?"

"No."

"Thank you, Inspector."

Kovalenko hesitated. "What do you intend to do with them?"

"Do with what?"

"The material, Chief Inspector."

"What material, Inspector Kovalenko?"

Kovalenko stared at her for a moment. "I see," he said and stood. "Good night, Chief Inspector."

"Good night, Inspector Kovalenko."

Kovalenko felt her eyes follow him as he crossed the cubicle and walked out the door.

There was no material. No computer disk, no plane ticket, no page from an appointment book. What Halliday had died for, what he and Marten had so carefully kept from Lenard, what he had given her, simply did not exist. And never had.

14

"You work for the CIA."

"No, I am a student."

"How did you penetrate the Russian inner circle?"

"I am a student."

"Who is Rebecca?"

"A girlfriend."

"Where is she now?"

"I don't know."

"You work for the CIA. Who is your handler? Where is your base?"

In the dark Marten had no idea where he was, or how long he had been there. Two days, three, four. A week. Maybe even more. The ride in the truck, bound and rolled up in the carpet, had seemed interminable but in reality had probably been no more than five or six hours. Afterward, he'd been taken out blindfolded. As in Rotterdam there had been stairs, four flights this time, and as in Rotterdam he'd been put alone into a small, windowless room. The only difference was that here he had a small water closet with a toilet and washbasin and a cot with a pillow and blankets. What had happened to the family who had saved him, he couldn't begin to imagine.

Over that same period his captors had bound his wrists and taken him blindfolded from the room at least a dozen times, walking him down a flight of stairs to a room where the man with the throaty voice and strong tobacco breath and thick accent waited to ask the same questions as before. Each time he gave the same answers. And when he did the questions began all over again.

"You work for the CIA. How did you penetrate the Russian inner circle?"

"My name is Nicholas Marten. I am a student—"

"You work for the CIA. Who is your handler? Where is your base?"

"My name is—"

"Who is Rebecca? Where is she now?"

"My name is—"

By now it had become a game of wills. Even though, as an LAPD homicide detective, Marten had been well schooled in the art of interrogation, he had not been taught what it was like to be on the other end of the stick, being interrogated instead of doing the interrogating, and certainly he had no defense lawyer to intervene on his behalf. He felt like a captured soldier giving name, rank, and serial number. And like a captured soldier, he knew that his first duty was to escape. But that had been impossible. He was under their control twenty-four hours a day, either alone, locked inside the room in the dark with balaclava-hooded guards outside his door, or—the door suddenly opening, the balaclavas storming in to bind his wrists and take him blindfolded down the stairs for more interrogation.

He had been given food and water and the means to keep himself more or less physically clean. Curiously, aside from the constant darkness—or blindfolds, which amounted to the same thing—and the interrogations that brought with them the odd shove or slap, he had not been harmed or physically mistreated. Yet, the endless passage of time aside, the worst thing was not knowing. For all his guessing, he had no idea who his captors were or what they were doing or plotting, or what they really expected to gain by keeping him imprisoned. Nor had he any idea how long it would go on—or if, at some point, they would tire of the interrogations and simply kill him.

Though he did his best not to show it, it was wearing him down. With no idea if it was day or night, with no sense of the passage of time, he was beginning to lose touch with reality. Worse, his nerves seemed filled with electricity and he knew he was edging into paranoia. The dark was bad enough, but increasingly he found himself listening for the slightest sound outside his door that would tell him they were coming again. Coming to take him and blindfold and bind him and take him down for more questioning. Sometimes he heard different sounds, or he thought he did. The worst were sharp and scratching. Always they began as one or two and then quickly became five, ten, fifty, a hundred until he was certain there were thousands of tiny scurrying feet outside his door, an army of rats scratching away at the woodwork trying to get in. How many times had he jumped from his cot and rushed to the door in the dark, yelling and banging on it to drive them away, only to stop a heartbeat later when he knew he had heard nothing at all?

Every so often, once a day, he believed, the door would open and the balaclavas would come in. There were always two of them, and they would leave food and then go back out without a word. Sometimes nothing else happened for days on end. Those were the times he actually wanted to be taken down and questioned. It was a human interaction, even though it was always accusatory and always the same.

By now the interrogator's voice had nearly become his own, with its familiar cadence and the accent he still could not place. The once nauseating smell of his tobacco breath had become almost welcome. A narcotic of some kind. To keep his sanity and survive, he knew, he had to wholly change his mind-set and focus not on his captors or the darkness but on something else entirely.

And he had.

It was Rebecca. How she had looked and been when he had last seen her at the villa in Davos. The adoring bride-to-be, the next Tsarina of Russia. He thought of her emotional condition then and what it would be now. If she thought he was dead, and how she would react to his death. And if she was still being innocently swept along in the wake of Cabrera's covert and bloody seizure of the Russian throne.

Swept along.

Because she loved him.

And knew he loved her.

And had no idea who he was.

Or what he had done.

"Who is Rebecca?"
"A girlfriend."

"You work for the CIA."

"No."

"How did you penetrate the Russian inner circle?"

"I am a student."

"Where is Rebecca now?"

"I don't know."

"You work for the CIA. Who is your handler? Where is your base?"

"No!" Marten said out loud. The interrogator's voice was inside his head battling him as if they were in the interrogation room. He was doing it to himself, as he knew they wanted, but it was a game he refused to play. Abruptly he pushed himself up from the cot where he sat in the dark and found his way to the tiny water closet. There he flushed the toilet and waited, listening to the water run down and the toilet basin refill. There was only one reason he'd done it. To keep the voice away. He flushed again, and then once more. Finally he went back and found the cot and lay down to stare into the darkness.

He knew his captors were using the dark and staggering the time between interrogations to deliberately disorient him, increasing his anxiety and making him fear their return all that much more. Their purpose was clear, to let him drive himself to the point where he would crumble and admit almost anything they demanded, which would allow them to use him as a huge playing card, especially if he confessed to being a CIA operative. And they wanted to make a political example of him. So crumbling was something he had to deny them. To do it he had to retain his sanity. The best way to do that, he realized, was to deliberately shift his thoughts from the present and focus on the past, replaying memories. And he had.

Mostly they were from long ago, of Rebecca growing up, of himself and Dan Ford as boys, riding bikes and teasing girls, and then he remembered what he had thought of after he had seen Dan's body in the Citroen as it was pulled from the Seine—the homemade rocket-launcher explosion that, at age ten, caused Dan to lose his right eye. And he wondered again whether, if Dan had had his full sight, he might have seen Raymond sooner, and in doing so would have had a chance to save himself. Tragically it was a question that would never be answered and only added to Marten's terrible and immense guilt.

With it came another thought, one he had continually tried to push away but that kept coming back. What if, in the auto body garage, with the squad watching, he had simply done what Valparaiso had urged and put his own Double Eagle Colt to Raymond's head and pulled the trigger? If he had done that, none of the rest would ever have happened.

15

The *rest*.

"The pieces."

"The pieces that will ensure the future."

Marten could still see Raymond on the Metrolink train in L.A. Hear his words as clearly as if he were saying them this moment.

"What pieces?" Marten had demanded.

He could still see Raymond's slow, calculated, arrogant smile as he answered. "That, you will have to find out for yourself."

Well, he had. He knew what the "pieces" were. The vintage Spanish Navaja switchblade and the 8 mm film. Film, he was certain, that had been taken of Raymond/Alexander killing his half brother in Paris twenty years earlier.

He knew what "ensure the future" meant, too. It was *Alexander's* future, because having the "pieces," the knife and the condemning film, meant he was no longer under threat from exposure to, or prosecution from, that murder.

Earlier, in surmising what might have happened in the park, he suggested to Kovalenko that perhaps someone had been taking home movies of the birthday party and had inadvertently filmed the murder. Now he wondered if that someone had been Alfred Neuss. If so, had he somehow come to take possession of the murder weapon afterward? And then, knowing full well who the killer had been—and as one of Peter Kitner's oldest friends—had said nothing to the police and given that friend both the knife and the film, which Kitner then asked him to be caretaker of?

And had Neuss, knowing who Kitner really was, quietly and clandestinely, and with Kitner's permission, divulged that information to the four handpicked Romanov family members living in the Americas and far from the tragedy in Paris? Swearing them to secrecy, had he asked them to be keepers of the safe deposit keys at the request of the true head of the imperial family? That possibility, and the way the victims had been tortured before they had been killed, made Marten think Neuss had not given a specific reason for his request or explained the why of the keys themselves, or told the location of the box they would open. Perhaps the people had not even known about the keys at all. Maybe each had simply been given a sealed package or envelope with the instructions that if anything were to happen to Kitner the envelopes or packages were to be sent immediately to a third party—the French police maybe, or perhaps to Neuss's or Kitner's legal representatives. Or maybe to some combination of all three?

Elaborate? Perhaps.

Unnecessary? Maybe.

But considering the cunning and reach of the Baroness, it might well have been a kind of fail-safe tactic to provide another level of protection against someone trying to retrieve the "pieces."

If Marten continued that line of reasoning and it had indeed been Neuss who had shot the film, it was clear he would have also been an eyewitness to the murder and therefore a very necessary subject for elimination. Why Alexander and the Baroness had waited for so many years to act, to retrieve the "pieces" and take care of Neuss was a mystery, unless—as Marten had suggested to Kovalenko before—the Baroness had used those years to carefully watch the course of history and, after the fall of the Soviet Union and sensing what was to come, had begun forcefully and deliberately courting the major power brokers inside Russia. Not just those in business and politics as he had thought earlier but also, as he had seen firsthand at the villa in Davos, those at the highest levels of the Orthodox Church and the Russian military.

With her influence in place, and knowing full well who Kitner really was, the Baroness would have bided her time until she was certain the social and economic conditions were primed for a return of the monarchy. When that time came, she made her move, quietly divulging to the proper persons Kitner's true identity and thus setting in motion the legal and technical apparatus to confirm beyond doubt who he was.

Once that was done, and perhaps even at the Baroness's further urging, Kitner was invited to meet with the Russian president and/or other top representatives of the Russian government, presented with the findings, and asked to head a new constitutional monarchy. When he had agreed and the plans and dates were firmly set—first, for his presentation to the Romanov family the day after he was knighted in London, and second, for the public announcement to be made several weeks later in Moscow—the Baroness and Alexander put their precisely timed, surgical plan into action. It would be done so swiftly that Kitner could suspect nothing until it was too late, because by then the Romanovs would already know who he was and that the Russian government had formally, if secretly, acknowledged him as the new monarch.

It was a move made, Marten saw, as a carefully calculated measure that not only announced the restoration of the monarchy with Kitner recognized as the rightful heir to the throne, but opened the door wide for his abdication to his eldest son. Even with all that had happened, Marten had to marvel at the Baroness's guile. By the very presence of the president of Russia, the Patriarch of the Orthodox Church, the mayor of Moscow, and the Russian Federation minister of defense at the villa in Davos, there was little doubt she had paved the way for Alexander as well, perhaps by convincing them that Alexander had the one thing Kitner did not, youth—and the huge public romance that went with it, especially when he was about to take as his bride a young, royally titled, educated, sophisticated beauty like Rebecca.

And each—president, patriarch, mayor, minister of defense—for his own reasons, and in one way or another, would have agreed, or he would not have come in the first place. How or when the Baroness had accomplished that, or the way in which she had presented Alexander to them, was impossible to know. The fact was she had. And Kitner, it seemed, was to have been the last to know of his own abdication. It was a fait accompli, done even before he signed it.

Judging from the Baroness's consummate planning and Raymond's lethal ability, it was a plot that should have gone off without a hitch—retrieve the safe deposit keys, eliminate the four Romanovs who possessed them, then kill Neuss and recover the condemning "pieces." Then, the day after Kitner was presented to the Romanov family in London, have the FSO colonel Murzin bring him to the house on Uxbridge Street, make it known they were in possession of the "pieces," and demand that he abdicate. And Kitner, terrified Alexander would kill him or one of his family, as he had so boldly proven he could do and would do and had done, even as a child, would comply—to protect his life and those of his wife and other children.

Neuss had been last on the list to be killed—when, as an eye-witness to Raymond/Alexander's murder of Paul, it would have seemed logical to eliminate him first. That might have been because they were afraid Neuss himself was part of the fail-safe plan and killing him could trigger a major alarm, causing the Romanovs to instantly send the safe deposit keys wherever they had been instructed to. So instead they had resolved those problems first, retrieving the keys and killing the Romanovs who had them. The killing of Neuss would then be the exclamation point to this part of their game, designed as much to terrify Kitner as to eliminate the jeweler. Of course, there was always the possibility that if Kitner learned about the killings of the Romanovs and Neuss and about the missing keys he would panic and stop the entire process—which, in retrospect, and with Neuss's arrival in London, was exactly what he had done—but, with Murzin and the FSO poised to take control the moment he was presented to the family and counting on Kitner's own eagerness to gain the throne, it was a chance they obviously had been willing to take.

Yet as much as Marten's analysis seemed reasonable, he knew there was no way to be certain he was right. There might have been other things at play entirely.

But the order of things aside, it was a plan that should have worked. Except that it didn't because fate had suddenly intervened and two wholly unforeseen things, one after the other, ran all of it straight into the ground. First, they failed to realize the keepers of the keys had no idea where the box was that the keys would open; second, the ice storm had put Alexander, as Raymond Thorne, on the same train as Frank Donlan.

Angry that it had taken him so long to understand what had been going on, and angry at his continued and forced confinement here, Marten again got up from the cot, this time not to go to the toilet but to pace the room in the dark. It was five strides from one wall to the other before he had to turn around and go back. He crossed it once and then again. As he crossed the third time his thoughts went to the knife Alexander had used to try to kill him on the mountain trail. Almost certainly it was the Spanish switchblade retrieved from Fabien Curtay's safe in Monaco and most probably the same knife used to kill Kitner's son twenty years earlier in Paris. And in all likelihood was the same razor-sharp weapon used to kill Halliday and Dan Ford and the printer's rep Jean-Luc Vabres and the Zurich printer Hans Lossberg. Kovalenko had said that at one time he thought what he was looking at was ritual killing, and maybe that was how it had begun—Alexander killing the younger Paul to throw fear and terror into Kitner's soul and at the same time removing his next eldest son, who might have become a rival to Alexander for the throne.

But then, as an adult, he had become a coldly dispassionate soldier, using a gun to commit the murders in the Americas and to kill Neuss and Curtay in Europe. With the "pieces" in his possession, that impersonal gun had suddenly been replaced by the very personal knife he had used to begin his journey. Why? Was it now, after everything, when he saw the throne nearly within his grasp, that there had come an almost primal need to prove to himself and to the Baroness, even to the world, that he was at the top of his game and worthy of being called Tsar of all Russia? With the abrupt casting aside of the gun for the very singular ritual of the knife he now had back in his possession, with the blood and the vicious slaughter of his victims, was he, consciously or subconsciously, demonstrating that he was indeed capable of presiding over Russia with an iron hand?

Kovalenko had thought that he might be looking at ritual murder, and Marten, at the same time, had suggested, based on the use of the knife and the manner of the slayings, that the killer seemed to be losing control. Now, seeing Alexander as some kind of warrior-king nearing the end of a murderous, exhausting, almost lifelong campaign (with his prize, the throne of Russia, finally in view), suddenly reunited with his symbolic knife and using it so savagely and emotionally to eradicate the last impediments to his goal—it appeared both of them had been right.

Yet for all that, there was something else. In remembering the way Alexander had looked at Rebecca that night at the villa in Davos with unconditional love in his eyes, Marten wondered if he wasn't being torn in another way as well. Perhaps too much ambition, too much battle, too much blood and violence were being intensely countered by his total love for Rebecca and the sea of calm that came with it. And that part of him wanted nothing at all to do with the sadistic whirlwind of murder and bloodshed that came with the quest for the throne or even the throne itself. If true, it would mean there was a monstrous psychotic conflict going on inside him that would rage all the more feverishly as the days wore on and his coronation drew ever nearer.

Then there was his mother, the Baroness, for years intricately acting the part of his guardian, the sister of his deceased mother, who, in truth, never existed.

Who was she in all of this?

16

Marten crossed the room again, this time stopping to listen at the door. He waited, listening intently, but he heard nothing. Finally he went to the washbasin and splashed cold water on his face, then rubbed his wet hands across the back of his neck and stood still, feeling the cool of it and taking a moment out of time. Sixty seconds later he sat down on his cot to cross his legs and lean back against the wall, determined to put more of the parts together, to make himself understand the whole of it. He knew that he if ever got away from his captors, the greater the understanding he had about what had gone on, the better he would be prepared to deal with what would come next—freeing Rebecca from the monster who held her.

Peter Kitner, it was apparent, governed his private life by imperial convention. His only publicly known marriage had been into royalty. His wife was the cousin of the King of Spain. It was a move to suggest Kitner himself had long ago prepared for some future time when the Russian throne might be restored and he, as the true head of the imperial family, would be made Tsar.

For Marten, knowing Kitner was Alexander's father and the Baroness was his mother, that raised the question—what had happened?

What if, years ago, Kitner and the Baroness had been lovers? Most certainly she would have learned who he was and about the same time become pregnant with Alexander. Possibly, and as a result, Kitner had married her and afterward there was a fight or a falling-out of some kind, which might have included his family, and they were divorced or the marriage had been annulled, maybe even before Alexander was born—and then not too long afterward Kitner married into Spanish royalty, a socially appropriate move for a man who was directly in line to become a monarch himself.

The Baroness might well have been enraged enough to spend the rest of her life seeking not only revenge but power, determined to have what she felt was rightfully hers in the event the imperial throne was ever restored to the man whose first male child she had borne. What if she had begun that long, determined, and hateful war by marrying into extreme wealth and social influence?

Later, when her son was old enough, she might have initiated a secret, conspiratorial partnership with him, telling him who his father really was and what he and his family had done to her and, in turn, to him, and vowing that if the day ever came when Russia restored the monarchy to the imperial family it would be he, Alexander, and not Peter Kitner who would become Tsar.

It was a goal she might have achieved without violence through the use of her position and vast wealth to gain influence with the necessary power brokers, but instead she had chosen blood. Why? Who knew? Maybe she felt it was the price a Tsar and his family—and the necessary others along the way—had to pay for casting her and her child out. Whatever the reason, violent and twisted as it was, it was the path she had pursued for years, slowly manipulating her son into the role and blood-spattered mind-set of the terrible Tsars of old, schooling him, in the process, in the fine art of killing. Finally, when he was a young teenager, she put his fingers to the fire, commanding him to take his first brutal steps toward the throne himself by eliminating his closest possible challenger, his own half brother, Paul.

And Kitner, shocked and horrified, afraid for the safety of the rest of his family, fearful of exposing his past for fear of damning his future, with the killing weapon and film of the event in his possession, had confronted both Alexander and the Baroness and made a pact. Instead of turning Alexander over to the police, he would send him into exile in Argentina, most probably with some kind of stipulation that Alexander would never reveal his true identity and therefore never be able to make claim to the throne.

Once again Marten pushed off of the cot to walk those five short paces back and forth in the inky darkness. Maybe he was wrong but he didn't think so. It might sound like an over-the-top scenario tailor-made for the movies, but in truth it wasn't all that different from cases Marten had seen on the streets of L.A. where the scorned woman found her former lover or husband in a bar and stabbed him to death with a knife or shot him five times in the head. What made this different was that such women did not use their children to do the deed. Maybe that was the distinction between ordinary people and those driven by hatred and maniacal ambition, or by the extreme seduction of the highest levels of power.

Suddenly he thought of Jura and the Rothfels and wondered if the Baroness had manipulated that, too. He remembered worrying to Rebecca's psychiatrist, Dr. Maxwell-Scot, that Jura was far too expensive for him, and he remembered being told that Rebecca's expenses, like those of all of the patients there, were covered in full by the foundation as stipulated by the grant from the benefactor who provided the facility.

"Who *is* the benefactor?" Marten had asked and was told that the patron preferred to remain anonymous. At the time he had accepted it, but now—

"Anonymous, hell!" he said angrily out loud in the dark. "It was the Baroness."

The abrupt sound of the key in the door lock made him freeze where he was, and then the door opened.

There were two of them as usual, with two more in the hallway outside. They were big and wore the balaclavas, and shut the door almost immediately, using flashlights to see by. One carried a large water bottle and had a loaf of black bread and cheese and an apple.

Suddenly Marten was swept with anger. He wanted to be free and he wanted to be free right now!

"I do not work for the CIA or anyone else!" Marten said abruptly and heatedly to the man closest to him. "I am a student, nothing else. When are you going to believe that? When?"

Abruptly the man who had brought him the food swung his flashlight, putting the beam directly in Marten's eyes.

"Be quiet," he grunted. "Be quiet." Immediately he turned the light toward the other man, who carried something Marten could not see and had moved to the far wall and was running the beam of his flashlight over the base of it looking for something. Then he found what he was looking for, an electrical socket. Kneeling, he plugged in a cord of some kind. Marten felt his heart skip with joy. They were giving him a lamp! Anything was better than the perpetual dark. Then he heard a click but no light came on. Instead something began to glow a grayish white and a small picture appeared. On it he saw a German shepherd racing across the screen in black and white. Immediately the picture cut and he saw a troop of U.S. cavalry charging across the desert following the dog.

"Rin Tin Tin," one of the balaclavas said in English, and then they left, closing the door behind them and locking it. They had brought him food and water and a television.

17

Why they had given it to him he didn't know. It didn't matter. The television was *Light*. After days in darkness he embraced it as if it were an icon. Within the hour it had become a companion, and within the day, a friend. That it received only one channel didn't matter, nor that the reception, depending on how he manipulated the wire antenna, was alternately clear and crisp or maddeningly impossible, with snowy images and heavily distorted sound. The sound was unimportant anyway because, for the most part, the broadcast was in German, a language he didn't understand at all. But it made no difference. The television was a connection, however slight, to a world outside his own mind. Never mind that it broadcast mainly old American television shows dubbed into German. For hours he sat fascinated by *Davy Crockett*, *Andy Griffith*, *Father Knows Best*, *Gunsmoke*, *Dobie Gillis*, *F Troop*, *The Three Stooges*, *Miami Vice*, *Magnum, P.I.*, more *Three Stooges*, *Hogan's Heroes*, *Gilligan's Island*, *Leave It to Beaver*, more *Three Stooges*—none of it mattered. For the first time in days there was something besides himself and his own anger and thoughts and inky darkness.

Then something totally different happened and everything changed—the evening news came on. Live and broadcast in German, it seemed to originate from Hamburg, but it showed video clips from around the world, many with interviews broadcast in the language of that country, with a German narrative explaining what was happening. Not only did he hear English, he saw stories from New York, Washington, San Francisco, London, Rome, Cairo, Tel Aviv, South Africa. Little by little he began to piece together the day and date, even the time.

It was 7:50 P.M., Friday, March 7, exactly seven weeks since he'd gone into the water above Villa Enkratzer. Suddenly he thought of Rebecca. Where was she right now and what had happened? By this time they must have given him up for dead.

How had she reacted to that? Was she alright or had she slipped back to the horrible state she'd been in before? And what about Alexander, or more rightly *Raymond!* Was he already Tsar? Was it possible they could have been married?

As if in divine answer, they suddenly appeared on the television screen— Rebecca, smiling warmly and dressed as elegantly as he'd ever seen her, and Raymond, his hair perfect, wearing a smartly cut business suit, his beard gone. And still wholly unrecognizable as Raymond Thorne. They were walking down a hallway inside Buckingham Palace with Her Majesty, the Queen of England. As quickly, the story cut to virtually the same scene in Washington, D.C., only this time they were in the White House rose garden and in the company of the President of the United States.

The German narrative overrode the bits of English he was getting as the president spoke, but even with the German he could understand, the information being given—the marriage between Alexander Nikolaevich Romanov, Tsarevich of Russia, and Alexandra Elisabeth Gabrielle Christian, Princess of Denmark, was to take place in Moscow on Wednesday, May 1, the old Soviet May Day, to be followed immediately by the coronation of the Tsar at the Kremlin.

Marten turned down the sound of the television to stand there stunned, staring blankly at the screen. He had to do something. But what? He was a prisoner and trapped in this room.

Suddenly emotion rose. He turned and went to the door and pounded on it, yelling for someone to open it. He had to get out. He had to get out *now!*

How long he stood there pounding and carrying on, he didn't know. But no one came, and finally he stopped and crossed back to stare at the television on the floor, its white glow faintly illuminating the room.

Click.

Angrily he turned it off. The glow faded and he went back to his cot and lay down, listening to his own deep breaths. Before, light had meant everything. Now, darkness had become equally welcome.

18

CORONATION/STATE DINNER
GRAND KREMLIN PALACE
St. George Hall/1 May—seating approximately 2,000
(to be confirmed)

Primary Menu

Soup—Ukrainian borscht
Fish—Braised sturgeon
Salad—salat izkrasnoy svykly (beet salad)
Entrée—Beef stroganoff with stuffed eggplant
Relevée—Braised rabbit with four-root purée
Dessert—Crêpes with lingonberries, honey, and brandy
Beverages—Russian vodka, Russian Champagne;
wines—Beaujolais, Moselle, Petsouka, Novysuet
Reserve, Burgundy, Château d'Yquem/Champagne; tea
and coffee

Alexander stood behind an antique desk in the eighth-floor
Presidential Suite studying the menu for his coronation dinner.
Other agendas awaited discussion: security; the Tsarevich's
itinerary for the next six weeks, which included travel plans and
housing arrangements for himself, Rebecca, and the Baroness;
television and other media interviews; plans for the wedding
and for the coronation itself, the seating, the route, the costumes, the carriages.

Across from him Colonel Murzin worked several telephones
at once, as did Igor Lukin, his newly appointed private secretary.
Farther across the room, a half-dozen secretaries huddled
around temporary desks, and these were only the immediate few.

The entire eighth floor had been taken over by the Tsarevich's staff of nearly three hundred. It was as if they were planning a presidential inauguration, the Olympics, the Super Bowl, the World Cup, and the Academy Awards all rolled into one. And in a way they were. It was a vast and huge undertaking—and, to all those personally involved, thrilling. It had never happened in their lifetimes and, barring illness or accident, probably never would again. On May 1 Alexander would become Tsar for life, and he was only thirty-four years old.

It seemed to matter little to anyone that the politics of it made his position merely titular. It was the sentiment of it that was magic, which of course was why the throne had been reinstated in the first place. It was an elixir to divert the attention of the Russian people from the world surrounding them—the endless, dismal poverty; the corruption; street crime; the bloody, rebellious turmoil of the breakaway states—and direct it toward a national conscience of hope and pride that reveled in the youth and glamour of a Russian Camelot, a picture-perfect image of wealth and joy and happiness, and the way life could and should be.

Abruptly Alexander put down the menu and looked toward his private secretary. "Do we have the revised guest list?"

"It has just been finished, Tsarevich." Igor Lukin walked to one of the secretaries, retrieved a typed list, and brought it to Alexander.

Alexander took it and walked over to stand in the large window warmed by bright sunshine to study it. Other details aside, it was the list of invited guests, gone over and revised any number of times, that really interested him.

He could feel his heartbeat pick up and sweat bead on his upper lip as he scanned the pages. There was one name in particular that kept reappearing, and each time he saw it he asked that it be deleted. He was sure it had been now but had to make certain.

Page ten, eleven. He scanned to the bottom of the twelfth page and then turned to the thirteenth. Eight lines down and—"*O gospodi!*" God!—he swore under his breath. It was still there.

NICHOLAS MARTEN.

"Why is Nicholas Marten still listed?" He said loudly, not hiding his anger. The secretaries looked up as one. Murzin did, too. "Nicholas Marten is deceased. I asked that his name be removed. Why is it still here?"

Igor Lukin came toward him. "It was removed, Tsarevich."

"Then why is it back?"

"The Tsarina, Tsarevich. She saw it missing and demanded it be put back."

"The Tsarina?"

"Yes."

Alexander glanced off, then looked at Murzin. "Where is she now?"

"With the Baroness."

"I want to see her, alone."

"Of course, Tsarevich. Where?"

Alexander hesitated. He wanted her away, isolated from anyone else. "Have her brought to my office at the Kremlin."

19

THE KREMLIN, TEREM PALACE—THE PRIVATE
CHAMBERS BUILT IN THE SEVENTEENTH CENTURY FOR
TSAR MIKHAIL ROMANOV, FIRST TSAR OF THE
ROMANOV DYNASTY. 11:55 A.M.

Rebecca was already there when he came in. She was sitting in a high-backed chair against a tapestried wall in the elaborate red and gold room that had been Tsar Mikhail's private study and that Alexander had taken as his own.

"You wanted to see me?" she asked quietly. "I was about to lunch with the Baroness."

"It's about the guest list, Rebecca." He still wanted to call her Alexandra. As Rebecca she was not of royal lineage, not worthy of becoming the wife of the head of the imperial family, but as European royalty, as Alexandra, daughter of the hereditary

Prince of Denmark, she was. Still, he followed her wishes, and besides, Rebecca was how the world knew her.

"I had your brother's name removed. You had it put back. Why?"

"Because he will come."

"Rebecca, I know how painful his death was for you and for all of us. How heartbreaking it still is. But the guest list will become a public document, and I cannot have a man who everyone knows is dead, and for whom the coroner's office in Davos formally filed a death certificate almost two months ago, be invited to the coronation. It is not only bad taste, it is bad luck."

"Bad luck? For whom?"

"Just—bad luck. Do I make myself clear? Do you understand?"

"Do what you want with the list. But he is not dead. I know that in here." She touched her heart. "Now, may I go? The Baroness is waiting."

Alexander's eyes locked on Rebecca's. He must have said yes or nodded or something, because a moment later she turned and left.

That his memory of actually seeing her leave the room was vague was understandable, because his mind had already drifted to something else, something he had felt before but never as strongly as now. The first time he'd noticed it had been during the search for Marten's body when they'd hunted hour after hour along the river near Villa Enkratzer and found no trace of him. It came again during the memorial service in Manchester. It was a rite without a body and only an assumption of death. The ceremony had been performed only after Alexander had convinced Lord Prestbury and Lady Clementine of the importance of bringing closure to Marten's death, saying he wanted to spare Rebecca any more pain than she had already suffered.

Her staunch refusal to accept the fact of her brother's death in the car immediately after the service struck the chord in him once again. And later, when she insisted on continuing to make the monthly rent payments on his Manchester flat. And her continuing defiance now, weeks later, and so publicly among the staff, with the guest list. And then again here, when he'd admonished her and she'd simply dismissed the guest list, emphasizing instead her enduring belief that Nicholas was alive.

Her belief troubled him as never before, gnawing and twisting inside him. He could see it like a dark spot on an X-ray, its tiny fibrous root starting to take hold in his organs, a disease beginning to spread. With it came a single word.

Fear.

Fear that Rebecca was right and that Marten was alive, and somewhere turning his eyes toward Moscow. Maybe not taking action yet, but soon, when his body was healed from the knife wounds and whatever beating he had taken in the river. What would happen if Marten came and laid bare who he really was and who he thought and could prove Alexander was? What if, as a result, Alexander were suddenly whisked from public view? The official account would be that he had suddenly taken ill and could no longer reign. And what if, afterward, they asked his father to retract his abdication and made him Tsarevich after all? And what if, because of it, Rebecca refused to marry him?

In the pit of his stomach a pulsating rhythm began. It was distant, even faint, but there nonetheless, like a metronome mimicking the beat of his heart.

Boom, boom, it went.

Boom, boom.

Boom, boom.

Boom, boom.

20

MONDAY, MARCH 31.

The glow of the television in the dark. Again. *The Three Stooges, Gilligan's Island, Miami Vice, The Ed Sullivan Show.*

Again.

The Three Stooges, Gilligan's Island, Miami Vice, The Ed Sullivan Show.

Again.

The Three Stooges, Gilligan's Island, Miami Vice, The Ed Sullivan Show.

Nicholas Marten dozed and woke and dozed. And then he got up and did the best he could trying to regain his physical strength and, afterward, keep it. An hour, two hours, three, every day. Sit-ups, push-ups, trunk twists, leg-lifts, single-leg balances, stretching, running in place. His broken ribs and bruises from the river were now all but healed. The same was true of his knife wounds.

How long he had been there he didn't know, but it felt as if it had been forever. It seemed like weeks since he'd last been interrogated. The intensity that had been there in the beginning had slowly subsided. It made him wonder what had happened. Maybe his raspy-voiced interrogator had gone to do other things, leaving a skeleton crew behind to keep watch on him. Or perhaps he'd been caught and arrested. Or perhaps he had gone to another part of the world to tell them about the American he had as a prisoner and to try and make a deal for him. Even if he wasn't CIA, they could still kill him and leave his body somewhere and claim he was, for whatever advantage it might give them.

Every day when they came with food, he pressed them, asking them *why?* Why were they keeping him? What did they plan to do with him? Every day he got the same answer. "Be quiet. Be quiet." Then they left his food and walked out. After that came the dreaded sound of the door as it was locked.

Again.

The Three Stooges, Gilligan's Island, Miami Vice, The Ed Sullivan Show. This time with *Rin Tin Tin* thrown in.

He was beginning to think maybe the shows weren't on at all. Maybe the screen was blank and the reruns were simply in his mind. Maybe he had switched the lone broadcast channel to a band with nothing on it just to keep the TV on for its light. He didn't know, didn't remember. Everything hung on the evening news, but it was increasingly difficult to get a sense of what time of day or night it was on or what the date was, because they had begun broadcasting the news the same as they did the series, over and over, the same thing as many as eight times a day. Moreover, the last story he'd seen about Alexander and Rebecca had been days earlier. Curiously, it had been funny and had made him laugh out loud—the first laughter he could remember in months.

The media, on a tear to learn about Rebecca, had shown her in the garden of a formal home in Denmark with two well-dressed, middle-aged, smiling people, Prince Jean Félix Christian and his wife Marie Gabrielle, who were her birth parents (or so he had been able to piece together as little by little he began to understand rudimentary German). They told the story of who she was, explaining she had been kidnapped as a child and that a ransom had been demanded. Afterward they'd waited in vain for further word while the police agencies searched, but nothing had ever happened. That was until now.

Then the tape had cut to the place she had spent her early years—Coles Corner, Vermont. Alexander well knew she had grown up in L.A. as Rebecca Barron, but wisely he let the story of her childhood in Vermont play as the truth, and it worked. At least a half-dozen townspeople had been interviewed and to a person they told of remembering Rebecca and her brother, Nicholas, as children. It was incredible, as if everyone there had some driving need to be part of this gigantic myth, and so they made up all kinds of personal anecdotes about the little township girl who was soon to become the darling Tsarina of Russia. School dances, Fourth of July parades, boyfriends and girlfriends, a third-grade teacher who helped her with her terribly flawed penmanship. "Oh, she was awful."

There was even a scene taped in the tiny family graveyard on the old Marten homestead; the television reporter stood directly over the unmarked spot where Hiram Ott had buried the real Nicholas Marten. Alfred Hitchcock couldn't have done it better, even to the final stroke of perfection: A reporter questioning a Coles Corner alderman about Rebecca's educational records was told that several years earlier the town's administrative hall that shared space with the fire department had burned to the ground and all of the township's records, including those of the school department, had gone up in flames.

At that Nicholas Marten, the new Nicholas Marten, the one in captivity, had burst out laughing, and afterward laughed and laughed until he cried and his belly hurt.

But all that had been days before, and since then he had seen nothing of them. Even the news seemed uneventful and blended in with the reruns. He was going crazy and he knew it.

Then, for the two millionth time, he heard the theme song from *Gilligan's Island* and suddenly he'd had enough. Anything was better than the television. At least in the dark he could lis-

ten to the city outside. Sirens. Traffic. Children playing. Trash
being collected. Once in a while, shouts of anger in German.

Abruptly he went toward the glow, his hand reaching passionately for the television's off switch, and then the station cut away
from *Gilligan's Island* to a German-speaking news anchor.
Marten heard the name Sir Peter Kitner and then the camera cut
from the studio to a country roadside in England. "Henley-on-
Thames," an identifying caption read. He saw police and rescue
workers and the terrible wreckage of an exploded Rolls-Royce.
There was no need for a translator. He understood the German
newscaster completely: The car had been blown up and five people were dead—Sir Peter Kitner, media mogul, former Tsarevich
of Russia, grandson of murdered Tsar Nicholas, son of the escaped Alexei; Kitner's wife, Luisa, cousin of King Juan Carlos
of Spain; their son Michael, heir-designate to Kitner's media empire; and Kitner's driver, his bodyguard, a Dr. Geoffrey Higgs.

"My God, he killed them, too," Marten breathed in horror.

Suddenly the horror turned to rage. "Raymond!" he blurted.
Abruptly he turned from the screen. Never mind that he had
killed Red, or Josef Speer, or Alfred Neuss, or Halliday or Dan
Ford, or Jean-Luc Vabres or the Zurich printer, Hans Lossberg.
Alexander/Raymond had turned against his own family once
again, this time murdering his father, as he had murdered his
half brother before. What would happen when he snapped and
unleashed his terror on Rebecca?

He couldn't let himself think about it. But he knew he had to
do something, and he had to do it quickly.

21

Once more Marten paced the room. This time his thoughts were
on his captors. Who they were, who they might be, what was
driving them. He was looking for a weak spot, something he
had missed, something he hadn't picked up on before, anyplace
where they might be vulnerable. Thinking back, he examined
their behavior from the moment they had taken control of him

in Rotterdam through the days and weeks until now. What stood out most clearly was what he had thought of before, that no matter how intense the interrogations or isolated his captivity, aside from a minor shove or slap, they had never resorted to physical punishment. Their practice had been simply to interrogate him and then isolate him in darkness and let his own mind do their work for them. Why they had given him the television he didn't know. Perhaps they were just being humane. Or maybe it was for some other reason he had no idea of. But the fact was he had not been physically abused and he had been fed and provided a toilet and washbasin that enabled him to keep himself clean. Looking at it that way made him begin to think that maybe they weren't terrorists or drug smugglers at all but instead were people like the "hauler" who trafficked in human beings, and who, by this stage, had determined he was not the big fish they thought he was and were wondering what to do with him.

Were they dangerous? Of course. They were engaged in the very risky and highly illegal business of transporting undocumented persons between countries on full terrorist alert, and doing it at a time when international police agencies were cooperating at a level never before seen. To do what they were doing, they would not be operating without strong connections to organized crime. So, not only would they be afraid of being caught, they would also be afraid of the gangsters they were paying to protect them.

He was certain they had done what they had with him because they thought they had a catch they could capitalize on, building both power and prestige. At the same time, he had little doubt that if they were pressed and thought the police were closing in, they would simply take him off and kill him and dump his body in the closest gutter or vacant lot they could find.

That aside, the thing was, if they were traffickers in human beings, they would be doing it for the money alone and not have the steely fanaticism of terrorists or the deadly mind-set of the killers who ran the drug trade.

Following that line of thinking, he had to assume their greatest fear, aside from running afoul of the gangsters they would be in bed with, was that they would be caught. Perhaps the thing to do would be to reveal what he had been so protective of before—tell them who Rebecca really was and ask them what they thought might happen if they were found to be holding the brother-in-law of the next Tsar of Russia captive. Ask them what might be the result if they were turned over to the Tsar's personal security force, the FSO, perhaps even naming Colonel Murzin in particular as evidence that he was telling the truth, then making the threat more fearsome by suggesting that Murzin in turn might hand them over to the Russian Federal Security Service, the FSB, the successor to the Soviet KGB. In that situation there would be no question at all of the outcome. They would be treated with extreme severity if not finality.

Taking that approach with them was a long shot at best because, other than the names he could drop and the fact that they knew he had been at the Tsarevich's dinner, he had absolutely nothing to back up his threat. It would be a bluff of the highest order, and if he was wrong and they were terrorists or drug traffickers after all, once he had told them who Rebecca was, and because of it who he was, he would simply be confirming what they had thought all along, that he was a major catch, and in a heartbeat he would find himself in far worse trouble than he would ever want to imagine.

On the other hand, if he was right and they were nothing more than smugglers of human cargo they might be frightened enough to simply let him go, if for no other reason than to get themselves out of a potentially disastrous if not deadly situation.

It wasn't much, but it was all he had. In the end it boiled down to two simple questions. Was he willing to bet his life and Rebecca's on his judgment of who these people were? And if he was, was he a good enough actor to pull it off?

The answer to both was the same.

He had no choice.

22

"I want to talk." Marten banged and pounded on the door, yelling through it. "I want to talk! I want to confess!"

Forty-five minutes later he sat bound and blindfolded in the interrogation room.

"What do you want to say?" his throaty-voiced interrogator asked, tobacco, as always, heavy on his breath. "What do you want to confess?"

"You wanted to know why I was at the dinner in Davos. You asked who Rebecca was. I lied about both because I was trying to protect her. The photograph in my wallet does not show her as she looks now. The reason I was in Davos was because I had been invited by the Tsarevich himself. Rebecca is not my girlfriend, she is my sister. She is formally known as Alexandra Elisabeth Gabrielle Christian, and she is to be married to the Tsarevich immediately after his coronation."

"If this is true, why did you not confess it before?" The interrogator's reply was calm, even detached. It was impossible for Marten to tell how he had reacted or what he was thinking. All he could do was continue with what he had begun.

"I was afraid you would realize that as a member of the Tsar's family I would be of political use. That you would find a way to exploit who I am. Even kill me if that would help your cause."

"We can do with you as we wish, the same as before." The interrogator's voice remained even and emotionless. "What did you hope to gain from telling us now?"

It was a question Marten had anticipated. This was where he had to carefully turn things so that the pressure was taken from him and put on the interrogator.

"What I hope to gain is not only for my benefit but yours."

"Mine?" The interrogator punched out an angry laugh. "You are the one bound and blindfolded. It is your life in question, not ours."

Marten smiled inwardly. His man was not only annoyed but

affronted. That was good because it put him on the defensive. Exactly what Marten wanted.

"I have been here a long time. Too long."

"Come to the point!" his interrogator snapped. Now he was becoming irritated. Better yet.

"The calendar is moving quickly toward the day Alexander Romanov is to be crowned Tsar. His future brother-in-law is missing and has been for too long. It is a situation that is healthy neither for his married life nor his position as monarch, and he will have become angry and impatient."

This was a point where Marten was afraid his interrogator would ask why there had been no media coverage of his disappearance, but he didn't. Still, it was something he had wondered about himself. He finally assumed Alexander had ordered it kept quiet, and as far as he could tell it had been.

"Since there has been no word of me and since they will have found no body, and because of the great unrest in the world, he and his people will assume I have been kidnapped and believe whoever has done it is waiting for the coronation to take some kind of terrorist-theater action that involves me. It is something they cannot allow to happen.

"You may know the Tsarevich has a personal guard called the Federalnaya Slujba Ohrani, the FSO. They are former Spetsnaz commandos led by a very capable man named Colonel Murzin. There is no doubt they will have been looking for me. And by now you can be certain other highly select and persuasive Russian security forces will have joined them.

"It won't be long before they find your door, and when they come through it they won't be smiling." Marten paused to give his interrogator a moment to think, but not too much of a moment.

"The clock is ticking, and the circle around you is tightening. If I were you I would take my men and get as far away from me and from this place as quickly as I possibly could."

For a long moment there was silence. Then Marten heard a distinct snap of fingers, and without a word he was taken back up the stairs to his room. His blindfold removed, he sat there in the dark with no idea what to expect. An hour passed and then another, and he began to wonder if he had been wrong in his judgment and even now they were making a deal for him and soon he would be on his way to some terrorist hideout where he would be dealt with in ways he didn't want to think about.

Another hour passed. Then he heard them coming up the stairs. Four, by the count. Seconds later the door burst open and they blindfolded him and bound his hands behind him. Then they were out the door and going down the stairs. One flight, then another, and then two more. He heard a door bang open, and he was taken out into cold air.

Shoved forward, he heard someone grunt, and then he was being lifted up and wrestled into what seemed like the back of a truck, the same way he had been brought there. He held his breath, waiting for them to push him to the floor and roll him into a carpet as they had before. Instead he heard the raspy voice of his interrogator.

"May God be kind to you," he said. Then he heard them leave. The doors were slammed shut and the slip-lock bolted from the outside. Next he heard the motor start. A second later there was the jamming of gears and the truck lurched forward.

23

Marten braced himself as the truck accelerated. Twenty seconds later it slowed and he had to brace himself again as the driver took a sharp turn, then once more. Where he had been or where they were taking him now, he had no idea, but it didn't matter. The cold, chilling words of his interrogator had been enough.

"May God be kind to you." It was a death sentence. He had wholly misjudged who they were. By trying to outsmart them he had outsmarted himself and given them a grand prize, more than they ever could have expected. Because of it he was on his way to Hell. These were brutal times, and he was all too aware of what had happened to others who were trophies of one kind or another. He was certain that within hours he would be handed over to some unknown group. He would be questioned and then tortured until he made whatever kind of political statement they demanded. Finally, he would be killed. All of it would most likely be done before a video camera, with a copy of the tape sent to any number of global news organizations to show what terrible and ruthless power the world had still to fear.

If Rebecca saw it, she would be horrified enough to go crashing back into the vegetative state she had been in in Los Angeles. And God only knew how the wholly unbalanced Alexander would react to that.

"May God be kind to you."

He'd tried to bluff his way out and they'd called him on it. Now he was sealed in the back of a truck, bound and blindfolded, an animal on his way to slaughter. And like an animal, there was absolutely nothing he could do to change it.

By Marten's guess it was nearly an hour before they slowed and stopped. A moment later the driver turned sharply right and drove perhaps another mile, then turned right again and then suddenly left. Another fifty yards and the truck stopped. He heard voices and the sound of the doors opening. Wherever they had taken him, they were there. He braced himself as the rear doors were thrown open and he heard two men climb up. Then hands grabbed him and he was rushed forward and hustled to the ground.

"May God be kind to you," an unfamiliar voice said close to him. This was their mantra, he knew, and he had the sense they were going to kill him right there. His only thought was *please make it quick*.

Then he heard a distinct *click* and waited for the cold steel of a pistol to be put against his head. Again he prayed that they would do it quickly. An instant later he felt something stuffed into his jacket pocket. Then the bonds tying his hands were cut. Abruptly came the scramble of feet and the sound of truck doors being slammed. Next came the rev of its motor and then the sound of it roaring away.

Marten ripped off the blindfold. It was night. He was alone on a darkened city street. The truck's taillights disappeared around a corner.

For a moment he stood frozen in sheer disbelief. Then ever so slowly a monstrous grin crossed his face. "Oh, my God," he said out loud. "Oh, my God!"

He'd been set free.

24

Marten turned and ran.

Fifty yards, a hundred. Ahead he saw a brightly lighted street. He heard music. Loud music, the kind that came from bars and nightclubs. He glanced over his shoulder. The street behind him was empty. Another thirty seconds and he turned onto a street alive with nighttime traffic. Pedestrians crowded the sidewalks, and he joined them, trying to blend in, in case, for some reason, his captors suddenly had a change of heart and came back looking for him.

Where he was, what city he was in, he didn't know. The snippets of passing conversation he heard were mostly German. The television channel he'd watched during his confinement had broadcast in German, the voices he'd heard on the street outside had spoken German, and so he'd assumed he was being held somewhere in that country. Now the chatter of the people around him seemed to confirm it. He had been in Germany and most likely was still in Germany. Or in a city that bordered it.

Now he saw a large digital clock in a shop window that read 1:22. A street sign at the end of the next block read REEPER-BAHN. Then he saw a large lighted billboard. It advertised the Hotel Hamburg International. At the same time a bus passed; on it he saw a transit ad for the Hamburger Golf Club. Wherever he had been, he was all but certain that now he was in Hamburg.

He kept walking, trying to get his bearings, unsure of exactly what to do next.

The street he was on seemed to consist of one nightclub after another. Music blasted from every doorway. There was everything. Rock, hip-hop, jazz, even country and western.

He was almost to the end of the block when the traffic light changed and the pedestrians around him stopped. He stopped with them and took a deep breath of the nighttime air. Absently he reached up and touched his growth of beard, then glanced down at the threadbare tuxedo he had all but lived in since Davos.

The traffic light changed, and he and the others moved off. Suddenly he remembered his captors stuffing something into the pocket of his jacket just before his bonds had been cut. He touched the pocket and felt a bulge, then reached in and took out a small brown paper bag. He had no idea what it was and stepped from the crowd to stop in the light of a shop window to open it. Inside he found his wallet and a palm-sized plastic packet. To his complete surprise everything that had been in his wallet still was, though clearly waterlogged and then dried out from his trip down the river—his English driver's license, his Manchester University student ID, the two credit cards, the roughly three hundred dollars in euros, and the photograph he had taken of Rebecca at the lakeside at Jura. For some reason he turned it over. Scrawled in a heavy hand in pencil on the back was a single word—*Tsarina*.

Once again the grin of before crept over him. This time it was not only from the sense that he had been freed but from triumph. Whoever his captors had been, they had taken his warning seriously, done some quick homework, and decided the last thing they needed was to be confronted by the FSO or the Russian secret police. After weeks of confinement, Marten had suddenly become a bastard child they wanted no part of, and they had literally dumped him out on the street, using the truck ride to ensure he could not lead anyone back to where he had been. Their "May God be kind to you" may have been a mantra, but it had been no death sentence. Instead it had been a salute to send him on his journey and, with returning his personal possessions intact, a prayer that *he* would "be kind to them" if one day they came face-to-face and their positions were reversed.

Laughter from a group of passing teenagers made Marten realize he was standing conspicuously alone, and he moved on. As he did, he put the wallet in his pocket and opened the plastic envelope. Inside he found a large coinlike engraving of the Romanov family crest, which was obviously meant to be a keepsake of the Davos occasion. With it was another memento, the thing his interrogator had been referring to—a now washed-out five-by-seven-inch cream-colored envelope. Inside would be the formal announcement of reinstatement of the Russian monarchy, naming Alexander as the new Tsar. Marten opened the envelope and slid out a simple but elegantly printed card that, like the envelope and the contents of his wallet, showed the beating it had taken from his time in the water.

Suddenly he felt the breath go out of him and he stopped cold in the middle of the sidewalk. People swore and shoved to get around him. He paid them no mind; his full concentration was on the card in his hand. Washed out or not, what was printed on the card was clearly legible. Printed in gold across the top were the words:

> *Villa Enkratzer*
> *Davos, Switzerland*
> *17 January*

Beneath it was the rest.

Commemorative Menu upon the Announcement of the Reinstatement of the Imperial Family Romanov to the Throne of Russia and the Appointing of Alexander Nikolaevich Romanov as Tsarevich of All Russia.

Marten shivered as he realized that what he held in his hand was not only a commemorative souvenir announcing the reinstatement of the monarchy, it was the thing he and Kovalenko had been searching for. It was the *second menu!*

MOSCOW, GORKY PARK. WEDNESDAY,
APRIL 2. 6:20 A.M.

The park was not open to the public until ten but available to a policeman wanting to lose weight and get in shape. And that was what Kovalenko was doing in the crisp early spring morning, running, passing the great Ferris wheel for the third time in an hour, working out. He was tired of his belly and the double chin under the beard. He was drinking less and eating better and getting up early. And running and running. Why, he wasn't sure, except maybe he was buying time, trying to stay ahead of middle age. Or maybe he was trying to forget the thing that had taken over every corner of the public consciousness—the incredible craze for Alexander and Rebecca, shamelessly exploited by the media and magnified by a feverish day-by-day countdown to their wedding and the coronation.

The warble of his cell phone inside the pocket of his warm-up jacket broke his concentration. It never rang at this hour. His had become a life of paperwork, not intrigue, and he only had the rarest contact with his chief inspector anymore, so it wasn't police business. The caller had to be his wife, or one of his children.

"*Da,*" he said breathlessly, huffing and puffing as he clicked on.

"The murder weapon was a knife," a familiar voice said.

"*Shto?*" What? Kovalenko stopped in his tracks.

"*The* knife. Your big Spanish switchblade, the one taken from Fabien Curtay's safe."

"Marten?"

"Yes, Marten."

"Mother of Christ, you are dead!"

"Is that what they think?"

Kovalenko glanced around, stepping aside as a park service truck passed. "How? What happened?"

"I need your help."

"Where are you?"

"In a bar, in Hamburg. Can you meet me?"

"I don't know. I will try."

"When?" Marten pressed him.

"Call me in an hour."

25

FUHLSBÜTTEL AIRPORT, HAMBURG, GERMANY.
SAME DAY, WEDNESDAY, APRIL 2. 5:30 P.M.

Marten saw Kovalenko exit the Lufthansa gate in a crowd of passengers and start down the corridor toward the coffee bar where he waited. He could see the Russian looking for him as he came, but he knew Kovalenko wouldn't recognize him. Not only was he bearded like Kovalenko, he had lost nearly thirty pounds and was bone thin. Moreover, in the hours he'd had to wait, he'd spent a hundred and sixty of his euros and shed his worn tuxedo for an inexpensive brown corduroy suit, tattersal shirt, and navy sweater. He looked the way Kovalenko did, like a professor. Academics meeting in an airport coffee bar, nothing unusual in that.

Kovalenko reached the bar and entered. He bought a cup of coffee at the counter and then sat down at a table near the back and took out a newspaper. A moment later Marten slid into a chair beside him.

"Tovarich," Marten said. Comrade.

"Tovarich." Kovalenko studied him carefully, as if to make sure it was really him. "How . . . ?" he said finally. "How did you survive? And how did you come to be here and so many weeks later?"

Within ten minutes they were on the Airport-City-Bus to Hamburg's Hauptbahnhof, its main train station. Fifteen minutes after that Kovalenko had guided them up Ernst-Merckstrasse to the restaurant Peter Lembcke. By the time they had finished their second glass of beer, the eel soup came and Kovalenko had the answer to his "How?"—at least as much of it as Marten could remember. The young girl finding him in the snow, the fugitive family, the "hauler," Rotterdam, the truck ride rolled up in a carpet, the captivity in dark rooms, the dreaded interrogations by people he never saw—and he still did not know who they were or where he had been held. The seemingly endless television. Seeing Rebecca and Alexander—with her birth parents in Denmark, with the Queen of England and the President of the United States. Seeing the wreckage of the car in which Peter Kitner had been killed. It was then Marten pulled out the envelope his captors had given him and handed it to Kovalenko.

"Open it," he said, and Kovalenko did, sliding from it the washed-out elegantly printed card that began:

> *Villa Enkratzer*
> *Davos, Switzerland,*
> *17 January*

Marten watched him as he studied it, saw his reaction as he realized what it was, saw him suddenly look up.

"The second menu," Marten said.

"Turn it over and look carefully at the bottom right-hand corner."

Kovalenko did, and Marten heard him grunt when he saw what was there. In miniscule print almost too small to be seen were the words *H. Lossberg, master printer. Zurich.*

"Lossberg's wife said her husband always kept a copy of what he printed." Marten was looking directly at Kovalenko. "But when she went to look for it she couldn't find it. She also said exactly two hundred menus were to be printed, no more, no less, and afterward the proofs were to be destroyed and the type disassembled. Lossberg and the sales rep Jean-Luc Vabres were close friends. This was big news. What if Lossberg gave his only copy of the menu to Vabres and in turn Vabres was going to pass it on to Dan Ford? Alexander couldn't have had it known that he was to become Tsar until after Kitner had been presented to the Romanov family and then, as Tsarevich, Kitner had abdicated to him."

"And somehow, through his connection in Zurich," Kovalenko picked up the reasoning, "he found out what Lossberg had done. He had Vabres followed, or his phone tapped, or both, and then when Vabres went to meet Dan Ford to give him the menu he was already there and waiting."

Marten leaned forward. "I have to get Rebecca away from him."

"Do you know what's happened? In weeks, how large a personality he has become?"

"Yes, I do know."

"I don't think you understand the scope of it. In Russia he is a star, a king, nearly a god. So is she."

Marten repeated slowly, "I have to get Rebecca away from him."

"He is surrounded by the FSO. Murzin has become his personal bodyguard. It would be like trying to take away the wife of the president of the United States."

"She is not his wife. Not yet."

Kovalenko put his hand on Marten's. "*Tovarich,* who knows if she would leave him, even if you asked her to. Things have changed immeasurably."

"She would if I went to her and told her who he was."

"Go to her? You couldn't get within a mile of her without being caught. Never mind you are here and not in Moscow."

"That's why I need your help."

"What do you want me to do? I am barely employed anymore, let alone have access on that level."

"Get me a cell phone, a passport, and a visa of some kind that will let me travel to and inside Russia. Use my name if you have to. I know it's dangerous, but that way you can simply have my U.S. passport renewed. It would be easier and faster."

"You are dead."

"That makes it even better. There has to be more than one Nicholas Marten in this world. Say I am a visiting landscape design professor at Manchester who wished to study formal gardens throughout Russia. If anyone checks, they will find nothing but confusion at the other end. Confusion we might be able to use. I'm dead. I'm someone else. I'm a professor, not a student. No one will know for sure. The university is a sprawling bureaucracy. People come and go all the time. It could take days, weeks to find out. Even then they might not know for sure." Marten looked at Kovalenko directly. "Can you do it?"

"I—" Kovalenko hesitated.

"Yuri—as a boy he killed his brother, and as a man he killed his father."

"The bombing of Sir Peter's car?"

"Yes."

"You think Alexander was responsible."

"It doesn't take much imagination."

Kovalenko stared at Marten, glancing up only as a waiter came near their table. "No, it doesn't." He leaned in and lowered his voice. "There were sophisticated explosives used, and the timing device was Russian. The investigation is quietly ongoing. But it still doesn't mean Alexander did it or had it done."

"If you had seen his eyes on the bridge above the villa when he tried to kill me, if you had seen the knife and the way he used it, you would understand. He's losing any control he might have had. It's what we thought when we saw Dan's body come out of the river. When we saw what he did to Vabres. It was the same with Lossberg in Zurich."

"And you are afraid that at some point he will unleash that same madness on your sister."

"Yes."

"Then, *tovarich,* you are right, we must do something."

26

PETER AND PAUL CATHEDRAL, THE CRYPT OF ST.
CATHERINE CHAPEL, ST. PETERSBURG, RUSSIA.
THURSDAY, APRIL 3. 11:00 A.M.

Lighted funeral candles held solemnly in their hands, Alexander and Rebecca stood alongside President Gitinov and King Juan Carlos of Spain as Gregor II, the Most Holy Patriarch of the Russian Orthodox Church, led the solemn funeral requiem. To their left in the ornate, marbled room were Peter Kitner's three grown daughters and their husbands. Aside from several priests attending the Patriarch, and the Baroness, dressed in black with a veil covering her face, that was all. The service was that private.

Before them rested three closed coffins bearing the remains of Peter Kitner, his son Michael, and his wife Luisa, Juan Carlos's cousin.

"Even in death, O Lord, Peter Mikhail Romanov returns greatness to the soul and the soil of All Russia." Gregor II's words echoed off the gold-crested columns and the great stone floors of the crypt where the remains of Alexander's great-grandfather, the murdered Tsar Nicholas, his wife, and three of his children were interred. The same grand and mournful chamber had been the final resting place of all Russian monarchs since the reign of Peter the Great, and here, by consent of the Russian parliament, Peter Mikhail Romanov Kitner and his family would be laid to rest, even though he had never taken the throne.

"Even in death, O Lord, his spirit endures."

Even in death—the Baroness smiled thinly behind her veil. Even in death you give power and credibility to Alexander;

more, perhaps, than you ever could have in life. Your death has made you beloved, even martyred, but you have made Alexander the last true male Romanov successor to the throne.

Even in death—

The same words resonated through Alexander, his mind not on the funeral but on the unceasing beat of the metronome inside him that became stronger and more unsettling with every passing hour. He glanced at Rebecca and saw calmness on her face and in her eyes. Her serenity, even here in the crypt with proof of the finality of death only feet away in the coffins before them, was maddening, and served only to increase the growing certainty inside him that Nicholas Marten was not dead. Not dead at all. He was somewhere out there, coming toward him like a tide.

"No," he said suddenly and out loud. "No!"

People turned to look at him, the Patriarch included. Abruptly he covered his mouth and coughed, as if that were what he had done before, then turned away to feign another.

Nick Marten/John Barron. What he called himself didn't matter. He thought he'd taken care of him on the trail above Villa Enkratzer. But he hadn't. Somehow Marten had survived and was coming after him now. Coming to expose who he was and, in doing so, turn Rebecca against him.

It was true. He knew it.

The metronome beat louder. He had to get Marten out of his mind. Feigning a last cough, he turned back to the service. Marten *was* dead. Everyone else who had searched with him agreed—Murzin, other FSO agents, Swiss army commandos, Kantonspolizei, mountain search and rescue teams that had included three doctors. These were experienced people who would not just guess but know. Moreover, he had walked what seemed every inch of that dark, snow-driven, God-forsaken mountain river edge himself. He was right, and they were right. It would have been impossible for anyone to have survived through the night, wounded and bleeding and in that horrid rush of icy water. Why did he think Marten had? No, Nicholas Marten was dead. There was no question. Just as his father was dead in the coffin before him. He glanced at the Baroness and she nodded toward him, reassuringly.

He turned back and looked around the room, the grand, ornate, and final resting place of his royal ancestors. The metronome quieted and his spirits rose at the thought of them. He was, in all truth, one of them, the great-grandson of Nicholas and Alexandra. *This* was his destiny and always had been. He and he alone was Tsarevich of All Russia. Nothing, least of all a dead man, could change it.

27

HAMBURG, GERMANY, FUHLSBÜTTEL AIRPORT, FRIDAY, APRIL 4. 10:10 A.M.

Nick Marten waited in a row of other passengers to board Air France flight 1411 to Charles de Gaulle Airport in Paris, where he would take a connecting flight to Moscow. He had used one of his credit cards to buy his ticket, something that had made him nervous at the time because Rebecca might have notified the issuing banks that he was dead and canceled them. Obviously she hadn't, because his card had been accepted and his ticket given to him without question. It had been the same with his other affairs. He had picked up his passport, a reissue of his original, late yesterday at the U.S. consular office in Hamburg. With it had been a small package. Inside it was a working cell phone, complete with battery charger, and a Russian business visa, good for three months and issued by the Department of Consular Service of the Russian Ministry of Foreign Affairs at the request of Lionsgate Landscapes, a Moscow-based U.K. landscape design company. His destination in Russia, the place where he would be staying— as required on all Russian visas—was the Hotel Marco-Polo Presnja, 9 Spiridonjevskij Pereulok, Moscow.

Marten wondered what Lionsgate Landscapes really was, or if it even existed, but it made no difference because his visa had been approved. Everything he had asked for he had been given, and in less than forty-eight hours. For someone who, in his own words, was "barely employed anymore," Kovalenko had done a remarkable job.

BALTSCHUG KEMPINSKI HOTEL, MOSCOW.
SAME DAY, FRIDAY, APRIL 4. 1:30 P.M.

Alexander, Rebecca, and the Baroness shared a small luncheon table in a corner of Alexander's private eighth-floor suite that overlooked a bright spring day and the bustle of Red Square. The food was simple, more like breakfast than lunch—*blini* (pancakes), red caviar, and coffee.

Their conversation, too, was uncomplicated and centered on two things: the final steps of Rebecca's conversion to Russian Orthodoxy—a must for any woman who would become Empress and bear royal children; and the choice of outfits she would wear for her wedding and for the coronation that followed almost immediately, and then for the coronation ball that evening. Both matters were important because time was quickly closing in and the events now less than a month away. Moreover, one of Paris's top couturiers and his staff were meeting them within the hour to take Rebecca's measurements and decide on the final selections. On that Alexander would defer to whatever Rebecca, the Baroness, and the designer finally chose. For him, other things pressed: a coronation costume fitting for himself, followed by a state television interview, and after it, a four o'clock appointment at the Kremlin with President Gitinov's chief of staff.

The meeting was to be about protocol and duty and was both political and social in nature. Russia had never before had a Tsar who was essentially a figurehead, and Alexander knew that because of his sudden, widespread popularity Gitinov wanted to rein him in and make certain he didn't attempt to turn that influence into power. It was something Gitinov would not do face-to-face because he was all too aware of the political potency of the triumvirate of powers that had brought back the monarchy, but he would make it clear through his chief of staff exactly how far Alexander was allowed to go. Or, more simply, give him his job description, to wit: a constitutional monarch is to be a public cheerleader, ceremonial host, and glad-handing representative of the new Russia at home and abroad. Nothing more. Period.

It was a role Alexander chafed at but was fully prepared to play, at least for a time, as he expanded his reach and began to build a power base. Then slowly, and in carefully calibrated stages, he would begin to take a more active role, first in politics, then with the military. The idea was to initiate a popular dream of national grandeur in which he became the irreplaceable centerpiece. In three years, parliament would be afraid to move without consulting him; in five it would be the president who was the figurehead; in seven the same would be said for parliament and the generals who commanded the armed forces. In a decade the word "constitutional" would no longer precede the word "monarchy," and Russia and the world would at last know the full meaning of the word "Tsar." Josef Stalin's opinion of Ivan the Terrible was that he had not been terrible enough. Alexander would have no such problem. There was already blood on his hands and he was prepared for more. The Baroness had schooled him in it since youth.

Alexander smiled at his contemplation and felt a peace settle over him he had not experienced in a long time. It was a feeling, he knew, caused by the simple realization that, with his father's death, the throne was finally and firmly his, and that Rebecca would be at his side for the rest of his life.

It made him realize, too, that his earlier gut-wrenching dread of Nicholas Marten's miraculously rising from the dead was nothing more than a nightmare of his own creation, driven by what he admitted was an almost primal, near psychotic fear of losing Rebecca. It was an emotion he had to watch carefully, because if he didn't, if he let it take him over, he could unravel in a blink.

"You had a gift with you when you went out with Nicholas." From somewhere far off, he heard Rebecca's voice. His muse vanished as he looked up and saw her staring across the table at him. They were alone; the Baroness had gone.

"What did you say?" he asked, puzzled.

"At the villa. You had a gift with you, a gaily wrapped package under your arm, when you and Nicholas went out for a walk. What was in it?"

"I don't know, I don't remember."

"Of course you remember. You brought it with you from the

library. You put it on the table in the ballroom where we were sitting. And then you took it with you when—"

"Rebecca. Why are we talking about gifts? Where is the Baroness?"

"She left to take a phone call."

"There was no need. She could have taken it here at the table."

"Perhaps it was confidential."

"Yes, perhaps."

From behind them came a knock, the door opened, and Colonel Murzin entered. He was dressed in the finely cut dark blue suit and crisply starched pale blue shirt that had become the everyday dress of the FSO who guarded Alexander.

"Tsarevich, the couturier from Paris has arrived and was greeted by the Baroness. She asked that the Tsarina join them." From Murzin's manner it was clear there was something he wanted to discuss with Alexander in private.

"Go on, darling." Alexander stood. "I will join you later this afternoon."

"Of course." Rebecca smiled and got up. Gathering her purse, she nodded pleasantly to Murzin and left.

Murzin waited for the door to close. "I thought you should know, Tsarevich, the consular service has issued a business visa to a man named Nicholas Marten."

"What?" Alexander felt his heart skip a beat.

"It was done yesterday in Hamburg. Arranged through the Ministry of Foreign Affairs at the request of a Moscow-based U.K. landscape design company."

"He is British?"

"No, American. He is arriving today from Germany. He has reservations at the Hotel Marco-Polo Presnja, here in Moscow."

Alexander stared at Murzin. "Is it him?"

"His visa will have his photograph. I have asked for an electronic copy. It has not yet arrived."

Alexander turned and crossed the room to look out. The day was still bright under a cloudless sky, the city alive with early afternoon traffic and a crush of pedestrians. But there in the room, with Murzin standing behind him, he could feel the darkness begin to creep back. And then, from far inside, the metronome began.

Boom, boom. Boom, boom.

The same as before. Unnerving and irrepressible. Like a monster emerging from within.

Boom, boom.
Boom, boom.
Boom, boom.

28

PARIS, CHARLES DE GAULLE AIRPORT. STILL FRIDAY, APRIL 4. 12:25 P.M.

Ticket in hand, Nicholas Marten followed the blue line on the polished floor, walking quickly from Terminal 2F where he had landed to Terminal 2C where Air France flight 2244 would take off for Moscow's Sheremetyevo Airport at 12:55, thirty minutes from now. He was thankful for the blue line on the floor. It made the transition from terminal to terminal quite simple, especially now, when his mind was elsewhere and his focus was on Rebecca and what to do about her.

Kovalenko had told him she was staying with the Baroness de Vienne in an eighth-floor suite at the Baltschug Kempinski Hotel. That entire floor and the one beneath it had been taken over by Alexander and the people planning the coronation. As a result the FSO would have both floors, if not the entire hotel, in virtual lockdown. It meant there was no practical way he could get to her himself, so he had to find a means of bringing her to him. How he would do that, he had no idea, but he had to trust he would find a way and that Kovalenko would be there to help him.

MOSCOW, THE KREMLIN. STILL FRIDAY, APRIL 4. 5:55 P.M.

Murzin had delivered Alexander to the office of Gitinov's chief of staff exactly at four. Afterward Alexander had been shown into a private study, given coffee, and asked to wait. The chief of staff, he was told, was with the president on a vital matter and would be with him as soon as possible. An hour later Alexander still waited. Finally, at five-fifteen, a secretary came in and Alexander was escorted down a back hallway and into Gitinov's private office, where the president himself waited. Alone.

"Please sit down," Gitinov said, escorting him to a comfortable sitting area where two overstuffed chairs faced a crackling fire. An aide came in and served tea and then left. As the door closed behind him, Alexander realized that although he had been with the Russian president numerous times, they had never once been entirely alone as they were now. For the first time he became conscious that Gitnov was far more physically fit than he appeared. The tailoring of his clothes hid a strong neck and powerful arms and a broad chest that slimmed quickly to a narrow waist. His thighs under his trousers were bulked and muscular, like those of a wrestler or cyclist. Beyond that, his manner was equally disconcerting. Even though his kind and personable actions at Davos in the aftermath of Marten's plunge into the mountain stream and subsequent disappearance had been politically driven, here in the intimacy of his office he seemed very relaxed, almost apolitical. He asked of Alexander's plans for the coronation and his wedding and where he and the Tsarina planned to honeymoon, giving some suggestions of favored resorts on the Black Sea. His open manner, the way he talked, the sparkle in his eyes, and the warmth of his smile would have put any visitor at ease, making him feel free to relax and return the conversation in a like manner, as if he were talking to an old friend. The trouble was, it was completely an act. In reality Gitinov had him under his microscope and was carefully scrutinizing every word and gesture, looking beneath the veneer to see if he was the person he appeared or if he had other designs or ambitions and should not be trusted.

For one astute enough to realize what was happening, the impact would be intimidating, if not frightening. Yet Alexander realized it and was neither intimidated nor frightened. After all, it was he who had the imperial birthright and was about to become Tsar, not Gitinov. It was he who should be feared and shrunk from and not the other way around. Yet he well knew this was hardly the time or the place to show his claws, and so he simply sat back and quietly and politely chatted about nothing, giving Gitinov the opportunity to judge him any way he chose.

Twenty minutes later it was over. They shook hands and Alexander was gone, with the president once again giving him personal condolences about the death of his father and then sending him on his way like a schoolboy.

In retrospect he should have predicted it; Gitinov showing him who was boss by making him wait, and then surprising him with a private meeting designed to feel him out and assess his character. But Alexander had given him nothing, purposely playing smiling jester instead of king. The end result had made Gitinov, despite his shrewdness, look small and inept, overplaying a hand that had not been necessary to play in the first place. Alexander had to smile to himself at the failing and to appreciate the side effect. The intrusion had, at least for a time, taken away his fixation on Nicholas Marten, and with it, the awful overpowering beat of the metronome.

"Tsarevich," Murzin turned the black Volga away from the Kremlin to negotiate rush hour traffic on the Prechistenskaya Naberezhnaya, the broad boulevard along the Moscow River. One hand on the wheel, he took a folded paper from his jacket and handed it over his shoulder to Alexander in the backseat. "A copy of the Marten visa."

Alexander opened it quickly to look at the bearded figure that stared out at him from the page. The face was painfully thin, the full beard covering most of his features. The eyes were diverted slightly, as if on purpose. Still, there was no doubt who it was, and at that moment Murzin confirmed it.

"His passport was a reissue of a previous one. He was born in Vermont, U.S.A. His current address is the University of Manchester in England. He *is* the Tsarina's brother."

The paper still in his hand, Alexander looked off and Moscow became a blur.

"Tsarevich." Murzin was watching him in the mirror. "Are you alright?"

For a long moment there was no reaction, and then Alexander's eyes swung toward him.

"Tsarskoe Selo," he said strongly. "Take the Tsarina and the

Baroness there now, tonight, by helicopter. They are to be told that I was called to an urgent meeting, and considering my increasingly difficult schedule and the escalating media attention for both me and the Tsarina I wished them to be free of it all. No one is to know where they have gone. Officially they have left the city for an unknown destination to rest before the coronation. Under no circumstance is anyone, especially the Tsarina, to be told about Marten."

"What do you want done about him?"

"I will see to that myself."

29

MOSCOW, SHEREMETYEVO AIRPORT. 6:50 P.M.

Once more Nick Marten waited in line. This time he was in Moscow and the queue was at passport control. Somewhere on the far side of the official booths and uniforms, Kovalenko waited. For now all Marten could do was stand with the hundred or so others waiting to pass through the official checkpoint.

So far the only person he had told he was alive was Kovalenko. He had been wary of telling anyone else, even Lady Clem, for fear the word would get back to Rebecca and, in turn, to Alexander. Now he knew he needed to call her, and standing there, inching along in the line toward passport control, gave him the time, so he took out the cell phone Kovalenko had given him, clicked on, and dialed. Wherever she was, whatever she was doing, he needed to talk to her. Not only did he want her to know he was alive and well, he wanted her with him and quickly.

MANCHESTER, ENGLAND. SAME TIME, 9:50 P.M.
LOCAL TIME.

She was in the bathroom of Leopold's flat preparing herself for Leopold. Leopold himself, a ruggedly handsome, muscular carpenter who had been renovating her flat, was waiting for her in the dark of his bedroom, sprawled naked and impatient on his oversized bed. He sat up at the distant chirp of a cell phone through the closed bathroom door. It wasn't his, so it had to be hers.

"Bloody Christ, not now," he moaned. "Say what you have to say and hang up, luv. Just hang up and get in here."

"Nicholas Marten!" Lady Clem whispered in absolute shock. "Wait." She straightened up, glancing at her nudity in the mirror. "Who is this really? Whoever it is, you are playing a very cruel joke." Suddenly Clem's face went beet red as she realized it really was Marten, and she grabbed Leopold's robe hanging on the back of the door as if Marten could see her and know what was going on.

"Nicholas Marten, you are a bastard!" she whispered, fuming, as she pulled on Leopold's robe. "How dare you call me like this, and here and now? And—Jesus God." She felt herself shiver with emotion as the truth of it hit. "Jesus God, you're alive! Are you alright? Where are you? Where?" Abruptly she shifted gears again. Emotion was everything.

"You couldn't have called sooner? Do you have any idea what I have been through? The worry! The despair! The awful sadness!—Do you have any idea what I was just about to—?"

"I am very sorry, Leopold, a family emergency." Fully dressed, Lady Clem kissed Leopold the carpenter on the forehead on her way out. "I will call you to say hello when I get back."

She reached the door and opened it.

"Back?" A muscular Leopold sat up. "Where the hell are you going?"

"Russia."

"Russia?"

"Russia."

30

Where was Marten?

Alexander rolled over in the dark. Maybe he'd slept, maybe not, he wasn't sure. Rebecca and the Baroness were already at Tsarskoe Selo, the immense imperial complex near St. Petersburg, which the wife of Peter the Great had established nearly three hundred years earlier as a retreat from the duties of government. Tonight, by putting it under the guard of the FSO, Alexander had made it a retreat of a different sort, a fortress to protect his treasured crown jewel from her brother.

Where was he?

Immigration records at Sheremetyevo Airport had Nicholas Marten clearing passport control at 7:08 P.M. Moscow time. By ten he had yet to arrive at the Hotel Marco-Polo Presnja, his stated destination as required by his visa. Nor had he been there at eleven or midnight. So where was he? Where had he gone? And how, and with whom?

Nicholas Marten leaned against the small pillow in the dim light, his hands behind his neck, watching Kovalenko sleep. Outside, beyond the pulled window curtain of their sleeping compartment, Russia passed in the dark.

Perhaps it was the swiftness of the train and the sound of the wheels over the tracks, but Marten found himself thinking of that night so far in the past when he boarded the Southwest Chief in the California desert, a young, wide-eyed detective filled with eagerness and anxiety on his first assignment as a member of the most fabled squad in the history of the Los Angeles Police Department. How long and dark and treacherous and deeply personal his road had become since.

Kovalenko snorted loudly twice in his sleep, then rolled over so that he faced the curtained window with his back toward Marten. They were here, rattling northwest through the Russian night, because Kovalenko had insisted they go straight from the airport to Leningradski Station instead of to the Hotel Marco-Polo Presnja to check in as his visa required. If they had, Kovalenko pointed out, it might well have been the last place Marten saw in this lifetime, because once his visa had been processed at Sheremetyevo Airport in Moscow, there was little doubt the Tsarevich would know about it. And finding out, he would know Marten's destination. And, having learned that—

"You see how it follows, *tovarich*. He knows you are going there and—to the world you are already dead anyway."

So instead of a bed in a hotel room in Moscow or in a hole in the ground, he was in a sleeping compartment on the Red Arrow with Kovalenko on their way to St. Petersburg. There Lady Clem would meet them, arriving on a flight from Copenhagen at 2:40 that afternoon, and not far from the vast imperial compound of Tsarskoe Selo, where Kovalenko had told him Rebecca was.

31

MOSCOW. BALTSCHUG KEMPINSKI HOTEL. SATURDAY, APRIL 5. 4:30 A.M.

Sleep was impossible.

Wearing boxer shorts and nothing else, Alexander paced the darkened bedroom of his suite, looking out at the city. A taxi passed below, a municipal truck, a police car. Marten was out there. Somewhere. But where?

So far neither Murzin nor any of his twenty-man detail knew what had happened after Marten cleared Sheremetyevo Airport passport control. He had simply gone out with the mass of faceless passengers and vanished, as if the city had swallowed him up.

It was, Alexander thought, the same as it must have been for John Barron in Los Angeles when he was searching every corner of the city for Raymond Oliver Thorne. But then Barron had the help of the media and the LAPD's nine thousand officers. The difference here was that Alexander could not sound the general alarm, which was why neither passport control nor the border police had been placed on alert. These were not Stalinist times, nor Soviet, nor were they yet Tsarist. The media might be under some restrictions, but unless they were critical of the government, the restrictions were relatively few. Moreover, like media anywhere, the reporters were very well connected. And there was the Internet. Let it be found out that the brother of the Tsarina was alive—and who would be one of the first to learn of it but Rebecca?

So the trackdown had to be done not only quickly but shrewdly and on the quiet. Promising a large and immediate cash reward to anyone revealing Marten's whereabouts, yet never revealing his name or why he was wanted, Murzin's men quickly printed up and handed out hundreds of copies of Marten's visa photograph to a collection of *avtoritet*, or leaders of Russian mafia groups who controlled airport and train station workers, hotel and restaurant employees, taxi drivers, and municipal and transport workers. As an extra measure they employed the *fartsovchik*, black market street-corner dealers, *blatnye*, street hoodlums, and *patsani*, young gang members who, like the others, could be trusted to keep their mouths shut and their eyes open and who would be only too eager to turn over a face for hard currency. Since most of these people carried cell phones, a fast if not immediate response was all but certain once he was seen.

32

Kovalenko lifted a cup of tea and glanced out the window, where the morning's early light touched a cold, gray countryside. It was all woods and water, rivers and streams with lakes and ponds in between. Here and there patches of snow still covered the ground, frozen beneath leafless trees still weeks from budding out.

"I was thinking about your friend, Detective Halliday." Kovalenko looked across the small compartment at Marten cradling his own cup of tea, courtesy of the *provodnik*, the train carriage's attendant, among whose jobs it was to maintain the carriage's samovar so that passengers had a constant supply of hot water for drinks.

"I told you I knew him," Marten said quietly. "I didn't say he was a friend." Kovalenko was pushing at him again as he had before in Switzerland. But why, and especially why now?

"Whatever you choose to call it, *tovarich*, he was still a remarkable man."

"How do you mean?"

"For one thing, an autopsy was done after he was killed. He had pancreatic cancer. He might have lived another month, two at most. But he came all the way to Paris, and with a fully purchased ticket to Buenos Aires, just to find out about Alfred Neuss and stay on the trail of Raymond Thorne."

"He cared."

"But about what?"

Marten shook his head. "I don't follow you."

"The famous Five-Two Squad, *tovarich*. He was a member of it long before anyone ever heard of Raymond Thorne. Its commander Arnold McClatchy was a most beloved man, yes?"

"I wouldn't know."

"Did you ever meet him?"

"McClatchy?"

"Yes." Kovalenko was watching him closely.

Marten hesitated, but only for an instant because he couldn't let the Russian sense he was unsure what to say. "Once, briefly."

"What was he like?"

"Tall and rugged, like a man who knew what to expect in the world."

"Yet Raymond, or rather our Tsarevich, killed him."

Marten nodded.

Kovalenko watched him a moment longer, then got off it. "Well, at any rate, Halliday obviously cared a great deal about the Five-Two. Even after it was disbanded and he was no longer a policeman, he cared enough to give it his last full measure. I have to wonder if I would do that, or if any other man would. What do you think, *tovarich?*"

"I'm a student learning how to design gardens. Garden designers are not usually put to that test."

"Unless they are trying to free their sister from a madman."

Marten took a sip of tea and sat back. Now it was he who studied Kovalenko. "Who do you work for?" he asked finally.

Kovalenko grinned. "The Ministry of Justice, who do you think?"

"No, *tovarich,* who do you *really* work for?"

Kovalenko grinned again. "I go to work, I get paid, I try not to ask too many questions. It only gets me in trouble."

Marten took another sip of tea and then looked away. Ahead he could see the big Czech-made Skoda engines as they eased the long train around a steep curve, the steady click-click of the wheels over the rails made all the more noticeable by the unhurried speed. Then the track straightened out and he could hear a distinct whine as the driver accelerated and the train picked up speed. It was six-forty-five, an hour and fifteen minutes before they would arrive in St. Petersburg.

"*Tovarich.*" Kovalenko stroked his beard purposefully.

Marten looked at him, puzzled. "What?"

"Once the Tsarevich finds you are not at the hotel, he will begin looking elsewhere. Passport control will confirm you entered the country. He will send people to look for you. They will be looking for a man who resembles the photograph on your visa."

"But they will be looking in Moscow."

"Will they?" Again Kovalenko stroked his beard.

"You think I should shave."

"And cut your hair."

33

MOSCOW, BALTSCHUG KEMPINSKI HOTEL. 7:20 A.M.

Where was he? Where was Marten?

Alexander was on the telephone to Murzin again, ignoring the ringing of his private cell phone. He knew from the number of times it had chirped in the past hours that it was the Baroness demanding to know why she and Rebecca had been spirited to Tsarskoe Selo without warning and without a personal explanation from him.

Why was there still no news? he demanded of Murzin. What was wrong? Marten had obviously come to Moscow; he thought his sister was there, so there was no reason to think he would go anywhere else. He *had* to be here. Somewhere! The *avtoritet* were useless. So were the other street criminals.

"They have not had enough time, Tsarevich," Murzin said quietly against Alexander's anxiety. "It was only late last night that they distributed his photograph. Today the sun is not even up."

"That is an excuse, not an answer." Alexander cut him off harshly, the way the Baroness would have.

"I promise you, Tsarevich," Murzin continued, unruffled, "by this time tomorrow they will have found him. There is no street corner in all of Moscow he can pass without being seen."

For a long moment Alexander held the phone in the silence, uncertain as to what to do or say next. Sitting and waiting was no good, but what else could he do? His mind raced. What if, in some way, Marten had gotten the number of Rebecca's cell phone? All he had to do was call her. But that was impossible. The numbers were changed every day, done after hackers had broken in twice, trying to talk with the new Tsarina. Since then Rebecca had been warned to use her cell phone only to make outgoing calls and the Tsarskoe Selo operators, as well as her two private secretaries, screened all incoming landline calls. So, no, Marten couldn't reach her by phone. Suddenly a new thought came to him and with it a chill that slid across his shoulders.

"What if," he said to Murzin, almost in a whisper, "he's not in Moscow? What if somehow he found out and is on his way to Tsarskoe Selo?"

"Tsarevich." Murzin tried to ease his concern. "It is impossible for him to know where she is. And even if he did, the palace is filled with FSO. There is no way he could even get onto the grounds, let alone to the apartments where she is."

Alexander's eyes flashed with anger and he could feel sweat on his palms.

"Colonel, you are not to tell me what Marten can or cannot do. Here is a man who has survived when everyone said he could not. He is dangerous and he is cunning. I have seen it first-hand." Alexander felt his stomach tighten and the metronome begin again. He shook it off. "I want the search expanded to include St. Petersburg and all the rail lines and roads and pathways leading to Tsarskoe Selo."

"Of course, Tsarevich," Murzin said quietly.

"And then I want a helicopter."

"For where, Tsarevich?"

"Tsarskoe Selo."

34

Marten stepped off the train, the fourth passenger behind Kovalenko, as if they were strangers, and followed him into the station in the crowd of other passengers. Marten was clean shaven and his hair a great deal shorter than it had been—courtesy of the *provodnik,* the same train attendant who had made sure the carriage samovar was steaming and provided their tea, and who, for a small wad of rubles pressed into his hand by Kovalenko, brought a razor, bar of soap, pair of old scissors, and hand mirror to the compartment. The rest had been Marten's personal labor, done over the sink in one of the car's two tiny lavatories. His hairstyle would win no prizes, but without a beard and with short hair, identifying him from his visa photograph would be a near impossibility.

Kovalenko saw the young man in the ragged blue jeans with the cigarette near the ticket windows. He was obviously high on something, sitting cross-legged on the floor with a guitar in his lap and strumming chords, as if just to make sound. Kovalenko knew a *fartsovchik,* a black market street-corner dealer, when he saw one. But this one was familiar. He either knew him or had seen him before, and shortly Kovalenko realized the dealer was an addict he had arrested several years earlier in Moscow as a suspect in the murder of another drug dealer. Later the addict had been cleared of the charge, but he obviously had learned nothing from the experience, because here he was back in business, only now it was St. Petersburg and not Moscow.

As Kovalenko drew closer he realized that, as stoned out as the addict seemed, he was clearly watching people come off the trains, looking for someone in particular. Whether he saw Kovalenko or not, or if he recognized him, there was no way to know.

Just ahead a corridor led to the right. Over it was a sign directing passengers toward a connection to the Trans-Siberian Express. Kovalenko reached it and turned quickly down it and out of the *fartsovchik*'s sight. Ten seconds later Marten caught up with him.

"They're here," Kovalenko said quietly.

"Who?"

"The Tsarevich's spies."

"Did they see us?"

"Maybe. Who knows. Just keep walking."

35

MOSCOW, THE BALTSCHUG KEMPINSKI HOTEL. 9:55 A.M.

His black hair combed straight back, strikingly handsome in sweater, dark slacks, and leather flight jacket, and wearing comfortable suede crepe-soled shoes, Alexander followed Murzin up the final steps to the roof heliport. At the top, Murzin pulled open the door and they stepped out into warm sunshine.

Directly across a Kamov Ka-60 Russian army helicopter waited, its rotors slowly churning. Thirty seconds later they were inside, the doors closed, clipping into safety harnesses. It was then that Murzin's cell phone rang. Quickly he clicked on, then immediately handed it to Alexander.

"For you, Tsarevich. The palace is calling."

"Rebecca?"

"The Baroness."

TSARSKOE SELO. SAME TIME.

Bright sunshine blazing through the windows in the palace's Great Library starkly illuminated both the Baroness and a room that, with its dark heavy furniture and its walls of unblemished, white artificial marble covered with mahogany bookcases that overflowed with almanacs, calendars, travel albums, and anthologies, was a vague remembrance of the past. But at the moment the past held no interest for the Baroness. What enraged her was the present.

"I've called for hours," she said into the phone, railing at Alexander in Russian as if he were a boy. "I left messages in twenty places. Why did you not answer?"

"I"—Alexander hesitated—"apologize. There are other things—"

"*What* other things? What is the meaning of sending us here in the middle of the night? Not a word from you. Just bundled off from Moscow by the FSO in the dark because you are busy and want us to powder our noses and do nothing."

Alexander motioned for Murzin to open the door, then unbuckled and got out. Murzin's cell phone in hand, he walked across the rooftop and away from the helicopter.

"Baroness, Rebecca's brother is alive. He arrived in Moscow last night. That's why I had you and her taken to Tsarskoe Selo."

"Where is he now?"

"We don't know."

"Are you certain it is him?"

"Yes."

"So, the Tsarina was right all along."

"Baroness, Rebecca can't know."

The Baroness de Vienne turned sharply from the center of the room and walked away toward the windows. "Rebecca be damned," she spat. "There are new things infinitely more important."

"What new things?"

"You met with President Gitinov yesterday."

"Yes. So?"

Abruptly she twisted a curl of black hair behind her ear and turned her back to the harsh sunlight. "He didn't like you."

"What do you mean?"

"He didn't like your demeanor. You were condescending."

"Baroness, I was polite. We talked. I said nothing. If that is condescending—"

"He saw through it. He thinks you are too strong. That you have other ambitions."

Alexander grinned confidently and looked out across the

roof toward the Moscow River and the Kremlin beyond it. "He's more perceptive than I gave him credit for."

"Gitinov did not become president because he is a fool. The fault is *yours,* not his!" The Baroness's voice cut like a razor.

Alexander turned his back to the helicopter as if Murzin or the crew might see his reaction, or worse, hear what was being said.

"Did you learn nothing in your life? To never, ever, reveal what's inside you!" The Baroness reached the library windows and immediately turned back, pacing angrily across the room.

"Have you no concept of what it took to get you to where you are? Not just the years of molding your temperament, or the years of physical and other very special and very personal training, all of which was designed to make you strong enough and forceful enough and brutal enough to be Tsar of All Russia, but manipulating the politics of it?" Her anger was building word by word.

"Who worked the triumvirate for nearly two decades, separately and together, gaining their confidence, getting inside their minds, listening to their problems, giving them money, a lot of money, for their causes? Who convinced them that the only way to stabilize the country and build a lasting national spirit was to reestablish the monarchy? Who convinced them to demand that Sir Peter Kitner step aside in favor of you?" Her anger crescendoed. *"Who?"*

"You," he whispered.

"Yes, *me.* And so you listen when I tell you that even now there remains great bitterness between the president and the triumvirate. I remind you it was they who pushed the members of both houses of parliament to restore the monarchy. They did it because I convinced each of them that doing so was not only in Russia's best interest but that of his own institution. And it was because of that that they, and their influence, settled it.

"The president, on the other hand, worried privately from the beginning that you would overshadow him in the public eye. And that fear has already been realized in the public attention paid to you. He knows what it means to be a celebrity, and he thinks you already command too much power.

"It is bad enough that three weeks before the coronation you have given him more cause for uneasiness. But if he can turn his own discomfort into a concern for national security by convincing them you are a conceited, disruptive force, and if that concern finds its way into the parliament or to any of the three, even with my influence and your popularity, everything could erode overnight, to the point where a new parliamentary election could be called that would effectively dissolve the monarchy before it even begins. It would be an election that for President Gitinov"—her voice became ice cold—"would be a godsend."

"What do you want me to do?"

"The president has graciously consented to take tea with you in the Kremlin at six this evening—where, he has been told, you will apologize for any misunderstanding yesterday and reassure him, in very direct terms, that you have no ambition whatsoever other than the good of the Russian people. Is that clear—" she hesitated and then softened, but only slightly—"my sweet?"

"Yes." Alexander was staring off, humiliated, seeing nothing.

"Then see it is done."

"Yes"—Alexander breathed—"Mother."

He heard her click off and for a moment just stood there, seething with anger. He hated her, hated Gitinov, hated them all. He was Tsarevich, not they. How dare they question him or his motives? Especially when he had done what they had requested and agreed on.

Across the roof he could see the dark silhouette of the helicopter, its door open, its blades slowly churning. What was he to do, forget about Marten and send the helicopter away? Suddenly he saw movement in the doorway; then Murzin stepped from it and came quickly toward him, a two-way radio in his hand. Clearly something had happened.

"What is it?"

"Kovalenko, the Ministry of Justice homicide inspector with Marten in Davos, was seen getting off the eight-twenty-five Moscow train in St. Petersburg."

"Was Marten with him?"

"At first he was alone, but then another man caught up with him inside the station."

"Marten?"

"Possibly, but this man was clean shaven and had short hair.

Marten came through passport control with a beard and long hair."

"How expensive are razor and scissors?" Alexander could feel the pound of his heart and with it the awful sweep of dread as he felt the metronome begin once again. "Where are Kovalenko and his friend now?"

"We don't know, Tsarevich. The *fartsovchik* that saw him didn't even know if sighting Kovalenko was worth reporting, let alone following him. After all, Kovalenko was not the man the *fartsovchik* was sent to look for. And a check with the Ministry of Justice shows Kovalenko is on holiday. His wife confirmed it, saying he went off unaccompanied yesterday to camp and hike in the Urals. It seems he is on some physical fitness program."

"St. Petersburg is not the Urals." Alexander reddened with anger. "We had Kovalenko removed from his assignment before. Why is he back?"

"I don't know, Tsarevich."

"Well, find out. And this time find out exactly what branch of the ministry he is in and the name of the person he reports to."

"Yes, Tsarevich."

Alexander stared at Murzin for the briefest moment; then he looked off and Murzin could see a grimace cross his face as if he were suffering some kind of internal pain. A heartbeat later Alexander looked back. "I want all *avtoritet, fartsovchik, blat-nye,* and *patsani* in St. Petersburg put on alert," he said coldly. "I want Kovalenko and the man with him found now."

36

10:57 A.M.

Moscow disappeared beneath puffy clouds as the Ka-60 helicopter banked sharply and then evened out to settle on a direct course for the palace at Tsarskoe Selo.

"Mother," Alexander had called the Baroness. It was a term he hadn't used since childhood, and he didn't know why he had done it now, except he had been angry and just had. But neither his anger nor hers, as she had lectured him about Gitinov, would be anything like the fury he could expect when she saw him arrive at Tsarskoe Selo. The reason he had come would not interest her at all, any more than Marten's sudden reappearance seemed to interest or even worry her. His personal feelings and concerns were nothing, and, as he thought about it, never had been. She had had her revenge on Peter Kitner. All that mattered now, and maybe always had, was the monarchy and only the monarchy.

"Rebecca be damned!" she had said. Well, Rebecca would not be damned. Not by the Baroness or anyone else. Nor would he lose her because of her brother.

Abruptly he turned to Murzin, raising his voice against the scream of the jet engines.

"The Tsarina's cell phone is to be taken from her immediately. If she asks why, she is to be told we are once again changing her number and need the instrument to reprogram it. Nor are any calls to be put through to her on any other telephone, cell or landline.

"Should she choose to place a call herself, she is to be informed there is a problem with the main switching terminal and repairs are being made. Under no circumstances is she to be in contact with anyone outside the palace, nor is she allowed to leave it.

"On the other hand, she is not to be alarmed or made to think anything out of the ordinary is happening. Is that clear?"

"Of course, Tsarevich."

"Next, quietly double the guard on the palace's perimeter walls and attach a canine unit to each section. At the same time, station four FSO agents at every palace entry and exit, two inside and two out. No one is to be permitted onto the grounds without prior clearance from either you or me, and even then only with full identification. That order is to include all purveyors, service people, palace staff, and FSO personnel, who are simply to be told we have increased security as the coronation date approaches. Any questions, Colonel?"

"No, Tsarevich, no questions." Murzin turned crisply to pick up the handset to his radio transmitter.

Alexander listened as Murzin contacted FSO headquarters at Tsarskoe Selo, then leaned back to absently touch the leather flight jacket he wore. The knife was there, in the inside pocket, and, as so many times in the past, its very closeness reassured him.

It was now a little after eleven. It would be nearly one-thirty when they reached the palace. His plan was straightforward and would, once she was calmed down and heard it, satisfy the Baroness.

He had sent Rebecca from Moscow to Tsarskoe Selo because her brother had been reported as being alive and in Moscow. Since Marten—he was certain the man with Kovalenko *was* Marten—was now in St. Petersburg, possibly even on his way to the palace, the most obvious thing was simply to fly her out of the compound and back to Moscow. The reason, too, was obvious—they had been invited to six o'clock tea with the president, and what better way to humble oneself before the president than to bring one's beautiful and utterly charming fiancée along.

It was an idea the Baroness would grasp instantly. It would immediately ease her rage, and at the same time physically remove Rebecca from the approach of her brother. Moreover it would all happen quickly because they would need to leave almost as soon as they arrived, to be back in Moscow in time to dress for the presidential tea.

Alexander glanced at Murzin and then out to the Russian countryside below. Huge expanses of still-raw land were cut here and there by rivers or lakes or forests, and the occasional roadway or rail line. Russia was a massive country, and flying over it like this made it feel even more so. Soon Russia would take all of his energy, touching this corner of it and that, as little by little he became its supreme ruler.

Still, for all his plans, despite everything that was already in motion, there remained the problem of Marten. Alexander should have killed him in Paris when he had the chance. Or before Paris, gone to his flat in Manchester and killed Marten there. But he hadn't because of Rebecca.

Earlier in the morning, as he stepped from a purposely cold shower, he had seen his reflection in the mirror and stood there transfixed. It was the first time in as long as he could remember that he had allowed himself to look at his body and the ugly patchwork of scars covering it. Some were surgical; others were from the L.A. policeman Polchak's horrific machine gun, bullets that would have killed him had it not been for his last-second twisting away and John Barron's Kevlar vest, which Raymond had put on, almost as an afterthought, before they left Barron's house for the Burbank Airport. And there, too, was the faint scar at his throat where Barron's shot had torn across, searing his flesh during his bloody escape from the Criminal Courts Building.

In truth he should have been dead. But he wasn't, because each time, a combination of his own ingenuity, skill, and luck had played a hand. So had God, who had given him strength and delivered him to his destiny as Tsar of All Russia. It was because of that God-guided destiny that he hadn't died in L.A., and wouldn't die during this Russian army helicopter ride to Tsarskoe Selo.

But Marten hadn't died either. He was still here, too, in spite of everything and at nearly every turn. The same as he had been in L.A. and Paris, and then in Zurich and Davos, and then Moscow, and now in St. Petersburg. He was always there. Why? What part of God's work was that? It was something Alexander didn't understand.

37

THE ST. PETERSBURG SEA AND RIVER YACHT CLUB,
NABEREZHNAYA MARTYNOVA. STILL SATURDAY,
APRIL 5. 12:50 P.M.

From where he stood with his collar turned up against a cold wind, peering in through a corner window, Marten could see Kovalenko at the bar, a glass in his hand, talking with a tall, sea-weathered man with a great mane of curly gray hair.

It had been nearly half an hour since Kovalenko had left him waiting in the beige Ford rental car, saying he'd only be a few minutes. But there he was, still talking and drinking as if he were on vacation, rather than trying to hire a boat.

Marten turned away and walked toward the pier, looking out at the stretch of islands and waterways across from him. To his left, in the distance, he could see the massive Kirov sports stadium, and beyond it, glinting in the sun, the Gulf of Finland. They were lucky, Kovalenko had told him. St. Petersburg harbor was usually full of ice at this time of year, but the Russian winter had been mild and the rivers and the harbor, and most probably the Finnish Sea itself, were virtually free of big ice fields, which meant the shipping lanes, while still hazardous, would be open.

The idea of using a boat as a means of getting Rebecca out of Russia had come to Marten on the train from Moscow as he watched Kovalenko sleep. Getting her away from Tsarskoe Selo was one thing—he knew that if Clem called Rebecca, calmly and matter-of-factly said she was coming to St. Petersburg, and asked her if there was some way she could sneak away from her courtly duties to meet her alone for an hour or so, Rebecca would do so without question. Once away from the palace, the two of them could get rid of the FSO protectors who would accompany Rebecca by simply saying they wanted to be alone. If Rebecca had trouble saying that, Lady Clem most certainly would not, and, if they chose the right location—a cathedral, an exclusive restaurant, a museum—once they were alone, there were any number of ways they could leave undetected.

The problem was what to do then. Rebecca, as the hugely popular Tsarina-to-be, was a world media darling whose face, along with Alexander's, was everywhere and on seemingly everything, from television to newspapers, to magazines, T-shirts, coffee mugs, even children's pajamas. As Rebecca, she could go nowhere without being recognized and, as a result, could hardly be expected to walk through a train station or airport without being mobbed, and without people asking, "Where is the Tsarina going, in public, without security, and without the Tsarevich?"

The authorities would ask the same question and immediately alert the FSO. Moreover, even if she wore some kind of disguise and eluded detection, tickets and passports were necessary even for a disguised Tsarina. Add to that timetables, weather, and late arrivals and departures, and public travel became far too complicated and time-consuming for a successful and swift escape. Therefore, Marten had had to think of an alternate means of transit that would get them not just out of St. Petersburg but out of Russia, quickly, out of public view, and on their own terms and schedule. A private aircraft was a possibility but far too costly. Moreover, a flight plan would have to be filed. Using Kovalenko's rental car was another alternative, but roadblocks could be hurriedly set up and every vehicle stopped and searched. Besides, it was a long way to the nearest border, Estonia to the west, or Finland to the north. However, hiring a private boat that could leave St. Petersburg immediately and sail rapidly out of Russian waters was as intriguing as it was attractive. When he broached the subject with Kovalenko, it seemed to be the ideal course, one made all the easier by Kovalenko's personal connections gained through years in law enforcement. Hence, the gray-haired man at the yacht club bar and Kovalenko's negotiation for a vessel and crew.

It might be crazy, but so far it was working. Clem, waiting to change planes in Copenhagen, had reached Marten on his cell phone to say she had spoken to Rebecca just before breakfast. She'd reached her simply by calling the Kremlin and saying who she was, and, after she'd given enough information for the Kremlin to verify her aristocratic identity, her call had been put through to Rebecca's secretary at Tsarskoe Selo. In no time Rebecca had eagerly agreed to meet her alone at the Hermitage Museum, where Lord Prestbury had long been a patron and where, as his daughter, Clem had special access to private rooms.

It was now nearly one o'clock. In just over ninety minutes Clem would arrive at Pulkovo Airport, and Marten and Kovalenko would pick her up in the rental car and drive her into St. Petersburg. At three-thirty she would meet Rebecca at the Hermitage Museum and begin to tour it. At four Rebecca and Clem would go to the Throne Room of Peter the Great, where Marten and Kovalenko would be waiting. If all went well, at four-fifteen they would leave by a side door and walk directly out to the boat landing across from the museum, where, assuming Kovalenko was successful with "Gray Hair," the man at the bar, a seaworthy boat would be waiting. Marten and Clem and Rebecca would board immediately and go into the cabin and out of sight. Within minutes the vessel would pull away from the landing, travel down the River Neva to the St. Petersburg harbor and out into the Gulf of Finland, and cross the sea in an overnight passage to Helsinki. Kovalenko would simply return the rental car and take the next train back to Moscow.

By the time the FSO realized Rebecca had gone and sounded the alarm it would be too late. They could alert every airport, search every train, and stop every car if they wanted, but they would find nothing. Even if they suspected she had left by boat, how could they know which of the hundreds of boats plying the waters she was on? What would they do, stop them all? Impossible. Even if they tried, by the time the warning was sounded and the Russian coast guard sent into action, night would be falling, and Rebecca, Clem, and Marten would either be in, or very close to, the safety of international waters.

So, with Clem on her way, and Kovalenko negotiating for a boat, the clock had started ticking down. The question now was how and if the remainder of the pieces would come together without breaking apart. In that, Rebecca was most problematical of all. The simple act of her leaving Tsarskoe Selo for a trip to St. Petersburg could become exceptionally difficult if the security people there protested. But assuming she did reach St. Petersburg without trouble, there was no way to predict what would happen once she arrived at the Hermitage Museum and met Lady Clem thinking she was there for a pleasant outing with a friend and instead was suddenly brought face to face with Nicholas. It was a moment that would pack a powerful emotional punch all its own. How she would react to the truth he would tell her about Alexander moments later, and if she would have the strength and courage to believe him and agree to leave St. Petersburg right then, was something else entirely. Yet it was something their escape fully depended upon.

"*Tovarich*, he wants you to pay now." Kovalenko was walking toward him, Gray Hair at his heels. "I thought he would take me on good faith and friendship and I could arrange for you to pay him later. He has a boat, and he has a crew who will not ask questions, but this is risky business and he's afraid that if something happens he will not get his money. And certainly I do not have the kind of money he is asking for."

"I—" Marten stammered. All he had were his two credit cards and, by now, less than a hundred euros in cash.

"How much does he want?"

"Two thousand U.S. dollars."

"Two thousand?"

"*Da.*" Gray Hair pushed up beside him. "Cash, up front," he said in English.

"Credit cards," Marten said flatly.

Gray Hair's face twisted and he shook his head. "*Nyet.* Cash dollars."

Marten looked to Kovalenko. "Tell him it's all I have."

Kovalenko turned to Gray Hair but never got the words out.

"ATM," Gray Hair said brusquely. "ATM."

"He wants—" Kovalenko started to explain.

"I know what he wants." Marten looked to Gray Hair. "ATM. Okay. Okay," he said, hoping to hell that between the two cards he had enough cash-advance balance available to cover it.

38

TSARSKOE SELO, 2:16 P.M.

Gardeners looked up at the sudden thud of heavy rotor blades as the Kamov Ka-60 came in just above the treetops to pass over the still-brown grass of the expansive lawns and early plantings of the massive formal gardens. Flying over a sea of fountains and obelisks, it turned abruptly over a corner of the enormous Catherine Palace, then flew directly over a dense copse of oak and maple to set down in a blast of prop-wash in front of the double-winged, colonnaded, hundred-room Alexander Palace.

Immediately the engines shut down and Alexander jumped

out. Ducking beneath the still-churning rotor blades, he ran anxiously toward the door leading to the building's left wing. In the last hour they had come up against particularly strong headwinds that used up fuel and slowed their airspeed, delaying their arrival time considerably and necessitating a refueling before they returned to Moscow. It meant he had little time to collect Rebecca and be on his way back for his meeting with Gitinov.

As he reached the entryway, the two newly posted FSO agents there came to attention. One of them pulled open the door and Alexander entered.

"Where is the Tsarina?" he said to the two FSO officers on post just inside. "Where?" he pressed.

"Tsarevich," the Baroness's voice echoed sharply down the long, white-walled hallway behind them. Immediately Alexander swung around. The Baroness stood in an open doorway, halfway down the long hallway, in a stark shaft of bright sunshine. Her dark hair turned up severely, she wore a light mink jacket over a designer pantsuit, yellow and white as always.

"Where is Rebecca?" He walked quickly toward her.

"Gone."

"What?" Horror stabbed across Alexander's face.

"I said, she has gone."

The Baroness led Alexander through a bedroom and then through heavily draped double doors into the Mauve Room, the favorite room of Tsar Nicholas II's wife, his own Alexandra. For the Baroness, the singular attraction of the room was neither its color nor its history, but that it could only be reached through the bedroom, then the draped double doors, and therefore was safe from roving eyes and ears. To be doubly safe, she closed the doors behind them as they came in.

"What do you mean she is not here?" Alexander had held his temper for as long as he could.

"She had the FSO drive her into St. Petersburg."

"St. Petersburg?"

"She left about thirty minutes before you arrived."

"Nicholas Marten is in St. Petersburg."

"You don't know that for certain. The only information you

have is that a detective from the Ministry of Justice arrived in St. Petersburg on the Moscow train, and someone may or may not have been with him."

"Where did you hear that?" Alexander was astonished.

"I try to take notice of what is going on around me."

"The FSO had specific orders she was not to leave the palace."

"She is strong-willed." A faint smile crossed the Baroness's face.

Alexander flared with sudden realization. "*You* are the only person strong-willed enough for that. It was *you* who gave permission for her to leave."

"She is not a prisoner of your imagination, or your"—the Baroness chose the word carefully—"worries."

Suddenly Alexander realized. "You *knew* I was coming."

"Yes, I knew, and I didn't want her here when you arrived because I knew her presence would complicate things further. That she wanted to go fit things perfectly." The Baroness's stare became ice. "The utter stupidity of your coming here. You are the Tsarevich, and with the most important encounter of your life only hours away, you act like some precious schoolboy who has an army helicopter to play with."

Alexander ignored her. "Where did she go?"

"Shopping. At least that's what she told me."

Abruptly Alexander turned for the door. "Colonel Murzin will radio the FSO agents with her and have her brought back."

"I think not."

"What?"

"There is every chance you will be late for your 'tea' with the president as it is. I will not have you jeopardizing everything we have worked for by standing around waiting for your 'Tsarina' to be brought back."

"She is shopping!" Alexander was outraged. "She will draw a crowd! People will know she is there. What if—"

"Her brother finds her?" Coldly, quietly, the Baroness finished his thought.

"Yes."

"Then Colonel Murzin would have to do something, wouldn't he?" she said directly, her eyes still riveted on him.

"Do you know what it means?" she asked in a voice that was suddenly soft, even distant, and had the quality of silk.

"What it means to be Tsar?" Her eyes held his for the longest moment, and then she turned and crossed to the window to stand there staring into the distance. "To know you have absolute power. To know that the land and everything in it—its cities, its people, its armies, its rivers and forests—all belong to you."

The Baroness let her words drift away. Then slowly she turned to face him. "Upon your coronation, my sweet, that power will be yours forever. Never again to be taken away, because you have had the training and the bloodletting, and will have the force and means, to ensure it.

"For me to have given you life, to have conceived you from Russia's noblest seed, was God's will. In time you will beget children of your own, and they in turn will beget theirs. They will be our children, all of them, my sweet, yours and mine. A dynasty has been reborn. A dynasty that will be feared and adored and obeyed without question. A dynasty that will one day make Russia the most formidable power on earth."

The faintest smile crossed the Baroness's lips. Then abruptly her eyes narrowed and her voice sharpened. "But for all of it, you are not yet Tsar. God still tests. Gitinov is his saber."

Slowly, almost imperceptibly, the Baroness started across the room toward Alexander, her eyes never leaving him. "A Tsar is a king, and a king must be wise enough to know his enemies. To understand he cannot risk his future and his children's future to the distrust or ambition of a mere politician. To realize that until the deal is done and the crown is fully upon his head, the king-in-waiting remains at the politician's mercy.

"President Gitinov is powerful and shrewd and very dangerous. He must be played like the cruel instrument he is. Coddled and stroked and twirled like a puppet until he fully believes that you are no threat to him whatsoever, that you will never be more than a figurehead monarch content to remain in his shadow."

The Baroness reached Alexander and stopped before him, her eyes still locked on his, powerful and unwavering. "Once that is done the crown will be ours," she whispered. "Do you understand, my sweet?"

Alexander wanted to turn and walk away from her, but he couldn't; the force of her was far too strong. "Yes, Baroness," he felt his lips move and his voice come in a hush, "I understand."

"Then leave Murzin here with me and return to Moscow at once," she said sharply.

For the longest moment Alexander did nothing, just stood there staring at her in numbed silence, his entire being overrun by two simple thoughts, one as vile as the other. Whose crown was it to be really? His or hers? And who was truly the puppet—Gitinov or himself?

"Did you hear me, my sweet?" The angry timbre of her voice rocked through him.

"I—" He started to speak, to react.

"What is it?" she demanded.

Alexander watched her a moment longer, wanting to have it out with her right then, tell her once and for all that he had had enough of her manipulations and everything that went with them. But he knew from a lifetime's experience that such a reaction would only bring on a further torrent. Here as always, against her, there was no such thing as winning.

"Nothing, Baroness," he said finally, then abruptly turned on his heel and left.

39

ST. PETERSBURG. 3:18 P.M.

The beige Ford crossed Anichkov Bridge and continued down the traffic-filled Nevsky Prospekt, St. Petersburg's Champs Elysées, its Fifth Avenue. The car was nondescript, one of thousands of vehicles on the move through the city. In minutes the gilded spire of the Admiralty building on the banks of the River Neva would come into view. And then, directly across from it, the huge Russian Baroque edifice that was the Hermitage Museum.

"Drop me on Dvortsovy Prospekt, just before the river." Lady Clem looked at Kovalenko behind the wheel from where she sat in the passenger seat. "There is a secondary entrance where I asked Rebecca to meet me. A personal guide will be waiting to take us on a private tour. That should be enough to get rid of the FSO, at least for a time."

"That's assuming she gets that far." Marten hunched forward anxiously from the backseat.

"*Tovarich*," Kovalenko said, as he slowed behind a crowded city bus, "at some point we must trust in fate."

"Yes," Marten said, and sat back. Clem sat back, too, and Kovalenko stayed intent on his driving.

Clem was even more beautiful than Marten remembered. He'd caught his breath as he'd seen her walk out of passport control at Pulkovo Airport and strut toward them in dark glasses, black cashmere turtleneck, black slacks, and tan Burberry raincoat, the big black leather handbag slung boldly over her shoulder.

Her reaction to him, as she'd seen them waiting, or rather as she had seen Kovalenko waiting alongside a barefaced, excruciatingly thin man with a very bad haircut, was quite different.

"Good Lord, Nicholas, you are a mess," she'd said with genuine concern, but that had been all she'd been able to say because Kovalenko quickly steered them out the door and toward the Ford on a breezy St. Petersburg afternoon, without giving them so much as a chance to embrace. What either of them felt at seeing the other after so long a time, and after all that had taken place, would have to be discussed later. What Clem also had to put aside for the moment was her not terribly fond sentiment for Kovalenko, remembering clearly the interrogation-hell he and Lenard had put her through in Paris.

What mattered most now, they all knew, as the clock clicked down and they approached the Hermitage, was Rebecca, how she would react when she saw her brother, then was informed about Alexander, and what she would do afterward. There was no discussion whatsoever about Marten's earlier concern, that a different kind of fate might intervene and she wouldn't arrive at all.

40

THE HERMITAGE MUSEUM. 3:25 P.M.

Clem got out of the Ford and walked directly toward the grand museum's secondary entrance on Dvortsovy Prospekt.

"Lady Clementine Simpson," she said in her best-clipped British accent to a uniformed guard at the door.

"Of course," the guard said in English and immediately opened the door.

Once inside, she followed a marble-floored corridor around to the Excursion Office. Again she introduced herself simply by reciting her name.

A moment later a door opened and a short, matronly woman in a neatly pressed uniform came out.

"I am your guide, Lady Clementine. My name is Svetlana."

"Thank you." Clem glanced around. It was three-thirty exactly. This was where and when she was to meet Rebecca. The plan was to tell the guide they wanted to see the Malachite Drawing Room on the second floor. Then they would dismiss the FSO, and with the guide leading them, they would take a private elevator to the second floor. A short walk down the corridor would lead them to the Malachite Drawing Room, where the windows provided an excellent view of the river and the boat landing directly in front of the museum. Gray Hair's boat was to arrive at three-fifty-five. When it did, Rebecca and Clem would go directly to the Small Throne Room, the Memorial Hall of Peter the Great, which Lord Prestbury had personally requested be closed off for the afternoon. Once there, they would ask the guide to wait outside the room while they had a private conversation. Then they would go in and close the door. Inside, Marten and Kovalenko would be waiting.

3:34 P.M.

Where was Rebecca?

Marten stood behind Kovalenko in the admission line at one of four ticket counters. Around them people waiting to get in jabbered in half a dozen languages. They inched forward.

"If you weren't with me, it would cost you almost eleven dollars U.S. to get in," Kovalenko said. "Russians pay just fifty-four cents. Today you are Russian. You are lucky, *tovarich*."

Suddenly there was a commotion behind them. The crowd around them turned. Three dark-blue-suited FSO were coming through the front doors. In their midst, resplendent in mink coat, pillbox hat, and dark veil, was Rebecca.

"The Tsarina!" a woman cried out.

"The Tsarina!" People's voices echoed in awe across the room.

And then she was gone, whisked away by the FSO.

Marten looked at Kovalenko. "You are right, *tovarich*, I am lucky."

3:40 P.M.

Rebecca and Lady Clem threw their arms around each other, hugging joyfully as the FSO shooed people from the Excursion Office. In a moment there were only the six of them, the three FSO, Lady Clem, Rebecca, and Svetlana Maslova, their tour guide.

Now came the hard part, and Clem walked Rebecca away to a corner of the room, smiling, chatting about nothing. When they were far enough away, she looked at Rebecca.

"I have a surprise for you," she said quietly. "We need to go to the second floor but without the FSO. Can you get rid of them?"

"Why?"

"It's important we be alone. I'll explain it to you when we are."

"I'm afraid it is not possible. Alexander radioed for them to stay with me until he got here."

Lady Clem tried to cover a gasp. "Alexander is coming here, to the Hermitage?"

"Yes, why? What's going on?"

"Rebecca—never mind, I'll take care of it." Immediately

Clem turned and crossed the room to where the FSO stood. Thankfully, they were all men.

"The Tsarina and I are going with the guide to the second floor, to the Malachite Drawing Room. We wish to be alone."

A tall, broad-shouldered FSO with eyes that were little more than dots stepped forward. "That is not possible," he said coldly.

"It's not—" Clem started to get mad, then realized it was the wrong approach. "Are you married?" she asked suddenly, dropping her voice and stepping back, away from the others, so he had to follow her.

"No," he said, joining her.

"A sister?"

"Three."

"Then you will appreciate that when a woman learns she is pregnant and she is not married, what to do about it is not something to be discussed in front of strangers, especially men, even if they are"—she used the full FSO designation respectfully and with solid Russian pronunciation—"Federalnaya Slujba Ohrani."

"The Tsarina is—?"

"Why do you think we went to all the trouble to meet away from the palace?"

"The Tsarevich does not know?"

"No, and he'd better not learn of it either. When he is told, the news will come from the Tsarina herself." Lady Clem glanced at the two FSO behind him. "This was conveyed to you in confidence. Do you understand?"

Dot-eyes shifted his feet uncomfortably. "Yes, of course."

"Now," Lady Clem said, indicating an elevator door near the back of the room, "we will go upstairs by private elevator. Svetlana will make certain that the Tsarina and I are not disturbed when we go into the room alone to talk. She has a radio. She can call you instantly if there is a problem."

"I—" He hesitated and Clem saw him wavering. This was no time to back off.

"The Tsarina is the most public woman in Russia. The wedding and coronation are barely three weeks off. She has asked for my help in a very delicate matter. Would you be the one to deny it?"

Still he hesitated, his dot-eyes boring into her, looking for the lie, the put-on, anything to tell him what she was saying was not true. But she held firm and he saw nothing.

"Go," he said finally, "go."

"*Spasiba*," Lady Clem whispered, "*spasiba*." Thank you.

41

3:45 P.M.

Alexander leaned anxiously forward, pulling against the seat harness, as his driver raced the black Volga through traffic and toward the city. Behind him was Rzhevka Airfield where the pilot had set the Kamov helicopter down for another refueling, while waiting for Alexander's return from the Hermitage Museum with Rebecca.

That he was here against the dictates of the Baroness was not an issue because she had no idea what he was doing. As far as she knew he had simply left Murzin behind as she had demanded and flown off for Moscow.

Flown off, but not for Moscow and not before having Murzin find out where Rebecca was at that time, and then personally radioing the FSO guarding her to stay at her side until Alexander arrived. As he left the palace, Murzin warned him not to draw a crowd by landing in the city proper. Such a maneuver would only complicate things when the Tsarevich and Rebecca left St. Petersburg. Rzhevka had been the pilot's call. They needed more fuel, the city was only a short drive from the airfield, and Murzin had arranged to have an FSO car waiting at the airfield for Alexander when he arrived.

Murzin himself had been instructed to inform the Baroness that he had located the Tsarina at the Hermitage in St. Petersburg and was taking a car from Tsarskoe Selo into the city to retrieve her and bring her back to the palace. Once back with Rebecca, Murzin was to tell the Baroness that the Tsarevich had requested that Rebecca be flown directly to Moscow for their six o'clock tea with the president. It was a simple and concise way to get the Baroness and her ceaseless meddling out of the picture.

3:50 P.M.

The Volga crossed Alexander Nevsky Bridge and turned onto Nevsky Prospekt into the growing congestion of rush hour traffic. The crush of vehicles was claustrophobic. Alexander felt trapped and unable to move, and right now, movement was everything because it kept the metronome stopped. If he moved, it didn't. But sitting there, all but helpless in the creep of trucks, buses, and automobiles, he could feel it begin to move inside him.

Boom, boom. Boom, boom.

The beat of his heart like a leitmotif of doom.

3:52 P.M.

Traffic crept.

He was the Tsarevich! Why was the roadway not cleared for him? Didn't people see his car, know who he was? No, how could they? He was riding in a simple black Volga, not a limousine. Nor was this a motorcade.

The booming beat of the metronome grew louder.

Why had Rebecca suddenly decided to go into the city? And if it was only for shopping, why had she gone to the Hermitage? To buy gifts? Maybe. But for whom? The government took care of state gifts, and if she wanted something personally, she could have asked for a consultant to come to the palace. She was Tsarina. All she had to do was ask.

Suddenly he thought of her question about the package he had taken with him when he went on his walk with Marten in Davos.

"You had a gift with you," she'd said, "a gaily wrapped package under your arm. What was in it?"

"I don't know, I don't remember," he'd lied.

But maybe she had known, and that was why she had asked, trying to get him to deny his knowledge. What if somehow

Marten had been in touch with her long before he returned to Russia, and told her about the knife? Perhaps that was the reason she had been so steadfast in her refusal to believe he was dead, because she had spoken to her brother afterward.

On the other hand, maybe she hadn't questioned him about the package at all. Maybe it was all in his mind. Maybe he was so terrified of losing her, he was creating imaginary scenarios. Maybe the Baroness was right and the man seen in the railway station with Kovalenko was someone else and not Marten at all.

Absently he touched his leather flight jacket, the way he had on the flight from Moscow to Tsarskoe Selo, to reassure himself that the knife was still in the inside pocket and close at hand.

"Pass the traffic! Pass it!" he suddenly commanded.

"Yes, Tsarevich," his FSO driver said, immediately pulling the Volga out of its lane and accelerating. He swerved around a large truck, then cut in front of a bus, just missing a young man on a bicycle coming toward them in the opposite direction. As quickly, the driver cut right and went up the inside as they reached the traffic circle at Vosstania Square.

3:55 P.M.

The knife. Why had he started using the Navaja again, after killing his half brother Paul with it twenty-one years before? Simply because he had it back after all that time? Was that it? Retribution for his own near-death at the hands of the LAPD? A furious reaction to the intricate game of keep-away his father and Alfred Neuss had played for decades? Or was it more? Was he using it to exorcise his demons? Instead of attacking his mother, who'd spent Alexander's lifetime single-mindedly and selfishly twisting, manipulating, and shaping her son into a weapon for her vengeance and an instrument for her ambitions, Alexander had released his homicidal rage and butchered his victims with increasing savagery.

And what about Marten, who was still alive only because of Alexander's love for Marten's sister?

He *had* to have been the man the *fartsovchik* had seen with Kovalenko in the railroad station. Alexander knew what Marten looked like the last time he had seen him in Davos. What would he look like now? Long haired and bearded like his visa photograph or thin and clean shaven as the *fartsovchik* had described? Would he even recognize Marten if they stood side by side? Maybe he could tell from Marten's eyes, as he had from the visa photo. But maybe not.

Suddenly a fearsome irony settled over him. He would not recognize Marten any more than Marten would have recognized him in Paris, if Marten had seen him, or had recognized him for the time they had been intimately face-to-face in Davos, both in the villa and on the mountain trail. If Marten was in St. Petersburg, if he was at the museum, he could be inches away and Alexander would never know it.

The metronome beat louder.

3:59 P.M.

42

THE MALACHITE DRAWING ROOM,
HERMITAGE MUSEUM. SAME TIME.

Svetlana and one of the old women whose job it was to guard the artworks kept a crush of people out of the room and gawking in from the doorway as the Tsarina and Lady Clementine Simpson privately toured what was possibly the museum's most imposing room—a hall of magnificent malachite columns, studded with gold-and-malachite figurines, bowls, and urns.

"Clem." Rebecca smiled. "What is going on? There was a surprise, what is it?" She was coy, even silly, as if she expected Clem to have something girlishly frivolous waiting for her.

"Be patient." Lady Clem smiled back and casually stepped to the window to look out at the River Neva. By now the sun of earlier had turned to a gray, sullen overcast. From where she stood she had a clear view of the river and the boat landing in front of the Hermitage. As she watched a lone vessel pulled from the river traffic and approached the landing. If that was the boat she had been told to expect it was hardly the kind of seagoing craft Marten had described. Instead, it was a simple river launch with open seating and a small, covered wheelhouse, and she looked past it and upriver for a larger boat. All she saw was the stream of river traffic and nothing approaching the landing, and she turned her attention back to the launch. As it neared she could see a lone man standing in the stern. He was tall and had a mass of thick, curly gray hair. He was the man she was looking for.

Clem suddenly crossed the room and opened the front door. "Svetlana, the Tsarina would like to see the Throne Room."

"Of course."

The walk down the hallway from the Malachite Drawing Room to the Throne Room was short and took almost no time. A sign in front advised that the room was closed for the afternoon.

"Svetlana." Lady Clem stopped at the door and turned to their guide. "The Tsarina and I would like to be alone for a few moments."

Svetlana hesitated and looked to Rebecca, who nodded in agreement.

"I will wait here," Svetlana said.

"*Spasiba.*" Lady Clem smiled, then opened the door, and she and Rebecca went inside.

43

Alexander could see the gilded spire of the huge and sprawling old Admiralty building ahead of them. On the far side of it was the River Neva, and directly across was the Palace Square, with a rear entrance to the Hermitage inside its circle of buildings.

"Radio the FSO guarding the Tsarina," he said to his driver. "Have them bring her down to the Invalid Entrance immediately."

"Yes, Tsarevich." The driver slowed, turning into the square and picking up his radio microphone.

Nicholas Marten saw a flurry of movement as the two women came in; then Clem closed the door and she and Rebecca looked at the waiting Marten and Kovalenko.

Marten could see the breath go out of Rebecca as she saw him. The moment was incredible, and for the briefest instant, time stood still.

"I knew it!" Rebecca cried out and suddenly was across the room. Holding him, hugging him. Crying, laughing. "Nicholas, Nicholas, how, Nicholas, how?"

Abruptly, as if she'd forgotten who she'd come with, she whirled to look at Lady Clem. "How did you know? When? Why did we have to keep this secret from the FSO?"

"We have to go." Kovalenko moved beside Marten. Getting into the Throne Room had been one thing—all he'd had to do was show his Ministry of Justice identification—but getting out and to the boat would be something else if they didn't move quickly.

Puzzlement crossed Rebecca's face as she saw him. "Who is he?" Her eyes went to her brother.

"Inspector Kovalenko. He is a homicide investigator for the Russian Ministry of Justice."

"Nicholas," Clem warned abruptly, "Alexander went to Tsarskoe Selo from Moscow a short while ago. He knows where Rebecca is. He is on his way here now."

Rebecca looked sharply from Marten to Clem. She could see fear and apprehension in both of them.

"What is it?"

Marten took her hand strongly. "In Paris I told you Raymond might still be alive."

"Yes—"

"Rebecca." Marten wanted to do this gently, but they didn't have the time. "Alexander is Raymond."

"What?" Rebecca reacted as if she hadn't heard.

"It's true."

"It cannot be." She took a step backward, horrified.

"Rebecca, please listen to me. We have almost no time before the FSO come through the door. Alexander carried a wrapped package with him when he and I went out on the trail above the villa in Davos. Do you remember?"

"Yes," Rebecca whispered. She remembered. She'd even asked Alexander about it. At the time it had simply been a thought that had come to her and made her curious, but he had reacted angrily, and so she'd dropped it and not brought it up again.

"When we were away from everyone and on the high bridge, he suddenly took the wrapping from it. Inside was a large knife." Abruptly Marten pulled back his corduroy jacket and lifted his sweater. "Look—"

"No." Rebecca turned away, shocked at the sight of the jagged, twisted scar just above Marten's waist. That was why Alexander had reacted as he had when she mentioned the package. He thought she had guessed what was in it.

"He tried to kill me, Rebecca. The same way he killed Dan Ford and Jimmy Halliday."

"What he is telling you is the truth," Kovalenko said gently.

Rebecca shivered. She was fighting it, desperate not to believe. She looked to Clem, wanting her to say they were wrong.

"I'm sorry, my dear," Clem said genuinely, loving her, "I'm so very sorry."

Rebecca's mouth twisted, and her eyes filled with pain and disbelief. All she could see was Alexander, how he looked at her, how he'd always looked at her. With kindness and respect and undying love.

The room where she stood whirled around her. Here, in this room, in this grand building, was the immense and imposing history of imperial Russia. Behind her, so close she could touch it, was the golden throne of Peter the Great. Everything, all of it, was Alexander's birthright. It was what he was and what she was to be part of. Yet in front of her stood her beloved brother, and with him, her best friend in the world. And with them both, a Russian policeman. Still, she didn't want to believe it. There had to be some other answer. Some other explanation. But she knew there wasn't.

Marten saw the pale fragility, the awful, agonized disquiet, the same look of horror and loss and terror he had seen at the warehouse massacre when Polchak had held her hostage as he tried to kill her brother. If Rebecca was going to collapse into that emotional, traumatized state for the third time in her life, it would be now, and he couldn't let it happen.

With a glance at Clem, he put his arm around Rebecca and led her toward the door. "We have a boat waiting," he said authoritatively. "It's going to take us out of here. You and Clem and me. Inspector Kovalenko is going to make sure that it does and that we are all safe."

"Maybe we have a boat, maybe we don't," Clem said quietly.

"What do you mean?" Marten started.

"It's not at the landing?" Kovalenko was incredulous.

"Oh, it's there, alright, and your gray-haired man is in it. But it's a river launch, and if you think Rebecca and I are going to take it across the Gulf of Finland filled with ice in the middle of the night, you'd better think again."

There was an abrupt knock at the door, and Svetlana came in.

"What is it?" Clem said.

"The FSO are coming to bring the Tsarina downstairs. The Tsarevich waits."

Suddenly Rebecca drew herself up. "Please leave us, and tell the FSO I will be right down," she said directly to Svetlana, regally and with no emotion whatsoever.

"Yes, Tsarina." Immediately Svetlana left, closing the door behind her.

Rebecca looked to Marten. "No matter what Alexander has done, I cannot leave him with nothing." Immediately she turned and walked toward the throne. Near it was an open guest book and beside it a pen. She went to the guest book and tore out a blank page, then picked up the pen.

Marten glanced at Kovalenko. "Watch the door," he said, then quickly went to his sister. "Rebecca, we don't have time. Forget it."

She looked up. Rebecca was strong and filled with her own will. "I shall not forget it, Nicholas. Please."

44

Alexander ran from the Volga toward the museum's Invalid Entrance.

Inside he found no one, not even the normally posted guard. He dashed up a corridor. Museum visitors stopped, open-mouthed, as they recognized him.

"The Tsarevich." Hushed voices resonated down the hallway. "The Tsarevich. The Tsarevich."

Alexander ignored the staring faces and the rolling murmur of his name and kept on. Where were the FSO, where was Rebecca? Just ahead he saw a woman in uniform step out from the gift shop.

"Where is the Tsarina?" he demanded, his face reddened with anger. "Where are the FSO?"

She didn't know, she stuttered, horrified that he was addressing her personally and in awe at the same time.

"Never mind!" He ran on. Where were they? Why had they disregarded his orders? The metronome beat louder. Something was terribly wrong. He was going to lose her, he knew it!

"Tsarevich!" a loud voice cried out from behind him. He stopped and turned.

"All the FSO have gone upstairs to the Throne Room!" His FSO driver ran toward him, the two-way radio in his hand crackling a storm of overlapping FSO communications.

"Why? Is she there? What is wrong?"

"I don't know, Tsarevich."

"This way!" Kovalenko said sharply as they came out of the museum's secondary entrance, the same door to the museum that Lady Clem had used to go in. The Russian was first, then Clem, and Marten with Rebecca. Marten had his arm around his sister, and Clem's Burberry raincoat was thrown over her head and shoulders, as much to keep her from public view as to protect her from the chill wind blowing in off the river.

In seconds Kovalenko had them across Dvortsovaya Naberezhnaya, the boulevard between the museum and the river, and hurrying toward the boat landing, where Gray Hair stood alongside a moored river launch, smoking a cigarette.

"Hey!" Kovalenko shouted as they neared.

Gray Hair waved, tossing his cigarette into the water and going quickly to the stern to unfasten the mooring line.

"You're not taking the Tsarina across open water with this!" Kovalenko was right in Gray Hair's face as they came up, jamming his finger at the launch. "Where the hell is the boat we negotiated for?"

"We have a trawler anchored in the harbor, but we couldn't very well tie it up here without every policeman in St. Petersburg wondering what the hell we were doing. You should know that, old friend." Gray Hair raised an eyebrow. "What's the matter, you don't trust me?"

The briefest smile crossed Kovalenko's face; then he abruptly looked to the others. "Get on board."

Gray Hair steadied the craft against the landing as Marten helped Rebecca and then Lady Clem across the gunwale and watched them go into the covered wheelhouse and out of sight. Then Gray Hair was casting off the bow line and climbing over the forward gunwale. "Come on," he shouted to Marten.

"By morning they will be in Helsinki." Kovalenko was standing so close to Marten that none of the others could hear, or see the Makarov automatic in his hand held out toward Marten, grip first. "What are you going to do?"

"What am *I*—?" Marten stared at him. So this was what it had been about all along. The probing into his past, the carefully developed friendship, the quickness and ease with which Kovalenko had arranged for his passport and visa, the talk about Halliday's terminal cancer and his extraordinary dedication to the squad. Alexander was Raymond, and he knew Kovalenko had been certain of it for a long time. But the only way to prove it was to match Alexander's fingerprints with those on Halliday's computer disk, and now that was gone, a victim of procedure and politics. Still, something had to be done about Raymond as the Tsarevich of All Russia; the *how* and *what* must have been churning over in Kovalenko's mind since Paris. That was why he had so carefully probed Marten about his past. With no choice but to answer, Marten had told little lies, pieces that could be checked. In the end he had given Kovalenko what he needed—a man protecting his true identity, who knew how to kill, and had any number of very personal reasons for executing Raymond.

"You know who I am." Marten's voice was barely a whisper.

Kovalenko nodded slowly. "I telephoned the University of California at Los Angeles. No Nicholas Marten attended the school when you said you were there. However, a John Barron did. Besides, *tovarich,* the squad had six men. Only five are accounted for. So what happened to the last man? Not difficult pieces to fit together—not if you stand where I do."

"Nicholas!" Rebecca called loudly behind them. At the same time, there was a shrill whine as Gray Hair started the launch's engine.

Kovalenko ignored both. "The Hermitage is filled with people. The Tsarevich will not know what you look like now; neither will the FSO."

Marten's eyes went to the automatic in Kovalenko's hand. It was as if, in one giant twist of time, he had been transported from a deserted auto body shop in Los Angeles to the heart of St. Petersburg, Russia.

Kovalenko might as well have demanded what Roosevelt Lee had. Might as well have said "For Red." Or "For Halliday" or "For Dan Ford" or even—"For the squad."

"Who the hell do you work for?" Marten breathed.

Kovalenko didn't answer. Instead he looked past him to the Hermitage. "He is in there, most probably in the Throne Room where we were, or at least near it. He will be upset about the Tsarina and berating the FSO assigned to guard her. Neither he nor they will be paying much attention to what is going on around them. The museum is filled with people. Not so difficult to escape in a crowd afterward, especially if one knows exactly where one is going. I will have the car waiting on Dvortsovy Prospekt at the door we just came out of."

Marten's stare cut the Russian in half. "You sonofabitch," he whispered.

"The choice is yours, *tovarich.*"

"Nicholas!" Rebecca cried again. "Come on!"

Abruptly Marten reached out, wrapped his hand around the Makarov's grip, and slid it into his belt under his jacket. Then he turned, looking first at Rebecca and then to Clem.

"Take her to Manchester, I'll meet you there!" Marten stared for a heartbeat longer, fixing them both in his memory. Then he turned and started back across the landing.

"Nicholas!" He heard Lady Clem yell behind him. "Get on the fucking boat!" But it was too late. He was already crossing Dvortsovaya Naberezhnaya and moving toward the Hermitage.

45

My Alexander,

It is with the greatest sadness I tell you I will not see you again. This destiny was not ours. I shall miss forever what might have been.

Rebecca

The beat of the metronome thundered. Alexander stood frozen, staring at the sheet torn from the guest book and the handwriting on it he knew so well.

The three FSO assigned to Rebecca, and the FSO who had driven him to the museum, stood back in silence watching, terrified about their futures. All they knew was that when they had arrived in the Throne Room, it was empty. A general alarm had been sounded and the building ordered searched by security personnel. The four FSO had been ordered to remain with the Tsarevich. God only knew what would happen next.

"Get out, all of you." The voice of the Baroness cracked through the room like a whip.

Alexander looked up to see her in the doorway, Murzin behind her.

"Get out, I said," she repeated.

Murzin nodded and the FSO quickly left.

"You, as well!" she snapped, and Murzin exited, closing the door behind him.

Three red-carpeted stairs led up to Peter the Great's golden throne, and Alexander stood at the top of them watching her approach.

"She's gone." Alexander's eyes were vacant, as if he saw nothing at all, or had no idea where he was. All there was, all that existed, was the awful *boom, boom, boom, boom,* of the metronome deep inside him.

"She will be found, of course." The Baroness's voice was calm, even soothing. "And when she is—" Her voice trailed off and she smiled thinly. "You know I love her like my own child, but if she were to die, the public would adore you even more."

"What?" Alexander was jolted into the present.

The Baroness came closer, to stand, finally, at the bottom of the stairs looking up at him.

"She was kidnapped, of course," she said assuredly. "The world's eyes will focus on the event. President Gitinov can say nothing, only share in the nation's horror. And then, in the end, her body will be found. Do you understand, my sweet? The hearts of the world will be in your hands. Nothing could be more fortunate."

Alexander was staring at her in disbelief. Trembling, unable to move, as if his feet had suddenly become part of the floor.

"It is all part of your destiny. We are the last true Romanovs. Do you know how many were destroyed after they became Tsar? Five." She moved up one step, coming closer to him, her voice soft as ever. "Alexander the First, Nicholas the First, Alexander the Second, Alexander the Third, and your great-grandfather, Nicholas the Second. But it will not happen to you. I shall not let it. You will be crowned as Tsar and you will not be destroyed. Tell me—" She moved up the second stair and smiled, softly, lovingly.

Alexander stared at her. "No," he whispered, "I won't."

"Tell me, my sweet—say it as you have since you could first talk, as you have forever. Tell me in Russian."

"I—"

"Tell me!"

"*Vsay,*" Alexander began the mantra. He was an automaton, helpless to do anything but her bidding. "*Vsay . . . ego . . . sudba . . . V rukah . . . Gospodnih.*"

Vsay ego sudba V rukah Gospodnih. All his destiny is in God's hands.

"Again, my sweet."

"*Vsay ego sudba V rukah Gospodnih,*" he repeated, a little boy giving in to the demands of his mother.

"Once more," she whispered, and moved up the final step to stand in front of him.

"*Vsay ego sudba V rukah Gospodnih!*" he said forcefully and compellingly, an allegiance to God and to himself. The way he had when he had been trapped by the police in Los Angeles. "*Vsay ego sudba V rukah Gospodnih!*"

Suddenly his eyes were wild and the knife was out of his jacket, the blade flashing in his hand. The first cut was across her throat. Then came the second cut. The third. The fourth. The fifth! Her blood was everywhere. On the floor. His hands. His jacket. His face. His trousers. He felt her slide down his body and heard her slump to the floor at his feet, one arm over the footrest of the golden throne.

Somehow he crossed the room and pulled open the door. Murzin stood there alone. Their eyes met. Alexander grabbed him by the jacket and pulled him into the room.

Murzin stared in horror. "My God—"

Again the knife flashed. Murzin's hand jumped to his throat. The final expression of his life was complete surprise.

Mechanically Alexander knelt and took Murzin's 9 mm Grach automatic from its belt holster. Then he stood, backed away, and went out the door, the pistol slipped into his belt, the bloody knife back inside his jacket.

46

Marten was going toward the Throne Room, climbing the Hermitage's main staircase with a large crowd of museumgoers, when he heard a woman's scream from the floor above. People stopped instantly and looked up.

"The Tsarevich," a man next to him whispered.

Alexander stood at the top of the stairs staring down, seemingly as startled as anyone else by whoever had cried out. His hands were held half in the air, like a surgeon waiting for the nurse to pull on his surgical gloves, and they were covered with blood. There was a large smear of blood on his face as well, and on the leather jacket he wore.

"Jesus God," Marten breathed, then started to move—slowly, carefully, easing up the staircase, using the people staring at Alexander to shield his move. Suddenly Alexander turned his head and his eyes locked on Marten's. For an instant they held there and then, as quickly, Alexander turned and was gone.

Alexander pushed through a door and rushed down an interior stairway. His heart pounding, his mind a blur, he barely felt the steps beneath his feet as he raced down them. At the bottom was another door. For the briefest second he hesitated, then pulled it open and stepped into a central corridor on the first floor. In one direction was the Invalid Entrance through which he had come in. In the other was the main staircase where the man he was certain was Marten had stood in a crowd staring up at him. In between were the toilets.

Alexander opened the stall door and went in. He closed it behind him and latched it, then, overcome, dropped to one knee over the toilet bowl itself and threw up. He knelt there gagging and vomiting, emptying everything in his stomach, for a full two minutes, maybe more. Finally, his throat raw, he managed to stand and flush the toilet, then wipe his mouth and nose with tissue. Afterward, he tried to drop the tissue in the toilet but he couldn't; it was stuck to his hands, and for the first time he became aware of the blood on them.

Suddenly there was a rush of excitement and he heard several people come into the toilet from the hallway outside. The Tsarevich had been seen in the building at the top of the main staircase, they said; he had had blood on him, or at least what appeared to be blood. There were rumors two people had been killed. Security people had sealed off the entire second floor. The killer could be anywhere.

Slowly Alexander bent to the toilet and put his hands into the cold water. Quickly, wildly, he rubbed them together, trying to get the blood off. In a way it seemed almost funny because he didn't know whose blood it was, Murzin's or the Baroness's, or both. He rubbed harder. The blood vanished in the wet, or most of it anyway. Good enough. He straightened and flushed again. Then he saw more blood on his trousers and on his leather flight jacket. He heard the restroom door open and one person and then another go out.

Alexander opened the stall door a crack. A lone man stood combing his hair in the mirror. He was in his thirties, of medium height and build, and was stylishly dressed in a brown plaid suit, with a long navy scarf twisted foppishly around his neck. Curiously, even in the toilet's muted light, he wore wraparound sunglasses.

"Excuse me," Alexander said in English as he came out of the stall.

"Yes?" the man answered. It was the last word he ever said.

47

Marten had tried to go up the staircase after Alexander, but a phalanx of FSO agents and uniformed security guards had suddenly closed off the second floor and were sending everyone back down. Minutes later a male voice came over a loudspeaker announcing in Russian and then in English, French, and German that the museum was being closed at once for security reasons and that no one would be allowed to leave until he or she had been cleared by police.

Quickly Marten had retreated back down the stairs with the others and walked swiftly down a long columned room toward the main entrance. He knew that with the scream, whatever had happened upstairs, and the suddenness of Alexander's retreat, things were moving too quickly for the security lockdown to be fully in place. If he got caught inside with the crowd, he could be hours in line before he was cleared and released—or not released at all, since he was carrying Kovalenko's automatic and a passport identifying him as Nicholas Marten—and by then Alexander would be long gone.

Ahead, he could see the main entrance.

Another twenty feet and—suddenly he pulled up short. The police were already there. The exit was sealed off and they were setting up their checking procedure.

To his left were the ticket booths, and beyond them, down a short hallway, was the Excursion Office, where Clem had gone to meet Rebecca. Anxiously, he pushed into the hallway, working his way through the pack of confused and frightened museumgoers. In a moment he was at the Excursion Office. Just past it he could see an emergency door leading out. It had a crash bar and maybe an alarm, but it was worth the chance. He reached it and was about to put his shoulder to it when he saw two FSO agents running down the hallway toward him. Immediately he turned and went back, fighting through the crowd, passing the ticket booths and the main entrance. Again the announcement came over the loudspeakers.

Now he was in the columned room once more, heading toward the main staircase. Then he saw a long corridor leading off to the right. He took it quickly, his eyes darting back and forth looking for an exit door. He passed a bookstore and an art shop. There were more people, more confusion. He kept on, passing the museum toilets. A dozen paces farther and something made him look down. He froze. On the black-and-white checkerboard floor in front of him was the bloody toe print of a shoe. A few paces more and he saw another. Immediately his hand went to the Makarov in his belt. Carefully he slipped it out and let his arm drop to his side. He walked on, keeping the automatic as hidden from view as possible.

Another bloody toe print and then another. It was the right foot, and whoever was leaving it was moving quickly. The strides were lengthening, and the prints becoming fainter as the blood wore off.

48

A gray, overcast sky hung above the city as a man dressed in a stylish plaid suit, navy scarf, and wraparound sunglasses stepped cautiously out of the Invalid Entrance and into the Palace Square at the rear of the building, his hand on Murzin's automatic under his jacket, ready to be challenged by police. But there were none. From the direction of the sirens they seemed, for the moment at least, to be concentrating their efforts on the crowds at the main entrance. Alexander hesitated a moment longer, then adjusted the sunglasses and moved forward.

In front of him was the black Volga. Where his FSO driver was or where the other FSO were, he had no idea. He had last seen them when they left the Throne Room after the Baroness had ordered them out.

Hurriedly he turned and looked across the wide square. In the center was the towering Alexander Column commemorating the defeat of Napoleon. On the far side the General Staff Building was linked to the Guard's Headquarters by a grand triumphal arch atop which sat a massive sixteen-ton sculpture of Victory riding in a chariot led by six horses. All were reminders of Russia's victories in the War of 1812. They should have given him the hope and courage of the Russian heart—and they might have, had he not glanced behind him and seen the faint but still visible bloody toe prints and realized he was leaving a trail.

Horrified, he moved on across the square, walking quickly, afraid to break into a run that would certainly draw attention. As he went he scuffed the sole of his right shoe on the pavement, trying desperately and awkwardly to wear off whatever blood was left, and at the same time trying to understand exactly what had happened in the stall of the *muzhskoy,* the men's toilet. He'd not had much time to strip off his clothes and change into the plaid suit of the man he had killed. In his haste he must have inadvertently stepped into the man's blood with his right foot, with the crepe of his shoe soaking it up like a sponge. Again, the specter of the knife haunted him. Why had he begun using it once more? If he hadn't, the Baroness would still be alive, and so would Murzin, to protect him.

He rushed on, passing the Alexander Column, his eyes on the triumphal arch in the distance. All around he could hear the scream of sirens. To his left he could see police cars sealing off the staff parking area. Fifty people, at least, had seen him at the top of the main stairway smeared with blood. In all the chaos and commotion there was no way to know how soon the police and the FSO would find the body in the men's toilet along with his jacket and trousers. But when they did, it would create even more confusion. No one would be sure what happened, why the Tsarevich's clothes were there, where he was, or what had happened to him. The first assumption—particularly after he had been seen blood-soaked in public—would have to be that he had been attacked by the same person or persons who had killed the Baroness and Murzin and was either dead or a prisoner or in hiding somewhere inside the cavernous building, which was where they would concentrate their search. Moreover, no one would know, at least right away, that the dead man had worn a plaid suit. Taken together, all of those things gave him the precious time and breathing room he needed. Another step and he looked back toward the museum. The square was empty. He kept on.

Suddenly he thought of Marten. He had been there on the staircase in the mass of others, coming up toward him. He was close shaven and thin, with short hair and in an inexpensive brown corduroy suit. It might have been someone else, but it wasn't, it was Marten without doubt, there, once again, as somehow he always was. Why he had thought he wouldn't recognize him he didn't know. He realized now he would know him anywhere. The reason was simple. His eyes. Marten would be looking straight at him, as if he were Alexander's soul and shadow at the same time.

"Stop it!" he told himself. "You need to think clearly. Stop this obsession with Marten." He looked up. He was nearly at the triumphal arch. Still there were no police, not here anyway. On the far side of the arch was St. Petersburg, and he knew that once he reached the city he could melt into it the way he had in Los Angeles. Again he looked back toward the Invalid Entrance. No one, nothing. Now he was at the arch. He turned back for one final glance. As he did, the door to the Invalid Entrance opened and a lone man stepped out. He was some distance away but there was no doubt at all who it was.

Nicholas Marten.

49

Marten saw the faint blood trail of the toe print just outside the door. And then, far across the square, he saw a man in a plaid suit suddenly turn and look back toward him, then dart into the shadows underneath a high arch between buildings.

Marten started to run, reaching for his cell phone as he did.

"He's alone and on the run!" Marten's voice jumped from Kovalenko's phone.

"Where is he? Where are you?" Kovalenko, parked by the museum's secondary entrance, was already starting the rental Ford's engine.

"Crossing the square behind the museum. He just cut under an archway on the far side."

"Stay with him, I'll meet you."

Alexander was clear of the triumphal arch and walking quickly toward the busy Nevsky Prospekt. He looked over his shoulder and saw no one. Then he reached Nevsky Prospekt and turned down it, going away from the museum and the river.

Marten came through the arch at a dead run. Ahead of him he saw three young women, walking and chatting animatedly among themselves. Quickly he crossed to them.

"Please, did you see a man in a plaid suit?" he asked.

"No English," one of the girls said awkwardly, and they stood staring at each other.

"Thanks, sorry." Marten pushed on, running toward the far end of the street. Thirty seconds later he reached Nevsky Prospekt just as Kovalenko's beige Ford slid to a stop.

"Lost him." Marten climbed in beside Kovalenko and slammed the door. "He was wearing a plaid suit."

"Okay." Kovalenko moved the Ford off. "This is *the* street in St. Petersburg, *tovarich,* maybe all of Russia. Millions of people are here every day. It will be very easy for him to hide, unless, of course, he is recognized. Then he can hide nowhere. You watch the right, I'll watch the left."

Suddenly the crackle of Russian police-speak came over the portable police radio Kovalenko had propped on the dash in front of him.

"What is it?" Marten asked.

"The museum. They've found another body in a downstairs toilet."

"What do you mean—another?"

"Two were dead upstairs. Colonel Murzin, the commander

of the Tsarevich's special FSO force, and"—Kovalenko hesitated—"the Baroness."

"The Baroness?"

"*Tovarich*, he killed his own mother."

50

Alexander pushed through the thick crowds milling along the Nevsky Prospekt sidewalk. So far, in the dead man's plaid suit and wraparound sunglasses, he was unnoticed; no one had even so much as turned to look as he passed. He glanced back, his eyes scanning both sidewalks. All he saw was a mass of faceless people, and the street in between, jammed with traffic. No sign of Marten. None. He kept on.

On the pavement in front of him was a crushed McDonald's takeout carton. Beside it, a crushed Coke container. A dozen paces later he walked by a Pizza Hut; another half block and he passed a store selling Nike and Adidas shoes, then one with American baseball caps in the window. He might as well have been in London, or Paris, or Manhattan. It didn't matter. The shops, the people, none of it mattered. Other than Marten, the only thing on his mind was the refueled Kamov helicopter at Rzhevka Airfield and its pilot waiting for him to return. Where he would go in it was not important. Maybe south to Moscow calling President Gitinov from the air to say that the Tsarina had been kidnapped and that he had escaped the massacre at the Hermitage and was on his way to Moscow and the safety of the Kremlin. Or west, to the Baroness's seventeenth-century manor in the mountainous Massif Central of France. Or maybe—his mind wandered as he thought of the possibilities—maybe he would go east, across Russia to Vladivostok, then Japan, and from Japan, south, using the Philippines, New Guinea, and French Polynesia for refueling stops across the southern Pacific on his way to his ranch in Argentina.

He looked back. Still no sign of Marten. He had to get to the airfield. What should he do? Stop a car and force the driver ou and take the car himself? No, there was too much traffic. He might get a block, two at most before he was caught. He looked up.

Ahead was a Metro station. It was perfect. Not just as a refuge but as a way to the airfield. Use the Metro the same way he had in Los Angeles when, as Josef Speer, he had taken the public bus to get to LAX. Suddenly he realized that to take the Metro he would need money. He put his hands in his jacket pockets.

Nothing.

He tried the pockets in the pants, front and back. Still nothing. What had he done with the dead man's personal things when he'd stripped him in the stall? He had no idea.

He needed money. Not much, just enough for a pass into the Metro. But where, how to get it quickly? Ten paces in front of him an elderly woman swaggered along, a large purse dangling from her arm.

He moved swiftly, decisively. In a moment he was next to her, grabbing the purse and ripping it free. He dashed forward through the crowd as she fell to the pavement. He heard her cry out behind him.

"Vor! Vor!" she yelled. Thief! Thief!

He kept on, pushing through the crowd. Suddenly he felt a hand grab him and start to pull him around.

"Vor!" a heavyset youth yelled, and threw a punch at him. Alexander ducked. And then another youth attacked him.

"Vor!" "Vor!" "Vor!" They screamed as they pummeled him with their fists and at the same time tried get the woman's purse for her.

Alexander threw up an arm and twisted away as a crowd began to close in.

"Vor! Vor!" the youths screamed and charged after him.

Suddenly Alexander turned back, Murzin's 9 mm Grach automatic in his hand.

Boom! He shot the first youth in the face point-blank.

Boom! Boom! The second youth was thrown sideways and staggered into the street in front of a bus, two-thirds of his head blown away.

People screamed in horror. Alexander stared for the briefest second, then turned and ran.

Marten and Kovalenko looked at each other. They were a block away, but the gunshots were thunderous. Suddenly traffic stopped short.

"There he is!" Marten caught a glimpse of plaid as Alexander darted across Nevsky Prospekt behind the bus and disappeared into the crowd on the far side of the street. In a blink Marten pushed open the door.

"*Tovarich*," Kovalenko warned, "if those shots came from him—"

"Means he's got a gun." Marten said and was gone, running up the center of the street dodging between the stopped vehicles.

Behind him, Kovalenko pulled the Ford to the curb and got out. In the rear seat was his traveling case. He reached in and flicked it open. In it was a second Makarov. He slid it into his belt, then locked the car and ran off in the direction Marten had taken.

51

Alexander crossed a bridge over a canal, then turned down one side street, and another. He looked back. He was alone. He stopped and looked around, unsure of where he was or which way he had come.

The world around him spun. Somewhere in the distance he heard sirens. To get to the airfield he needed to find a Metro station. Again he looked around. Nothing was familiar. He needed a street sign, a building he recognized, anything at all to tell him where he was.

He started walking.

Ahead an elderly couple was coming toward him walking a dog. He clutched the stolen purse to him so they wouldn't see it. A moment later they passed. There was no recognition at all, not even a glance, the same as it had been on Nevsky Prospekt. He looked behind him. Where was Marten? Where was his shadow?

He saw nothing.

If Marten could find Alexander's trail in the museum, he could find him on the street. Why had he fallen in love with Marten's sister in the first place? It had only served to draw the man to him. Again he thought, if only he had killed him before, in Paris or Manchester or even in L.A., but he hadn't.

The helicopter.

He opened the stolen purse and took out the woman's wallet. There was cash, more than enough for the Metro, certainly enough to take a taxi. That was it, a cab. That way he would only have to deal with the driver and not the public.

The street was narrow; he couldn't tell where it led. Here and there people passed. Still no one recognized him. He was one of them, he was no one.

He glanced up at the gray sky. It was getting dark. There was maybe an hour of daylight left, certainly no more than that.

He turned a corner. A canal was directly in front of him. He walked toward it. Which one was it? He reached it and saw a sign on a protective iron balustrade—EKATERININSKY CANAL. Now he knew exactly where he was. Across it, to his right, was the familiar majestic Cathedral of Our Lady of Kazan, and just beyond it the Kazansky Bridge and Nevsky Prospekt. Taxis passed there every few minutes. The shooting had happened farther down. Time had passed; he had to take the chance no one would recognize him. He started along the canal on the run. The bridge was a hundred yards away. When he reached it he would take the stairs leading up to the street. On Nevsky Prospekt, he would find a taxi that would take him to Rzhevka Airfield and the waiting helicopter. It would be alright. Everything was going to be alright.

Marten walked back along Nevsky Prospekt the way he'd come. He'd seen Alexander dash over a bridge and then disappear. Marten had followed, crossing the same bridge less than a minute later. He'd run two more blocks before he realized he'd lost Alexander. He continued for a little way, passing several side streets that were all but deserted, then he'd turned back. Why, he wasn't sure. It was just a sense that Alexander hadn't gone quite that far and was somewhere nearby. But where?

Marten's eyes searched faces as he walked. Alexander could be any one of them. To kill for a change of clothes or another appearance meant nothing to him. Life meant nothing to him. Except—Marten remembered the villa in Davos and the look in Alexander's eyes when he was with Rebecca. The devotion, the absolute love, they were something Marten had been certain Alexander was wholly incapable of. But he'd been wrong, because he had been there and seen it.

He passed more faces. Men, women, Alexander could be either. Suddenly Marten thought of Alexander's tricks and deadly guile in Los Angeles. At the same time he remembered Dan Ford's warning in Paris. *You won't know what he's doing until it's too late. Because by then you'll already be in the cave and then—there he is.*

Marten put his hand on the Makarov in his belt and kept walking, his eyes shifting from one stranger to the next. Alexander was here somewhere, he knew it.

Suddenly the steely overcast sky that had hovered over St. Petersburg for most of the afternoon gave way to brilliant sunshine as the sun sank low on the horizon. In seconds the entire city was bathed in a breathtaking golden light. It caught Marten unaware, and he stopped to look at it. Then he realized he was standing on the same bridge he had seen Alexander cross, and he looked around. Movement below caught his eye, and he saw a man in a plaid suit moving quickly along the canal beneath him and nearly to the steps leading up to the bridge on which Marten stood.

Alexander had his hand on the stair railing and was starting up when he froze. Marten stood at the top of the steps, looking down at him. A light wind ruffled Marten's hair, and he and the city and the sky were colored a brilliant yellow.

Coolly, even coldly, Alexander turned and started back the way he had come. On the far side of the canal, the Cathedral of Our Lady of Kazan glowed in the same golden light. Steps led down from the bridge on that side, too, and he thought he saw someone vaguely familiar come down them.

He picked up his pace. There was no need to look. He knew Marten was coming down the steps behind him. He was walking, not running, his steps deliberate, keeping him in sight, but not forcing it. If he ran, Marten would run. Yes, there was a chance he might lose him, but there was also an even greater chance that two running men would attract attention, and he knew the police were there because he could still hear the sirens. They were looking for the person who had killed the Baroness and the FSO colonel Murzin and the man in the Hermitage men's toilet. They would have no idea who that was, or whether it was a man or a woman, or what he or she might look like. But now they would be looking for someone else as well, a man in a plaid suit who had just shot two men on Nevsky Prospekt.

So just keep walking, he thought, let Marten come. Finally he understood. Marten was here now, the same as he had been at every turn. Here because he was supposed to be. It was why they had gone up against each other in L.A., why Alexander had fallen in love with Marten's sister, perhaps even why he had left the bloody footprints. Marten was an integral part of his *sudba*, his destiny. Rebecca had told him more than once how alike he and her brother were. Their skills and daring were on the same extraordinary level; so, too, were their courage and will and tenacity. And both had come back from the dead. Marten was God's last fiery gauntlet, the ultimate test of his ability to reach the greatness God commanded of him.

This time, and once and for all, Alexander would achieve it, prove to God that he could bring himself back from the edge of the oblivion where he stood.

It should be simple. He still had the gun and the Navaja switchblade. Marten had been in the Hermitage. All he had to do was kill him, then put his fingerprints on the knife and the knife in his pocket, and the people of Russia would see what their Tsarevich was made of. He would be the hero who, alone, had tracked the murderer of the Baroness and Colonel Murzin through the streets of St. Petersburg and finally slain him. After that there would be no questions about the plaid suit or the dead men on Nevsky Prospekt and in the men's toilet at the museum—all of whom, he would say, were accomplices of the murderer and had tried to kill him. Nor would there be any need to go to the helicopter. The helicopter would come to him.

Ahead another bridge crossed the canal. It was a footbridge. Bankovski Most, Bank Bridge, it was called. It was lovely, ancient, classic, with two huge griffins sporting great gold wings guarding either side. To his left was a series of three- and four-story stone and brick buildings. Nothing else. He kept on, his back to Marten.

Before long he would reach the bridge. As he did he would slide Murzin's Grach automatic from his waistband, then drop the purse as a distraction and turn and fire.

Marten was twenty yards behind him when he saw Alexander shift the stolen purse from his right hand to his left and look to the footbridge directly ahead of him that crossed the canal to the other side. It was then he saw Kovalenko. He was on the far side and staying just behind them, keeping pace. Marten knew Kovalenko was smart, but he had never seen him use a gun and didn't know if he was aware of Alexander's deadly quick speed and extreme accuracy with a firearm. If Alexander took the bridge and recognized Kovalenko, he would kill him in the bat of an eye.

"Raymond!"

Alexander heard Marten cry out behind him. He kept walking. Another five paces and he would be at the bridge. The griffins were huge bronze statues and would be excellent cover. Marten would be alone on the walkway with no cover whatsoever. The Grach felt light, even nimble in his hand. It would only take one shot, and it would be between the eyes.

Marten stopped and raised the Makarov in two hands, training its sight on the back of Alexander's head. "Raymond! Freeze! Now!"

Alexander half smiled and kept walking.

"Raymond!" Marten commanded again. "Last chance! Freeze! I'll kill you right there!"

Again the half smile. Alexander kept walking. A deaf man out for a stroll.

For the briefest moment Marten did nothing. Then slowly his finger closed on the Makarov's trigger. A single thundering boom echoed off the canal and the surrounding buildings. Shards of jagged pavement exploded at Alexander's feet.

Alexander ignored it and kept on. He was almost to the bridge. In his mind Marten was already dead. His right hand slid into his belt and he took hold of the Grach at his waist.

Three paces, two.

He was at the bridge.

He let the purse drop from his hand.

Marten was already on the ground and rolling sideways when Alexander turned, the Grach in his hand. Marten came up on both elbows, the Makarov full on Alexander, staccato thoughts spitting through him, all the buttons Kovalenko had pushed before—*For Red. For Dan. For Halliday. For the squad.*

He squeezed the trigger just as Alexander fired. There was a thundering roar of gunshots. Pieces of concrete sprayed up in his face and for an instant he was blinded. Then his vision cleared and he saw Alexander staggering back, his left leg a shattered mass of plaid and blood. He saw him try to raise the Grach, but he couldn't. Then his leg gave way and he collapsed, the automatic skittering away on the pavement.

Alexander saw Marten push up and start toward him, the Makarov held in both hands. At the same time, he realized he was on the pavement and the Grach was on the ground in front of him. He tried to get up and reach for it. He couldn't. Everything beneath him felt soft, as if he had landed on a bed of dry leaves. Suddenly he saw Marten stop where he was and look past him. As quickly he turned to see what had Marten's attention.

The vaguely familiar figure he had seen coming down the steps on the far side of the canal was now crossing the footbridge coming toward him. It was the Russian policeman, Kovalenko. A Makarov was in his hand, and his eyes were like ice. Puzzlement crossed Alexander's face. Why was Kovalenko coming at him with the gun raised like that? Why was he looking at him the way he was when he was down and unarmed and helpless? Suddenly he knew. *This* was his destiny, and had been from the day he plunged the Navaja knife into his half brother's chest in the park in Paris.

"Kovalenko, don't!" he heard Marten scream behind him.

It was too late. The Russian policeman was right next to him.

"No! No! Don't!" he heard Marten scream again.

Then he saw the Russian policeman's eyes harden and felt the push of the Makarov against his head. His finger tightened on the trigger. A thundering boom was cut short by a terrible onrush of searing white light. It washed over everything like a ferocious tide. Becoming brighter and brighter and brighter. And then. Finally.

It went out.

52

THE GULF OF FINLAND. SAME TIME.

Rebecca and Lady Clem stood outside the wheelhouse of the sixty-foot herring trawler number 67730, looking back at St. Petersburg awash in a golden hue. The ship was twenty minutes out of the harbor and traveling at eight knots through a gentle swell dotted with intermittent patches of ice. The golden light held for a few moments longer and then, as if a curtain had been abruptly lowered, vanished as the sun sank beneath the clouds on the horizon.

Darkness settled, and, as if drawn by the same force that had brought the radiant light to St. Petersburg, the women turned to each other.

"Time will pass and it will become a little more bearable," Clem said quietly, "and in more time, less and less on your mind. It's something we will work toward, the two of us, you and I. We will, I promise you."

Rebecca studied her for a moment, trying to believe her, wanting to believe. Finally she closed her eyes and, with a monstrous sob, the tears came.

Lady Clem put her arms around Rebecca and held her, silently crying with her, the sorrow of it, perhaps, most painful of all. After minutes, or hours, who knew, and feeling the roll of the sea beneath them, Clem glanced back toward St. Petersburg and led Rebecca inside, into the light and warmth of the wheelhouse.

ST. PETERSBURG. STILL SATURDAY,
APRIL 5. 7:40 P.M.

Kovalenko accelerated through Sennaya Square in the darkness, taking them quickly away from the bridge and the canal, away from Nevsky Prospekt.

"He was down. His gun was out of reach. There was no reason to kill him." Marten was furious.

"Tovarich." Kovalenko kept his eyes on the traffic in front of them. "I save your life and this is how you respond?"

"He was harmless."

"There was always the knife, maybe another gun. Who knew what? A man like that is never harmless until he is dead."

"You didn't have to execute him."

"How would you like to meet your ladies for breakfast?" Kovalenko turned the Ford down Moskovsky Prospekt and accelerated once more, heading toward Pulkovo Airport. "There is a flight out for Helsinki in little more than an hour."

Marten glared at him, then abruptly stared off, the lights of oncoming traffic illuminating his face, changing it from light to dark and back again.

"You carefully work to build a trust, even a friendship between us." Marten's voice was filled with bitterness. "And in the meantime you search for a way to find out who I am. You ask questions trying to trip me up, and when you finally figure it out, you start to play on my guilt—for what happened to the squad, for all the people that Raymond killed in L.A. and later in Paris—and on my love for my sister. You provide a passport and a visa, even a cell phone. And then when the time is right you give me a gun and send me in to do the dirty work. And I did, for all the reasons you preyed on and more. And then I got him and he was down and out. You could have arrested him, but you killed him instead." Marten's eyes swung to Kovalenko. "It was an assassination, wasn't it?"

Kovalenko watched the road as the Ford's headlights alternately illuminated the entrances to potato farms and thick stands of still-leafless birch and maple trees, and, in between, even thicker forests of lighted billboards advertising Fords and Hondas, Volvos and Toyotas.

"This is what will happen, *tovarich*." Kovalenko looked to Marten and then back to the road. "By now they will have found his body. They will be horrified when they discover who he is. For a while they won't realize what really happened at the Hermitage. And then they will, especially when they put it together with the knife still in his jacket pocket.

"Shortly afterward official word will come from Moscow that the Tsarevich is dead, murdered while trying to apprehend the killers of the Baroness and his FSO chief Colonel Murzin at the Hermitage. The three people he killed along the way will be identified as conspirators, and an all-out search will be made for his killer or killers. In all probability the blame will fall on some Communist faction because the democrats are still at war with the Communists. Eventually, to protect the integrity of law enforcement, there may even be an arrest and a trial.

"Your sister, the Tsarina, beloved by the Tsarevich who was murdered before he could be crowned, beloved by the Russian people, will be out of contact, sent away for a period of bereavement with her good friend and confidant, the daughter of the Earl of Prestbury, Lady Clementine Simpson.

"Next will come several days of public mourning. Alexander's body will lie in state at the Kremlin, and he will be acclaimed as a national hero. After that will be a state funeral, and he will be buried alongside his father and the other Russian emperors in the crypt of the St. Catherine Chapel of the Peter and Paul Cathedral in St. Petersburg. Your sister will be expected to attend, and no doubt you as well."

"That doesn't answer—"

"Why I killed him? He was a madman, and Russia could not very well have a Tsar who was a madman."

Marten was still angry. "What you're saying is that if this madman was alive and under arrest, you would have had to put him on trial and in the end be forced to either put him in prison for life or execute him. It's not the kind of thing the Russian government would have wanted. So you took care of it yourself."

Kovalenko smiled just a little. "That's part of it."

"What's the rest?"

"As I suggested, there was always the possibility of the knife or another gun. What if, when you came up on him, he tried to kill you? We know his work all too well. His move would have been quick, and you would have had no choice but to kill him or die yourself. Yes?"

"Maybe."

Kovalenko's eyes narrowed and he looked at Marten. "No, *tovarich*, not maybe, certainly." He stared for a moment longer, letting his point sink in, then looked back to the road. "First I will say it is true I had you marked by the time we left Paris, and yes, I sent you into the museum to kill Alexander because I knew you were capable of doing it and had a reason and because I didn't have to include anyone else.

"But when I was waiting for you outside I remembered what had happened when you and your sister were reunited, how she reacted to seeing you, and to what you told her. I realized my decision had been wrong. If you had been the one to kill the Tsarevich, you could never again look at her without the fear that she would see the truth of what you had done in your eyes, and you would have had to live the rest of your life like that, knowing you had killed the man she loved more than life itself, even if he was what he was.

"And then, *tovarich*, there is something else, and it is a basic truth. Some men, no matter how skillful or dedicated they are, or force themselves to be, are not meant to be policemen. The sometimes necessary cruelty of it, killing without remorse and in disregard for the law they have sworn to uphold when the circumstance requires it, is not in their blood." Kovalenko looked over and smiled gently. "You are such a man, *tovarich*. You are still young. Go back to your English gardens. It is a much better life."

EPILOGUE

The sea was brilliant turquoise and the white sand blazing hot. Away from the sand and beneath the ocean's surface were colors unimaginable. Unearthly whites, stripes of radiant coral and dazzling magenta, oranges never seen on land, hues of black not on any chart, all in the magic of tropical fish that reached out to nibble the sea-damp crumbs of bread Marten took from his small plastic bag to feed them while he swam, watching this world through his mask as he took in fresh air through his snorkel.

Later, toward sundown, he left his snorkeling gear in the trunk of his rental car and walked along the deserted beach at Kekaha.

The sale of a short article on the use of fieldstone in the design of private gardens to an international house-and-garden magazine had brought him an advance contract to provide a series of similar pieces monthly. The sum, while by no means large, allowed him to pay off his credit card debt for the rental of the trawler, with enough left over to indulge his sanity, or what little there was left of it, without tapping into his savings. He had come here to Kauai seven days ago, some seven thousand miles from England, his long-overdue paper, like his semester's studies, finally completed, his examinations taken and passed with honors.

Thin and sunburned with a five-day growth of beard and dressed in only faded shorts and an equally washed-out University of Manchester T-shirt, he could easily have been taken for a world-hopping beach bum.

Kekaha was the same beach he and Rebecca had come to every few years as children with their mother and father. It was a place he knew well and remembered fondly. That was why he had come to it now, alone, to drift and think, and to try to get some reasonable perspective on what had happened. And maybe, finally, some tiny morsel of peace of mind. But it was a goal that was difficult, even elusive. Its context was as raw and obscene as ever, its reality, the stuff not of dreams but nightmares.

Alexander Nikolaevich Romanov, Tsarevich of All Russia, had been buried five days after his death, as Kovalenko had predicted, a national hero. Rebecca and Clem had gone to St. Petersburg; so had he—officially invited as a member of Rebecca's family—to support her emotionally. He had stood in the great crypt of the Peter and Paul Cathedral alongside Rebecca's birth parents and the presidents of Russia and the United States and the prime ministers of a dozen countries.

The massive presence of foreign dignitaries and the media coverage accompanying it was exceeded only by the enormous outpouring of sympathy from people around the world. The Kremlin alone received tens of thousands of cards of condolence and twice that many e-mails. Even though the wedding between Alexander and Rebecca had never taken place, twenty thousand handwritten notes addressed to the Tsarina were delivered to the Kremlin's central post office. Hundreds of bouquets of flowers had been left on the footbridge over the Ekaterininsky Canal where Alexander had been slain. People in tears lit candles and left flowers and photographs of him in front of Russian embassies on every continent.

All of it had eaten at Marten's soul, twisting him in rage at its terrible irony. How could the world know, or begin to comprehend if it did, that the tearful, solemn state pageantry honoring the romantic, charismatic figure who would have been the first Tsar of Russia in modern times was really nothing more than a grand funeral for the heinous multiple murderer Raymond Oliver Thorne?

A small package arriving in Manchester some five weeks after the funeral in St. Petersburg helped Marten realize that, upset as he was, he was not alone in his feelings.

The package, mixed in with his regular mail, had no return address but was postmarked Moscow. Inside it he'd found a lone sheet of paper, typed single-spaced and folded in quarters. With it had been two five-by-seven black-and-white photographs. One had carried an LAPD date/time code; the other had a handwritten designation, *State Morgue, Moscow.* The photographs were digital reproductions of fingerprints. The first, he knew, were Raymond's LAPD booking prints. The second, he didn't know but guessed, had been taken during Alexander's autopsy. The prints, like those matching Dan Ford's killer with Raymond, were identical.

The typed sheet had the following:

(1) FSO Colonel Murzin: Former Spetsnaz soldier. Two years prior to Moscow assignment spent eight months sick leave recovering from injuries sustained in a special training exercise. Seven of those eight months spent out of country. Destination country, Argentina.

(2) FSO Colonel Murzin: Personal account at Credit Suisse bank, Luxembourg. $10,000 U.S. dollars deposited monthly for past three years. Deposits were from payroll account of CKK, AG, personal security firm, Frankfurt, FRG. CKK legal affairs handled by Zurich-based attorney, Jacques Bertrand.

(3) J. Bertrand placed the printing order for the Davos menu with deceased Zurich printer, H. Lossberg.

(4) J. Bertrand was personal attorney for Baroness de Vienne.

(5) Former Spetsnaz soldier, I. Maltsev. Employed as chief security officer at Alexander Cabrera's ranch in Argentina for past ten years. Member of hunting party concurrent with Cabrera's shooting accident. In Spetsnaz, specialist in firearms and hand-to-hand combat training, special proficiency, knife fighting; also expert in explosives and sabotage. Arrived in U.K. three days before Kitner automobile blast. Current whereabouts unknown.

(6) Banque Privée, 17 Bis Avenue Robert Schuman, Marseilles, France. Safe deposit box #8989 visited by Alfred Neuss, three hours before he met with Fabien Curtay in Monaco.

That was it. No cover note, no signature. Just what was there. But obviously Kovalenko had sent it. Marten had never told him of I. M. or of the safe deposit keys, but the information was there anyway. I. Maltsev was obviously the I. M. Raymond/Alexander was to have met at Penrith's Bar in London. Maltsev's lethal specialties made it very clear that the original plan developed by the Baroness and Alexander, a year earlier, had been to have Maltsev kill Kitner and his family very soon after he had been formally presented to the Romanov family and then forced to abdicate, thereby permanently ending any challenge or reversal of thought that might possibly have come later.

Even without an identifying note, Kovalenko had revealed himself as a man who was thorough and caring. It was his way of tying things up and giving documentary credence to what they had been through together. How he had managed to get the LAPD fingerprint copy there was no way to know, except that it had to have come from Halliday's disk, which Kovalenko had been forced to hand over to his superior. The probability was that he had thought something like that might happen and so had prepared for it by making a copy of the disk beforehand, telling no one, not even Marten.

The how or when or why of Kovalenko's actions made no difference. It was the information and his generosity in sharing it that mattered. The result was that Marten had in his possession proof beyond doubt that Alexander Cabrera and Raymond Oliver Thorne were one and the same. Additionally he knew that, in all probability, Alexander had been trained in killing by both Murzin and Maltsev and that Murzin and maybe Maltsev were in the direct employ of the Baroness. That led Marten—and, he was sure, Kovalenko—to believe it had been the Baroness who had ordered the murder of Peter Kitner and his family, to say nothing of directing Alexander to murder Neuss and Curtay and the Romanovs in the Americas.

What had Marten said to Kovalenko those four months ago when the Russian had seen him through passport control at Pulkovo Airport for his night flight to Helsinki? "There's one thing I don't understand. Why did he steal the woman's purse? Money? How much could he have gotten, and what did he need it for? If he hadn't done it, just kept going, there's every chance he would have gotten away."

Kovalenko had simply looked at him and replied, "Why did he kill his mother?"

Those thoughts and questions led to another—and what Kovalenko had said at very nearly the same time. It was about what it takes to be a policeman and *the sometimes necessary cruelty of it, killing without remorse and in disregard for the law they have sworn to uphold when the circumstances require it.*

Kovalenko had spoken about police officers in general. But Marten knew he did not mean it that way. Most cops, the ones he knew and had worked with in Los Angeles, first in patrol cars and then as a detective in Robbery-Homicide, believed as he did, that they were there to enforce the law and not to make their own. In doing so they worked long, hard, and sometimes thankless hours during which they were often seen by the media and the public as either corrupt or ineffectual, or both. Most were neither. They just had an incredibly difficult and dangerous job to do under an unreasonably cruel spotlight. What Kovalenko had been talking about was something else and was driven by the same kind of thinking that belonged to Red McClatchy. It was deep and complex and very dark. And even though they were separated by thousands of miles and operated in hugely different political spheres, both men dealt with what they saw as the same truth—that there were persons and situations the law and the public and the lawmakers were not prepared to deal with, and so the burden of what to do about it fell to men like them. Men like McClatchy and Polchak and Lee and Valparaiso, and even Halliday, and, of course, Kovalenko, who took on that kind of responsibility for themselves and stepped outside the law to do it. In that, Kovalenko was right when he said Marten was not that kind of policeman. He hadn't been then and he never would be. It wasn't who he was.

That in itself raised a question of its own—who was Kovalenko really, and who did he work for? He doubted he would ever know, and maybe he didn't want to. He wondered, too, if things hadn't turned out as they had in St. Petersburg and Alexander hadn't escaped as he had, if Marten had killed him in the Hermitage as Kovalenko had wished and then come out the side door where Kovalenko was waiting, whether the Russian might not have shot him on the spot, killing the Tsarevich's assassin as he tried to escape and thereby ending all of it. It was something, he thought now, he would ask him to his face if they ever met again.

It was growing dark, and Marten felt the pull of the tide at his feet as he walked in the shallow water at the ocean's edge. The only light there was came from the last streaks of sun on the horizon, and he turned in the surf and started back for his car. Rebecca had come through with remarkable strength. She had even appeared before both houses of the Russian parliament to thank them for their kindness and support in the terrible aftermath of the Tsarevich's assassination. Later she had had a private session with President Gitinov himself where she had received his personal condolences and thanked him as well. Afterward she had simply asked to return to her previous life in Switzerland, and she had done just that. She was safely there now, protected by special agents of the Neuchâtel Kantonspolizei and caring once again for the Rothfels children.

After everything, Marten knew he should be grateful, and he was. Yet one thing remained that was still difficult for him to accept, and that was Rebecca's true heritage. The confirmation of it was all there in Alexander's office in Lausanne as he had promised, the complete file—obtained, as he had said, with "money and persistence"—that followed her trail backward from the stored files of the now-defunct House of Sarah home for unwed mothers in Los Angeles. It led to someone named Marlene J. in a place unknown, and then to a person called Houdremont in Port of Spain, Trinidad, then to a Ramon in Palma, Majorca, and then to a Gloria, also in Palma. And, finally, to her royal family in Copenhagen. The DNA report was there, too, and he'd read enough of those to know it was authentic, or at least it looked to be authentic. Still, knowing Alexander or Raymond or whatever you wanted to call him, and knowing the Baroness and what she had done and was capable of, who could be sure of anything? It might all be true or it might all have been cannily put together to give Rebecca the royal lineage necessary to become the wife of the Tsar of All Russia. But what would he do now, ask for Rebecca and the Prince and his wife to submit to a new DNA test? To what end other than his own? Rebecca had a mother and father she believed were hers and loved, and two people who had lost a daughter had received what they thought was a miracle. How could he chance destroying that? The answer was, he couldn't.

He walked on, and his thoughts went to Clem. It was she, after all, who, when he told her of the beach here at Kekaha and the fond memories from childhood, had suggested he come here after his examinations to reflect and renew. It was an idea he'd embraced right away, and he'd wanted her to come with him, but she'd said no, this was something he needed to do alone and for himself. As much as he missed her, she'd been right, and the combination of solitude, long walks, and snorkeling had given him an inner peace he hadn't felt for as long as he could remember.

Clem was a marvel, a delightful, sometimes frightful, loving, caring woman with a huge and courageous heart. He could picture her now in Manchester in her haphazard flat on Palatine Road, books and papers scattered everywhere as she prepared for the upcoming semester, and all the while still nose to claw with her father, the same as she had been the whole time he'd known her.

He loved her and he was sure she loved him, yet he knew she sensed there was some part of him he hadn't shared with her. She'd never pressed him about it. It was as if she knew he would tell her in his own time and she was willing to wait until he did. And he knew one day he would, when he'd earned his degree and was gainfully employed and could truly contemplate spending the rest of his life with her, perhaps even with children. That was a year off, though, maybe two. By then, he hoped and prayed, the danger of his past would have faded to nothing and he would feel comfortable enough to tell her about it. Tell her who he really was, and who he had been, and the truth of what had happened.

Marten stepped out of the surf and walked alone across the sand toward his rental car, happy in the fact that in the morning he would go back to Manchester and to Clem and to the green and peaceful world that had become his. What was it Kovalenko had told him? *Go back to your English gardens. It is a much better life.*

Just ahead was his car, and as he approached he could see something scrawled across the windshield in big bold letters, as if it had been done with a bar of soap. In the dim light he couldn't make out exactly what it was, or imagine who had done it, or why. Who cared? It might be a nuisance, but in the scheme of things it meant nothing. Then he was closer and saw what it was. His heart went to his throat and a chill rifled down his spine. Scrawled in an angry hand, covering most of the windshield and accentuated by an exclamation mark, were the four most terrifying letters he could imagine.

LAPD!

They'd found him.

ACKNOWLEDGMENTS

For technical information and advice I am especially grateful to Paul Tippin, former Los Angeles Police Department homicide investigator; Tony Fitzpatrick, Detective Inspector, Murder Investigations Unit, West Midlands Police, England; David Davidson, M.D.; Pete Noyes, investigative television reporter; Olga Gottlieb; Gillian Hush; Lorcan Sirr; Antonia Bailey Camilleri; Ian Trenwith; and Norton F. Kristy, Ph.D. For suggestions and corrections to the manuscript, I am particularly thankful to Robert Gleason, Hilary Hale, and Marion Rosenberg.

I am especially indebted to Tom Doherty for his faith in the project; and to Robert Gottlieb, who managed to keep me directed and on keel during the long and arduous process of taking *The Exile* from idea to manuscript.